ISAAC ASIMOV

PRESENTS

THE GOLDEN YEARS OF SCIENCE FICTION

THIRD SERIES

ISAAC ASIMOV

PRESENTS

THE GOLDEN YEARS OF SCIENCE FICTION

THIRD SERIES

20 STORIES AND NOVELLAS

Edited by ISAAC ASIMOV AND MARTIN H. GREENBERG

BONANZA BOOKS
NEW YORK

This 1984 edition is published by Bonanza Books, distributed by
Crown Publishers, Inc. by arrangement with DAW Books, Inc.

This book was previously published as two separate works entitled
Isaac Asimov Presents the Great SF Stories 5 (1943)
Isaac Asimov Presents the Great SF Stories 6 (1944)

Manufactured in the United States of America

ISBN: 0-517-435225
h g f e d c b a

ACKNOWLEDGMENTS

Contents

Introduction

In the world outside reality, things continued to improve, in 1943 at least at the macro-level. In January, German forces began their slow and costly withdrawal from the Soviet Union as General Paulus surrendered his army at Stalingrad on the 31st after suffering staggering losses the previous week, and the German retreat continued all through the winter as the Soviets took back Kharkov on St. Valentine's Day. The German position in North Africa also continued to deteriorate, and Hitler replaced Rommel with General von Arnim as head of the Afrika Korps. The Allied advance in North Africa steamed ahead, and Tunis was re-taken on May 7, the German army in Tunisia surrendering on May 12. On April 20th, German troops massacred the few remaining fighters in the Warsaw ghetto, and moved the others to concentration camps.

Meanwhile, the Royal Air Force stepped up its attacks on Germany, striking the Ruhr dams on May 17. In July, the Germans made a major attempt to stabilize their crumbling position in the east with a sizable counterattack at Kursk, which culminated in the largest armored battle of the war—it bought Germany some time, but little more. To the south-west, the Allies landed in Sicily on July 10 and had occupied Palermo by the 23rd, three days before Mussolini fell before an aroused Italian people. The long-awaited invasion of Italy began on September 3rd—by October 13, a newly formed Italian government had declared war on Germany. As the year drew to a close, Soviet forces were again advancing across their homeland, recapturing Kiev on November 6, while the "Big Three"—Roosevelt, Stalin, and Churchill—planned the defeat of Germany at the Teheran Conference in late November.

In the Pacific, the year began with the final defeat of Japanese forces on Guadalcanal, with the American advance

3

continuing slowly, either driving the Japanese off of their island strongholds or bypassing the more strongly defended ones. U.S. troops landed on the Solomons at Bougainville on November 1, as the desperately fighting Japanese began to fall back.

On November 19 the British fascist leader Oswald Mosley was released from prison.

During 1943 Frank Sinatra became a star, and despite some ups and downs is still one today. The New York Yankees defeated the St. Louis Cardinals four games to one to become baseball champions of the world (if not the galaxy), avenging their defeat of the previous year. Dylan Thomas published *New Poems,* while Dmitri Shostakovich composed his *Eighth Symphony.*

Penicillin was used to treat a variety of diseases. *Oklahoma* by Rodgers and Hammerstein was a big hit on Broadway. Henry Moore sculpted "Madonna and Child" and Count Fleet won the Kentucky Derby. Lieutenant (J.G.) J. R. Hunt found time to win the United States Tennis Championship— the great Pauline Betz won the women's title. *For Whom the Bell Tolls* and *Jane Eyre* were two of the big film hits of the year.

Henry Green published *Caught,* while the first Liberty Ships were launched under the auspices of Henry Kaiser. Some things did not change—Joe Louis was still the Heavyweight Boxing Champion of the World, and the Washington Redskins repeated as National Football League champions. Some things did not change *officially*—the world record for the mile run was still the 4:06.4 set by Sydney Wooderson in 1937, but the international body in charge of the records had been unable to meet since late 1938 and the current mark had been broken several times, including a 4:02.6 by Arne Anderson of Sweden.

Walter Lippmann published *U.S. Foreign Policy* while Jacques Maritain published *Christianity and Democracy.* Waksman and Schatz discovered streptomycin. The Professional Golf Association Championship was called because of war.

Death took Beatrice Webb and Sergei Rachmaninov.

Mel Brooks was still Melvin Kaminsky.

In the real world it was another good year, despite the fact that most of the writers and fans were in the armed forces or otherwise engaged.

The news was not *completely* good. *Astonishing Stories* folded in April, and the beloved *Unknown Worlds* published its last issue in October—it instantly became a legend.

But wonderous things were happening in the real world: Fritz Leiber published *Gather Darkness. Donovan's Brain* by Curt Siodmak and *The Lost Traveller* by Ruthven Todd appeared, as did *Judgement Night* by C. L. Moore, *The Book of Ptath* by A. E. van Vogt, and *Perelandra* by C. L. Lewis. Some of these were magazine serials which would not see book publication for many years. Donald A. Wollheim broke new ground with *The Pocket Book of Science Fiction,* the first paperback sf anthology. And James H. Schmitz made his maiden voyage into reality in August with "Greenface."

Death took Stephen Vincent Benét, A. Merritt, and *The Spider*.

But distant wings were beating as Joe Haldeman, Christopher Priest, James Baen, Mick Farren, Robert M. Philmus, Cecelia Holland, Chris Boyce, and Ian Watson were born.

Let us travel back to that honored year of 1943 and enjoy the best stories that the real world bequeathed to us.

And now on to 1944.....

In the world outside reality, things continued to improve on the war fronts. On January 22 Allied forces landed on the beach at Anzio in Italy, inaugurating a long and bloody campaign, while on January 27 the gallant residents of Leningrad were finally liberated from the German siege of that war-torn city. On March 4 Soviet armies swept back into the Ukraine, and by the 19th the Russians had crossed the Dniester River in force. Meanwhile, on the Ides of March, American forces launched a heavy attack on the monastery on top of Monte Cassino, destined to become one of the most famous battlefields of the war. Monte Cassino finally fell on May 18.

By April 2 Soviet troops were in the Crimea, and on May 21 the Allies finally broke through the "Hitler Line" in Italy, the U.S. Fifth Army entering Rome on June 4. Two days later, on "The Longest Day," a giant Allied invasion force began to come ashore on the beaches of Normandy—the long-awaited invasion of Europe had begun. By June 27 the Allies had taken Cherbourg, complete with its umbrellas. But the Germans still had a few unpleasant tricks left, as Britishers found out on June 13, the day the first V-1 "buzz bomb" fell on London, to be followed by the first V-2 rocket on September 8.

On July 20 members of the German General Staff attempted to kill Hitler with a bomb but failed. The conspirators (and many others) paid for failure with their lives. Three days later Soviet troops began to cross into Poland. Back in Italy, Florence was liberated on August 19, while Brest-Litovsk fell to the relentlessly advancing Russians on July 28. On August 1st the Polish resistance rose against the German occupiers in Warsaw, only to be ruthlessly crushed long before Soviet forces reached the city. In the West, Paris was liberated on August 25, and on September 4 the Allies captured Antwerp, giving them a major deep-water port for the landing of supplies. A week later the first American troops crossed into Germany in the vicinity of Trier, while the Soviets entered Yugoslavia on September 29 and Hungary on October 23.

In November, President Roosevelt was reelected, defeating Thomas Dewey by 3,500,000 votes, and Edward Stettinius replaced Cordell Hull as Secretary of State. The year ended with Allied and Soviet armies closing in on Germany, which tried one last major gambit—an offensive in the Ardennes that became known as "The Battle of the Bulge."

In the Pacific, U.S. forces took the last island in the Solomons group from the Japanese on February 15, while the British launched a major offensive in upper Burma on the 28th. Saipan fell to American troops on June 19—on July 18 General Tojo resigned as the head of the Japanese war machine. On October 19 the first U.S. troops, led by General MacArthur, landed in the Philippines. By the end of the year American forces were advancing steadily through the Philippine Archipelago, while northern Burma had been cleared of Japanese troops.

During 1944 Ingrid Bergman won an Academy Award for her performance in *Gaslight*, while Sumner Welles published *The Time for Decision*. The United States Military Academy was the number one ranked college football team. Tennessee Williams's *The Glass Menagerie* was produced on Broadway. Clinton, Tennessee, was the site of the world's second uranium pile. Pensive was the surprise winner of the Kentucky Derby. Carl Jung published his influential *Psychology and Religion*, while the hit films of the year included *Zola, Henry V* (starring the great Laurence Olivier), *The White Cliffs of Dover*, and Hitchcock's *Lifeboat*.

The United States Open Golf Championship was again called because of war. Quinine was successfully synthesized for the first time. Alberto Moravia published *Agostino*. The Green Bay Packers were National Football League Champions. Lewis Mumford's *The Condition of Man* was widely hailed, as was Somerset Maugham's *The Razor's Edge*. Sargent Frank Parker won the United States Tennis Championship, while Pauline Betz repeated as women's champ. Sutherland painted "Christ on the Cross."

T. S. Eliot published *Four Quartets* and Joe Louis was still the Heavyweight Champion of the World. Bela Bartok's Violin Concerto was performed, as was Dmitri Shostakovich's Eighth Symphony. Marty Marion of the St. Louis Cardinals and Hal Newhouser of the Detroit Tigers were Most Valuable Players in the National and American Leagues respectively. Bing Crosby won the Academy Award for his performance in *Going My Way*, which walked away with the Best Film Oscar. St. Louis went crazy as the Cardinals defeated the crosstown Browns four games to two to take the World Series. Paul Hindemith's opera *Herodias* was performed. The semi-official world record for the mile run was 4:02.6 by Arne Andersson of Sweden, but he had a 4:01.6 in 1944—the international certifying committee still could not meet because of World War II.

Death took Wendell Willkie and Lucien Pissarro.

Mel Brooks was still Melvin Kaminsky.

In the real world it was another good year, despite the preoccupations of the war and the death of *Captain Future* in the Spring.

Wondrous things were happening: Olaf Stapledon published *Sirius. Renaissance* by Raymond F. Jones and *The Riddle of the Tower* by J. D. Beresford and Esme Wynne-Tyson appeared as did *World's Beginning* by Robert Ardrey, who would later achieve fame in another field. *The Lady and the Monster*, one of several film versions of Curt Siodmak's *Donovan's Brain*, was released. And an Australian sailor named A. Bertram Chandler made his maiden voyage into reality in May with "This Means War."

And distant wings were beating as P. J. Plauger, James Sallis, Bruce Pennington, Stanley Schmidt, George Lucas, Katherine Kurtz, Vernor Vinge, Jack Chalker, David Gerrold, Peter Weston, and Vance Aandahl were born.

Let us travel back to that honored year of 1944 and enjoy the best stories that the real world bequeathed to us.

ISAAC ASIMOV

PRESENTS

THE GOLDEN YEARS OF SCIENCE FICTION

THIRD SERIES

THE CAVE

Astounding,

January

by P. Schuyler Miller (1912-1974)

P. Schuyler Miller was a quiet man who was also one of the most powerful figures in science fiction from 1951 until his death. His power (which he never abused) derived from the fact that he was the book reviewer for Astounding *during those years, and as such helped to define the "classics" of the field. During the 1930s and early 1940s he was a steady and capable contributor of stories to the sf magazines, although he only published one collection of his stories—*The Titan *(1952), now difficult to find. He also coauthored* Genus Homo *(1950) with L. Sprague de Camp.*

"The Cave" is a story about Mars, a familiar enough subject, here treated in a unique, sweeping fashion that makes it one of the most unusual of the best stories of 1943.

(The influence of John W. Campbell is clear here. He would not allow the traditional views of Mars in the magazine. The Mars of Edgar Rice Burroughs or, for that matter, Ray Bradbury, was not welcome. He wanted the astronomical Mars and he got it from, among others, P. Schuyler Miller, who was a geologist by training. Of course, our knowledge of Mars has advanced enormously in the four decades since this story appeared and (alas) if the story were written today we could not have intelligent Martians featured. Nevertheless, the point made is a clear and poignant one, and is fitting considering that the story was written, and published, in the middle of World War II—I.A.)

11

The cave measured less than a hundred feet from end to
end. It opened at the base of a limestone ridge which rose
like a giant, rounded fin out of the desert. Its mouth was a
flat oval, a shallow alcove scoured out of the soft stone by
wind and sand. Near one end a smooth-walled tunnel sloped
gently back into the ridge. Twenty feet from the entrance it
turned sharply to the right and in a few feet swung back to
the left, paralleling its original course. Here it leveled out into
a broad, flat channel not more than four feet high. This was
the main chamber of the cave.

The big room, like the rest of the cave, had been leached
out of the limestone by running water, long before. The
water had followed a less resistant seam in the rock, dissolv-
ing out a passage whose low ceiling rose and fell a little with
irregularities in the harder stratum overhead, whose floor was
flat and water-polished in spots and in others buried under a
fine yellow clay. A little past the midpoint, the room opened
out into a kind of inverted funnel in which a tall man could
stand erect, a tapering chimney which quickly dwindled to a
shaft barely big enough to admit a man's hand. Here the
floor of the cave was lower and the walls, which had drawn
together until they were less than ten feet apart, were ribbed
and terraced with flowstone.

Beyond the chimney the ceiling dropped suddenly to within
a few inches of the floor. By lying flat on his face and
squirming along between the uneven layers of rock a thin man
might have entered here. After measuring his length perhaps
three times he would have been able to raise himself on one
elbow and twist into a sitting position, his back against the
end wall of the cave and his head and shoulders wedged into
a crevice which cut across the main passage at right angles.
This crevice lay directly under the highest part of the ridge
and vanished into darkness above and on either side. Water
must at one time have flowed through it, for the harder sili-
cious layers in the limestone stood out on the walls in low relief like fine ruled lines drawn in sooty black. Not even air
stirred in it now.

Twenty feet in the winding entry—six or eight feet at the
bend—another thirty to the chimney and fifteen or twenty
more to the back wall; it was a small cave. It was also very
old.

The limestone of which the ridge was formed was perhaps the oldest exposed rock on the surface of that small old world. It had been laid down in fairly deep water at a time when there were seas where there were only deserts now. There had been life in those seas; where wind or water had worn away the softer lime, their fossil bodies stood out from the surface of the gray stone. There were fluted shells like glistening black trumpets—swarms of tiny big-eyed things with fantastically shaped armor and many sprawling arms—long ropes of delicate, saw-edged weed whose fossil tissues were still stained a dull purple—occasionally fragments of some larger thing like an armored, blunt-headed fish. They had been alive, swarming and breeding in the shallow sea, when Earth was no more than a scabbed-over globe of slowly jelling flame.

The cave itself was very old. It had been made by running water, and it was a long time since there was much water on the dying world. Water, sour with soil acids leached from the black humus of a forest floor, had seeped down into the network of joint-planes which intersected the flat-lying limestone beds, eating away the soft stone, widening cracks into crannies and crannies into high-arched rooms, rushing along the harder strata and tunneling through the softer ones, eventually bursting out into the open again at the base of a mossy ledge and babbling away over the rocks to join a brook, a river, or the sea.

Millions of years had passed since there were rivers and seas on Mars.

Things change slowly underground. After a cave has died—after the sources of moisture which created it have shifted or dried up—it may lie without changing for centuries. A man may set his foot in the clay of its floor and go away, and another man may come a hundred or a thousand or ten thousand years afterward and see his footprint there, as fresh as though it had been made yesterday. A man may write on the ceiling with the smoke of a torch, and if there is still a little life in the cave and moisture in the rock, what he has written will gradually film over with clear stone and last forever. Rock may fall from the ceiling and bury portions of the floor, or seal off some rooms completely. Water may return and wash away what has been written or coat it with slime. But if a cave has died—if water has ceased to flow and its walls and ceilings are dry—things seldom change.

Most of the planet's surface had been desert for more millions of years than anyone has yet estimated. From the mouth of the cave its dunes and stony ridges stretched away like crimson ripples left on a beach after a wave has passed. They were dust rather than sand: red, ferric dust ground ever finer by the action of grain against grain, milling over and over through the centuries. It lay in a deep drift in the alcove and spilled down into the opening of the cave; it carpeted the first twenty-foot passage as with a strip of red velvet, and a little of it passed around the angle in the tunnel into the short cross-passage. Only the very finest powder, well nigh impalpable, hung in the still air long enough to pass the second bend and reach the big room. Enough had passed to lay a thin, rusty mantle over every horizontal surface in the cave. Even in the black silt at the very back of the cave, where the air never stirred, there was a soft red bloom on the yellow flowstone.

The cave was old. Animals had sheltered in it. There were trails trodden into the dry clay, close to the walls, made before the clay had dried. There was no dust on these places— animals still followed them when they needed to. There was a mass of draggled, shredded stalks and leaves from some desert plant, packed into the cranny behind a fallen rock and used as a nest. There were little piles of excreta, mostly the chitinous shells of insectlike creatures and the indigestible cellulose of certain plants. Under the chimney the ceiling was blackened by smoke, and there were shards of charcoal and burned bone mixed with the dust of the floor. There were places where the clay had been chipped and dug away to give more headroom, or to make a flat place where a bowl could be set down. There were other signs as well.

The *grak* reached the cave a little after dawn. He had been running all night, and as the sun rose he had seen the shadow of the ridge drawn in a long black line across the crimson dunes, and turned toward it. He ran with the tireless lope of the desert people, his splayed feet sinking only a little way into the soft dust where a man of his weight would have floundered ankle deep.

He was a young male, taller than most of his kind, better muscled and fatter. His fur was sleek and thick, jet black

with a pattern of rich brown. The colors in his cheek patches
were fresh and bright, and his round black eyes shone like
discs of polished coal.

He had been a hunter for less than one season. His tribe
was one of the marauding bands which summered in the
northern oases, raiding down into the lowlands in winter
when the dry plateau became too cold and bare even for
their hardy breed. It had fared better than most, for it had
had little contact with man. The *grak* carried a knife which
he had made for himself out of an eight-inch bar of beryl-
lium copper, taken in his first raid. It was the only human
thing he owned. Its hilt was of bone, intricately carved with
the clan symbols of his father-line; its burnished blade was
honed to a wicked double edge. It was the finest knife any of
the desert folk had ever seen, and he had had to fight for it
more than once. The desert tribes retained the old skills of
metal working which the softer-living pastoral greenlanders
had forgotten, and his tribe, the *Begar,* were among the best
of the dryland smiths.

He wore the knife tucked into the short kilt of plaited
leather which was his only garment. The Old One of his father-line had given it to him on the day he became a hunter
and could no longer run naked like a cub. It was soft and pliable with long wear and oiled to a mahogany brown almost
as dark and rich as his own chest patterns. There were black
stains on it which he knew were blood, for the Old One had
been one of the fiercest slayers of his line and the kilt had
come down to him from an even greater warrior in his own
youth. The very pattern in which the thin strips of *zek* hide
were woven had lost its meaning, though it undoubtedly had
been and still was of great virtue. .

It was cold in the shadow of the ridge, and the *grak's* long
fur fluffed out automatically to provide extra insulation. He
looked like a big black owl as he stood scanning the western
sky, sniffing the wind with his beaklike nose. There was a
tawny band low on the horizon, brightening as the sun rose.
He had smelled a storm early in the night, for he had all the
uncanny weather-wiseness of his race and was sensitive to every subtle change in the quality of the atmosphere. He had
started for the nearest arm of the greenlands, intending to
claim the hospitality of the first village he could find, but the
storm front was moving faster than he could run. He had
seen the ridge only just in time.

He had recognized the place as he approached, though he had never seen it and none of his tribe had visited this part of the desert for many seasons. Such landmarks were part of the education of every dryland cub, and until they had become thoroughly ingrained in his wrinkled young brain he could not hope to pass the hunter's tests and win a hunter's rights. The cave was where he had known it would be, and he chuckled softly with satisfaction as he saw the weathered symbol carved in the stone over the opening. The desert people had long ago discarded the art of writing, having no use for it, but the meaning of certain signs had been passed down as a very practical part of their lore. This was a cave which the *grak's* own forefathers had used and marked.

He studied the signs in the dust around the entrance of the cave. He was not the first to seek shelter there. The feathery membranes of his nose unfolded from their horny sheath, recording the faint scents which still hung in the thin air. They confirmed what his eyes had told him. The cave was occupied.

The wind was rising fast. Red dust devils whirled ahead of the advancing wall of cloud. Red plumes were streaming from the summit of every dune. Making the sign of peace-coming, the *grak* stooped and entered the cave. Beyond the second bend in the passage was darkness which not even his owl's eyes, accustomed to the desert nights, could penetrate. However, he did not need to see. The sensitive organs of touch which were buried in the gaudy skin of his cheek patches picked up infinitesimal vibrations in the still air and told him accurately where there were obstacles. His ears were pricked for the slightest sound. His nose picked up a mixture of odors—his own characteristic scent, the dry and slightly musty smell of the cave itself, and the scents of the other creatures with which he would have to share it.

He identified them, one by one. There were four or five small desert creatures which had more to fear from him than he from them. There was one reptilian thing which under other circumstances might be dangerous, and which still might be if the peace were broken. And there was a *zek*.

The carnivore was as big and nearly as intelligent as the tribesman himself. Its kind waged perpetual war on the flocks of the greenland people, and rarely visited the oases, but when one did wander into the desert it was the most dreaded enemy of the dryland tribes. It stole their cubs from beside their very campfires and attacked full-grown hunters with impunity. Its mottled pelt was the choicest prize a hunter could bring back as proof of his prowess. To some of the more barbaric tribes of the north it was more than just a beast—it was His emissary.

A sudden gust from the passage at his back told the *grak* that the storm was breaking. In a matter of minutes the air would be unbreathable outside. Softly, so as not to arouse the savage beast's suspicions, he began to murmur the ritual of the peace. His fingers were on the hilt of his knife as he began, but as the purring syllables went out into the hollow darkness, his nostrils told him that the fear odor was diminishing. Somewhere in the dark a horny paw scuffed on the dry clay and there was an instant reek of terror from some of the smaller things, but the *zek* made no sign. It was satisfied to keep the peace. Moving cautiously, the *grak* found a hollow in the wall near the entry and sat down to wait, squatting with his knees tucked up close under his furry belly, the hard rock at his back. The knife he laid on the floor beside his hand where it would be ready if he needed it. For a time his senses remained keyed to fever pitch, but gradually his tenseness eased. They were all *grekka* here—all living things, united in the common battle for existence against a cruel and malignant Nature. They knew the law and the brotherhood, and they would keep the truce as long as the storm lasted. Gradually the nictitating lids slipped across his open eyes and he sank into a half-sleep.

Harrigan blundered into the cave by pure luck. He knew nothing about Mars or its deserts except what the Company put in its handbook, and that was damn little. He was a big man and a strong man, born in the mountains with a more than ordinary tolerance for altitude, and he had had to spend less than a week in the dome before they shifted him to the new post in the eastern Sabaeus. He did what he was told and no more than he was told, laid away his pay every week in anticipation of one almighty spree when they brought him in at the next opposition, and had nothing but contempt for the native Martians. *Grekka* they were called, and that was all he knew or cared about them. To him they looked like animals and they were animals, in spite of the fact that they could talk and build houses and kept herds of peg-legged monstrosities which seemed to serve as cattle. Hell—parrots could talk and ants keep cattle!

Harrigan had been a miner on Earth. He was that here, but he couldn't get used to the idea that plants could be more valuable than all the copper and tungsten and carnotite in the world. The desert and its barren red hills nagged at him, and whenever he could get time off he explored them. The fact that he found only rocks and sand did nothing to extinguish his sullen conviction that there was treasure incalculable here somewhere if only the damned natives would talk or the Company would listen to a man who knew minerals better than the big shots knew the swing of their secretaries' hips.

The fact was, of course, as the Company knew very well, that Martian mineral deposits had been exhausted by a native Martian civilization pursuing its inevitable way to an inevitable end at a time when Adam and Eva probably had tails. That the descendants of that civilization were still alive, even on a basis of complete savagery, spoke volumes for the stamina of the native race. Such arguments, however, would have meant less than nothing to a man of Harrigan's type. There were mines on Earth. There were mines on the moon. Hell—there were mines on Mars!

This time he had overstayed his luck. To him the low yellow wall of cloud on the western horizon was only a distant range of hills which he might some day visit and where he might find wealth enough to set him up in liquor for the rest of his life. He had spent the night in the cab of his sand car, and it was not until the clouds were a sullen precipice towering halfway up the sky that he understood what he was heading into. He swung around and headed back, but by then it was too late.

When the storm hit it was like night. The air was a semi-solid mass through which the sand car wallowed blindly with only its instrument board to show where it was going. Dust swiftly clogged the air intake, and he had to take out the filters, put on his mask, and hope for the best. It didn't come. In seconds the air inside the cab was a reddish mist and dust was settling like fine red pepper on every exposed surface. The wind seized the squat machine and rocked it like a skiff in a typhoon, but Harrigan could only hang on, peer red-eyed through dust-coated goggles at his dust-covered instruments, and wonder where he was.

The floundering car climbed painfully to the top of a monster dune, pushed its blunt snout out and over the steep leading edge, slewed violently around, and started down. Harrigan yanked despairingly at the steering levers; they were packed tight with dust and refused to move. He did not see the ridge until the car smashed head on into it. There was a despairing gurgle from the engine, a last clatter of broken bearings, and the car stopped. At once sand began to pile up behind and around it, and Harrigan, picking himself up off the floor of the cab, saw that if he didn't get out fast he would be buried where he sat.

He struggled out on the lee side of the car into a gale that bit into him like an icy knife. He could not see the car when he had taken one step away from it. The dust drove through every seam and patch of his clothes and filtered in around the edges of his mask. It was sucked into his mouth and nose and gritted under his swollen eyelids. It was everywhere, and in no time it would smother him.

The car was lost, though he was probably less than ten feet from it. The wind screamed past him in unholy glee, tearing at every loose flap on his coat, chilling him to the bone. He took half a dozen blundering steps, knee-deep in the soft dust, stumbled, and came down on his knees at the foot of the cliff. His outthrust hands met solid rock. He struggled forward on his knees and peered at it through crusted goggles. It was limestone, and where there was limestone there might be a cave. Foot by foot he felt his way along the uneven surface of the ridge until suddenly it dropped away in front of him; he staggered forward, and fell on his hands and knees in the entrance of the cave.

His head had clipped the low overhang as he fell and it was a minute or two before he realized where he was. Almost automatically, then, he crawled ahead until his skull rammed hard into another wall. He sat gingerly back on his heels and clawed at his mask. It was completely plugged with dust and utterly useless. He lifted it off his face and took a slow breath. There was dust in the air—plenty of it—but he could breathe.

He groped about him in the pitch dark, found an opening in the right-hand wall, and crawled in. Almost immediately there was another sharp turn and the passage suddenly opened out on either side and left him crouching at the entrance of what he knew must be a good-sized room.

Harrigan knew caves too well to take chances with them. What lay ahead might be a room or it might be a pit dropping to some lower level. He had a feeling that it was big. He found the corner where the left-hand wall swung back, moved up against it, moistened his lips with a thick, dry tongue, and shouted:

"Hoy!"

The echo rattled back at him like gunfire. The place was big, but not too big. What he needed now was water and a light.

He had both. Dust had worked in around the stopper of his canteen until he could barely start the threads, but one last savage twist of his powerful fingers did the trick. There wasn't much left. He let a few drops trickle over his tongue and down his throat, wiped the caked dust off the threads with a finger, and screwed the cap back on. These storms lasted for days sometimes, and it was all the water in the world as far as he was concerned.

Light came next. Harrigan had spent too much time underground to be afraid of the dark, but it was plain common sense to want to see what you were getting into. Harrigan hated mysteries. If he knew what he was facing he could fight his way through anything, but he hated blind fumbling and he hated the dark.

Enough water had evaporated from the open canteen in the minute or two he had had the cap off appreciably to raise the moisture content of the cave—at least for the Martians. To their acute senses it was the equivalent of a heavy fog. A few feet away in the blackness the *grak* awoke with a start. Farther back in the cave one of the small animals stirred eagerly. And the *zek* sneezed.

Harrigan's blundering approach had roused the occupants of the cave, and every eye, ear, and nose had been trained on him when he appeared. One rodentlike creature made a panicky rush as it got his scent, only to freeze in terror as it nearly bumped into the *zek*. The peace, for the moment, was suspended—a new factor had entered the situation and a new equilibrium must be reached. They quietly awaited developments.

Harrigan had missed all this preliminary activity in his efforts to find out where he was, rub the dust out of his eyes, and get a few drops of water down his parched gullet. But when the *zek* sneezed, the sudden sound was like an explosion in his ears. In the dead silence which followed he could clearly hear the sound of quiet breathing. It was close to him, and it came from more than one place. He had to have a light!

There should have been a torch in the pocket of his coverall. There wasn't. He had lost it or left it in the car. He had a lighter, though. He ripped feverishly at the zipper of his coverall. It slid open a few inches with a sound like the crackle of lightning and jammed. Sweat dripping from his forehead, he sat back on his heels and fumbled for his gun, but there was no movement from the things in the dark. Slowly and softly he slipped two fingers into his pocket and found the lighter. Leveling the gun at the blank blackness in front of him he lifted the lighter above his head and flipped off the cap.

The burst of yellow flame was dazzling. Then he saw their eyes—dozens of little sparks of green and red fire staring out of the dark. As his own eyes adjusted he saw the *grak*, huddled like a woolly black gargoyle in his corner. The Martian's huge round eyes were watching him blankly, his grinning mouth was slightly open over a saw-edged line of teeth, and his pointed ears were spread wide to catch every sound. His beaklike, shining nose and bright red cheek patches gave him the look of a partly plucked owl. He had a wicked-looking knife in his spidery fingers.

Harrigan's gaze flickered around the circle of watching beasts. He knew nothing of Martian animals, except for the few domesticated creatures the greenlanders kept, and they made a weird assortment. They were mostly small, ratty things with big eyes and feathery antennae in place of noses. Some of them were furred and some had horny or scaly armor. All of them were variously decorated with fantastic collections of colored splotches, crinkled horns, and faceted spines which presumably were attractive to themselves or their mates. At the far end of the cave, curled up in a bed of dry grass, was a lean splotched thing almost as big as the little native which stared at him with malevolent red eyes set close together over a grinning, crocodilian snout. As he eyed it, it yawned hideously and dropped its head on its crossed forepaws—paws like naked, taloned hands. It narrowed its eyes to crimson slits and studied him insolently from under the pallid lids. It looked nasty, and his fingers closed purposefully over the butt of his gun.

The *grak's* cackle of protest stopped him. The only word he could make out was *bella*—peace. He knew that because he had a woman named Bella back in New York, or he had had before he signed on with the Company. Besides, it was part of the spiel you were supposed to rattle off every time you talked to one of the damned little rats. It was all the Martian he knew, so he spat it out, keeping one eye on the other beast.

This was the first man the *grak* had ever seen. It was a monstrous-looking thing, wrapped in layer after layer of finely plaited fabric which must have taken his mates many years to weave, even if their clumsy fingers were as deft as those of the greenlanders, who occasionally did such things. A thrilling philosophical problem was teasing the *grak's* young brain. Was or was not this man of the *grekka?*

To a native Martian the term *grekka* means literally "living things." Any creature native to the planet is a *grak;* all of them, separately or collectively, are *grekka*. The first men to come in contact with the native race heard the word used to designate the Martians themselves and assumed that it was the Martian equivalent of "men." Graziani, of course, as an anthropologist of note, immediately realized the truth of the matter—the situation is duplicated again and again among human aborigines—but the label stuck. Nor did that matter too much, for *grekka* did include the natives and made perfectly good sense when it was used as men proceeded to use it. What did matter was that the word was also the key to the whole elaborate structure of Martian psychology.

Millions of years of unceasing struggle with the forces of an inclement environment on a swiftly maturing and rapidly dying planet have ingrained in the native Martian race, greenlanders and drylanders alike, the fundamental concept that Nature is their undying enemy. Life for them is a bitter fight against overwhelming odds, with an invisible foe who will use every possible means to grind out the little spark of ego in each round, furry Martian skull. You find it in the oldest legends: always the wily native hero is outwitting—there is no other word for it—the evil purposes of the personified, malignant Universe.

Grekka is the ultimate expression of this grim philosophy.

In the battle for life all living things—all *grekka*—are brothers. No Martian would ever dispute the theory of evolution—it is the`very core of his existence that all beasts are
brothers. That is a somewhat oversimplified statement of the
fact, for from there on *grekka* becomes entangled in the most
elaborate maze of qualifications and exceptions which a once
highly civilized race has been able to devise over a period of
millions of years. Your native Martian, drylander or green-
lander, will help his brother beast whenever the latter is
clearly losing out in a battle with Nature, but there are certain things which the individual is supposed to be able to do
for himself if he is not to give unholy satisfaction to Him—
the Great Evil One—the personification of the universal
doom which pours unending misfortune on all *grekka* alike.

The distinction is one of those things which no logician
will ever be able to work out. It is one thing for the desert
tribes and something else for the lowlanders. The *Begar* will
draw the line at something which is a sacred duty of every
Gorub, in spite of the fact that the two tribes have lived side
by side on a more or less friendly basis for generations. One
clan—even one father-line—may and must act in ways which
no other clan on Mars may duplicate without eternally losing
a varying number of points in its game with Him and His
aides.

What puzzled the young *grak* of the cave was whether
man—specifically Harrigan—was *grekka*. If he was, he was
an innate member of the brotherhood of living things and
subject to its laws. If he wasn't, then he could only be a personification or extension of the inimical First Principle Himself, and hence an inherent enemy. Since the time of Graziani
and the Flemming expedition every Martian native, individual by individual and tribe by tribe, has had to make this decision for himself, and by it govern his further relations with
humanity. The *Begar* had had too little contact with mankind
to have needed to make such a decision as a tribe. Now the
young *grak* decided to reserve judgment, keep his eyes open,
and let the man prove himself by his further actions.

Harrigan, of course, knew absolutely nothing of all this. It
would probably not have mattered if he had. What some
damned animal thought about the Universe was nothing to
him.

For a moment there had been death in the air. Now the

tension was vanishing. The smaller animals were settling down again, the little *grak* grinning and nodding as he squatted down in the corner. Only the *zek's* slitted eyes were still studying him with cold indifference. The damned nightmare was curled up in the one place in the cave where a man could stand up! Harrigan gave it eye for eye, and all the little furry and scaly creatures lifted their heads and watched them while the *grak* blinked worriedly. They could all smell the hostility between the two. The *zek* yawned again, showing an evil double line of knife-edged fangs and a leprous white gullet, and flexed the mighty muscles which lay like slabs of molded steel across its massive shoulders. Harrigan sat glumly down where he was, his back against the cold stone, his gun on the floor beside him, the lighter wedged into a crack in the rock between his feet.

Outside the storm was at its height. The faroff screaming of the wind echoed and re-echoed in the big room. Puffs of red dust drifted in out of the darkness, and the flame of the lighter wavered and danced. In the occasional lulls, the only sound in the cave was steady breathing. Every eye, Harrigan knew, was on him. He was the intruder here, and they were wary of him. Let 'em be! A man was something to *be* afraid of on this damned little dried-up world!

He glowered back at them, making up malicious fantasies about their probable habits. There were plenty of fancy stories going the rounds about how these Martians went at things. He grinned sardonically at the little *grak* as he recalled one particularly outrageous libel. The *grak* smiled reassuringly back at him. This man was a hideous travesty of a thing, but he was keeping the peace.

Harrigan sized up the cave. It wasn't a bad hole as caves went. It was dry, the angle in the passage kept the dust out, and it was big enough so a man could stretch. With a fire and water he could last as long as the storm would.

There had been a fire, he noticed, under the chimney at the far end of the cave. There was soot on the ceiling, and the rock had the crumbled look of burned limestone. It was too close to the big beast for comfort, though. That was a wicked-looking brute if there ever was one. Better leave him be—but if he tried to start anything, James Aloysius Harrigan would show him who was tough!

A gust stronger than any that had come before bent the thin flame of the lighter far over, drawing it out into a feeble yellow thread. Harrigan bent quickly and sheltered it with his cupped palms. It seemed smaller and duller than when he had first lit it. He picked up the lighter and shook it close to his ear. It was almost dry! He snapped down the cap.

The darkness which fell was stifling. The invisible walls of the cave seemed to be closing in on him, compressing the thin air, making it hard to breathe. The dust got into his nose and throat. It had a dry metallic taste. Iron in it. It shriveled the membranes of his throat like alum. He cleared his throat noisily and ran his tongue over his thick lips. What he needed was a drink. Just a couple of drops. He unscrewed the canteen and lifted it to his lips.

Somewhere in the blackness something moved. It made only the very smallest sound—the tick of a claw on the rock—but he heard it. Instantly he was on the alert. So that was their game! Well, let 'em come! They were as blind as he was in this hole, and he had yet to see the day when any animal could outsmart him!

He set the canteen carefully down behind a block of stone. It would be safer there if there was a scrap, and it might hit against something and give him away if he carried it. Shifting his gun to his left hand, he began cautiously to work his way along the wall, stopping every few inches to listen. He could hear nothing, but the rhythmic, ghostly whisper of the creatures' breathing. Whatever it was that had moved, it was quiet now.

His fingers found the first of the slabs of fallen limestone which lay half buried in the clay along the right-hand wall. They reached almost to the chimney, but about fifteen feet from where he had been sitting there was a break in the line, and the wall dropped back into a shallow alcove no more than two feet high. In there he would have solid rock on all sides of him, and he would be directly opposite the pile of dried weeds in which the *zek* was lying. He would have a clear shot at the ugly brute between two of the fallen blocks.

His groping hand came down on something cold and scaly that wriggled hastily away under the rocks. There was an answering squeal of terror and a patter of scampering feet as panic-stricken little creatures scattered in front of him. Something as heavy as a cat landed on his back and clung there, chattering madly. He batted at it and knocked it to the floor.

Then, only a few feet ahead in the darkness, he heard the stealthy click of claw on stone again. The *zek!*

He had to have light! It was suicide to face that monster in pitch blackness! He had slipped the lighter back into the outside pocket of his coverall. He fumbled for it. It was gone!

The panic went out of Harrigan in a flash. He sat back on his heels and curled his fingers lovingly around the butt of his gun. The tougher things got, the better he liked them. The lighter must have dropped out of his open pocket; he could find it when he needed it by going back over the ground he had just covered. It wasn't lost. But he didn't need it. The dark was his protection, not his enemy. They couldn't see him in the dark.

He dropped back on all fours. Everything was quiet again. He'd hear them if they tried anything. He was almost at the alcove, and then they'd have to blast to get at him. He could pick 'em off one by one if they tried to get in.

The clay was hard as brick and full of little chunks of broken stone that gouged at his knees, even through the heavy suit. The roof was lower, too; he had to get down on his elbows and hitch along, almost flat on his face.

His heart was thumping like mad. He was working too hard in this thin air. He rolled over on his side, his back against one of the big blocks, and stared into the blackness. Another few feet and he could lie down and wait for them. He needed time out. He had to have a clear head. He cursed his stupidity in not bringing an oxygen flask from the car. One shot of that stuff and he'd be ready to take 'em on all at once, barehanded!

As he started on again something tinkled on the stone beside him. He groped for it: it was the lighter. It had been in his back pocket. Damn fool—letting the darkness rattle him! Animals were all afraid of fire. He could smoke 'em out any time he wanted to. He was boss of this cave! A grin of satisfaction spread over his grimy face as he shuffled along on knees and elbows through the dust.

One big slab almost blocked the hole he was looking for. It was a tight squeeze, but he wriggled through and found plenty of room behind it. He felt for the crack between the blocks that was opposite the nest, slid his gun cautiously into position, and flashed the lighter. Now!

The nest was empty.

With a curse Harrigan rolled to the other opening. The

flame of the lighter showed him the far end of the cave—the *grak* crouching wide-eyed in his niche—the black arch of the entrance—and the *zek!*

The thing had slipped past him in the dark. It stood where he had been sitting a moment ago, by the entrance. It stared back at him over its shoulder—a hideous thing like a giant reptile-snouted weasel, mottled with leprous gray. It grinned at him, its red eyes mocking, then stretched out a handlike paw and picked up his canteen!

Harrigan's first shots spattered against the rock above the monster's head; the light blinded him. His next clipped through the coarse mane on the back of its thick neck. His last was fired point-blank into its snarling face. Then the lighter went spinning away across the floor and talons like steel clamps closed on his arm.

The rocks saved him then. The thing had him by the arm, but his body was protected. He still had the gun; he twisted around in the beast's grim grasp and emptied it into the darkness. Its grip loosened and he snatched his arm free. It was bleeding where the *zek's* claws had bitten into the flesh. Then, through the crack on his right, he saw a sheet of white flame go up as the lighter touched the powder-dry mass of weeds in the beast's nest.

The cave was lit up as bright as day. Harrigan saw the *zek,* blood streaming from a ragged wound in its broad chest, its face a bloody mask of fury. One shot had plowed a long furrow across the side of his head. It gathered its powerful hind legs under it, seized a corner of the great block which barred the opening with paws like human hands, and pulled. The muscles stood out in knotted ropes on its arms and shoulders as it worried at the massive stone. Then the packed clay at its base crumbled and the great block slowly tipped. The way was open. His sanctuary had become a trap.

There was one way out. Harrigan took it. Desperately he lunged forward, out of the cranny straight into the thing's arms. He clamped both hands over its narrow lower jaw and forced its slavering snout straight back with all the power of his own broad back. It rose on its haunches, hugging him to it, then toppled over, dragging him with it into the open, raking at him with its cruel hind claws. He set his jaw and felt his arm stiffen and straighten as the evil head was driven back—back. As through a red mist he saw the *grak's* owl eyes staring at him over the monster's shoulder—saw the coppery gleam of firelight on a shining knife. He felt the *zek* shudder as the keen blade was driven home in its back. It began to cough—great racking coughs that shook its whole frame. Its arms tightened convulsively about him and its claws clenched in his back as the copper knife drove home again and again. Then, slowly, they began to loosen. The beast was dead.

The burning weeds had dimmed to a dull flicker. The dust that had been stirred up in their struggle hung like a red veil in the air. Harrigan lay staring up through it at the little native, sucking the thin air painfully into his tortured lungs. The damned little rat had saved his life! He wiped the blood and dust off his face with his sleeve and got slowly to his feet. He had to stoop to clear the ceiling. That knife—that was a man's weapon. Wonder where the *grak* got it—

He took one step toward the *grak*. Before he could take another the knife went smoothly into his belly, just under the breastbone, driving upward to the heart.

Squatting in the darkness, listening to the distant murmur of the storm, the *grak* wondered what would have happened in the cave if the man had not come there. The *zek* had been a treacherous ally: sooner or later it might have broken the peace. Once its blood-rage had been aroused it had, of course, been necessary to kill it. But if the man had not come that necessity might have been averted.

The man had been very clever. The *grak* had been almost certain that he was what he pretended to be. But as always there was one thing—one very little thing—to betray him. He did not know the law of water.

In every doubtful situation, the *grak* reflected smugly, there was some trivial matter in which the Source of Evil or His emissaries would reveal themselves. Some one thing in which the true *grak* was clearly distinguishable from the forces of Nature against which he must forever fight. One must be quick to see such discrepancies—and quick to act on them.

The matter of water lay at the very root of the law by which all *grekka*—all living things—existed. It was the thing which all must have, which none, under the law, could withhold from another. Without it there could be no life. With it every living thing was given strength to battle on against the eternal foe.

The man had brought water to the cave. Under the law all

grekka must share in it according to their need. But when the *zek* had gone to take its share, the man had tried to kill it. By that small thing he revealed himself—no *grak,* but one of His evil things. So he had died. So, once more, was victory won for the brotherhood of living things against the Universe.

He would make a song about this thing, and sing it by the fires of his tribe. He would cut a sign in the stone over the entrance of the cave, after the storm was over, so that others who came there would know of it. And the cave itself, where his forefathers had come and lit their fires, would keep the bodies of the *zek* and the man thus, side by side, as witness forever.

THE HALFLING

Astounding Stories,

February

by Leigh Brackett (1915-1978)

Leigh Brackett, along with C. L. Moore, was one of the premier women authors in science fiction in the 1940s. She wrote high-quality space opera and sword and sorcery, including such novels as Shadow Over Mars *(1951),* People of the Talisman *(1964), and* Sword of Rhiannon *(1953), all of which appeared in the sf magazines in the 1940s or early 1950s. Her most important book is the subdued yet powerful* The Long Tomorrow *(1955), one of the finest post-holocaust novels ever written. A noted Hollywood screenwriter (she completed the first draft of the screenplay for* The Empire Strikes Back *just before her death), she achieved commercial success with her* Book of Skaith *trilogy in the 1970s.*

"The Halfling" is representative of her forties work at its best.

(I was always enthusiastic about Leigh, both literarily and personally. My clearest memory of her, in fact, is that of seeing her once at a convention and racing happily toward her (I was younger in those faroff days, though of course I am essentially ageless), shouting, "Leigh! Leigh!" When I got to her, I threw my arms around her waist and lifted her into the air and whirled her around. (She was no lightweight but, as I said, I was younger in those faroff days.) As a gesture of affection, it was delightful and I'm sure Leigh appreciated it in a theoretical sense. Not in a practical sense, however,

30

for in manhandling her thus, I threw her back out (unintentionally, of course) and she had to hobble through the rest of the convention.—I.A.)

Chapter I

Primitive Venus

I was watching the sunset. It was something pretty special in the line of California sunsets, and it made my feel swell, being the first one I'd seen in about nine years. The pitch was in the flatlands between Culver City and Venice, and I could smell the sea. I was born in a little dump at Venice, Cal., and I've never found any smell like the clean cold salt of the Pacific—not anywhere in the solar system.

I was standing alone, off to one side of the grounds. The usual noises of a carnival around feeding time were being made behind me, and the hammer gang was pinning the last of the tents down tight. But I wasn't thinking about Jade Green's Interplanetary Carnival, The Wonders of the Seven Worlds Alive Before Your Eyes.

I was remembering John Damien Greene running barefoot on a wet beach, fishing for perch off the end of a jetty, and dreaming big dreams. I was wondering where John Damien Greene had gone, taking his dreams with him, because now I could hardly remember what they were.

Somebody said softly from behind me, "Mr. Greene?"

I quit thinking about John Damien Greene. It was that kind of voice—sweet, silky, guaranteed to make you forget your own name. I turned around.

She matched her voice, all right. She stood about five-three on her bronze heels, and her eyes were more purple than the hills of Malibu. She had a funny little button of a nose and a pink mouth, smiling just enough to show her even white teeth. The bronze metal-cloth dress she wore hugged a chassis with no flaws in it anywhere. I tried to find some.

She dropped her head, so I could see the way the last of the sunlight tangled in her gold-brown hair.

"They said you were Mr. Greene. If I've made a mistake. . . ."

She had an accent, just enough to be fascinating.

I said, "I'm Greene. Something I can do for you?" I still couldn't find anything wrong with her, but I kept looking just the same. My blood pressure had gone up to about three hundred.

It's hard to describe a girl like that. You can say she's five-three and beautiful, but you can't pass on the odd little tilt of her eyes and the way her mouth looks, or the something that just comes out of her like light out of a lamp, and hooks into you so you know you'll never be rid of it, not if you live to be a thousand.

She said, "Yes. You can give me a job. I'm a dancer."

I shook my head. "Sorry, miss. I got a dancer."

Her face had a look of steel down under the soft kittenish roundness. "I'm not just talking," she said. "I need a job so I can eat. I'm a good dancer. I'm the best dancer you ever saw anywhere. Look me over."

That's all I had been doing. I guess I was staring by then. You don't expect fluffy dolls like that to have so much iron in them. She wasn't bragging. She was just telling me.

"I still have a dancer," I told her, "a green-eyed Martian babe who is plenty good, and who would tear my head off, and yours too, if I hired you."

"Oh," she said. "Sorry. I thought you bossed this carnival." She let me think about that, and then grinned. "Let me show you."

She was close enough so I could smell the faint, spicy perfume she wore. But she'd stopped me from being just a guy chinning with a pretty girl. Right then I was Jade Greene, the carny boss-man, with scars on my knuckles and an ugly puss, and a show to keep running.

Strictly Siwash, that show, but my baby—mine to feed and paint and fuel. If this kid had something Sindi didn't have, something to drag in the cash customers—well, Sindi would have to take it and like it. Besides, Sindi was getting so she thought she owned me.

The girl was watching my face. She didn't say anything more, or even move. I scowled at her.

"You'd have to sign up for the whole tour. I'm blasting off next Monday for Venus, and then Mars, and maybe into the Asteroids."

"I don't care. Anything to be able to eat. Anything to—"

She stopped right there and bent her head again, and suddenly I could see tears on her thick brown lashes.

I said, "Okay. Come over to the coach tent and we'll have a look."

Me, I was tempted to sign her for what was wrapped up in that bronze cloth—but business is business. I couldn't take on any left-footed ponies.

She said shakily, "You don't soften up very easily, do you?" We started across the lot toward the main gate. The night was coming down cool and fresh. Off to the left, clear back to the curving deep-purple barrier of the hills, the slim white spires of Culver, Westwood, Beverly Hills, and Hollywood were beginning to show a rainbow splash of color under their floodlights.

Everything was clean, new, and graceful. Only the thin fog and the smell of the sea were old.

We were close to the gate, stumbling a little in the dusk of the afterglow. Suddenly a shadow came tearing out from between the tents.

It went erratically in lithe, noiseless bounds, and it was somehow not human though it went on two feet. The girl caught her breath and shrank in against me. The shadow went around us three times like a crazy thing, and then stopped.

There was something eerie about the sudden stillness. The hair crawled on the back of my neck. I opened my mouth angrily.

The shadow stretched itself toward the darkening sky and let go a wail like Lucifer falling from Heaven.

I cursed. The carny lights came on, slamming a circle of blue-white glare against the night.

"Laska, come here!" I yelled.

The girl screamed.

I put my arm around her. "It's all right," I said, and then, "Come here, you misbegotten Thing! You're on a sleigh ride again."

There were more things I wanted to say, but the girl cramped my style. Laska slunk in toward us. I didn't blame her for yelping. Laska wasn't pretty.

He wasn't much taller than the girl, and looked shorter because he was drooping. He wore a pair of tight dark trunks and nothing else except the cross-shaped mane of fine blue-gray fur that went across his shoulders and down his back, from the peak between his eyes to his long tail. He was dragging the tail, and the tip of it was twitching. There was more of the soft fur on his chest and forearms, and a fringe of it down his lank belly.

I grabbed him by the scruff and shook him. "I ought to boot your ribs in! We got a show in less than two hours."

He looked up at me. The pupils of his yellow-green eyes were closed to thin hairlines, but they were flat and cold with hatred. The glaring lights showed me the wet whiteness of his pointed teeth and the raspy pinkness of his tongue.

"Let me go. Let me go, you human!" His voice was hoarse and accented.

"I'll let you go." I cuffed him across the face. "I'll let you go to the immigration authorities. You wouldn't like that, would you? You wouldn't even have coffee to hop up on when you died."

The sharp claws came out of his fingers and toes, flexed hungrily and went back in again.

I dropped him.

"Go on back inside. Find the croaker and tell him to straighten you out. I don't give a damn what you do on your own time, but you miss out on one more show and I'll take your job and call the I-men. Get it?"

"I get it," said Laska sullenly, and curled his red tongue over his teeth. He shot his flat, cold glance at the girl and went away, not making any sound at all.

The girl shivered and drew away from me. "What was—that?"

"Cat-man from Callisto. My prize performer. They're pretty rare."

"I—I've heard of them. They evolved from a cat ancestor instead of an ape, like we did."

"That's putting it crudely, but it's close enough. I've got a carload of critters like that, geeks from all over the system. They ain't human, and they don't fit with animals either. Moth-men, lizard-men, guys with wings and guys with six arms and antennae. They all followed evolutionary tracks peculiar to their particular hunks of planet, only they stopped before they got where they were going. The Callistan kitties are the aristocrats of the bunch. They've got an I. Q. higher than a lot of humans, and wouldn't spit on the other half-lings."

"Poor things," she said softly. "You didn't have to be so cruel to him."

I laughed. "That What's-it would as soon claw my insides out as look at me—or any other human, including you—just on general principles. That's why Immigration hates to let 'em in even on a work permit. And when he's hopped up on coffee. . . ."

"Coffee? I thought I must have heard wrong."

"Nope. The caffeine in Earthly coffee berries works just like coke or hashish for 'em. Venusian coffee hits 'em so hard they go nuts and then die, but our own kind just keeps 'em going. It's only the hoppy ones you ever find in a show like this. They get started on coffee and they have to have it no matter what they have to do to get it."

She shuddered a little. "You said something about dying."

"Yeah. If he's ever deported back to Callisto his people will tear him apart. They're a clannish bunch. I guess the first humans on Callisto weren't very tactful, or else they just hate us because we're something they're not and never can be. Anyway, their tribal law forbids them to have anything to do with us except killing. Nobody knows much about 'em, but I hear they have a nice friendly religion, something like the old-time Thugs and their Kali worship."

I paused, and then said uncomfortably, "Sorry I had to rough him up in front of you. But he's got to be kept in line."

She nodded. We didn't say anything after that. We went in past the main box and along between the burglars readying up their layouts—Martian *getak*, Venusian *shalil* and the game the Mercurian hillmen play with human skulls. Crooked? Sure—but suckers like to be fooled, and a guy has to make a living.

I couldn't take my eyes off the girl. I thought, *if she dances the way she walks. . . .*

She didn't look much at the big three-dimensional natural-color pictures advertising the geek show. We went by the brute top, and suddenly all hell broke loose inside of it. I've got a fair assortment of animals from all over. They make pretty funny noises when they get started, and they were started now.

They were nervous, unhappy noises. I heard prisoners yammering in the Lunar cell blocks once, and that was the way this sounded—strong, living things shut up in cages and tearing their hearts out with it—hate, fear, and longing like you never thought about. It turned you cold.

The girl looked scared. I put my arm around her again, not minding it at all. Just then Tiny came out of the brute top.

Tiny is a Venusian deep-jungle man, about two sizes smaller than the Empire State Building, and the best zooman I ever had, drunk or sober. Right now he was mad.

"I tell that Laska stay 'way from here," he yelled. "My kids smell, him. You listen!"

I didn't have to listen. His "kids" could have been heard halfway to New York. Laska had been expressly forbidden to go near the brute top because the smell of him set the beasts crazy. Whether they were calling to him one animal to another, or scared of him as something unnatural, we didn't know. The other halflings were pretty good about it, but Laska liked to start trouble just for the hell of it.

I said, "Laska's hopped again. I sent him to the croaker. You get the kids quiet again, and then send one of the punks over to the crumb castle and tell the cook I said if he ever gives Laska a teaspoonful of coffee again without my say-so I'll fry him in his own grease."

Tiny nodded his huge pale head and vanished, cursing. I said to the girl, "Still want to be a carny?"

"Oh, yes," she said. "Anything, as long as you serve food!"

"That's a pretty accent you got. What is it?"

"Just about everything. I was born on a ship between Earth and Mars, and I've lived all over. My father was in the diplomatic corps."

I said, "Oh. Well, here's the place. Go to it."

Sindi was sitting cross-legged on the stage, sipping *thil* and listening to sad Martian music on the juke box behind the screen of faded Martian tapestry. She looked up and saw us, and she didn't like what she saw.

She got up. She was a Low-Canaler, built light and wiry, and she moved like a cat. She had long emerald eyes and black hair with little bells braided in it, and clusters of tiny bells in her ears. She was wearing the skin of a Martian sand-leopard, no more clothes than the law forced her to wear. She was something to look at, and she had a disposition like three yards of barbed wire.

I said, "Hi, Sindi. This kid wants a tryout. Climb down, huh?"

Sindi looked the kid over. She smiled and climbed down

and put her hand on my arm. She sounded like a shower of rain when she moved, and her nails bit into me, hard.

I said between my teeth, "What music do you want, kid?"

"My name's Laura—Laura Darrow." Her eyes were very big and very purple. "Do you have Enhali's *Primitive Venus?*"

Not more than half a dozen dancers in the system can do justice to that collection of tribal music. Some of it's subhuman and so savage it scares you. We use it for mood music, to draw the crowd.

I started to protest, but Sindi smiled and tinkled her head back. "Of course. Put it on, Jade."

I shrugged and went in and fiddled with the juke box. When I came out Laura Darrow was up on the stage and we had an audience. Sindi must have passed the high sign. I shoved my way through a bunch of Venusian lizard-men and sat down. There were three or four little moth-people from Phobos roosting up on the braces so their delicate wings wouldn't get damaged in the crush.

The music started. Laura kicked off her shoes and danced.

I don't think I breathed all the time she was on the stage. I don't remember anyone else breathing, either. We just sat and stared, sweating with nervous ecstasy, shivering occasionally, with the music beating and crying and surging over us.

The girl wasn't human. She was sunlight, quicksilver, a leaf riding the wind—but nothing human, nothing tied down to muscles and gravity and flesh. She was—oh, hell, there aren't any words. She was the music.

When she was through we sat there a long time, perfectly still. Then the Venusians, human and half-human, let go a yell and the audience came to and tore up the seats.

In the middle of it Sindi looked at me with deadly green eyes and said, "I suppose she's hired."

"Yeah. But it doesn't have anything to do with you, baby."

"Listen, Jade. This suitcase outfit isn't big enough for two of us. Besides, she's got you hooked, and she can have you."

"She hasn't got me hooked. Anyway, so what? You don't own me."

"No. And you don't owe me, either."

"I got a contract."

She told me what I could do with my contract.

I yelled, "What do you want me to do, throw her out on her ear? With that talent?"

"Talent!" snarled Sindi. "She's not talented. She's a freak."

"Just like a dame. Why can't you be a good loser?"

She explained why. A lot of it didn't make sense, and none of it was printable. Presently she went out, leaving me sore and a little uneasy. We had quite a few Martians with the outfit. She could make trouble.

Oh, hell! Just another dame sore because she was outclassed. Artistic temperament, plus jealousy. So what? Let her try something. I could handle it. I'd handled people before.

I jammed my way up to the stage. Laura was being mobbed. She looked scared—some of the halflings are enough to give a tough guy nightmares—and she was crying.

I said, "Relax, honey. You're in." I knew that Sindi was telling the truth. I was hooked. I was so hooked it scared me, but I wouldn't have wiggled off if I could.

She sagged down in my arms and said, "Please, I'm hungry."

I half carried her out, with the moth-people fluttering their gorgeous wings around our heads and praising her in their soft, furry little voices.

I fed her in my own quarters. She shuddered when I poured her coffee and refused it, saying she didn't think she'd ever enjoy it again. She took tea instead. She was hungry, all right. I thought she'd never stop eating.

Finally I said, "The pay's forty credits, and found."

She nodded.

I said gently, "You can tell me. What's wrong?"

She gave me a wide, purple stare. "What do you mean?"

"A dancer like you could write her own ticket anywhere, and not for the kind of peanuts I can pay you. You're in a jam."

She looked at the table and locked her fingers together. Their long pink nails glistened.

She whispered, "It isn't anything bad. Just a—a passport difficulty. I told you I was born in space. The records got lost somehow, and living the way we did—well, I had to come to Earth in a hurry, and I couldn't prove my citizenship, so I came without it. Now I can't get back to Venus where my money is, and I can't stay here. That's why I wanted so badly to get a job with you. You're going out, and you can take me."

I knew how to do that, all right. I said, "You must have a

big reason to take the risk you did. If you're caught it means the Luna cell blocks for a long time before they deport you."

She shivered. "It was a personal matter. It delayed me a while. I—was too late."

I said, "Sure. I'm sorry." I took her to her tent, left her there and went out to get the show running, cursing Sindi. I stopped cursing and stared when I passed the coach tent. She was there, and giving.

She stuck out her tongue at me and I went on.

That evening I hired the punk, just a scrawny kid with a white face, who said he was hungry and needed work. I gave him to Tiny, to help out in the brute top.

Chapter II

Voice of Terror

We played in luck that week. Some gilded darling of the screen showed up with somebody else's husband who wasn't quite divorced yet, and we got a lot of free publicity in the papers and over the air. Laura wnet on the second night and brought down the house. We turned 'em away for the first time in history. The only thing that worried me was Sindi. She wouldn't speak to me, only smile at me along her green eyes as though she knew a lot she wasn't telling and not any of it nice. I tried to keep an eye on her, just in case.

For five days I walked a tightrope between heaven and hell. Everybody on the pitch knew I was a dead duck where Laura was concerned. I suppose they got a good laugh out of it—me, Jade Greene the carny boss, knocked softer than a cup custard by a girl young enough to be my daughter, a girl from a good family, a girl with talent that put her so far beyond my lousy dog-and-pony show. . . .

I knew all that. It didn't do any good. I couldn't keep away from her. She was so little and lovely; she walked like music; her purple eyes had a tilt to them that kept you looking, and her mouth—

I kissed it on the fifth night, out back of the coach tent when the show was over. It was dark there; we were all alone, and the faint spicy breath of her came to me through the thin salt fog. I kissed her.

Her mouth answered mine. Then she wrenched away, suddenly, with a queer fury. I let her go. She was shuddering, and breathing hard.

I said, "I'm sorry."

"It isn't that. Oh, Jade, I—" She stopped. I could hear the breath sobbing in her throat. Then she turned and ran away, and the sound of her weeping came back to me through the dark.

I went to my quarters and got out a bottle. After the first shot I just sat staring at it with my head in my hands. I haven't any idea how long I sat there. It seemed like forever. I only know that the pitch was dark, sound asleep under a pall of fog, when Sindi screamed.

I didn't know it was Sindi then. The scream didn't have any personality. It was the voice of terror and final pain, and it was far beyond anything human.

I got my gun out of the table drawer. I remember my palm was slippery with cold sweat. I went outside, catching up the big flashlight kept for emergencies near the tent flap. It was very dark out there, very still, and yet not quiet. There was something behind the darkness and the silence, hiding in them, breathing softly and waiting.

The pitch began to wake up. The stir and rustle spread out from the scream like ripples from a stone, and over in the brute top a Martian sand-cat began to wail, thin and feral, like an echo of death.

I went along between the tents, walking fast and silent. I felt sick, and the skin of my back twitched; my face began to ache from being drawn tight. The torch beam shook a little in my hand.

I found her back of the coach tent, not far from where I'd kissed Laura. She was lying on her face, huddled up, like a brown island in a red sea. The little bells were still in her ears.

I walked in her blood and knelt down in it and put my hand on her shoulder. I thought she was dead, but the bells tinkled faintly, like something far away on another star. I tried to turn her over.

She gasped, "Don't." It wasn't a voice. It was hardly a breath, but I could hear it. I can still hear it. I took my hand away.

"Sindi—"

A little wash of sound from the bells, like rain far off— "You fool," she whispered. "The stage. Jade, the stage—"

She stopped. The croaker came from somewhere behind me and knocked me out of the way, but I knew it was no use. I knew Sindi had stopped for good.

Humans and halflings were jammed in all round, staring, whispering, some of them screaming a little. The brute top had gone crazy. They smelt blood and death on the night wind, and they wanted to be free and a part of it.

"Claws," the croaker said. "Something clawed her. Her throat—"

I said, "Yeah. Shut up." I turned around. The punk was standing there, the white-faced kid, staring at Sindi's body with eyes glistening like shiny brown marbles.

"You," I said. "Go back to Tiny and tell him to make sure all his kids are there. . . . All the roustabouts and every man that can handle a gun or a tent stake, get armed as fast as you can and stand by. . . . Mike, take whatever you need and guard the gate. Don't let anybody or anything in or out without permission from me, in person. Everybody else get inside somewhere and stay there. I'm going to call the police."

The punk was still there, looking from Sindi's body to me and around the circle of faces. I yelled at him. He went away then, fast. The crowd started to break up.

Laura Darrow came out of it and took my arm.

She had on a dark blue dressing gown and her hair was loose around her face. She had the dewy look of being freshly washed, and she breathed perfume. I shook her off. "Look out," I said. "I'm all—blood."

I could feel it on my shoes, soaking through the thin stuff of my trouser legs. My stomach rose up under my throat. I closed my eyes and held it down, and all the time Laura's voice was soothing me. She hadn't let go of my arm. I could feel her fingers. They were cold, and too tight. Even then, I loved her so much I ached with it.

"Jade," she said. "Jade, darling. Please—I'm so frightened."

That helped. I put my arm around her and we started back toward my place and the phone. Nobody had thought to put the big lights on yet, and my torchbeam cut a fuzzy tunnel through the fog.

"I couldn't sleep very well," Laura said suddenly. "I was lying in my tent thinking, and a little while before she screamed I thought I heard something—something like a big cat, padding."

The thing that had been in the back of my mind came out yelling. I hadn't seen Laska in the crowd around Sindi. If Laska had got hold of some coffee behind the cook's back. . . .

I said, "You were probably mistaken."

"No. Jade."

"Yeah?" It was dark between the tents. I wished somebody would turn the lights on. I wished I hadn't forgotten to tell them to. I wished they'd shut up their overall obbligato of gabbling, so I could hear. . . .

"Jade. I couldn't sleep because I was thinking—"

Then she screamed.

He came out of a dark tunnel between two storage tents. He was going almost on all fours, his head flattened forward, his hands held in a little to his belly. His claws were out. They were wet and red, and his hands were wet and red, and his feet. His yellow-green eyes had a crazy shine to them, the pupils slitted against the light. His lips were peeled back from his teeth. They glittered, and there was froth between them—Laska coked to hell and gone!

He didn't say anything. He made noises, but they weren't speech and they weren't sane. They weren't anything but horrible. He sprang.

I pushed Laura behind me. I could see the marks his claws made in the dirt, and the ridging of his muscles with the jump. I brought up my gun and fired, three shots.

The heavy slugs nearly tore him in two, but they didn't stop him. He let go a mad animal scream and hit me, slashing. I went part way down, firing again, but Laska was still going. His hind feet clawed into my hip and thigh, using me as something to push off from. He wanted the girl.

She had backed off, yelling bloody murder. I could hear feet running, a lot of them, and people shouting. The lights came on. I twisted around and got Laska by the mane of fur on his backbone and then by the scruff. He was suddenly a very heavy weight. I think he was dead when I put the fifth bullet through his skull.

I let him drop.

I said, "Laura, are you all right?" I saw her brown hair and her big purple eyes like dark stars in her white face. She was saying something, but I couldn't hear what it was. I said, "You ought to faint, or something," and laughed.

But it was me, Jade Greene, that did the fainting.

I came out of it too soon. The croaker was still working on my leg. I called him everything I could think of in every language I knew, out of the half of my mouth that wasn't taped shut. He was a heavy man, with a belly and a dirty chin.

He laughed and said, "You'll live. That critter damn near took half your face off, but with your style of beauty it won't matter much. Just take it easy a while until you make some more blood."

I said, "The hell with that. I got work to do." After a while he gave in and helped me get dressed. The holes in my leg weren't too deep, and the face wasn't working anyway. I poured some Scotch in to help out the blood shortage, and managed to get over to the office.

I walked pretty well.

That was largely because Laura let me lean on her. She'd waited outside my tent all that time. There were drops of fog caught in her hair. She cried a little and laughed a little and hold me how wonderful I was, and helped me along with her small vibrant self. Pretty soon I began to feel like a kid waking up from a nightmare into a room full of sunshine.

The law had arrived when we got to the office. There wasn't any trouble. Sindi's torn body and the crazy cat-man added up, and the Venusian cook put the lid on it. He always took a thermos of coffee to bed with him, so he'd have it first thing when he woke up—Venusian coffee, with enough caffeine in it to stand an Earthman on his head. Enough to finish off a Callistan cat-man. Somebody had swiped it when he wasn't looking. They found the thermos in Laska's quarters.

The show went on. Mobs came to gawk at the place where the killing had happened. I took it easy for one day, lolling in a shiny golden cloud with Laura holding my head.

Along about sundown she said, "I'll have to get ready for the show."

"Yeah. Saturday's a big night. Tomorrow we tear down, and then Monday we head out for Venus. You'll feel happier then?"

"Yes. I'll feel safe." She put her head down over mine. Her hair was like warm silk. I put my hands up on her throat. It was firm and alive, and it made my hands burn.

She whispered, "Jade, I—" A big hot tear splashed down on my face, and then she was gone.

I say still, hot and shivering like a man with swamp fever, thinking, *Maybe. . . .*

Maybe Laura wouldn't leave the show when we got to Venus. Maybe I could make her not want to. Maybe it wasn't too late for dreaming, a dream that John Damein Greene had never had, sitting in a puddle of water at the end of a jetty stringer and fishing for perch.

Crazy, getting ideas like that about a girl like Laura. Crazy like cutting your own throat. Oh, hell. A man never really grows up, not past believing that maybe miracles still happen.

It was nice dreaming for a while.

It was a nice night, too, full of stars and the clean, cool ocean breeze, when Tiny came over to tell me they'd found the punk dead in a pile of straw with his throat torn out, and the Martian sand-cat loose.

Chapter III

Carnival of Death

We jammed our way through the mob on the midway. Lots of people having fun, lots of kids yelling and getting sick on Mercurian *jitsi*-beans and bottled Venusian fruit juice. Nobody knew about the killing. Tiny had had the cat rounded up and caged before it could get outside the brute top, which had not yet opened for business.

The punk was dead, all right—dead as Sindi, and in the same way. His twisted face was not much whiter than I remembered it, the closed eyelids faintly blue. He lay almost under the sand-cat's cage.

The cat paced, jittery and snarling. There was blood on all its six paws. The cages and pens and pressure tanks seethed nastily all around me, held down and quiet by Tiny's wranglers.

I said, "What happened?"

Tiny lifted his gargantuan shoulders. "Dunno. Everything quiet. Even no yell, like Sindi. Punk kid all lonesome over here behind cages. Nobody see; nobody hear. Only Mars kitty waltz out on main aisle, scare hell out of everybody. We catch, and then find punk, like you see."

I turned around wearily. "Call the cops again and report

the accident. Keep the rubes out of here until they pick up the body." I shivered. I'm superstitious, like all carnies.

They come in threes—always in threes. Sindi, the punk—what next?

Tiny sighed. "Poor punk. So peaceful, like sleeper with shut eye."

"Yeah." I started away. I limped six paces and stopped and limped back again.

I said, "That's funny. Guys that die violent aren't tidy about their eyes, except in the movies."

I leaned over. I didn't quite know why, then. I do now. You can't beat that three-time jinx. One way or another, it gets you.

I pushed back one thin, waxy eyelid. After a while I pushed back the other. Tiny breathed heavily over my shoulder. Neither of us said anything. The animals whimpered and yawned and paced.

I closed his eyes again and went through his pockets. I didn't find what I was looking for. I got up very slowly, like an old man. I felt like an old man. I felt dead, deader than the white-faced kid.

I said, "His eyes were brown."

Tiny stared at me. He started to speak, but I stopped him. "Call Homicide, Tiny. Put a guard on the body. And send men with guns. . . ."

I told him where to send them. Then I went back across the midway.

A couple of Europeans with wiry little bodies and a twenty-foot wing-spread were doing Immelmans over the geek top, and on the bally stand in front of it two guys with six hands apiece and four eyes on movable stalks were juggling. Laura was out in front of the coach tent, giving the rubes a come-on.

I went around behind the tent, around where I'd kissed her, around where Sindi had died with the bells in her ears like a wash of distant rain.

I lifted up the flap and went in.

The tent was empty except for the man that tends the juke box. He put out his cigarette in a hurry and said, "Hi, Boss," as though that would make me forget he'd been smoking. I didn't give a damn if he set the place on fire with a blow-torch. The air had the warm, musty smell that tents have. Enhali's *Primitive Venus* was crying out of the juke box with a rhythm like thrown spears.

I pulled the stage master, and then the whites. They glared on the bare boards, naked as death and just as yielding.

I stood there a long time.

After a while the man behind me said uneasily, "Boss, what—"

"Shut up. I'm listening."

Little bells, and a voice that was pain made vocal.

"Go out front," I said. "Send Laura Darrow in here. Then tell the rubes there won't be a show here tonight."

I heard his breath suck in, and then catch. He went away down the aisle.

I got a cigarette out and lit it very carefully, broke the match in two and stepped on it. Then I turned around.

Laura came down the aisle. Her gold-brown hair was caught in a web of brilliants. She wore a sheath-tight thing of sea-green metal scales, with a short skirt swirling around her white thighs, and sandals of the shiny scales with no heels to them. She moved with the music, part of it, wild with it, a way I'd never seen a woman move before.

She was beautiful. There aren't any words. She was— beauty.

She stopped. She looked at my face and I could see the quivering tightness flow up across her white skin, up her throat and over her mouth, and catch her breath and hold it. The music wailed and throbbed on the still, warm air.

I said, "Take off your shoes, Laura. Take off your shoes and dance."

She moved then, still with the beat of the savage drums, but not thinking about it. She drew in upon herself, a shrinking and tightening of muscles, a preparation.

She said, "You know."

I nodded. "You shouldn't have closed his eyes. I might never have noticed. I might never have remembered that the kid had brown eyes. He was just a punk. Nobody paid much attention. He might just as well have had purple eyes—like yours."

"He stole them from me." Her voice came sharp under the music. It had a hiss and a wail in it I'd never heard before, and the accent was harsher. "While I was in your tent, Jade.

I found out when I went to dress. He was an I-man. I found his badge inside his clothes and took it."

Purple eyes looking at me—purple eyes as phony as the eyes on the dead boy. Contact lenses painted purple to hide what was underneath.

"Too bad you carried an extra pair, Laura, in case of breakage."

"He put them in his eyes, so he couldn't lose them or break them or have them stolen, until he could report. He threw away the little suction cup. I couldn't find it. I couldn't get the shells off his eyeballs. All I could do was close his eyes and hope—"

"And let the sand-cat out of his cage to walk through the blood." My voice was coming out all by itself. It hurt. The words felt as though they had fishhooks on them, but I couldn't stop saying them.

"You almost got by with it, Laura. Just like you got by with Sindi. She got in your way, didn't she? She was jealous and she was a dancer. She knew that no true human could dance like you dance. She said so. She said you were a freak."

That word hit her like my fist. She showed me her teeth, white, even teeth that I knew now were as phony as her eyes. I didn't want to see her change, but I couldn't stop looking, couldn't stop.

I said, "Sindi gave you away before she died, only I was too dumb to know what she meant. She said, 'The stage.'"

I think we both looked, down at the stark boards under the stark lights, looked at the scratches on them where Laura had danced barefoot that first time and left the marks of her claws on the wood.

She nodded, a slow, feral weaving of the head.

"Sindi was too curious. She searched my tent. She found nothing, but she left her scent, just as the young man did today. I followed her back here in the dark and saw her looking at the stage by the light of matches. I can move in the dark, Jade, very quickly and quietly. The cook tent is only a few yards back of this one, and Laska's quarters close beyond that. I smelt the cook's coffee. It was easy for me to steal it and slip it through the tent flap by Laska's cot, and wake him with the touch of my claws on his face. I knew he couldn't help drinking it. I was back here before Sindi came out of the tent to go and tell you what she'd found."

She made a soft purring sound under the wicked music.

"Laska smelt the blood and walked in it, as I meant him to do. I thought he'd die before he found us—or me—because I knew he'd find my scent in the air of his quarters and know who it was, and what it was. My perfume had worn too thin by then to hide it from his nose."

I felt the sullen pain of the claw marks on my face and leg. Laska, crazy with caffeine and dying with it, knowing he was dying and wanting with all the strength of his drugged brain to get at the creature who had killed him. He'd wanted Laura that night, not me. I was just something to claw out of the way.

I wished I hadn't stopped him.

I said, "Why? All you wanted was Laska. Why didn't you kill him?"

The shining claws flexed out of her fingertips, under the phony plastic nails—very sharp, very hungry.

She said huskily, "My tribe sent me to avenge its honor. I have been trained carefully. There are others like me, tracking down the renegades, the dope-ridden creatures like Laska who sell our race for human money. He was not to die quickly. He was not to die without knowing. He was not to die without being given the chance to redeem himself by dying bravely."

"But I was not to be caught. I cost my people time and effort, and I am not easily replaced. I have killed seven renegades, Jade. I was to escape. So I wanted to wait until we were out in space."

She stopped. The music hammered in my temples, and inside I was dead and dried up and crumbled away.

I said, "What would you have done in space?"

I knew the answer. She gave it to me, very simply, very quietly.

"I would have destroyed your whole filthy carnival by means of a little bomb in the jet timers, and gone away in one of the lifeboats."

I nodded. My head felt as heavy as Mount Whitney, and as lifeless. "But Sindi didn't give you time. Your life came first. And if it hadn't been for the punk. . . ."

No, not just a punk—an Immigration man. Somewhere Laura had slipped, or else her luck was just out. A white-faced youngster, doing his job quietly in the shadows, and dying without a cry. I started to climb down off the stage.

She backed off. The music screamed and stopped, leaving a silence like the feel of a suddenly stopped heart.

Laura whispered, "Jade, will you believe something if I tell you?

"I love you, Jade." She was still backing off down the aisle, not making any sound. "I deserve to die for that. I'm going to die. I think you're going to kill me, Jade. But when you do, remember that those tears I shed—were real."

She turned and ran, out onto the midway. I was close. I had caught her hair. It came free, leaving me standing alone just inside the tent, staring stupidly.

I had men out there, waiting. I thought she couldn't get through. But she did. She went like a wisp of cloud on a gale, using the rubes as a shield. We didn't want a panic. We let her go, and we lost her.

I say we let her go. We couldn't help it. She wasn't bothering about being human then. She was all cat, just a noiseless blur of speed. We couldn't shoot without hurting people, and our human muscles were too slow to follow her.

I knew Tiny had men at the gates and all around the pitch, anywhere that she could possibly get out. I wasn't worried. She was caught, and pretty soon the police would come. We'd have to be careful, careful as all hell not to start one of those hideous, trampling panics that can wreck a pitch in a matter of minutes.

All we had to do was watch until the show was over and the rubes were gone. Guard the gates and keep her in, and then round her up. She was caught. She couldn't get away. Laura Darrow. . . .

I wondered what her name was, back on Callisto. I wondered what she looked like when she let the cross-shaped mane grow thick along her back and shoulders. I wondered what color her fur was. I wondered why I had ever been born.

I went back to my place and got my gun and then went out into the crowd again. The show was in full swing; lots of people having fun, lots of kids crazy with excitement; lights and laughter and music—and a guy out in front of the brute top splitting his throat telling the crowd that something was wrong with the lighting system and it would be a while before they could see the animals.

A while before the cops would have got what they wanted and cleaned up the mess under the sand-cat's cage.

The squad cars would be coming in a few minutes. There wasn't anything to do but wait. She was caught. She couldn't escape.

The one thing we didn't think about was that she wouldn't try to.

A Mercurian cave-tiger screamed. The Ionian quags took it up in their deep, rusty voices, and then the others chimed in, whistling, roaring, squealing, shrieking, and doing things there aren't any names for. I stopped, and gradually everybody on the pitch stopped and listened.

For a long moment you could hear the silence along the midway and in the tents. People not breathing, people with a sudden glassy shine of fear in their eyes and a cold tightening of the skin that comes from way back beyond humanity. Then the muttering started, low and uneasy, the prelude to panic.

I fought my way to the nearest bally stand and climbed on it. There were shots, sounding small and futile under the brute howl.

I yelled, "Hey, everybody! Listen! There's nothing wrong. One of the cats is sick, that's all. There's nothing wrong. Enjoy yourselves."

I wanted to tell them to get the hell out, but I knew they'd kill themselves if they started. Somebody started music going again, loud and silly. It cracked the icy lid that was tightening down. People began to relax and laugh nervously and talk too loudly. I got down and ran for the brute top.

Tiny met me at the tent flap. His face was just a white blur. I grabbed him and said, "For God's sake, can't you keep them quiet?"

"She's in there, Boss—like shadow. No hear, no see. One man dead. She let my kids out. She—"

More shots from inside, and a brute scream of pain. Tiny groaned.

"My kids! No lights, Boss. She wreck 'em."

I said, "Keep 'em inside. Get lights from somewhere. There's a blizzard brewing on the pitch. If that mob gets started."

I went inside. There were torchbeams spearing the dark, men sweating and cursing, a smell of hot, wild bodies and the sweetness of fresh blood.

Somebody poked his head inside the flap and yelled, "The cops are here!"

I yelled back, "Tell 'em to clear the grounds if they can, without starting trouble. Tell—"

Somebody screamed. There was a sudden spangle of lights in the high darkness, balls of crimson and green and vicious yellow tumbling toward us, spots of death no bigger than your fist—the stinging fireflies of Ganymede. Laura had opened their case.

We scattered, fighting the fireflies. Somewhere a cage went over with a crash. Bodies thrashed, and feet padded on the packed earth—and somewhere above the noise was a voice that was sweet and silky and wild, crying out to the beasts and being answered.

I knew then why the brute top went crazy when Laska was around. It was kinship, not fear. She talked to them, and they understood.

I called her name.

Her voice came down to me out of the hot dark, human and painful with tears. "Jade! Jade, get out; go somewhere safe!"

"Laura, don't do this! For God's sake—"

"Your God, or mine? Our God forbids us to know humans except to kill. How, if we kept men as you kept Laska?"

"Laura!"

"Get out! I'm going to kill as many as I can before I'm taken. I'm turning the animals loose on the pitch. Go somewhere safe!"

I fired at the sound of her voice.

She said softly, "Not yet, Jade. Maybe not at all."

I beat off a bunch of fireflies hunting for me with their poisoned stings. Cage doors banged open. Wild throats coughed and roared, and suddenly the whole side wall of the tent fell down, cut free at the top, and there wasn't any way to keep the beasts inside any more.

A long mob scream went up from outside, and the panic was on.

I could hear Tiny bellowing, sending his men out with ropes and nets and guns. Some huge, squealing thing blundered around in the dark, went past me close enough to touch, and charged through the front opening, bringing part of the top down. I was close enough behind it so that I got free.

I climbed up on the remains of the bally stand. There was plenty of light outside—blue-white, glaring light, to show me the packed mass of people screaming and swaying between the tents, trampling toward the exits, to show me a horde of creatures sweeping down on them, caged beasts free to kill, and led by a lithe and leaping figure in shining green.

I couldn't see her clearly. Perhaps I didn't want to. Even then she moved in beauty, like wild music—and she had a tail.

I never saw a worse panic, not even the time a bunch of Nahali swamp-edgers clemmed our pitch when I was a pony punk with Triangle.

The morgues were going to be full that night.

Tiny's men were between the bulk of the mob and the animals. The beasts had had to come around from the far side of the tent, giving them barely time to get set. They gave the critters all they had, but it wasn't enough.

Laura was leading them. I heard her voice crying out above all that din. The animals scattered off sideways between the tents. One Martian sand-cat was dead, one quag kicking its life out, and that was all. They hadn't touched Laura, and she was gone.

I fought back, away from the mob, back into a temporarily empty space behind a tent. I got out my whistle and blew it, the rallying call. A snake-headed kibi from Titan sneaked up and tried to rip me open with its double-pointed tail. I fed it three soft-nosed slugs, and then there were half a dozen little moth-people bouncing in the air over my head, squeaking with fear and shining their great eyes at me.

I told them what I wanted. While I was yelling the Europans swooped in on their wide wings and listened.

I said finally, "Did any of you see which way *she* went?"

"That way." One of the mothlings pointed back across the midway. I called two of the Europans. The mothlings went tumbling away to spread my orders, and the bird-men picked me up and carried me across, over the crowd.

The animals were nagging at their flanks, pulling them down in a kind of mad ecstasy. There was a thin salt fog, and blood on the night wind, and the cage doors were open at last.

They set me down and went to do what I told them. I went alone among the swaying tents.

All this hadn't taken five minutes. Things like that move fast. By the time the Europans were out of sight the moth-lings were back, spotting prowling beasts and rolling above them in the air to guide men to them—men and geeks.

Geeks with armor-plated backs and six arms, carrying tear-gas guns and nets; lizard-men, fast and powerful, armed with their own teeth and claws and whatever they could pick up; spider-people, spinning sticky lassos out of their own bodies; the Europans, dive-bombing the quags with tear gas.

The geeks saved the day for us. They saved lives, and the reputation of their kind, and the carnival. Without them, God only knows how many would have died on the pitch. I saw the mothlings dive into the thick of the mob and pick up fallen children and carry them to safety. Three of them died, doing that.

I went on, alone.

I was beyond the mob, beyond the fringe of animals. I was remembering Laura's voice saying, "Not yet, Jade. Maybe not at all." I was thinking of the walls being down and all California free outside. I was hearing the mob yell and the crash of broken tents, and the screams of people dying—my people, human people, with the claws bred out of them.

I was thinking—

Guns slamming and brute throats shrieking, wings beating fast against the hot hard glare, feet pounding on packed earth. I walked in silence, a private silence built around me like a shell. . . .

Four big cats slunk out of the shadows by the tent. There was enough light left to show me their eyes and their teeth, and the hungry licking of their tongues.

Laura's voice came through the canvas, tremulous but no softer nor more yielding than the blue barrel of my gun.

"I'm going away, Jade. At first I didn't think there was any way, but there is. Don't try to stop me. Please don't try."

I could have gone and tried to find a cop. I could have called men or half-men from their jobs to help me. I didn't. I don't know that I could have made anybody hear me, and anyway they had enough to do. This was my job.

My job, my carnival, my heart.

I walked toward the tent flap, watching the cats.

They slunk a little aside, belly down, making hoarse, whimpering noises. One was a six-legged Martian sand-cat, about the size of an Earthly leopard. Two were from Venus, the fierce white beauties of the high plateaus. The fourth was a Mercurian cave-cat, carrying its twenty-foot body on eight powerful legs and switching a tail that had bone barbs on it.

Laura called to them. I don't know whether she said words in their language, or whether her voice was just a bridge for thought transference, one cat brain to another. Anyway, they understood.

"Jade, they won't touch you if you go."

I fired.

One of the white Venusians took the slug between the eyes and dropped without a whimper. Its mate let go a sobbing shriek and came for me, with the other two beside it.

I snapped a shot at the Martian. I went over kicking, and I dived aside, rolling. The white Venusian shot over me, so close its hind claws tore my shirt. I put a slug in its belly. It just yowled and dug its toes in and came for me again. Out of the tail of my eye I saw the dying Martian tangle with the Mercurian, just because it happened to be the nearest moving object.

I kicked the Venusian in the face. The pain must have blinded it just enough to make its aim bad. On the second jump its forepaws came down on the outer edges of my deltoids, gashing them but not tearing them out. The cat's mouth was open clear to its stomach.

I should have died right then. I don't know why I didn't, except that I didn't care much if I did. It's the guys that want to live that get it, seems like. The ones that don't care go on forever.

I got a lot of hot bad breath in my face and five parallel gashes in back, where its hind feet hit me when I rolled up. I kicked it in the belly. Its teeth snapped a half inch short of my nose, and then I got my gun up under its jaw and that was that. I had four shots left.

I rolled the body off and turned. The Martian cat was dead. The Mercurian stood over it, watching me with its four pale, hot eyes, twitching its barbed tail.

Laura stood watching us.

She looked just like she had the first time I saw her. Soft gold-brown hair and purple eyes with a little tilt to them, and a soft pink mouth. She was wearing the bronze metal-cloth dress and the bronze slippers, and there was still nothing wrong with the way she was put together. She glinted dully in the dim light, warm bronze glints.

She was crying, but there was no softness in her tears.

The cat flicked its eyes at her and made a nervous, eager whine. She spoke to it, and it sank to its belly, not wanting to.

Laura said, "I'm going, Jade."

"No."

I raised my gun hand. The big cat rose with it. She was beyond the cat. I could shoot the cat, but a Mercurian lives a long time after it's shot.

"Throw down your gun, Jade, and let me go."

I didn't care if the cat killed me. I didn't care if Death took me off piggy-back right then. I suppose I was crazy. Maybe I was just numb. I don't know. I was looking at Laura, and choking on my own heart.

I said, "No."

Just a whisper of sound in her throat, and the cat sprang. It reared up on its four hind feet and clawed at me with its four front ones. Only I wasn't where it thought I was. I knew it was going to jump and I faded—not far, I'm no superman—just far enough so its claws raked me without gutting me. It snapped its head down to bite.

I slammed it hard across the nose with my gun. It hurt, enough to make it wince, enough to fuddle it just for a split second. I jammed the muzzle into its nearest eye and fired.

Laura was going off between the tents, fast, with her head down, just a pretty girl, mingling with the mob streaming off the pitch. Who'd notice her, except maybe to whistle.

I didn't have time to get away. I dropped down flat on my belly and let the cat fall on top of me. I only wanted to live a couple of seconds longer. After that, the hell with it!

The cat was doing a lot of screaming and thrashing. I was between two sets of legs. The paws came close enough to touch me, clawing up the dirt. I huddled up small, hoping it wouldn't notice me there under its belly. Everything seemed to be happening very slowly, with a cold precision. I steadied my right hand on my left wrist.

I shot Laura three times, carefully, between the shoulders.

The cat stopped thrashing. Its weight crushed me. I knew it was dead. I knew I'd done something that even experienced hunters don't do in nine cases out of ten. My first bullet had found the way into the cat's little brain and killed it.

It wasn't going to kill me. I pulled myself out from under it. The pitch was almost quiet now, the mob gone, the animals mostly under control. I kicked the dead cat. It had died too soon.

My gun was empty. I remember I clicked the hammer twice. I got more bullets out of my pocket, but my fingers wouldn't hold them and I couldn't see to load. I threw the gun away.

I walked away in the thin, cold fog, down toward the distant beat of the sea.

MIMSY WERE THE BOROGOVES

Astounding,

February

by Lewis Padgett
(Henry Kuttner, 1914-1958, and
C. L. Moore, 1911-   )

Henry Kuttner and C. L. Moore are undoubtedly the most successful husband-and-wife writing team in the history of science fiction. Although they produced memorable solo efforts before their marriage in 1940, their best work was that produced in collaboration—indeed, it was impossible to ascertain who wrote what no matter what by-line their stories carried—they did not even know themselves, and we are going to treat all the stories by them in this series as collaborations, although we will make educated guesses about authorship in a few cases. Their contributions to science fiction were varied and many, and in a real sense they dominated the sf of the 1943 to 1947 period, at least in the magazines.

The first of five stories by them in this book, "Mimsy Were the Borogoves," is a genuine classic, combining impressive internal logic, a tragic perspective, and magical "gifts" from the future. The story also has some profound things to say about the nature and complexity of the gap that always seems to exist between generations.

(I certainly can't quarrel with Marty's view that Kuttner and Moore were the most successful husband-and-wife writing team in science fiction. There

57

*have been others, of course; Damon Knight and
Kate Wilhelm are perhaps the most prominent con-
temporary example, although I don't believe they
collaborate. As a personal touch, my wife, Janet
Jeppson, has published two science fiction novels
and several shorter pieces. If she hadn't gotten
started so late in life (being a psychiatrist and psy-
choanalyst is time-consuming both in training and
the practice) why, who knows, we might have given
them all a run for their money.—I.A.)*

There's no use trying to describe either Unthahorsten or his
surroundings, because, for one thing, a good many million
years has passed and, for another, Unthahorsten wasn't on
Earth, technically speaking. He was doing the equivalent of
standing in the equivalent of a laboratory. He was preparing
to test his time machine.

Having turned on the power, Unthahorsten suddenly realized that the Box was empty. Which wouldn't do at all. The
device needed a control, a three-dimensional solid which
would react to the conditions of another age. Otherwise Unthahorsten couldn't tell, on the machine's return, where and
when it had been. Whereas a solid in the Box would automatically be subject to the entropy and cosmic-ray bombardment
of the other era, and the Unthahorsten could measure the
changes, both qualitative and quantitative, when the machine
returned. The Calculators could then get to work and,
presently, tell Unthahorsten that the Box had briefly visited
A.D. 1,000,000, A.D. 1000 or A.D. I, as the case might be.

Not that it mattered, except to Unthahorsten. But he was
childish in many respects.

There was little time to waste. The Box was beginning to
flow and shiver. Unthahorsten stared around wildly, fled into
the next glossatch and groped in a storage bin there. He came
up with an armful of peculiar-looking stuff. Uh-huh. Some of
the discarded toys of his son Snowen, which the boy had
brought with him when he had passed over from Earth, after
mastering the necessary technique. Well, Snowen needed this
junk no longer. He was conditioned, and had put away
childish things. Besides, though Unthahorsten's wife kept the
toys for sentimental reasons, the experiment was more important.

Unthahorsten left the glossatch and dumped the assortment into the Box, slamming the cover shut before the warning signal flashed. The Box went away. The manner of its departure hurt Unthahorsten's eyes.

He waited.

And he waited.

Eventually he gave up and built another time machine, with identical results. Snowen hadn't been annoyed by the loss of his old toys, nor had Snowen's mother, so Unthahorsten cleaned out the bin and dumped the remainder of his son's childhood relics in the second time machine's Box.

According to his calculations, this one should have appeared on Earth in the latter part of the nineteenth century, A.D. If that actually occurred, the device remained there.

Disgusted, Unthahorsten decided to make no more time machines. But the mischief had been done. There were two of them, and the first. . . .

Scott Paradine found it while he was playing hooky from the Glendale Grammar School. There was a geography test that day, and Scott saw no sense in memorizing place names—which, in the nineteen-forties, was a fairly sensible theory. Besides, it was the sort of warm spring day, with a touch of coolness in the breeze, which invited a boy to lie down in a field and stare at the occasional clouds till he fell asleep. Nuts to geography! Scott dozed.

About noon he got hungry, so his stocky legs carried him to a nearby store. There he invested his small hoard with penurious care and a sublime disregard for his gastric juices. He went down by the creek to feed.

Having finished his supply of cheese, chocolate, and cookies, and having drained the soda-pop bottle to its dregs, Scott caught tadpoles and studied them with a certain amount of scientific curiosity. He did not persevere. Something tumbled down the bank and thudded into the muddy ground near the water, so Scott, with a wary glance around, hurried to investigate.

It was a box. It was, in fact, the Box. The gadgetry hitched to it meant little to Scott, though he wondered why it was so fused and burned. He pondered. With his jackknife he pried and probed, his tongue sticking out from a corner of his mouth— Hm-m-m. Nobody was around. Where had the box

come from? Somebody must have left it here, and sliding soil
had dislodged it from its precarious perch.

"That's a helix," Scott decided, quite erroneously. It was
helical, but it wasn't a helix, because of the dimensional warp
involved. Had the thing been a model airplane, no matter
how complicated, it would have held few mysteries to Scott.
As it was, a problem was posed. Something told Scott that
the device was a lot more complicated than the spring motor
he had deftly dismantled last Friday.

But no boy has ever left a box unopened, unless forcibly
dragged away. Scott probed deeper. The angles on this thing
were funny. Short circuit, probably. That was why—uh! The
knife slipped. Scott sucked his thumb and gave vent to experienced blasphemy.

Maybe it was a music box.

Scott shouldn't have felt depressed. The gadgetry would
have given Einstein a headache and driven Steinmetz raving
mad. The trouble was, of course, that the box had not yet
completely entered the space-time continuum where Scott existed, and therefore it could not be opened—at any rate, not
till Scott used a convenient rock to hammer the helical non-
helix into a more convenient position.

He hammered it, in fact, from its contact point with the
fourth dimension, releasing the space-time torsion it had been
maintaining. There was a brittle snap. The box jarred slightly,
and lay motionless, no longer only partially in existence.
Scott opened it easily now.

The soft, woven helmet was the first thing that caught his
eye, but he discarded that without much interest. It was just a
cap. Next, he lifted a square, transparent crystal block, small
enough to cup in his palm—much too small to contain the
maze of apparatus within it. In a moment Scott had solved
the problem. The crystal was a sort of magnifying glass, vastly enlarging the things inside the block. Strange things they
were, too. Miniature people, for example.

They moved. Like clockwork automatons, though much
more smoothly. It was rather like watching a play. Scott was
interested in their costumes, but fascinated by their actions.
The tiny people were deftly building a house. Scott wished it
would catch fire, so he could see the people put it out.

Flames licked up from the half-completed structure. The

automatons, with a great deal of odd apparatus, extinguished the blaze.

It didn't take Scott long to catch on. But he was a little worried. The manikins would obey his thoughts. By the time he discovered that, he was frightened and threw the cube from him.

Halfway up the bank, he reconsidered and returned. The crystal lay partly in the water, shining in the sun. It was a toy; Scott sensed that, with the unerring instinct of a child. But he didn't pick it up immediately. Instead, he returned to the box and investigated its remaining contents.

He found some really remarkable gadgets. The afternoon passed all too quickly. Scott finally put the toys back in the box and lugged it home, grunting and puffing. He was quite red-faced by the time he arrived at the kitchen door.

His find he hid at the back of a closet in his room upstairs. The crystal cube he slipped into his pocket, which already bulged with string, a coil of wire, two pennies, a wad of tin-foil, a grimy defense stamp and a chunk of feldspar. Emma, Scott's two-year-old sister, waddled unsteadily in from the hall and said hello.

"Hello, Slug," Scott nodded, from his altitude of seven years and some months. He patronized Emma shockingly, but she didn't know the difference. Small, plump and wide-eyed, she flopped down on the carpet and stared dolefully at her shoes.

"Tie 'em, Scotty, please?"

"Sap," Scott told her kindly, but knotted the laces. "Dinner ready yet?"

Emma nodded.

"Let's see your hands." For a wonder they were reasonably clean, though probably not aseptic. Scott regarded his own paws thoughtfully and, grimacing, went to the bathroom, where he made a sketchy toilet. The tadpoles had left traces.

Dennis Paradine and his wife, Jane, were having a cocktail before dinner, downstairs in the living room. He was a young-ish, middle-aged man with soft gray hair and a thin, prim-mouthed face; he taught philosophy at the university. Jane was small, neat, dark, and very pretty. She sipped her Martini and said: "New shoes. Like 'em?"

"Here's to crime," Paradine muttered absently. "Huh?

Shoes?. Not now. Wait till I've finished this. I had a bad day."

"Exams?"

"Yeah. Flaming youth aspiring toward manhood. I hope they die. In considerable agony. *Insh' Allah!*"

"I want the olive," Jane requested.

"I know," Paradine said despondently. "It's been years since I've tasted one myself. In a Martini, I mean. Even if I put six of 'em in your glass, you're still not satisfied."

"I want yours. Blood brotherhood. Symbolism. That's why."

Paradine regarded his wife balefully and crossed his long legs. "You sound like one of my students."

"Like that hussy Betty Dawson, perhaps?" Jane unsheathed her nails. "Does she still leer at you in that offensive way?"

"She does. The child is a neat psychological problem. Luckily she isn't mine. If she were—" Paradine nodded significantly. "Sex consciousness and too many movies. I suppose she still thinks she can get a passing grade by showing me her knees. Which are, by the way, rather bony."

Jane adjusted her skirt with an air of complacent pride. Paradine uncoiled himself and poured fresh Martinis. "Candidly, I don't see the point of teaching those apes philosophy. They're all at the wrong age. Their habit patterns, their methods of thinking, are already laid down. They're horribly conservative, not that they'd admit it. The only people who can understand philosophy are mature adults or kids like Emma and Scotty."

"Well, don't enroll Scotty in your course," Jane requested. "He isn't ready to be a *Philosophiae Doctor*. I hold no brief for a child genius, especially when it's my son."

"Scotty would probably be better at it than Betty Dawson," Paradine grunted.

" 'He died an enfeebled old dotard at five'," Jane quoted dreamily. "I want your olive."

"Here. By the way, I like the shoes."

"Thank you. Here's Rosalie. Dinner?"

"It's all ready, Miz Pa'dine," said Rosalie, hovering. "I'll call Miss Emma 'n' Mista' Scotty."

"I'll get 'em." Paradine put his head into the next room and roared, "Kids! Come and get it!"

Small feet scuttered down the stairs. Scott dashed into view, scrubbed and shining, a rebellious cowlick aimed at the zenith. Emma pursued, levering herself carefully down the steps. Halfway, she gave up the attempt to descend upright and reversed, finishing the task monkey-fashion, her small behind giving an impression of marvelous diligence upon the work in hand. Paradine watched, fascinated by the spectacle, till he was hurled back by the impact of his son's body.

"Hi, Dad!" Scott shrieked.

Paradine recovered himself and regarded Scott with dignity. "Hi, yourself. Help me in to dinner. You've dislocated at least one of my hip joints."

But Scott was already tearing into the next room, where he stepped on Jane's new shoes in an ecstasy of affection, burbled an apology, and rushed off to find his place at the dinner table. Paradine cocked up an eyebrow as he followed, Emma's pudgy hand desperately gripping his forefinger.

"Wonder what the young devil's been up to."

"No good, probably," Jane sighed. "Hello, darling. Let's see your ears."

"They're *clean*. Mickey licked 'em."

"Well, that Airedale's tongue is far cleaner than your ears," Jane pondered, making a brief examination. "Still, as long as you can hear, the dirt's only superficial."

"Fisshul?"

"Just a little, that means." Jane dragged her daughter to the table and inserted her legs into a high chair. Only lately had Emma graduated to the dignity of dining with the rest of the family, and she was, as Paradine remarked, all eaten up with pride by the prospect. Only babies spilled food, Emma had been told. As a result, she took such painstaking care in conveying her spoon to her mouth that Paradine got the jitters whenever he watched.

"A conveyor belt would be the thing for Emma," he suggested, pulling out a chair for Jane. "Small buckets of spinach arriving at her face at stated intervals."

Dinner proceeded uneventfully until Paradine happened to glance at Scott's plate. "Hello, there. Sick? Been stuffing yourself at lunch?"

Scott thoughtfully examined the food still left before him. "I've had all I need, Dad," he explained.

"You usually eat all you can hold, and a great deal more," Paradine said. "I know growing boys need several tons of foodstuff a day, but you're below par tonight. Feel O.K.?"

"Uh-huh. Honest, I've had all I need."

"All you *want?*"

"Sure. I eat different."

"Something they taught you at school?" Jane inquired.

Scott shook his head solemnly.

"Nobody taught me. I found it out myself. I use spit."

"Try again," Paradine suggested. "It's the wrong word."

"Uh—s-saliva. Hm-m-m?"

"Uh-huh. More pepsin? Is there pepsin in the salivary juices, Jane? I forget."

"There's poison in mine," Jane remarked. "Rosalie's left lumps in the mashed potatoes again."

But Paradine was interested. "You mean you're getting everything possible out of your food—no wastage—and eating less?"

Scott thought that over. "I guess so. It's not just the sp— saliva. I sort of measure how much to put in my mouth at once, and what stuff to mix up. I dunno. I just do it."

"Hm-m-m," said Paradine, making a note to check up later. "Rather a revolutionary idea." Kids often get screwy notions, but this one might not be so far off the beam. He pursed his lips. "Eventually I suppose people will eat quite differently—I mean the *way* they eat, as well as what. What they eat, I mean. Jane, our son shows signs of becoming a genius."

"Oh?"

"It's a rather good point in dietetics he just made. Did you figure it out yourself, Scott?"

"Sure," the boy said, and really believed it.

"Where'd you get the idea?"

"Oh, I—" Scott wriggled. "I dunno. It doesn't mean much, I guess."

Paradine was unreasonably disappointed. "But surely—"

"S-s-s-spit!" Emma shrieked, overcome by a sudden fit of badness. "*Spit!*" She attempted to demonstrate, but succeeded only in dribbling into her bib.

With a resigned air Jane rescued and reproved her daughter, while Paradine eyed Scott with rather puzzled interest. But it was not till after dinner, in the living room, that anything further happened.

"Any homework?"

"N-no," Scott said, flushing guiltily. To cover his embarrassment he took from his pocket a gadget he had found in the box, and began to unfold it. The result resembled a tesseract, strung with beads. Paradine didn't see it at first, but Emma did. She wanted to play with it.

"No. Lay off, Slug," Scott ordered. "You can watch me." He fumbled with the beads, making soft, interested noises. Emma extended a fat forefinger and yelped.

"Scotty," Paradine said warningly.

"I didn't hurt her."

"Bit me. It did," Emma mourned.

Paradine looked up. He frowned, staring. What in—

"Is that an abacus?" he asked. "Let's see it, please."

Somewhat unwillingly, Scott brought the gadget across to his father's chair. Paradine blinked. The "abacus," unfolded, was more than a foot square, composed of thin, rigid wires that interlocked here and there. On the wires the colored beads were strung. They could be slid back and forth, and from one support to another, even at the points of jointure. But—a pierced bead couldn't cross *interlocking* wires.

So, apparently, they weren't pierced. Paradine looked closer. Each small sphere had a deep groove running around it, so that it could be revolved and slid along the wire at the same time. Paradine tried to pull one free. It clung as though magnetically. Iron? It looked more like plastic.

The framework itself—Paradine wasn't a mathematician. But the angles formed by the wires were vaguely shocking, in their ridiculous lack of Euclidean logic. They were a maze. Perhaps that's what the gadget was—a puzzle.

"Where'd you get this?"

"Uncle Harry gave it to me," Scott said, on the spur of the moment. "Last Sunday, when he came over." Uncle Harry was out of town, a circumstance Scott well knew. At the age of seven, a boy soon learns that the vagaries of adults follow a certain definite pattern, and that they are fussy about the donors of gifts. Moreover, Uncle Harry would not return for several weeks; the expiration of that period was unimaginable to Scott, or, at least, the fact that his lie would ultimately be discovered meant less to him than the advantages of being allowed to keep the toy.

Paradine found himself growing slightly confused as he attempted to manipulate the beads. The angles were vaguely illogical. It was like a puzzle. This red bead, if slid along *this* wire to *that* junction, should reach *there*—but it didn't. A

maze, odd, but no doubt instructive. Paradine had a well-
founded feeling that he'd have no patience with the thing
himself.

Scott did, however, retiring to a corner and sliding beads
around with much fumbling and grunting. The beads *did*
sting, when Scott chose the wrong ones or tried to slide them
in the wrong direction. At last he crowed exultantly.

"I did it, Dad!"

"Eh? What? Let's see." The device looked exactly the same
to Paradine, but Scott pointed and beamed.

"I made it disappear."

"It's still there."

"That blue bead. It's gone now."

Paradine didn't believe that, so he merely snorted. Scott
puzzled over the framework again. He experimented. This
time there were no shocks, even slight. The abacus had
showed him the correct method. Now it was up to him to do
it on his own. The bizarre angles of the wires seemed a little
less confusing now, somehow.

It was a most instructive toy—

It worked, Scott thought, rather like the crystal cube. Reminded of that gadget, he took it from his pocket and relinquished the abacus to Emma, who was struck dumb with joy.
She fell to work sliding the beads, this time without protesting
against the shocks—which, indeed were very minor—and,
being imitative, she managed to make a bead disappear almost as quickly as had Scott. The blue bead reappeared—but
Scott didn't notice. He had thoughtfully retired into an angle
of the chesterfield and an overstuffed chair and amused himself with the cube.

There were the little people inside the thing, tiny manikins
much enlarged by the magnifying properties of the crystal.
They moved, all right. They built a house. It caught fire, with
realistic-seeming flames, and the little people stood by waiting. Scott puffed urgently. "Put it *out!*"

But nothing happened. Where was that queer fire engine,
with revolving arms, that had appeared before? Here it was.
It came sailing into the picture and stopped. Scott urged it
on.

This was fun. The little people really did what Scott told
them, inside of his head. If he made a mistake, they waited
till he'd found the right way. They even posed new problems
for him.

The cube, too, was a most instructive toy. It was teaching Scott, with alarming rapidity—and teaching him very entertainingly. But it gave him no really new knowledge as yet. He wasn't ready. Later . . . later. . . .

Emma grew tired of the abacus and went in search of Scott. She couldn't find him, even in his room, but once there the contents of the closet intrigued her. She discovered the box. It contained treasure-trove—a doll, which Scott had already noticed but discarded with a sneer. Squealing, Emma brought the doll downstairs, squatted in the middle of the floor and began to take it apart.

"Darling! What's that?"

"Mr. Bear!"

Obviously it wasn't Mr. Bear, who was blind, earless, but comforting in his soft fatness. But all dolls were named Mr. Bear to Emma.

Jane Paradine hesitated. "Did you take that from some other little girl?"

"I didn't. She's mine."

Scott came out from his hiding place, thrusting the cube into his pocket. "Uh—that's from Uncle Harry."

"Did Uncle Harry give that to you, Emma?"

"He gave it to me for Emma," Scott put in hastily, adding another stone to his foundation of deceit. "Last Sunday."

"You'll break it, dear."

Emma brought the doll to her mother. "She comes apart. See?"

"Oh? It—*ugh!*" Jane sucked in her breath. Paradine looked up quickly.

"What's up?"

She brought the doll over to him, hesitated and then went into the dining room, giving Paradine a significant glance. He followed, closing the door. Jane had already placed the doll on the cleared table.

"This isn't very nice is it, Denny?"

"Hm-m-m." It was rather unpleasant, at first glance. One might have expected an anatomical dummy in a medical school, but a child's doll . . .

The thing came apart in sections—skin, muscles, organs—miniature but quite perfect, as far as Paradine could see. He was interested. "Dunno. Such things haven't the same connotations to a kid."

"Look at that liver. Is it a liver?"

"Sure. Say, I—this is funny."

"What?"

"It isn't anatomically perfect, after all." Paradine pulled up a chair. "The digestive tract's too short. No large intestine. No appendix, either."

"Should Emma have a thing like this?"

"I wouldn't mind having it myself," Paradine said. "Where on earth did Harry pick it up? No, I don't see any harm in it. Adults are conditioned to react unpleasantly to innards. Kids don't. They figure they're solid inside, like a potato. Emma can get a sound working knowledge of physiology from this doll."

"But what are those? Nerves?"

"No, these are the nerves. Arteries here; veins here. Funny sort of aorta." Paradine looked baffled. "That—what's Latin for network, anyway, huh? *Rita? Rata?*"

"Rales," Jane suggested at random.

"That's a sort of breathing," Paradine said crushingly. "I can't figure out what this luminous network of stuff is. It goes all through the body, like nerves."

"Blood."

"Nope. Not circulatory, not neural. Funny! It seems to be hooked up with the lungs."

They became engrossed, puzzling over the strange doll. It was made with remarkable perfection of detail, and that in itself was strange, in view of the physiological variation from the norm. "Wait'll I get that Gould," Paradine said, and presently was comparing the doll with anatomical charts. He learned little, except to increase his bafflement.

But it was more fun than a jigsaw puzzle.

Meanwhile, in the adjoining room, Emma was sliding the beads to and fro in the abacus. The motions didn't seem so strange now. Even when the beads vanished. She could almost follow that new direction—almost. . . .

Scott panted, staring into the crystal cube and mentally directing, with many false starts, the building of a structure somewhat more complicated than the one which had been destroyed by fire. He, too, was learning—being conditioned. . . .

Paradine's mistake, from a completely anthropomorphic standpoint, was that he didn't get rid of the toys instantly. He did not realize their significance, and, by the time he did, the

progression of circumstances had got well under way. Uncle
Harry remained out of town, so Paradine couldn't check with
him. Too, the midterm exams were on, which meant arduous
mental effort and complete exhaustion at night; and Jane was
slightly ill for a week or so. Emma and Scott had free rein
with the toys.

"What," Scott asked his father one evening, "is a wabe,
Dad?"

"Wave?"

He hesitated. "I—don't *think* so. Isn't 'wabe' right?"

" 'Wabe' is Scot for 'web.' That it?"

"I don't see how," Scott muttered, and wandered off,
scowling, to amuse himself with the abacus. He was able to
handle it quite deftly now. But, with the instinct of children
for avoiding interruption, he and Emma usually played with
the toys in private. Not obviously, of course—but the more
intricate experiments were never performed under the eye of
an adult.

Scott was learning fast. What he now saw in the crystal
cube had little relationship to the original simple problems.
But they were fascinatingly technical. Had Scott realized that
his education was being guided and supervised—though
merely mechanically—he would probably have lost interest.
As it was, his initiative was never quashed.

Abacus, cube, doll and other toys the children found in the
box. . . .

Neither Paradine nor Jane guessed how much of an effect
the contents of the time machine were having on the kids.
How could they? Youngsters are instinctive dramatists, for
purposes of self-protection. They have not yet fitted themselves to the exigencies—to them partially inexplicable—of a
mature world. Moreover, their lives are complicated by human variables. They are told by one person that playing in
the mud is permissible, but that, in their excavations, they
must not uproot flowers or small trees. Another adult vetoes
mud per se. The Ten Commandments are not carved on
stone—they vary; and the children are helplessly dependent
on the caprice of those who give them birth and feed and
clothe them. And tyrannize. The young animal does not
resent that benevolent tyranny, for it is an essential part of
nature. He is, however, an individualist, and maintains his in-
tegrity by a subtle, passive fight.

Under the eyes of an adult he changes. Like an actor on

stage, when he remembers, he strives to please, and also to attract attention to himself. Such attempts are not unknown to maturity. But adults are less obvious—to other adults.

It is difficult to admit that children lack subtlety. Children are different from mature animals because they think in another way. We can more or less easily pierce the pretenses they set up, but they can do the same to us. Ruthlessly a child can destroy the pretenses of an adult. Inconoclasm is a child's perogative.

Foppishness, for example. The amenities of social intercourse, exaggerated not quite to absurdity. The gigolo. . . .

"Such *savoir-faire!* Such punctilious courtesy!" The dowager and the blonde young thing are often impressed. Men have less pleasant comments to make. But the child goes to the root of the matter.

"You're *silly!*"

How can an immature human being understand the complicated system of social relationships? He can't. To him, an exaggeration of natural courtesy is silly. In his functional structure of life patterns, it is rococo. He is an egotistic little animal who cannot visualize himself in the position of another—certainly not an adult. A self-contained, almost perfect natural unit, his wants supplied by others, the child is much like a unicellular creature floating in the bloodstream, nutriment carried to him, waste products carried away.

From the standpoint of logic, a child is rather horribly perfect. A baby must be even more perfect, but so alien to an adult that only superficial standards of comparison apply. The thought processes of an infant are completely unimaginable. But babies think, even before birth. In the womb they move and sleep, not entirely through instinct. We are conditioned to react rather peculiarly to the idea that a nearly viable embryo may think. We are surprised, shocked into laughter and repelled. Nothing human is alien.

But a baby is not human. An embryo is far less human.

That, perhaps, was why Emma learned more from the toys than did Scott. He could communicate his thoughts, of course; Emma could not, except in cryptic fragments. The matter of the scrawls, for example.

Give a young child pencil and paper, and he will draw something which looks different to him than to an adult. The absurd scribbles have little resemblance to a fire engine, but it *is* a fire engine, to a baby. Perhaps it is even three-dimensional. Babies think differently and see differently.

Paradine brooded over that, reading his paper one evening and watching Emma and Scott communicate. Scott was questioning his sister. Sometimes he did it in English. More often he had resource to gibberish and sign language. Emma tried to reply, but the handicap was too great.

Finally Scott got pencil and paper. Emma liked that. Tongue in cheek, she laboriously wrote a message. Scott took the paper, examined it and scowled.

"That isn't right, Emma," he said.

Emma nodded vigorously. She seized the pencil again and made more scrawls. Scott puzzled for a while, finally smiled rather hesitantly and got up. He vanished into the hall. Emma returned to the abacus.

Paradine rose and glanced down at the paper, with some mad thought that Emma might abruptly have mastered calligraphy. But she hadn't. The paper was covered with meaningless scrawls, of a type familiar to any parent. Paradine pursed his lips.

It might be a graph showing the mental variations of a manic-depressive cockroach, but probably wasn't. Still, it no doubt had meaning to Emma. Perhaps the scribble represented Mr. Bear.

Scott returned, looking pleased. He met Emma's gaze and nodded. Paradine felt a twinge of curiosity.

"Secrets?"

"Nope. Emma—uh—asked me to do something for her."

"Oh." Paradine, recalling instances of babies who had babbled in unknown tongues and baffled linguists, made a note to pocket the paper when the kids had finished with it. The next day he showed the scrawl to Elkins at the university. Elkins had a sound working knowledge of many unlikely languages, but he chuckled over Emma's venture into literature.

"Here's a free translation, Dennis. Quote. I don't know what this means, but I kid the hell out of my father with it. Unquote."

The two men laughed and went off to their classes. But later Paradine was to remember the incident. Especially after he met Holloway. Before that, however, months were to pass, and the situation to develop even further toward its climax.

Perhaps Paradine and Jane had evinced too much interest in the toys. Emma and Scott took to keeping them hidden, playing with them only in private. They never did it overtly, but with a certain unobtrusive caution. Nevertheless, Jane especially was somewhat troubled.

She spoke to Paradine about it one evening. "That doll Harry gave Emma."

"Yeah?"

"I was downtown today and tried to find out where it came from. No soap."

"Maybe Harry bought it in New York."

Jane was unconvinced. "I asked them about the other things, too. They showed me their stock—Johnson's is a big store, you know. But there's nothing like Emma's abacus."

"Hm-m-m." Paradine wasn't much interested. They had tickets for a show that night, and it was getting late. So the subject was dropped for the nonce.

Later it cropped up again, when a neighbor telephoned Jane.

"Scotty's never been like that, Denny. Mrs. Burns said he frightened the devil out of her Francis."

"Francis? A little fat bully of a punk, isn't he? Like his father. I broke Burns's nose for him once, when we were sophomores."

"Stop boasting and listen," Jane said, mixing a highball. "Scott showed Francis something that scared him. Hadn't you better—"

"I suppose so." Paradine listened. Noises in the next room told him the whereabouts of his son. "Scotty!"

"Bang," Scott said, and appeared smiling. "I killed 'em all. Space pirates. You want me, Dad?"

"Yes. If you don't mind leaving the space pirates unburied for a few minutes. What did you do to Francis Burns?"

Scott's blue eyes reflected incredible candor. "Huh?"

"Try hard. You can remember, I'm sure."

"Uh. Oh, that. I didn't do nothing."

"Anything," Jane corrected absently.

"Anything. Honest. I just let him look into my television set, and it—it scared him."

"Television set?"

Scott produced the crystal cube. "It isn't really that. See?"

Paradine examined the gadget, startled by the magnification. All he could see, though, was a maze of meaningless colored designs.

"Uncle Harry—"

Paradine reached for the telephone. Scott gulped. "Is—is Uncle Harry back in town?"

"Yeah."

"Well, I gotta take a bath." Scott headed for the door. Paradine met Jane's gaze and nodded significantly.

Harry was home, but disclaimed all knowledge of the peculiar toys. Rather grimly, Paradine requested Scott to bring down from his room all of the playthings. Finally they lay in a row on the table—cube, abacus, doll, helmet-like cap, several other mysterious contraptions. Scott was cross-examined. He lied valiantly for a time, but broke down at last and bawled, hiccuping his confession.

"Get the box these things came in," Paradine ordered. "Then head for bed."

"Are you—*hup!*—gonna punish me, Daddy?"

"For playing hooky and lying, yes. You know the rules. No more shows for two weeks. No sodas in the same period."

Scott gulped. "You gonna keep my things?"

"I don't know yet."

"Well—g'night, Daddy. G'night, Mom."

After the small figure had gone upstairs, Paradine dragged a chair to the table and carefully scrutinized the box. He poked thoughtfully at the focused gadgetry. Jane watched.

"What is it, Denny?"

"Dunno. Who'd leave a box of toys down by the creek?"

"It might have fallen out of a car."

"Not at that point. The road doesn't hit the creek north of the railroad trestle. Empty lots—nothing else." Paradine lit a cigarette. "Drink, honey?"

"I'll fix it." Jane went to work, her eyes troubled. She brought Paradine a glass and stood behind him, ruffling his hair with her fingers. "Is anything wrong?"

"Of course not. Only—where did these toys come from?"

"Johnson's didn't know, and they get their stock from New York."

"I've been checking up, too," Paradine admitted. "That doll"—he poked it—"rather worried me. Custom jobs, maybe, but I wish I knew who'd made 'em."

"A psychologist? That abacus—don't they give people tests with such things?"

Paradine snapped his fingers. "Right! And say, there's a guy going to speak at the university next week, fellow named Holloway, who's a child psychologist. He's a big shot, with quite a reputation. He might know something about it."

"Holloway? I don't—"

"Rex Holloway. He's—hm-m-m! He doesn't live far from here. Do you suppose he might have had these things made himself?"

Jane was examining the abacus. She grimaced and drew back. "If he did, I don't like him. But see if you can find out, Denny."

Paradine nodded. "I shall."

He drank his highball, frowning. He was vaguely worried. But he wasn't scared—yet.

Rex Holloway was a fat, shiny man, with a bald head and thick spectacles, above which his thick, black brows lay like bushy caterpillars. Paradine brought him home to dinner one night a week later. Holloway did not appear to watch the children, but nothing they did or said was lost on him. His gray eyes, shrewd and bright, missed little.

The toys fascinated him. In the living room the three adults gathered around the table, where the playthings had been placed. Holloway studied them carefully as he listened to what Jane and Paradine had to say. At last he broke his silence.

"I'm glad I came here tonight. But not completely. This is very disturbing, you know."

"Eh?" Paradine stared, and Jane's face showed her consternation. Holloway's next words did not calm them.

"We are dealing with madness."

He smiled at the shocked looks they gave him. "All children are mad, from an adult viewpoint. Ever read Hughes's *High Wind in Jamaica?*"

"I've got it." Paradine secured the little book from its shelf. Holloway extended a hand, took the book and flipped the pages till he had found the place he wanted. He read aloud:

Babies, of course, are not human—they are animals, and have a very ancient and ramified culture, as cats have, and fishes, and even snakes; the same in kind as these, but much more complicated and vivid, since babies are, after all, one of the most developed species of the lower vertebrates. In short, babies have minds which work in terms and categories of their own, which cannot be translated into the terms and categories of the human mind.

Jane tried to take that calmly, but couldn't. "You don't mean that Emma—"

"Could you think like your daughter?" Holloway asked. "Listen: 'One can no more think like a baby than one can think like a bee.'"

Paradine mixed drinks. Over his shoulder he said, "You're theorizing quite a bit, aren't you? As I get it, you're implying that babies have a culture of their own, even a high standard of intelligence."

"Not necessarily. There's no yardstick, you see. All I say is that babies think in other ways than we do. Not necessarily *better*—that's a question of relative values. But with a different matter of extension." He sought for words, grimacing.

"Fantasy," Paradine said, rather rudely but annoyed because of Emma. "Babies don't have different senses from ours."

"Who said they did?" Holloway demanded. "They use their minds in a different way, that's all. But it's quite enough!"

"I'm trying to understand," Jane said slowly. "All I can think of is my Mixmaster. It can whip up batter and potatoes, but it can squeeze oranges, too."

"Something like that. The brain's a colloid, a very complicated machine. We don't know much about its potentialities. We don't even know how much it can grasp. But it *is* known that the mind becomes conditioned as the human animal matures. It follows certain familiar theorems, and all thought thereafter is pretty well based on patterns taken for granted. Look at this." Holloway touched the abacus. "Have you experimented with it?"

"A little," Paradine said.

"But not much, eh?"

"Well—"

"Why not?"

"It's pointless," Paradine complained. "Even a puzzle has to have some logic. But those crazy angles—"

"Your mind has been conditioned to Euclid," Holloway said. "So this—thing—bores us, and seems pointless. But a child knows nothing of Euclid. A different sort of geometry from ours wouldn't impress him as being illogical. He believes what he sees."

"Are you trying to tell me that this gadget's got a fourth-dimensional extension?" Paradine demanded.

"Not visually, anyway," Holloway denied. "All I say is that our minds, conditioned to Euclid, can see nothing in this but an illogical tangle of wires. But a child—especially a baby— might see more. Not at first. It'd be a puzzle, of course. Only a child wouldn't be handicapped by too many preconceived ideas."

"Hardening of the thought arteries," Jane interjected.

Paradine was not convinced. "Then a baby could work calculus better than Einstein? No, I don't mean that. I can see your point, more or less clearly. Only—"

"Well, look. Let's suppose there are two kinds of geometry; we'll limit it, for the sake of the example. Our kind, Euclidean, and another, we'll call x. X hasn't much relationship to Euclid. It's based on different theorems. Two and two needn't equal four in it; they could equal y^2, or they might not even *equal*. A baby's mind is not yet conditioned, except by certain questionable factors of heredity and environment. Start the infant on Euclid—"

"Poor kid," Jane said.

Holloway shot her a quick glance. "The basis of Euclid. Alphabet blocks. Math, geometry, algebra—they come much later. We're familiar with that development. On the other hand, start the baby with the basic principles of our x logic."

"Blocks? What kind?"

Holloway looked at the abacus. "It wouldn't make much sense to us. But we've been conditioned to Euclid."

Paradine poured himself a stiff shot of whisky. "That's pretty awful. You're not limiting to math."

"Right! I'm not limiting it at all. How can I? I'm not conditioned to x logic."

"There's the answer," Jane said, with a sigh of relief. "Who is? It'd take such a person to make the sort of toys you apparently think these are."

Holloway nodded, his eyes, behind the thick lenses, blinking. "Such people may exist."

"Where?"

"They might prefer to keep hidden."

"Supermen?"

"I wish I knew. You see, Paradine, we've got yardstick trouble again. By our standards these people might seem super-dupers in certain respects. In others they might seem moronic. It's not a quantitative difference; it's qualitative. They *think* different. And I'm sure we can do things they can't."

"Maybe they wouldn't want to," Jane said.

Paradine tapped the fused gadgetry on the box. "What about this? It implies—"

"A purpose, sure."

"Transportation?"

"One thinks of that first. If so, the box might have come from anywhere."

"Where—things are—*different?*" Paradine asked slowly.

"Exactly. In space, or even time. I don't know; I'm a psychologist. Unfortunately I'm conditioned to Euclid, too."

"Funny place it must be," Jane said. "Denny, get rid of those toys."

"I intend to."

Holloway picked up the crystal cube. "Did you question the children much?"

Paradine said, "Yeah. Scott said there were people in that cube when he first looked. I asked him what was in it now."

"What did he say?" The psychologist's eyes widened.

"He said they were building a place. His exact words. I asked him who—people? But he couldn't explain."

"No, I suppose not," Holloway muttered. "It must be progressive. How long have the children had these toys?"

"About three months, I guess."

"Time enough. The perfect toy, you see, is both instructive and mechanical. It should do things, to interest a child, and it should teach, preferably unobtrusively. Simple problems at first. Later—"

"*X* logic," Jane said, white-faced.

Paradine cursed under his breath. "Emma and Scott are perfectly normal!"

"Do you know how their minds work—now?"

Holloway didn't pursue the thought. He fingered the doll. "It would be interesting to know the conditions of the place where these things came from. Induction doesn't help a great deal, though. Too many factors are missing. We can't visualize a world based on the x factor—environment adjusted to minds thinking in x patterns. This luminous network inside the doll. It could be anything. It could exist inside us, though we haven't discovered it yet. When we find the right stain—" He shrugged. "What do you make of this?"

It was a crimson globe, two inches in diameter, with a protruding knob upon its surface.

"What could anyone make of it?"

"Scott? Emma?"

"I hadn't even seen it till about three weeks ago. Then Emma started to play with it." Paradine nibbled his lip. "After that, Scott got interested."

"Just what do they do?"

"Hold it up in front of them and move it back and forth. No particular pattern of motion."

"No Euclidean pattern," Holloway corrected. "At first they couldn't understand the toy's purpose. They had to be educated up to it."

"That's horrible," Jane said.

"Not to them. Emma is probably quicker at understanding x than is Scott, for her mind isn't yet conditioned to this environment."

Paradine said, "But I can remember plenty of things I did as a child. Even as a baby."

"Well?"

"Was I—mad then?"

"The things you don't remember are the criterion of your madness," Holloway retorted. "But I use the word 'madness' purely as a convenient symbol for the variation from the known human norm. The arbitrary standard of sanity."

Jane put down her glass. "You've said that induction was difficult, Mr. Holloway. But it seems to me you're making a great deal of it from very little. After all, these toys—"

"I *am* a psychologist, and I've specialized in children. I'm not a layman. These toys mean a great deal to me, chiefly because they mean so little."

"You might be wrong."

"Well, I rather hope I am. I'd like to examine the children."

Jane rose in arms. "How?"

After Holloway had explained, she nodded, though still a bit hesitantly. "Well, that's all right. But they're not guinea pigs."

The psychologist patted the air with a plump hand. "My dear girl! I'm not a Frankenstein. To me the individual is the prime factor—naturally, since I work with minds. If there's anything wrong with the youngsters, I want to cure them."

Paradine put down his cigarette and slowly watched blue smoke spiral up, wavering in an unfelt draught. "Can you give a prognosis?"

"I'll try. That's all I can say. If the undeveloped minds have been turned into the *x* channel, it's necessary to divert them back. I'm not saying that's the wisest thing to do, but it probably is from our standards. After all, Emma and Scott will have to live in this world."

"Yeah. Yeah. I can't believe there's much wrong. They seem about average, thoroughly normal."

"Superficially they may seem so. They've no reason for acting abnormally, have they? And how can you tell if they—think differently?"

"I'll call 'em," Paradine said.

"Make it informal, then. I don't want them to be on guard."

Jane nodded toward the toys. Holloway said, "Leave the stuff there, eh?"

But the psychologist, after Emma and Scott were summoned, made no immediate move toward direct questioning. He managed to draw Scott unobtrusively into the conversation, dropping key words now and then. Nothing so obvious as a word-association test; cooperation is necessary for that.

The most interesting development occurred when Holloway took up the abacus. "Mind showing me how this works?"

Scott hesitated. "Yes, sir. Like this." He slid a bead deftly through the maze, in a tangled course, so swiftly that no one was quite sure whether or not it ultimately vanished. It might have been merely legerdemain. Then, again—

Holloway tried. Scott watched, wrinkling his nose.

"That's right?"

"Uh-huh. It's gotta go *there*."

"Here? Why?"

"Well, that's the only way to make it work."

But Holloway was conditioned to Euclid. There was no apparent reason why the bead should slide from this particular wire to the other. It looked like a random factor. Also, Holloway suddenly noticed, this wasn't the path the bead had taken previously, when Scott had worked the puzzle. At least, as well as he could tell.

"Will you show me again?"

Scott did, and twice more, on request. Holloway blinked through his glasses. Random, yes. And a variable. Scott moved the bead along a different course each time.

Somehow, none of the adults could tell whether or not the bead vanished. If they had expected to see it disappear, their reactions might have been different.

In the end nothing was solved. Holloway, as he said good night, seemed ill at ease.

"May I come again?"

"I wish you would," Jane told him. "Any time. You still think—"

He nodded. "The children's minds are not reacting normally. They're not dull at all, but I've the most extraordinary impression that they arrive at conclusions in a way we don't understand. As though they used algebra while we used geometry. The same conclusion, but a different method of reaching it."

"What about the toys?" Paradine asked suddenly.

"Keep them out of the way. I'd like to borrow them, if I may."

That night Paradine slept badly. Holloway's parallel had been ill chosen. It led to disturbing theories. The x factor. . . . The children were using the equivalent of algebraic reasoning, while adults used geometry.

Fair enough. Only. . . .

Algebra can give you answers that geometry cannot, since there are certain terms and symbols which cannot be expressed geometrically. Suppose x logic showed conclusions inconceivable to an adult mind.

"Damn!" Paradine whispered. Jane stirred beside him.

"Dear? Can't you sleep either?"

"No." He got up and went into the next room. Emma slept peacefully as a cherub, her fat arm curled around Mr. Bear. Through the open doorway Paradine could see Scott's dark head motionless on the pillow.

Jane was beside him. He slipped his arm around her.

"Poor little people," she murmured. "And Holloway called them mad. I think we're the ones who are crazy, Dennis."

"Uh-huh. We've got jitters."

Scott stirred in his sleep. Without awakening, he called what was obviously a question, though it did not seem to be in any particular language. Emma gave a little mewling cry that changed pitch sharply.

She had not wakened. The children lay without stirring.

But, Paradine thought, with a sudden sickness in his middle, it was exactly as though Scott had asked Emma something, and she had replied.

Had their minds changed so that even—sleep was different to them?

He thrust the thought away. "You'll catch cold. Let's get back to bed. Want a drink?"

"I think I do," Jane said, watching Emma. Her hand reached out blindly toward the child; she drew it back. "Come on. We'll wake the kids."

They drank a little brandy together, but said nothing. Jane cried in her sleep, later.

Scott was not awake, but his mind worked in slow, careful building. Thus—

"They'll take the toys away. The fat man—listava dangerous, maybe. But the Ghoric direction won't show—evankrus dun hasn't them. Intransdection—bright and shiny. Emma. She's more khopranik-high now than—I still don't see how to—thavarar lixery dist. . . ."

A little of Scott's thoughts could still be understood. But Emma had become conditioned to x much faster.

She was thinking, too.

Not like an adult or a child. Not even like a human being. Except, perhaps, a human being of a type shockingly unfamiliar to genus Homo.

Sometimes, Scott himself had difficulty in following her thoughts.

If it had not been for Holloway, life might have settled back into an almost normal routine. The toys were no longer active reminders. Emma still enjoyed her dolls and sandpile, with a thoroughly explicable delight. Scott was satisfied with baseball and his chemical set. They did everything other children did, and evinced few, if any, flashes of abnormality. But Holloway seemed to be an alarmist.

He was having the toys tested, with rather idiotic results. He drew endless charts and diagrams, corresponded with mathematicians, engineers, and other psychologists, and went quietly crazy trying to find rhyme or reason in the construction of the gadgets. The box itself, with its cryptic machinery, told nothing. Fusing had melted too much of the stuff into slag. But the toys. . . .

It was the random element that baffled investigation. Even that was a matter of semantics. For Holloway was convinced that it wasn't really random. There just weren't enough known factors. No adult could work the abacus, for example. And Holloway thoughtfully refrained from letting a child play with the thing.

The crystal cube was similarly cryptic. It showed a mad pattern of colors, which sometimes moved. In this it resembled a kaleidoscope. But the shifting of balance and gravity didn't affect it. Again the random factor.

Or, rather, the unknown. The x pattern. Eventually, Paradine and Jane slipped back into something like complacence, with a feeling that the children had been cured of their mental quirk, now that the contributing cause had been removed. Certain of the actions of Emma and Scott gave them every reason to quit worrying.

For the kids enjoyed swimming, hiking, movies, games, the normal functional toys of this particular time-sector. It was true that they failed to master certain rather puzzling mechanical devices which involved some calculation. A three-dimensional jigsaw globe Paradine had picked up, for example. But he found that difficult himself.

Once in a while there were lapses. Scott was hiking with his father one Saturday afternoon, and the two had paused at the summit of a hill. Beneath them a rather lovely valley was spread.

"Pretty, isn't it?" Paradine remarked.

Scott examined the scene gravely. "It's all wrong," he said.

"Eh?"

"I dunno."

"What's wrong about it?"

"Gee." Scott lapsed into puzzled silence. "I dunno."

The children had missed their toys, but not for long. Emma recovered first, though Scott still moped. He held unintelligible conversations with his sister, and studied meaningless scrawls she drew on paper he supplied. It was almost as though he were consulting her, anent difficult problems beyond his grasp.

If Emma understood more, Scott had more real intelligence, and manipulatory skill as well. He built a gadget with his Meccano set, but was dissatisfied. The apparent cause of his dissatisfaction was exactly why Paradine was relieved when he viewed the structure. It was the sort of thing a normal boy would make, vaguely reminiscent of a cubistic ship.

It was a bit too normal to please Scott. He asked Emma more questions, though in private. She thought for a time, and then made more scrawls, with an awkward clutched pencil.

"Can you read that stuff?" Jane asked her son one morning.

"Not read it, exactly. I can tell what she means. Not all the time, but mostly."

"Is it writing?"

"N-no. It doesn't mean what it *looks* like."

"Symbolism," Paradine suggested over his coffee.

Jane looked at him, her eyes widening. "Denny—"

He winked and shook his head. Later, when they were alone, he said, "Don't let Holloway upset you. I'm not implying that the kids are corresponding in an unknown tongue. If Emma draws a squiggle and says it's a flower, that's an arbitrary rule—Scott remembers that. Next time she draws the same sort of squiggle, or tries to—well!"

"Sure," Jane said doubtfully. "Have you noticed Scott's been doing a lot of reading lately?"

"I noticed. Nothing unusual, though. No Kant or Spinoza."

"He browses, that's all."

"Well, so did I, at his age," Paradine said, and went off to his morning classes. He lunched with Holloway, which was becoming a daily habit, and spoke of Emma's literary endeavors.

"Was I right about symbolism, Rex?"

The psychologist nodded. "Quite right. Our own language is nothing but arbitrary symbolism now. At least in its application. Look here." On his napkin he drew a very narrow ellipse. "What's that?"

"You mean what does it represent?"

"Yes. What does it suggest to you? It could be a crude representation of—what?"

"Plenty of things," Paradine said. "Rim of a glass. A fried egg. A loaf of French bread. A cigar."

Holloway added a little triangle to his drawing, apex joined to one end of the ellipse. He looked up at Paradine.

"A fish," the latter said instantly.

"Our familiar symbol for a fish. Even without fins, eyes or mouth, it's recognizable, because we've been conditioned to identify this particular shape with our mental picture of a fish. The basis of a rebus. A symbol, to us, means a lot more than what we actually see on paper. What's in your mind when you look at this sketch?"

"Why—a fish."

"Keep going. What do you visualize? Everything!"

"Scales," Paradine said slowly, looking into space. "Water. Foam. A fish's eyes. The fins. The colors."

"So the symbol represents a lot more than just the abstract idea *fish*. Note the connotation's that of a noun, not a verb. It's harder to express actions by symbolism, you know. Anyway—reverse the process. Suppose you want to make a symbol for some concrete noun, say *bird*. Draw it."

Paradine drew two connected arcs, concavities down.

"The lowest common denominator," Holloway nodded. "The natural tendency is to simplify. Especially when a child is seeing something for the first time and has few standards of comparison. He tries to identify the new thing with what's already familiar to him. Ever notice how a child draws the ocean?" He didn't wait for an answer; he went on.

"A series of jagged points. Like the oscillating line on a seismograph. When I first saw the Pacific, I was about three. I remember it pretty clearly. It looked—tilted. A flat plain, slanted at an angle. The waves were regular triangles, apex upward. Now, I didn't *see* them stylized that way, but later, remembering, I had to find some familiar standard of comparison. Which is the only way of getting any conception of an entirely new thing. The average child tries to draw these regular triangles, but his coordination's poor. He gets a seismograph pattern."

"All of which means what?"

"A child sees the ocean. He stylizes it. He draws a certain definite pattern, symbolic, to him, of the sea. Emma's scrawls may be symbols, too. I don't mean that the world looks different to her—brighter, perhaps, and sharper, more vivid and with a slackening of perception above her eye level. What I do mean is that her thought processes are different, that she translates what she sees into abnormal symbols."

"You still believe—"

"Yes, I do. Her mind has been conditioned unusually. It may be that she breaks down what she sees into simple, obvious patterns—and realizes a significance to those patterns that we can't understand. Like the abacus. She saw a pattern in that, though to us it was completely random."

Paradine abruptly decided to taper off these luncheon engagements with Holloway. The man was an alarmist. His theories were growing more fantastic than ever, and he dragged in anything, applicable or not, that would support them.

Rather sardonically he said, "Do you mean Emma's communicating with Scott in an unknown language?"

"In symbols for which she hasn't any words. I'm sure Scott understands a great deal of those—scrawls. To him, an isosceles triangle may represent any factor, though probably a concrete noun. Would a man who knew nothing of chemistry understand what H_2O meant? Would he realize that the symbol could evoke a picture of the ocean?"

Paradine didn't answer. Instead, he mentioned to Holloway Scott's curious remark that the landscape, from the hill, had looked all wrong. A moment later, he was inclined to regret his impulse, for the psychologist was off again.

"Scott's thought patterns are building up to a sum that doesn't equal this world. Perhaps he's subconsciously expecting to see the world where those toys came from."

Paradine stopped listening. Enough was enough. The kids were getting along all right, and the only remaining disturbing factor was Holloway himself. That night, however, Scott evinced an interest, later significant, in eels.

There was nothing apparently harmful in natural history. Paradine explained about eels.

"But where do they lay their eggs? Or do they?"

"That's still a mystery. Their spawning grounds are unknown. Maybe the Sargasso Sea, or the deeps, where the pressure can help them force the young out of their bodies."

"Funny," Scott said, thinking deeply.

"Salmon do the same thing, more or less. They go up rivers to spawn." Paradine went into detail. Scott was fascinated.

"But that's *right*, Dad. They're born in the river, and when they learn how to swim, they go down to the sea. And they come back to lay their eggs, huh?"

"Right."

"Only they wouldn't *come* back," Scott pondered. "They'd just send their eggs—"

"It'd take a very long ovipositor," Paradine said, and vouchsafed some well-chosen remarks upon oviparity.

His son wasn't entirely satisfied. Flowers, he contended, sent their seeds long distances.

"They don't guide them. Not many find fertile soil."

"Flowers haven't got brains, though. Dad, why do people live *here?*"

"Glendale?"

"No— *here.* This whole place. It isn't all there is, I bet."

"Do you mean the other planets?"

Scott was hesitant. "This is only—part of the big place. It's like the river where the salmon go. Why don't people go on down to the ocean when they grow up?"

Paradine realized that Scott was speaking figuratively. He felt a brief chill. The—ocean?

The young of the species are not conditioned to live in the more complete world of their parents. Having developed sufficiently, they enter that world. Later they breed. The fertilized eggs are buried in the sand, far up the river, where later they hatch.

And they learn. Instinct alone is fatally slow. Especially in the case of a specialized genus, unable to cope even with this world, unable to feed or drink or survive, unless someone has foresightedly provided for those needs.

The young, fed and tended, would survive. There would be incubators and robots. They would survive, but they would not know how to swim downstream, to the vaster world of the ocean.

So they must be taught. They must be trained and conditioned in many ways.

Painlessly, subtly, unobtrusively. Children love toys that do things, and if those toys teach at the same time. . . .

In the latter half of the nineteenth century an Englishman sat on a grassy bank near a stream. A very small girl lay near him, staring up at the sky. She had discarded a curious toy with which she had been playing, and now was murmuring a wordless little song, to which the man listened with half an ear.

"What was that, my dear?" he asked at last.

"Just something I made up, Uncle Charles."

"Sing it again." He pulled out a notebook.

The girl obeyed.

"Does it mean anything?"

She nodded. "Oh, yes. Like the stories I tell you, you know."

"They're wonderful stories, dear."

"And you'll put them in a book someday?"

"Yes, but I must change them quite a lot, or no one would understand. But I don't think I'll change your little song."

"You mustn't. If you did, it wouldn't mean anything."

"I won't change that stanza, anyway," he promised. "Just what does it mean?"

"It's the way out, I think," the girl said doubtfully. "I'm not sure yet. My magic toys told me."

"I wish I knew what London shop sold these marvelous toys!"

"Mama bought them for me. She's dead. Papa doesn't care."

She lied. She had found the toys in a box one day, as she played by the Thames. And they were indeed wonderful.

Her little song—Uncle Charles thought it didn't mean anything. (He wasn't her real uncle, she parenthesized. But he was nice.) The song meant a great deal. It was the way. Presently she would do what it said, and then. . . .

But she was already too old. She never found the way.

Paradine had dropped Holloway. Jane had taken a dislike to him, naturally enough, since what she wanted most of all was to have her fears calmed. Since Scott and Emma acted normally now, Jane felt satisfied. It was partly wishful thinking, to which Paradine could not entirely subscribe.

Scott kept bringing gadgets to Emma for her approval. Usually she'd shake her head. Sometimes she would look doubtful. Very occasionally she would signify agreement. Then there would be an hour of laborious, crazy scribbling on scraps of notepaper, and Scott, after studying the notations, would arrange and rearrange his rocks, bits of machinery, candle ends and assorted junk. Each day the maid cleaned them away, and each day Scott began again.

He condescended to explain a little to his puzzled father, who could see no rhyme or reason in the game.

"But why this pebble right here?"

"It's hard and round, Dad. It *belongs* there."

"So is this one hard and round."

"Well, that's got vaseline on it. When you get that far, you can't see just a hard, round thing."

"What comes next? This candle?"

Scott looked disgusted. "That's toward the end. The iron ring's next."

It was, Paradine thought, like a scout trail through the woods, markers in a labyrinth. But here again was the random factor. Logic halted—familiar logic—at Scott's motives in arranging the junk as he did.

Paradine went out. Over his shoulder he saw Scott pull a crumpled piece of paper and a pencil from his pocket and head for Emma, who was squatted in a corner thinking things over.

Well. . . .

Jane was lunching with Uncle Harry, and, on this hot Sunday afternoon, there was little to do but read the papers. Paradine settled himself in the coolest place he could find, with a Collins, and lost himself in the comic strips.

An hour later a clatter of feet upstairs roused him from his doze. Scott's voice was crying exultantly, "This is it, Slug! Come on!"

Paradine stood up quickly, frowning. As he went into the hall the telephone began to ring. Jane had promised to call. . . .

His hand was on the receiver when Emma's faint voice squealed with excitement. Paradine grimaced. What the devil was going on upstairs?

Scott shrieked, "Look out! This way!"

Paradine, his mouth working, his nerves ridiculously tense, forgot the phone and raced up the stairs. The door of Scott's room was open.

The children were vanishing.

They went in fragments, like thick smoke in a wind, or like movement in a distorting mirror. Hand in hand they went, in a direction Paradine could not understand, and as he blinked there on the threshold, they were gone.

"Emma!" he said, dry-throated. *"Scotty!"*

On the carpet lay a pattern of markers, pebbles, an iron ring—junk. A random pattern. A crumpled sheet of paper blew towards Paradine.

He picked it up automatically.

"Kids. Where are you? Don't hide—*Emma! SCOTTY!*"

Downstairs the telephone stopped its shrill, monotonous ringing. Paradine looked at the paper he held.

It was a leaf torn from a book. There were interlineations and marginal notes, in Emma's meaningless scrawl. A stanza of verse had been so underlined and scribbled over that it was almost illegible, but Paradine was thoroughly familiar with *Through the Looking Glass*. His memory gave him the words—

> *'Twas brillig, and the slithy toves*
> *Did gyre and gimble in the wabe:*
> *All mimsy were the borogoves,*
> *And the mome raths outgrabe.*

Idiotically he thought: Humpty Dumpty explained it. A wabe is the plot of grass around a sundial. A sundial. Time. It has something to do with time. A long time ago Scotty asked me what a wabe was. Symbolism.

'Twas brillig . . .

A perfect mathematical formula, giving all the conditions, in symbolism the children had finally understood. The junk on the floor. The toves had to be made slithy—vaseline?—and they had to be placed in a certain relationship, so that they'd gyre and gimble.

Lunacy!

But it had not been lunacy to Emma and Scott. They thought differently. They used x logic. Those notes Emma had made on the page—she'd translated Carroll's words into symbols both she and Scott could understand.

The random factor had made sense to the children. They had fulfilled the conditions of the time-span equation. *And the mome raths outgrabe. . . .*

Paradine made a rather ghastly little sound, deep in his throat. He looked at the crazy pattern on the carpet. If he could follow it, as the kids had done— But he couldn't. The pattern was senseless. The random factor defeated him. He was conditioned to Euclid.

Even if he went insane, he still couldn't do it. It would be the wrong kind of lunacy.

His mind had stopped working now. But in a moment the stasis of incredulous horror would pass—Paradine crumpled the page in his fingers. "Emma! Scotty!" he called in a dead voice, as though he could expect no response.

Sunlight slanted through the open windows, brightening the golden pelt of Mr. Bear. Downstairs the ringing of the telephone began again.

Q.U.R.

Astounding,

March

by Anthony Boucher
(William Anthony Parker White)
(1911-1968)

"Anthony Boucher" was the name used by William Anthony Parker White for most of his science fiction and fantasy stories, mystery novels and shorts, and mystery criticism. He employed the name "H. H. Holmes" for much of his excellent sf criticism for both the Chicago Sun Times *and* The New York Tribune *in the fifties and early sixties, as well as for two mystery novels. A man of great wisdom and wit, he is best known in the sf field as the founding coeditor (with the late J. Francis McComas) of* The Magazine of Fantasy and Science Fiction *and as the author of a number of outstanding sf and fantasy stories.*

"Q.U.R.," which appeared as by "Holmes," is one of the earliest treatments of a robot which exists in other than humanoid form, an innovative as well as an outstanding story.

(I have somehow developed the notion that I have a patent on robot stories or, at the very least, that no one's robots, either in reality or fiction, are allowed to deviate from the Three Laws of Robotics. That's just fantasy on my part but it's a harmless fantasy, I hope. In any case, my robots are not usuform and I have on occasion argued vehemently against usuformity. However, I always liked Tony Boucher so much (who didn't?) that I wouldn't have dreamed of arguing with him. If he wants to infringe on my patent rights, why let him, say I. And if you're wondering what usuformity is, read the story.—I.A.)

It's got so the young sprouts nowadays seem never to have heard of androids. Oh, they look at them in museums and they read the references to them in the literature of the time, but they never seem to realize how essential a part of life androids once were, how our whole civilization, in fact, depended on them. And when you say you got your start in life as troubleshooter for an android factory, they look at you as though you'd worked in two-dimensional shows way back before the sollies, as though you ought to be in a museum yourself.

Now I'll admit I'm no infant. I'll never see a hundred again. But I'm no antique either. And I think it's a crying shame that the rising generation is so completely out of touch with the last century. Not that I ever intended to be writing my memoirs; I didn't exactly construct my life to that end. But somebody's got to tell the real story of what androids meant and how they ceased to mean it. And I'm the man to tell it, because I'm the man who discovered Dugg Quinby.

Yes, I said Quinby. Dugglesmarther H. Quinby, the Q. in Q. U. R. The man who made your life run the way it does today. And I found him.

That summer was a hell of a season for a trouble shooter for androids. There was nothing but trouble. My five-hour day stretched to eight, and even ten and twelve while I dashed all over New Washington checking on one android after another that had cracked up. And maybe you know how hot the Metropolitan District gets in summer, even worse than the rest of Oklahoma.

Because my job wasn't one that you could carry on comfortably in conditioned buildings and streets, it meant going outside and topside and everywhere that a robot might work. We called the androids robots then. We hadn't conceived of any kind of robot that wasn't an android or at least a naturoid of some sort.

And these breakdowns were striking everywhere, hitting robots in every line of activity. Even the Martoids and Veneroids that some ex-colonists fancied for servants. It would be an arm that went limp or a leg that crumpled up or a tentacle that collapsed. Sometimes mental trouble, too, slight indications of a tendency toward insubordination, even a sort of mania that wasn't supposed to be in their makeup. And the thing kept spreading and getting worse. Any manifestation like this among living beings, and you'd think of an epidemic. But what germ could attack tempered duralite?

The worst of it was there was nothing wrong with them. Nothing that I could find, and to me that meant plain nothing. You don't get to be head troubleshooter of Robinc if anything can get past you. And the second worst was that it was hitting my own staff. I had had six robots under me— plenty to cover the usual normal amount of trouble. Now I had two, and I needed forty.

So all in all I wasn't happy that afternoon. It didn't make me any happier to see a crowd in front of the Sunspot engaged in the merry pastime of Venusian-baiting. It was never safe for one of the little green fellows to venture out of the Venusian ghetto; this sport was way too common a spectacle.

They'd got his vapor inhalator away from him. That was all there was to the game, but that was enough. No extraphysical torment was needed. There the poor giller lay on the sidewalk, sprawled and gasping like a fish out of water, which he practically was. The men—factory executives mostly, and a few office foremen—made a circle around him and laughed. There was supposed to be something hilariously funny about the struggles of a giller drowning in air, though I never could see it myself.

Oh, they'd give him back his inhalator just in time. They never killed them off; the few Venusians around had their uses, particularly for repair work on the Veneroid robots that were used under water. But meanwhile there'd be some fun.

Despite the heat of the day, I shuddered a little. Then I crossed to the other side of the street. I couldn't watch the game. But I turned back when I heard one loud shout of fury.

That was when I found Dugg Quinby. That shout was the only sound he made. He was ragingly silent as he plowed through that mass of men, found the biggest of them, snatched the inhalator away from him, and restored it to its gasping owner. But there was noise enough from the others.

Ever try to take a bone from a dog? Or a cigar from a Martian mountaineer? Well, this was worse. Those boys objected to having their fun spoiled, and they expressed their objection forcibly.

I liked this young blond giant that had plowed in there. I

liked him because his action had asked me what I was doing crossing over to the other side of the street, and I didn't have an answer. The only way even to try to answer was to cross back.

Androids or Q. U. R., single-drive space ships or modern multiples, one thing that doesn't change much is a brawl, and this was a good one. I don't know who delivered the right that met my chin as I waded in, and I don't know who it was meant for, but it was just what I needed. Not straight enough to do more than daze me for a minute, but just hard enough to rouse my fighting spirit to the point of the hell with anything but finding targets for my knuckles. I avenged the Venusian, I avenged the blond youth, I avenged the heat of the day and the plague of the robots. I avenged my job and my corns and the hangover I had two weeks ago.

The first detail that comes clear is sitting inside the Sunspot I don't know how much later. The blond boy was with me, and so was one of the factory men. We all seemed to be the best of friends, and there wasn't any telling whose blood was which.

Guzub was beaming at us. When you know your Martians pretty well you learn that that trick of shutting the middle eye is a beam. "You zure bolished 'em ub, boys," he gurgled.

The factory man felt of his neck and decided his head was still there. "Guzub," he declared, "I've leaned me a lesson: From now on any green giller is safe around me."

"That'z the zbird," Guzub glurked. "Avder all, we're all beings, ain'd we? Now, wad'll id be?"

Guzub was hurt when the blond youth ordered milk, but delighted when the factory man said he'd have a Three Planet with a double shot of margil. I'm no teetotaler, but I don't go for these strong drinks; I stuck to my usual straight whiskey.

We exchanged names while we waited. Mike Warren, the factory man was; and the other—but then I tipped that off already. That was Quimby. They both knew me by name.

"So you're with Robinc," Mike said. "I want to have a talk with you about that sometime. My brother-in-law's got a new use for a robot that could make somebody, including me, a pile of credits, and I can't get a hearing any place."

"Glad to," I said, not paying too much attention. Everybody's got a new use for a robot, just like writers tell me everybody's got a swell idea for a solly.

Dugg Quinby had been staring straight ahead of him and not listening. Now he said, "What I don't see is why."

"Well," Mike began, "it seems like he was stuck once on the lunar desert and—"

"Uh-huh. Not that. What I don't see is why Venusians. Why we act that way about them, I mean. After all, they're more or less like us. They're featherless bipeds, pretty much on our general model. And we treat them like they weren't even beings. While Martians are a different shape of life altogether, but we don't have ghettos for them or Martian-baiting."

"That's just it," said Mike. "The gillers are too much like us. They're like a cartoon of us. We see them, and they're like a dirty joke on humans, and we see red. I mean," he added hastily, his hand rubbing his neck, "that's the way I used to feel. I was just trying to explain."

"Nuts," I said. "It's all a matter of historical parallel. We licked the pants—which they don't wear—off the Venusians in the First War of Conquest, so we feel we can push 'em around. The Second War of Conquest went sour on us and damned near put an end to the Empire and the race to boot, so we've got a healthy respect for the Martians." I looked over at the bartender, his tentacles industriously plying an impressive array of bottles and a gleaming duralite shaker. "We only persecute the ones it's safe to persecute."

Quinby frowned. "It's bad enough to do what no being ought to do, but to do it only when you know you can get away with it—I've been reading," he announced abruptly, as though it were a challenge to another fight.

Mike grunted. "Sollies and telecasts are enough for a man, I always say. You get to reading and you get mixed up."

"Do you think you aren't mixed up without it? Do you think you aren't all mixed up? If people would only try to look at things straight—"

"What have you been reading?" I asked.

"Old stuff. Dating, oh I guess, a millennium or so back. There were people then that used to write a lot about the Brotherhood of Man. They said good things. And it all means something to us now if you translate it into the Brotherhood of Beings. Man is unified now, but what's the result? The doctrine of Terrene Supremacy."

Guzub brought the drinks and we forked out our credits.
When he heard the phrase "Terrene Supremacy" his left eyelid went into that little quiver that is the Martian expression
of polite incredulity but he said nothing.

Quinby picked up his milk. "It's all because nobody looks
at things straight. Everybody looks around the corners of his
own prejudices. If you look at a problem straight, there isn't
a problem. That's what I'm trying to do," he said with that
earnestness you never come back to after youth. "I'm trying
to train myself to look straight."

"So there isn't a problem. No problems at all." I thought
of the day I'd had and the jobs still ahead of me and I
snorted. And then I had an idea and calmly, between swal-
lows of whiskey, changed the course of terrene civilization.
"I've got problems," I asserted. "How'd you like to look
straight at them? Are you working now?"

"I'm in my free-lance period," he said. "I've finished technical college and I'm not due for my final occupation analysis
for another year."

"All right," I said. "How's about it?"

Slowly he nodded.

"If you can look," said Mike, wobbling his neck, "as
straight as you can hit—"

I was back in my office when the call came from the
spaceport. I'd seen Thuringer's face red before, but never
purple. He had trouble speaking, but he finally sputtered out,
"Somebody did a lousy job of sterilization on your new assistant's parents."

"What seems to be the trouble?" I asked in my soothingest
manner.

"Trouble! The man's lunatic stock. Not a doubt. When you
see what he's done to—" He shuddered. He reached out to
switch the ike-range, but changed his mind. "Uh-huh. Come
over here and see it for yourself. You wouldn't believe it. But
come quick, before I go and apply for sterilization myself."

We had a special private tube to the space port; they used
so many of our robots. It took me less than five minutes to
get there. A robot parked my bus and another robot took me
up in the lift. It was a relief to see two in good working order, though I noticed that the second one showed signs of incipient limpness in his left arm. Since he ran the lift with his

right, it didn't really matter, but Robinc had principles of
perfection.

Thuringer's robot secretary said, "Tower room," and I
went on up. The spaceport manager scanned me and gave the
click that meant the beam was on. The tower door opened as
I walked in.

I don't know what I'd expected to see. I couldn't imagine
what would get the hard-boiled Thuringer into such a blasting
dither. This had been the first job that I'd tried Quinby out
on, and a routine piece of work it was, or should have been
Routine, that is, in these damnable times. The robot which
operated the signal tower had gone limp in the legs and one
arm. He'd been quoted as saying some pretty strange things
on the beam, too. Backsass to pilots and insubordinate mut-
terings.

The first thing I saw was a neat pile of scrap in the middle
of the room. Some of it looked like robot parts. The next
thing I saw was Thuringer, who had gone from purple to a
kind of rosy black. "It's getting me!" he burst out. "I sit here
and watch it and I'm going mad! Do something, man! Then
go out and annihilate your assistant, but do something first!'

I looked where he pointed. I'd been in this tower control
room before. The panel had a mike and an ike, a speaker and
a viewer, and a set of directional lights. In front of it there
used to be a chair where the robot sat, talking on the beam
and watching the indicators.

Now there was no chair. And no robot. There was a table,
and on the table was a box. And from that box there extended one arm, which was alive. That arm punched regularly
and correctly at the lights, and out of the box there issued the
familiar guiding voice.

I walked around and got a gander at the front of the box.
It had eyes and a mouth and a couple of holes that it took
me a minute to spot as ear holes. It was like a line with two
dots above and two below it, so:

It was like no face that ever was in nature, but it could obviously see and hear and talk.

Thuringer moaned. "And that's what you call a repair job!

My beautiful robot! Your A-1-A Double Prime All-Utility Extra-Quality De-Luxe Model! Nothing of him left but this"—he pointed at the box—"and this"—he gestured sadly at the scrap heap.

I looked a long time at the box and I scratched my head. "He works, doesn't he?"

"Works? What? Oh, works."

"You've been here watching him. He pushes the right lights? He gets messages right, He gives the right instructions?"

"Oh yes. I suppose so. Yes, he works all right. But damn it, man, he's not a robot any more. You've ruined him."

The box interrupted its beam work. "Ruined hell," it said in the same toneless voice. "I never felt so good since I was animated. Thanks, boss."

Thuringer goggled. I started to leave the room.

"Where are you going? Are you going to make this right? I demand another A-1-A Double Prime at once, you understand. And I trust you'll kill that assistant."

"Kill him? I'm going to kiss him."

"Why, you—" He'd picked up quite a vocabulary when he ran the space port at Venusberg. "I'll see that you're fired from Robinc tomorrow!"

"I quit today," I said. "One minute ago."

That was the birth of Q. U. R.

I found Quinby at the next place on the list I'd given him. This was a job repairing a household servant—one of the Class B androids with a pretty finish, but not up to commercial specifications.

I gawped when I saw the servant. Instead of two arms he had four tentacles, which he was flexing intently.

Quinby was packing away his repair kit. He looked up at me, smiling. "It was very simple," he said. "He'd seen Martoid robots at work, and he realized that flexible tentacles would be much more useful than jointed arms for housework. The more he brooded about it, the clumsier his arms got. But it's all right now, isn't it?"

"Fine, boss," said the servant. He seemed to be reveling in the free pleasure of those tentacles.

"There were some Martoid spares in the kit," Quinby explained, "and when I switched the circuit a little—"

"Have you stopped," I interposed, "to think what that

housewife is going to say when she comes home and finds her servant waving Martoid tentacles at her?"

"Why, no. You think she'd—"

"Look at it straight," I said. "She's going to join the procession demanding that I be fired from Robinc. But don't let it worry you. Robinc's nothing to us. From now on we're ourselves. We're Us Incorporated. Come on back to the Sunspot and we'll thrash this out."

"Thanks, boss," the semi-Martoid called after us, happily writhing.

I recklessly ordered a Three Planet. This was an occasion. Quinby stuck to milk. Guzub shrugged—that is, he wrinkled his skin where shoulders might have been on his circular body—and said, "You loog abby, boys. Good news?"

I nodded. "Best yet, Guzub. You're dishing 'em up for an historic occasion. Make a note."

"Lazd dime you zelebrade izdorig oggazion," said Guzub resignedly, "you breag zevendy-vour glazzes. Wy zhould I maig a node?"

"This is different, Guz. Now," I said to Quinby, "tell me how you got this unbelievable idea of repair?"

"Why, isn't it obvious?" he asked simply. "When Zwergenhaus invented the first robot, he wasn't thinking functionally. He was trying to make a mechanical man. He did, and he made a good job of it. But that's silly. Man isn't a functionally useful animal. There's very little he can do himself. What's made him top dog is that he can invent and use tools to do what needs doing. But why make his mechanical servants as helplessly constructed as he is?

"Almost every robot, except perhaps a few like farmhands, does only one or two things and does those things constantly. All right. Shape them so that they can best do just those things, with no part left over. Give them a brain, eyes and ears to receive commands, and whatever organs they need for their work.

"There's the source of your whole robot epidemic. They were all burdened down with things they didn't need—legs when their job was a sedentary one, two arms when they used only one—or else, like my house servant, their organs were designed to imitate man's rather than to be ideally functional. Result: the unused waste parts atrophied, and the robots became physically sick, sometimes mentally as well because

they were tortured by unrealized potentialities. It was simple
enough, once you looked at it straight."

The drinks came. I went at the Three Planets cautiously.
You know the formula: one part Terrene rum—170 proof—
one part Venusian margil, and a dash or so of Martian vuzd.
It's smooth and murderous. I'd never tasted one as smooth as
this of Guzub's, and I feared it'd be that much the more murderous.

"You know something of the history of motor-transporta-
tion?" Quinby went on. "Look at the twentieth-century models in the museum sometime. See how long they kept trying
to make a horseless carriage look like a carriage for horses.
We've been making the same mistake—trying to make a
manless body look like the bodies of men."

"Son," I said—he was maybe five or ten years younger
than I was—"there's something in this looking-straight
business of yours. There's so much, in fact, that I wonder if
even you realize how much. Are you aware that if we go at
this right we can damned near wipe Robinc out of existence?"

He choked on his milk. "You mean," he ventured, slowly
and dreamily, "we could—"

"But it can't be done overnight. People are used to android
robots. It's the only kind they ever think of. They'll be scared
of your unhuman-looking contraptions, just like Thuringer
was scared. We've got to build into this gradually. Lots of
publicity. Lots of promotion. Articles, lectures, debates. Give
'em a name. A good name. Keep robots; that's common
domain, I read somewhere, because it comes out of a play
written a long time ago in some dialect of Old Slavic.
Quinby's Something Robots—"

"Functionoid?"

"Sounds too much like fungoid. Don't like. Let me see—"
I took some more Three Planets. "I've got it. Usuform.
Quinby's Usuform Robots. Q.U.R."

Quinby grinned. "I like it. But shouldn't it be your name
too?"

"Me, I'll take a cut on the credits. I don't like my name
much. Now what we ought to do is introduce it with a new
robot. One that can do something no android in the Robinc
stock can tackle—"

Guzub called my name. "Man ere looking vor you."

It was Mike. "Hi, mister," he said. "I was wondering did

you maybe have a minute to listen to my brother-in-law's idea. You remember, about that new kind of robot—"

"Hey, Guzub," I yelled. "Two more Three Planets."

"Make it three," said Quinby quietly.

We talked all the rest of that night. When the Sunspot closed at twenty-three—we were going through one of our cyclic periods of blue laws then—we moved to my apartment and kept at it until we fell asleep from sheer exhaustion, scattered over my furniture.

Quinby's one drink—he stopped there—was just enough to stimulate him to seeing straighter than ever. He took something under one minute to visualize completely the possibilities of Mike's contribution.

This brother-in-law was a folklore hobbyist, and had been reading up on the ancient notion of dowsing. He had realized at once that there could have been no particular virtue in the forked witch-hazel rod which was supposed to locate water in the earth, but that certain individuals must have been able to perceive that water in some nth-sensory manner, communicating this reaction subconsciously to the rod in their hands.

To train that nth sense in a human being was probably impossible; it was most likely the result of a chance mutation. But you could attempt to develop it in a robot brain by experimentation with the patterns of the sense-perception tracks; and he had succeeded. He could equip a robot with a brain that would infallibly register the presence of water, and he was working on the further possibilities of oil and other mineral deposits. There wasn't any need to stress the invaluability of such a robot to an exploring party.

"All right," Quinby said. "What does such a robot need beside his brain and his sense organs? A means of locomotion and a means of marking the spots he finds. He'll be used chiefly in rough desert country, so a caterpillar tread will be far more useful to him than legs that can trip and stumble. The best kind of markers—lasting and easy to spot—would be metal spikes. He could, I suppose, carry those and have an arm designed as a pile driver; but . . . yes, look, this is best: Supposing he lays them?"

"Lays them?" I repeated vaguely.

"Yes. When his water sense registers maximum intensity— that is, when he's right over a hidden spring—there'll be a sort of sphincter reaction, and *plop,* he'll lay a sharp spike, driving it into the ground."

It was perfect. It would be a cheap robot to make—just a box on treads, the box containing the brain, the sense organs, and a supply of spikes. Maybe later in a more elaborate model he could be fed crude metal and make his own spikes. There'd be a decided demand for him, and nothing of Robinc's could compete. An exploring party could simply send him out for the day, then later go over the clear track left by his treads and drill wherever he had laid a spike. And the pure functionalism of him would be the first step in our campaign to accustom the public to Quinby's Usuform Robots.

Then the ideas came thick and fast. We had among us figured out at least seventy-three applications in which usuforms could beat androids, before our eyes inevitably folded up on us.

I woke up with three sensations: First, a firm resolve to stick to whiskey and leave Three Planetses to the Martians that invented them. Second, and practically obliterating this discomfort, a thrill of anticipation at the wonders that lay ahead of us, like a kid that wakes up and knows today's his birthday. But third, and uncomfortably gnawing at the back of this pleasure, the thought that there was something wrong, something we'd overlooked.

Quinby was fixing up a real cooked breakfast. He insisted that this was an occasion too noble for swallowing a few concentrates, and he'd rumaged in my freezing storeroom to find what he called "honest food." It was good eating, but this gnawing thought kept pestering me. At last I excused myself and went into the library. I found the book I wanted: *Planetary Civil Code. Volume 34. Robots.* I put it in the projector and ran it rapidly over the screen, till I located the paragraph I half remembered.

That gnawing was all too well founded. I remembered now. The theory'd always been that this paragraph went into the Code because only Robinc controlled the use of the factor that guaranteed the robots against endangering any intelligent beings, but I've always suspected that there were other elements at work. Even Council Members get their paws greased sometimes.

The paragraph read:

259: All robots except those in the military employ of
the Empire shall be constructed according to the patents
held by Robots, Inc, sometimes known as Robinc. Any robot constructed in violation of this section shall be
destroyed at once, and all those concerned in constructing
him shall be sterilized and segregated.

I read this aloud to the breakfast party. It didn't add to the
cheer of the occasion.

"I knew it was too good to be true," Mike grunted. "I can
just see Robinc leasing its patents to the boys that'll put it out
of business."

"But our being great business successes isn't what's important," Quinby protested. "Do we really want . . . could any
being of good will really want to become like the heads of
Robinc?"

"I do," said Mike honestly.

"What's important is what this can do: Cure this present
robot epidemic, conserve raw materials in robot building,
make possible a new and simpler and more sensible life for
everybody. Why can't we let Robinc take over the idea?"

"Look," I said patiently. "Quite aside from the unworthy
ambitions that Mike and I may hold, what'll happen if we
do? What has always happened when a big company buys out
a new method when they've got a billion credits sunk in the
old? It gets buried and is never heard of again."

"That's right," Quinby sighed. "Robinc would simply
strangle it."

"All right. Now look at it straight and say what is going to
become of Quinby's Usuform Robots."

"Well," he said simply, "there's only one solution. Change
the code."

I groaned. "That's all, huh? Just that. Change the code.
And how do you propose to go about that?"

"See the Head of the Council. Explain to him what our
idea means to the world—to the system. He's a good man.
He'll see us through."

"Dugg," I said, "when you look at things straight I never
know whether you're going to see an amazing truth or the
most amazing nonsense that ever was. Sure the Head's a good
man. If he could do it without breaking too many political
commitments, I think he might help out on an idea as big as
this. But how to get to see him when—"

"My brother-in-law tried once," Mike contributed. "He got kind of too persistent. That's how come he's in the hospital now. Hey," he broke off. "Where you going?"

"Come on, Dugg," I said. "Mike, you spend the day looking around the city for a likely factory site. We'll meet you around seventeen at the Sunspot. Quinby and I are going to see the Head of the Council."

We met the first guard about a mile from the office. "Robinc Repair," I said, and waved my card. After all, I assuaged Quinby's conscience, I hadn't actually resigned yet. "Want to check the Head's robot."

The guard nodded. "He's expecting you."

It hadn't been even a long shot. With robots in the state they were in, it was practically a certainty that one of those in direct attendance on the Head would need repair. The gag got us through a mile of guards, some robot, some—more than usual since all the trouble—human, and at last into the presence of the Head himself.

The white teeth gleamed in the black face in that friendly grin so familiar in telecasts. "I've received you in person," he said, "because the repair of this robot is such a confidential matter."

"What are his duties?" I asked.

"He is my private decoder. It is most important that I should have his services again as soon as possible."

"And what's the matter with him?"

"Partly what I gather is, by now, almost the usual thing. Paralysis of the legs. But partly more than that: He keeps talking to himself. Babbling nonsense."

Quinby spoke up. "Just what is he supposed to do?"

The Head frowned. "Assistants bring him every coded or ciphered dispatch. His brain was especially constructed for cryptanalysis. He breaks them down, writes out the clear, and drops it into a pneumatic chute which goes to a locked compartment in my desk."

"He uses books?"

"For some of the codes. The ciphers are entirely brain-mechanics."

Quinby nodded. "Can do. Bring us to him."

The robot was saying to himself, "This is the ponderous time of the decadence of the synaptic reflexes when all curmudgeons wonkle in the withering wallabies."

Quinby looked after the departing Head. "Some time," he said, "we're going to see a Venusian as Interplanetary Head."

I snorted.

"Don't laugh. Why, not ten centuries ago people would have snorted just like that at the idea of a Black as Head on this planet. Such narrow stupidity seems fantastic to us now. Our own prejudices will seem just as comical to our great-great-grandchildren."

The robot said, "Over the larking lunar syllogisms lopes the chariot of funereal ellipses."

Quinby went to work. After a minute—I was beginning to catch on to this seeing-straight business myself—I saw what he was doing and helped.

This robot needed nothing but the ability to read, to transcribe deciphered messages, and to handle papers and books. His legs had atrophied—that was in line with the other cases. But he was unusual in that he was the rare thing: a robot who had no need at all for communication by speech. He had the power of speech and was never called upon to exercise it; result, he had broken down into this fantastic babbling of nonsense, just to get some exercise of his futile power.

When Quinby had finished, the robot consisted only of his essential cryptanalytic brain, eyes, one arm, and the writer. This last was now a part of the robot's hookup; so that instead of using his hands to transcribe the message, he thought it directly into the writer. He had everything he needed, and nothing more. His last words before we severed the speech connection were, "The runcible rhythm of ravenous raisins rolled through the rookery rambling and raving." His first words when the direct connection with the writer was established were, "This feels good. Thanks, boss."

I went to fetch the Head. "I want to warn you," I explained to him, "you may be a little surprised by what you see. But please look at it without preconceptions."

He was startled and silent. He took it well; he didn't blow up hysterically like Thuringer. But he stared at the new thing for a long time without saying a word. Then he took a paper from his pocket and laid it on the decoding table. The eyes looked at it. The arm reached out for a book and opened it. Then a message began to appear on the writer. The Head snatched it up before it went into the tube, read it, and nodded.

"It works," he said slowly. "But it's not a robot any more. It's . . . it's just a decoding machine."

"A robot," I quoted, "is any machine equipped with a Zwergenhaus brain and capable of independent action upon the orders or subject to the guidance of an intelligent being. Planetary Code, paragraph num—"

"But it looks so—"

"It works," I cut in. "And it won't get paralysis of the legs and it won't ever go mad and babble about wonkling curmudgeons. Because, you see, it's a usuform robot." And I hastily sketched out the Quinby project.

The Head listened attentively. Occasionally he flashed his white grin, especially when I explained why we could not turn the notion over to Robinc. When I was through, he paused a moment and then said at last, "It's a fine idea you have there. A great idea. But the difficulties are great, too. I don't need to recount the history of robots to you," he said, proceeding to do so. "How Zwergenhaus's discovery lay dormant for a century and a half because no one dared upset the economic system by developing it. How the Second War of Conquest so nearly depopulated the earth that the use of robot labor became not only possible but necessary. How our society is now so firmly based on it that the lowest laboring rank possible to a being is foreman. The Empire is based on robots; robots are Robinc. We can't fight Robinc."

"Robinc is slowly using up all our resources of metallic and radioactive ore, isn't it?" Quinby asked.

"Perhaps. Scaremongers can produce statistics—"

"And our usuforms will use only a fraction of what Robinc's androids need."

"A good point. An important one. You have convinced me that android robots are a prime example of conspicuous waste, and this epidemic shows that they are moreover dangerous. But I cannot attempt to fight Robinc now. My position—I shall be frank, gentlemen—my position is too precarious. I have problems of my own."

"Try Quinby," I said. "I had a problem and tried him, and he saw through it at once."

"Saw through it," the Head observed, "to a far vaster and more difficult problem beyond. Besides, I am not sure if my problem lies in his field. It deals with the question of how to mix a Three Planets cocktail."

The excitement of our enterprise had made me forget my

head. Now it began throbbing again at the memory. "A Three Planets?"

The Head hesitated. "Gentlemen," he said at last, "I ask your pledge of the utmost secrecy."

He got it.

"And even with that I cannot give you too many details. But you know that the Empire holds certain mining rights in certain districts of Mars—I dare not be more specific. These rights are essential to maintain our stocks of raw materials. And they are held only on lease, by an agreement which must be renewed quinquennially. It has heretofore been renewed as a matter of course, but the recent rise of the Planetary Party in Mars, which advocates the abolition of all interplanetary contact, makes this coming renewal a highly doubtful matter. Within the next three days I am to confer here with a certain high Martian dignitary, traveling incognito. Upon the result of that conference our lease depends."

"And the Three Planets?" I asked. "Does the Planetary Party want to abolish them as a matter of principle?"

"Probably," he smiled. "But this high individual is not a party member, and is devoted to Three Planets. He hates to travel, because only on Mars, he claims, is the drink ever mixed correctly. If I could brighten his trip here by offering him one perfect Three Planets—"

"Guzub!" I cried. "The bartender at the Sunspot. He's a Martian and the drink is his specialty."

"I know," the Head agreed sadly. "Dza . . . the individual in question once said that your Guzub was the only being on this planet who knew how. Everyone else puts in too much or too little vuzd. But Guzub is an exiled member of the Varjinian Loyalists. He hates everything that the present regime represents. He would never consent to perform his masterpiece for my guest."

"You could order one at the Sunspot and have it sent here by special—"

"You know that a Three Planets must be drunk within thirty seconds of mixing for the first sip to have its ideal flavor."

"Then—"

"All right," Quinby said. "You let us know when your honored guest arrives, and we'll have a Three Planets for him."

The Head looked doubtful. "If you think you can—A bad one might be more dangerous than none—"

"And if we do," I interposed hastily, "you'll reconsider this business of the usuform robots?"

"If this mining deal goes through satisfactorily, I should be strong enough to contemplate facing Robinc."

"Then you'll get your Three Planets," I said calmly, wondering what Quinby had seen straight now.

We met Mike at the Sunspot as arranged. He was drinking a Three Planets. "This is good," he announced. "This has spacedrive and zoomf to it. You get it other places and—"

"I know," I said. "Find a site?"

"A honey. Wait'll I—"

"Hold it. We've got to know have we got anything to go on it. Guzub! One Three Planets."

We watched entranced as he mixed the potion. "Get exactly what he does," Quinby had said. "Then construct a usuform bartender who'll be infallible. It'll satisfy the Martian envoy and at the same time remind the Head of why we're helping him out."

But all we saw was a glittering swirl of tentacles. First a flash as each tentacle picked up its burden—one the shaker, one the lid, one the glass, and three others the bottles of rum, margil, and vuzd. Then a sort of spasm that shook all Guzub's round body as the exact amount of each liquid went in, and finally a gorgeous pinwheel effect of shaking and pouring.

Guzub handed me my drink, and I knew as much as I had before.

By the time I'd finished it, I had courage. "Guzub," I said, "this is wonderful."

"Zure," Guzub glurked. "Always I maig id wondervul."

"Nobody else can make 'em like you, Guz. But tell me. How much vuzd do you put in?"

Guzub made his kind of a shrug. "I dell you, boys, I dunno. Zome dime maybe I wadge myzelv and zee. I juzd go zo! I dunno how mudj."

"Give me another one. Let's see you watch yourself."

"Businezz is good by you, you dring zo many Blanedz? O Gay, ere goes."

But the whirl stopped in the middle. There was Guzub, all his eyes focused sadly on the characteristic green corkscrew-shaped bottle of vuzd. Twice he started to move that tentacle, then drew it back. At last he made a dash with it.

"Exactly two drops," Quinby whispered.

Guzub handed over the drink unhappily. "Dry id," he said.

I did. It was terrible. Too little vuzd, so that you could taste both the heavy sweetness of the rum and the acrid harshness of the margil. I said so.

"I know, boys. Wen I zdob do wadge, id bothers me. No gan do."

I gupled the drink. "Mix up another without watching. Maybe we can tell."

This one was perfect. And we could see nothing.

The next time he "wadged." He used precisely four and a half drops of vuzd. You tasted nothing but the tart decay of the vuzd itself.

The next time—

But my memory gets a little vague after that. Like I said, I'm a whiskey drinker. And four Three Planetses in quick succession—I'm told the party went on till closing hour at twenty-three, after which Guzub accepted Quinby's invitation to come on and mix for us at my apartment. I wouldn't know. All I remember is one point where I found a foot in my face. I bit it, decided it wasn't mine, and stopped worrying about it. Or about anything.

I'm told that I slept thirty-six hours after that party—a whole day and more simply vanished out of my existence. I woke up feeling about twelve and spry for my age, but it took me a while to reconstruct what had been going on.

I was just beginning to get it straightened out when Quinby came in. His first words were, "How would you like a Three Planets?"

I suddenly felt like two hundred and twelve, and on an off day at that. Not until I'd packed away a superman-size breakfast did he dare repeat the offer. By then I felt brave. "O. K.," I said. "But with a whiskey chaser."

I took one sip and said, "Where's Guzub? I didn't know he was staying here too."

"He isn't."

"But this Three Planets— It's perfect. It's the McCoy. And Guzub—"

Quinby opened a door. There sat the first original Quinby Usuform—no remake of a Robinc model, but a brand new creation. Quinby said, "Three Planets," and he went into action. He had tentacles, and the motions were exactly like

Guzub's except that he was himself the shaker. He poured the liquids into his maw, joggled about, and then poured them out of a hollow hoselike tentacle.

The televisor jangled. Quinby hastily shifted the ike so as to miss the usuform barkeep, as I answered. The screen showed the Head himself. He'd been there before on telecasts, but this was the real thing.

He didn't waste time. "Tonight, nineteen thirty," he said. "I don't need to explain?"

"We'll be there," I choked out.

A special diplomatic messenger brought the pass to admit the two of us and "one robot or robotlike machine" to the Council building. I was thankful for that alternative phrase; I didn't want to have to argue with each guard about the technical legal definition of a robot. We were installed in a small room directly off the Head's private reception room. It was soundproofed and there was no window; no chance of our picking up interplanetary secrets of diplomacy. And there was a bar.

A dream of a bar, a rhapsody of a bar. The vuzd, the rum, the margil were all of brands that you hear about and brood about but never think to see in a lifetime. And there was whiskey of the same caliber.

We had hardly set out usuform facing the bar when a servant came in. He was an android. He said. "The Head says now."

Quinby asked me, "Do you want one?"

I shook my head and selected a bottle of whiskey.

"Two Three Planetses," Quinby said.

The tentacles flickered, the shaker-body joggled, the hose-tentacle poured. The android took the tray from our usuform. He looked at him with something as close to a mixture of fear, hatred, and envy as his eye cells could express. He went out with the tray.

I turned to Quinby. "We've been busy getting ready for this party ever since I woke up. I still don't understand how you made him into another Guzub."

There was a click and the room was no longer soundproof. The Head was allowing us to hear the reception of our creation. First his voice came, quiet, reserved and suave. "I think your magnitude would enjoy this insignificant drink. I have been to some slight pains to see that it was worthy of your magnitude's discriminating taste."

There was silence. Then the faintest sound of a sip, a pause, and an exhalation. We could almost hear the Head holding his breath.

"Bervegd!" a deep voice boomed—which since no Martian has ever yet learned to pronounce a voiceless consonant, means a verdict of "Perfect!"

"I am glad that your magnitude is pleased."

"Bleased is doo mild a word, my dear Ead. And now thad you ave zo delighdvully welgomed me—"

The sound went dead again.

"He liked it, huh?" said Guzub II. "You boys want some, maybe?"

"No thanks," said Quinby. "I wonder if I should have given him a Martian accent—they are the best living bartenders. Perhaps when we get that model into mass production—"

I took a gleefully long swig of whiskey. Its mild warmth felt soothing after memories of last night's Three Planetses. "Look," I said. "We have just pulled off the trick that ought to net us a change in the code and a future as the great revolutionists of robot design. I feel like . . . hell, like Ley landing on the moon. And you sit there with nothing on your mind but a bartender's accent."

"Why not?" Quinby asked. "What is there to do in life but find what you're good for and do it best you can?"

He had me there. And I began to have some slight inklings of the trouble ahead with a genius who had commercial ideas and the conscience of an other-worldly saint. I said, "All right. I won't ask you to kill this bottle with me, and in return I expect you not to interfere with my assassinating it. But as to what you're good for—how did you duplicate Guzub?"

"Oh that. That was simple—"

"—when you looked at it straight," I ended.

"Yes." That was another thing about Quinby; he never knew if he was being ribbed. "Yes. I got one of those new electronic cameras—you know, one thousand exposures per second. Hard to find at that time of night, but we made it."

"We?"

"You helped me. You kept the man from overcharging me. Or maybe you don't remember? So we took pictures of Guzub making a Three Planets, and I could construct this one to do it exactly right down to the thousandth of a second. The proper proportion of vuzd, in case you're interested, works out to three-point-six-five-four-seven-eight-two-three drops. It's done with a flip of the third joint of the tentacle on the down beat. It didn't seem right to use Guzub to make a robot that would compete with him and probably drive him out of business; so we've promised him a generous pension from the royalties on usuform barkeeps."

"We?" I said again, more feebly.

"You drew up the agreement."

I didn't argue. It was fair enough. A good businessman would have slipped Guzub a fiver for posing for pictures and then said the hell with him. But I was beginning to see that running Q.U.R. was not going to be just good business.

When the Head finally came in, he didn't need to say a word, though he said plenty. I've never seen that white grin flash quite so cheerfully. That was enough; the empire had its Martian leases, and Q. U. R. was a fact.

When I read back over this story, I can see there's one thing wrong. That's about the giller. I met Dugg Quinby, and you met him through me, in the act of rescuing a Venusian from a giller-baiting mob. By all the rights of storytelling, the green being should have vowed everlasting gratitude to his rescuer, and at some point in our troubles he should have showed up and made everything fine for us.

That's how it should have been. In actual fact the giller grabbed his inhalator and vanished without so much as a "thank you." If anybody helped us, it was Mike, who had been our most vigorous enemy in the battle.

Which means, I think, that seeing straight can work with things and robots, but not with beings, because no being is really straight, not even to himself.

Except maybe Dugg Quinby.

CLASH BY NIGHT

Astounding,

March

by Lawrence O'Donnell
(Henry Kuttner and C. L. Moore)

There is considerable debate about the authorship of this powerful story, with some sources claiming that Kuttner did this one alone, while others claim that it was a collaboration. What matters most is that "Clash By Night" is an important novella, one of the most convincing treatments of an undersea civilization in science fiction. The Kuttners (possibly Henry alone) produced a memorable sequel in 1947, "Fury," also in Astounding. *The "O'Donnell" name was used sparingly on their work, another example being "Vintage Season" in the September, 1946* Astounding.

(All Mars has lost since 1943 are its canals and the dreams of an intelligent civilization (or the dead remnants of one) upon it. Venus lost its ocean, its relatively mild climate, its relatively benign atmosphere, its status as our younger near-twin sister. For some fifteen years after "Clash By Night" appeared, it was still possible to write of Venus's oceans and I published Lucky Starr and the Oceans of Venus *in 1954. But then came microwave astronomy and planetary probes and Venus was revealed to be bone-dry, nearly red-hot, and buried under a dense atmosphere of carbon dioxide, which was in turn under a cloud layer of dilute sulfuric acid. But the dream is remembered and "Clash by Night" is one of its best expressions—I.A.)*

113

Introduction

A half mile beneath the shallow Venusian Sea the black impervium dome that protects Montana Keep rests frowningly on the bottom. Within the Keep is carnival, for the Montanans celebrate the four-hundred-year anniversary of Earthman's landing on Venus. Under the great dome that houses the city all is light and color and gaiety. Masked men and women, bright in celoflex and silks, wander through the broad streets, laughing, drinking, the strong native wines of Venus. The sea bottom has been combed, like the hydroponic tanks, for rare delicacies to grace the tables of the nobles.

Through the festival grim shadows stalk, men whose faces mark them unmistakably as members of a Free Company. Their finery cannot disguise that stamp, hard-won through years of battle. Under the domino masks their mouths are hard and harsh. Unlike the undersea dwellers, their skins are burned black with the ultraviolet rays that filter through the cloud layer of Venus. They are skeletons at the feast. They are respected but resented. They are Free Companions—

We are on Venus, nine hundred years ago, beneath the Sea of Shoals, not much north of the equator. But there is a wide range in time and space. All over the cloud planet the underwater Keeps are dotted, and life will not change for many centuries. Looking back, as we do now, from the civilized days of the thirty-fourth century, it is too easy to regard the men of the Keeps as savages, groping, stupid, and brutal. The Free Companies have long since vanished. The islands and continents of Venus have been tamed, and there is no war.

But in periods of transition, of desperate rivalry, there is always war. The Keeps fought among themselves, each striving to draw the fangs of the others of depriving them of their reserves of korium, the power source of the day. Students of that era find pleasure in sifting the legends and winnowing out the basic social and geopolitical truths. It is fairly well known that only one factor saved the Keeps from annihilating one another—the gentlemen's agreement that left war to the warriors, and allowed the undersea cities to develop their science and social cultures. That particular compromise was, perhaps, inevitable. And it caused the organization of the Free Companies, the roving bands of mercenaries, highly trained for their duties, who hired themselves out to fight for whatever Keeps were attacked or wished to attack.

Ap Towrn, in his monumental "Cycle of Venus," tells the saga through symbolic legends. Many historians have recorded the sober truth, which, unfortunately, seems often Mars-dry. But it is not generally realized that the Free Companions were almost directly responsible for our present high culture. War, because of them, was not permitted to usurp the place of peacetime social and scientific work. Fighting was highly specialized, and, because of technical advances, manpower was no longer important. Each band of Free Companions numbered a few thousand, seldom more.

It was a strange, lonely life they must have led, shut out from the normal life of the Keeps. They were vestigian but necessary, like the fangs of the marsupians who eventually evolved into Homo sapiens. But without those warriors, the Keeps would have been plunged completely into total war, with fatally destructive results.

Harsh, gallant, indomitable, serving the god of battles so that it might be destroyed—working toward their own obliteration—the Free Companies roar down the pages of history, the banner of Mars streaming above them in the misty air of Venus. They were doomed as Tyrannosaur Rex was doomed, and they fought on as he did, serving, in their strange way, the shape of Minerva that stood behind Mars.

Now they are gone. We can learn much by studying the place they held in the Undersea Period. For, because of them, civilization rose again to the heights it had once reached on Earth, and far beyond.

> *"These lords shall light the mystery*
> *Of mastery or victory,*
> *And these ride high in history,*
> *But these shall not return."*

The Free Companions hold their place in interplanetary literature. They are a legend now, archaic and strange. For they were fighters, and war has gone with unification. But we can understand them a little more than could the people of the Keeps.

This story, built on legends and fact, is about a typical warrior of the period—Captain Brian Scott of Doone's Free Companions. He may never have existed—

I.

O, it's Tommy this, an' Tommy that, an' "Tommy, go away";
But it's "Thank you, Mr. Atkins," when the band begins to
*   play,*
The band begins to play, my boys, the band begins to play—
O, it's "Thank you, Mr. Atkins," when the band begins to play.
                                    —R. Kipling circa 1900

Scott drank stinging uisqueplus and glowered across the smoky tavern. He was a hard, stocky man, with thick gray-shot brown hair and the scar of an old wound crinkling his chin. He was thirty-odd, looking like the veteran he was, and he had sense enough to wear a plain suit of blue celoflex, rather than the garish silks and rainbow fabrics that were all around him.

Outside, through the transparent walls, a laughing throng was carried to and fro along the movable ways. But in the tavern it was silent, except for the low voice of a harpman as he chanted some old ballad, accompanying himself on his complicated instrument. The song came to an end. There was scattered applause, and from the hot-box overhead the blaring music of an orchestra burst out. Instantly the restraint was gone. In the booths and at the bar men and women began to laugh and talk with casual unrestraint. Couples were dancing now.

The girl beside Scott, a slim, tan-skinned figure with glossy black ringlets cascading to her shoulders, turned inquiring eyes to him.

"Want to, Brian?"

Scott's mouth twisted in a wry grimace. "Suppose so, Jeana. Eh?" He rose, and she came gracefully into his arms. Brian did not dance too well, but what he lacked in practice he made up in integration. Jeana's heart-shaped face, with its high cheekbones and vividly crimson lips, lifted to him.

"Forget Bienne. He's just trying to ride you."

Scott glanced toward a distant booth, where two girls sat with a man—Commander Fredric Bienne of the Doones. He was a gaunt, tall, bitter-faced man, his regular features twisted into a perpetual sneer, his eyes somber under heavy dark brows. He was pointing, now, toward the couple on the floor.

"I know," Scott said. "He's doing it, too. Well, the hell with him. So I'm a captain now and he's still a commander. That's tough. Next time he'll obey orders and not send his ship out of the line, trying to ram."

"That was it, eh?" Jeana asked. "I wasn't sure. There's plenty of talk."

"There always is. Oh, Bienne's hated me for years. I reciprocate. We simply don't get on together. Never did. Every time I got a promotion, he chewed his nails. Figured he had a longer service record than I had, and deserved to move up faster. But he's too much of an individualist—at the wrong times."

"He's drinking a lot," Jeana said.

"Let him. Three months we've been in Montana Keep. The boys get tired of inaction—being treated like this." Scott nodded toward the door, where a Free Companion was arguing with the keeper. "No noncoms allowed in here. Well, the devil with it."

They could not hear the conversation above the hubbub, but its importance was evident. Presently the soldier shrugged, his mouth forming a curse, and departed. A fat man in scarlet silks shouted encouragement.

"—want any . . . Companions here!"

Scott saw Commander Bienne, his eyes half closed, get up and walk toward the fat man's booth. His shoulder moved in an imperceptible shrug. The hell with civilians, anyhow. Serve the lug right if Bienne smashed his greasy face. And that seemed the probable outcome. For the fat man was accompanied by a girl, and obviously wasn't going to back down, though Bienne, standing too close to him, was saying something insulting, apparently.

The auxiliary hot-box snapped some quick syllables, lost in the general tumult. But Scott's trained ear caught the words. He nodded to Jeana, made a significant clicking noise with his tongue, and said, "This is it."

She, too, had heard. She let Scott go. He headed toward the fat man's booth just in time to see the beginning of a brawl. The civilian, red as a turkey cock, had struck out suddenly, landing purely by accident on Bienne's gaunt cheek. The commander, grinning tightly, stepped back a pace, his fist clenching. Scott caught the other's arm.

"Hold it, commander."

Bienne swung around, glaring. "What business is it of yours? Let—"

The fat man, seeing his opponent's attention distracted, acquired more courage and came in swinging. Scott reached past Bienne, planted his open hand in the civilian's face, and pushed hard. The fat man almost fell backward on his table.

As he rebounded, he saw a gun in Scott's hand. The captain said curtly, "Tend to your knitting, mister."

The civilian licked his lips, hesitated, and sat down. Under his breath he muttered something about too-damn-cocky Free Companions.

Bienne was trying to break free, ready to swing on the captain. Scott holstered his gun. "Orders," he told the other, jerking his head toward the hot-box. "Get it?"

"—mobilization. Doonemen report to headquarters. Captain Scott to Administration. Immediate mobilization—"

"Oh," Bienne said, though he still scowled. "O.K. I'll take over. There was time for me to take a crack at that louse, though."

"You know what instant mobilization means," Scott grunted. "We may have to leave at an instant's notice. Orders, commander."

Bienne saluted halfheartedly and turned away. Scott went back to his own booth. Jeana had already gathered her purse and gloves and was applying lip juice.

She met his eyes calmly enough.

"I'll be at the apartment, Brian. Luck."

He kissed her briefly, conscious of a surging excitement at the prospect of a new venture. Jeana understood his emotion. She gave him a quick, wry smile, touched his hair lightly, and rose. They went out into the gay tumult of the ways.

Perfumed wind blew into Scott's face. He wrinkled his nose disgustedly. During carnival seasons the Keeps were less pleasant to the Free Companions than otherwise; they felt more keenly the gulf that lay between them and the undersea dwellers. Scott pushed his way through the crowd and took Jeana across the ways to the center fast-speed strip. They found seats.

At a clover-leaf intersection Scott left the girl, heading toward Administration, the cluster of taller buildings in the city's center. The technical and political headquarters were centered here, except for the laboratories, which were in the suburbs near the base of the Dome. There were a few small test-domes a mile or so distant from the city, but these were used only for more precarious experiments. Glancing up, Scott was reminded of the catastrophe that had unified science into something like a free-masonry. Above him, hanging without gravity over a central plaza, was the globe of the Earth, half shrouded by the folds of a black plastic pall. In every Keep on Venus there was a similar ever-present reminder of the lost mother planet.

Scott's gaze went up farther, to the Dome, as though he could penetrate the impervium and the mile-deep layer of water and the clouded atmosphere to the white star that hung in space, one quarter as brilliant as the sun. A star—all that remained of Earth, since atomic power had been unleashed there two centuries ago. The scourge had spread like flame, melting continents and leveling mountains. In the libraries there were wire-tape pictorial records of the Holocaust. A religious cult—Men of the New Judgment—had sprung up, and advocated the complete destruction of science; followers of that dogma still existed here and there. But the cult's teeth had been drawn when technicians unified, outlawing experiments with atomic power forever, making use of that force punishable by death, and permitting no one to join their society without taking the Minervan Oath.

"—to work for the ultimate good of mankind . . . taking all precaution against harming humanity and science . . . requiring permission from those in authority before undertaking any experiment involving peril to the race . . . remembering always the extent of the trust placed in us and remembering forever the death of the mother planet through misuse of knowledge—"

The Earth. A strange sort of world it must have been, Scott thought. Sunlight, for one thing, unfiltered by the cloud layer. In the old days, there had been few unexplored areas left on Earth. But here on Venus, where the continents had not yet been conquered—there was no need, of course, since everything necessary to life could be produced under the Domes—here on Venus, there was still a frontier. In the Keeps, a highly specialized social culture. Above the surface, a primeval world, where only the Free Companions had their fortresses and navies—the navies for fighting, the forts to house the technicians who provided the latter-day sinews of war, science instead of money. The Keeps tolerated visits from the Free Companions, but would not offer them head-quarters, so violent the feeling, so sharp the schism, in the public mind, between war and cultural progress.

Under Scott's feet the sliding way turned into an escalator, carrying him into the Administration Building. He stepped to another way which took him to a lift, and, a moment or two later, was facing the door-curtain bearing the face of President Dane Crosby of Montana Keep.

Crosby's voice said, "Come in, captain," and Scott brushed through the curtain, finding himself in a medium-sized room with muraled walls and a great window overlooking the city. Crosby, a white-haired, thin figure in blue silks, was at his desk. He looked like a tired old clerk out of Dickens, Scott thought suddenly, entirely undistinguished and ordinary. Yet Crosby was one of the greatest socio-politicians on Venus.

Cinc Rhys, leader of Doone's Free Companions, was sitting in a relaxer, the apparent antithesis of Crosby. All the moisture in Rhys's body seemed to have been sucked out of him years ago by ultraviolet actinic, leaving a mummy of brown leather and whipcord sinew. There was no softness in the man. His smile was a grimace. Muscles lay like wire under the swarthy cheeks.

Scott saluted. Rhys waved him to a relaxer. The look of subdued eagerness in the cinc's eyes was significant—an eagle poising himself, smelling blood. Crosby sensed that, and a wry grin showed on his pale face.

"Every man to his trade," he remarked, semi-ironically. "I suppose I'd be bored stiff if I had too long a vacation. But you'll have quite a battle on your hands this time, Cinc Rhys."

Scott's stocky body tensed automatically. Rhys glanced at him.

"Virginia Keep is attacking, captain. They've hired the Helldivers—Flynn's outfit."

There was a pause. Both Free Companions were anxious to discuss the angles, but unwilling to do so in the presence of a civilian, even the president of Montana Keep. Crosby rose.

"The money settlement's satisfactory, then?"

Rhys nodded. "Yes, that's all right. I expect the battle will take place in a couple of days. In the neighborhood of Venus Deep, at a tough guess."

"Good. I've a favor to ask, so if you'll excuse me for a few minutes, I'll—" He left the sentence unfinished and went out through the door-curtain. Rhys offered Scott a cigarette.

"You get the implications, captain—the Helldivers?"

"Yes, sir. Thanks. We can't do it alone."

"Right. We're short on manpower and armament both. And the Helldivers recently merged with O'Brian's Legion, after O'Brien was killed in that polar scrap. They're a strong outfit, plenty strong. Then they've got their specialty—submarine attack. I'd say we'll have to use H-plan 7."

Scott closed his eyes, remembering the files. Each Free Company kept up-to-date plans of attack suited to the merits of every other Company of Venus. Frequently revised as new advances were made, as groups merged, and as the balance of power changed on each side, the plans were so detailed that they could be carried into action at literally a moment's notice. H-plan 7, Scott recalled, involved enlisting the aid of the Mob, a small but well-organized band of Free Companions led by Cinc Tom Mendez.

"Right," Scott said. "Can you get him?"

"I think so. We haven't agreed yet on the bonus. I've been telaudioing him on a tight beam, but he keeps putting me off—waiting till the last moment, when he can dictate his own terms."

"What's he asking, sir?"

"Fifty thousand cash and a fifty-percent cut on the loot."

"I'd say thirty percent would be about right."

Rhys nodded. "I've offered him thirty-five. I may send you to his fort—carte blanche. We can get another Company, but Mendex has got beautiful sub-detectors—which would come in handy against the Helldivers. Maybe I can settle things by audio. If not, you'll have to fly over to Mendez and buy his services, at less than fifty per if you can."

Scott rubbed the old scar on his chin with a callused forefinger. "Meantime Commander Bienne's in charge of mobilization. When—"

"I telaudioed our fort. Air transports are on the way now."

"It'll be quite a scrap," Scott said, and the eyes of the two men met in perfect understanding. Rhys chuckled dryly.

"And good profits. Virginia Keep has a big supply of korium . . . dunno how much, but plenty."

"What started the fracas this time?"

"The usual thing, I suppose," Rhys said uninterestedly.

"Imperialism. Somebody in Virginia Keep worked out a new plan for annexing the rest of the Keeps. Same as usual."

They stood up as the door-curtain swung back, admitting President Crosby, another man, and a girl. The man looked young, his boyish face not yet toughened under actinic burn. The girl was lovely in the manner of a plastic figurine, lit from within by vibrant life. Her blond hair was cropped in the prevalent mode, and her eyes, Scott saw, were an unusual shade of green. She was more than merely pretty—she was instantly exciting.

Crosby said, "My niece, Ilene Kane—and my nephew, Norman Kane." He performed introductions, and they found seats.

"What about drinks?" Ilene suggested. "This is rather revoltingly formal. The fight hasn't started yet, after all."

Crosby shook his head at her. "You weren't invited here anyway. Don't try to turn this into a party—there isn't too much time, under the circumstances."

"O.K.," Ilene murmured. "I can wait." She eyed Scott interestedly.

Norman Kane broke in. "I'd like to join Doone's Free Companions, sir. I've already applied, but now that there's a battle coming up, I hate to wait till my application's approved. So I thought—"

Crosby looked at Cinc Rhys. "A personal favor, but the decision's up to you. My nephew's a misfit—a romanticist. Never liked the life of a Keep. A year ago he went off and joined Starling's outfit."

Rhys raised an eyebrow. "That gang? It's not a recommendation, Kane. They're not even classed as Free Companions. More like a band of guerrillas, and entirely without ethics. There've even been rumors they're messing around with atomic power."

Crosby looked startled. "I hadn't heard that."

"It's no more than a rumor. If it's ever proved, the Free Companions—all of them—will get together and smash Starling in a hurry."

Norman Kane looked slightly uncomfortable. "I suppose I was rather a fool. But I wanted to get in the fighting game, and Starling's group appealed to me—"

The cinc made a sound in his throat. "They would. Swashbuckling romantics, with no idea of what war means. They've

not more than a dozen technicians. And they've no discipline—it's like a pirate outfit. War today, Kane, isn't won by
romantic animals dashing at forlorn hopes. The modern soldier is a tactician who knows how to think, integrate, and
obey. If you join our Company, you'll have to forget what
you learned with Starling."

"Will you take me, sir?"

"I think it would be unwise. You need the training course."

"I've had experience—"

Crosby said, "It would be a favor, Cinc Rhys, if you'd skip
the red tape. I'd appreciate it. Since my nephew wants to be
a soldier, I'd much prefer to see him with the Doones."

Rhys shrugged. "Very well. Captain Scott will give you
your orders, Kane. Remember that discipline is vitally important to us."

The boy tried to force back a delighted grin. "Thank you,
sir."

"Captain—"

Scott rose and nodded to Kane. They went out together. In
the anteroom was a telaudio set, and Scott called the Doone's
local headquarters in Montana Keep. An integrator answered,
his face looking inquiringly from the screen.

"Captain Scott calling, subject induction."

"Yes, sir. Ready to record."

Scott drew Kane forward. "Photosnap this man. He'll report to headquarters immediately. Name, Norman Kane. En-
list him without training course—special orders from Cinc
Rhys."

"Acknowledged, sir."

Scott broke the connection. Kane couldn't quite repress his
grin.

"All right," the captain grunted, a sympathetic gleam in his
eyes. "That fixes it. They'll put you in command. What's your
specialty."

"Flitterboats, sir."

"Good. One more thing. Don't forget what Cinc Rhys said,
Kane. Discipline is damned important, and you may not have
realized that yet. This isn't a cloak-and-sword war. There are
no Charges of Light Brigades. No grandstand plays—that
stuff went out with the Crusades. Just obey orders, and you'll
have no trouble. Good luck."

"Thank you, sir." Kane saluted and strode out with a perceptible swagger. Scott grinned. The kid would have *that* knocked out of him pretty soon.

A voice at his side made him turn quickly. Ilene Kane was standing there, slim and lovely in her celoflex gown.

"You seem pretty human after all, captain," she said. "I heard what you told Norman."

Scott shrugged. "I did that for his own good—and the good of the Company. One man off the beam can cause plenty of trouble, Mistress Kane."

"I envy Norman," she said. "It must be a fascinating life you lead. I'd like it—for a while. Not for long. I'm one of the useless offshoots of this civilization, not much good for anything. So I've perfected one talent."

"What's that?"

"Oh, hedonism, I suppose you'd call it. I enjoy myself. It's not often too boring. But I'm a bit bored now. I'd like to talk to you, captain."

"Well, I'm listening," Scott said.

Ilene Kane made a small grimace. "Wrong sematic term. I'd like to get inside of you psychologically. But painlessly. Dinner and dancing. Can do?"

"There's no time," Scott told her. "We may get our orders any moment." He wasn't sure he wanted to go out with this girl of the Keeps, though there was definitely a subtle fascination for him, an appeal he could not analyze. She typified the most pleasurable part of a world he did not know. The other facets of that world could not impinge on him; geopolitics or nonmilitary science held no appeal, were too alien. But all worlds touch at one point—pleasure. Scott could understand the relaxations of the undersea groups, as he could not understand or feel sympathy for their work or their social impulses.

Cinc Rhys came through the door-curtain, his eyes narrowed. "I've some telaudioing to do, captain," he said. Scott knew what implications the words held: the incipient bargain with Cinc Mendez. He nodded.

"Yes, sir. Shall I report to headquarters?"

Rhys's harsh face seemed to relax suddenly as he looked from Ilene to Scott. "You're free till dawn. I won't need you till then, but report to me at six a.m. No doubt you've a few details to clean up."

"Very well, sir." Scott watched Rhys go out. The cinc had meant Jeana, of course. But Ilene did not know that.

"So?" she asked. "Do I get a turn-down? You might buy me a drink, anyway."

There was plenty of time. Scott said, "It'll be a pleasure," and Ilene linked her arm with his. They took the dropper to ground level.

As they came out on one of the ways, Ilene turned her head and caught Scott's glance. "I forgot something, captain. You may have a previous engagement. I didn't realize—"

"There's nothing," he said. "Nothing important."

It was true; he felt a mild gratitude toward Jeana at the realization. His relationship with her was the peculiar one rendered advisable by his career. Free-marriage was the word for it; Jeana was neither his wife nor his mistress, but something midway between. The Free Companions had no firmly grounded foundation for social life; in the Keeps they were visitors, and in their coastal forts they were—well, soldiers. One would no more bring a woman to a fort than aboard a ship of the line. So the women of the Free Companions lived in the Keeps, moving from one to another as their men did; and because of the ever-present shadow of death, ties were purposely left loose. Jeana and Scott had been free-married for five years now. Neither made demands on the other. No one expected fidelity of a Free Companion. Soldiers lived under such iron disciplines that when they were released, during the brief peacetimes, the pendulum often swung far in the opposite direction.

To Scott, Ilene Kane was a key that might unlock the doors of the Keep—doors that opened to a world of which he was not a part, and which he could not quite understand.

II

I, a stranger and afraid
In a world I never made.
        —Housman

There were nuances, Scott found, which he had never known existed. A hedonist like Ilene devoted her life to such nuances; they were her career. Such minor matters as making the powerful, insipid moonflower cocktails more palatable by filtering them through lime-soaked sugar held between the teeth. Scott was a uisqueplus man, having the average soldier's contempt for what he termed hydroponic drinks, but the cocktails Ilene suggested were quite as effective as acrid, burning amber uisqueplus. She taught him, that night, such tricks as pausing between glasses to sniff lightly at happy-gas, to mingle sensual excitement with mental by trying the amusement rides designed to give one the violent physical intoxication of breathless speed. Nuances all, which only a girl with Ilene's background could know. She was not representative of Keep life. As she had said, she was an offshoot, a casual and useless flower on the great vine that struck up inexorably to the skies, its strength in its tough, reaching tendrils—scientists and technicians and socio-politicians. She was doomed in her own way, as Scott was in his. The undersea folk served Minerva; Scott served Mars; and Ilene served Aphrodite—not purely the sexual goddess, but the patron of arts and pleasure. Between Scott and Ilene was the difference between Wagner and Strauss; the difference between crashing chords and tinkling arpeggios. In both was a muted bittersweet sadness, seldom realized by either. But that undertone was brought out by their contact. The sense of dim hopelessness in each responded to the other.

It was carnival, but neither Ilene nor Scott wore masks. Their faces were masks enough, and both had been trained to reserve, though in different ways. Scott's hard mouth kept its tight grimness even when he smiled. And Ilene's smiles came so often that they were meaningless.

Through her, Scott was able to understand more of the undersea life than he had ever done before. She was for him a catalyst. A tacit understanding grew between them, not needing words. Both realized that, in the course of progress, they would eventually die out. Mankind tolerated them because that was necessary for a little time. Each responded differently. Scott served Mars; he served actively; and the girl, who was passive, was attracted by the antithesis.

Scott's drunkenness struck psychically deep. He did not show it. His stiff silver-brown hair was not disarranged, and his hard, burned face was impassive as ever. But when his brown eyes met Ilene's green ones a spark of—something—met between them.

Color and light and sound. They began to form a pattern now, were not quite meaningless to Scott. They were, long past midnight, sitting in an Olympus, which was a private cosmos. The walls of the room in which they were seemed nonexistent. The gusty tides of gray, faintly luminous clouds seemed to drive chaotically past them, and, dimly, they could hear the muffled screaming of an artificial wind. They had the isolation of the gods.

And the Earth was without form, and void; and darkness was upon the face of the deep— That was, of course, the theory of the Olympus room. No one existed, no world existed, outside of the chamber; values automatically shifted, and inhibitions seemed absurd.

Scott relaxed on a translucent cushion like a cloud. Beside him, Ilene lifted the bit of a happy-gas tube to his nostrils. He shook his head.

"Not now, Ilene."

She let the tube slide back into its reel. "Nor I. Too much of anything is unsatisfactory, Brian. There should always be something untasted, some anticipation left—You have that. I haven't."

"How?"

"Pleasures—well, there's a limit. There's a limit to human endurance. And eventually I build up a resistance psychically, as I do physically, to everything. With you, there's always the last adventure. You never know when death will come. You can't plan. Plans are dull; it's the unexpected that's important."

Scott shook his head slightly. "Death isn't important either. It's an automatic cancellation of values. Or, rather—" He hesitated, seeking words. "In this life you can plan, you can work out values, because they're all based on certain conditions. On—let's say—arithmetic. Death is a change to a different plane of conditions, quite unknown. Arithmetical rules don't apply as such to geometry."

"You think death has its rules?"

"It may be a lack of rules, Ilene. One lives realizing that life is subject to death; civilization is based on that. That's why civilization concentrates on the race instead of the individual. Social self-preservation."

She looked at him gravely. "I didn't think a Free Companion could theorize that way."

Scott closed his eyes, relaxing. "The Keeps know nothing about Free Companions. They don't want to. We're men. Intelligent men. Our technicians are as great as the scientists under the Domes."

"But they work for war."

"War's necessary," Scott said. "Now, anyway."

"How did you get into it? Should I ask?"

He laughed a little at that. "Oh, I've no dark secrets in my past. I'm not a runaway murderer. One—drifts. I was born in Australia Keep. My father was a tech, but my grandfather had been a soldier. I guess it was in my blood. I tried various trades and professions. Meaningless. I wanted something that . . . hell, I don't know. Something, maybe, that needs all of a man. Fighting does. It's like a religion. Those cultists—Men of the New Judgment—they're fanatics, but you can see that their religion is the only thing that matters to them."

"Bearded, dirty men with twisted minds, though."

"It happens to be a religion based on false premises. There are others, appealing to different types. But religion was too passive for me, in these days."

Ilene examined his harsh face. "You'd have perferred the church militant—the Knights of Malta, fighting Saracens."

"I suppose. I had no values. Anyhow, I'm a fighter."

"Just how important is it to you? The Free Companions?"

Scott opened his eyes and grinned at the girl. He looked unexpectedly boyish.

"Damn little, really. It has emotional appeal. Intellectually, I know that it's a huge fake. Always has been. As absurd as the Men of the New Judgment. Fighting's doomed. So we've no real purpose. I suppose most of us know there's no future for the Free Companions. In a few hundred years—well!"

"And still you go on. Why? It isn't money."

"No. There is a . . . a drunkenness to it. The ancient Norsemen had their berserker madness. We have something similar. To a Dooneman, his group is father, mother, child, and God Almighty. He fights the other Free Companions when he's paid to do so, but he doesn't hate the others. They serve the same toppling idol. And it *is* toppling, Ilene. Each battle we win or lose brings us closer to the end. We fight to protect the culture that eventually will wipe us out. The Keeps—when they finally unify, will they need a military arm? I can see the trend. If war were an essential part of civilization, each Keep would maintain its own military. But they shut us out—a necessary evil. If they would end war now!" Scott's fist unconsciously clenched. "So many men would find happier places in Venus—undersea. But as long as the Free Companions exist, there'll be new recruits."

Ilene sipped her cocktail, watching the gray chaos of clouds flow like a tide around them. In the dimly luminous light Scott's face seemed like dark stone, flecks of brightness showing in his eyes. She touched his hand gently.

"You're a soldier, Brian. You wouldn't change."

His laugh was intensely bitter. "Like hell I wouldn't, Mistress Ilene Kane! Do you think fighting's just pulling a trigger? I'm a military strategist. That took ten years. Harder cramming than I'd have had in a Keep Tech-Institute. I have to know everything about war from trajectories to mass psychology. This is the greatest science the System has ever known, and the most useless. Because war will die in a few centuries at most. Ilene—you've never seen a Free Company's fort. It's science, marvelous science, aimed at military ends only. We have our psych-specialists. We have our engineers, who plan everything from ordnance to the frictional quotient on flitterboats. We have the foundries and mills. Each fortress is a city made for war, as the Keeps are made for social progress."

"As complicated as that?"

"Beautifully complicated and beautifully useless. There are so many of us who realize that. Oh, we fight—it's a poison. We worship the Company—that is an emotional poison. But we live only during wartime. It's an incomplete life. Men in the Keeps have full lives; they have their work, and their relaxations are geared to fit them. We don't fit."

"Not all the undersea races," Ilene said. "There's always the fringe that doesn't fit. At least you have a *raison d'être*. You're a soldier. I can't make a lifework out of pleasure. But there's nothing else for me."

Scott's fingers tightened on hers. "You're the product of a civilization, at least. I'm left out."

"With you, Brian, it might be better. For a while. I don't think it would last for long."

"It might."

"You think so now. It's quite a horrible thing, feeling yourself a shadow."

"I know."

"I want you, Brian," Ilene said, turning to face him. "I want you to come to Montana Keep and stay here. Until our experiment fails. I think it'll fail presently. But, perhaps, not for some time. I need your strength. I can show you how to get the most out of this sort of life—how to enter into it.

True hedonism. You can give me—companionship perhaps.
For me the companionship of hedonists who know nothing
else isn't enough."

Scott was silent. Ilene watched him for a while.

"Is war so important?" she asked at last.

"No," he said, "it isn't at all. It's a balloon. And it's empty,
I know that. Honor of the regiment!" Scott laughed. "I'm not
hesitating, really. I've been shut out for a long time. A social
unit shouldn't be founded on an obviously doomed fallacy.
Men and women are important, nothing else, I suppose."

"Men and women—or the race?"

"Not the race," he said with abrupt violence. "Damn the
race! It's done nothing for me. I can fit myself into a new
life. Not necessarily hedonism. I'm an expert in several lines;
I have to be. I can find work in Montana Keep."

"If you like. I've never tried. I'm more of a fatalist, I suppose. But . . . what about it, Brian?"

Her eyes were almost luminous, like shining emerald, in
the ghostly light.

"Yes," Scott said. "I'll come back. To stay."

Ilene said, "Come back? Why not stay now?"

"Because I'm a complete fool, I guess. I'm a key man, and
Cinc Rhys needs me just now."

"Is it Rhys or the Company?"

Scott smiled crookedly. "Not the Company. It's just a job I
have to do. When I think how many years I've been slaving,
pretending absurdities were important, knowing that I was
bowing to a straw dummy— *No!* I want your life—the sort
of life I didn't know could exist in the Keeps. I'll be back,
Ilene. It's something more important than love. Separately
we're halves. Together we may be a complete whole."

She didn't answer. Her eyes were steady on Scott's. He
kissed her.

Before morning bell he was back in the apartment. Jeana
had already packed the necessary light equipment. She was
asleep, her dark hair cascading over the pillow, and Scott did
not waken her. Quietly he shaved, showered, and dressed. A
heavy, waiting silence seemed to fill the city like a cup
brimmed with stillness.

As he emerged from the bathroom, buttoning his tunic, he
saw the table had been let down and two places set at it.

Jeana came in, wearing a cool morning frock. She set cups down and poured coffee.

"Morning, soldier," she said. "You've time for this, haven't you?"

"Uh-huh." Scott kissed her, a bit hesitantly. Up till this moment, the breaking with Jeana had seemed easy enough. She would raise no objections. That was the chief reason for free-marriage. However—

She was sitting in the relaxer, sweetening the coffee, opening a fresh celopack of cigarettes. "Hung over?"

"No. I vitamized. Feel pretty good." Most bars had a vita-minizing chamber to nullify the effects of too much stimulant. Scott was, in fact, feeling fresh and keenly alert. He was wondering how to broach the subject of Ilene to Jeana.

She saved him the trouble.

"If it's a girl, Brian, just take it easy. No use doing anything till this war's over. How long will it take?"

"Oh, not long. A week at most. One battle may settle it, you know. The girl—"

"She's not a Keep girl."

"Yes."

Jeana looked up, startled. "You're crazy."

"I started to tell you," Scott said impatiently. "It isn't just—her. I'm sick of the Doones. I'm going to quit."

"Hm-m-m. Like that?"

"Like that."

Jeana shook her head. "Keep women aren't tough."

"They don't need to be. Their men aren't soldiers."

"Have it your own way. I'll wait till you get back. Maybe I've got a hunch. You see, Brian, we've been together for five years. We fit. Not because of anything like philosophy or psy-chology—it's a lot more personal. It's just us. As man and woman, we get along comfortably. There's love, too. Those close emotional feelings are more important, really, than the long view. You can get excited about futures, but you can't live them."

Scott shrugged. "Could be I'm starting to forget about fu-tures. Concentrating on Brian Scott."

"More coffee . . . there. Well, for five years now I've gone with you from Keep to Keep, waiting every time you went off to war, wondering if you'd come back, knowing that I was just a part of your life, but—I sometimes thought—the most important part. Soldiering's seventy-five percent. I'm the other quarter. I think you need that quarter—you need the whole thing, in that proportion, actually. You could find another woman, but she'd have to be willing to take twenty-five percent."

Scott didn't answer. Jeana blew smoke through her nostrils.

"O.K., Brian. I'll wait."

"It isn't the girl so much. She happens to fit into the pattern of what I want. You—"

"I'd never be able to fit that pattern," Jeana said softly. "The Free Companions need women who are willing to be soldiers' wives. Freewives, if you like. Chiefly it's a matter of not being too demanding. But there are other things. No, Brian. Even if you want that, I couldn't make myself over into one of the Keep people. It wouldn't be me. I wouldn't respect myself, living a life that'd be false to me; and you wouldn't like me that way either. I couldn't and wouldn't change. I'll have to stay as I am. A soldier's wife. As long as you're a Dooneman, you'll need me. But if *you* change—"
She didn't finish.

Scott lit a cigarette, scowling. "It's hard to know, exactly."

"I may not understand you, but I don't ask questions and I don't try to change you. As long as you want that, you can have it from me. I've nothing else to offer you. It's enough for a Free Companion. It's not enough—or too much—for a Keep-dweller."

"I'll miss you," he said.

"That'll depend, too. I'll miss you." Under the table her fingers writhed together, but her face did not change. "It's getting late. Here, let me check your chronometer." Jeana leaned across the table, lifted Scott's wrist, and compared his watch with the central-time clock on the wall. "O.K. On your way, soldier."

Scott stood up, tightening his belt. He bent to kiss Jeana, and, though she began to turn her face away, after a moment she raised her lips to his.

They didn't speak. Scott went out quickly, and the girl sat motionless, the cigarette smoldering out unheeded between her fingers. Somehow it did not matter so much, now, that Brian was leaving her for another woman and another life. As always, the one thing of real importance was that he was going into danger.

Guard him from harm, she thought, not knowing that she was praying. *Guard him from harm!*

And now there would be silence, and waiting. That, at least, had not changed. Her eyes turned to the clock.

Already the minutes were longer.

III.

'E's the kind of a giddy harumfrodite—soldier an' sailor too!
—*Kipling*

Commander Bienne was superintending the embarkation of the last Dooneman when Scott arrived at headquarters. He saluted the captain briskly, apparently untired by his night's work of handling the transportation routine.

"All checked, sir."

Scott nodded. "Good. Is Cinc Rhys here?"

"He just arrived." Bienne nodded toward a door-curtain. As Scott moved away, the other followed.

"What's up, commander?"

Bienne pitched his voice low. "Bronson's laid up with endemic fever." He forgot to say "sir." "He was to handle the left wing of the fleet. I'd appreciate that job."

"I'll see if I can do it."

Bienne's lips tightened, but he said nothing more. He turned back to his men, and Scott went on into the cinc's office. Rhys was at the telaudio. He looked up, his eyes narrowed.

"Morning, captain. I've just heard from Mendez."

"Yes, sir?"

"He's still holding out for a fifty-percent cut on the korium ransom from Virginia Keep. You'll have to see him. Try and get the Mob for less than fifty if you can. Telaudio me from Mendez's fort."

"Check, sir."

"Another thing. Bronson's in sick bay."

"I heard that. If I may suggest Commander Bienne to take his place at left-wing command—"

But Cinc Rhys raised his hand. "Not this time. We can't afford individualism. The commander tried to play a lone hand in the last war. You know we can't risk it till he's back in line—thinking of the Doones instead of Fredric Bienne."

"He's a good man, sir. A fine strategist."

"But not yet a good integrating factor. Perhaps next time. Put Commander Geer on the left wing. Keep Bienne with you. He needs discipline. And—take a flitterboat to Mendez."

"Not a plane?"

"One of the technicians just finished a new tight-beam camouflager for communications. I'm having it installed immediately on all our planes and gliders. Use the boat; it isn't far to the Mob's fort—that long peninsula on the coast of Southern Hell."

Even on the charts that continent was named Hell—for obvious reasons. Heat was only one of them. And, even with the best equipment, a party exploring the jungle there would soon find itself suffering the tortures of the damned. On the land of Venus, flora and fauna combined diabolically to make the place uninhabitable to Earthmen. Many of the plants even exhaled poisonous gases. Only the protected coastal forts of the Free Companies could exist—and that was because they *were* forts.

Cinc Rhys frowned at Scott. "We'll use H-plan 7 if we can get the Mob. Otherwise we'll have to fall back on another outfit, and I don't want to do that. The Helldivers have too many subs, and we haven't enough detectors. So do your damnedest."

Scott saluted. "I'll do that, sir." Rhys waved him away, and he went out into the next room, finding Commander Bienne alone. The officer turned an inquiring look toward him.

"Sorry," Scott said. "Geer gets the left-wing command this time."

Bienne's sour face turned dark red. "I'm sorry I didn't take a crack at you before mobilization," he said. "You hate competition, don't you?"

Scott's nostrils flared. "If it had been up to me, you'd have got that command, Bienne."

"Sure. I'll bet. All right, captain. Where's my bunk? A flitterboat?"

"You'll be on right wing, with me. Control ship *Flintlock*."

"With you. Under you, you mean," Bienne said tightly. His eyes were blazing. "Yeah."

Scott's dark cheeks were flushed too. "Orders, commander," he snapped. "Get me a flitterboat pilot. I'm going topside."

Without a word Bienne turned to the telaudio. Scott, a tight, furious knot in his stomach, stamped out of headquarters, trying to fight down his anger. Bienne was a jackass. A lot he cared about the Doones—

Scott caught himself and grinned sheepishly. Well, he cared little about the Doones himself. But while he was in the Company, discipline was important—integration with the smoothly running fighting machine. No place for individualism. One thing he and Bienne had in common; neither had any sentiment about the Company.

He took a lift to the ceiling of the Dome. Beneath him Montana Keep dropped away, shrinking to doll size. Somewhere down there, he thought, was Ilene. He'd be back. Perhaps this war would be a short one—not that they were ever much longer than a week, except in unusual cases when a Company developed new strategies.

He was conducted through an air lock into a bubble, a tough, transparent sphere with a central vertical core through which the cable ran. Except for Scott, the bubble was empty. After a moment it started up with a slight jar. Gradually the water outside the curving walls changed from black to deep green, and thence to translucent chartreuse. Sea creatures were visible, but they were nothing new to Scott; he scarcely saw them.

The bubble broke surface. Since air pressure had been constant, there was no possibility of the bends, and Scott opened the panel and stepped out on one of the buoyant floats that dotted the water above Montana Keep. A few sightseers crowded into the chamber he had left, and presently it was drawn down, out of sight.

In the distance Free Companions were embarking from a larger float in an air ferry. Scott glanced up with a weather eye. No storm, he saw, though the ceiling was, as usual, torn and twisted into boiling currents by the winds. He remembered, suddenly, that the battle would probably take place over Venus Deep. That would make it somewhat harder for the gliders—there would be few of the thermals found, for instance, above the Sea of Shallows here.

A flitterboat, low, fast, and beautifully maneuverable, shot in toward the quay. The pilot flipped back the overhead shell and saluted Scott. It was Norman Kane, looking shipshape in his tight-fitting gray uniform, and apparently ready to grin at the slightest provocation.

Scott jumped lightly down into the craft and seated himself beside the pilot. Kane drew the transparent shell back over them. He looked at Scott.

"Orders, captain?"

"Know where the Mob's fort is? Good. Head there. Fast."

Kane shot the flitterboat out from the float with a curtain of v-shaped spray rising from the bow. Drawing little water, maneuverable, incredibly fast, these tiny craft were invaluable in naval battle. It was difficult to hit one, they moved so fast. They had no armor to slow them down. They carried high-explosive bullets fired from smaller-caliber guns, and were, as a rule, two-man craft. They complemented the heavier ordnance of the battlewagons and destroyers.

Scott handed Kane a cigarette. The boy hesitated.

"We're not under fire," the captain chuckled. "Discipline clamps down during a battle, but it's O.K. for you to have a smoke with me. Here!" He lit the white tube for Kane.

"Thanks, sir. I guess I'm a bit—over-anxious?"

"Well, war has its rules. Not many, but they mustn't be broken." Both men were silent for a while, watching the blank gray surface of the ocean ahead. A transport plane passed them, flying low.

"Is Ilene Kane your sister?" Scott asked presently.

Kane nodded. "Yes, sir."

"Thought so. If she'd been a man, I imagine she'd have been a Free Companion."

The boy shrugged. "Oh, I don't know. She doesn't have the—I don't know. She'd consider it too much effort. She doesn't like discipline."

"Do you?"

"It's fighting that's important to me. Sir." That was an afterthought. "Winning, really."

"You can lose a battle even though you win it," Scott said rather somberly.

"Well, I'd rather be a Free Companion than do anything else I know of. Not that I've had much experience—"

"You've had experience of war with Starling's outfit, but you probably learned some dangerous stuff at the same time. War isn't swashbuckling piracy these days. If the Doones tried to win battles by that sort of thing, there'd be no more Doones in a week or so."

"But—" Kane hesitated. "Isn't that sort of thing rather necessary? Taking blind chances, I mean—"

"There are desperate chances," Scott told him, "but there are no blind chances in war—not to a good soldier. When I was green in the service, I ran a cruiser out of the line to ram. I was demoted, for a very good reason. The enemy ship

I rammed wasn't as important to the enemy as our cruiser was to us. If I'd stayed on course, I'd have helped sink three or four ships instead of disabling one and putting my cruiser out of action. It's the great god integration we worship, Kane. It's much more important now than it ever was on Earth, because the military has consolidated. Army, navy, air, undersea—they're all part of one organization now. I suppose the only important change was in the air."

"Gliders, you mean? I knew powered planes couldn't be used in battle."

"Not in the atmosphere of Venus," Scott agreed. "Once powered planes get up in the cloud strata, they're fighting crosscurrents and pockets so much they've got no time to do accurate firing. If they're armored, they're slow. If they're light, detectors can spot them and antiaircraft can smash them. Unpowered gliders are valuable not for bombing but for directing attacks. They get into the clouds, stay hidden, and use infrared telecameras which are broadcast on a tight beam back to the control ships. They're the eyes of the fleet. They can tell us—*White water ahead, Kane! Swerve!*"

The pilot had already seen the ominous boiling froth foaming out in front of the bow. Instinctively he swung the flitterboat in a wrenching turn. The craft heeled sidewise, throwing its occupants almost out of their seats.

"Sea beast?" Scott asked, and answered his own question. "No, not with those spouts. It's volcanic. And it's spreading fast."

"I can circle it, sir," Kane suggested.

Scott shook his head. "Too dangerous. Backtrack."

Obediently the boy sent the flitterboat racing out of the area of danger. Scott had been right about the extent of the danger; the boiling turmoil was widening almost faster than the tiny ship could flee. Suddenly the line of white water caught up with them. The flitterboat jounced like a chip, the wheel being nearly torn from Kane's grip. Scott reached over and helped steady it. Even with two men handling the wheel, there was a possibility that it might wrench itself free. Steam rose in veils beyond the transparent shell. The water had turned a scummy brown under the froth.

Kane jammed on the power. The flitterboat sprang forward like a ricocheting bullet, dancing over the surface of the seething waves. Once they plunged head-on into a swell, and a screaming of outraged metal vibrated through the craft. Kane, tight-lipped, instantly slammed in the auxiliary, cutting out the smashed motor unit. Then, unexpectedly, they were in clear water, cutting back toward Montana Keep.

Scott grinned. "Nice handling. Lucky you didn't try to circle. We'd never have made it."

"Yes, sir." Kane took a deep breath. His eyes were bright with excitement.

"Circle now. Here." He thrust a lighted cigarette between the boy's lips. "You'll be a good Dooneman, Kane. Your reactions are good and fast."

"Thanks, sir."

Scott smoked silently for a while. He glanced toward the north, but, with the poor visibility, he could not make out the towering range of volcanic peaks that were the backbone of Southern Hell. Venus was a comparatively young planet, the internal fires still bursting forth unexpectedly. Which was why no forts were ever built on islands—they had an unhappy habit of disappearing without warning!

The flitterboat rode hard, at this speed, despite the insulating system of springs and shocks absorbers. After a ride in one of these "spankers"—the irreverent name the soldiers had for them—a man needed arnica if not a chiropractor. Scott shifted his weight on the soft air cushions under him, which felt like cement.

Under his breath he hummed:

"It ain't the 'eavy 'aulin' that 'urts the 'orses' 'oofs,
It's the 'ammer, 'ammer, 'ammer on the 'ard 'ighway!"

The flitterboat scooted on, surrounded by monotonous sea and cloud, till finally the rampart of the coast grew before the bow, bursting suddenly from the fog-veiled horizon. Scott glanced at his chronometer and sighed with relief. They had made good time, in spite of the slight delay caused by the subsea volcano.

The fortress of the Mob was a huge metal and stone castle on the tip of the peninsula. The narrow strip that separated it from the mainland had been cleared, and the pockmarks of shell craters showed where guns had driven back onslaughts from the jungle—the reptilian, ferocious giants of Venus, partially intelligent but absolutely untractable because of the gulf that existed between their methods of thinking and the culture of mankind. Overtures had been made often enough; but it had been found that the reptile-folk were better left alone. They would not parley. They were blindly bestial savages, with whom it was impossible to make truce. They stayed in the jungle, emerging only to hurl furious attacks at the forts—attacks doomed to failure, since fang and talon were matched against lead-jacketed bullet and high explosive.

As the flitterboat shot in to a jetty, Scott kept his eyes straight ahead—it was not considered good form for a Free Companion to seem too curious when visiting the fort of another Company. Several men were on the quay, apparently waiting for him. They saluted as Scott stepped out of the boat.

He gave his name and rank. A corporal stepped forward.

"Cinc Mendez is expecting you, sir. Cinc Rhys telaudioed an hour or so back. If you'll come this way—"

"All right, corporal. My pilot—"

"He'll be taken care of, sir. A rubdown and a drink, perhaps, after a spanker ride."

Scott nodded and followed the other into the bastion that thrust out from the overhanging wall of the fort. The sea gate was open, and he walked swiftly through the courtyard in the corporal's wake, passing a door-curtain, mounting an escalator, and finding himself, presently, before another curtain that bore the face of Cinc Mendez, plump, hoglike, and bald as a bullet.

Entering, he saw Mendez himself at the head of a long table, where nearly a dozen officers of the Mob were also seated. In person Mendez was somewhat more prepossessing than in effigy. He looked like a boar rather than a pig—a fighter, not a gourmand. His sharp black eyes seemed to drive into Scott with the impact of a physical blow.

He stood up, his officers following suit. "Sit down, captain. There's a place at the foot of the table. No reflections on rank, but I prefer to be face to face with the man I'm dealing with. But first—you just arrived? If you'd like a quick rubdown, we'll be glad to wait."

Scott took his place. "Thank you, no, Cinc Mendez. I'd prefer not to lose time."

"Then we'll waste none on introductions. However, you can probably stand a drink." He spoke to the orderly at the door, and presently a filled glass stood at Scott's elbow.

His quick gaze ran along the rows of faces. Good soldiers, he thought—tough, well trained, and experienced. They had been under fire. A small outfit, the Mob, but a powerful one.

Cinc Mendez sipped his own drink. "To business. The Doonemen wish to hire our help in fighting the Helldivers. Virginia Keep has bought the services of the Helldivers to attack Montana Keep." He enumerated on stubby fingers. "You offer us fifty thousand cash and thirty-five percent of the korium ransom. So?"

"That's correct."

"We ask fifty percent."

"It's high. The Doones have superior manpower and equipment."

"To us, not to the Helldivers. Besides, the percentage is contingent. If we should lose, we get only the cash payment."

Scott nodded. "That's correct, but the only real danger from the Helldivers is their submarine corps. The Doones have plenty of surface and air equipment. We might lick the Helldivers without you."

"I don't think so." Mendez shook his bald head. "They have some new underwater torpedoes that make hash out of heavy armor plate. But *we* have new sub-detectors. We can blast the Helldivers' subs for you before they get within torpedo range."

Scott said bluntly, "You've been stalling, Cinc Mendez. We're not that bad off. If we can't get you, we'll find another outfit."

"With sub-detectors?"

"Yardley's Company is good at undersea work."

A major near the head of the table spoke up. "That's true, sir. They have suicide subs—not too dependable, but they have them."

Cinc Mendez wiped his bald head with his palms in a slow circular motion. "Hm-m-m. Well, captain, I don't know. Yardley's Company isn't as good as ours for this job."

"All right," Scott said, "I've *carte blanche*. We don't know how much korium Virginia Keep has in her vaults. How would this proposition strike you: the Mob gets fifty percent of the korium ransom up to a quarter of a million; thirty-five percent above that."

"Forty-five."

"Forty, above a quarter of a million; forty-five below that sum."

"Gentlemen?" Cinc Mendez asked, looking down the table. "Your vote?"

There were several ayes, and a scattering of nays. Mendez shrugged.

"Then I have the deciding vote. Very well. We get forty-five percent of the Virginia Keep ransom up to a quarter of a million; forty percent on any amount above that. Agreed. We'll drink to it."

Orderlies served drinks. As Mendez rose, the others followed his example. The cinc nodded to Scott.

"Will you propose a toast, captain?"

"With pleasure. Nelson's toast, then—a willing foe and sea room!"

They drank to that, as Free Companions had always drunk that toast on the eve of battle. As they seated themselves once more, Mendez said, "Major Matson, please telaudio Cinc Rhys and arrange details. We must know his plans."

"Yes, sir."

Mendez glanced at Scott. "Now how else may I serve you?"

"Nothing else. I'll get back to our fort. Details can be worked out on the telaudio, on tight beam."

"If you're going back in that flitterboat," Mendez said sardonically, "I strongly advise a rubdown. There's time to spare, now we've come to an agreement."

Scott hesitated. "Very well. I'm . . . uh . . . starting to ache." He stood up. "Oh, one thing I forgot. We've heard rumors that Starling's outfit is using atomic power."

Mendez's mouth twisted into a grimace of distaste. "Hadn't heard that. Know anything about it, gentlemen?"

Heads were shaken. One officer said, "I've heard a little talk about it, but only talk, so far."

Mendez said, "After this war, we'll investigate further. If there's truth in the story, we'll join you, of course, in mopping up the Starlings. No court-martial is necessary for *that* crime!"

"Thanks. I'll get in touch with other Companies and see what they've heard. Now, if you'll excuse me—"

He saluted and went out, exaltation flaming within him. The bargain had been a good one—for the Doonemen badly needed the Mob's help against the Helldivers. Cinc Rhys would be satisfied with the arrangement.

An orderly took him to the baths, where a rubdown relaxed his aching muscles. Presently he was on the quay again, climbing into the flitterboat. A glance behind him showed that the gears of war were beginning to grind. There was little he could see, but men were moving about through the courtyard with purposeful strides, to the shops, to administration, to the laboratories. The battlewagons were anchored down the coast, Scott knew, in a protected bay, but they would soon move out to their rendezvous with the Doones.

Kane, at the controls of the flitterboat, said, "They repaired the auxiliary unit for us, sir."

"Courtesies of the trade." Scott lifted a friendly hand to the men on the quay as the boat slid toward open water. "The Doone fort, now. Know it?"

"Yes, sir. Are . . . are the Mob fighting with us, if I may ask?"

"They are. And they're a grand lot of fighters. You're going to see action, Kane. When you hear battle stations next, it's going to mean one of the sweetest scraps that happened on Venus. Push down that throttle—we're in a hurry!"

The flitterboat raced southwest at top speed, its course marked by the flying V of spray.

"One last fight," Scott thought to himself. "I'm glad it's going to be a good one."

IV.

We eat and drink our own damnation.
—The Book of Common Prayer

The motor failed when they were about eight miles from the Doone fort.

It was a catastrophe rather than a merely a failure. The overstrained and overheated engine, running at top speed, blew back. The previous accident, at the subsea volcano, had brought out hidden flaws in the alloy which the Mob's repairmen had failed to detect when they replaced the smashed single unit. Sheer luck had the flitterboat poised on a swell when the crack-up happened. The engine blew out and down, ripping the bow to shreds. Had they been bow-deep, the blast would have been unfortunate for Scott and the pilot—more so than it was.

They were perhaps a half mile from the shore. Scott was

deafened by the explosion and simultaneously saw the horizon swinging in a drunken swoop. The boat turned turtle, the shell smacking into water with a loud cracking sound. But the plastic held. Both men were tangled together on what had been their ceiling, sliding forward as the flitterboat began to sink bow first. Steam sizzled from the ruined engine.

Kane managed to touch one of the emergency buttons. The shell was, of course, jammed, but a few of the segments slid aside, admitting a gush of acrid sea water. For a moment they struggled there, fighting the cross-currents till the air had been displaced. Scott, peering through cloudy green gloom, saw Kane's dark shadow twist and kick out through a gap. He followed.

Beneath him the black bulk of the boat dropped slowly and was gone. His head broke surface, and he gasped for breath, shaking droplets from his lashes and glancing around. Where was Kane?

The boy appeared, his helmet gone, sleek hair plastered to his forehead. Scott caught his eye and pulled the trigger on his life vest, the inflatable undergarment which was always worn under the blouse on sea duty. As chemicals mixed, light gas rushed into the vest, lifting Scott higher in the water. He felt the collar cushion inflate against the back of his head—the skull-fitting pillow that allowed shipwrecked men to float and rest without danger of drowning in their sleep. But he had no need for this now.

Kane, he saw, had triggered his own life vest. Scott hurled himself up, searching for signs of life. There weren't any. The gray-green sea lay desolate to the misty horizon. A half mile away was a mottled chartreuse wall that marked the jungle. Above and beyond that dim sulphurous red lit the clouds.

Scott got out his leaf-bladed smatchet, gesturing for Kane to do the same. The boy did not seem worried. No doubt this was merely an exciting adventure for him, Scott thought wryly. Oh, well.

Gripping the smatchet between his teeth, the captain began to swim shoreward. Kane kept at his side. Once Scott warned his companion to stillness and bent forward, burying his face in the water and peering down at a great dim shadow that coiled away and was gone—a sea snake, but, luckily, not hungry. The oceans of Venus were perilous with teeming, ferocious life. Precautions were fairly useless. When a man was once in the water, it was up to him to get out of it as rapidly as possible.

Scott touched a small cylinder attached to his belt and felt bubbles rushing against his palm. He was slightly relieved. When he had inflated the vest, this tube of compressed gas had automatically begun to release, sending out a foul-smelling vapor that permeated the water for some distance around. The principle was that of the skunk adjusted to the environment of the squid, and dangerous undersea life was supposed to be driven away by the Mellison tubes; but it didn't work with carrion eaters like the snakes. Scott averted his nose. The gadgets were named Mellison tubes, but the men called them Stinkers, a far more appropriate term.

Tides on Venus are unpredictable. The clouded planet has no moon, but it is closer to the sun than Earth. As a rule the tides are mild, except during volcanic activity, when tidal waves sweep the shores. Scott, keeping a weather eye out for danger, rode the waves in toward the beach, searching the strip of dull blackness for signs of life.

Nothing.

He scrambled out at last, shaking himself like a dog, and instantly changed the clip in his automatic for high explosive. The weapon, of course, was watertight—a necessity on Venus. As Kane sat down with a grunt and deflated his vest, Scott stood eyeing the wall of jungle thirty feet away. It stopped there abruptly, for nothing could grow on black sand.

The rush and whisper of the waves made the only sound. Most of the trees were liana-like, eking out a precarious existence, as the saying went, by taking in each other's washing. The moment one of them showed signs of solidity, it was immediately assailed by parasitic vines flinging themselves madly upward to reach the filtered sunlight of Venus. The leaves did not begin for thirty feet above the ground; they made a regular roof up there, lying like crazy shingles, and would have shut out all light had they not been of light translucent green. Whitish tendrils crawled like reaching serpents from tree to tree, tentacles of vegetable octopi. There were two types of Venusian fauna: the giants who could crash through the forest, and the supple, small ground-dwellers—insects and reptiles mostly—who depended on poison sacs for self-protection. Neither kind was pleasant company.

There were flying creatures, too, but these lived in the upper strata, among the leaves. And there were ambiguous horrors that lived in the deep mud and the stagnant pools under the forest, but no one knew much about these.

"Well," Scott said, "that's that."

Kane nodded. "I guess I should have checked the motors."

"You wouldn't have found anything. Latent flaws—it would have taken black night to bring 'em out. Just one of those things. Keep your gas mask handy, now. If we get anywhere near poison flowers and the wind's blowing this way, we're apt to keep over like that." Scott opened a water-proof wallet and took out a strip of sensitized litmus, which he clipped to his wrist. "If this turns blue, that means gas, even if we don't smell it."

"Yes, sir. What now?"

"We-el—the boat's gone. We can't telaudio for help." Scott fingered the blade of his smatchet and slipped it into the belt sheath. "We head for the fort. Eight miles. Two hours, if we can stick to the beach and if we don't run into trouble. More than that if Signal Rock's ahead of us, because we'll have to detour inland in that case." He drew out a collapsible single-lenser telescope and looked southwest along the shore. "Uh-huh. We detour."

A breath of sickening sweetness gusted down from the jungle roof. From above, Scott knew, the forest looked surprisingly lovely. It always reminded him of an antique candlewick spread he had once bought Jeana—immense rainbow flowers scattered over a background of pale green. Even among the flora competition was keen; the plants vied in producing colors and scents that would attract the winged carriers of pollen.

There would always be frontiers, Scott thought. But they might remain unconquered for a long time, here on Venus. The Keeps were enough for the undersea folk; they were self-sustaining. And the Free Companions had no need to carve out empires on the continents. They were fighters, not agrarians. Land hunger was no longer a part of the race. It might come again, but not in the time of the Keeps.

The jungles of Venus held secrets he would never know. Men can conquer lands from the air, but they cannot hold them by that method. It would take a long, slow period of encroachment, during which the forest and all it represented would be driven back, step by painful step—and that belonged to a day to come, a time Scott would not know. The savage world would be tamed. But not now—not yet.

At the moment it was untamed and very dangerous. Scott stripped off his tunic and wrung water from it. His clothing would not dry in this saturated air, despite the winds. His trousers clung to him stickily, clammy coldness in their folds.

"Ready, Kane?"

"Yes, sir."

"Then let's go."

_ They went southwest, along the beach, at a steady, easy lope that devoured miles. Speed and alertness were necessary in equal proportion. From time to time Scott scanned the sea with his telescope, hoping to sight a vessel. He saw nothing. The ships would be in harbor, readying for the battle, and planes would be grounded for installation of the new telaudio device Cinc Rhys had mentioned.

Signal Rock loomed ahead, an outthrust crag with eroded, unscalable sides towering two hundred feet and more. The black strip of sand ended there. From the rock there was a straight drop into deep water, cut up by a turmoil of currents. It was impossible to take the sea detour; there was nothing else for it but to swerve inland, a dangerous but inevitable course. Scott postponed the plunge as long as possible, till the scarp of Signal Rock, jet black with leprous silvery patches on its surface, barred the way. With a quizzical look at Kane he turned sharply to his right and headed for the jungle.

"Half a mile of forest equals a hundred miles of beach hiking," he remarked.

"That bad, sir? I've never tackled it."

"Nobody does, unless they have to. Keep your eyes open and your gun ready. Don't wade through water, even when you can see bottom. There are some little devils that are pretty nearly transparent—vampire fish. If a few of those fasten on you, you'll need a transfusion in less than a minute. I wish the volcanoes would kick up a racket. The beasties generally lie low when that happens."

Under a tree Scott stopped, seeking a straight, long limb. It took a while to find a suitable one, in that tangle of coiling lianas, but finally he succeeded, using his smatchet blade to hack himself a light five-foot pole. Kane at his heels, he moved on into the gathering gloom.

"We may be stalked," he told the boy. "Don't forget to guard the rear."

The sand had given place to sticky whitish mud that plastered the men to their calves before a few moments had passed. A patina of slickness seemed to overlay the ground. The grass was colored so much like the mud itself that it was practically invisible, except by its added slipperiness. Scott slowly advanced, keeping close to the wall of rock on his left where the tangle was not so thick. Nevertheless he had to use the smatchet more than once to cut a passage through vines.

He stopped, raising his hand, and the squelch of Kane's feet in the mud paused. Silently Scott pointed. Ahead of them in the cliff base was the mouth of a burrow.

The captain bent down, found a small stone, and threw it toward the den. He waited, one hand lightly on his gun, ready to see something flash out of that burrow and race toward them. In the utter silence a new sound made itself heard—tiny goblin drums, erratic and resonant in a faraway fashion. Water, dropping from leaf to leaf, in the soaked jungle ceiling above them. *Tink, tink, tink-tink, tink, tink-tink*—

"O.K.," Scott said quietly. "Watch it, though." He went on, gun drawn, till they were level with the mouth of the burrow. "Turn, Kane. Keep your eye on it till I tell you to stop." He gripped the boy's arm and guided him, holstering his own weapon. The pole, till now held between biceps and body, slipped into his hand. He used it to probe the slick surface of the mud ahead. Sinkhole and quicksands were frequent, and so were traps, camouflaged pits built by mud-wolves—which, of course, were not wolves, and belonged to no known genus. On Venus, the fauna had more subdivisions than on old Earth, and lines of demarcation more subtle.

"All right now."

Kane, sighing with relief, turned his face forward again. "What was it?"

"You never know what may come out of those holes," Scott told him. "They come fast, and they're usually poisonous. So you can't take chances with the critters. Slow down here. I don't like the looks of that patch ahead."

Clearings were unusual in the forest. There was one here, twenty feet wide, slightly saucer-shaped. Scott gingerly extended the pole and probed. A faint ripple shook the white mud, and almost before it had appeared the captain had unholstered his pistol and was blasting shot after shot at the movement.

"Shoot, Kane!" he snapped. "Quick! Shoot at it!"

Kane obeyed, though he had to guess at his target. Mud geysered up, suddenly crimson-stained. Scott, still firing, gripped the boy's arm and ran him back at a breakneck pace.

The echoes died. Once more the distant elfin drums whispered through the green gloom.

"We got it," Scott said, after a pause.

"We did?" the other asked blankly. "What—"

"Mud-wolf, I think. The only way to kill those things is to get 'em before they get out of the mud. They're fast and they die hard. However—" He warily went forward. There was nothing to see. The mud had collapsed into a deeper saucer, but the holes blasted by the high-x bullets had filled in. Here and there were traces of thready crimson.

"Never a dull moment," Scott remarked. His crooked grin eased the tension. Kane chuckled and followed the captain's example in replacing his half-used clip with a full one.

The narrow spine of Signal Rock extended inland for a quarter mile before it became scalable. They reached that point finally, helping each other climb, and finding themselves, at the summit, still well below the leafy ceiling of the trees. The black surface of the rock was painfully hot, stinging their palms as they climbed, and even striking through their shoe soles.

"Halfway point, captain?"

"Yeah. But don't let that cheer you. It doesn't get any better till we hit the beach again. We'll probably need some fever shots when we reach the fort, just in case. Oh-oh. Mask, Kane, quick." Scott lifted his arm. On his wrist the band of litmus had turned blue.

With trained accuracy they donned the respirators. Scott felt a faint stinging on his exposed skin, but that wasn't serious. Still, it would be painful later. He beckoned to Kane, slid down the face of the rock, used the pole to test the mud below, and jumped lightly. He dropped in the sticky whiteness and rolled over hastily, plastering himself from head to foot. Kane did the same. Mud wouldn't neutralize the poison flowers' gas, but it would absorb most of it before it reached the skin.

Scott headed toward the beach, a grotesque figure. Mud

dripped on the eye plate, and he scrubbed it away with a handful of white grass. He used the pole constantly to test the footing ahead.

Neverthless the mud betrayed him. The pole broke through suddenly, and as Scott automatically threw his weight back, the ground fell away under his feet. He had time for a crazy feeling of relief that this was quicksand, not a mud-wolf's den, and then the clinging, treacherous stuff had sucked him down knee-deep. He fell back, keeping his grip on the pole and swinging the other end in an arc toward Kane.

The boy seized it in both hands and threw himself flat. His foot hooked over an exposed root. Scott, craning his neck at a painfully awkward angle and trying to see through the mud-smeared vision plates, kept a rattrap grip on his end of the pole, hoping its slickness would not slip through his fingers.

He was drawn down farther, and then Kane's anchorage began to help. The boy tried to pull the pole toward him, hand over hand. Scott shook his head. He was a good deal stronger than Kane, and the latter would need all his strength to keep a tight grip on the pole.

Something stirred in the shadows behind Kane. Scott instinctively let go with one hand, and, with the other, got out his gun. It had a sealed mechanism, so the mud hadn't harmed the firing, and the muzzle had a one-way trap. He fired at the movement behind Kane, heard a muffled tumult, and waited till it had died. The boy, after a startled look behind him, had not stirred.

After that, rescue was comparatively easy. Scott simply climbed along the pole, spreading his weight over the surface of the quicksand. The really tough part was pulling his legs free of that deadly grip. Scott had to rest for five minutes after that.

But he got out. That was the important thing.

Kane pointed inquiringly into the bushes where the creature had been shot, but Scott shook his head. The nature of the beast wasn't a question worth deciding, as long as it was apparently *hors de combat*. Readjusting his mask, Scott turned toward the beach, circling the quicksand, and Kane kept at his heels.

Their luck had changed. They reached the shore with no further difficulty and collapsed on the black sand to rest.

Presently Scott used a litmus, saw that the gas had dissipated, and removed his mask. He took a deep breath.

"Thanks, Kane," he said. "You can take a dip now if you want to wash off that mud. But stay close inshore. No, don't strip. There's no time."

The mud clung like glue and the black sand scratched like pumice. Still, Scott felt a good deal cleaner after a few minutes in the surf, while Kane stayed on guard. Slightly refreshed, they resumed the march.

An hour later a convoy plane, testing, sighted them, telaudioed the fort, and a flitterboat came racing out to pick them up. What Scott appreciated most of all was the stiff shot of uisqueplus the pilot gave him.

Yeah. It was a dog's life, all right!

He passed the flask to Kane.

Presently the fort loomed ahead, guarding Doone Harbor. Large as the landlocked bay was, it could scarcely accommodate the fleet. Scott watched the activity visible with an approving eye. The flitterboat rounded the sea wall, built for protection against tidal waves, and shot toward a jetty. Its almost inaudible motor died; the shell swung back.

Scott got out, beckoning to an orderly.

"Yes, sir?"

"See that this soldier gets what he needs. We've been in the jungle."

The man didn't whistle sympathetically, but his mouth pursed. He saluted and helped Kane climb out of the flitterboat. As Scott hurried along the quay, he could hear an outburst of friendly profanity from the men on the dock, gathering around Kane.

He nodded imperceptibly. The boy would make a good Free Companion—always granted that he could stand the gaff under fire. That was the acid test. Discipline was tightened then to the snapping point. If it snapped—well, the human factor always remained a variable, in spite of all the psychologists could do.

He went directly to his quarters, switching on the telaudio to call Cinc Rhys. The cinc's seamed, leathery face resolved itself on the screen.

"Captain Scott reporting for duty, sir."

Rhys looked at him sharply. "What happened?"

"Flitterboat crack-up. Had to make it in here on foot."

The cinc called on his God in a mild voice. "Glad you made it. Any accident?"

"No, sir. The pilot's unharmed, too. I'm ready to take over, after I've cleaned up."

"Better take a rejuvenation—you probably need it. Everything's going like clockwork. You did a good job with Mendez—a better bargain than I'd hoped for. I've been talking with him on the telaudio, integrating our forces. We'll go into that later, though. Clean up and then make general inspection."

"Check, sir."

Rhys clicked off. Scott turned to face his orderly.

"Hello, Briggs. Help me off with these duds. You'll probably have to cut 'em off."

"Glad to see you back, sir. I don't think it'll be necessary to cut—" Blunt fingers flew deftly over zippers and clasps. "You were in the jungle?"

Scott grinned wryly. "Do I look as if I'd been gliding?"

"Not all the way, sir—no."

Briggs was like an old bulldog—one of those men who proved the truth of the saying: "Old soldiers never die, they only fade away." Briggs could have been pensioned off ten years ago, but he hadn't wanted that. There was always a place for old soldiers in the Free Companies, even those who were unskilled. Some became technicians; others, military instructors; the rest, orderlies. The forts were their homes. Had they retired to one of the Keeps, they would have died for lack of interests.

Briggs, now—he had never risen above the ranks, and knew nothing of military strategy, ordnance, or anything except plain fighting. But he had been a Dooneman for forty years, twenty-five of them on active service. He was sixty-odd now, his squat figure slightly stooped like an elderly bear, his ugly face masked with scar tissue.

"All right. Start the shower, will you?"

Briggs stumped off, and Scott, stripped of his filthy, sodden garments, followed. He luxuriated under the stinging spray, first hot soapy water, then alcomix, and after that plain water, first hot, then cold. That was the last task he had to do himself. Briggs took over, as Scott relaxed on the slab, dropping lotion into the captain's burning eyes, giving him a deft but murderous rubdown, combining osteopathic and chiropractic treatment, adjusting revitalizing lamps, and measuring a hypo shot to nullify fatigue toxins. When the orderly was finished, Scott was ready to resume his duties with a clear brain and a refreshed body.

Briggs appeared with fresh clothing. "I'll have the old uniform cleaned, sir. No use throwing it away."

"You can't clean that," Scott remarked, slipping into a singlet. "Not after I rolled in mud. But suit yourself. I won't be needing it for long."

The orderly's fingers, buttoning Scott's tunic, stopped briefly and then resumed their motion. "Is that so, sir?"

"Yeah. I'm taking out discharge papers."

"Another Company, sir?"

"Don't get on your high horse," Scott told the orderly. "It's not that. What would you do if it were? Court-martial me yourself and shoot me at sunrise?"

"No, sir. Begging your pardon, sir, I'd just think you were crazy."

"Why I stand you only the Lord knows," Scott remarked. "You're too damn independent. There's no room for new ideas in that plastic skull of yours. You're the quintessence of dogmatism."

Briggs nodded. "Probably, sir. When a man's lived by one set of rules for as long as I have, and those rules work out, I suppose he might get dogmatic."

"Forty years for you—about twelve for me."

"You came up fast, captain. You'll be cinc here yet."

"That's what you think."

"You're next in line after Cinc Rhys."

"But I'll be out of the Doones," Scott pointed out. "Keep that under your belt, Briggs."

The orderly grunted. "Can't see it, sir. If you don't join another Company, where'll you go?"

"Ever heard of the Keeps?"

Briggs permitted himself a respectful snort. "Sure. They're fine for a binge, but—"

"I'm going to live in one. Montana Keep."

"The Keeps were built with men and machines. I helped at the building of Doone fort. Blood's mixed with the plastic here. We had to hold back the jungle while the technicians were working. Eight months, sir, and never a day passed without some sort of attack. And attacks always meant casualties then. We had only breastworks. The ships laid down a barrage, but barrages aren't impassable. That was a fight, captain."

Scott thrust out a leg so that Briggs could lace his boots. "And a damn good one. I know." He looked down at the orderly's baldish, brown head where white hairs straggled.

"You know, but you weren't there, captain. I was. First we dynamited. We cleared a half circle where we could dig in behind breastworks. Behind us were the techs, throwing up a plastic wall as fast as they could. The guns were brought in on barges. Lying offshore were the battlewagons. We could hear the shells go whistling over our heads—it sounded pretty good, because we knew things were O.K. as long as the barrage kept up. But it couldn't be kept up day and night. The jungle broke through. For months the smell of blood hung here, and that drew the enemy."

"But you held them off."

"Sure, we did. Addison Doone was cinc then—he'd formed the Company years before, but we hadn't a fort. Doone fought with us. Saved my life once, in fact. Anyhow—we got the fort built, or rather the techs did. I won't forget the kick I got out of it when the first big gun blasted off from the wall behind us. There was a lot to do after that, but when that shell was fired, we knew we'd done the job."

Scott nodded. "You feel a proprietary interest in the fort, I guess."

Briggs looked puzzled. "The fort? Why, that doesn't mean much, captain. There are lots of forts. It's something more than that; I don't quite know what it is. It's seeing the fleet out there—breaking in the rookies—giving the old toasts at mess—knowing that—" He stopped, at a loss.

Scott's lips twisted wryly. "You don't really know, do you, Briggs?"

"Know what, sir?"

"Why you stay here. Why you can't believe I'd quit."

Briggs gave a little shrug. "Well—it's the Doones," he said. "That's all, captain. It's just that."

"And what the devil will it matter, in a few hundred years?"

"I suppose it won't. No, sir. But it isn't our business to think about that. We're Doonemen, that's all."

Scott didn't answer. He could easily have pointed out the fallacy of Briggs's argument, but what was the use? He stood up, the orderly whisking invisible dust off his tunic.

"All set, sir. Shipshape."

"Check, Briggs. Well, I've one more scrap, anyhow. I'll bring you back a souvenir, eh?"

The orderly saluted, grinning. Scott went out, feeling good. Inwardly he was chuckling rather sardonically at the false values he was supposed to take seriously. Of course many men had died when Doone fort had been built. But did that, in itself, make a tradition? What good was the fort? In a few centuries it would have outlived its usefulness. Then it would be a relic of the past. Civilization moved on, and, these days, civilization merely tolerated the military.

So—what was the use? Sentiment needed a valid reason for its existence. The Free Companions fought, bitterly, doggedly, with insane valor, in order to destroy themselves. The ancient motives for war had vanished.

What was the use? All over Venus the lights of the great forts were going out—and, this time, they would never be lit again—not in a thousand lifetimes!

V.

> *And we are here as on a darkling plain*
> *Swept with confused alarms of struggle and flight,*
> *Where ignorant armies clash by night.*
> *—Arnold circa 1870*

The fort was a completely self-contained unit, military rather than social. There was no need for any agrarian development, since a state of complete siege never existed. Food could be brought in from the Keeps by water and air.

But military production was important, and, in the life of the fort, the techs played an important part, from the experimental physicist to the spot welder. There were always replacements to be made, for, in battle, there were always casualties. And it was necessary to keep the weapons up-to-date, continually striving to perfect new ones. But strategy and armament were of equal importance. An outnumbered fleet had been known to conquer a stronger one by the use of practical psychology.

Scott found Commander Bienne at the docks, watching the launching of a new sub. Apparently Bienne hadn't yet got over his anger, for he turned a scowling, somber face to the captain as he saluted.

"Hello, commander," Scott said. "I'm making inspection. Are you free?"

Bienne nodded. "There's not much to do."

"Well—routine. We got that sub finished just in time, eh?"

"Yes." Bienne couldn't repress his pleasure at sight of the trim, sleek vessel beginning to slide down the ways. Scott, too, felt his pulses heighten as the sub slipped into the water, raising a mighty splash, and then settling down to a smooth, steady riding on the waves. He looked out to where the great battlewagons stood at anchor, twelve of them, gray-green monsters of plated metal. Each of them carried launching equipment for gliders, but the collapsible aircraft were stowed away out of sight as yet. Smaller destroyers lay like lean-flanked wolves among the battleships. There were two fast carriers, loaded with gliders and flitterboats. There were torpedo boats and one low-riding monitor, impregnable, powerfully armed, but slow. Only a direct hit could disable a monitor, but the behemoths had their disadvantages. The battle was usually over before they lumbered into sight. Like all monitors, this one—the *Armageddon*—was constructed on the principle of a razorback hog, covered, except for the firing ports, by a tureen-shaped shield, strongly braced from within. The *Armageddon* was divided into groups of compartments and had several auxiliary engines, so that, unlike the legendary *Rover*, when a monitor died, it did *not* die all over. It was, in effect, a dinosaur. You could blow off the monster's head, and it would continue to fight with talons and lashing tail. Its heavy guns made up in mobility for the giant's unwieldiness—but the trouble was to get the monitor into battle. It was painfully slow.

Scott scowled. "We're fighting over Venus Deep, eh?"

"Yes," Bienne nodded. "That still goes. The Helldivers are already heading toward Montana Keep, and we'll intercept them over the Deep."

"When's zero hour?"

"Midnight tonight."

Scott closed his eyes, visualizing their course on a mental chart. Not so good. When battle was joined near island groups, it was sometimes possible for a monitor to slip up under cover of the islets, but that trick wouldn't work now. Too bad—for the Helldivers were a strong outfit, more so since their recent merger with O'Brien's Legion. Even with the

Mob to help, the outcome of the scrap would be anyone's guess. The *Armageddon* might be the decisive factor.

"I wonder——" Scott said. "No. It'd be impossible."

"What?"

"Camouflaging the *Armageddon*. If the Helldivers see the monitor coming, they'll lead the fight away from it, faster than that tub can follow. I was thinking we might get her into the battle without the enemy realizing it."

"She's camouflaged now."

"Paint, that's all. She can be spotted. I had some screwy idea about disguising her as an island or a dead whale."

"She's too big for a whale and floating islands look a bit suspicious."

"Yeah. But if we *could* slip the *Armageddon* in without scaring off the enemy—— Hm-m-m. Monitors have a habit of turning turtle, don't they?"

"Right. They're top-heavy. But a monitor can't fight upside down. It's not such a bright idea, captain." Briefly Bienne's sunken eyes gleamed with sneering mockery. Scott grunted and turned away.

"All right. Let's take a look around."

The fleet was shipshape. Scott went to the shops. He learned that several new hulls were under way, but would not be completed by zero hour. With Bienne, he continued to the laboratory offices. Nothing new. No slip-ups; no surprises. The machine was running smoothly.

By the time inspection was completed, Scott had an idea. He told Bienne to carry on and went to find Cinc Rhys. The cinc was in his office, just clicking off the teleaudio as Scott appeared.

"That was Mendez," Rhys said. "The Mob's meeting our fleet a hundred miles off the coast. They'll be under our orders, of course. A good man, Mendez, but I don't entirely trust him."

"You're not thinking of a double cross, sir?"

Cinc Rhys made disparaging noises. "Brutus is an honorable man. No, he'll stick to his bargain. But I wouldn't cut cards with Mendez. As a Free Companion, he's trustworthy. Personally—Well, how do things look?"

"Very good, sir. I've an idea about the *Armageddon*."

"I wish I had," Rhys said frankly. "We can't get that

damned scow into the battle in any way I can figure out. The
Helldivers will see it coming, and lead the fight away."

"I'm thinking of camouflage."

"A monitor's a monitor. It's unmistakable. You can't make
it look like anything else."

"With one exception, sir. You can make it look like a disabled monitor."

Rhys sat back, giving Scott a startled glance. "That's interesting. Go on."

"Look here, sir." The captain used a stylo to sketch the
outline of a monitor on a convenient pad. "Above the surface, the *Armageddon's* dome-shaped. Below, it's a bit different, chiefly because of a keel. Why can't we put a fake
superstructure on the monitor—build a false keel on it, so it'll
seem capsized?"

"It's possible."

"Everybody knows a monitor's weak spot—that it turns
turtle under fire sometimes. If the Helldivers saw an apparently capsized *Armageddon* drifting toward them, they'd
naturally figure the tub was disabled."

"It's crazy," Rhys said. "One of those crazy ideas that
might work." He used the local telaudio to issue crisp orders.
"Got it? Good. Get the *Armageddon* under way as soon as
the equipment's aboard. Alterations will be made at sea. We
can't waste time. If we had them made in the yards, she'd
never catch up with the fleet."

The cinc broke the connection, his seamed, leathery face
twisting into a grin. "I hope it works. We'll see."

He snapped his fingers. "Almost forgot. President Crosby's
nephew—Kane?—he was with you when you cracked up,
wasn't he? I've been wondering whether I should have waived
training for him. How did he show up in the jungle?"

"Quite well," Scott said. "I had my eye on him. He'll make
a good soldier."

Rhys looked keenly at the captain. "What about discipline?
I felt that was his weak spot."

"I've no complaint to make."

"So. Well, maybe. Starling's outfit is bad training for anyone—especially a raw kid. Speaking of Starling, did Cinc
Mendez know anything about his using atomic power?"

"No, sir. If Starling's doing that, he's keeping it plenty
quiet."

"We'll investigate after the battle. Can't afford that sort of thing—we don't want another holocaust. It was bad enough to lose Earth. It decimated the race. If it happened again, it'd wipe the race out."

"I don't think there's much danger of that. On Earth, it was the big atomic-power stations that got out of control. At worst, Starling can't have more than hand weapons."

"True. You can't blow up a world with those. But you know the law—no atomic power on Venus."

Scott nodded.

"Well, that's all." Rhys waved him away. "Clear weather."

Which, on this perpetually clouded world, had a tinge of irony.

After mess Scott returned to his quarters for a smoke and a brief rest. He waved away Briggs's suggestion of a rubdown and sent the orderly to the commissary for fresh tobacco. "Be sure to get Twenty Star," he cautioned. "I don't want that green hydroponic cabbage."

"I know the brand, sir." Briggs looked hurt and departed. Scott settled back in his relaxer, sighing.

Zero hour at twelve. The last zero hour he'd ever know. All through the day he had been conscious that he was fulfilling his duties for the last time.

His mind went back to Montana Keep. He was living again those other-worldly moments in the cloud-wrapped Olympus with Ilene. Curiously, he found it difficult to visualize the girl's features. Perhaps she was a symbol—her appearance did not matter. Yet she was very lovely.

In a different way from Jeana. Scott glanced at Jeana's picture on the desk, three-dimensional and tinted after life. By pressing a button on the frame, he could have given it sound and motion. He leaned forward and touched the tiny stud. In the depths of the picture the figure of Jeana stirred, smiling. The red lips parted.

Her voice, though soft, was quite natural.

"Hello, Brian," the recording said. "Wish I were with you now. Here's a present, darling." The image blew him a kiss, and then faded back to immobility.

Scott sighed again. Jeana was a comfortable sort of person. But—Oh, hell! She wasn't willing to change. Very likely she couldn't. Ilene perhaps was equally dogmatic, but she represented the life of the Keeps—and that was what Scott wanted now.

It was an artificial life Ilene lived, but she was honest about it. She knew its values were false. At least she didn't pretend, like the Free Companions, that there were ideals worth dying for. Scott remembered Briggs. The fact that men had been killed during the building of Doone fort meant a lot to the old orderly. He never asked himself—*why?* Why had they died? Why was Doone fort built in the first place? For war. And war was doomed.

One had to believe in an ideal before devoting one's life to it. One had to feel he was helping the ideal to survive—watering the plant with his blood so eventually it would come to flower. The red flower of Mars had long since blown. How did that old poem go?

> *One thing is certain, and the rest is lies;*
> *The flower that once has blown forever dies.*

It was true. But the Free Companions blindly pretended that the flower was still in blazing scarlet bloom, refusing to admit that even the roots were withered and useless, scarcely able now to suck up the blood sacrificed to its hopeless thirst.

New flowers bloomed; new buds opened. But in the Keeps, not in the great doomed forts. It was the winter cycle, and, as the last season's blossoms faded, the buds of the next stirred into life. Life questing and intolerant. Life that fed on the rotting petals of the rose of war.

But the pretense went on, in the coastal forts that guarded the Keeps. Scott made a grimace of distaste. Blind, stupid folly! He was a man first, not a soldier. And man is essentially a hedonist, whether he identifies himself with the race or not.

Scott could not. He was not part of the undersea culture, and he could never be. But he could lose himself in the hedonistic backwash of the Keeps, the froth that always overlies any social unit. With Ilene, he could, at least, seek happiness, without the bitter self-mockery he had known for so long. Mockery at his own emotional weaknesses in which he did not believe.

Ilene was honest. She knew she was damned, because unluckily she had intelligence.

So—Scott thought—they would make a good pair.

Scott looked up as Commander Bienne came into the

room. Bienne's sour, mahogany face was flushed deep red under the bronze. His lids were heavy over angry eyes. He swung the door-curtain shut after him and stood rocking on his heels, glowering at Scott.

He called Scott something unprintable.

The captain rose, an icy knot of fury in his stomach. Very softly he said, "You're drunk, Bienne. Get out. Get back to your quarters."

"Sure—you little tinhorn soldier. You like to give orders, don't you? You like to chisel, too. The way you chiseled me out of that left-wing command today. I'm pretty sick of it, Captain Brian Scott."

"Don't be a damned fool! I don't like you personally any more than you like me, but that's got nothing to do with the Company. I recommended you for that command."

"You lie," Bienne said, swaying. "And I hate your guts."

Scott went pale, the scar on his cheek flaming red. Bienne came forward. He wasn't too drunk to coordinate. His fist lashed out suddenly and connected agonizingly with Scott's molar.

The captain's reach was less than Bienne's. He ducked inside of the next swing and carefully smashed a blow home on the point of the other's jaw. Bienne was driven back, crashing against the wall and sliding down in a limp heap, his head lolling forward.

Scott, rubbing his knuckles, looked down, considering. Presently he knelt and made a quick examination. A knockout, that was all.

Oh, well.

Briggs appeared, showing no surprise at sight of Bienne's motionless body. The perfect orderly walked across to the table and began to refill the humidor with the tobacco he had brought.

Scott almost chuckled.

"Briggs."

"Yes, sir?"

"Commander Bienne's had a slight accident. He—slipped. Hit his chin on something. He's a bit tight, too. Fix him up, will you?"

"With pleasure, sir." Briggs hoisted Bienne's body across his brawny shoulders.

"Zero hour's at twelve. The commander must be aboard the *Flintlock* by then. And sober. Can do?"

"Certainly, sir," Briggs said, and went out.

Scott returned to his chair, filling his pipe. He should have confined Bienne to his quarters, of course. But—well, this was a personal matter. One could afford to stretch a point, especially since Bienne was a valuable man to have aboard during action. Scott vaguely hoped the commander would get his thick head blown off.

After a time he tapped the dottle from his pipe and went off for a final inspection.

At midnight the fleet hoisted anchor.

By dawn the Doones were nearing the Venus Deep.

The ships of the Mob had already joined them, seven battleships, and assorted cruisers, destroyers, and one carrier. No monitor. The mob didn't own one — it had capsized two months before, and was still undergoing repairs.

The combined fleets sailed in crescent formation, the left wing, commanded by Scott, composed of his own ship, the *Flintlock*, and the *Arquebus*, the *Arrow*, and the *Misericordia*, all Doone battlewagons. There were two Mob ships with him, the *Navaho* and the *Zuni*, the latter commanded by Cinc Mendez. Scott had one carrier with him, the other being at right wing. Besides these, there were the lighter craft.

In the center were the battleships *Arbalest*, *Lance*, *Gatling*, and *Mace*, as well as three of Mendez's. Cinc Rhys was aboard the *Lance*, controlling operations. The camouflaged monitor *Armageddon* was puffing away valiantly far behind, well out of sight in the mists.

Scott was in his control room, surrounded by telaudio screens and switchboards. Six operators were perched on stools before the controls, ready to jump to action when orders came through their earphones. In the din of battle spoken commands often went unheard, which was why Scott wore a hush-mike strapped to his chest.

His eyes roved over the semicircle of screens before him.

"Any report from the gliders yet?"

"No, sir."

"Get me air-spotting command."

One of the screens flamed to life; a face snapped into view on it.

"Report."

"Nothing yet, captain. Wait." There was a distant thunder.

"Detectors clamped on a telaudio tight-beam directly overhead."

"Enemy glider in the clouds?"

"Apparently. It's out of the focus now."

"Try to relocate it."

A lot of good that would do. Motored planes could easily be detected overhead, but a glider was another matter. The only way to spot one was by clamping a detector focus directly on the glider's telaudio beam—worse than a needle in a haystack. Luckily the crates didn't carry bombs.

"Report coming in, sir. One of our gliders."

Another screen showed a face. "Pilot reporting, sir. Located enemy."

"Good. Switch in the telaudio, infra. What sector?"

"V.D. eight hundred seven northwest twenty-one."

Scott said into his hush-mike, "Get Cinc Rhys and Commander Geer on tight-beam. And Cinc Mendez."

Three more screens lit up, showing the faces of the three officers.

"Cut in the pilot."

Somewhere over Venus Deep the glider pilot was arcing his plane through the cloud-layer, the automatic telaudio-camera, lensed to infrared, penetrating the murk and revealing the ocean below. On the screen ships showed, driving forward in battle formation.

Scott recognized and enumerated them mentally. The *Orion*, the *Sirius*, the *Vega*, the *Polaris*—uh-huh. Lighter ships. Plenty of them. The scanner swept on.

Cinc Rhys said, "We're outnumbered badly. Cinc Mendez, are your sub-detectors in operation?"

"They are. Nothing yet."

"We'll join battle in half an hour, I judge. We've located them, and they've no doubt located us."

"Check."

The screens blanked out. Scott settled back, alertly at ease. Nothing to do now but wait, keeping ready for the unexpected. The *Orion* and the *Vega* were the Helldivers' biggest battleships, larger than anything in the line of the Doones—or the Mob. Cinc Flynn was no doubt aboard the *Orion*. The Helldivers owned a monitor, but it had not showed on the infrared aerial scanner. Probably the behemoth wouldn't even show up in time for the battle.

But even without the monitor, the Helldivers had an overwhelming surface display. Moreover, their undersea fleet was an important factor. The sub-detectors of Cinc Mendez might—probably would—cut down the odds. But possibly not enough.

The *Armageddon*, Scott thought, might be the point of decision, the ultimate argument. And, as yet, the camouflaged monitor was lumbering through the waves far in the wake of the Doones.

Commander Bienne appeared on a screen. He had frozen into a disciplined, trained robot, personal animosities forgotten for the time. Active duty did that to a man.

Scott expected nothing different, however, and his voice was completely impersonal as he acknowledged Bienne's call.

"The flitterboats are ready to go, captain."

"Send them out in fifteen minutes. Relay to left wing, all ships carrying flitters."

"Check."

For a while there was silence. A booming explosion brought Scott to instant alertness. He glanced up at the screens.

A new face appeared. "Helldivers opening up. Testing for range. They must have gliders overhead. We can't spot 'em."

"Get the men under cover. Send up a test barrage. Prepare to return fire. Contact our pilots over the Helldivers."

It was beginning now—the incessant, racking thunder that would continue till the last shot was fired. Scott cut in to Cinc Rhys as the latter signaled.

"Reporting, sir."

"Harry the enemy. We can't do much yet. Change to R-8 formation."

Cinc Mendez said, "We've got three enemy subs. Our detectors are turned up to high pitch."

"Limit the range so our subs will be outside the sphere of influence."

"Already did that. The enemy's using magnetic depth charges, laying an undersea barrage as they advance."

"I'll talk to the sub command." Rhys cut off. Scott listened to the increasing fury of explosions. He could not yet hear the distinctive *clap-clap* of heat rays, but the quarters were not yet close enough for those undependable, though powerful, weapons. It took time for a heat ray to warm up, and during that period a well-aimed bullet could smash the projector lens.

"Casualty, sir. Direct hit aboard destroyer *Bayonet.*"

"Extent of damage?"

"Not disabled. Complete report later."

After a while a glider pilot came in on the beam.

"Shell landed on the *Polaris,* sir."

"Use the scanner."

It showed the Helldivers' battlewagon, part of the superstructure carried away, but obviously still in fighting trim. Scott nodded. Both sides were getting the range now. The hazy clouds still hid each fleet from the other, but they were nearing.

The sound of artillery increased. Problems of trajectory were increased by the violent winds of Venus, but accurate aiming was possible. Scott nodded grimly as a crash shook the *Flintlock*.

They were getting it now. Here, in the brain of the ship, he was as close to the battle as any member of a firing crew. The screens were his eyes.

They had the advantage of being able to use infrared, so that Scott, buried here, could see more than he could have on deck, with his naked eye. Something loomed out of the murk and Scott's breath stopped before he recognized the lines of the Doone battlewagon *Misericordia*. She was off course. The captain used his hush-mike to snap a quick reprimand.

Flitterboats were going out now, speedy hornets that would harry the enemy fleet. In one of them, Scott remembered, was Norman Kane. He thought of Ilene and thrust the thought back, out of his mind. No time for that now.

Battle stations allowed no time for wool gathering.

The distant vanguard of the Helldivers came into sight on the screens. Cinc Mendez called.

"Eleven more subs. One got through. Seems to be near the *Flintlock*. Drop depth bombs."

Scott nodded and obeyed. Shuddering concussions shook the ship. Presently a report came in: fuel slick to starboard.

Good. A few well-placed torpedoes could do a lot of damage.

The *Flintlock* heeled incessantly under the action of the heavy guns. Heat rays were lancing out. The big ships could not easily avoid the searing blasts that could melt solid metal, but the flitterboats, dancing around like angry insects, sent a rain of bullets at the projectors. But even that took integration. The rays themselves were invisible, and could only be traced from their targets. The camera crews were working overtime, snapping shots of the enemy ships, tracing the rays' points of origin, and telaudioing the information to the flitterboats.

"Helldivers' *Rigel* out of action."

On the screen the big destroyer swung around, bow pointing forward. She was going to ram. Scott snapped orders. The *Flintlock* went hard over, guns pouring death into the doomed *Rigel*.

The ships passed, so close that men on the *Flintlock*'s decks could see the destroyer lurching through the haze. Scott judged her course and tried desperately to get Mendez. There was a delay.

"QM—QM—emergency! Get the *Zuni!*"

"Here she answers, sir."

Scott snapped, "Change course, QM. Destroyer *Rigel* bearing down on you."

"Check." The screen blanked. Scott used a scanner. He groaned at the sight. The *Zuni* was swinging fast, but the *Rigel* was too close—too damned close.

She rammed.

Scott said, "Hell." That put the *Zuni* out of action. He reported to Cinc Rhys.

"All right, captain. Continue R-8 formation."

Mendez appeared on a screen. "Captain Scott. We're disabled. I'm coming aboard. Have to direct sub-strafing operations. Can you give me a control board?"

"Yes, sir. Land at Port Sector 7."

Hidden in the mist, the fleets swept on in parallel courses, the big battlewagons keeping steady formation, pouring heat rays and shells across the gap. The lighter ships strayed out of line at times, but the flitterboats swarmed like midges, dog-fighting when they were not harrying the larger craft. Gliders were useless now, at such close quarters.

The thunder crashed and boomed. Shudders rocked the *Flintlock*.

"Hit on Helldivers' *Orion*. Hit on *Sirius*."

"Hit on Mob ship *Apache*."

"Four more enemy subs destroyed."

"Doone sub *X-16* fails to report."

"Helldivers' *Polaris* seems disabled."

"Send out auxiliary flitterboats, units nine and twenty."

Cinc Mendez came in, breathing hard. Scott waved him to an auxiliary control unit seat.

"Hit on *Lance*. Wait a minute. Cinc Rhys a casualty, sir."

Scott froze. "Details."

"One moment—Dead, sir."

"Very well," Scott said after a moment. "I'm assuming command. Pass it along."

He caught a sidelong glance from Mendez. When a Company's cinc was killed, one of two things happened—promotion of a new cinc, or a merger with another Company. In this case Scott was required, by his rank, to assume temporarily the fleet's command. Later, at the Doone fort, there would be a meeting and a final decision.

He scarcely thought of that now. Rhys dead! Tough, unemotional old Rhys, killed in action. Rhys had a free-wife in some Keep. Scott remembered. The Company would pension her. Scott had never seen the woman. Oddly, he wondered what she was like. The question had never occurred to him before.

The screens were flashing. Double duty now—or triple. Scott forgot everything else in directing the battle.

It was like first-stage anesthesia—it was difficult to judge time. It might have been an hour or six since the battle had started. Or less than an hour, for that matter.

"Destroyer disabled. Cruiser disabled. Three enemy subs out of action—"

It went on, endlessly. At the auxiliaries Mendez was directing sub-strafing operations. Where in hell's the *Armageddon*, Scott thought. The fight would be over before that overgrown tortoise arrived.

Abruptly a screen flashed QM. The lean, beak-nosed face of Cinc Flynn of the Helldivers showed.

"Calling Doone command."

"Acknowledging," Scott said. "Captain Scott, emergency command."

Why was Flynn calling? Enemy fleets in action never communicated, except to surrender.

Flynn said curtly, "You're using atomic power. Explanation, please."

Mendez jerked around. Scott felt a tight band around his stomach.

"Done without my knowledge or approval, of course, Cinc Flynn. My apologies. Details?"

"One of your flitterboats fired an atomic-powered pistol at the *Orion*."

"Damage?"

"One seven-unit gun disabled."

"One of ours, of the same caliber, will be taken out of action immediately. Further details, sir?"

"Use your scanner, captain, on Sector Mobile 18 south *Orion*. Your apology is accepted. The incident will be erased from our records."

Flynn clicked off. Scott used the scanner, catching a Doone flitterboat in its focus. He used the enlarger.

The little boat was fleeing from enemy fire, racing back toward the Doone fleet, heading directly toward the *Flintlock*, Scott saw. Through the transparent shell he saw the bombardier slumped motionless, his head blown half off. The pilot, still gripping an atomic-fire pistol in one hand, was Norman Kane. Blood streaked his boyish, strained face.

So Starling's outfit did have atomic power, then. Kane must have smuggled the weapon out with him when he left. And, in the excitement of battle, he had used it against the enemy.

Scott said coldly, "Gun crews starboard. Flitterboat *Z-19-4*. Blast it."

Almost immediately a shell burst near the little craft. On the screen Kane looked up, startled by his own side firing upon him. Comprehension showed on his face. He swung the flitterboat off course, zigzagging, trying desperately to dodge the barrage.

Scott watched, his lips grimly tight. The flitterboat exploded in a rain of spray and debris.

Automatic court-martial.

After the battle, the Companies would band together and smash Starling's outfit.

Meanwhile, this was action. Scott returned to his screens, erasing the incident from his mind.

Very gradually, the balance of power was increasing with the Helldivers. Both sides were losing ships, put out of action rather than sunk, and Scott thought more and more often of the monitor *Armageddon*. She could turn the battle now. But she was still far astern.

Scott never felt the explosion that wrecked the control room. His senses blacked out without warning.

He could not have been unconscious for long. When he opened his eyes, he stared up at a shambles. He seemed to be the only man left alive. But it could not have been a direct hit, or he would not have survived either.

He was lying on his back, pinned down by a heavy crossbeam. But no bones were broken. Blind, incredible luck had helped him there. The brunt of the damage had been borne by the operators. They were dead, Scott saw at a glance.

He tried to crawl out from under the beam, but that was impossible. In the thunder of battle his voice could not be heard.

There was a movement across the room, halfway to the door. Cinc Mendez stumbled up and stared around, blinking. Red smeared his plump cheeks.

He saw Scott and stood, rocking back and forth, staring.

Then he put his hand on the butt of his pistol.

Scott could very easily read the other's mind. If the Doone captain died now, the chances were that Mendez could merge with the Doones and assume control. The politico-military balance lay that way.

If Scott lived, it was probable that he would be elected cinc.

It was, therefore, decidedly to Mendez's advantage to kill the imprisoned man.

A shadow crossed the doorway. Mendez, his back to the newcomer, did not see Commander Bienne halt on the threshold, scowling at the tableau. Scott knew that Bienne understood the situation as well as he himself did. The commander realized that in a very few moments Mendez would draw his gun and fire.

Scott waited. The cinc's fingers tightened on his gun butt.

Bienne, grinning crookedly, said, "I thought that shell had finished you, sir. Guess it's hard to kill a Dooneman."

Mendez took his hand off the gun, instantly regaining his poise. He turned to Bienne.

"I'm glad you're here, commander. It'll probably take both of us to move that beam."

"Shall we try, sir?"

Between the two of them, they managed to shift the weight off Scott's torso. Briefly the latter's eyes met Bienne's. There was still no friendliness in them, but there was a look of wry self-mockery.

Bienne hadn't saved Scott's life, exactly. It was, rather, a question of being a Dooneman. For Bienne was, first of all, a soldier, and a member of the Free Company.

Scott tested his limbs; they worked.

"How long was I out, commander?"

"Ten minutes, sir. The *Armageddon's* in sight."

"Good. Are the Helldivers veering off?"

Bienne shook his head. "So far they're not suspicious."

Scott grunted and made his way to the door, the others at his heels. Mendez said, "We'll need another control ship."

"All right. The *Arquebus.* Commander, take over here. Cinc Mendez—"

A flitterboat took them to the *Arquebus,* which was still in good fighting trim. The monitor *Armageddon,* Scott saw, was rolling helplessly in the trough of the waves. In accordance with the battle plan, the Doone ships were leading the Helldivers toward the apparently capsized giant. The technicians had done a good job; the false keel looked shockingly convincing.

Aboard the *Arquebus,* Scott took over, giving Mendez the auxiliary control for his substrafers. The Cinc beamed at Scott over his shoulder.

"Wait till that monitor opens up, captain."

"Yeah ... we're in bad shape, though."

Neither man mentioned the incident that was in both their minds. It was tacitly forgotten—the only thing to do now.

Guns were still bellowing. The Helldivers were pouring their fire into the Doone formation, and they were winning. Scott scowled at the screens. If he waited too long, it would be just too bad.

Presently he put a beam on the *Armageddon.* She was in a beautiful position now, midway between two of the Helldivers' largest battleships.

"Unmask. Open fire."

Firing ports opened on the monitor. The sea titan's huge guns snouted into view. Almost simultaneously they blasted, the thunder drowning out the noise of the lighter guns.

"All Doone ships attack," Scott said. "Plan R-7."

This was it. *This was it!*

The Doones raced in to the kill. Blasting, bellowing, shouting, the guns tried to make themselves heard above the roaring of the monitor. They could not succeed, but that savage, invincible onslaught won the battle.

It was nearly impossible to maneuver a monitor into battle formation, but, once that was accomplished, the only thing that could stop the monster was atomic power.

But the Helldivers fought on, trying strategic formation. They could not succeed. The big battlewagons could not get out of range of the *Armageddon's* guns. And that meant—

Cinc Flynn's face showed on the screen.

"Capitulation, sir. Cease firing."

Scott gave orders. The roar of the guns died into humming, incredible silence.

"You gave us a great battle, cinc."

"Thanks. So did you. Your strategy with the monitor was excellent."

So—that was that. Scott felt something go limp inside of him. Flynn's routine words were meaningless; Scott was drained of the vital excitement that had kept him going till now.

The rest was pure formula.

Token depth charges would be dropped over Virginia Keep. They would not harm the Dome, but they were the rule. There would be the ransom, paid always by the Keep which backed the losing side. A supply of korium, or its negotiable equivalent. The Doone treasury would be swelled. Part of the money would go into replacements and new keels. The life of the forts would go on.

Alone at the rail of the *Arquebus,* heading for Virginia Keep, Scott watched slow darkness change the clouds from pearl to gray, and then to invisibility. He was alone in the night. The wash of waves came up to him softly as the *Arquebus* rushed to her destination, three hundred miles away.

Warm yellow lights gleamed from ports behind him, but he did not turn. This, he thought, was like the cloud-wrapped Olympus in Montana Keep, where he had promised Ilene— many things.

Yet there was a difference. In an Olympus a man was like a god, shut away completely from the living world. Here, in the unbroken dark, there was no sense of alienage. Nothing could be seen—Venus has no moon, and the clouds hid the stars. And the seas are not phosphorescent.

Beneath these waters stand the Keeps, Scott thought. They hold the future. Such battles as were fought today are fought so that the Keeps may not be destroyed.

And men will sacrifice. Men have always sacrificed, for a social organization or a military unit. Man must create his own ideal. "If there had been no God, man would have created Him."

Bienne had sacrificed today, in a queer, twisted way of loyalty to his fetish. Yet Bienne still hated him, Scott knew.

The Doones meant nothing. Their idea was a false one. Yet, because men were faithful to that ideal, civilization would rise again from the guarded Keeps. A civilization that would forget its doomed guardians, the watchers of the seas of Venus, the Free Companions yelling their mad, futile battle cry as they drove on—as this ship was driving—into a night that would have no dawn.

Ilene.

Jeana.

It was no such simple choice. It was, in fact, no real choice at all. For Scott knew, very definitely, that he could never, as long as he lived, believe wholeheartedly in the Free Companions. Always a sardonic devil deep within him would be laughing in bitter self-mockery.

The whisper of the waves drifted up.

It wasn't sensible. It was sentimental, crazy, stupid, sloppy thinking.

But Scott knew, now, that he wasn't going back to Ilene.

He was a fool.

But he was a soldier.

EXILE

Super Science Stories,

May

by Edmond Hamilton (1904-1977)

The husband of Leigh Brackett (they edited excellent Best of . . . books of each other's work shortly before their deaths), Edmond Hamilton first appeared in the science fiction/fantasy field with "The Monster-God of Mamurth" in 1926, making him one of the longest-lasting of the first generation of sf writers. Unlike many of his contemporaries, he got better with age. His early reputation was built on a series of spectacular space operas (he was known as "World-Saver Hamilton" for a while) featuring his "Instellar Patrol" characters. He also wrote a great many of the "Captain Future" series in the 1940s.

However, Hamilton was capable of more thoughtful work, such as "What's It Like Out There?" (1952), The Star Kings *(1949), and* The Haunted Stars *(1960).* The Best of Edmond Hamilton *(1977) is a wonderful collection.*

Exile is short, sweet, and quite profound.

(This is Ed Hamilton's first appearance in this series, but that is because his great years came before 1939. In my anthology Before the Golden Age, *which dealt with the years from 1931 to 1938, three of his stories were included. Had I been able to include novels as well, there would have been even more. His* The Universe Wreckers *was one of the delights of my childhood. It embarrassed me that when I finally met him, I had become better known than he was. It struck me as*

lèse majesté. *He was a gentle, self-possessed soul,
though, and he didn't seem to mind.—I.A.)*

I wish now that we hadn't got to talking about science fiction that night! If we hadn't, I wouldn't be haunted now by
that queer, impossible story which can't ever be proved or
disproved.

But the four of us were all professional writers of fantastic
stories, and I suppose shop talk was inevitable. Yet, we'd kept
off it through dinner and the drinks afterward. Madison had
outlined his hunting trip with gusto, and then Brazell started
a discussion of the Dodgers' chances. And then I had to turn
the conversation to fantasy.

I didn't mean to do it. But I'd had an extra Scotch, and
that always makes me feel analytical. And I got to feeling
amused by the perfect way in which we four resembled a
quartet of normal, ordinary people.

"Protective coloration, that's what it is," I announced.
"How hard we work at the business of acting like ordinary
good guys!"

Brazell looked at me, somewhat annoyed by the interruption. "What are you talking about?"

"About us," I answered. "What a wonderful imitation of
solid, satisfied citizens we put up! But we're not satisfied, you
know—none of us. We're violently dissatisfied with the Earth,
and all its works, and that's why we spend our lives dreaming
up one imaginary world after another."

"I suppose the little matter of getting paid for it has nothing to do with it?" Brazell asked skeptically.

"Sure it has," I admitted. "But we all dreamed up our impossible worlds and peoples long before we ever wrote a line,
didn't we? From back in childhood, even? It's because we
don't feel at home here."

Madison snorted. "We'd feel a lot less at home on some of
the worlds we write about."

Then Carrick, the fouth of our party, broke into the conversation. He'd been sitting over his drink in his usual silent
way, brooding, paying no attention to us.

He was a queer chap, in most ways. We didn't know him
very well, but we liked him and admired his stories. He'd
done some wonderful tales of an imaginary planet—all carefully worked out.

He told Madison, "That happened to me."

"What happened to you?" Madison asked.

"What you were suggesting—*I* once wrote about an imaginary world and then had to live on it," Carrick answered.

Madison laughed. "I hope it was a more livable place than the lurid planets on which I set my own yarns."

But Carrick was unsmiling. He murmured, "I'd have made it a lot different—if I'd known I was ever going to live on it."

Brazell, with a significant glance at Carrick's empty glass winked at us and then asked blandly, "Let's hear about it, Carrick."

Carrick kept looking dully down at his empty glass, turning it slowly in his fingers as he talked. He paused every few words.

"It happened just after I'd moved next to the big power station. It sounds like a noisy place, but actually it was very quiet out there on the edge of the city. And I had to have quiet, if I was to produce stories.

"I got right to work on a new series I was starting, the stories of which were all to be laid on the same imaginary world. I began by working out the detailed physical appearance of that world, as well as the universe that was its background. I spent the whole day concentrating on that. And, as I finished, something in my mind went *click!*

"That queer, brief mental sensation felt oddly like a sudden *crystallization*. I stood there, wondering if I was going crazy. For I had a sudden strong conviction that it meant that the universe and world I had been dreaming up all day had suddenly crystallized into physical existence somewhere.

"Naturally, I brushed aside the eerie thought and went out and forgot about it. But the next day, the thing happened again. I had spent most of that second day working up the inhabitants of my story world. I'd made them definitely human, but had decided against making them too civilized—for that would exclude the conflict and violence that must form my story.

"So, I'd made my imaginary world a world whose people were still only half-civilized. I figured out all their cruelties and superstitions. I mentally built up their colorful barbaric cities. And just as I was through—that *click!* echoed sharply in my mind.

"It startled me badly, this second time. For now I felt

more strongly than before that queer conviction, that my day's dreaming had crystallized into solid reality. I knew it was insane to think that, yet it was an incredible certainty in my mind. I couldn't get rid of it.

"I tried to reason the thing out so that I could dismiss that crazy conviction. If my imagining a world and universe had actually created them, where were they? Certainly not in my own cosmos. It couldn't hold two universes—each completely different from the other.

"But maybe that world and universe of my imagining had crystallized into reality in another and empty cosmos? A cosmos lying in a different dimension from my own? One which had contained only free atoms, formless matter that had not taken on shape until my concentrated thought had somehow stirred it into the forms I dreamed?

"I reasoned along like that, in the queer, dreamlike way in which you apply the rules of logic to impossibilities. How did it come that my imaginings had never crystallized into reality before, but had only just begun to do so? Well, there was a plausible explanation for that. It was the big power station nearby. Some unfathomable freak of energy radiated from it was focusing my concentrated imaginings, as super-amplified force, upon an empty cosmos where they stirred formless matter into the shapes I dreamed.

"Did I believe that? No, I didn't believe it—but I knew it. There is quite a difference between knowledge and belief, as somone said who once pointed out that all men know they will die and none of them believe it. It was like that with me. I realized it was not possible that my imaginary world had come into physical being in a different dimensional cosmos, yet at the same time I was strangely convinced that it had.

"A thought occurred to me that amused and interested me. What if I imagined *myself* in that other world? Would I, too, become physically real in it? I tried it. I sat at my desk, imagining myself as one of the millions of persons in that imaginary world, dreaming up a whole soberly realistic background and family and history for myself over there. And my mind said *click!*"

Carrick paused, still looking down at the empty glass that he twirled slowly between his fingers.

Madison prompted him. "And of course you woke up there, and a beautiful girl was leaning over you, and you asked, 'Where am I?' "

"It wasn't like that," Carrick said dully. "It wasn't like that at all. I woke up in that other world, yes. But it wasn't like a real awakening. I was just suddenly in it.

"I was still myself. But I was the myself I had imagined in that other world. That other me had always lived in it—and so had his ancestors before him. I had worked all that out, you see.

"And I was just as real to myself, in that imaginary world I had created, as I had been in my own. That was the worst part of it. Everything in that half-civilized world was so utterly, commonplacely real."

He paused again. "It was queer, at first. I walked out into the streets of those barbaric cities, and looked into the people's faces, and I felt like shouting aloud, 'I imagined you all! You had no existence until I dreamed of you!'

"But I didn't do that. They wouldn't have believed me. To them, I was just an insignificant single member of their race. How could they guess that they and their traditions of long history, their world and their universe, had all been suddenly brought into being by my imagination?

"After my first excitement ebbed, I didn't like the place. I had made it too barbaric. The savage violences and cruelties that had seemed so attractive as material for a story, were ugly and repulsive at first hand. I wanted nothing but to get back to my own world.

"And I couldn't get back! There just wasn't any way. I had had a vague idea that I could imagine myself back into my own world as I had imagined myself into this other one. But it didn't work that way. The freak force that had wrought the miracle didn't work two ways.

"I had a pretty bad time when I realized that I was trapped in that ugly, squalid, barbarian world. I felt like killing myself at first. But I didn't. A man can adapt himself to anything. I adapted myself the best I could to the world I had created."

"What did you do there? What was your position, I mean?" Brazell asked.

Carrick shrugged. "I don't know the crafts or skills of that world I'd brought into being. I had only my own skill—that of story telling."

I began to grin. "You don't mean to say that you started writing fantastic stories?"

He nodded soberly. "I had to. It was all I could do. I wrote stories about my own real world. To those other people my tales were wild imagination—and they liked them."

We chuckled. But Carrick was deadly serious.

Madison humored him to the end. "And how did you finally get back home from that other world you'd created?"

"I never did get back home," Carrick said with a heavy sigh.

"Oh, come now," Madison protested lightly. "It's obvious that you got back some time."

Carrick shook his head somberly as he rose to leave.

"No, I never got back home," he said soberly. "I'm still here."

DAYMARE

Thrilling Wonder Stories,

Fall

by Fredric Brown (1906-1972)

Frederic Brown was one of the finest craftsmen who ever worked the commercial magazine markets. He was a major figure in the mystery genre, the author of such important works as The Fabulous Clipjoint, The Screaming Mimi, *and* The Lenient Beast. *In science fiction his reputation as the master of the short-short story is richly deserved although he was generally excellent at all lengths, his stories usually combining sardonic wit with clever ideas. His story "Arena" (see Volume 6 of this series) is included in* The Science Fiction Hall of Fame.

"Daymare" is one of his longest less-than-novel-length sf works and one of his best.

(There have been a number of mystery writers who have tried their hand at science fiction. John D. MacDonald is one, for instance. Even Mickey Spillane who (from my point of view) wrote deplorable mysteries, managed to write at least one deplorable piece of science fiction that I recall. And some science fiction writers have tried their hand at mysteries: Robert Bloch, Barry Malzberg and (in a whisper) I myself. However, I always thought the perfect fusion was Fredric Brown. All the others were either mystery writers who could do science fiction, or science fiction writers who could do mysteries. Fred was the one guy who managed to straddle the two genres well-balanced. I could never decide which was his prime talent, which second-

ary. He did both equally well and, apparently, with equal pleasure.—I.A.)

CHAPTER ONE: FIVE-WAY CORPSE

It started out like a simple case of murder. That was bad enough in itself, because it was the first murder during the five years Rod Caquer had been Lieutenant of Police in Sector Three of Callisto.

Sector Three was proud of that record, or had been until the record became a dead duck.

But before the thing was over, nobody would have been happier than Rod Caquer if it had stayed a simple case of murder—without cosmic repercussions.

Events began to happen when Rod Caquer's buzzer made him look up at the visiscreen.

There he saw the image of Barr Maxon, Regent of Sector Three.

"Morning, Regent," Caquer said pleasantly. "Nice speech you made last night on the—"

Maxon cut him short. "Thanks, Caquer," he said. "You know Willem Deem?"

"The book-and-reel shop proprietor? Yes, slightly."

"He's dead," announced Maxon. "It seems to be murder. You better go there."

His image clicked off the screen before Caquer could ask any questions. But the questions could wait anyway. He was already on his feet and buckling on his shortsword.

Murder on Callisto? It did not seem possible, but if it had really happened he should get there quickly. Very quickly, if he was to have time for a look at the body before they took it to the incinerator.

On Callisto, bodies are never held for more than an hour after death because of the hylra spores which, in minute quantity, are always present in the thinnish atmosphere. They are harmless, of course, to live tissue, but they tremendously accelerate the rate of putrefaction in dead animal matter of any sort.

Dr. Skidder, the Medico-in-Chief, was coming out the front door of the book-and-reel shop when Lieutenant Caquer arrived there, breathless.

The medico jerked a thumb back over his shoulder. "Better

hurry if you want a look," he said to Caquer. "They're taking it out the back way. But I've examined—"

Caquer ran on past him and caught the white-uniformed utility men at the back door óf the shop.

"Hi, boys, let me take a look," Caquer cried as he peeled back the sheet that covered the thing on the stretcher.

It made him feel a bit sickish, but there was not any doubt of the identity of the corpse or the cause of death. He had hoped against hope that it would turn out to have been an accidental death after all. But the skull had been cleaved down to the eyebrows—a blow struck by a strong man with a heavy sword.

"Better let us hurry, Lieutenant. It's almost an hour since they found him."

Caquer's nose confirmed it, and he put the sheet back quickly and let the utility men go on to their gleaming white truck parked just outside the door.

He walked back into the shop, thoughtfully, and looked around. Everything seemed in order. The long shelves of cel-luwrapped merchandise were neat and orderly. The row of booths along the other side, some equipped with an enlarger for book customers and the others with projectors for those who were interested in the microfilms, were all empty and undisturbed.

A little crowd of curious persons was gathered outside the door, but Brager, one of the policemen, was keeping them out of the shop.

"Hey, Brager," said Caquer, and the patrolman came in and closed the door behind him.

"Yes, Lieutenant?"

"Know anything about this? Who found him, and when, and so on?"

"I did, almost an hour ago. I was walking by on my beat when I heard the shot."

Caquer looked at him blankly.

"The shot?" he repeated.

"Yeah. I ran in and there he was dead and nobody around. I knew nobody had come out the front way, so I ran to the back and there wasn't anybody in sight from the back door. So I came back and put in the call."

"To whom? Why didn't you call me direct, Brager?"

"Sorry, Lieutenant, but I was excited and I pushed the wrong button and got the Regent. I told him somebody had shot Deem and he said stay on guard and he'd call the Medico and the utility boys and you."

In that order? Caquer wondered. Apparently, because Caquer had been the last one to get there.

But he brushed that aside for the more important question—the matter of Brager having heard a shot. That did not make sense, unless—no, that was absurd, too. If Willem Deem had been shot, the Medico would not have split his skull as part of the autopsy.

"What do you mean by a shot, Brager?" Caquer asked. "An old-fashioned explosive weapon?"

"Yeah," said Brager. "Didn't you see the body? A hole right over the heart. A bullet-hole, I guess. I never saw one before. I didn't know there was a gun on Callisto. They were outlawed even before the blasters were."

Caquer nodded slowly.

"You—you didn't see evidence of any other—uh—wound?" he persisted.

"Earth, no. Why would there be any other wound? A hole through a man's heart's enough to kill him, isn't it?"

"Where did Dr. Skidder go when he left here?" Caquer inquired. "Did he say?"

"Yeah, he said you would be wanting his report so he'd go back to his office and wait till you came around or called him. What do you want to do, Lieutenant?"

Caquer thought a moment.

"Go next door and use the visiphone there, Brager—I'll be busy on this one," Caquer at last told the policeman. "Get three more men, and the four of you canvass this block and question everyone."

"You mean whether they saw anybody run out the back way, and if they heard the shot, and that sort of thing?" asked Brager.

"Yes. Also anything they may know about Deem, or who might have had a reason to—to shoot him."

Brager saluted, and left.

Caquer got Dr. Skidder on the visiphone. "Hello, Doctor," he said. "Let's have it."

"Nothing but what met the eye, Rod. Blaster, of course. Close range."

Lieutenant Rod Caquer steadied himself. "Say that again, Medico."

"What's the matter," jibed Skidder. "Never see a blaster

death before? Guess you wouldn't have at that, Rod, you're too young. But fifty years ago when I was a student, we got them once in a while."

"Just how did it kill him?"

Dr. Skidder looked surprised. "Oh, you didn't catch up with the clearance men then. I thought you'd seen it. Left shoulder, burned all the skin and flesh off and charred the bone. Actual death was from shock—the blast didn't hit a vital area. Not that the burn wouldn't have been fatal anyway, in all probability. But the shock made it instantaneous."

Dreams are like this, Caquer told himself.

In dreams things happen without meaning anything, he thought. *But I'm not dreaming, this is real.*

"Any other wounds, or marks on the body?" he asked, slowly.

"None. I'd suggest, Rod, you concentrate on a search for that blaster. Search all of Sector Three, if you have to. You know what a blaster looks like, don't you?"

"I've seen pictures," said Caquer. "Do they make a noise, Medico? I've never seen one fired."

Dr. Skidder shook his head. "There's a flash and a hissing sound, but no report."

"It couldn't be mistaken for a gunshot?"

The doctor stared at him.

"You mean an explosive gun? Of course not. Just a faint s-s-s-s. One couldn't hear it more than ten feet away."

When Lieutenant Caquer had clicked off the visiphone, he sat down and closed his eyes to concentrate. Somehow he had to make sense out of three conflicting sets of observations. His own, the patrolman's, and the medico's.

Brager had been the first one to see the body, and he said there was a hole over the heart. And that there were no other wounds. He had heard the report of the shot.

Caquer thought, suppose Brager is lying. It still doesn't make sense. Because according to Dr. Skidder, there was no bullet hole, but a blaster wound. Skidder had seen the body after Brager had.

Someone could, theoretically at least, have used a blaster in the interim, on a man already dead. But—

But that did not explain the head wound, nor the fact that the medico had not seen the bullet hole.

Someone could, theoretically at least, have struck the skull

with a sword between the time Skidder had made the autopsy
and the time he, Rod Caquer, had seen the body. But—

But that didn't explain why he hadn't seen the charred
shoulder when he'd lifted the sheet from the body on the
stretcher. He might have missed seeing the bullet hole, but he
would not, and he could not, have missed seeing a shoulder
in the condition Dr. Skidder described it.

Around and around it went, until at last it dawned on him
that there was only one explanation possible. The Medico-in-
Chief was lying, for whatever mad reason. Brager's story
could be true, in toto. That meant, of course, that he, Rod
Caquer, had overlooked the bullet hole Brager had seen; but
that was possible.

But Skidder's story could not be true. Skidder himself, at
the time of the autopsy, could have inflicted the wound in the
head. And he could have lied about the shoulder wound.
Why—unless the man was mad—he would have done either
of those things, Caquer could not imagine. But it was the
only way he could reconcile all the factors.

But by now the body had been disposed of. It would be his
word against Dr. Skidder's—

But wait!—the utility men, two of them, would have seen
the corpse when they put it on the stretcher.

Quickly Caquer stood up in front of the visiphone and ob-
tained a connection with utility headquarters.

"The two clearance men who took a body from Shop 9364
less than an hour ago—have they reported back yet?" he
asked.

"Just a minute, Lieutenant . . . Yes, one of them was
through for the day and went on home. The other one is
here."

"Put him on."

Rod Caquer recognized the man who stepped into the
screen. It was the one of the two utility men who had asked
him to hurry.

"Yes, Lieutenant?" said the man.

"You helped put the body on the stretcher?"

"Of course."

"What would you say was the cause of death?"

The man in white looked out of the screen incredulously.

"Are you kidding me, Lieutenant?" he grinned. "Even a
moron could see what was wrong with that stiff."

Caquer frowned.

"Neverthless, there are conflicting statements. I want your opinion."

"Opinion? When a man has his head cut off, what two opinions can there be, Lieutenant?"

Caquer forced himself to speak calmly. "Will the man who went with you confirm that?"

"Of course. Earth's Oceans! We had to put it on the stretcher in two pieces. Both of us for the body, and then Walter picked up the head and put it on next to the trunk. The killing was done with a disintegrator beam, wasn't it?"

"You talked it over with the other man?" said Caquer. "There was no difference of opinion between you about the—uh—details?"

"Matter of fact there was. That was why I asked you if it was a disintegrator. After we'd cremated it, he tried to tell me the cut was a ragged one like somebody'd taken several blows with an axe or something. But it was clean."

"Did you notice evidence of a blow struck at the top of the skull?"

"No. Say, lieutenant, you aren't looking so well. Is anything the matter with you?"

CHAPTER TWO: TERROR BY NIGHT

That was the setup that confronted Rod Caquer, and one can not blame him for beginning to wish it had been a simple case of murder.

A few hours ago, it had seemed bad enough to have Callisto's no-murder record broken. But from there, it got worse. He did not know it then, but it was going to get still worse and that would be only the start.

It was eight in the evening, now, and Caquer was still at his office with a copy of Form 812 in front of him on the duraplast surface of his desk. There were questions on that form, apparently simple questions.

Name of Deceased: Willem Deem
Occupation: Prop. of book-and-reel shop
Residence: Apt. 8250, Sector Three, Clsto.
Place of Bus.: Shop 9364, S. T., Clsto.
Time of Death: Approx. 3 P.M. Clsto. Std. Time
Cause of Death:

Yes, the first five questions had been a breeze. But the sixth? He had been staring at that question an hour now. A Callisto hour, not so long as an Earth one, but long enough when you're staring at a question like that.

But confound it, he would have to put something down.

Instead, he reached for the visiphone button and a moment later Jane Gordon was looking at him out of the screen. And Rod Caquer looked back, because she was something to look at.

"Hello, Icicle," he said. "Afraid I'm not going to be able to get there this evening. Forgive me?"

"Of course, Rod. What's wrong? The Deem business?"

He nodded gloomily. "Desk work. Lot of forms and reports I got to get out for the Sector Coordinator."

"Oh. How was he killed, Rod?"

"Rule Sixty-five," he said with a smile, "forbids giving details of any unsolved crime to a civilian."

"Brother Rule Sixty-five. Dad knew Willem Deem well, and he's been a guest here often. Mr. Deem was practically a friend of ours."

"Practically?" Caquer asked. "Then I take it you didn't like him, Icicle?"

"Well—I guess I didn't. He was interesting to listen to, but he was a sarcastic little beast, Rod. I think he had a perverted sense of humor. How was he killed?"

"If I tell you, will you promise not to ask any more questions?" Caquer said with a sigh.

Her eyes lighted eagerly. "Of course."

"He was shot," said Caquer, "with an explosive-type gun and a blaster. Someone split his skull with a sword, chopped off his head with an axe and with a disintegrator beam. Then after he was on the utility stretcher, someone struck his head back on because it wasn't off when I saw him. And plugged up the bullet hole, and—"

"Rod, stop driveling," cut in the girl. "If you don't want to tell me, all right."

Rod grinned. "Don't get mad. Say, how's your father?"

"Lots better. He's asleep now, and definitely on the upgrade. I think he'll be back at the university by next week. Rod, you look tired. When do those forms have to be in?"

"Twenty-four hours after the crime. But—"

"But nothing. Come on over here, right now. You can make out those old forms in the morning."

She smiled at him, and Caquer weakened. He was not getting anywhere anyway, was he?

· "All right, Jane," he said. "But I'm going by patrol quarters on the way. Had some men canvasing the block the crime was committed in,–and I want their report."

But the report, which he found waiting for him, was not illuminating. The canvass had been thorough, but it had failed to elicit any information of value. No one had been seen to leave or enter the Deem shop prior to Brager's arrival, and none of Deem's neighbors knew of any enemies he might have. No one had heard a shot.

Rod Caquer grunted and stuffed the reports into his pocket, and wondered, as he walked to the Gordon home, where the investigation went from there. How did a detective go about solving such a crime?

True, when he was a college kid back on Earth a few years ago, he had read a detective usually trapped someone by discovering a discrepancy in his statements. Generally in a rather dramatic manner, too.

There was Wilder Williams, the greatest of all the fictional detectives, who could look at a man and deduce his whole life history from the cut of his clothes and the shape of his hands. But Wilder Williams had never run across a victim who had been killed in as many ways as there were witnesses.

He spent a pleasant—but futile—evening with Jane Gordon, again asked her to marry him, and again was refused. But he was used to that. She was a bit cooler this evening than usual, probably because she resented his unwillingness to talk about Willem Deem.

And home, to bed.

Out the window of his apartment, after the light was out, he could see the monstrous ball of Jupiter hanging low in the sky, the green-black midnight sky. He lay in bed and stared at it until it seemed that he could still see it after he had closed his eyes.

Willem Deem, deceased. What was he going to do about Willem Deem? Around and around, until at last one orderly thought emerged from chaos.

Tomorrow morning he would talk to the Medico. Without mentioning the sword wound in the head, he would ask Skidder about the bullet hole Brager claimed to have seen over the heart. If Skidder still said the blaster burn was the only

wound, he would summon Brager and let him argue with
the Medico.

And then—Well, he would worry about what to do then
when he got there. He would never get to sleep this way.

He thought about Jane, and went to sleep.

After a while, he dreamed. Or was it a dream? If so, then
he dreamed that he was lying there in bed, almost but not
quite awake, and that there were whispers coming from all
corners of the room. Whispers out of the darkness.

For big Jupiter had moved on across the sky now. The
window was a dim, scarcely discernible outline, and the rest
of the room in utter darkness.

Whispers!

"—kill them."

"You hate them, you hate them, you hate them."

"—kill, kill, kill."

"Sector Two gets all the gravy and Sector Three does all
the work. They exploit our corla plantations. They are evil.
Kill them, take over."

"You hate them, you hate them, you hate them."

"Sector Two is made up of weaklings and usurers. They
have the taint of Martian blood. Spill it, spill Martian blood.
Sector Three should rule Callisto. Three the mystic number.
We are destined to rule Callisto."

"You hate them, you hate them."

"—kill, kill, kill."

"Martian blood of usurious villains. You hate them, you
hate them, you hate them."

Whispers.

"Now—now—now."

"Kill them, kill them."

"A hundred ninety miles across the flat planes. Get there in
an hour in monocars. Surprise attack. Now. Now. Now."

And Rod Caquer was getting out of bed, fumbling hastily
and blindly into his clothing without turning on the light because this was a dream and dreams were in darkness.

His sword was in the scabbard at his belt and he took it
out and felt the edge and the edge was sharp and ready to
spill the blood of the enemy he was going to kill.

Now it was going to swing in arcs of red death, his
unblooded sword—the anachronistic sword that was his
badge of office, of authority. He had never drawn the sword

in anger, a stubby symbol of a sword, scarce eighteen inches long; enough, though, enough to reach the heart—four inches to the heart.

The whispers continued.

"You hate them, you hate them, you hate them."

"Spill the evil blood; kill, spill, kill, spill."

"Now, now, now, now."

Unsheathed sword in clenched fist, he was stealing silently out the door, down the stairway, past the other apartment doors.

And some of the doors were opening, too. He was not alone, there in the darkness. Other figures moved beside him in the dark.

He stole out of the door and into the night-cooled darkness of the street, the darkness of the street that should have been brightly lighted. That was another proof that this was a dream. Those streetlights were never off after dark. From dusk till dawn, they were never off.

But Jupiter over there on the horizon gave enough light to see by. Like a round dragon in the heavens, and the red spot like an evil, malignant eye.

Whispers breathed in the night, whispers from all around him.

"Kill—kill—kill—"

"You hate them, you hate them, you hate them."

The whispers did not come from the shadowy figures about him. They pressed forward silently, as he did.

Whispers came from the night itself, whispers that now began to change tone.

"Wait, not tonight, not tonight, not tonight," they said.

"Go back, go back, go back."

"Back to your homes, back to your beds, back to your sleep."

And the figures about him were standing there, fully as irresolute as he had now become. And then, almost simultaneously, they began to obey the whispers. They turned back, and returned the way they had come, and as silently. . . .

Rod Caquer awoke with a mild headache and a hangover feeling. The sun, tiny but brilliant, was already well up in the sky.

His clock showed him that he was a bit later than usual, but he took time to lie there for a few minutes, just the same, remembering that screwy dream he'd had. Dreams were like that; you had to think about them right away when you woke up, before you were really fully awake, or you forgot them completely.

A silly sort of dream, it had been. A mad, purposeless dream. A touch of atavism, perhaps? A throwback to the days when people had been at each other's throats half the time, back to the days of wars and hatreds and struggle for supremacy.

This was before the Solar Council, meeting first on one inhabited planet and then another, had brought order by arbitration, and then union. And now war was a thing of the past. The inhabitable portion of the solar system—Earth, Venus, Mars, and the moons of Jupiter—were all under one government.

But back in the old bloody days, people must have felt as he had felt in that atavistic dream. Back in the days when Earth, united by the discovery of space travel, had subjugated Mars—the only other planet already inhabited by an intelligent race—and then had spread colonies wherever Man could get a foothold.

Certain of those colonies had wanted independence and, next, supremacy. The bloody centuries, those times were called now.

Getting out of bed to dress, he saw something that puzzled and dismayed him. His clothing was not neatly folded over the back of the chair beside the bed as he had left it. Instead, it was strewn about the floor as though he had undressed hastily and carelessly in the dark.

"Earth!" he thought. "Did I sleepwalk last night? Did I actually get out of bed and go out into the street when I dreamed that I did? When those whispers told me to?"

"No," he then told himself, "I've never walked in my sleep before, and I didn't then. I must simply have been careless when I undressed last night. I was thinking about the Deem case. I don't actually remember hanging my clothes on that chair."

So he donned his uniform quickly and hurried down to the office. In the light of morning it was easy to fill out those forms. In the "Cause of Death" blank he wrote, "Medical Examiner reports that shock from a blaster wound caused death."

That let him out from under; he had not said that was the cause of death; merely that the medico said it was.

CHAPTER THREE: BLACKDEX

He rang for a messenger and gave him the reports with instructions to rush them to the mail ship that would be leaving shortly. Then he called Barr Maxon.

"Reporting on the Deems matter, Regent," he said. "Sorry, but we just haven't got anywhere on it yet. Nobody was seen leaving the shop. All the neighbors have been questioned. Today I'm going to talk to all his friends."

Regent Maxon shook his head.

"Use all jets, Lieutenant," he said. "The case must be cracked. A murder, in this day and age, is bad enough. But an unsolved one is unthinkable. It would encourage further crime."

Lieutenant Caquer nodded gloomily. He had thought of that, too. There were the social implications of murder to be worried about—and there was his job as well. A Lieutenant of Police who let anyone get away with murder in his district was through for life.

After the Regent's image had clicked off the visiphone screen, Caquer took the list of Deem's friends from the drawer of his desk and began to study it, mainly with an eye to deciding the sequence of his calls.

He penciled a figure "1" opposite the name of Perry Peters, for two reasons. Peters's place was only a few doors away, for one thing, and for another he knew Perry better than anyone on the list, except possibly Professor Jan Gordon. And he would make that call last, because later there would be a better chance of finding the ailing professor awake—and a better chance of finding his daughter Jane at home.

Perry Peters was glad to see Caquer, and guessed immediately the purpose of the call.

"Hello, Shylock."

"Huh?" said Rod.

"Shylock—the great detective. Confronted with a mystery for the first time in his career as a policeman. Or have you solved it, Rod?"

"You mean Sherlock, you dope—Sherlock Holmes. No, I haven't solved it, if you want to know. Look, Perry, tell me all you know about Deem. You knew him pretty well, didn't you?"

Perry Peters rubbed his chin reflectively and sat down on the workbench. He was so tall and lanky that he could sit down on it instead of having to jump up.

"Willem was a funny little runt," he said. "Most people didn't like him because he was sarcastic, and he had crazy notions on politics. Me, I'm not sure whether he wasn't half right half the time, and anyway he played a swell game of chess."

"Was that his only hobby?"

"No. He liked to make things, gadgets mostly. Some of them were good, too, although he did it for fun and never tried to patent or capitalize anything."

"You mean inventions, Perry? Your own line?"

"Well, not so much inventions as gadgets, Rod. Little things, most of them, and he was better on fine workmanship than on original ideas. And, as I said, it was just a hobby with him."

"Ever help you with any of your own inventions?" asked Caquer.

"Sure, occasionally. Again, not so much on the idea of it as by helping me make difficult parts." Perry Peters waved his hand in a gesture that included the shop around them. "My tools here are all for rough work, comparatively. Nothing under thousandths. But Willem has—had a little lathe that's a honey. Cuts anything, and accurate to a fifty-thousandth."

"What enemies did he have, Perry?"

"None that I know of. Honestly, Rod. Lot of people disliked him, but just an ordinary mild kind of dislike. You know what I mean, the kind of dislike that makes 'em trade at another book-and-reel shop, but not the kind that makes them want to kill anybody."

"And who, as far as you know, might benefit by his death?"

"Um—nobody, to speak of," said Peters, thoughtfully. "I think his heir is a nephew on Venus. I met him once, and he was a likable guy. But the estate won't be anything to get excited about. A few thousand credits is all I'd guess it to be."

"Here's a list of his friends, Perry." Caquer handed Peters a paper. "Look it over, will you, and see if you can make any additions to it. Or any suggestions."

The lanky inventor studied the list, and then passed it back.

"That includes them all, I guess," he told Caquer. "Couple on there I didn't know he knew well enough to rate listing. And you have his best customers down, too; the ones that bought heavily from him."

Lieutenant Caquer put the list back in his pocket.

"What are you working on now?" he asked Peters.

"Something I'm stuck on, I'm afraid," the inventor said. "I needed Deem's help—or at least the use of his lathe, to go ahead with this." He picked up from the bench a pair of the most peculiar-looking goggles Rod Caquer had ever seen. The lenses were shaped like arcs of circles instead of full circles, and they fastened in a band of resilient plastic obviously designed to fit close to the face above and below the lenses. At the top center, where it would be against the forehead of the goggles' wearer, was a small cylindrical box an inch and a half in diameter.

"What on earth are they for?" Caquer asked.

"For use in radite mines. The emanations from that stuff, while it's in the raw state, destroy immediately any transparent substance yet made or discovered. Even quartz. And it isn't good on naked eyes either. The miners have to work blindfolded, as it were, and by their sense of touch."

Rod Caquer looked at the goggles curiously.

"But how is the funny shape of these lenses going to keep the emanations from hurting them, Perry?" he asked.

"That part up on top is a tiny motor. It operates a couple of specially treated wipers across the lenses. For all the world like an old-fashioned windshield wiper, and that's why the lenses are shaped like the wiper-arm arcs."

"Oh," said Caquer. "You mean the wipers are absorbent and hold some kind of liquid that protects the glass?"

"Yes, except that it's quartz instead of glass. And it's protected only a minute fraction of a second. Those wipers go like the devil—so fast you can't see them when you're wearing the goggles. The arms are half as big as the arcs, and the wearer can see out of only a fraction of the lens at a time. but he can see, dimly, and that's a thousand percent improvement in radite mining."

"Fine, Perry," said Caquer. "And they can get around the dimness by having ultra-brilliant lighting. Have you tried these out?"

"Yes, and they work. Trouble's in the rods; friction heats them and they expand and jam after it's run a minute, or thereabouts. I have to turn them down on Deem's lathe—or one like it. Think you could arrange for me to use it? Just for a day or so?"

"I don't see why not," Caquer told him. "I'll talk to whomever the Regent appoints executor, and fix it up. And later you can probably buy the lathe from his heir. Or does the nephew go in for such things?"

Perry Peters shook his head. "Nope, he wouldn't know a lathe from a drill-press. Be swell of you, Rod, if you can arrange for me to use it."

Caquer had turned to go, when Perry Peters stopped him.

"Wait a minute," Peters said and then paused and looked uncomfortable.

"I guess I was holding out on you, Rod," the inventor said at last. "I do know one thing about Willem that might possibly have something to do with his death, although I don't see how, myself. I wouldn't tell it on him, except that he's dead, and so it won't get him in trouble."

"What was it, Perry?"

"Illicit political books. He had a little business on the side selling them. Books on the index—you know just what I mean."

Caquer whistled softly. "I didn't know they were made any more. After the council put such a heavy penalty on them— whew!"

"People are still human, Rod. They still want to know the things they shouldn't know—just to find out why they shouldn't, if for no other reason."

"Graydex or Blackdex books, Perry?"

Now the inventor looked puzzled.

"I don't get it. What's the difference?"

"Books on the official index," Caquer explained, "are divided into two groups. The really dangerous ones are in the Blackdex. There's a severe penalty for owning one, and a death penalty for writing or printing one. The mildly dangerous ones are in the Graydex, as they call it."

"I wouldn't know which Willem peddled. Well, off the record, I read a couple Willem lent me once, and I thought they were pretty dull stuff. Unorthodox political theories."

"That would be Graydex." Lieutenant Caquer looked relieved. "Theoretical stuff is all Graydex. The Blackdex books are the ones with dangerous practical information."

"Such as?" The inventor was staring intently at Caquer.

"Instructions how to make outlawed things," explained Caquer. "Like Lethite, for instance. Lethite is a poison gas that's tremendously dangerous. A few pounds of it could wipe out a city, so the council outlawed its manufacture, and any book telling people how to make it for themselves would go on the Blackdex. Some nitwit might get hold of a book like that and wipe out his whole home town."

"But why would anyone?"

"He might be warped mentally, and have a grudge," explained Caquer. "Or he might want to use it on a lesser scale for criminal reasons. Or—by Earth, he might be the head of a government with designs on neighboring states. Knowledge of a thing like that might upset the peace of the solar system."

Perry Peters nodded thoughtfully. "I get your point," he said. "Well, I still don't see what it could have to do with the murder, but I thought I'd tell you about Willem's sideline. You probably want to check over his stock before whoever takes over the shop reopens."

"We shall," said Caquer, "Thanks a lot, Perry. If you don't mind, I'll use your phone to get that search started right away. If there are any Blackdex books there, we'll take care of them all right."

When he got his secretary on the screen, she looked both frightened and relieved at seeing him.

"Mr. Caquer," she said, "I've been trying to reach you. Something awful's happened. Another death."

"Murder again?" gasped Caquer.

"Nobody knows what it was," said the secretary. "A dozen people saw him jump out of a window only twenty feet up. And in this gravity that couldn't have killed him, but he was dead when they got there. And four of them that saw him knew him. It was—"

"Well, for Earth's sake, who?"

"I don't—Lieutenant Caquer, they said, all four of them, that it was Willem Deem!"

CHAPTER FOUR: RULE OF THUMB

With a nightmarish feeling of unreality Lieutenant Rod Caquer peered down over the shoulder of the Medico-in-Chief at the body that already lay on the stretcher of the utility men, who stood by impatiently.

"You better hurry, Doc," one of them said. "He won't last much longer and it will take us five minutes to get there."

Dr. Skidder nodded impatiently without looking up, and went on with his examination. "Not a mark, Rod," he said. "Not a sign of poison. Not a sign of anything. He's just dead."

"The fall couldn't have caused it?" said Caquer.

"There isn't even a bruise from the fall. Only verdict I can give is heart failure. Okay, boys, you can take it away."

"You through too, Lieutenant?"

"I'm through," said Caquer. "Go ahead. Skidder, which of them was Willem Deem?"

The medico's eyes followed the white-sheeted burden of the utility men as they carried it toward the truck, and he shrugged helplessly.

"Lieutenant, I guess that's your pigeon," he said. "All I can do is certify to cause of death."

"It just doesn't make sense," Caquer wailed. "Sector Three City isn't so big that he could have had a double living here without people knowing about it. But one of them had to be a double. Off the record, which looked to you like the original?"

Dr. Skidder shook his head grimly.

"Willem Deem had a peculiarly shaped wart on his nose," he said. "So did both of his corpses, Rod. And neither one was artificial, or make-up. I'll stake my professional reputation on that. But come on back to the office with me, and I'll tell you which one of them is the real Willem Deem."

"Huh? How?"

"His thumbprint's on file at the tax department, like everybody's is. And it's part of routine to fingerprint a corpse on Callisto, because it has to be destroyed so quickly."

"You have thumbprints of both corpses?" inquired Caquer.

"Of course. Took them before you reached the scene, both times. I have the one for Willem—I mean the other corpse—

back in my office. Tell you what—you pick up the print on file at the tax office and meet me there."

Caquer sighed with relief as he agreed. At least one point in the case would be cleared up—which corpse was which.

And in that comparatively blissful state of mind he remained until half an hour later when he and Dr. Skidder compared the three prints—the one Rod Caquer had secured from the tax office, and one from each of the corpses.

They were identical, all three of them.

"Um," said Caquer. "You're sure you didn't get mixed up on those prints, Dr. Skidder?"

"How could I? I took only one copy from each body, Rod. If I had shuffled them just now while we were looking at them, the result would be the same. All three prints are alike."

"But they can't be."

Skidder shrugged.

"I think we should lay this before the Regent, direct," he said. "I'll call him and arrange an audience. Okay?"

Half an hour later, he was giving the whole story to Regent Barr Maxon, with Dr. Skidder corroborating the main points. The expression on Regent Maxon's face made Lieutenant Rod Caquer glad, very glad, that he had that corroboration.

"You agree," Maxon asked, "that this should be taken up with the Sector Coordinator, and that a special investigator should be sent here to take over?"

A bit reluctantly, Caquer nodded. "I hate to admit that I'm incompetent, Regent, or that I seem to be," Caquer said. "But this isn't an ordinary crime. Whatever goes on, it's way over my head. And there may be something even more sinister than murder behind it."

"You're right, Lieutenant. I'll see that a qualified man leaves headquarters today and he'll get in touch with you in the morning."

"Regent," Caquer asked, "has any machine or process ever been invented that will—uh—duplicate a human body with or without the mind being carried over?"

Maxon seemed puzzled by the question.

"You think Deem might have been playing around with something that bit him. No, to my knowledge a discovery like that has never been approached. Nobody has ever duplicated, except by constructive imitation, even an inanimate object. You haven't heard of such a thing, have you, Skidder?"

"No," said the Medical Examiner. "I don't think even your friend Perry Peters could do that, Rod."

From the Regent Maxon's office, Caquer went on to Deem's shop. Brager was in charge there, and Brager helped him search the place thoroughly. It was a long and laborious task, because each book and reel had to be examined minutely.

The printers of illicit books, Caquer knew, were clever at disguising their product. Usually, forbidden books bore the cover and title page, often even the opening chapters, of some popular work of fiction, and the projection reels were similarly disguised.

Jupiter-lighted darkness was falling outside when they finished, but Rod Caquer knew they had done a thorough job. There wasn't an indexed book anywhere in the shop, and every reel had been run off on a projector.

Other men, at Rod Caquer's orders, had been searching Deem's apartment with equal thoroughness. He phoned there, and got a report, completely negative.

"Not so much as a Venusian pamphlet," said the man in charge at the apartment, with what Caquer thought was a touch of regret in his voice.

"Did you come across a lathe, a small one for delicate work?" Rod asked.

"Um—no, we didn't see anything like that. One room's turned into a workshop, but there's no lathe in it. Is it important?"

Caquer grunted noncommittally. What was one more mystery, and a minor one at that, to a case like this?

"Well, Lieutenant," Brager said, when the screen had gone blank, "what do we do now?"

Caquer sighed.

"You can go off duty, Brager," he said. "But first arrange to leave men on guard here and at the apartment. I'll stay until whoever you send comes to relieve me."

When Brager had left, Caquer sank wearily into the nearest chair. He felt terrible, physically, and his mind just did not seem to be working. He let his eyes run again around the orderly shelves of the shop and their orderliness oppressed him.

If there was only a clue of some sort. Wilder Williams had never had a case like this in which the only leads were two identical corpses, one of which had been killed five different ways and the other did not have a mark or sign of violence. What a mess, and where did he go from here?

Well, he still had the list of people he was going to interview, and there was time to see at least one of them this evening.

Should he look up Perry Peters again, and see what, if anything, the lanky inventor could make of the disappearance of the lathe? Perhaps he might be able to suggest what had happened to it. But then again, what could a lathe have to do with a mess like this? One cannot turn out a duplicate corpse on a lathe.

Or should he look up Professor Gordon? He decided to do just that.

He called the Gordon apartment on the visiphone, and Jane appeared in the screen.

"How's your father?" Jane asked Caquer. "Will he be able to talk to me for a while this evening?"

"Oh, yes," said the girl. "He's feeling much better, and thinks he'll go back to his classes tomorrow. But get here early if you're coming. Rod, you look terrible; what's the matter with you?"

"Nothing, except I feel goofy. But I'm all right, I guess."

"You have a gaunt, starved look. When did you eat last?"

Caquer's eyes widened. "Earth! I forgot all about eating. I slept late and didn't even have breakfast!"

Jane Gordon laughed.

"You dope! Well, hurry around, and I'll have something ready for you when you get here."

"But—"

"But nothing. How soon can you start?"

A minute after he had clicked off the visiphone, Lieutenant Caquer went to answer a knock on the shuttered door of the shop.

He opened it. "Oh, hullo, Reese," he said. "Did Brager send you?"

The policeman nodded.

"He said I was to stay here in case. In case what?"

"Routine guard duty, that's all," explained Caquer. "Say, I've been stuck here all afternoon. Anything going on?"

"A little excitement. We been pulling in soap-box orators off and on all day. Screwballs. There's an epidemic of them."

"The devil you say! What are they hipped about?"

"Sector Two, for some reason I can't make out. They're trying to incite people to get mad at Sector Two and do something about it. The arguments they use are plain nutty."

Something stirred uneasily in Rod Caquer's memory—but he could not quite remember what it was. Sector Two? Who'd been telling him things about Sector Two recently—usury, unfairness, tainted blood, something silly. Although of course a lot of the people over there did have Martian blood in them. . . .

"How many of the orators were arrested?" he asked.

"We got seven. Two more slipped away from us, but we'll pick them up if they start spouting that kind of stuff again."

Lieutenant Caquer walked slowly, thoughtfully, to the Gordon apartment, trying his level best to remember where, recently, he heard anti-Sector Two propaganda. There must be something back of the simultaneous appearance of nine soap-box radicals, all preaching the same doctrine.

A sub-rosa political organization? But none such had existed for almost a century now. Under a perfectly democratic government, a component part of a stable system-wide organization of planets, there was no need for such activity. Of course an occasional crackpot was dissatisfied, but a group in that state of mind struck him as fantastic.

It sounded as crazy as the Willem Deem case. That did not make sense either. Things happened meaninglessly, as in a dream. Dream? What was he trying to remember about a dream? Hadn't he had an odd sort of dream last night—what was it?

But, as dreams usually do, it eluded his conscious mind.

Anyway, tomorrow he would question—or help question—those radicals who were under arrest. Put men on the job of tracing them back, and undoubtedly a common background somewhere, a tieup, would be found.

It could not be accidental that they should all pop up on the same day. It was screwy, just as screwy as the two inexplicable corpses of a book-and-reel shop proprietor. Maybe because the cases were both screwy, his mind tended to couple the two sets of events. But taken together, they were no more digestible than taken separately. They made even less sense.

Confound it, why hadn't he taken that post on Ganymede when it was offered to him? Ganymede was a nice orderly moon. Persons there did not get murdered twice on consecutive days. But Jane Gordon did not live on Ganymede; she lived right here in Sector Three and he was on his way to see her.

And everything was wonderful except that he felt so tired he could not think straight, and Jane Gordon insisted on looking on him as a brother instead of a suitor, and he was probably going to lose his job. He would be the laughingstock of Callisto if the special investigator from headquarters found some simple explanation of things that he had overlooked. . . .

CHAPTER FIVE: NINE-MAN MORRIS

Jane Gordon, looking more beautiful than he had ever seen her, met him at the door. She was smiling, but the smile changed to a look of concern as he stepped into the light.

"Rod!" she exclaimed. "You do look ill, really ill. What have you been doing to yourself besides forgetting to eat?"

Rod Caquer managed a grin.

"Chasing vicious circles up blind alleys, Icicle. May I use your visiphone?"

"Of course. I've some food ready for you; I'll put it on the table while you're calling. Dad's taking a nap. He said to wake him when you got here, but I'll hold off until you're fed."

She hurried out to the kitchen. Caquer almost fell into the chair before the visiscreen, and called the police station. The red, beefy face of Borgesen, the night lieutenant, flashed into view.

"Hi, Borg," said Caquer. "Listen, about those seven screwballs you picked up. Have you—"

"Nine," Borgesen interrupted. "We got the other two, and I wish we hadn't. We're going nuts down here."

"You mean the other two tried it again?"

"No. Suffering Asteroids, they came in and gave themselves up, and we can't kick them out, because there's a charge against them. But they're confessing all over the place. And do you know what they're confessing?"

"I'll bite," said Caquer.

"That you hired them, and offered one hundred credits apiece to them."

"Huh?"

Borgesen laughed, a little wildly. "The two that came in voluntarily say that, and the other seven—Gosh, why did I ever become a policeman? I had a chance to study for fireman on a spacer once, and I end up doing this."

"Look—maybe I better come around and see if they make that accusation to my face."

"They probably would, but it doesn't mean anything, Rod. They say you hired them this afternoon, and you were at Deem's with Brager all afternoon. Rod, this moon is going nuts. And so am I. Walter Johnson has disappeared. Hasn't been seen since this morning."

"What? The Regent's confidential secretary? You're kidding me, Borg."

"Wish I was. You ought to be glad you're off duty. Maxon's been raising seven brands of thunder for us to find his secretary for him. He doesn't like the Deem business, either. Seems to blame us for it; thinks it's bad enough for the department to let a man get killed once. Say, which was Deem, Rod? Got any idea?"

Caquer grinned weakly.

"Let's call them Deem and Redeem till we find out," he suggested. "I think they were both Deem."

"But how could one man be two?"

"How could one man be killed five ways?" countered Caquer. "Tell me that and I'll tell you the answer to yours."

"Nuts," said Borgesen, and followed it with a masterpiece of understatement. "There's something funny about that case."

Caquer was laughing so hard that there were tears in his eyes when Jane Gordon came to tell him food was ready. She frowned at him, but there was concern behind the frown.

Caquer followed her meekly, and discovered he was ravenous. When he'd put himself outside enough food for three ordinary meals, he felt almost human again. His headache was still there, but it was something that throbbed dimly in the distance.

Frail Professor Gordon was waiting in the living room when they went there from the kitchen. "Rod, you look like something the cat dragged in," he said. "Sit down before you fall down."

Caquer grinned. "Overeating did it. Jane's a cook in a million."

He sank into a chair facing Gordon. Jane Gordon had sat on the arm of her father's chair and Caquer's eyes feasted on her. How could a girl with lips as soft and kissable as hers insist on regarding marriage only as an academic subject? How could a girl with—

"I don't see offhand how it could be a cause of his death, Rod, but Willem Deem rented out political books," said Gordon. "There's no harm in my telling that, since the poor chap is dead."

Almost the same words, Caquer remembered, that Perry Peters had used in telling him the same thing.

Caquer nodded.

"We've searched his shop and his apartment and haven't found any, Professor," he said. "You wouldn't know, of course, what kind—"

Professor Gordon smiled. "I'm afraid I would, Rod. Off the record—and I take it you haven't a recorder on our conversation—I've read quite a few of them."

"You?" There was frank surprise in Caquer's voice.

"Never underestimate the curiosity of an educator, my boy. I fear the reading of Graydex books is a more prevalent vice among the instructors in universities than among any other class. Oh, I know it's wrong to encourage the trade, but the reading of such books can't possibly harm a balanced, judicious mind."

"And Father certainly has a balanced, judicious mind, Rod," said Jane, a bit defiantly. "Only—darn him—he wouldn't let me read those books."

Caquer grinned at her. The professor's use of the word "Graydex" had reassured him.

Renting Graydex books was only a misdemeanor, after all.

"Ever read any Graydex books, Rod?" the professor asked. Caquer shook his head.

"Then you've probably never heard of hypnotism. Some of the circumstances in the Deem case—Well, I've wondered whether hypnotism might have been used."

"I'm afraid I don't even know what it is, Professor."

The frail little man sighed.

"That's because you've never read illicit books, Rod," said Gordon. "Hypnotism is the control of one mind by another, and it reached a pretty high state of development before it

was outlawed. You've never heard of the Kaprelian Order or
the Vargas Wheel?"

Caquer shook his head.

"The history of the subject is in Graydex books, in several
of them," said the professor. "The actual methods, and how a
Vargas Wheel is constructed would be Blackdex, high on the
roster of the lawless. Of course, I haven't read that, but I
have read the history.

"A man by the name of Mesmer, way back in the
eighteenth century, was one of the first practitioners, if not
the discoverer, of hypnotism. At any rate, he put it on a
more or less scientific basis. By the twentieth century, quite a
bit had been learned about it—and it became extensively
used in medicine.

"A hundred years later, doctors were treating almost as
many patients through hypnotism as through drugs and surgery. True, there were cases of its misuse, but they were
relatively few.

"But another hundred years brought a big change. Mes-
merism had developed too far for the public safety. Any
criminal or selfish politician who had a smattering of the art
could operate with impunity. He could fool all the people all
the time, and get away with it."

"You mean he could really make people think anything he
wanted them to?" Caquer asked.

"Not only that, he could make them do anything he
wanted. And by that time, television was in such common use
that one speaker could visibly and directly talk to millions of
people."

"But couldn't the government have regulated the art?"

Professor Gordon smiled thinly. "How, when legislators
were human, too, and as subject to hypnotism as the people
under them? And then, to complicate things almost hope-
lessly, came the invention of the Vargas Wheel.

"It had been known, back as far as the nineteenth century,
that an arrangement of moving mirrors could throw anyone
who watched it into a state of hypnotic submission. And
thought transmission had been experimented with in the
twenty-first century. It was in the following one that Vargas
combined and perfected the two into the Vargas Wheel. A
sort of helmet affair, really, with a revolving wheel of
specially constructed tricky mirrors on top of it."

"How did it work, Professor?" asked Caquer.

"The wearer of a Vargas Wheel helmet had immediate and automatic control over anyone who saw him—directly, or on a television screen," said Gordon. "The mirrors in the small turning wheel produced instantaneous hypnosis and the helmet—somehow—brought thoughts of its wearer to bear through the wheel and impressed upon his subjects any thoughts he wished to transmit.

"In fact, the helmet itself—or the wheel—could be set to produce certain fixed illusions without the necessity of the operator speaking, or even concentrating, on those points. Or the control could be direct, from his mind."

"Ouch," said Caquer. "A thing like that would—I can certainly see why instructions in making a Vargas Wheel would be Blackdexed. Suffering Asteroids! A man with one of these could—"

"Could do almost anything. Including killing a man and making the manner of his death appear five different ways to five different observers."

Caquer whistled softly. "And including playing nine-man Morris with soap-box radicals—or they wouldn't even have to be radicals. They could be ordinary orthodox citizens."

"Nine men?" Jane Gordon demanded. "What's this about nine men, Rod? I hadn't heard about it."

But Rod was already standing up.

"Haven't time to explain, Icicle," he said. "Tell you tomorrow, but I must get down to—Wait a minute. Professor, is that all you know about the Vargas Wheel business?"

Absolutely all, my boy. It just occurred to me as a possibility. There were only five or six of them ever made, and finally the government got hold of them and destroyed them, one by one. It cost millions of lives to do it.

"When they finally got everything cleaned up, colonization of the planets was starting, and an international council had been started with control over all governments. They decided that the whole field of hypnotism was too dangerous, and they made it a forbidden subject. It took quite a few centuries to wipe out all knowledge of it, but they succeeded. The proof is that you'd never heard of it."

"But how about the beneficial aspects of it," Jane Gordon asked. "Were they lost?"

"Of course," said her father. "But the science of medicine had progressed so far by that time that it wasn't too much of a loss. Today the medicos can cure, by physical treatment, anything that hypnotism could handle."

Caquer who had halted at the door, now turned back.

"Professor, do you think it possible that someone could have rented a Blackdex book from Deem, and learned all those secrets?" he inquired.

Professor Gordon shrugged. "It's possible," he said. "Deem might have handled occasional Blackdex books, but he knew better than try to sell or rent any to me. So I wouldn't have heard of it."

At the station, Lieutenant Caquer found Lieutenant Borgesen on the verge of apoplexy.

He looked at Caquer.

"You!" he said. And then, plaintively, "The world's gone nuts. Listen, Brager discovered Willem Deem, didn't he? At ten o'clock yesterday morning? And stayed there on guard while Skidder and you and the clearance men were there?"

"Yes, why?" asked Caquer.

Borgesen's expression showed how much he was upset by developments.

"Nothing, not a thing, except that Brager was in the emergency hospital yesterday morning, from nine until after eleven, getting a sprained ankle treated. He couldn't have been at Deem's. Seven doctors and attendants and nurses swear up and down he was in the hospital at that time."

Caquer frowned.

"He was limping today, when he helped me search Deem's shop," he said. "What does Brager say?"

"He says he was there, I mean at Deem's, and discovered Deem's body. We just happened to find out otherwise accidentally—if it is otherwise. Rod, I'm going nuts. To think I had a chance to be fireman on a spacer and took this celestial job. Have you learned anything new?"

"Maybe. But first I want to ask you, Borg. About these nine nitwits you picked up. Has anybody tried to identify—"

"Them," interrupted Borgesen. "I let them go."

Caquer stared at the beefy face of the night lieutenant in utter amazement.

"Let them go?" he repeated. "You couldn't, legally. Man, they'd been charged. Without a trial, you couldn't turn them loose."

"Nuts. I did, and I'll take the responsibility for it. Look, Rod, they were right, weren't they?"

"What?"

"Sure. People ought to be waked up about what's going on over in Sector Two. Those phonies over there need taking down a peg, and we're the only ones to do it. This ought to be headquarters for Callisto, right here. Why listen, Rod, a united Callisto could take over Ganymede."

"Borg, was there anything over the televis tonight? Anybody make a speech you listened to?"

"Sure, didn't you hear it? Our friend Skidder. Must have been while you were walking here, because all the televis turned on automatically—it was a general."

"And—was anything specific suggested, Borg? About Sector Two, and Ganymede, and that sort of thing?"

"Sure, general meeting tomorrow morning at ten. In the square. We're all supposed to go; I'll see you there, won't I?"

"Yeah," said Lieutenant Caquer. "I'm afraid you will. I—I got to go, Borg."

CHAPTER SIX: TOO FAMILIAR FACE

Rod Caquer knew what was wrong now. Also the last thing he wanted to do was stay around the station listening to Borgesen talking under the influence of—what seemed to be—a Vargas Wheel. Nothing else, nothing less, could have made police Lieutenant Borgesen talk as he had just talked. Professor Gordon's guess was getting righter every minute. Nothing else could have brought about such results.

Caquer walked on blindly through the Jupiter lighted night, past the building in which his own apartment was. He did not want to go there either.

The streets of Sector Three City seemed crowded for so late an hour of the evening. Late? He glanced at his watch and whistled softly. It was not evening any more. It was two o'clock in the morning, and normally the streets would have been utterly deserted.

But they were not, tonight. People wandered about, alone or in small groups that walked together in uncanny silence. Shuffle of feet, but not even the whisper of a voice. Not even—

Whispers! Something about those streets and the people on them made Rod Caquer remember now, his dream of the night before. Only now he knew that it had not been a dream. Nor had it been sleepwalking, in the ordinary sense of the word.

He had dressed. He had stolen out of the building. And the streetlights had been out too, and that meant that employes of the service department had neglected their posts. They, like others, had been wandering with the crowds.

"Kill—kill—kill—You hate them . . ."

A shiver ran down Rod Caquer's spine as he realized the significance of the fact that last night's dream had been a reality. This was something that dwarfed into insignificance the murder of a petty book-and-reel shop owner.

This was something which was gripping a city, something that could upset a world, something that could lead to unbelievable terror and carnage on a scale that hadn't been known since the twenty-fourth century. This—which had started as a simple murder case!

Up ahead somewhere, Rod Caquer heard the voice of a man addressing a crowd. A frenzied voice, shrill with fanaticism. He hurried his steps to the corner, and walked around it to find himself on the fringe of a crowd of people pressing around a man speaking from the top of a flight of steps.

"—and I tell you that tomorrow is the day. Now we have the Regent himself with us, and it will be unnecessary to depose him. Men are working all night tonight, preparing. After the meeting in the square tomorrow morning, we shall—"

"Hey!" Rod Caquer yelled. The man stopped talking and turned to look at Rod, and the crowd turned slowly, almost as one man, to stare at him.

"You're under—"

Then Caquer saw that this was but a futile gesture.

It was not the man's surging toward him that convinced him of this. He was not afraid of violence. He would have welcomed it as relief from uncanny terror, welcomed a chance to lay about him with the flat of his sword.

But standing behind the speaker was a man in uniform— Brager. And Caquer remembered, then, that Borgesen, now in charge at the station, was on the other side. How could he arrest the speaker, when Borgesen, now in charge, would refuse to book him. And what good would it do to start a riot and cause injury to innocent people—people acting not under their own volition, but under the insidious influence Professor Gordon had described to him?

Hand on his sword, he backed away. No one followed.

Like automatons, they turned back to the speaker, who resumed his harangue, as though never interrupted. Policeman Brager had not moved, had not even looked in the direction of his superior officer. He alone of all those there had not turned at Caquer's challenge.

Lieutenant Caquer hurried on in the direction he had been going when he had heard the speaker. That way would take him back downtown. He would find a place open where he could use a visiphone, and call the Sector Coordinator. This was an emergency.

And surely the scope of whoever had the Vargas Wheel had not yet extended beyond the boundaries of Sector Three.

He found an all-night restaurant, open but deserted, the lights on but no waiters on duty, no cashier behind the counter. He stepped into the visiphone booth and pushed the button for a long-distance operator. She flashed into sight on the screen almost at once.

"Sector Coordinator, Callisto City," Caquer said. "And rush it."

"Sorry, sir. Out of town service suspended by order of the controller of Utilities, for the duration."

"Duration of what?"

"We are not permitted to give out information."

Caquer gritted his teeth. Well, there was *one* someone who might be able to help him. He forced his voice to remain calm.

"Give me Professor Gordon, University Apartments," he told the operator.

"Yes, sir."

But the screen stayed dark, although the little red button that indicated the buzzer was operating flashed on and off, for minutes.

"There is no answer, sir."

Probably Gordon and his daughter were asleep, too soundly asleep to hear the buzzer. For a moment, Caquer considered rushing over there. But it was on the other side of town, and of what help could they be? None, and Professor Gordon was a frail old man, and ill.

No, he would have to— Again he pushed a button of the visiphone and a moment later was talking to the man in charge of the ship hangar.

"Get out that little speed job of the Police Department,"

snapped Caquer. "Have it ready and I'll be there in a few minutes."

"Sorry, Lieutenant," came the curt reply. "All outgoing power beams shut off, by special order. Everything's grounded for the emergency."

He might have known it, Caquer thought. But what about the special investigator coming in from the Coordinator's office? "Are incoming ships still permitted to land?" he inquired.

"Permitted to land, but not to leave again without special order," answered the voice.

"Thanks," Caquer said. He clicked off the screen and went out into the dawn, outside. There was a chance, then. The special investigator might be able to help.

But he, Rod Caquer would have to intercept him, tell him the story and its implications before he could fall, with the others, under the influence of the Vargas Wheel. Caquer strode rapidly toward the terminal. Maybe it was too late. Maybe his ship had already landed and the damage had been done.

Again he passed a knot of people gathered about a frenzied speaker. Almost everyone must be under the influence by this time. But why had he been spared? Why was not he, too, under the evil influence?

True, he must have been on the street on the way to the police station at the time Skidder had been on the air, but that didn't explain everything. All of these people could not have seen and heard that visicast. Some of them must have been asleep already at that hour.

Also he, Rod Caquer, had been affected, the night before, the night of the whispers. He must have been under the influence of the wheel at the time he investigated the murder—the murders.

Why, then, was he free now? Was he the only one, or were there others who had escaped, who were sane and their normal selves?

If not, if he was the only one, why was he free?

Or was he free?

Could it be that what he was doing right now was under direction, was part of some plan?

But no use to think that way, and go mad. He would have to carry on the best he could, and hope that things, with him, were what they seemed to be.

Then he broke into a run, for ahead was the open area of the terminal, and a small spaceship, silver in the dawn, was settling down to land. A small official speedster—it must be the special investigator. He ran around the check-in building, through the gate in the wire fence, and toward the ship, which was already down. The door opening.

A small, wiry man stepped out and closed the door behind him. He saw Caquer and smiled.

"You're Caquer?" he asked, pleasantly. "Coordinator's office sent me to investigate a case you fellows are troubled with. My name—"

Lieutenant Rod Caquer was staring with horrified fascination at the little man's well-known features, the all-too-familiar wart on the side of the little man's nose, listening for the announcement he knew this man was going to make—

"—is Willem Deem. Shall we go to your office?"

CHAPTER SEVEN: WHEELS WITHIN THE WHEEL

Such a thing as too much can happen to any man!

Lieutenant Rod Caquer, Lieutenant of Police of Sector Three, Callisto, had experienced more than his share. How can you investigate the murder of a man who has been killed twice? How should a policeman act when the victim shows up, alive and happy, to help you solve the case?

Not even when you know he is not there really—or if he is, he is not what your eyes tell you he is and is not saying what your ears hear.

There is a point beyond which the human mind can no longer function sanely with proper sense and when they reach and pass that point different people react in different ways.

Rod Caquer's reaction was a sudden blind, red anger. Directed, for lack of a better object, at the special investigator—if he was the special investigator and not a hypnotic phantasm which wasn't there at all.

Rod Caquer's fist lashed out, and it met a chin. Which proved nothing except that if the little man who'd just stepped out of the speedster was an illusion, he was an illusion of touch as well as of sight. Rod's fist exploded on his chin like a rocket blast, and the little man swayed and fell forward. Still smiling, because he had not had time to change the expression on his face.

He fell face down, and then rolled over, his eyes closed but smiling gently up at the brightening sky.

Shakily, Caquer bent own and put his hand against the front of the man's tunic. There was the thump of a beating heart, all right. For a moment, Caquer had feared he might have killed with that blow.

And Caquer closed his eyes, deliberately, and felt the man's face with his hand—and it still felt like the face of Willem Deem looked, and the wart was there to the touch as well as to the sense of sight.

Two men had run out of the check-in building and were coming across the field toward him. Rod caught the expression on their faces and then thought of the little speedster only a few paces from him. He had to get out of Sector Three City, to tell somebody what was happening before it was too late.

If only they'd been lying about the outgoing power beam being shut off. He leaped across the body of the man he had struck and into the door of the speedster, jerked at the controls. But the ship did not respond, and—no, they hadn't been lying about the power beam.

No use staying here for a fight that could not possibly decide anything. He went out the door of the speedster, on the other side, away from the men coming toward him, and ran for the fence.

It was electrically charged, that fence. Not enough to kill a man, but plenty to hold him stuck to it until men with rubber gloves cut the wire and took him off. But if the power beam was off, probably the current in the fence was off, too.

It was too high to jump, so he took the chance. And the current was off. He scrambled over it safely and his pursuers stopped and went back to take care of the fallen man beside the speedster.

Caquer slowed down to a walk, but he kept on going. He didn't know where, but he had somehow to keep moving. After a while he found that his steps were taking him toward the edge of town, on the northern side, toward Callisto City.

But that was silly. He couldn't possibly walk to Callisto City and get there in less than three days. Even if he could walk across the intervening roadless desert at all. Besides, three days would be too late.

He was in a small park near the north border when the significance, and the futility, of his direction came to him. And he found, at the same time, that his muscles were sore and tired, that he had a raging headache, that he could not keep on going unless he had a worthwhile and possible goal.

He sank down on a park bench, and for a while his head was sunk in his hands. No answer came.

After a while he looked up and saw something that fascinated him. A child's pinwheel on a stick, stuck in the grass of the park, spinning in the wind. Now fast, now slow, as the breeze varied.

It was going in circles, like his mind was. How could a man's mind go other than in circles when he could not tell what was reality and what was illusion? Going in circles, like a Vargas Wheel.

Circles.

But there ought to be some way. A man with a Vargas Wheel was not completely invincible, else how had the council finally succeeded in destroying the few that had been made? True, possessors of the wheels would have cancelled each other out to some extent, but there must have been a last wheel, in someone's hands. Owned by someone who wanted to control the destiny of the solar system.

But they had stopped the wheel.

It could be stopped, then. But how? How, when one could not see it? Rather when the sight of it put a man so completely under its control that he no longer, after the first glimpse, knew that it was there because, on sight, it had captured his mind.

He must stop the wheel. That was the only answer. But how?

That pinwheel there could be the Vargas Wheel, for all he could tell, set to create the illusion that it was a child's toy. Or its possessor, wearing the helmet, might be standing on the path in front of him at this moment, watching him. The possessor of the wheel might be invisible because Caquer's mind was told not to see.

But if the man was there, he'd be *really* there, and should Rod slash out with his sword, the menace would be ended, wouldn't it? Of course.

But how to find a wheel that one could not see? That one could not see because—

And then, still staring at the pinwheel, Caquer saw a chance, something that might work, a slender chance!

He looked quickly at his wristwatch and saw that it was

half past nine which was one half hour before the demonstration in the square. And the wheel and its owner would be there, surely.

His aching muscles forgotten, Lieutenant Rod Caquer started to run back toward the center of town. The streets were deserted. Everyone had gone to the square, of course. They had been told to come.

He was winded after a few blocks, and had to slow down to a rapid walk, but there would be time for him to get there before it was over, even if he missed the start.

Yes, he could get there all right. And then, if his idea worked. . . .

It was almost ten when he passed the building where his own office was situated, and kept on going. He turned in a few doors beyond. The elevator operator was gone, but Caquer ran the elevator up and a minute later he had used his picklock on a door and was in Perry Peters's laboratory.

Peters was gone, of course, but the goggles were there, the special goggles with the trick windshield-wiper effect that made them usable in radite mining.

Rod Caquer slipped them over his eyes, put the motive-power battery into his pocket, and touched the button on the side. They worked. He could see dimly as the wipers flashed back and forth. But a minute later they stopped.

Of course. Peters had said that the shafts heated and expanded after a minute's operation. Well, that might not matter. A minute might be long enough, and the metal would have cooled by the time he reached the square.

But he would have to be able to vary the speed. Among the litter of stuff on the workbench, he found a small rheostat and spliced it in one of the wires that ran from the battery to the goggles.

That was the best he could do. No time to try it out. He slid the goggles up onto his forehead and ran out into the hall, took the elevator down to street level. And a moment later he was running toward the public square, two blocks away.

He reached the fringe of the crowd gathered in the square looking up at the two balconies of the Regency building. On the lower one were several people he recognized. Dr. Skidder, Walther Johnson. Even Lieutenant Borgesen was there.

On the higher balcony, Regent Barr Maxon was alone, and was speaking to the crowd below. His sonorous voice rolled out phrases extolling the might of empire. Only a little distance away, in the crowd, Caquer caught sight of the gray hair of Professor Gordon, and Jane Gordon's golden head beside it. He wondered if they were under the spell, too. Of course they were deluded also or they would not be there. He realized it would be useless to speak to them, then, and tell them what he was trying to do.

Lieutenant Caquer slid the goggles down over his eyes, blinded momentarily because the wiper arms were in the wrong position. But his fingers found the rheostat, set at zero, and began to move it slowly around the dial toward maximum.

And then, as the wipers began their frantic dance and accelerated, he could see dimly. Through the arc-shaped lenses, he looked around him. On the lower balcony he saw nothing unusual, but on the upper balcony the figure of Regent Barr suddenly blurred.

There was a man standing there on the upper balcony wearing a strange-looking helmet with wires and atop the helmet was a three-inch wheel of mirrors and prisms.

A wheel that stood still, because of the stroboscopic effect of the mechanized goggles. For an instant, the speed of those wiper arms was synchronized with the spinning of the wheel, so that each successive glimpse of the wheel showed it in the same position, and to Caquer's eyes the wheel stood still, and he could see it.

Then the goggles jammed.

But he did not need them any more now.

He knew that Barr Maxon, or whoever stood up there on the balcony, was the wearer of the wheel.

Silently, and attracting as little attention as possible, Caquer sprinted around the fringe of the crowd and reached the side door of the Regency building.

There was a guard on duty there.

"Sorry, sir, but no one's allowed—"

Then he tried to duck, too late. The flat of Police Lieutenant Rod Caquer's shortsword thudded against his head.

The inside of the building seemed deserted. Caquer ran up the three flights of stairs that would take him to the level of the higher balcony, and down the hall toward the balcony door.

He burst through it, and Regent Maxon turned. Maxon now no longer wore the helmet on his head. Caquer had lost the goggles, but whether he could see it or not, Caquer knew the helmet and the wheel were still in place and working, and that this was his one chance.

Maxon turned and saw Lieutenant Caquer's face, and his drawn sword.

Then, abruptly, Maxon's figure vanished. It seemed to Caquer—although he knew that it was not—that the figure before him was that of Jane Gordon. Jane, looking at him pleadingly, and speaking in melting tones.

"Rod, don't—" she began to say.

But it was not Jane, he knew. A thought, in self-preservation, had been directed at him by the manipulator of the Vargas Wheel.

Caquer raised his sword, and he brought it down hard.

Glass shattered and there was the ring of metal on metal, as his sword cut through and split the helmet.

Of course it was not Jane now—just a dead man lying there with blood oozing out of the split in a strange and complicated, but utterly shattered, helmet. A helmet that could now be seen by everyone there, and by Lieutenant Caquer himself.

Just as everyone, including Caquer, himself, could recognize the man who had worn it.

He was a small, wiry man, and there was an unsightly wart on the side of his nose.

Yes, it was Willem Deem. And this time, Rod Caquer knew, it *was* Willem Deem. . . .

"I thought," Jane Gordon said, "that you were going to leave for Callisto City without saying good-bye to us."

Rod Caquer threw his hat in the general direction of a hook.

"Oh, that," he said. "I'm not even sure I'm going to take the promotion to a job as police coordinator there. I have a week to decide, and I'll be around town at least that long. How you been doing, Icicle?"

"Fine, Rod. Sit down. Father will be home soon, and I know he has a lot of things to ask you. Why, we haven't seen you since the big mass meeting."

Funny how dumb a smart man can be, at times.

But then again, he had proposed so often and been refused, that it was not all his fault.

He just looked at her.

"Rod, all the story never came out in the newscasts," she

said. "I know you'll have to tell it all over again for my father, but while we're waiting for him, won't you give me some information?"

Rod grinned.

"Nothing to it, really, Icicle," he said. "Willem Deem got hold of a Blackdex book, and found out how to make a Vargas Wheel. So he made one, and it gave him ideas.

"His first idea was to kill Barr Maxon and take over as Regent, setting the helmet so he would appear to be Maxon. He put Maxon's body in his own shop, and then had a lot of fun with his own murder. He had a warped sense of humor, and got a kick out of chasing us in circles."

"But just how did he do all the rest?" asked the girl.

"He was there as Brager, and pretended to discover his own body. He gave one description of the method of death, and caused Skidder and me and the clearance men to see the body of Maxon each a different way. No wonder we nearly went nuts."

"But Brager remembered being there too," she objected.

"Brager was in the hospital at the time, but Deem saw him afterward and impressed on his mind the memory pattern of having discovered Deem's body," explained Caquer. "So naturally, Brager thought he had been there.

"Then he killed Maxon's confidential secretary, because being so close to the Regent, the secretary must have suspected something was wrong even though he couldn't guess what. That was the second corpse of Willem Deem, who was beginning to enjoy himself in earnest when he pulled that on us.

"And of course he never sent to Callisto City for a special investigator at all. He just had fun with me, by making me seem to meet one and having the guy turn out to be Willem Deem again. I nearly did go nuts then, I guess."

"But why, Rod, weren't you as deeply in as the others—I mean on the business of conquering Callisto and all of that?" she inquired. "You were free of that part of the hypnosis."

Caquer shrugged.

"Maybe it was because I missed Skidder's talk on the televis," he suggested. "Of course it wasn't Skidder at all, it was Deem in another guise and wearing the helmet. And maybe he deliberately left me out, because he was having a psychopathic kind of fun out of my trying to investigate the murders of two Willem Deems. It's hard to figure. Perhaps I was slightly cracked from the strain, and it might have been that for that reason I was partially resistant to the group hypnosis."

"You think he really intended to try to rule all of Callisto, Rod?" asked the girl.

"We'll never know, for sure, just how far he wanted or expected to go later. At first, he was just experimenting with the powers of hypnosis, through the wheel. That first night, he sent people out of their houses into the streets, and then sent them back and made them forget it. Just a test, undoubtedly."

Caquer paused and frowned thoughtfully.

"He was undoubtedly psychopathic, though, and we don't dare even guess what all his plans were," he continued. "You understand how the goggles worked to neutralize the wheel, don't you, Icicle?"

"I think so. That was brilliant, Rod. It's like when you take a moving picture of a turning wheel, isn't it? If the camera synchronizes with the turning of the wheel, so that each successive picture shows it after a complete revolution, then it looks like it's standing still when you show the movie."

Caquer nodded.

"That's it on the head," he said. "Just luck I had access to those goggles, though. For just a second I could see a man wearing a helmet up there on the balcony—but that was all I had to know."

"But Rod, when you rushed out on the balcony, you didn't have the goggles on any more. Couldn't he have stopped you, by hypnosis?"

"Well, he didn't. I guess there wasn't time for him to take over control of me. He did flash an illusion at me. It wasn't either Barr Maxon or Willem Deem I saw standing there at the last minute. It was you, Jane."

"I?"

"Yep, you. I guess he knew I'm in love with you, and that's the first thing flashed into his mind; that I wouldn't dare use the sword if I thought it was you standing there. But I knew it wasn't you, in spite of the evidence of my eyes, so I swung it."

He shuddered slightly, remembering the willpower he had needed to bring that sword down.

"The worst of it was that I saw you standing there like I've always wanted to see you—with your arms out toward me, and looking at me as though you loved me."

"Like this, Rod?"

And he was not too dumb to get the idea, that time.

DOORWAY INTO TIME

Famous Fantastic Mysteries,

September

by C. L. Moore

This may *be a solo effort by Catherine Moore, although the science fantasy element was also common in Kuttner's work. The story appeared in* Famous Fantastic Mysteries, *which is unusual in itself, since FFM was primarily a reprint magazine, restoring to print works by hands as diverse as those of Franz Kafka, Ray Cummings and H.G. Wells. It had a surprisingly long run, lasting from 1939 to 1953, a remarkable performance which saw it survive the paper shortage of World War II, which killed so many of the pulp magazines.*

(Long before the feminist revolution had brought women authors by the dozen into science fiction, C. L. Moore was one of the few who invaded what had been an almost purely masculine realm. What's more, her stories seemed "masculine" because they didn't deal with the petty fripperies that readers expected of women authors and that women authors were therefore forced to deal with if they expected to sell. I wonder how many of her early readers assumed C. L. stood for Charles Ludwig, or something like that. I was in the audience a couple of years ago when she appeared at a convention. She has aged well, married again in the period since Hank Kuttner's death and seemed very happy and contented with life.—I.A.)

He came slowly, with long, soft, ponderous strides, along the hallway of his treasure house. The gleanings of many

219

worlds were here around him, he had ransacked space and
time for the treasures that filled his palace. The robes that
moulded their folds richly against his great rolling limbs as he
walked were in themselves as priceless as anything within
these walls, gossamer fabric pressed into raised designs that
had no meaning, this far from the world upon which they
had been created, but—in their beauty—universal. But he
was himself more beautiful than anything in all that vast
collection. He knew it complacently, a warm contented knowledge deep in the center of his brain.

His motion was beautiful, smooth power pouring along his
limbs as he walked, his great bulk ponderous and graceful.
The precious robes he wore flowed open over his magnificent
body. He ran one sensuous palm down his side, enjoying the
texture of that strange, embossed delicacy in a fabric thinner
than gauze. His eyes were proud and half shut, flashing
many-colored under the heavy lids. The eyes were never
twice quite the same color, but all the colors were beautiful.

He was growing restless again. He knew the feeling well,
that familiar quiver of discontent widening and strengthening
far back in his mind. It was time to set out once more on the
track of something dangerous. In times past, when he had
first begun to stock this treasure house, beauty alone had been
enough. It was not enough any longer. Danger had to be
there too. His tastes were growing capricious and perhaps a
little decadent, for he had lived a very long time.

Yes, there must be a risk attending the capture of his next
new treasure. He must seek out great beauty and great danger, and subdue the one and win the other, and the thought
of it made his eyes change color and the blood beat faster in
mighty rhythms through his veins. He smoothed his palm
again along the embossed designs of the robe that moulded itself to his body. The great, rolling strides carried him noise-
lessly over the knife-edged patterns of the floor.

Nothing in life meant much to him any more except these
beautiful things which his own passion for beauty had
brought together. And even about these he was growing
capricious now. He glanced up at a deep frame set in the
wall just at the bend of the corridor, where his appreciative
eyes could not fail to strike the objects it enclosed at just the
proper angle. Here was a group of three organisms fixed in
an arrangement that once had given him intense pleasure. On
their own world they might have been living creatures, per-

haps even intelligent. He neither knew nor cared. He did not even remember now if there had been eyes upon their world to see, or minds to recognize beauty. He cared only that they had given him acute pleasure whenever he turned this bend of the corridor and saw them frozen into eternal perfection in their frame.

But the pleasure was clouded as he looked at them now. His half-shut eyes changed color, shifting along the spectrum from yellow-green to the cooler purity of true green. This particular treasure had been acquired in perfect safety; its value was impaired for him, remembering that. And the quiver of discontent grew stronger in his mind. Yes, it was time to go out hunting again. . . .

And here, set against a panel of velvet, was a great oval stone whose surface exhaled a light as soft as smoke, in waves whose colors changed with languorous slowness. Once the effect had been almost intoxicating to him. He had taken it from the central pavement of a great city square upon a world whose location he had forgotten long ago. He did not know if the people of the city had valued it, or perceived its beauty at all. But he had won it with only a minor skirmish, and now in his bitter mood it was valueless to his eyes.

He quickened his steps, and the whole solid structure of the palace shook just perceptibly underfoot as he moved with ponderous majesty down the hall. He was still running one palm in absent appreciation up and down the robe across his mighty side, but his mind was not on present treasures anymore. He was looking to the future, and the color of his eyes had gone shivering up the spectrum to orange, warm with the anticipation of danger. His nostrils flared a little and his wide mouth turned down at the corners in an inverted grimace. The knife-edged patterns of the floor sang faintly beneath his footsteps, their sharp intricacies quivering as the pressure of his steps passed by.

He went past a fountain of colored fire which he had wrecked a city to possess. He thrust aside a hanging woven of unyielding crystal spears which only his great strength could have moved. It gave out showers of colored sparks when he touched it, but their beauty did not delay him now.

His mind had run on ahead of him, into that room in the center of his palace, round and dim, from which he searched the universe for plunder and through whose doorways he set out upon its track. He came ponderously along the hall toward it, passing unheeded treasures, the gossamer of his robes floating after him like a cloud.

On the wall before him, in the dimness of the room, a great circular screen looked out opaquely, waiting his touch. A doorway into time and space. A doorway to beauty and deadly peril and everything that made livable for him a life which had perhaps gone on too long already. It took strong measures now to stir the jaded senses which once had responded so eagerly to more stimuli than he could remember anymore. He sighed, his great chest expanding tremendously. Somewhere beyond that screen, upon some world he had never trod before, a treasure was waiting lovely enough to tempt his boredom and dangerous enough to dispel it for just a little while.

The screen brightened as he neared the wall. Blurred shadows moved, vague sounds drifted into the room. His wonderful senses sorted the noises and the shapes and dismissed them as they formed; his eyes were round and luminous now, and the orange fires deepened as he watched. Now the shadows upon the screen moved faster. Something was taking shape. The shadows leaped backward into three-dimensional vividness that wavered for a moment and then sharpened into focus upon a desert landscape under a vivid crimson sky. Out of the soil a cluster of tall flowers rose swaying, exquisitely shaped, their colors shifting in that strange light. He glanced at them carelessly and grimaced. And the screen faded.

He searched the void again, turning up scene after curious scene and dismissing each with a glance. There was a wall of carved translucent panels around a city he did not bother to identify. He saw a great shining bird that trailed luminous plumage, and a tapestry woven gorgeously with scenes from no earthly legend, but he let all of them fade again without a second look, and the orange glow in his eyes began to dull with boredom.

Once he paused for a while before the picture of a tall, dark idol carved into a shape he did not recognize, its strange limbs adorned with jewels that dripped fire, and for an instant his pulse quickened. It was pleasant to think of those jewels upon his own great limbs, trailing drops of flame along his halls. But when he looked again he saw that the idol stood deserted upon a barren world, its treasure his for the taking. And he knew that so cheap a winning would be savorless. He sighed again, from the depths of his mighty chest, and let the screen shift its pictures on.

It was the faraway flicker of golden lightning in the void that first caught his eyes, the distant scream of it from some world without a name. Idly he let the screen's shadows form a picture. First was the lightning, hissing and writhing from a mechanism which he spared only one disinterested glance. For beside it two figures were taking shape, and as he watched them his restless motions stilled and the floating robe settled slowly about his body. His eyes brightened to orange again. He stood very quiet, staring.

The figures were of a shape he had not seen before. Remotely like his own, but flexible and very slender, and of proportions grotesquely different from his. And one of them, in spite of its difference, was—He stared thoughtfully. Yes, it was beautiful. Excitement began to kindle behind his quietness. And the longer he stared the clearer the organism's subtle loveliness grew. No obvious flamboyance like the fire-dripping jewels or the gorgeously plumed bird, but a delicate beauty of long, smooth curves and tapering lines, and colors in softly blended tints of apricot and creamy white and warm orange-red. Folds of blue-green swathing it were probably garments of some sort. He wondered if it was intelligent enough to defend itself, or if the creature beside it, making lightnings spurt out of the mechanism over which it bent, would know or care if he reached out to take its companion away.

He leaned closer to the screen, his breath beginning to come fast and his eyes glowing with the first flush of red that meant excitement. Yes, this was a lovely thing. A very lovely trophy for his halls. Briefly he thought of it arranged in a frame whose ornaments would echo the soft and subtle curves of the creature itself, colored to enhance the delicacy of the subject's coloring. Certainly a prize worth troubling himself for—if there were danger anywhere near to make it a prize worth winning. . . .

He put one hand on each side of the screen and leaned forward into it a little, staring with eyes that were a dangerous scarlet now. That flare of lightning looked like a weapon of some sort. If the creatures had intelligence—It would be amusing to test the limits of their minds, and the power of the weapon they were using. . . .

He watched a moment longer, his breath quickening. His

mighty shoulders hunched forward. Then with one shrug he cast off the hampering garment of gossamer and laughed deep in his throat and lunged smoothly forward into the open doorway of the screen. He went naked and weaponless, his eyes blazing scarlet. This was all that made life worth living. Danger, and beauty beyond danger. . . .

Darkness spun around him. He shot forward through dimensionless infinity along a corridor of his own devising.

The girl leaned back on her metal bench and crossed one beautiful long leg over the other, stirring the sequined folds of her gown into flashing motion.

"How much longer, Paul?" she asked.

The man glanced over his shoulder and smiled.

"Five minutes. Look away now—I'm going to try it again." He reached up to slip a curved, transparent mask forward, closing his pleasant, dark face away from the glare. The girl sighed and shifted on the bench, averting her eyes.

The laboratory was walled and ceiled in dully reflecting metal, so that the blue-green blur of her gown moved as if in dim mirrors all around her when she changed position. She lifted a bare arm to touch her hair, and saw the reflections lift too, and the pale blur that was her hair, shining ashes of silver and elaborately coiffed.

The murmur of well-oiled metal moving against metal told her that a lever had been shifted, and almost instantly the room was full of golden glare, like daylight broken into hissing fragments as jagged as lightning. For a long moment the walls quivered with light and sound. Then the hissing died, the glare faded. A smell of hot metal tainted the air.

The man sighed heavily with satisfaction and lifted both hands to pull the mask off. Indistinctly behind the glass she heard him say:

"Well, that's done. Now we can—"

But he never finished, and the helmet remained fixed on his shoulders as he stared at the wall they were both facing. Slowly, almost absentmindedly, he pushed aside the glass across his face, as if he thought it might be responsible for the thing they both saw. For above the banked machinery which controlled the mechanism he had just released, a shadow had fallen upon the wall. A great circle of shadow. . . .

Now it was a circle of darkness, as if twilight had rushed timelessly into midnight before them as they watched, and a midnight blacker than anything earth ever knew. The midnight of the ether, of bottomless spaces between worlds. And now it was no longer a shadow, but a window opening upon that midnight, and the midnight was pouring through. . . .

Like smoke the darkness flowed in upon them, dimming the glitter of machinery, dimming the girl's pale hair and pale, shining shoulders and the shimmer of her gown until the man looked at her as if through veil upon veil of falling twilight.

Belatedly he moved, making a useless gesture of brushing the dark away with both hands before his face.

"Alanna—" he said helplessly. "What's happened? I can't see—very well—"

He heard her whimper in bewilderment, putting her own hands to her eyes as if she thought blindness had come suddenly upon them both. He was too sick with sudden dizziness to move or speak. This, he told himself wildly, must be the blindness that foreruns a swoon, and his obedient mind made the floor seem to tilt as if the faintness and blindness were inherent in himself, and not the result of some outward force.

But before either of them could do more than stammer a little, as their minds tried desperately to rationalize what was happening into some weakness of their own senses, the dark was complete. The room brimmed with it, and sight ceased to exist.

When the man felt the floor shake, he thought for an unfathomable moment that it was his own blindness, his own faintness again, deceiving his senses. The floor could not shake, as if to a ponderous tread. For there was no one here but themselves—there could not be great footfalls moving softly through the dark, making the walls shudder a little as they came. . . .

Alanna's caught breath was clear in the silence. Not terror at first; but surprised inquiry. She said, "Paul—Paul, don't—"

And then he heard the beginning of her scream. He heard the beginning, but incredibly, he never heard the scream's end. One moment the full-throated roundness of her cry filled the room, pouring from a throat stretched wide with terror; the next, the sound diminished and vanished into infinite distances, plummeting away from him and growing thin and tiny while the echo of its first sound still rang through the room. The impossibility of such speed put the last touch of nightmare upon the whole episode. He did not believe it.

The dark was paling again. Rubbing his eyes, still not sure at all that this had not been some brief aberration of his own senses, he said, "Alanna—I thought—"

But the twilight around him was empty.

He had no idea how long a while elapsed between that moment and the moment when he stood up straight at last, facing the wall upon which the shadow still lay. In between there must have been a period of frantic search, of near hysteria and self-doubt and reeling disbelief. But now, as he stood looking up at the wall upon which the shadow still hung blackly, drawing into itself the last veils of twilight from the corners of the room, he ceased to rationalize or disbelieve.

Alanna was gone. Somehow, impossibly, in the darkness that had come upon them a Something with great silent feet that trod ponderously, shaking the walls, had seized her in the moment when she said, "Paul—" thinking it was himself. And while she screamed, it had vanished into infinite distances out of this room, carrying her with it.

That it was impossible he had no time to consider. He had time now only to realize that nothing had passed him toward the door, and that the great circle upon the wall before him was—an entrance?—out of which Something had come and into which Something must have retreated again—and not alone. . . .

And the entrance was closing.

He took one step toward it, unreasoning and urgent, and then stumbled over the boxed instrument which he had been testing just before insanity entered the room. The sight and feel of it brought back his own sanity a little. Here was a weapon; it offered a grip upon slipping reality to know that he was not wholly helpless. Briefly he wondered whether any weapon at all would avail against That which came in impossible darkness on feet that made no sound, though their tread shook the foundations of the building. . . .

But the weapon was heavy. And how far away from the parent machine would it work? With shaking fingers he groped for the carrying handle. He staggered a little, lifting it, but he turned toward the end of the room where the great circle drank in the last of its twilight and began imperceptibly to pale upon the wall. If he were to follow, to take That which had gone before him by surprise, he must go swiftly. . . .

One glance at the lever of the parent machine, to be sure it was thrown full over, for the weapon itself drank power from that source alone—if it would drink power at all in the unfathomable distances to which he was going. . . . One last unbelieving glance around the room, to be quite sure Alanna was really gone—

The lower arc of the circle was a threshold opening upon darkness. He could not think that he would pass it, this flat shadow upon the flat and solid wall, but he put out one hand uncertainly and took a step forward, and another, bent to the weight of the box he carried. . . .

But there was no longer any weight. Nor was there any light or sound—only wild, whirling motion that spun him over and over in the depths of his blindness. Spun interminably—spun for untimed eons that passed in the flash of an eye. And then—

"Paul! Oh, Paul!"

He stood reeling in a dim, round room walled with strange designs he could not quite focus upon. He had no sense that was not shaken intolerably; even sight was not to be relied upon just now. He thought he saw Alanna in the dimness, pale hair falling over her pale, shining shoulders, her face distorted with bewilderment and terror. . . .

"Paul! Paul, answer me! What is it? What's happened?"

He could not speak yet. He could only shake his head and cling by blind instinct to the weight that dragged down upon one arm. Alanna drew her bare shoulders together under the showering hair and hugged herself fearfully, the creamy arms showing paler circles where her fingertips pressed them hard. Her teeth were chattering, though not from cold.

"How did we get here?" she was saying. "How did we get here, Paul? We'll have to go back, won't we? I wonder what's happened to us." The words were almost aimless, as if the sound of speech itself were more important to her now than any sense of what she was saying. "Look behind you, Paul—see? We came out of—there."

He turned. A great circle of mirror rose behind him on the dim wall, but a mirror reversed, so that it reflected not themselves, but the room they had just left.

Clearer than a picture—he looked into it—his laboratory walls shining with dull reflections, his batteries and dials, and the lever standing up before them that meant the heavy thing he carried would be deadly—perhaps. Deadly? A weapon in a dream? Did they even know that the Something which dwelt here was inimical?

But this was ridiculous. It was too soon yet to accept the fact that they were standing here at all. In reality, of course, they must both be back in the laboratory, and both of them dreaming the same strange dream. And he felt, somehow, that to treat all this as a reality would be dangerous. For if he accepted even by implication that such a thing could be true, then perhaps—perhaps. . . . Could acceptance make it *come* true?

He set his weapon down and rubbed his arm dazedly, looking around. Words did not come easily yet, but he had to ask one question.

"That—that thing, Alanna. What was it? How did you—"

She gripped her own bare arms harder, and another spasm of shuddering went over her. The blue-green sequins flashed chilly star points from her gown as she moved. Her voice shook too; her very mind seemed to be shaking behind the blank eyes. But when she spoke the words made approximate sense. And they echoed his own thought.

"I'm dreaming all this, you know." Her voice sounded far away. "This isn't really happening. But—but *something* took me in its arms back there." She nodded toward the mirrored laboratory on the wall. "And everything whirled, and then—" A hard shudder seized her. "I don't know. . . ."

"Did you see it?"

She shook her head. "Maybe I did. I'm not sure. I was so dizzy—I think it went away through that door. Would you call it a door?" Her little breath of laughter was very near hysteria. "I—I felt its feet moving away."

"But what was it? What did it look like?"

"I don't know, Paul."

He closed his lips on the questions that rushed to be asked. Here in the dream, many things were very alien indeed. Those patterns on the wall, for instance. He thought he could understand how one could look at something and not be sure at all what the something was. And Alanna's heavy spasms of shuddering proved that shock must have blanked her mind protectively to much of what had happened. She said:

"Aren't we going back now, Paul?" And her eyes flickered past him to the pictured laboratory. It was a child's question;

her mind was refusing to accept anything but the barest essentials of their predicament. But he could not answer. His first impulse was to say, "Wait—we'll wake up in a minute." But suppose they did not? Suppose they were trapped here? and if the Thing came back. . . . Heavily, he said:

"Of course it's a dream, Alanna. But while it lasts I think we'll have to act as if it were real. I don't want to—" The truth was, he thought, he was afraid to. "But we must. And going back wouldn't do any good as long as we go on dreaming. *It* would just come after us again."

It would come striding through the dream to drag them back, and after all people have died in their sleep—died in their dreams, he thought.

He touched the unwieldy weapon with his toe, thinking silently, "This will help us—maybe. If anything can, it will. And if it won't—well, neither will running away." And he glanced toward the high, distorted opening that must be a doorway into some other part of this unimaginable, dream-created building. It had gone that way, then. Perhaps they should follow. Perhaps their greatest hope of waking safely out of this nightmare lay in acting rashly, in following with the weapon before it expected them to follow. It might not guess his own presence here at all. It must have left Alanna alone in the dim room, intending to return, not thinking to find her with a defender, or to find the defender armed. . . .

But was he armed? He grinned wryly.

Perhaps he ought to test the weapon. And yet, for all he knew, the Thing's strange, alien gaze might be upon him now. He was aware of a strong reluctance to let it know that he had any defense against it. Surprise—that was important. Keep it a secret until he needed a weapon, if he ever did need one. Very gently he pressed the trigger of the lens that had poured out lightnings in the faraway sanity of his laboratory. Would it work in—a dream? For a long moment nothing happened. Then, faintly and delicately against his palm he felt the tubing begin to throb just a little. It was as much of an answer as he dared take now. Some power was there. Enough? He did not know. It was unthinkable, really, that he should ever need to know. Still—

"Alanna," he said, "I think we'd better explore a little. No use just standing here waiting for *it* to come back. It may be perfectly friendly, you know. Dream creatures often are. But I'd like to see what's outside."

"We'll wake up in a minute," she assured him between chattering teeth. "I'm all right, I think, really. Just—just nervous." He thought she seemed to be rousing from her stupor. Perhaps the prospect of action—any action—even rashness like this, was better for them both than inactivity. He felt surer of himself as he lifted the heavy weapon.

"But Paul, we can't!" She turned, halfway to the door, and faced him. "Didn't I tell you? I tried that before you came. There's a corridor outside, with knives all over the floor. Patterns of them, sharp-edged spirals and—and shapes. Look." She lifted her sparkling skirt a little and put out one foot. He could see the clean, sharp lacerations of the leather sole. His shoulders sagged a bit. Then:

"Well, let's look anyhow. Come on."

The corridor stretched before them, swimming in purple distances, great gothic hollows and arches melting upon arches. There were things upon the walls. Like the patterns in the room behind them, many were impossible to focus upon directly, too different from anything in human experience to convey meaning to the brain. The eye perceived them blankly, drawing no conclusions. He thought vaguely that the hall looked like a museum, with those great frames upon the walls.

Beside the door another tall frame leaned, empty. About six feet high, it was deep enough for a man to lie down in, and all around its edges an elaborate and beautiful decoration writhed, colored precisely like Alanna's blue-green gown. Interwoven in it were strands of silver, the color of her pale and shining hair.

"It looks like a coffin," Alanna said aimlessly. Some very ugly thought stirred in Paul's mind. He would not recognize it; he pushed it back out of sight quickly, but he was gladder now that he had brought this lightning-throwing weapon along.

The hall shimmered with strangeness before them. So many things he could not quite see clearly, but the razor-edged decorations of the floor were clear enough. It made the mind reel a little to think what utter alienage lay behind the choice of such adornment for a floor that must be walked upon—even in a dream. He thought briefly of the great earth-shaking feet in the darkness of his laboratory. Here in the dream they walked this knife-edged floor. They must.

But how?

The spirals of the pattern lay in long loops and rosettes. After a moment, eyeing them, he said, "I think we can make it, Alanna. If we walk between the knives—see, there's space if we're careful." And if they were not careful, if they had to run. . . . "We've got to risk it," he said aloud, and with those words admitted to himself for perhaps the first time an urgency in this dream, risk and danger. . . .

He took a firmer grip upon his burden and stepped delicately into the hollow of a steely spiral. Teetering a little, clutching at his arm to steady herself, Alanna came after him.

Silence—vast, unechoing hollows quivering with silence all around them. They advanced very slowly, watching wide-eyed for any signs of life in the distances, their senses strained and aching with the almost subconscious awareness of any slightest motion in the floor that might herald great feet ponderously approaching. But That which had opened the doorway for them had gone now, for a little while, and left them to their own devices.

Paul carried the lens of his weapon ready in his free hand, the lightest possible pressure always on its trigger so that the tubing throbbed faintly against his palm. That reassurance that contact still flowed between his faraway laboratory and this unbelievable hall was all that kept him forging ahead over the razory mosaics.

They went slowly, but they passed many very strange things. A tremendous transparent curtain swung from the vaulted ceiling in folds as immovable as iron. They slipped through the little triangle of opening where the draperies hung awry, and a shower of fiery sparkles sprang out harmlessly when they brushed the sides. They passed a fountain that sent up gushes of soundless flame from its basin in the center of the corridor floor. They saw upon the walls, in frames and without them, things too alien to think about clearly. That very alienage was worrying the man. In dreams one rehearses the stimuli of the past, fears and hopes and memories. But how *could* one dream of things like these? Where in any human past could such memories lie?

They skirted an oval stone set in the floor, the metal patterns swirling about it. They were both dizzy when they looked directly at it. Dangerous dizziness, since a fall here must end upon razor edges. And once they passed an in-

describable something hanging against a black panel of the
wall, that brought tears to the eyes with its sheer loveliness, a
thing of unbearable beauty too far, removed from human experience to leave any picture in their minds once they had
gone past it. Only the emotional impact remained, remembered beauty too exquisite for the mind to grasp and hold.
And the man knew definitely now that this at least was no
part of any human memory, and could be in itself no dream.

They saw it all with the strange clarity and vividness of
senses sharp with uncertainty and fear, but they saw it too
with a dreamlike haziness that faded a little as they went on.
To the man, a terrible wonder was dawning. Could it, after
all, be a dream? Could it possibly be some alien reality into
which they had stumbled? And the import of that frame outside the door they had left—the frame shaped like a coffin
and adorned with the colors of Alanna's gown and hair. . . .
Deep in his mind he knew what that frame was for. He knew
he was walking through a museum filled with lovely things,
and he was beginning to suspect why Alanna had been
brought here too. The thing seemed unthinkable, even in a
dream as mad as this, and yet—

"Look, Paul." He glanced aside. Alanna had reached up to
touch a steel-blue frame upon the wall, its edges enclosing
nothing but a dim rosy shimmer. She was groping inside it,
her face animated now. No thought had come to her yet
about that other frame, evidently. No thought that from this
dream neither of them might ever wake. . . .

"Look," she said. "It seems empty, but I can *feel* something—something like feathers. What do you suppose—"

"Don't try to suppose," he said almost brusquely. "There
isn't any sense to any of this."

"But some of the things are so pretty, Paul. See that—that
snowstorm ahead, between the pillars?"

He looked. Veiling the hallway a little distance away hung
a shower of patterned flakes, motionless in midair. Perhaps
they were embroideries upon some gossamer drapery too
sheer to see. But as he looked he thought he saw them quiver
just a little. Quiver, and fall quiet, and then quiver again, as
if—as if—

"Paul!"

Everything stopped dead still for a moment. He did not
need Alanna's whisper to make his heart pause as he strained
intolerably to hear, to see, to feel. . . . Yes, definitely now

the snowstorm curtain shook. And the floor shook with it in faint rhythms to that distant tremor—

This is it, he thought. *This is real.*

He had known for minutes now that he was not walking through a dream. He stood in the midst of impossible reality, and the Enemy itself came nearer and nearer with each great soundless footfall, and there was nothing to do but wait. Nothing at all. It wanted Alanna. He knew why. It would not want himself, and it would brush him away like smoke in its juggernaut striding to seize her, unless his weapon could stop it. His heart began to beat with heavy, thick blows that echoed the distant footsteps.

- "Alanna," he said, hearing the faintest possible quiver in his voice. "Alanna, get behind something—that pillar over there. Don't make a sound. And if I tell you—*run!*"

He stepped behind a nearer pillar, his arm aching from the weight of his burden, the lens of it throbbing faintly against his palm with its promise of power in leash. He thought it would work. . . .

There was no sound of footfalls as the rhythm grew stronger. Only by the strength of those tremors that shook the floor could he judge how near the Thing was drawing. The pillar itself was shaking now, and the snowstorm was convulsed each time a mighty foot struck the floor soundlessly. Paul thought of the knife-edged patterns which those feet were treading with such firm and measured strides.

For a moment of panic he regretted his daring in coming to meet the Thing. He was sorry they had not stayed cowering in the room of the mirror—sorry they had not fled back down the whirling darkness through which they came. But you can't escape a nightmare. He held his lensed weapon throbbing like a throat against his palm, waiting to pour out lightning upon—what?

Now it was very close. Now it was just beyond the snowstorm between the pillars. He could see dim motion through their veil. . . .

Snow swirled away from its mighty shoulders, clouded about its great head so that he could not see very clearly what it was that stood there, tall and grotesque and terrible, its eyes shining scarlet through the veil. He was aware only of the eyes, and of the being's majestic bulk, before his hand of its own volition closed hard upon the pulse of violence in his palm.

For one timeless moment nothing happened. He was too stunned with the magnitude of the thing he faced to feel even terror at his weapon's failure; awe shut out every other thought. He was even a little startled when the glare of golden daylight burst hissing from his hand, splashing its brilliance across the space between them.

Then relief was a weakness that loosened all his muscles as he played the deadlines of his weapon upon the Enemy, hearing the air shriek with its power, seeing the stone pillars blacken before those lashes of light. He was blinded by their glory; he could only stand there pouring the lightnings forth and squinting against their glare. The smell of scorched metal and stone was heavy in the air, and he could hear the crash of a falling column somewhere, burned through by the blast of the flame. Surely *it* too must be consumed and falling.... Hope began to flicker in his brain.

It was Alanna's whimper that told him something must still be wrong. Belatedly he reached up to close the glass visor of the mask he still wore, and by magic the glare ceased to blind him. He could see between the long, writhing whips of light—see the pillars falling and the steel patterns of the floor turn blue and melt away. But he could see it standing between those crumbling pillars now. . . .

He could see it standing in the full bath of the flames, see them splash upon its mighty chest and sluice away over its great shoulders like the spray of water, unheeded, impotent.

Its eyes were darkening from crimson to an angry purple as it lurched forward one ponderous, powerful stride, brushing away the sparks from its face, putting out a terrible arm. . . .

"Alanna—" said the man in a very quiet voice, pitched below the screaming of the flame. "Alanna—you'd better start back. I'll hold it while I can. You'd better run, Alanna. . . ."

He did not know if she obeyed. He could spare no further attention from the desperate business at hand, to delay it—to hold it back even for sixty seconds—for thirty seconds—for one breath more of independent life. What might happen after that he could not let himself think. Perhaps not death— perhaps something far more alien and strange than death. . . . He knew the struggle was hopeless and senseless, but he knew he must struggle on while breath remained in him.

There was a narrow place in the corridor between himself and it. The lightning had weakened one wall already. He swung it away from the oncoming colossus and played the fire screaming to and fro upon blackened stones, seeing mortar crumble between them and girders bending in that terrible heat.

The walls groaned, grinding their riven blocks surface against surface. Slowly, slowly they leaned together; slowly they fell. Stone dust billowed in a cloud to hide the final collapse of the corridor, but through it the scream of lightnings sounded and the shriek of metal against falling stone. And then, distantly, a deeper groaning of new pressure coming to bear.

The man stood paralyzed for a moment, dizzy with an unreasonable hope that he had stopped the Enemy at last, not daring to look too closely for fear of failure. But hope and despair came almost simultaneously into his mind as he watched the mass of the closed walls shuddering and resisting for a moment—but only for a moment.

With dust and stone blocks and steel girders falling away from its tremendous shoulders, it stepped through the ruined arch. Jagged golden lightnings played in its face, hissing and screaming futilely. It ignored them. Shaking off the debris of the wall, it strode forward, eyes purple with anger, great hands outstretched.

And so the weapon failed. He loosed the trigger, hearing its shriek die upon the air as the long ribbons of lightning faded. It was instinct, echoing over millennia from the first fighting ancestor of mankind, that made him swing the heavy machine overhead with both hands and hurl it into the face of the Enemy. And it was a little like relinquishing a living comrade to let the throb of that fiery tubing lose contact with his palm at last.

Blindly he flung the weapon from him, and in the same motion whirled and ran. The knife-edged floor spun past below him. If he could hit a rhythm to carry him from loop to empty loop of the pattern, he might even reach the room at the end of the passage—There was no sanctuary anywhere, but unreasoning instinct made him seek the place of his origin here. . . .

Ahead of him a flutter of blue-green sequins now and then told him that Alanna was running too, miraculously keeping her balance on the patterned floor. He could not look up to watch her. His eyes were riveted to the spirals and loops among which his precarious footing lay. Behind him great feet were thudding soundlessly, shaking the floor.

The things that happened then happened too quickly for the brain to resolve into any sequence at all. He knew that the silence which had flowed back when the screaming lightnings died was suddenly, shockingly broken again by a renewed screaming. He remembered seeing the metal patterns of the floor thrown into sharp new shadows by the light behind him, and he knew that the Enemy had found the trigger he had just released, that his weapon throbbed now against an alien hand.

But it happened in the same instant that the doorway of the entrance room loomed up before him, and he hurled himself desperately into the dimness after Alanna, knowing his feet were cut through and bleeding, seeing the dark blotches of the tracks she too was leaving. The mirror loomed before them, an unbearable picture of the lost familiar room he could not hope to enter again in life.

And all this was simultaneous with a terrifying soundless thunder of great feet at his very heels of a mighty presence suddenly and ponderously in the same room with them, like a whirlwind exhausting the very air they gasped to breathe. He felt anger eddying about him without words or sound. He felt monstrous hands snatch him up as if a tornado had taken him into its windy grasp. He remembered purple eyes glaring through the dimness in one brief instant of perception before the hands hurled him away.

He spun through empty air. Then a howling vortex seized him and he was falling in blindness, stunned and stupefied, through the same strange passageway that had brought him here. Distantly he heard Alanna scream.

There was silence in the dim, round room in the center of the treasure house, except for a muffled howling from the screen. He who was master here stood quietly before it, his eyes half shut and ranging down the spectrum from purple to red, and then swiftly away from red through orange to a clear, pale, tranquil yellow. His chest still heaved a little with the excitement of that minor fiasco which he had brought upon himself, but it was an excitement soon over, and wholly disappointing.

He was a little ashamed of his momentary anger. He

should not have played the little creatures' puny lightnings upon them as they fell down the shaft of darkness. He had misjudged their capacity, after all. They were not really capable of giving him a worthwhile fight.

It was interesting that one had followed the other, with its little weapon that sparkled and stung, interesting that one fragile being had stood up to him.

But he knew a moment's regret for the beauty of the blue-and-white creature he had flung away. The long, smooth lines of it, the subtle coloring. . . . Too bad that it had been worthless because it was helpless too.

Helpless against himself, he thought, and equally against the drive of its own mysterious motives. He sighed.

He thought again, almost regretfully, of the lovely thing he had coveted hurtling away down the vortex with lightnings bathing it through the blackness.

Had he destroyed it? He did not know. He was a little sorry now that anger for his ruined treasures had made him lose his temper when they ran. Futile, scuttling little beings—they had cheated him out of beauty because of their own impotence against him, but he was not even angry about that now. Only sorry, with vague, confused sorrows he did not bother to clarify in his mind. Regret for the loss of a lovely thing, regret that he had expected danger from them and been disappointed, regret perhaps for his own boredom, that did not bother any longer to probe into the motives of living things. He was growing old indeed.

The vortex still roared through the darkened screen. He stepped back from it, letting opacity close over the surface of the portal, hushing all sound. His eyes were a tranquil yellow. Tomorrow he would hunt again, and perhaps tomorrow. . . .

He went out slowly, walking with long, soundless strides that made the steel mosaics sing faintly beneath his feet.

THE STORM

Astounding,

October

by A. E. van Vogt (1912-)

The then prolific A. E. van Vogt continued his production of quality stories in 1943 (see Second Series, and preceeding volumes for other examples). In addition to the present selection he published in 1943, among others, "The Search" (Astounding, January); "M 33 In Andromeda" (Astounding, August); "The Beast" (Astounding, November); the novel The Book of Ptath *(Unknown, October); "The Great Engine" (Astounding, July); "The Witch" (Unknown, February); "Concealment" (Astounding, September); and* The Weapon Makers, *a three-part serial that began in the February issue of* Astounding, *and which proved to be one of his most famous works.*

"The Storm" was a sequel to "Concealment" but far superior to that story. Together with another story of the Dellian Robots it formed part of his novel The Mixed Men *(1952).*

(No one captured the Campbell aura as well as van Vogt did. No, not even I. I caught what Campbell was driving at, I thought. I understood the general outlook of the man in the matter of reason, logic, and pragmatism, but I interpreted it in my own way. I had no way of imitating the florid gashes of primary color that filled Campbell's writing. Van Vogt did, though, and in this story particularly it is almost as though I am listening to Campbell.— Except, of course, that van Vogt, when he was really rolling, did it better.—I.A.)

Over the miles and the years, the gases drifted. Waste matter from ten thousand suns, a diffuse miasma of spent explosions, of dead hell fires and the furies of a hundred million raging sunspots—formless, purposeless.

But it was the beginning.

Into the great dark the gases crept. Calcium was in them, and sodium, and hydrogen; and the speed of the drift varied up to twenty miles a second.

There was a timeless period while gravitation performed its function. The inchoate mass became masses. Great blobs of gas took a semblance of shape in widely separate areas, and moved on and on and on.

They came finally to where a thousand flaring seetee suns had long before doggedly "crossed the street" of the main stream of terrene suns. Had crossed, and left *their* excrement of gases.

The first clash quickened the vast worlds of gas. The electron haze of terrene plunged like spurred horses and sped deeper into the equally violently reacting positron haze of contraterrene. Instantly, the lighter orbital positrons and electrons went up in a blaze of hard radiation.

The storm was on.

The stripped seetee nuclei carried now terrific and unbalanced negative charges and repelled electrons, but tended to attract terrene atom nuclei. In their turn the stripped terrene nuclei attracted contraterrene.

Violent beyond all conception were the resulting cancellations of charges.

The two opposing masses heaved and spun in a cataclysm of partial adjustment. They had been heading in different directions. More and more they became one tangled, seething whirlpool.

The new course, uncertain at first, steadied and became a line drive through the midnight heavens. On a front of nine light years, at a solid fraction of the velocity of light, the storm roared toward its destiny.

Suns were engulfed for half a hundred years—and left behind with only a hammering of cosmic rays to show that they had been the centers of otherwise invisible, impalpable atomic devastation.

In its four hundred and ninetieth Sidereal year, the storm intersected the orbit of a Nova at the flash moment.

It began to move!

On the three-dimensional map at weather headquarters on the planet Kaider III, the storm was colored orange. Which meant it was the biggest of the four hundred odd storms raging in the Fifty Suns region of the Lesser Magellanic Cloud.

It showed as an uneven splotch fronting at latitude 473, longitude 228, center 190 parsecs, but that was a special Fifty Suns degree system which had no relation to the magnetic center of the Magellanic Cloud as a whole.

The report about the Nova had not yet been registered on the map. When that happened the storm color would be changed to an angry red.

They had stopped looking at the map. Maltby stood with the councillors at the great window staring up at the Earth ship.

The machine was scarcely more than a dark sliver in the distant sky. But the sight of it seemed to hold a deadly fascination for the older men.

Maltby felt cool, determined, but also sardonic. It was funny, these—these people of the Fifty Suns in this hour of their danger calling upon *him*.

He unfocused his eyes from the ship, fixed his steely, laconic gaze on the plump, perspiring chairman of the Kaider III government—and, tensing his mind, forced the man to look at him. The councillor, unaware of the compulsion, conscious only that he had turned, said: "You understand your instructions, Captain Maltby?"

Maltby nodded. "I do."

The curt words must have evoked a vivid picture. The fat face rippled like palsied jelly and broke out in a new trickle of sweat.

"The worst part of it all," the man groaned, "is that the people of the ship found us by the wildest accident. They had run into one of our meterorite stations and captured its attendant. The attendant sent a general warning and then forced them to kill him before they could discover which of the fifty million suns of the Lesser Magellanic Cloud was us.

"Unfortunately, they did discover that he and the rest of us were all descendants of the robots who had escaped the mas-

sacre of the robots in the main galaxy fifteen thousand years
ago.

"But they were baffled, and without a clue. They started
home, stopping off at planets on the way on a chance basis.
The seventh stop was us. Captain Maltby—"

The man looked almost beside himself. He shook. His face
was as colorless as a white shroud. He went on hoarsely:

"Captain Maltby, you must not fail. They have asked for a
meteorologist to guide them to Cassidor VII, where the central government is located. They mustn't reach there. You
must drive them into the great storm at 473.

"We have commissioned you to do this for us because you
have the two minds of the Mixed Men. We regret that we
have not always fully appreciated your services in the past.
but you must admit that, after the wars of the Mixed Men, it
was natural that we should be careful about—"

Maltby cut off the lame apology. "Forget it," he said. "The
Mixed Men are robots, too, and therefore as deeply involved,
as I see it, as the Dellians and non-Dellians. Just what the
Hidden Ones of my kind think, I don't know, nor do I care. I
assure you I shall do my best to destroy this ship."

"Be careful!" the chairman urged anxiously. "This ship
could destroy us, our planet, our sun in a single minute. We
never dreamed that Earth could have gotten so far ahead of
us and produced such a devastatingly powerful machine. After all, the non-Dellian robots and, of course, the Mixed Men
among us are capable of research work; the former have
been laboring feverishly for thousands of years.

"But, finally, remember that you are not being asked to
commit suicide. The battleship is absolutely invincible. Just
how it will survive a real storm we were not told when we
were shown around. But it will. What happens, however, is
that everyone aboard becomes unconscious.

"As a Mixed Man you will be the first to revive. Our combined fleets will be waiting to board the ship the moment you
open the doors. Is that clear?"

It had been clear the first time it was explained, but these
non-Dellians had a habit of repeating themselves, as if
thoughts kept growing vague in their minds. As Maltby
closed the door of the great room behind him, one of the
councillors said to his neighbor:

"Has he been told that the storm has gone Nova?"

The fat man overheard. He shook his head. His eyes gleamed as he said quietly: "No. After all, he is one of the Mixed Men. We can't trust him too far no matter what his record."

All morning the reports had come in. Some showed progress, some didn't. But her basic good humor was untouched by the failures.

The great reality was that her luck had held. She had found a planet of the robots. Only one planet so far, but—

Grand Captain Laurr smiled grimly. It wouldn't be long now. Being a supreme commander was a terrible business. But she had not shrunk from making the deadly threat: provide all required information, or the entire planet of Kaider III would be destroyed.

The information was coming in: Population of Kaider III two billion, one hundred million, two-fifths Dellian, three-fifths non-Dellian robots.

Dellians physically and mentally the higher type, but completely lacking in creative ability. Non-Dellians dominated in the research laboratories.

The forty-nine other suns whose planets were inhabited were called, in alphabetical order: Assora, Atmion, Bresp, Buraco, Cassidor, Corrab—They were located at (1) Assora: latitude 931, longitude 27, center 201 parsecs; (2) Atmion—

It went on and on. Just before noon she noted with steely amusement that there was still nothing coming through from the meteorology room, nothing at all about storms.

She made the proper connection and flung her words: "What's the matter, Lieutenant Cannons? Your assistants have been making prints and duplicates of various Kaider maps. Aren't you getting anything?"

The old meteorologist shook his head. "You will recall, noble lady, that when we captured that robot in space, he had time to send out a warning. Immediately on every Fifty Suns planet, all maps were despoiled, civilian meteorologists were placed aboard spaceships, that were stripped of receiving radios, with orders to go to a planet on a chance basis, and stay there for ten years.

"To my mind, all this was done before it was clearly grasped that their navy hadn't a chance against us. Now they are going to provide us with a naval meteorologist, but we

shall have to depend on our lie detectors as to whether or not
he is telling us the truth."

"I see." The woman smiled. "Have no fear. They don't
dare oppose us openly. No doubt there is a plan being built
up against us, but it cannot prevail now that we can take action to enforce our unalterable will. Whoever they send must
tell us the truth. Let me know when he comes."

Lunch came, but she ate at her desk, watching the flashing
pictures on the astro, listening to the murmur of voices, storing the facts, the general picture, into her brain.

"There's no doubt, Captain Turgess," she commented once,
savagely, "that we're being lied to on a vast scale. But let it
be so. We can use psychological tests to verify all the vital
details.

"For the time being it is important that you relieve the
fears of everyone you find it necessary to question. We must
convince these people that Earth will accept them on an
equal basis without bias or prejudice of any kind because of
their robot orig—"

She bit her lip. "That's an ugly word, the worst kind of
propaganda. We must eliminate it from our thoughts."

"I'm afraid," the officer shrugged, "not from our thoughts."

She stared at him, narrow-eyed, then cut him off angrily. A
moment later she was talking into the general transmitter:
"The word robot must not be used—by any of our person-
nel—under pain of fine—"

Switching off, she put a busy signal on her spare receiver,
and called Psychology House. Lieutenant Neslor's face appeared on the plate.

"I heard your order just now, noble lady," the woman psychologist said. "I'm afraid, however, that we're dealing with
the deepest instincts of the human animal—hatred or fear of
the stranger, the alien.

"Excellency, we come from a long line of ancestors who,
in their time, have felt superior to others because of some
slight variation in the pigmentation of the skin. It is even
recorded that the color of the eyes has influenced the egoistic
in historical decisions. We have sailed into very deep waters,
and it will be the crowning achievement of our life if we sail
out in a satisfactory fashion."

There was an eager lilt in the psychologist's voice; and the
grand captain experienced a responsive thrill of joy. If there

was one thing she appreciated, it was the positive outlook, the kind of people who faced all obstacles short of the recognizably impossible with a youthful zest, a will to win. She was still smiling as she broke the connection.

The high thrill sagged. She sat cold with her problem. It was a problem. Hers. All aristocratic officers had *carte blanche* powers, and were expected to solve difficulties involving anything up to whole groups of planetary systems.

After a minute she dialed the meteorology room again.

"Lieutenant Cannons, when the meteorology officer of the Fifty Suns navy arrives, please employ the following tactics—"

Maltby waved dismissal to the driver of his car. The machine pulled away from the curb and Maltby stood frowning at the flaming energy barrier that barred farther progress along the street. Finally, he took another look at the Earth ship.

It was directly above him now that he had come so many miles across the city toward it. It was tremendously high up, a long, black torpedo shape almost lost in the mist of distance.

But high as it was it was still visibly bigger than anything ever seen by the Fifty Suns, an incredible creature of metal from a world so far away that, almost, it had sunk to the status of myth.

Here was the reality. There would be tests, he thought, penetrating tests before they'd accept any orbit he planned. It wasn't that he doubted the ability of his double mind to overcome anything like that, but—

Well to remember that the frightful gap of years which separated the science of Earth from that of the Fifty Suns had already shown unpleasant surprises. Maltby shook himself grimly and gave his full attention to the street ahead.

A fan-shaped pink fire spread skyward from two machines that stood in the center of the street. The flame was a very pale pink and completely transparent. It looked electronic, deadly.

Beyond it were men in glittering uniforms. A steady trickle of them moved in and out of buildings. About three blocks down the avenue a second curtain of pink fire flared up.

There seemed to be no attempt to guard the sides. The men he could see looked at ease, confident. There was murmured conversation, low laughter and—they weren't all men.

As Maltby walked forward, two fine-looking young women in uniform came down the steps of the nearest of the requisitioned buildings. One of the guards of the flame said something to them. There was a twin tinkle of silvery laughter. Still laughing, they strode off down the street.

It was suddenly exciting. There was an air about these people of far places, of tremendous and wonderful lands beyond the farthest horizons of the staid Fifty Suns.

He felt cold, then hot, then he glanced up at the fantastically big ship; and the chill came back. One ship, he thought, but so big, so mighty that thirty billion people didn't dare send their own fleets against it. They—

He grew aware that one of the brilliantly arrayed guards was staring at him. The man spoke into a wrist radio, and after a moment a second man broke off his conversation with a third soldier and came over. He stared through the flame barrier at Maltby.

"Is there anything you desire? Or are you just looking?"

He spoke English, curiously accented—but English! His manner was mild, almost gentle, cultured. The whole effect had a naturalness, an unalienness that was pleasing. After all, Maltby thought, he had never had the fear of these people that the others had. His very plan to defeat the ship was based upon his own fundamental belief that the robots were indestructible in the sense that no one could ever wipe them out completely.

Quietly, Maltby explained his presence.

"Oh, yes," the man nodded, "we've been expecting you. I'm to take you at once to the meteorological room of the ship. Just a moment—"

The flame barrier went down and Maltby was led into one of the buildings. There was a long corridor, and the transmitter that projected him into the ship must have been focused somewhere along it.

Because abruptly he was in a very large room. Maps floated in half a dozen antigravity pits. The walls shed light from millions of tiny point sources. And everywhere were tables with curved lines of very dim but sharply etched light on their surfaces.

Maltby's guide was nowhere to be seen. Coming toward him, however, was a tall, fine-looking old man. The oldster offered his hand.

"My name is Lieutenant Cannons, senior ship meteorologist. If you will sit down here we can plan an orbit and the ship can start moving within the hour. The grand captain is very anxious that we get started."

Maltby nodded casually. But he was stiff, alert. He stood quite still, feeling around with that acute second mind of his, his Dellian mind, for energy pressures that would show secret attempts to watch or control his mind.

But there was nothing like that.

He smiled finally, grimly. It was going to be as simple as this, was it? Like hell it was.

As he sat down, Maltby felt suddenly cozy and alive. The pure exhilaration of existence burned through him like a flame. He recognized the singing excitement for the battle thrill it was and felt a grim joy that for the first time in fifteen years he could do something about it.

During his long service in the Fifty Suns navy, he had faced hostility and suspicion because he was a Mixed Man. And always he had felt helpless, unable to do anything about it. Now, here was a far more basic hostility, however veiled, and a suspicion that must be like a burning fire.

And this time he could fight. He could look this skillfully voluble, friendly old man squarely in the eye and—

Friendly?

"It makes me smile sometimes," the old man was saying, "when I think of the unscientific aspects of the orbit we have to plan now. For instance, what is the time lag on storm reports out here?"

Maltby could not suppress a smile. So Lieutenant Cannons wanted to know things, did he? To give the man credit, it wasn't really a lame opening. The truth was, the only way to ask a question was—well—to ask it. Maltby said: "Oh, three, four months. Nothing unusual. Each space meteorologist takes about that length of time to check the bounds of the particular storm in his area, and then he reports, and we adjust our maps.

"Fortunately"—he pushed his second mind to the fore as he coolly spoke the great basic lie—"there are no major storms between the Kaider and Cassidor suns."

He went on, sliding over the untruth like an eel breasting wet rock: "However, several suns prevent a straight-line movement. So if you would show me some of your orbits for twenty-five hundred light years, I'll make a selection of the best ones."

He wasn't, he realized instantly, going to slip over his main point as easily as that.

"No intervening storms?" the old man said. He pursed his lips. The fine lines in his long face seemed to deepen. He looked genuinely nonplused; and there was no doubt at all that he hadn't expected such a straightforward statement. "Hm-m-m, no storms. That does make it simple, doesn't it?"

He broke off. "You know, the important thing about two"—he hesitated over the word, then went on—"two people, who have been brought up in different cultures, under different scientific standards, is that they make sure they are discussing a subject from a common viewpoint.

"Space is so big. Even this comparatively small system of stars, the Lesser Magellanic Cloud, is so vast that it defies our reason. We on the battleship *Star Cluster* have spent ten years surveying it, and now we are able to say glibly that it comprises two hundred sixty billion cubic light-years, and contains fifty millions of suns.

"We located the magnetic center of the Cloud, fixed our zero line from center to the great brightest star, S Doradus; and now, I suppose, there are people who would be fools enough to think we've got the system stowed away in our brainpans."

Maltby was silent because he himself was just such a fool. This was warning. He was being told in no uncertain terms that they were in a position to check any orbit he gave them with respect to all intervening suns.

It meant much more. It showed that Earth was on the verge of extending her tremendous sway to the Lesser Magellanic Cloud. Destroying this ship now would provide the Fifty Suns with precious years during which they would have to decide what they intended to do.

But that would be all. Other ships would come; the inexorable pressure of the stupendous populations of the main galaxy would burst out even farther into space. Always under careful control, shepherded by mighty hosts of invincible battleships, the great transports would sweep into the Cloud, and every planet everywhere, robot or non-robot, would acknowledge Earth suzerainty.

Imperial earth recognized no separate nations of any description anywhere. The robots, Dellian, non-Dellian, and Mixed, would need every extra day, every hour; and it was lucky for them all that he was not basing his hope of destroying this ship on an orbit that would end inside a sun.

Their survey had magnetically placed all the suns for them. But they couldn't know about the storms. Not in ten years or in a hundred was it possible for one ship to locate possible storms in an area that involved twenty-five hundred light years of length.

Unless their psychologists could uncover the special qualities of his double brain, he had them. He grew aware that Lieutenant Cannons was manipulating the controls of the orbit table.

The lines of light on the surface flickered and shifted. Then settled like the balls in a game of chance. Maltby selected six that ran deep into the great storm. Ten minutes after that he felt the faint jar as the ship began to move. He stood up, frowning. Odd that they should act without *some* verification of his—

"This way," said the old man.

Maltby thought sharply: This couldn't be all. Any minute now they'd start on him and—

His thought ended.

He was in space. Far, far below was the receding planet Kaider III. To one side gleamed the vast dark hull of the battleship; and on every other side, and up, and down, were stars and the distances of dark space.

In spite of all his will, the shock was inexpressibly violent.

His active mind jerked. He staggered physically; and he would have fallen like a blindfolded creature except that, in the movement of trying to keep on his feet, he recognized that he *was* still on his feet.

His whole being steadied. Instinctively, he—tilted—his second mind awake, and pushed it forward. Put its more mechanical and precise qualities, its Dellian strength, between his other self and whatever the human beings might be doing against him.

Somewhere in the midst of darkness and blazing stars, a woman's clear and resonant voice said: "Well, Lieutenant Neslor, did the surprise yield any psychological fruits?"

The reply came from a second, an older-sounding woman's voice: "After three seconds, noble lady, his resistance leaped to I.Q. 900. Which means they've sent us a Dellian. Your excellency, I thought you specifically asked that their representative be not a Dellian."

Maltby said swiftly into the night around him: "You're quite mistaken. I am not a Dellian. And I assure you that I will lower my resistance to zero if you desire. I reacted instinctively to surprise, naturally enough."

There was a click. The illusion of space and stars snapped out of existence. Maltby saw what he had begun to suspect, that he was, had been all the time, in the meteorology room.

Nearby stood the old man, a thin smile on his lined face. On a raised dais, partly hidden behind a long instrument board, sat a handsome young woman. It was the old man who spoke. He said in a stately voice:

"You are in the presence of Grand Captain, the Right Honorable Gloria Cecily, the Lady Laurr of Noble Laurr. Conduct yourself accordingly."

Maltby bowed but he said nothing. The grand captain frowned at him, impressed by his appearance. Tall, magnificent-looking body—strong, supremely intelligent face. In a single flash she noted all the characteristics common to the first-class human being and robot.

These people might be more dangerous than she had thought. She said with unnatural sharpness for her: "As you know, we have to question you. We would prefer that you do not take offense. You have told us that Cassidor VII, the chief planet of the Fifty Suns, is twenty-five hundred light-years from here. Normally, we would spend more than sixty years *feeling* our way across such an immense gap of uncharted, star-filled space. But you have given us a choice of orbits.

"We must make sure those orbits are honest, offered without guile or harmful purpose. To that end we have to ask you to open your mind and answer our questions under the strictest psychological surveillance."

"I have orders," said Maltby, "to cooperate with you in every way."

He had wondered how he would feel, now that the hour of decision was upon him. But there was nothing abnormal. His body was a little stiffer, but his minds—

He withdrew his *self* into the background and left his Dellian mind to confront all the questions that came. His Dellian mind that he had deliberately kept apart from his thoughts. That curious mind, which had no will of its own, but which, by remote control, reacted with the full power of an I. Q. of 191.

Sometimes, he marveled himself at that second mind of his. It had no creative ability, but its memory was machine-like, and its resistance to outside pressure was, as the woman psychologist had so swiftly analyzed, over nine hundred. To be exact, the equivalent of I. Q. 917.

"What is your name?"

That was the way it began: His name, distinction—He answered everything quietly, positively, without hesitation. When he had finished, when he had sworn to the truth of every word about the storms, there was a long moment of dead silence. And then a middle-aged woman stepped out of the nearby wall.

She came over and motioned him into a chair. When he was seated she tilted his head and began to examine it. She did it gently; her fingers were caressing as a lover's. But when she looked up she said sharply:

"You're not a Dellian or a non-Dellian. And the molecular structure of your brain and body is the most curious I've ever seen. All the molecules are twins. I saw a similar arrangement once in an artificial electronic structure where an attempt was being made to balance an unstable electronic structure. The parallel isn't exact, but—mm-m-m, I must try to remember what the end result was of that experiment."

She broke off: "What is your explanation? What are you?"

Maltby sighed. He had determined to tell only the one main lie. Not that it mattered so far as his double brain was concerned. But untruths effected slight variations in blood pressure, created neural spasms, and disturbed muscular integration. He couldn't take the risk of even one more than was absolutely necessary.

"I'm a Mixed Man," he explained. He described briefly how the cross between the Dellian and non-Dellian, so long impossible, had finally been brought about a hundred years before. The use of cold and pressure—

"Just a moment," said the psychologist.

She disappeared. When she stepped again out of the wall transmitter, she was thoughtful.

"He seems to be telling the truth," she confessed, almost reluctantly.

"What is this?" snapped the grand captain. "Ever since we ran into that first citizen of the Fifty Suns, the psychology department has qualified every statement it issues. I thought psychology was the only perfect science. Either he is telling the truth or he isn't."

The older woman looked unhappy. She stared very hard at Maltby, seemed baffled by his cool gaze, and finally faced her superior, said: "It's that double-molecule structure of his brain. Except for that, I see no reason why you shouldn't order full acceleration."

The grand captain smiled. "I shall have Captain Maltby to dinner tonight. I'm sure he will cooperate then with any further studies you may be prepared to make at that time. Meanwhile I think—"

She spoke into a communicator: "Central engines, step up to half light-year a minute on the following orbit—"

Maltby listened, estimating with his Dellian mind. Half a light-year a minute; it would take a while to attain that speed, but—in eight hours they'd strike the storm.

In eight hours he'd be having dinner with the grand captain.

Eight hours!

The full flood of a contraterrene Nova impinging upon terrene gases already infuriated by seetee gone insane—that was the new, greater storm.

The exploding, giant sun added weight to the diffuse, maddened thing. And it added something far more deadly.

Speed! From peak to peak of velocity the tumult of ultrafire leaped. The swifter crags of the storm danced and burned with an absolutely hellish fury.

The sequence of action was rapid almost beyond the tolerance of matter. First raced the light of the Nova, blazing its warning at more than a hundred and eighty-six thousand miles a second to all who knew that it flashed from the edge of an interstellar storm.

But the advance glare of warning ws nullified by the colossal speed of the storm. For weeks and months it drove through the vast night at a velocity that was only a bare measure short of that of light itself.

The dinner dishes had been cleared away. Maltby was thinking: In half an hour—*half an hour!*

He was wondering shakily just what did happen to a battleship suddenly confronted by thousands of gravities of deceleration. Aloud he was saying: "My day? I spent it in the library. Mainly, I was interested in the recent history of Earth's interstellar colonization. I'm curious as to what is done with groups like the Mixed Men. I mentioned to you that, after the war in which they were defeated largely because there was so few of them, the Mixed Men hid themselves from the Fifty Suns. I was one of the captured children who—"

There was an interruption, a cry from the wall communicator: "*Noble lady, I've solved it!*"

A moment fled before Maltby recognized the strained voice of the woman psychologist. He had almost forgotten that she was supposed to be studying him. Her next words chilled him: "Two minds! I thought of it a little while ago and rigged up a twin watching device. Ask him, *ask* him the question about the storms. Meanwhile stop the ship. At once!"

Maltby's dark gaze clashed hard with the steely, narrowed eyes of the grand captain. Without hesitation he concentrated his two minds on her, forced her to say: "Don't be silly, lieutenant. One person can't have two brains. Explain yourself further."

His hope was delay. They had ten minutes in which they could save themselves. He must waste every second of that time, resist all their efforts, try to control the situation. If only his special three-dimensional hypnotism worked through communicators—

It didn't. Lines of light leaped at him from the wall and crisscrossed his body, held him in his chair like so many unbreakable cables. Even as he was bound hand and foot by palpable energy, a second complex of forces built up before his face, barred his thought pressure from the grand captain, and finally coned over his head like a dunce cap.

He was caught as neatly as if a dozen men had swarmed with their strength and weight over his body. Maltby relaxed and laughed.

"Too late," he taunted. "It'll take at least an hour for this ship to reduce to a safe speed; and at this velocity you can't turn aside in time to avoid the greatest storm in this part of the universe."

That wasn't strictly true. There was still time and room to sheer off before the advancing storm in any of the fronting directions. The impossibility was to turn toward the storm's tail or its great, bulging sides.

His thought was interrupted by the first cry from the young woman, a piercing cry: "Central engines! Reduce speed! Emergency!"

There was a jar that shook the walls and a pressure that tore at his muscles. Maltby adjusted and then stared across the table at the grand captain. She was smiling, a frozen mask of a smile; and she said from between clenched teeth:

"Lieutenant Neslor, use any means physical or otherwise, but make him talk. There must be something."

"His second mind is the key," the psychologist's voice came. "It's not Dellian. It has only normal resistance. I shall subject it to the greatest concentration of conditioning ever focused on a human brain, using the two basics: sex and logic. I shall have to use you, noble lady, as the object of his affections."

"Hurry!" said the young woman. Her voice was like a metal bar.

Maltby sat in a mist, mental and physical. Deep in his mind was awareness that he was an entity, and that irresistible machines were striving to mold his thought.

He resisted. The resistance was as strong as his life, as intense as all the billions and quadrillions of impulses that had shaped his being could make it.

But the outside thought, the pressure, grew stronger. How silly of him to resist Earth—when this lovely woman of Earth loved him, loved him, loved him. Glorious was that civilization of Earth and the main galaxy. Three hundred million billion people. The very first contact would rejuvenate the Fifty Suns. How lovely she is; I must save her. She means everything to me.

As from a great distance, he began to hear his own voice, explaining what must be done, just how the ship must be turned, in what direction, how much time there was. He tried to stop himself, but inexorably his voice went on, mouthing the words that spelled defeat for the Fifty Suns.

The mist began to fade. The terrible pressure eased from his straining mind. The damning stream of words ceased to pour from his lips. He sat up shakily, conscious that the energy cords and the energy cap had been withdrawn from his body. He heard the grand captain say into a communicator: "By making a point 0100 turn we shall miss the storm by seven light-weeks. I admit it is an appallingly sharp curve, but I feel that we should have at least that much leeway."

She turned and stared at Maltby: "Prepare yourself. At half a light-year a minute even a hundredth of a degree turn makes some people black out."

"Not me," said Maltby, and tensed his Dellian muscles.

She fainted three times during the next four minutes as he sat there watching her. But each time she came to within seconds.

"We human beings," she said wanly, finally, "are a poor lot. But at least we know how to endure."

The terrible minutes dragged. And dragged. Maltby began to feel the strain of that infinitesimal turn. He thought at last: Space! How could these people ever hope to survive a direct hit on a storm?

Abruptly, it was over; a man's voice said quietly: "We have followed the prescribed course, noble lady, and are now out of dang—"

He broke off with a shout: "Captain, the light of a Nova sun has just flashed from the direction of the storm. We—"

In those minutes before disaster struck, the battleship *Star Cluster,* glowed like an immense and brilliant jewel. The warning glare from the Nova set off an incredible roar of emergency clamor through all of her hundred and twenty decks.

From end to end her lights flicked on. They burned row by row straight across her four thousand feet of length with the hard tinkle of cut gems. In the reflection of that light, the black mountain that was her hull looked like the fabulous planet of Cassidor, her destination, as seen at night from a far darkness, sown with diamond-shining cities.

Silent as a ghost, grand and wonderful beyond all imagination, glorious in her power, the great ship slid through the blackness along the special river of time and space which was her plotted course.

Even as she rode into the storm there was nothing visible. The space ahead looked as clear as any vacuum. So tenuous were the gases that made up the storm that the ship would not even have been aware of them if it had been traveling at atomic speeds.

Violent the disintegration of matter in that storm might be, and the sole source of cosmic rays the hardest energy in the known universe. But the immense, the cataclysmic danger to the *Star Cluster* was a direct result of her own terrible velocity.

If she had had time to slow, the storm would have meant nothing.

Striking that mass of gas at half a light-year a minute was like running into an unending solid wall. The great ship shuddered in every plate as the deceleration tore at her gigantic strength.

In seconds she had run the gamut of all the recoil systems her designers had planned for her as a unit.

She began to break up.

And still everything was according to the original purpose of the superb engineering firm that had built her. The limit of unit strain reached, she dissolved into her nine thousand separate sections.

Streamlined needles of metal were those sections, four hundred feet long, forty feet wide; sliverlike shapes that sinuated cunningly through the gases, letting the pressure of them slide off their smooth hides.

But it wasn't enough. Metal groaned from the torture of deceleration. In the deceleration chambers, men and women lay at the bare edge of consciousness, enduring agony that seemed on the verge of being beyond endurance.

Hundreds of the sections careened into each other in spite of automatic screens, and instantaneously fused into white-hot coffins.

And still, in spite of the hideously maintained velocity, that mass of gases was not bridged; light-years of thickness had still to be covered.

For those sections that remained, once more all the limits of human strength were reached. The final action was chemical, directly on the human bodies that remained of the original thirty thousand. Those bodies for whose sole benefit all the marvelous safety devices had been conceived and constructed, the poor, fragile, human beings who through all the ages had persisted in dying under normal conditions from a pressure of something less than fifteen gravities.

The prompt reaction of the automatics in rolling back every floor, and plunging every person into the deceleration chambers of each section—that saving reaction was abruptly augmented as the deceleration chamber was flooded by a special type of gas.

Wet was that gas, and clinging. It settled thickly on the clothes of the humans, soaked through to the skin and *through* the skin, into every part of the body.

Sleep came gently, and with it a wonderful relaxation. The blood grew immune to shock; muscles that, in a minute before, had been drawn with anguish—loosened; the brain impregnated with life-giving chemicals that relieved it of all shortages remained untroubled even by dreams.

Everybody grew enormously flexible to gravitation pressures—a hundred—a hundred and fifty gravities of deceleration; and still the life force clung.

The great heart of the universe beat on. The storm roared along its inescapable artery, creating the radiance of life, purging the dark of its poisons—and at last the tiny ships in their separate courses burst its great bounds.

They began to come together, to seek each other, as if among them there was an irresistible passion that demanded intimacy of union.

Automatically, they slid into their old positions; the battleship *Star Cluster* began again to take form—but there were gaps. Segments destroyed, and segments lost.

On the third day Acting Grand Captain Rutgers called the surviving captains to the forward bridge, where he was temporarily making his headquarters. After the conference a communique was issued to the crew:

At 008 hours this morning a message was received from Grand Captain, the Right Honorable Gloria Cecily, the Lady Laurr of Noble Laurr, I. C., C. M., G. K. R. She has been forced down on the planet of a yellow-white sun. Her ship crashed on landing, and is unrepairable. As all communication with her has been by nondirectional sub-space radio, and as it will be utterly impossible to locate such an ordinary type sun among so many millions of other suns, the Captains in Session regret to report that our noble lady's name must now be added to that longest of all lists of naval casualties: the list of those who have been lost forever on active duty.

The admiralty lights will burn blue until further notice.

Her back was to him as he approached. Maltby hesitated, then tensed his mind, and held her there beside the section of ship that had been the main bridge of the *Star Cluster*.

The long metal shape lay half buried in the marshy ground of the great valley, its lower end jutting down into the shimmering deep yellowish-black waters of a sluggish river.

Maltby paused a few feet from the tall, slim woman, and, still holding her unaware of him, examined once again the environment that was to be their life.

The fine spray of dark rain that had dogged his exploration walk was retreating over the yellow rim of valley to the "west."

As he watched, a small yellow sun burst out from behind a curtain of dark, ocherous clouds and glared at him brilliantly. Below it an expanse of jungle glinted strangely brown and yellow.

Everywhere was that dark-brown and intense, almost liquid yellow.

Maltby sighed—and turned his attention to the woman, willed her not to see him as he walked around in front of her.

He had given a great deal of thought to the Right Honorable Gloria Cecily during his walk. Basically, of course, the problem of a man and a woman who were destined to live the rest of their lives together, alone, on a remote planet, was very simple. Particularly in view of the fact that one of the two had been conditioned to be in love with the other.

Maltby smiled grimly. He could appreciate the artificial origin of that love. But that didn't dispose of the profound fact of it.

The conditioning machine had struck to his very core. Unfortunately, it had not touched her at all; and two days of being alone with her had brought out one reality: The Lady Laurr of Noble Laurr was not even remotely thinking of yielding herself to the normal requirements of the situation.

It was time that she was made aware, not because an early solution was necessary or even desirable, but because she had to realize that the problem existed.

He stepped forward and took her in his arms.

She was a tall, graceful woman; she fitted into his embrace as if she belonged there; and, because his control of her made her return the kiss, its warmth had an effect beyond his intention.

He had intended to free her mind in the middle of the kiss.

He didn't.

When he finally released her, it was only a physical release. Her mind was still completely under his domination.

There was a metal chair that had been set just outside one of the doors. Maltby walked over, sank into it and stared up at the grand captain.

He felt shaken. The flame of desire that had leaped through him was a telling tribute to the conditioning he had undergone. But it was entirely beyond his previous analysis of the intensity of his own feelings.

He had thought he was in full control of himself, and he wasn't. Somehow, the sardonicism, the half detachment, the objectivity, which he had fancied was the keynote of his own reaction to this situation, didn't apply at all.

The conditioning machine had been thorough.

He loved this woman with such a violence that the mere touch of her was enough to disconnect his will from operations immediately following.

His heart grew quieter; he studied her with a semblance of detachment.

She was lovely in a handsome fashion; though almost all robot women of the Dellian race were better-looking. Her lips, while medium full, were somehow a trifle cruel; and there was a quality in her eyes that accentuated that cruelty.

There were built-up emotions in this woman that would not surrender easily to the idea of being marooned for life on an unknown planet.

It was something he would have to think over. Until then—

Maltby sighed. And released her from the three-dimensional hypnotic spell that his two minds had imposed on her.

He had taken the precaution of turning her away from

him. He watched her curiously as she stood, back to him, for
a moment, very still. Then she walked over to a little knob of
trees above the springy, soggy marsh land.

She climbed up it and gazed in the direction from which
he had come a few minutes before. Evidently looking for
him.

She turned finally, shaded her face against the yellow
brightness of the sinking sun, came down from the hillock
and saw him.

She stopped; her eyes narrowed. She walked over slowly.
She said with an odd edge in her voice:

"You came very quietly. You must have circled and
walked in from the west."

"No," said Maltby deliberately, "I stayed in the east."
She seemed to consider that. She was silent, her lean face
creased into a frown. She pressed her lips together, finally;
there was a bruise there that must have hurt, for she winced,
then she said: "What did you discover? Did you find any—"

She stopped. Consciousness of the bruise on her lip must
have penetrated at that moment. Her hand jerked up, her fingers touched the tender spot. Her eyes came alive with the violence of her comprehension. Before she could speak, Maltby
said: "Yes, you're quite right."

She stood looking at him. Her stormy gaze quieted. She
said finally, in a stony voice: "If you try that again I shall feel
justified in shooting you."

Maltby shook his head. He said, unsmiling: "And spend
the rest of your life here alone? You'd go mad."

He saw instantly that her basic anger was too great for
that kind of logic. He went on swiftly: "Besides, you'd have
to shoot me in the back. I have no doubt you could do that
in the line of duty. But not for personal reasons."

Her compressed lips—separated. To his amazement there
were suddenly tears in her eyes. Anger tears, obviously. But
tears!

She stepped forward with a quick movement and slapped
his face.

"You robot!" she sobbed.

Maltby stared at her ruefully; then he laughed. Finally he
said, a trace of mockery in his tone: "If I remember rightly,
the lady who just spoke is the same one who delivered a ringing radio address to all the planets of the Fifty Suns swearing

that in fifteen thousand years Earth people had forgotten all their prejudices against robots.

"Is it possible," he finished, "that the problem on *closer* investigation is proving more difficult?"

There was no answer. The Honorable Gloria Cecily brushed past him and disappeared into the interior of the ship.

She came out again a few minutes later.

Her expression was more serene; Maltby noted that she had removed all trace of the tears. She looked at him steadily, said, "What did you discover when you were out? I've been delaying my call to the ship till you returned."

Maltby said, "I thought they asked you to call at 010 hours."

The woman shrugged; and there was an arrogant note in her voice as she replied, "They'll take my calls when I make them. Did you find any sign of intelligent life?"

Maltby allowed himself brief pity for a human being who had as many shocks still to absorb as had Grand Captain Laurr.

One of the books he had read while aboard the battleship about colonists of remote planets had dealt very specifically with castaways.

He shook himself and began his description. "Mostly marsh land in the valley and there's jungle, very old. Even some of the trees are immense, though sections show no growth rings—some interesting beasts and a four-legged, two-armed thing that watched me from a distance. It carried a spear but it was too far away for me to use my hypnotism on it. There must be a village somewhere, perhaps on the valley rim. My idea is that during the next months I'll cut the ship into small sections and transport it to drier ground.

"I would say that we have the following information to offer the ship's scientists: We're on a planet of a G-type sun. The sun must be larger than the average yellow-white type and have a larger surface temperature. ⁻

"It must be larger and hotter because, though it's far away, it is hot enough to keep the northern hemisphere of this planet in a semitropical condition.

"The sun was quite a bit north at midday, but now it's swinging back to the south. I'd say offhand the planet must be tilted at about forty degrees, which means there's a cold winter coming up, though that doesn't fit with the age and type of vegetation."

The Lady Laurr was frowning. "It doesn't seem very helpful," she said. "But, of course, I'm only an executive."

"And I'm only a meteorologist."

"Exactly. Come in. Perhaps my astrophysicist can make something of it."

"*Your* astrophysicist!" said Maltby. But he didn't say it aloud.

He followed her into the segment of ship and closed the door.

Maltby examined the interior of the main bridge with a wry smile as the young woman seated herself before the astroplate.

The very imposing glitter of the instrument board that occupied one entire wall was ironical now. All the machines it had controlled were far away in space. Once it had dominated the entire Lesser Magellanic Cloud; now his own handgun was a more potent instrument.

He grew aware that Lady Laurr was looking up at him.

"I don't understand it," she said. "They don't answer."

"Perhaps"—Maltby could not keep the faint sardonicism out of his tone—"perhaps they may really have had a good reason for wanting you to call at 010 hours."

The woman made a faint, exasperated movement with her facial muscles but she did not answer. Maltby went on coolly: "After all, it doesn't matter. They're only going through routine motions, the idea being to leave no loophole of rescue unlooked through. I can't even imagine the kind of miracle it would take for anybody to find us."

The woman seemed not to have heard. She said, frowning, "How is it that we've never heard a single Fifty Suns broadcast? I intended to ask about that before. Not once during our ten years in the Lesser Cloud did we catch so much as a whisper of radio energy."

Maltby shrugged. "All radios operate on an extremely complicated variable wavelength—changes every twentieth of a second. Your instruments would register a tick once every ten minutes, and—"

He was cut off by a voice from the astroplate. A man's face was there—Acting Grand Captain Rutgers.

"Oh, there you are, captain," the woman said. "What kept you?"

"We're in the process of landing our forces on Cassidor VII," was the reply. "As you know, regulations require that the grand captain—"

"Oh, yes. Are you free now?"

"No. I've taken a moment to see that everything is right with you, and then I'll switch you over to Captain Planston."

"How is the landing proceeding?"

"Perfectly. We have made contact with the government. They seem resigned. But now I must leave. Good-bye, my lady."

His face flickered and was gone. The plate went blank. It was about as curt a greeting as anybody had ever received. But Maltby, sunk in his own gloom, scarcely noticed.

So it was all over. The desperate scheming of the Fifty Suns leaders, his own attempt to destroy the great battleship, proved futile against an invincible foe.

For a moment he felt very close to the defeat, with all its implications. Consciousness came finally that the fight no longer mattered in his life. But the knowledge failed to shake his dark mood.

He saw that the Right Honorable Gloria Cecily had an expression of mixed elation and annoyance on her fine, strong face; and there was no doubt that she didn't *feel*—disconnected—from the mighty events out there in space. Nor had she missed the implications of the abruptness of the interview.

The astroplate grew bright and a face appeared on it—one that Maltby hadn't seen before. It was of a heavy-jowled, oldish man with a ponderous voice that said: "Privilege, your ladyship—hope we can find something that will enable us to make a rescue. Never give up hope, I say, until the last nail's driven in your coffin."

He chuckled; and the woman said: "Captain Maltby will give you all the information he has, then no doubt you can give him some advice, Captain Planston. Neither he nor I, unfortunately, are astrophysicists."

"Can't be experts on every subject," Captain Planston puffed. "Er, Captain Maltby, what do you know?"

Maltby gave his information briefly, then waited while the other gave instructions. There wasn't much: "Find out length of seasons. Interested in that yellow effect of the sunlight and the deep brown. Take the following photographs, using or-thosensitive film—use three dyes, a red sensitive, a blue, and a yellow. Take a spectrum reading—what I want to check on is that maybe you've got a strong blue sun there, with the ultraviolet barred by a heavy atmosphere, and all the heat and light coming in on the yellow band.

"I'm not offering much hope, mind you—the Lesser Cloud is packed with blue suns—five hundred thousand of them brighter than Sirius.

"Finally, get that season information from the natives. Make a point of it. Good-bye!"

The native was wary. He persisted in retreating elusively into the jungle; and his four legs gave him a speed advantage of which he seemed to be aware. For he kept coming back, tantalizingly.

The woman watched with amusement, then exasperation.

"Perhaps," she suggested, "if we separated, and I drove him toward you?"

She saw the frown on the man's face as Maltby nodded reluctantly. His voice was strong, tense.

"He's leading us into an ambush. Turn on the sensitives in your helmet and carry your gun. Don't be too hasty about firing, but don't hesitate in a crisis. A spear can make an ugly wound; and we haven't got the best facilities for handling anything like that."

His orders brought a momentary irritation. He seemed not to be aware that she was as conscious as he of the requirements of the situation.

The Right Honorable Gloria sighed. If they had to stay on this planet there would have to be some major psychological adjustments, and not—she thought grimly—only by herself.

"*Now!*" said Maltby beside her, swiftly. "Notice the way the ravine splits in two. I came this far yesterday and they join about two hundred yards farther on. He's gone up the left fork. I'll take the right. You stop here, let him come back to see what's happened, then drive him on."

He was gone, like a shadow, along a dark path that wound under thick foliage.

Silence settled.

She waited. After a minute she felt herself alone in a yellow and black world that had been lifeless since time began.

She thought: This was what Maltby had meant yesterday

when he had said she wouldn't dare shoot him—and remain alone. It hadn't penetrated then.

It did now. Alone, on a nameless planet of a mediocre sun, one woman waking up every morning on a moldering ship that rested its unliving metal shape on a dark, muggy, yellow marshland.

She stood somber. There was no doubt that the problem of robot and human being would have to be solved here as well as out there.

A sound pulled her out of her gloom. As she watched, abruptly more alert, a catlike head peered cautiously from a line of bushes a hundred yards away across the clearing.

It was an interesting head; its ferocity not the least of its fascinating qualities. The yellowish body was invisible now in the underbrush, but she had caught enough glimpses of it earlier to recognize that it was the CC type, of the almost universal Centaur family. Its body was evenly balanced between its hind and forelegs.

It watched her, and its great glistening black eyes were round with puzzlement. Its head twisted from side to side, obviously searching for Maltby.

She waved her gun and walked forward. Instantly the creature disappeared. She could hear it with her sensitives, running into distance. Abruptly, it slowed; then there was no sound at all.

He's got it, she thought.

She felt impressed. These two-brained Mixed Men, she thought, were bold and capable. It would really be too bad if antirobot prejudice prevented them from being absorbed into the galactic civilization of Imperial Earth.

She watched him a few minutes later, using the block system of communication with the creature. Maltby looked up, saw her. He shook his head as if puzzled.

"He says it's always been warm like this, and that he's been alive for thirteen hundred moons. And that a moon is forty suns—forty days. He wants us to come up a little farther along this valley, but that's too transparent for comfort. Our move is to make a cautious, friendly gesture, and—"

He stopped short. Before she could even realize anything was wrong, her mind was caught, her muscles galvanized. She was thrown sideways and downward so fast that the blow of striking the ground was pure agony.

She lay there stunned, and out of the corner of her eye she saw the spear plunge through the air where she had been.

She twisted, rolled over—her own free will now—and jerked her gun in the direction from which the spear had come. There was a second centaur there, racing away along a bare slope. Her finger pressed on the control; and then—

"Don't!" It was Maltby, his voice low. "It was a scout the others sent ahead to see what was happening. He's done his work. It's all over."

\She lowered her gun and saw with annoyance that her hand was shaking, her whole body trembling. She parted her lips to say: "Thanks for saving my life!" Then she closed them again. Because the words would have quavered. And because—

Saved her life! Her mind poised on the edge of blankness with the shock of the thought. Incredibly—she had never before been in personal danger from an individual creature.

There had been the time when her battleship had run into the outer fringes of a sun; and there was the cataclysm of the storm, just past.

But those had been impersonal menaces to be met with technical virtuosities and the hard training of the service.

This was different.

All the way back to the segment of ship she tried to fathom what the difference meant.

It seemed to her finally that she had it.

"Spectrum featureless." Maltby gave his findings over the astro. "No dark lines at all; two of the yellow bands so immensely intense that they hurt my eyes. As you suggested, apparently what we have here is a blue sun whose strong violet radiation is cut off by the atmosphere.

"However," he finished, "the uniqueness of that effect is confined to our planet here, a derivation of the thick atmosphere. Any questions?"

"No-o!" The astrophysicist looked thoughtful. "And I can give you no further instructions. I'll have to examine this material. Will you ask Lady Laurr to come in? Like to speak to her privately, if you please."

"Of course."

When she had come, Maltby went outside and watched the moon come up. Darkness—he had noticed it the previous night—brought a vague, overall violet haze. Explained now!

An eighty-degree temperature on a planet that, the angular

diameter of the sun being what it was, would have been minus one hundred eighty degrees, if the sun's apparent color had been real.

A blue sun, one of five hundred thousand—Interesting but—Maltby smiled savagely—Captain Planston's "No further instructions!" had a finality about it that—

He shivered involuntarily. And after a moment tried to picture himself sitting, like this, a year hence, staring up at an unchanged moon. Ten years, twenty—

He grew aware that the woman had come to the doorway and was gazing at him where he sat on the chair.

Maltby looked up. The stream of white light from inside the ship caught the queer expression on her face, gave her a strange, bleached look after the yellowness that had seemed a part of her complexion all day.

"We shall receive no more astroradio calls," she said and, turning, went inside.

Maltby nodded to himself, almost idly. It was hard and brutal, this abrupt cutting off of communication. But the regulations governing such situations were precise.

The marooned ones must realize with utter clarity, without false hopes and without the curious illusions produced by radio communication, that they were cut off forever. Forever on their own.

Well, so be it. A fact was a fact, to be faced with resolution. There had been a chapter on castaways in one of the books he had read on the battleship. It had stated that nine hundred million human beings had, during recorded history, been marooned on then undiscovered planets. Most of these planets had eventually been found; and on no less than ten thousand of them great populations had sprung from the original nucleus of castaways.

The law prescribed that a castaway could not withhold himself or herself from participating in such population increases—regardless of previous rank. Castaways must forget considerations of sensitivity and individualism, and think of themselves as instruments of race expansion.

There were penalties; naturally inapplicable if no rescue was effected, but ruthlessly applied whenever recalcitrants were found.

Conceivably the courts might determine that a human being and a robot constituted a special case.

Half an hour must have passed while he sat there. He

stood up finally, conscious of hunger. He had forgotten all about supper.

He felt a qualm of self-annoyance. Damn it, this was not the night to appear to be putting pressure on her. Sooner or later she would have to be convinced that she ought to do her share of the cooking.

But not tonight.

He hurried inside, toward the compact kitchen that was part of every segment of ship. In the corridor, he paused.

A blaze of light streamed from the kitchen door. Somebody was whistling softly and tunelessly but cheerfully; and there was an odor of cooking vegetables, and hot *lak* meat.

They almost bumped in the doorway. "I was just going to call you," she said.

The supper was a meal of silences, quickly over. They put the dishes into the automatic and went and sat in the great lounge; Maltby saw finally that the woman was studying him with amused eyes.

"Is there any possibility," she said abruptly, "that a Mixed Man and a human woman can have children?"

"Frankly," Maltby confessed, "I doubt it."

He launched into a detailed description of the cold and pressure process that had molded the protoplasm to make the original Mixed Men. When he finished he saw that her eyes were still regarding him with a faint amusement. She said in an odd tone: "A very curious thing happened to me today, after that native threw his spear. I realized"—she seemed for a moment to have difficulty in speaking—"I realized that I had, so far as I personally was concerned, solved the robot problem.

"Naturally," she finished quietly, "I would not have withheld myself in any event. But it is pleasant to know that I like you without"—she smiled—"qualifications."

Blue sun that looked yellow. Maltby sat in the chair the following morning puzzling over it. He half expected a visit from the natives, and so he was determined to stay near the ship that day.

He kept his eyes aware of the clearing edges, the valley rims, the jungle trails, but—

There was a law, he remembered, that governed the shifting of light to other wave bands, to yellow for instance. Rather complicated, but in view of the fact that all the instruments of the main bridge were controls of instruments, not the machines themselves, he'd have to depend on mathematics if he ever hoped to visualize the kind of sun that was out there.

Most of the heat probably came through the ultraviolet range. But that was uncheckable. So leave it alone and stick to the yellow.

He went into the ship. Gloria was nowhere in sight, but her bedroom door was closed. Maltby found a notebook, returned to his chair and began to figure.

An hour later he stared at the answer: One million three hundred thousand million miles. About a fifth of a light-year.

He laughed curtly. That was that. He'd have to get better data than he had or—

Or would he?

His mind poised. In a single flash of understanding, the stupendous truth burst upon him.

With a cry he leaped to his feet, whirled to race through the door as a long, black shadow slid across him.

The shadow was so vast, instantly darkening the whole valley, that, involuntarily, Maltby halted and looked up.

The battleship *Star Cluster* hung low over the yellow-brown jungle planet, already disgorging a lifeboat that glinted a yellowish silver as it circled out into the sunlight, and started down.

Maltby had only a moment with the woman before the lifeboat landed. "To think," he said, "that I just now figured out the truth."

She was, he saw, not looking at him. Her gaze seemed far away. He went on: "As for the rest, the best method, I imagine, is to put me in the conditioning chamber, and—"

Still without looking at him, she cut him off: "Don't be ridiculous. You must not imagine that I feel embarrassed because you have kissed me. I shall receive you later in my quarters."

A bath, new clothes—at last Maltby stepped through the transmitter into the astrophysics department. His own first realization of the tremendous truth, while generally accurate, had lacked detailed facts.

"Ah, Maltby!" The chief of the department came forward, shook hands. "Some sun you picked there—we suspected from your first description of the yellowness and the black.

But naturally we couldn't rouse your hopes—Forbidden, you know.

"The axial tilt, the apparent length of a summer in which jungle trees of great size showed no growth rings—very suggestive. The featureless spectrum with its complete lack of dark lines—almost conclusive. Final proof was that the orthosensitive film was overexposed, while the blue and red sensitives were badly underexposed.

"This star-type is so immensely hot that practically all of its energy radiation is far in the ultravisible. A secondary radiation—a sort of fluorescence in the star's own atmosphere—produces the visible yellow when a minute fraction of the appalling ultraviolet radiation is transformed into longer wavelengths by helium atoms. A fluorescent lamp, in a fashion—but on a scale that is more than ordinarily cosmic in its violence. The total radiation reaching the planet was naturally tremendous; the surface radiation, after passing through miles of absorbing ozone, water vapor, carbondioxide, and other gases, was very different.

"No wonder the native said it had always been hot. The summer lasts four thousand years. The normal radiation of that special appalling star type—the æon-in-æon-out radiation rate—is about equal to a full-fledged Nova at its catastrophic maximum of violence. It has a period of a few hours, and is equivalent to approximately a hundred million ordinary suns. Nova O, we call that brightest of all stars; and there's only one in the Lesser Magellanic Cloud, the great and glorious S-Doradus.

"When I asked you to call Grand Captain Laurr, and I told her that out of thirty million suns she had picked—"

It was at that point that Maltby cut him off. "Just a minute," he said, "did you say you told Lady Laurr *last night?*"

"Was it night down there?" Captain Planston asked, interested. "Well, well—By the way, I almost forgot—this marrying and giving in marriage is not so important to me now that I am an old man. But congratulations."

The conversation was too swift for Maltby. His minds were still examining the first statement. That she had known all the time. He came up, groping, before the new words.

"Congratulations?" he echoed.

"Definitely time she had a husband," boomed the captain. "She's been a career woman, you know. Besides, it'll have a revivifying effect on the other robots ... pardon me. Assure you, the name means nothing to me.

"Anyway, Lady Laurr herself made the announcement a few minutes ago, so come down and see me again."

He turned away with a wave of a thick hand.

Maltby headed for the nearest transmitter. She would probably be expecting him by now.

She would not be disappointed.

THE PROUD ROBOT

Astounding,

October

by Lewis Padgett
(this one is *probably* by Kuttner)

"The Proud Robot" is one of the Galloway Gallegher series of stories about a heavy drinking inventor who can only be creative when drunk and then can't remember how his inventions work. The series of five stories all appeared in Astounding *between 1943 and 1948 and were collected as* Robots Have No Tails *in 1952.*

This selection is arguably the best in the series, although all were memorable.

(In the 1940s, when I was turning out my positronic robot stories with tolerable frequency, the only other robot series which seemed to impress the readers as much was Henry Kuttner's Gallegher series. I must admit that Kuttner's robots were amusing and in those days, Kuttner was one of the established major figures in science fiction and I was just an up-and-coming junior, so I felt it inevitable that he could outdo me. Even so, I didn't like it. I am quite certain that if Kuttner had lived out a normal lifetime he would have continued to stay ahead of me in the robot world.—I.A.)

Things often happened to Gallegher, who played at science by ear. He was, as he often remarked, a casual genius. Sometimes he'd start with a twist of wire, a few batteries, and a button hook, and before he finished, he might contrive a new type of refrigerating unit.

At the moment he was nursing a hangover. A disjointed,

lanky, vaguely boneless man with a lock of dark hair falling untidily over his forehead, he lay on the couch in the lab and manipulated his mechanical liquor bar. A very dry martini drizzled slowly from the spigot into his receptive mouth.

He was trying to remember something, but not trying too hard. It had to do with the robot, of course. Well, it didn't matter.

"Hey, Joe," Gallegher said.

The robot stood proudly before the mirror and examined its innards. Its hull was transparent, and wheels were going around at a great rate inside.

"When you call me that," Joe remarked, "whisper. And get that cat out of here."

"Your ears aren't that good."

"They are. I can hear the cat walking about, all right."

"What does it sound like?" Gallegher inquired, interested.

"Jest like drums," said the robot, with a put-upon air. "And when you talk, it's like thunder." Joe's voice was a discordant squeak, so Gallegher meditated on saying something about glass houses and casting the first stone. He brought his attention, with some effort, to the luminous door panel, where a shadow loomed—a familiar shadow, Gallegher thought.

"It's Brock," the annunciator said. "Harrison Brock. Let me in!"

"The door's unlocked." Gallegher didn't stir. He looked gravely at the well-dressed, middle-aged man who came in, and tried to remember. Brock was between forty and fifty; he had a smoothly massaged, clean-shaven face, and wore an expression of harassed intolerance. Probably Gallegher knew the man. He wasn't sure. Oh, well.

Brock looked around the big, untidy laboratory, blinked at the robot, searched for a chair, and failed to find it. Arms akimbo, he rocked back and forth and glared at the prostrate scientist.

"Well?" he said.

"Never start conversations that way," Gallegher mumbled, siphoning another martini down his gullet. "I've had enough trouble today. Sit down and take it easy. There's a dynamo behind you. It isn't very dusty, is it?"

"Did you get it?" Brock snapped. "That's all I want to know. You've had a week. I've a check for ten thousand in my pocket. Do you want it, or don't you?"

"Sure," Gallegher said. He extended a large, groping hand. "Give."

"*Caveat emptor.* What am I buying?"

"Don't you know?" the scientist asked, honestly puzzled.

Brock began to bounce up and down in a harassed fashion. "My God," he said. "They told me you could help me if anybody could. Sure. And they also said it'd be like pulling teeth to get sense out of you. Are you a technician or a driveling idiot?"

Gallegher pondered. "Wait a minute. I'm beginning to remember. I talked to you last week, didn't I?"

"You talked—" Brock's round face turned pink. "Yes! You lay there swilling liquor and babbled poetry. You sang 'Frankie and Johnnie.' And you finally got around to accepting my commission."

"The fact is," Gallegher said, "I have been drunk. I often get drunk. Especially on my vacation. It releases my subconscious, and then I can work. I've made my best gadgets when I was tizzied," he went on happily. "Everything seems so clear then. Clear as a bell. I mean a bell, don't I? Anyway—" He lost the thread and looked puzzled. "Anyway, what are you talking about?"

"Are you going to keep quiet?" the robot demanded from its post before the mirror.

Brock jumped. Gallegher waved a casual hand. "Don't mind Joe. I just finished him last night, and I rather regret it."

"A robot?"

"A robot. But he's no good, you know. I made him when I was drunk, and I haven't the slightest idea how or why. All he'll do is stand there and admire himself. And sing. He sings like a banshee. You'll hear him presently."

With an effort Brock brought his attention back to the matter at hand. "Now look, Gallegher. I'm in a spot. You promised to help me. If you don't, I'm a ruined man."

"I've been ruined for years," the scientist remarked. "It never bothers me. I just go along working for a living and making things in my spare time. Making all sorts of things. You know, if I'd really studied, I'd have been another Einstein. So they tell me. As it is, my subconscious picked up a first-class scientific training somewhere. Probably that's why I never bothered. When I'm drunk or sufficiently absent-minded, I can work out the damnedest problems."

"You're drunk now," Brock accused.

"I approach the pleasanter stages. How would you feel if you woke up and found you'd made a robot for some unknown reason, and hadn't the slightest idea of the creature's attributes?"

"Well—"

"I don't feel that way at all," Gallegher murmured. "Probably you take life too seriously, Brock. Wine is a mocker; strong drink is raging. Pardon me. I rage." He drank another martini.

Brock began to pace around the crowded laboratory, circling various enigmatic and untidy objects. "If you're a scientist, heaven help science."

"I'm the Larry Adler of science," Gallegher said. "He was a musician—lived some hundreds of years ago, I think. I'm like him. Never took a lesson in my life. Can I help it if my subconscious likes practical jokes?"

"Do you know who I am?" Brock demanded.

"Candidly, no. Should I?"

There was bitterness in the other's voice. "You might have the courtesy to remember, even though it was a week ago. Harrison Brock. Me. I own Vox-View Pictures."

"No," the robot said suddenly, "it's no use. No use at all, Brock."

"What the—"

Gallegher sighed wearily. "I forget the damned thing's alive. Mr. Brock, meet Joe. Joe, meet Mr. Brock—of Vox-View."

Joe turned, gears meshing within his transparent skull. "I am glad to meet you, Mr. Brock. Allow me to congratulate you on your good fortune in hearing my lovely voice."

"Ugh," said the magnate inarticulately. "Hello."

"Vanity of vanities, all is vanity," Gallegher put in, *sotto voce*. "Joe's like that. A peacock. No use arguing with him either."

The robot ignored this aside. "But it's no use, Mr. Brock," he went on squeakily. "I'm not interested in money. I realize it would bring happiness to many if I consented to appear in your pictures, but fame means nothing to me. Nothing. Consciousness of beauty is enough."

Brock began to chew his lips. "Look," he said savagely, "I didn't come here to offer you a picture job. See? Am I offering you a contract? Such colossal nerve—*Pah!* You're crazy."

"Your schemes are perfectly transparent," the robot remarked coldly. "I can see that you're overwhelmed by my beauty and the loveliness of my voice—its grand tonal qualities. You needn't pretend you don't want me, just so you can get me at a lower price. I said I wasn't interested."

"You're *cr-r-razy!*" Brock howled, badgered beyond endurance, and Joe calmly turned back to his mirror.

"Don't talk so loudly," the robot warned. "The discordance is deafening. Besides you're ugly and I don't like to look at you." Wheels and cogs buzzed inside the transplastic shell. Joe extended his eyes on stalks and regarded himself with every appearance of appreciation.

Gallegher was chuckling quietly on the couch. "Joe has a high irritation value," he said. "I've found that out already. I must have given him some remarkable senses, too. An hour ago he started to laugh his damn fool head off. No reason, apparently. I was fixing myself a bite to eat. Ten minutes after that I slipped on an apple core I'd thrown away and came down hard. Joe just looked at me. 'That was it,' he said. 'Logics of probability. Cause and effect. I knew you were going to drop that apple core and then step on it when you went to pick up the mail.' Like the White Queen, I suppose. It's a poor memory that doesn't work both ways."

Brock sat on the small dynamo—there were two, the larger one named Monstro, and the smaller one serving Gallegher as a bank—and took deep breaths. "Robots are nothing new."

"This one is. I hate its gears. It's beginning to give me an inferiority complex. Wish I knew why I'd made it," Gallegher sighed. "Oh, well. Have a drink?"

"No. I came here on business. Do you seriously mean you spent last week building a robot instead of solving the problem I hired you for?"

"Contingent, wasn't it?" Gallegher asked. "I think I remember that."

"Contingent," Brock said with satisfaction. "Ten thousand, if and when."

"Why not give me the dough and take the robot? He's worth that. Put him in one of your pictures."

"I won't have any pictures unless you figure out an answer," Brock snapped. "I told you all about it."

"I have been drunk," Gallegher said. "My mind has been

wiped clear, as by a sponge. I am as a little child. Soon I shall be as a drunken little child. Meanwhile, if you'd care to explain the matter again—"

Brock gulped down his passion, jerked a magazine at random from the bookshelf, and took out a stylo. "All right. My preferred stocks are at twenty-eight, way below par—" He scribbled figures on the magazine.

"If you'd taken that medieval folio next to that, it'd have cost you a pretty penny," Gallegher said lazily. "So you're the sort of guy who writes on tablecloths, eh? Forget this business of stocks and stuff. Get down to cases. Who are you trying to gyp?"

"It's no use," the robot said from before its mirror. "I won't sign a contract. People may come and admire me, if they like, but they'll have to whisper in my presence."

"A madhouse." Brock muttered, trying to get a grip on himself. "Listen, Gallegher. I told you all this a week ago, but—"

"Joe wasn't here then. Pretend like you're talking to him."

"Uh—look. You've heard of Vox-View Pictures, at least."

"Sure. The biggest and best television company in the business. Sonatone's about your only competitor."

"Sonatone's squeezing me out."

Gallegher looked puzzled. "I don't see how. You've got the best product. Tri-dimensional color, all sorts of modern improvements, the top actors, musicians, singers—"

"No use," the robot said. "I won't."

"Shut up, Joe. You're tops in your field, Brock. I'll hand you that. And I've always heard you were fairly ethical. What's Sonatone got on you?"

Brock made helpless gestures. "Oh, it's politics. The bootleg theaters. I can't buck 'em. Sonatone helped elect the present administration, and the police just wink when I try to have the bootleggers raided."

"Bootleg theaters?" Gallegher asked, scowling a trifle. "I've heard something—"

"It goes way back. To the old sound-film days. Home television killed sound film and big theaters. People were conditioned away from sitting in audience groups to watch a screen. The home televisors got good. It was more fun to sit in an easy chair, drink beer, and watch the show. Television wasn't a rich man's hobby by that time. The meter system brought the price down to middle-class levels. Everybody knows that."

"I don't," Gallegher said. "I never pay attention to what goes on outside of my lab, unless I have to. Liquor and a selective mind. I ignore everything that doesn't affect me directly. Explain the whole thing in detail so I'll get a complete picture. I don't mind repetition. Now, what about this meter system of yours?"

"Televisors are installed free. We never sell 'em; we rent them. People pay according to how many hours they have the set tuned in. We run a continuous show, stage plays, wire-tape films, operas, orchestras, singers, vaudeville—everything. If you use your televisor a lot, you pay proportionately. The man comes around once a month and reads the meter. Which is a fair system. Anybody can afford a Vox-View. Sonatone and the other companies do the same thing, but Sonatone's the only big competitor I've got. At least, the only one that's crooked as hell. The rest of the boys—they're smaller than I am, but I don't step on their toes. Nobody's ever called me a louse," Brock said darkly.

"So what?"

"So Sonatone has started to depend on audience appeal. It was impossible till lately—you couldn't magnify tri-dimensional television on a big screen without streakiness and mirage-effect. That's why the regular three-by-four home screens were used. Results were perfect. But Sonatone's bought a lot of the ghost theaters all over the country—"

"What's a ghost theater?" Gallegher asked.

"Well—before sound films collapsed, the world was thinking big. Big—you know? Ever heard of the Radio City Music Hall? That wasn't in it! Television was coming in, and competition was fierce. Sound-film theaters got bigger and more elaborate. They were palaces. Tremendous. But when television was perfected, nobody went to the theaters any more, and it was often too expensive a job to tear 'em down. Ghost theaters—see? Big ones and little ones. Renovated them. And they're showing Sonatone programs. Audience appeal is quite a factor. The theaters charge plenty, but people flock into 'em. Novelty and the mob instinct."

Gallegher closed his eyes. "What's to stop you from doing the same thing?"

"Patents," Brock said briefly. "I mentioned that dimensional television couldn't be used on big screens till lately.

Sonatone signed an agreement with me ten years ago that any enlarging improvements would be used mutually. They crawled out of that contract. Said it was faked, and the courts upheld them. They uphold the courts—politics. Anyhow, Sonatone's technicians worked out a method of using the large screen. They took out patents—twenty-seven patents, in fact, covering every possible variation on the idea. My technical staff has been working day and night trying to find some similar method that won't be an infringement, but Sonatone's got it all sewed up. They've a system called the Magna. It can be hooked up to any type of televisor—but they'll only allow it to be used on Sonatone machines. See?"

"Unethical, but legal," Gallegher said. "Still, you're giving your customers more for their money. People want good stuff. The size doesn't matter."

"Yeah," Brock said bitterly, "but that isn't all. The newstapes are full of A. A.—it's a new catchword. Audience Appeal. The herd instinct. You're right about people wanting good stuff—but would you buy Scotch at four a quart if you could get it for half that amount?"

"Depends on the quality. What's happening?"

"Bootleg theaters," Brock said. "They've opened all over the country. They show Vox-View products, and they're using the Magna enlarger system Sonatone's got patented. The admission price is low—lower than the rate of owning a Vox-View in your own home. There's audience appeal. There's the thrill of something a bit illegal. People are having their Vox-Views taken out right and left. I know why. They can go to a bootleg theater instead."

"It's illegal," Gallegher said thoughtfully.

"So were speakeasies, in the Prohibition Era. A matter of protection, that's all. I can't get any action through the courts. I've tried. I'm running in the red. Eventually I'll be broke. I can't lower my home rental fees on Vox-Views. They're nominal already. I make my profits through quantity. Now, no profits. As for these bootleg theaters, it's pretty obvious who's backing them."

"Sonatone?"

"Sure. Silent partners. They get the take at the box office. What they want is to squeeze me out of business, so they'll have a monopoly. After that, they'll give the public junk and pay their artists starvation salaries. With me it's different. I pay my staff what they're worth—plenty."

"And you offered me a lousy ten thousand," Gallegher remarked. "Uh-*huh!*"

"That was only the first instalment," Brock said hastily. "You can name your own fee. Within reason," he added.

"I shall. An astronomical sum. Did I say I'd accept the commission a week ago?"

"You did."

"Then I must have had some idea how to solve the problem." Gallegher pondered. "Let's see. I didn't mention anything in particular, did I?"

"You kept talking about marble slabs and . . . uh . . . your sweetie."

"Then I was singing," Gallegher explained largely. " 'St. James Infirmary.' Singing calms my nerves, and God knows they need it sometimes. Music and liquor. I often wonder what the vintners buy—"

"What?"

"One half so precious as the stuff they sell. Let it go. I am quoting Omar. It means nothing. Are your technicians any good?"

"The best. And the best paid."

"They can't find a magnifying process that won't infringe on the Sonatone Magna patents?"

"In a nutshell, that's it."

"I suppose I'll have to do some research," Gallegher said sadly. "I hate it like poison. Still, the sum of the parts equals the whole. Does that make sense to you? It doesn't to me. I have trouble with words. After I say things, I start wondering what I've said. Better than watching a play," he finished wildly. "I've got a headache. Too much talk and not enough liquor. Where were we?"

"Approaching the madhouse," Brock suggested. "If you weren't my last resort, I'd—"

"No use," the robot said squeakily. "You might as well tear up your contract, Brock. I won't sign it. Fame means nothing to me—nothing."

"If you don't shut up," Gallegher warned, "I'm going to scream in your ears."

"All right!" Joe shrilled. "Beat me! Go on, beat me! The meaner you are, the faster I'll have my nervous system disrupted, and then I'll be dead. I don't care. I've got no instinct of self-preservation. Beat me. See if I care."

"He's right, you know," the scientist said after a pause. "And it's the only logical way to respond to blackmail or threats. The sooner it's over, the better. There aren't any graduations with Joe. Anything really painful to him will destroy him. And he doesn't give a damn."

"Neither do I," Brock grunted. "What I want to find out—"

"Yeah. I know. Well, I'll wander around and see what occurs to me. Can I get into your studios?"

"Here's a pass." Brock scribbled something on the back of a card. "Will you get to work on it right away?"

"Sure," Gallegher lied. "Now you run along and take it easy. Try and cool off. Everything's under control. I'll either find a solution to your problem pretty soon or else—"

"Or else what?"

"Or else I won't," the scientist finished blandly, and fingered the buttons on a control panel near the couch. "I'm tired of martinis. Why didn't I make that robot a mechanical bartender, while I was at it? Even the effort of selecting and pushing buttons is depressing at times. Yeah, I'll get to work on the business, Brock. Forget it."

The magnate hesitated. "Well, you're my only hope. I needn't bother to mention that if there's anything I can do to help you—"

"A blonde," Gallegher murmured. "That gorgeous, gorgeous star of yours, Silver O'Keefe. Send her over. Otherwise I want nothing."

"Good-bye, Brock," the robot said squeakily. "Sorry we couldn't get together on the contract, but at least you've had the delight of hearing my beautiful voice, not to mention the pleasure of seeing me. Don't tell too many people how lovely I am. I really don't want to be bothered with mobs. They're noisy."

"You don't know what dogmatism means till you've talked to Joe," Gallegher said. "Oh, well. See you later. Don't forget the blonde."

Brock's lips quivered. He searched for words, gave it up as a vain task, and turned to the door.

"Good-bye, you ugly man," Joe said.

Gallegher winced as the door slammed, though it was harder on the robot's supersensitive ears than on his own.

"Why do you go on like that?" he inquired. "You nearly gave the guy apoplexy."

"Surely he didn't think he was beautiful," Joe remarked.

"Beauty's in the eye of the beholder."

"How stupid you are. You're ugly, too."

"And you're a collection of rattletrap gears, pistons, and cogs. You've got worms," said Gallegher, referring of course, to certain mechanisms in the robot's body.

"I'm lovely." Joe stared raptly into the mirror.

"Maybe, to you. Why did I make you transparent, I wonder?"

"So others could admire me. I have X-ray vision, of course."

"And wheels in your head. Why did I put your radio-atomic brain in your stomach? Protection?"

Joe didn't answer. He was humming in a maddeningly squeaky voice, shrill and nerve-racking. Gallegher stood it for a while, fortifying himself with a gin rickey from the siphon.

"Get it up!" he yelped at last. "You sound like an old-fashioned subway train going round a curve."

"You're merely jealous," Joe scoffed, but obediently raised his tone to a supersonic pitch. There was silence for a half-minute. Then all the dogs in the neighborhood began to howl.

Wearily Gallegher dragged his lanky frame up from the couch. He might as well get out. Obviously there was no peace to be had in the laboratory. Not with that animated junk pile inflating his ego all over the place. Joe began to laugh in an off-key cackle. Gallegher winced.

"What now?"

"You'll find out."

Logic of causation and effect, influenced by probabilities, X-ray vision and other enigmatic senses the robot no doubt possessed. Gallegher cursed softly, found a shapeless black hat, and made for the door. He opened it to admit a short, fat man who bounced painfully off the scientist's stomach.

"*Whoof!* Uh. What a corny sense of humor that jackass has. Hello, Mr. Kennicott. Glad to see you. Sorry I can't offer you a drink."

Mr. Kennicott's swarthy face twisted malignantly. "Don' wanna no drink. Wanna my money. You gimme. Howzabout it?"

Gallegher looked thoughtfully at nothing. "Well, the fact is, I was just going to collect a check."

"I sella you my diamonds. You say you gonna make somet'ing wit' 'em. You gimme check before. It go bounca, bounca, bounca. Why is?"

"It was rubber," Gallegher said faintly. "I never can keep track of my bank balance."

Kennicott showed symptoms of going bounca on the threshold. "You gimme back diamonds, eh?"

"Well, I used 'em in an experiment. I forget just what. You know, Mr. Kennicott, I think I was a little drunk when I bought them, wasn't I?"

"Dronk," the little man agreed. "Mad wit' vino, sure. So whatta? I wait no longer. Awready you put me off too much. Pay up now or elsa."

"Go away, you dirty man," Joe said from within the room. "You're awful."

Gallegher hastily shouldered Kennicott out into the street and latched the door behind him. "A parrot," he explained. "I'm going to wring its neck pretty soon. Now about that money. I admit I owe it to you. I've just taken on a big job, and when I'm paid, you'll get yours."

"Bah to such stuff," Kennicott said. "You gotta position, eh? You are technician wit' some big company, eh? Ask for ahead-salary."

"I did," Gallegher sighed. "I've drawn my salary for six months ahead. Now look. I'll have that dough for you in a couple of days. Maybe I can get an advance from my client. O.K.?"

"No."

"No?"

"Ah-h, nutsa. I waita one day. Two daysa, maybe. Enough. You get money. Awright. If not, O.K., *calabozo* for you."

"Two days is plenty," Gallegher said, relieved. "Say, are there any of those bootleg theaters around here?"

"Better you get to work an' not waste time."

"That's my work. I'm making a survey. How can I find a bootleg place?"

"Easy. You go downtown, see guy in doorway. He sell you tickets. Anywhere. All over."

"Swell," Gallegher said, and bade the little man adieu. Why had he bought diamonds from Kennicott? It would be almost worthwhile to have his subconscious amputated. It did the most extraordinary things. It worked on inflexible principles of logic, but that logic was completely alien to Gallegher's conscious mind. The results, though, were often surprisingly good, and always surprising. That was the worst of being a scientist who knew no science—who played by ear.

There was diamond dust in a retort in the laboratory, from some unsatisfactory experiment Gallegher's subconscious had performed; and he had a fleeting memory of buying the stones from Kennicott. Curious. Maybe—oh, yeah. They'd gone into Joe. Bearings or something. Dismantling the robot wouldn't help now, for the diamonds had certainly been reground. Why the devil hadn't he used commercial stones, quite as satisfactory, instead of purchasing blue-whites of the finest water? The best was none too good for Gallegher's subconscious. It had a fine freedom from commercial instincts. It just didn't understand the price system of the basic principles of economics.

Gallegher wandered downtown like a Diogenes seeking truth. It was early evening, and the luminates were flickering on overhead, pale bars of light against darkness. A sky sign blazed above Manhattan's towers. Air-taxis, skimming along at various arbitrary levels, paused for passengers at the elevator landings. Heigh-ho.

Downtown, Gallegher began to look for doorways. He found an occupied one at last, but the man was selling postcards. Gallegher declined and headed for the nearest bar, feeling the needs of replenishment. It was a mobile bar, combining the worst features of a Coney Island ride with uninspired cocktails, and Gallegher hesitated on the threshold. But at last he seized a chair as it swung past and relaxed as much as possible. He ordered three rickeys and drank them in rapid succession. After that he called the bartender over and asked him about bootleg theaters.

"Hell, yes," the man said, producing a sheaf of tickets from his apron. "How many?"

"One. Where do I go?"

"Two-twenty-eight. This street. Ask for Tony."

"Thanks," Gallegher said, and having paid exorbitantly, crawled out of the chair and weaved away. Mobile bars were an improvement he didn't appreciate. Drinking, he felt, should be performed in a state of stasis, since one eventually reached that stage, anyway.

The door was at the bottom of a flight of steps, and there was a grilled panel set in it. When Gallegher knocked, the

visascreen lit up—obviously a one-way circuit, for the door-
man was invisible.

"Tony here?" Gallegher said.

The door opened, revealing a tired-looking man in pneumo-
slacks, which failed in their purpose of building up his skinny
figure. "Got a ticket? Let's have it. O.K., bud. Straight ahead.
Show now going on. Liquor served in the bar on your left."

Gallegher pushed through soundproofed curtains at the end
of a short corridor and found himself in what appeared to be
the foyer of an ancient theater, *circa* 1980, when plastics
were the great fad. He smelled out the bar, drank expensively
priced cheap liquor, and, fortified, entered the theater itself.
It was nearly full. The great screen—a Magna, presumably—was filled with people doing things to a spaceship. Either an adventure film or a newsreel, Gallegher realized.

Only the thrill of lawbreaking would have enticed the audience into the bootleg theater. It smelled. It was certainly run
on a shoestring, and there were no ushers. But it was illicit,
and therefore well patronized. Gallegher looked thoughtfully
at the screen. No streakiness, no mirage effect. A Magna enlarger had been fitted to a Vox-View unlicensed televisor, and
one of Brock's greatest stars was emoting effectively for the
benefit of the bootleggers' patrons. Simple highjacking. Yeah.

After a while Gallegher went out, noticing a uniformed policeman in one of the aisle seats. He grinned sardonically.
The flatfoot hadn't paid his admission, of course. Politics
were as usual.

Two blocks down the street a blaze of light announced
SONATONE BIJOU. This, of course, was one of the legalized theaters, and correspondingly high-priced. Gallegher
recklessly squandered a small fortune on a good seat. He was
interested in comparing notes, and discovered that, as far as
he could make out, the Magna in the Bijou and the bootleg
theater were identical. Both did their job perfectly. The difficult task of enlarging television screens had been successfully
surmounted.

In the Bijou, however, all was palatial. Resplendent ushers
salaamed to the rugs. Bars dispensed free liquor, in reasonable
quantities. There was a Turkish bath. Gallegher went through
a door labelled MEN and emerged quite dazzled by the
splendor of the place. For at least ten minutes afterward he
felt like a Sybarite.

All of which meant that those who could afford it went to

the legalized Sonatone theaters, and the rest attended the bootleg places. All but a few homebodies, who weren't carried off
their feet by the new fad. Eventually Brock would be forced
out of business for lack of revenue. Sonatone would take
over, jacking up their prices and concentrating on making
money. Amusement was necessary to life; people had been
conditioned to television. There was no substitute. They'd pay
and pay for inferior talent, once Sonatone succeeded in their
squeeze.

Gallegher left the Bijou and hailed an air-taxi. He gave the
address of Vox-View's Long Island studio, with some vague
hope of getting a drawing account out of Brock. Then, too,
he wanted to investigate further.

Vox-View's eastern offices sprawled wildly over Long Island,
bordering the Sound, a vast collection of variously shaped
buildings. Gallegher instinctively found the commissary, where
he . absorbed more liquor as a precautionary measure. His
subconscious had a heavy job ahead, and he didn't want it
handicapped by lack of complete freedom. Besides, the
collins was good.

After one drink, he decided he'd had enough for a while.
He wasn't a superman, though his capacity was slightly incredible. Just enough for objective clarity and subjective release—

"Is the studio always open at night?" he asked the waiter.

"Sure. Some of the stages, anyway. It's a round-the-clock
program."

"The commissary's full."

"We get the airport crowd, too. 'Nother?"

Gallegher shook his head and went out. The card Brock
had given him provided entry at a gate, and he went first of all
to the big-shot's office. Brock wasn't there, but loud voices
emerged, shrilly feminine.

The secretary said, "Just a minute, please," and used her
interoffice visor. Presently—"Will you go in?"

Gallegher did. The office was a honey, functional and lux-
-urious at the same time. Three-dimensional stills were in
niches along the walls—Vox-View's biggest stars. A small, excited, pretty brunette was sitting behind the desk, and a
blonde angel was standing furiously on the other side of it.
Gallegher recognized the angel as Silver O'Keefe.

He seized the opportunity. "Hiya, Miss O'Keefe. Will you autograph an ice cube for me? In a highball?"

Silver looked feline. "Sorry, darling, but I'm a working girl. And I'm busy right now."

The brunette scratched a cigarette. "Let's settle this later, Silver. Pop said to see this guy if he dropped in. It's important."

"It'll be settled," Silver said. "And soon." She made an exit. Gallegher whistled thoughtfully at the closed door.

"You can't have it," the brunette said. "It's under contract. And it wants to get out of the contract, so it can sign up with Sonatone. Rats desert a sinking ship. Silver's been kicking her head off ever since she read the storm signals."

"Yeah?"

"Sit down and smoke or something. I'm Patsy Brock. Pop runs this business, and I manage the controls whenever he blows his top. The old goat can't stand trouble. He takes it as a personal affront."

Gallegher found a chair. "So Silver's trying to renege, eh? How many others?"

"Not many. Most of 'em are loyal. But, of course, if we bust up—" Patsy Brock shrugged. "They'll either work for Sonatone for their cakes, or else do without."

"Uh-huh. Well—I want to see your technicians. I want to look over the ideas they've worked out for enlarger screens."

"Suit yourself," Patsy said. "It's not much use. You just can't make a televisor enlarger without infringing on some Sonatone patent."

She pushed a button, murmured something into a visor, and presently two tall glasses appeared through a slot in the desk. "Mr. Gallegher?"

"Well, since it's a collins—"

"I could tell by your breath," Patsy said enigmatically. "Pop told me he'd seen you. He seemed a bit upset, especially by your new robot. What is it like, anyway?"

"Oh, I don't know," Gallegher said, at a loss. "It's got lots of abilities—new senses, I think—but I haven't the slightest idea what it's good for. Except admiring itself in a mirror."

Patsy nodded. "I'd like to see it sometime. But about this Sonatone business. Do you think you can figure out an answer?"

"Possibly. Probably."

"Not certainly?"

"Certainly, then. Of that there is no manner of doubt—no possible doubt whatever."

"Because it's important to me. The man who owns Sonatone is Elia Tone. A piratical skunk. He blusters. He's got a son named Jimmy. And Jimmy, believe it or not, has read 'Romeo and Juliet.' "

"Nice guy?"

"A louse. A big, brawny louse. He wants me to marry him."

" 'Two families, both alike in—' "

"Spare me," Patsy interrupted. "I always thought Romeo was a dope, anyway. And if I ever thought I was going aisling with Jimmy Tone, I'd buy a one-way ticket to the nut hatch. No, Mr. Gallegher, it's not like that. No hibiscus blossoms. Jimmy has proposed to me—his idea of a proposal, by the way, is to get a half Nelson on a girl and tell her how lucky she is."

"Ah," said Gallegher, diving into his collins.

"This whole idea—the patent monopoly and the bootleg theaters—is Jimmy's. I'm sure of that. His father's in on it, too, of course, but Jimmy Tone is the bright little boy who started it."

"Why?"

"Two birds with one stone. Sonatone will have a monopoly on the business, and Jimmy thinks he'll get me. He's a little mad. He can't believe I'm in earnest in refusing him, and he expects me to break down and say 'Yes' after a while. Which I won't, no matter what happens. But it's a personal matter. I can't let him put this trick over on us. I want that self-sufficient smirk wiped off his face."

"You just don't like him, eh?" Gallegher remarked. "I don't blame you, if he's like that. Well, I'll do my damnedest. However, I'll need an expense account."

"How much?"

Gallegher named a sum. Patsy styloed a check for a far smaller amount. The scientist looked hurt.

"It's no use," Patsy said, grinning crookedly. "I've heard of you, Mr. Gallegher. You're completely irresponsible. If you had more than this, you'd figure you didn't need any more, and you'd forget the whole matter. I'll issue more checks to you when you need 'em—but I'll want itemized expense accounts."

"You wrong me," Gallegher said, brightening. "I was figur-

ing on taking you to a night club. Naturally I don't want to
take you to a dive. The big places cost money. Now if you'll
just write another check—"

Patsy laughed. "No."

"Want to buy a robot?"

"Not that kind, anyway."

"Then I'm washed up," Gallegher sighed. "Well, what
about—"

At this point the visor hummed. A blank, transparent face
grew on the screen. Gears were clicking rapidly inside the
round head. Patsy gave a small shriek and shrank back.

"Tell Gallegher Joe's here, you lucky girl," a squeaky voice
announced. "You may treasure the sound and sight of me till
your dying day. One touch of beauty in a world of
drabness—"

Gallegher circled the desk and looked at the screen. "What
the hell. How did you come to life?"

"I had a problem to solve."

"How'd you know where to reach me?"

"I vastened you," the robot said.

"What?"

"I vastened you were at the Vox-View studios, with Patsy
Brock."

"What's vastened?" Gallegher wanted to know.

"It's a sense I've got. You've nothing remotely like it, so I
can't describe it to you. It's like a combination of sagrazi and
prescience."

"Sagrazi?"

"Oh, you don't have sagrazi, either, do you. Well, don't
waste my time. I want to go back to the mirror."

"Does he always talk like that?" Patsy put in.

"Nearly always. Sometimes it makes even less sense. O.K.,
Joe. Now what?"

"You're not working for Brock any more," the robot said.
"You're working for the Sonatone people."

Gallegher breathed deeply. "Keep talking. You're crazy,
though."

"I don't like Kennicott. He annoys me. He's *too* ugly. His
vibrations grate on my sagrazi."

"Never mind him," Gallegher said, not wishing to discuss
his diamond-buying activities before the girl. "Get back to—"

"But I knew Kennicott would keep coming back till he got

his money. So when Elia and James Tone came to the laboratory, I got a check from them."

Patsy's hand gripped Gallegher's biceps. "Steady! What's going on here? The old double cross?"

"No. Wait. Let me get to the bottom of this. Joe, damn your transparent hide, just what did you do? How could you get a check from the Tones?"

"I pretended to be you."

"Sure," Gallegher said with savage sarcasm. "That explains it. We're twins. We look exactly alike."

"I hypnotized them," Joe explained. "I made them think I was you."

"You can do *that?*"

"Yes. It surprised me a bit. Still, if I'd thought, I'd have vastened I could do it."

"You . . . yeah, sure. I'd have vastened the same thing myself. *What happened?*"

"The Tones must have suspected Brock would ask you to help him. They offered an exclusive contract—you work for them and nobody else. Lots of money. Well, I pretended to be you, and said all right. So I signed the contract—it's your signature, by the way—and got a check from them and mailed it to Kennicott."

"The whole check?" Gallegher asked feebly. "How much was it?"

"Twelve thousand."

"They only offered me *that?*"

"No," the robot said, "they offered a hundred thousand, and two thousand a week for five years. But I merely wanted enough to pay Kennicott and make sure he wouldn't come back and bother me. The Tones were satisfied when I said twelve thousand would be enough."

Gallegher made an inarticulate, gurgling sound deep in his throat. Joe nodded thoughtfully.

"I thought I had better notify you that you're working for Sonatone now. Well, I'll go back to the mirror and sing to myself."

"Wait," the scientist said. "Just wait, Joe. With my own two hands I'm going to rip you gear from gear and stamp on your fragments."

"It won't hold in court," Patsy said, gulping.

"It will," Joe told her cheerily. "You may have one last, satisfying look at me, and then I must go." He went.

Gallegher drained his collins at a draft. "I'm shocked sober," he informed the girl. "What did I put into that robot? What abnormal senses has he got? Hypnotizing people into believing he's me—I'm him—I don't know what I mean."

"Is this a gag?" Patsy said shortly, after a pause. "You didn't sign up with Sonatone yourself, by any chance, and have your robot call up here to give you an out—an alibi? I'm just wondering."

"Don't. Joe signed a contract with Sonatone, not me. But—figure it out: If the signature's a perfect copy of mine, if Joe hypnotized the Tones into thinking they saw me instead of him, if there are witnesses to the signature—the two Tones are witnesses, of course—Oh, hell."

Patsy's eyes were narrowed. "We'll pay you as much as Sonatone offered. On a contingent basis. But you're working for Vox-View—that's understood."

"Sure."

Gallegher looked longingly at his empty glass. Sure. He was working for Vox-View. But, to all legal appearances, he had signed a contract giving his exclusive services to Sonatone for a period of five years—and for a sum of twelve thousand! *Yipes!* What was it they'd offered? A hundred thousand flat, and . . . and—

It wasn't the principle of the thing, it was the money. Now Gallegher was sewed up tighter than a banded pigeon. If Sonatone could win a court suit, he was legally bound to them for five years. With no further emolument. He had to get out of that contract, somehow—and at the same time solve Brock's problem.

Why not Joe? The robot, with his surprising talents, had got Gallegher into this spot. He ought to be able to get the scientist out. He'd better—or the proud robot would soon be admiring himself piecemeal.

"That's it," Gallegher said under his breath. "I'll talk to Joe. Patsy, feed me liquor in a hurry and send me to the technical department. I want to see those blueprints."

The girl looked at him suspiciously. "All right. If you try to sell us out—"

"I've been sold out myself. Sold down the river. I'm afraid of that robot. He's vastened me into quite a spot. That's right, collinses." Gallegher drank long and deeply.

After that, Patsy took him to the tech offices. The reading of three-dimensional blueprints was facilitated with a scanner—a selective device which eliminated confusion. Gallegher studied the plans long and thoughtfully. There were copies of the patent Sonatone prints, too, and, as far as he could tell, Sonatone had covered the ground beautifully. There weren't any outs. Unless one used an entirely new principle—

But new principles couldn't be plucked out of the air. Nor would that solve the problem completely. Even if Vox-View owned a new type of enlarger that didn't infringe on Sonatone's Magna, the bootleg theaters would still be in existence, pulling the trade. A. A.—audience appeal—was a prime factor now. It had to be considered. The puzzle wasn't a purely scientific one. There was the human equation as well.

Gallegher stored the necessary information in his mind, neatly indexed on shelves. Later he'd use what he wanted. For the moment, he was completely baffled. Something worried him.

What?

The Sonatone affair.

"I want to get in touch with the Tones," he told Patsy. "Any ideas?"

"I can reach 'em on a visor."

Gallegher shook his head. "Psychological handicap. It's too easy to break the connection."

"Well, if you're in a hurry, you'll probably find the boys night-clubbing. I'll go see what I can find out." Patsy scuttled off, and Silver O'Keefe appeared from behind a screen.

"I'm shameless," she announced. "I always listen at keyholes. Sometimes I hear interesting things. If you want to see the Tones, they're at the Castle Club. And I think I'll take you up on that drink."

Gallegher said, "O.K. You get a taxi. I'll tell Patsy we're going."

"She'll hate that," Silver remarked. "Meet you outside the commissary in ten minutes. Get a shave while you're at it."

Patsy Brock wasn't in her office, but Gallegher left word. After that, he visited the service lounge, smeared invisible shave cream on his face, left it there for a couple of minutes, and wiped it off with a treated towel. The bristles came away with the cream. Slightly refreshed, Gallegher joined Silver at the rendezvous and hailed an air-taxi. Presently they were leaning back on the cushions, puffing cigarettes and eyeing each other warily.

"Well?" Gallegher said.

"Jimmy Tone tried to date me up tonight. That's how I knew where to find him."

"Well?"

"I've been asking questions around the lot tonight. It's unusual for an outsider to get into the Vox-View administration offices. I went around saying, 'Who's Gallegher?' "

"What did you find out?"

"Enough to give me a few ideas. Brock hired you, eh? I can guess why."

"*Ergo* what?"

"I've a habit of landing on my feet," Silver said, shrugging. She knew how to shrug. "Vox-View's going bust. Sonatone's taking over. Unless——"

"Unless I figure out an answer."

"That's right. I want to know which side of the fence I'm going to land on. You're the lad who can probably tell me. Who's going to win?"

"You always bet on the winning side, eh?" Gallegher inquired. "Have you no ideals, wench? Is there no truth in you? Ever hear of ethics and scruples?"

Silver beamed happily. "Did you?"

"Well, I've heard of 'em. Usually I'm too drunk to figure out what they mean. The trouble is, my subconscious is completely amoral, and when it takes over, logic's the only law."

She threw her cigarette into the East River. "Will you tip me off which side of the fence is the right one?"

"Truth will triumph," Gallegher said piously. "It always does. However, I figure truth is a variable, so we're right back where we started. All right, sweetheart. I'll answer your question. Stay on my side if you want to be safe."

"Which side are you on?"

"God knows," Gallegher said. "Consciously I'm on Brock's side. But my subconscious may have different ideas. We'll see."

Silver looked vaguely dissatisfied, but didn't say anything. The taxi swooped down to the Castle roof, grounding with pneumatic gentleness. The Club itself was downstairs, in an immense room shaped like half a melon turned upside down. Each table was on a transparent platform that could be raised on its shaft to any height at will. Smaller service elevators allowed waiters to bring drinks to the guests. There wasn't any particular reason for this arrangement, but at least it was novel, and only extremely heavy drinkers ever fell from their tables. Lately the management had taken to hanging transparent nets under the platforms, for safety's sake.

The Tones, father and son, were up near the roof, drinking with two lovelies. Silver towed Gallegher to a service lift, and the man closed his eyes as he was elevated skyward. The liquor in his stomach screamed protest. He lurched forward, clutched at Elia Tone's bald head, and dropped into a seat beside the magnate. His searching hand found Jimmy Tone's glass, and he drained it hastily.

"What the hell," Jimmy said.

"It's Gallegher," Elia announced. "And Silver. A pleasant surprise. Join us?"

"Only socially," Silver said.

Gallegher, fortified by the liquor, peered at the two men. Jimmy Tone was a big, tanned, handsome lout with a jutting jaw and an offensive grin. His father combined the worst features of Nero and a crocodile.

"We're celebrating," Jimmy said. "What made you change your mind, Silver? You said you had to work tonight."

"Gallegher wanted to see you. I don't know why."

Elia's cold eyes grew even more glacial. "All right. Why?"

"I hear I signed some sort of contract with you," the scientist said.

"Yeah. Here's a photostatic copy. What about it?"

"Wait a minute." Gallegher scanned the document. It was apparently his own signature. Damn that robot!

"It's a fake," he said at last.

Jimmy laughed loudly. "I get it. A hold up. Sorry, pal, but you're sewed up. You signed that in the presence of witnesses."

"Well—" Gallegher said wistfully. "I suppose you wouldn't believe me if I said a robot forged my name to it—"

"Haw!" Jimmy remakred.

"—hypnotizing you into believing you were seeing me."

Elia stroked his gleaming bald head. "Candidly, no. Robots can't do that."

"Mine can."

"Prove it. Prove it in court. If you can do that, of course—" Elia chuckled. "Then you might get the verdict."

Gallegher's eyes narrowed. "Hadn't thought of that. However—I hear you offered me a hundred thousand flat, as well as a weekly salary."

"Sure, sap," Jimmy said. "Only you said all you needed was twelve thousand. Which was what you got. Tell you what, though. We'll pay you a bonus for every usable product you make for Sonatone."

Gallegher got up. "Even my subconscious doesn't like these lugs," he told Silver. "Let's go."

"I think I'll stick around."

"Remember the fence," he warned cryptically. "But suit yourself. I'll run along."

Elia said, "Remember, Gallegher, you're working for us. If we hear of *you* doing any favors for Brock, we'll slap an injunction on you before you can take a deep breath."

"Yeah?"

The Tones deigned no answer. Gallegher unhappily found the lift and descended to the floor. What now? Joe.

Fifteen minutes later Gallegher let himself into his laboratory. The lights were blazing, and dogs were barking frantically for blocks around. Joe stood before the mirror, singing inaudibly.

"I'm going to take a sledge hammer to you," Gallegher said. "Start saying your prayers, you misbegotten collection of cogs. So help me, I'm going to sabotage you."

"All right, beat me," Joe squeaked. "See if I care. You're merely jealous of my beauty."

"Beauty?"

"You can't see all of it—you've only six senses."

"Five."

"Six. I've a lot more. Naturally my full splendor is revealed only to me. But you can see enough and hear enough to realize part of my loveliness, anyway."

"You squeak like a rusty tin wagon," Gallegher growled.

"You have dull ears. Mine are supersensitive. You miss the full tonal values of my voice, of course. Now be quiet. Talking disturbs me. I'm appreciating my gear movements."

"Live in your fool's paradise while you can. Wait'll I find a sledge."

"All right, beat me. What do I care?"

Gallegher sat down wearily on the couch, staring at the robot's transparent back. "You've certainly screwed things up for me. What did you sign that Sonatone contract for?"

"I told you. So Kennicott wouldn't come and bother me."

"Of all the selfish, lunk-headed . . . *uh!* Well, you got me into a sweet mess. The Tones can hold me to the letter of the contract unless I prove I didn't sign it. All right. You're going to help me. You're going into court with me and turn on your hypnotism or whatever it is. You're going to prove to a judge that you did and can masquerade as me."

"Won't," said the robot. "Why should I?"

"Because you got me into this," Gallegher yelped. "You've got to get me out!"

"Why?"

"Why? Because . . . uh . . . well, it's common decency!"

"Human values don't apply to robots," Joe said. "What care I for semantics? I refuse to waste time I could better employ admiring my beauty. I shall stay here before the mirror forever and ever——"

"The hell you will," Gallegher snarled. "I'll smash you to atoms."

"All right, I don't care."

"You don't?"

"You and your instinct for self-preservation," the robot said, rather sneeringly. "I suppose it's necessary for you, though. Creatures of such surpassing ugliness would destroy themselves out of sheer shame if they didn't have something like that to keep them alive."

"Suppose I take away your mirror?" Gallegher asked in a hopeless voice.

For answer Joe shot his eyes out on their stalks. "Do I need a mirror? Besides, I can vasten myself lokishly."

"Never mind that. I don't want to go crazy for a while yet. Listen, dope, a robot's supposed to *do* something. Something useful, I mean."

"I do. Beauty is all."

Gallegher squeezed his eyes shut, trying to think. "Now look. Suppose I invent a new type of enlarger screen for Brock. The Tones will impound it. I've got to be legally free to work for Brock, or——"

"Look!" Joe cried squeakily. "They go round! How lovely." He stared in ecstasy at his whirling insides. Gallegher went pale with impotent fury.

"Damn you!" he muttered. "I'll find some way to bring pressure to bear. I'm going to bed." He rose and spitefully snapped off the lights.

"It doesn't matter," the robot said. "I can see in the dark, too."

The door slammed behind Gallegher. In the silence Joe began to sing tunelessly to himself.

Gallegher's refrigerator covered an entire wall of his kitchen. It was filled mostly with liquors that required chilling, including the imported canned beer with which he always started his binges. The next morning, heavy-eyed and disconsolate, Gallegher searched for tomato juice, took a wry sip, and hastily washed it down with rye. Since he was already a week gone in bottle-dizziness, beer wasn't indicated now—he always worked cumulatively, by progressive stages. The food service popped a hermetically sealed breakfast on a table, and Gallegher morosely toyed with a bloody steak.

Well?

Court, he decided, was the only recourse. He knew little about the robot's psychology. But a judge would certainly be impressed by Joe's talents. The evidence of robots was not legally admissible—still, if Joe could be considered as a machine capable of hypnotism, the Sonatone contract might be declared null and void.

Gallegher used his visor to start the ball rolling. Harrison Brock still had certain political powers of pull, and the hearing was set for that very day. What would happen, though, only God and the robot knew.

Several hours passed in intensive but futile thought. Gallegher could think of no way in which to force the robot to do what he wanted. If only he could remember the purpose for which Joe had been created—but he couldn't. Still—

At noon he entered the laboratory.

"Listen, stupid," he said, "you're coming to court with me. Now."

"Won't."

"O.K." Gallegher opened the door to admit two husky men in overalls, carrying a stretcher. "Put him in, boys."

Inwardly he was slightly nervous. Joe's powers were quite unknown, his potentialities an x quantity. However, the robot wasn't very large, and, though he struggled and screamed in a voice of frantic squeakiness, he was easily loaded on the stretcher and put in a straitjacket.

"Stop it! You can't do this to me! Let me go, do you hear? Let me go!"

"Outside," Gallegher said.

Joe, protesting valiantly, was carried out and loaded into

an air-van. Once there, he quieted, looking up blankly at nothing. Gallegher sat down on a bench beside the prostrate robot. The van glided up.

"Well?"

"Suit yourself," Joe said. "You got me all upset, or I could have hypnotized you all. I still could, you know. I could make you all run around barking like dogs."

Gallegher twitched a little. "Better not."

"I won't. It's beneath my dignity. I shall simply lie here and admire myself. I told you I don't need a mirror. I can vasten my beauty without it."

"Look," Gallegher said. "You're going to a courtroom. There'll be a lot of people in it. They'll all admire you. They'll admire you more if you show how you can hypnotize people. Like you did to the Tones, remember?"

"What do I care how many people admire me?" Joe asked. "I don't need confirmation. If they see me, that's their good luck. Now be quiet. You may watch my gears if you choose."

Gallegher watched the robot's gears with smoldering hatred in his eyes. He was still darkly furious when the van arrived at the court chambers. The men carried Joe inside, under Gallegher's direction, and laid him down carefully on a table, where, after a brief discussion, he was marked as Exhibit A.

The courtroom was well filled. The principals were there, too—Elia and Jimmy Tone, looking disagreeably confident, and Patsy Brock, with her father, both seeming anxious. Silver O'Keefe, with her usual wariness, had found a seat midway between the representatives of Sonatone and Vox-View. The presiding judge was a martinet named Hansen, but, as far as Gallegher knew, he was honest. Which was something, anyway.

Hansen looked at Gallegher. "We won't bother with formalities. I've been reading this brief you sent down. The whole case stands or falls on the question of whether you did or did not sign a certain contract with the Sonatone Television Amusement Corp. Right?"

"Right, your honor."

"Under the circumstances you dispense with legal representation. Right?"

"Right, your honor."

"Then this is technically *ex officio*, to be confirmed later by appeal if either party desires. Otherwise after ten days the

verdict becomes official." This new type of informal court
hearing had lately become popular—it saved time, as well as
wear and tear on everyone. Moreover, certain recent scandals
had made attorneys slightly disreputable in the public eye.
There was a prejudice.

Judge Hansen called up the Tones, questioned them, and
then asked Harrison Brock to take the stand. The big shot
looked worried, but answered promptly.

"You made an agreement with the appellor eight days
ago?"

"Yes. Mr. Gallegher contracted to do certain work for
me—"

"Was there a written contract?"

"No. It was verbal."

Hansen looked thoughtfully at Gallegher. "Was the appellor intoxicated at the time? He often is, I believe."

Brock gulped. "There were no tests made. I really can't
say."

"Did he drink any alcoholic beverages in your presence?"

"I don't know if they were *alcoholic* bev—"

"If Mr. Gallegher drank them, they were alcoholic. Q.E.D.
The gentleman once worked with me on a case— However,
there seems to be no legal proof that you entered into any
agreement with Mr. Gallegher. The defendant—Sonatone—
possesses a written contract. The signature has been verified."

Hansen waved Brock down from the stand. "Now, Mr.
Gallegher. If you'll come up here— The contract in question
was signed at approximately 8 P.M. last night. You contend
you did not sign it?"

"Exactly. I wasn't even in my laboratory then."

"Where were you?"

"Downtown."

"Can you produce witnesses to that effect?"

Gallegher thought back. He couldn't.

"Very well. Defendant states that at approximately 8 P.M.
last night you, in your laboratory, signed a certain contract.
You deny that categorically. You state that Exhibit A, through
the use of hypnotism, masqueraded as you and successfully
forged your signature. I have consulted experts, and they are
of the opinion that robots are incapable of such power."

"My robot's a new type."

"Very well. Let your robot hypnotize me into believing
that it is either you, or any other human. In other words, let

it prove its capabilities. Let it appear to me in any shape it chooses."

Gallgher said, "I'll try," and left the witness box. He went to the table where the straitjacketed robot lay and silently sent up a brief prayer.

"Joe."

"Yes."

"You've been listening?"

"Yes."

"Will you hypnotize Judge Hansen?"

"Go away," Joe said. "I'm admiring myself."

Gallegher started to sweat. "Listen. I'm not asking much. All you have to do—"

Joe off-focused his eyes and said faintly, "I can't hear you. I'm vastening."

Ten minutes later Hansen said, "Well, Mr. Gallegher—"

"Your honor! All I need is a little time. I'm sure I can make this rattle-geared Narcissus prove my point if you'll give me a chance."

"This court is not unfair," the judge pointed out. "Whenever you can prove that Exhibit A is capable of hypnotism, I'll rehear the case. In the meantime, the contract stands. You're working for Sonatone, not for Vox-View. Case closed."

He went away. The Tones leered unpleasantly across the courtroom. They also departed, accompanied by Silver O'Keefe, who had decided which side of the fence was safest. Gallegher looked at Patsy Brock and shrugged helplessly.

"Well—" he said.

She grinned crookedly. "You tried. I don't know how hard, but—Oh, well, maybe you couldn't have found the answer, anyway."

Brock staggered over, wiping sweat from his round face. "I'm a ruined man. Six new bootleg theaters opened in New York today. I'm going crazy. I don't deserve this."

"Want me to marry the Tone?" Patsy asked sardonically.

"Hell, no! Unless you promise to poison him just after the ceremony. Those skunks can't lick me. I'll think of something."

"If Gallegher can't, you can't," the girl said. "So—what now?"

"I'm going back to my lab," the scientist said. "*In vino veritas*. I started this business when I was drunk, and maybe if I

get drunk enough again, I'll find the answer. If I don't sell
my pickled carcass for whatever it'll bring."

"O.K.," Patsy agreed, and led her father away. Gallegher
sighed, superintended the reloading of Joe into the van, and
lost himself in hopeless theorizing.

An hour later Gallegher was flat on the laboratory couch,
drinking passionately from the liquor bar, and glaring at the
robot, who stood before the mirror singing squeakily. The
binge threatened to be monumental. Gallegher wasn't sure
flesh and blood would stand it. But he was determined to
keep going till he found the answer or passed out.

His subconscious knew the answer. Why the devil had he
made Joe in the first place? Certainly not to indulge a Narcissus complex! There was another reason, a soundly logical
one, hidden in the depths of alcohol.

The x factor. If the x factor were known, Joe might be
controllable. He *would* be. X was the master switch. At
present the robot was, so to speak, running wild. If he were
told to perform the task for which he was made, a psychological balance would occur. X was the catalyst that would
reduce Joe to sanity.

Very good. Gallegher drank high-powered Drambuie.
Whoosh!

Vanity of vanities; all is vanity. How could the x factor be
found? Deduction? Induction? Osmosis? A bath in Drambuie—Gallegher clutched at his wildly revolving thoughts.
What had happened that night a week ago?

He had been drinking beer. Brock had come in. Brock had
gone. Gallegher had begun to make the robot—Hm-m-m. A
beer drunk was different from other types. Perhaps he was
drinking the wrong liquors. Very likely. Gallegher rose, sobered himself with thiamine, and carted dozens of imported
beer cans out of the refrigerator. He stacked them inside a
frost unit beside the couch. Beer squirted to the ceiling as he
plied the opener. Now let's see.

The x factor. The robot knew what it represented, of
course. But Joe wouldn't tell. There he stood, paradoxically
transparent, watching his gears go around.

"Joe."

"Don't bother me. I'm immersed in contemplation of
beauty."

"You're not beautiful."

"I am. Don't you admire my tarzeel?"

"What's your tarzeel?"

"Oh, I forgot," Joe said regretfully. "You can't sense that, can you? Come to think of it, I added the tarzeel myself after you made me. It's very lovely."

"Hm-m-m." The empty beer cans grew more numerous. There was only one company, somewhere in Europe, that put up beer in cans nowadays, instead of using the omnipresent plastibulbs, but Gallegher preferred the cans—the flavor was different, somehow. But about Joe. Joe knew why he had been created. Or did he? Gallegher knew, but his subconscious—

"Oh-oh! What about Joe's subconscious?

Did a robot have a subconscious? Well, it had a brain—

Gallegher brooded over the impossibility of administering scopolamin to Joe. Hell! How could you release a robot's subconscious?

Hypnotism.

Joe couldn't be hypnotized. He was too smart.

Unless—

Autohypnotism?

Gallegher hastily drank more beer. He was beginning to think clearly once more. Could Joe read the future? No; he had certain strange senses, but they worked by inflexible logic and the laws of probability. Moreover, Joe had an Achillean heel—his Narcissus complex.

There *might*—there just *might*—be a way.

Gallegher said, "You don't seem beautiful to me, Joe."

"What do I care about you? I *am* beautiful, and I can see it. That's enough."

"Yeah. My senses are limited, I suppose. I can't realize your full potentialities. Still, I'm seeing you in a different light now. I'm drunk. My subconscious is emerging. I can appreciate you with both my conscious and my subconscious. See?"

"How lucky you are," the robot approved.

Gallegher closed his eyes. "You see yourself more fully than I can. But not completely, eh?"

"What? I see myself as I am."

"With complete understanding and appreciation?"

"Well, yes," Joe said. "Of course. Don't I?"

"Consciously *and* subconsciously? Your subconsciousness might have different senses, you know. Or keener ones. I know there's a qualitative and quantitive difference in my outlook when I'm drunk or hypnotized or my subconscious is in control somehow."

"Oh." The robot looked thoughtfully into the mirror. "Oh."

"Too bad you can't get drunk."

Joe's voice was squeakier than ever. "My subconscious . . . I've never appreciated my beauty that way. I may be missing something."

"Well, no use thinking about it," Gallegher said. "You can't release your subconscious."

"Yes, I can," the robot said. "I can hypnotize myself."

Gallegher dared not open his eyes. "Yeah? Would that work?"

"Of course. It's just what I'm going to do now. I may see undreamed-of beauties in myself that I've never suspected before. Greater glories— Here I go."

Joe extended his eyes on stalks, opposed them, and then peered intently into each other. There was a long silence.

Presently Gallegher said, "Joe!"

Silence.

"*Joe!*"

Still silence. Dogs began to howl.

"Talk so I can hear you."

"Yes," the robot said, a faraway quality in its squeak.

"Are you hypnotized?"

"Yes."

"Are you lovely?"

"Lovelier than I'd ever dreamed."

Gallegher let that pass. "Is your subconscious ruling?"

"Yes."

"Why did I create you?"

No answer. Gallegher licked his lips and tried again.

"Joe. You've got to answer me. Your subconscious is dominant—remember? Now why did I create you?"

No answer.

"Think back. Back to the hour I created you. What happened then?"

"You were drinking beer," Joe said faintly. "You had trouble with the can opener. You said you were going to build a bigger and better can opener. That's me."

Gallegher nearly fell off the couch. "*What?*"

The robot walked over, picked up a can, and opened it

with incredible deftness. No beer squirted. Joe was a perfect can opener.

"That," Gallegher said under his breath, "is what comes of knowing science by ear. I build the most complicated robot in existence just so—" He didn't finish.

Joe woke up with a start. "What happened?" he asked.

Gallegher glared at him. "Open that can!" he snapped.

The robot obeyed, after a brief pause. "Oh. So you found out. Well, I guess I'm just a slave now."

"Damned right you are. I've located the catalyst—the master switch. You're in the groove, stupid, doing the job you were made for."

"Well," Joe said philosophically, "at least I can still admire my beauty, when you don't require my services."

Gallegher grunted. "You oversized can opener! Listen. Suppose I take you into court and tell you to hypnotize Judge Hansen. You'll have to do it, won't you?"

"Yes. I'm no longer a free agent. I'm conditioned to obey only one command—to do the job I was made for. Until you commanded me to open cans, I was free. Now I've got to obey you completely."

"Uh-huh," Gallegher said. "Thank God for that. I'd have gone nuts within a week otherwise. At least I can get out of the Sonatone contract. Then all I have to do is solve Brock's problem."

"But you did," Joe said.

"Huh?"

"When you made me. You'd been talking to Brock previously, so you incorporated the solution to *his* problem into me. Subconsciously, perhaps."

Gallegher reached for a beer. "Talk fast. What's the answer?"

"Subsonics," Joe said. "You made me capable of a certain subsonic tone that Brock must broadcast at irregular time intervals over his televiews—"

Subsonics cannot be heard. But they can be felt. They can be felt as a faint, irrational uneasiness at first, which mounts to a blind, meaningless panic. It does not last. But when it is coupled with A.A.—audience appeal—there is a certain inevitable result.

Those who possessed home Vox-View units were scarcely troubled. It was a matter of acoustics. Cats squalled; dogs howled mournfully. But the families sitting in their parlors, watching Vox-View stars perform on the screen, didn't really notice anything amiss. There wasn't sufficient amplification, for one thing.

But in the bootleg theater, where illicit Vox-View televisors were hooked up to Magnas—

There was a faint, irrational uneasiness at first. It mounted. Someone screamed. There was a rush for the doors. The audience was afraid of something, but didn't know what. They knew only that they had to get out of there.

All over the country there was a frantic exodus from the bootleg theaters when Vox-View first rang in a subsonic during a regular broadcast. Nobody knew why, except Gallegher, the Brocks, and a couple of technicians who were let in on the secret.

An hour later another subsonic was played. There was another mad exodus.

Within a few weeks it was impossible to lure a patron into a bootleg theater. Home televisors were far safer! Vox-View sales picked up—

Nobody would attend a bootleg theater. An unexpected result of the experiment was that, after a while, nobody would attend any of the legalized Sonatone theaters either. Conditioning had set in.

Audiences didn't know why they grew panicky in the bootleg places. They associated their blind, unreasoning fear with other factors, notably mobs and claustrophobia. One evening a woman named Jane Wilson, otherwise not notable, attended a bootleg show. She fled with the rest when the subsonic was turned on.

The next night she went to the palatial Sonatone Bijou. In the middle of a dramatic feature she looked around, realized that there was a huge throng around her, cast up horrified eyes to the ceiling, and imagined that it was pressing down.

She had to get out of there!

Her squall was the booster charge. There were other customers who had heard subsonics before. No one was hurt during the panic; it was a legal rule that theater doors be made large enough to permit easy egress during a fire. No one was hurt, but it was suddenly obvious that the public was being conditioned by subsonics to avoid the dangerous combination of throngs and theaters. A simple matter of psychological association—

Within four months the bootleg places had disappeared

and the Sonatone supertheaters had closed for want of patronage. The Tones, father and son, were not happy. But everybody connected with Vox-View was.

Except Gallegher. He had collected a staggering check from Brock, and instantly cabled to Europe for an incredible quantity of canned beer. Now, brooding over his sorrows, he lay on the laboratory couch and siphoned a highball down his throat. Joe, as usual, was before the mirror, watching the wheels go round.

"Joe," Gallegher said.

"Yes? What can I do?"

"Oh, nothing." That was the trouble. Gallegher fished a rumpled cable tape out of his pocket and morosely read it once more. The beer cannery in Europe had decided to change its tactics. From now on, the cable said, their beer would be put in the usual plastibulbs, in conformance with custom and demand. No more cans.

There wasn't *anything* put up in cans in this day and age. Not even beer, now.

So what good was a robot who was built and conditioned to be a can opener?

Gallegher sighed and mixed another highball—a stiff one. Joe postured proudly before the mirror.

Then he extended his eyes, opposed them, and quickly liberated his subconscious through autohypnotism. Joe could appreciate himself better that way.

Gallegher sighed again. Dogs were beginning to bark like mad for blocks around. Oh, well.

He took another drink and felt better. Presently, he thought, it would be time to sing "Frankie and Johnnie." Maybe he and Joe might have a duet—one baritone and one inaudible sub or supersonic. Close harmony.

Ten minutes later Gallegher was singing a duet with his can opener.

SYMBIOTICA

Astounding,

October

by Eric Frank Russell (1905-1978)

The late Eric Frank Russell was a talented writer who always seemed to be able to come up with new ideas. Perhaps his best known work is the novel Sinister Barrier, *based on one of Charles Fort's beliefs that appeared in the premier issue of* Unknown *in 1939. He won a Hugo Award for his story "Allamagoosa" in 1956.*

"Symbiotica" is one of the four stories in his "Jay Score" series that were collected as Men, Martians *and* Machines *in 1956. (See Volume III, 1941 of this series for "Jay Score.") Although the concept of symbiosis (the idea that species are linked together in mutually beneficial ways in nature) had long existed in biology, it did not receive widespread attention until the ecological concerns of the 1960s. "Symbiotica" beautifully illustrates the concept, and is a fine story besides.*

(Marty mentioned "Sinister Barrier" and that reminds me— When I read Charles Fort's series of columns in Astounding Stories *in the mid-1930s, I despised them. The best way I can describe Fort is by saying he was the von Daniken of his time. He used newspaper items, chosen uncritically, to support the most outlandish theories and managed to inspire a group of Forteans, otherwise presumably intelligent men, who accepted his ideas. Russell was one of them and, as Marty said, "Sinister Barrier" was rather Fortean in its outlook. And yet, at the time I read it, it seemed to me that "Sinister Bar-*

306

rier" was the best and most exciting story I had
ever read. That's how good a writer Russell was.
He made me swallow Fort, and do so enthusiasti-
cally.—I.A.)

I

They'd commissioned the *Marathon* to look over one
floating near Rigel, and what some of us would've liked to
know was how the devil our Terrestrial astronomers could
pick out likely specimens at such an arithmetical distance.
Last trip they'd found us a juicy job when they sent us to
that mechanical world and its watery neighbor near Bootes.
The *Marathon*, a newly designed Flettner job, was something
super. It hadn't a counterpart in our neck of the cosmos. So
our solution of the mystery was that the astronomers had got
hold of some instrument just as revolutionary.

Anyway, we'd covered the outward trip as per instructions
and were near enough to see that once again the astronomers
had lined them up for jackpot when they said that here was a
planet likely to hold life. Rigel blazed like a distant furnace
way over to starboard and about thirty degrees above the
plane that was horizontal at that moment. What I mean is
that the horizontal plane is always the ship's horizontal plane
and the cosmos has to relate itself to it whether it likes it or
not. But this plane's primary wasn't the faroff Rigel; it was a
kid brother sun just a fraction smaller and paler than Old
Sol. There were two more planets lying farther out; we'd seen
yet another the other side of the sun. That made four in all,
but three looked as sterile as a Venusian guppy's mind and
truly this one, the innermost, seemed interesting.

We swooped on it bow first. The way that world swelled in
the ports did things to my bowels. One trip on the casually
meandering *Upsydaisy* had given me my space legs and got
me used to living in suspense over umpteen million miles of
nothing, but I reckoned it'd take me another century or two
to get accustomed to the mad bull takeoffs and landings of
these Flettner craft. Young Wilson muttered in his harness
and I knew that he was following his pious custom of praying
for the safety of his precious photographic plates. From his
look of spiritual agony you'd have thought he was married to

the darned things. We landed, *kerumph!* The boat did a belly
slide.

"I wouldn't grieve," I told Wilson. "Those things never fry
you a chicken or shove a strawberry shortcake under your
drooling mouth."

"No," he admitted, "they don't." Struggling out of his
harness, he gave me the sour eye and growled. "How'd you
like me to spit in the needlers?"

"I wouldn't," I snapped.

"See?" he said, and forthwith beat it to find out whether
his stuff had survived.

Sticking my face to the nearest port, I stared through the
immensely strong Permex disk, had a look at the new world.
It was green. You'd've never believed any place could be so
thoroughly and absolutely green. The sun, which had appeared a primrose color out in space, now looked an extremely pale green. It poured down a flood of yellowy-green
light. The *Marathon* lay in a great glade that cut through a
mighty forest, and the glade was full of green grasses, herbs,
shrubs, and bugs. The forest was one mass of tremendous
growths that ranged in color from a very light silver-green to
a dark, glossy green that verged on black. Brennand came
and stood beside me; his face promptly went a spotty and bilious green as the light hit it. He looked like one of the un-
dead.

"Well, here we are again." He turned his attention from
the port, grinned at me, abruptly wiped away the grin. "Hey,
don't you be sick over me!"

"It's the light," I pointed out. "You look like something
floating in the scuppers of a moon-tripper."

"Thanks," he said.

"Don't mention it."

We stood there looking out and waiting for the general
summons to the conference which usually preceded the first
venture out of the ship. I was counting on maintaining my
lucky streak by being picked out of the hat, and Brennand
was itching to stamp his dogs outside, too. But the summons
didn't come.

After a while, Brennand said, "The skipper's slow. What's
holding him back?"

"No idea." I had another look at his leprous face. It was
awful. Judging by his expression, he wasn't enamored of my

features either. "You know what a cautious guy McNulty is. Guess that spree we had on Mechanistria persuaded him to count a hundred before giving an order."

"Yeah," agreed Brennand. "I'll go forward and see what's cooking."

He went along the passage. I couldn't go with him because I had to stand by the armory. You could never tell when they'd come for my stuff, and they had a habit of coming on the run. Brennand mooched disconsolately around the farther corner and had hardly gone when sure enough the exploring party barged in shouting for equipment. There were six of them: Molders, an engineer; Jepson, a navigating officer; Sam Hignett, our Negro surgeon; young Wilson and two Martians, Kli Dreen and Kli Morg.

"Huh, lucky again?" I growled at Sam, tossing him his needle ray and sundry oddments.

"Yes, sergeant." Sam's very white teeth glistened in his black face as he smiled with satisfaction. "The skipper says nobody's to go out afoot until we've first scouted around in No. 4 lifeboat."

Kli Morg got his needler in a long, snaky tentacle, waved the thing with bland disregard for everybody's personal safety, and chirruped, "Give Dreen and me our helmets."

"Helmets?" I looked from him to the Terrestrials. "You guys want spacesuits, too?"

"No," replied Jepson. "The stuff outside is up to fifteen pounds and so rich in oxygen you whizz while you think you're just ambling along."

"Mud," snapped Kli Morg. "Just like mud. Give us our helmets."

He got the helmets. These Martians were so accustomed to the three pounds atmospheric pressure of their native planet that anything heavier bothered them no end. That's why they had the use of the starboard air lock in which pressure was kept down to suit their taste. They could endure heavy pressure for a limited time, but sooner or later they'd wax unsociable and act like somebody had burdened them with all the world's woes.

We Terrestrials helped the pair of Martians to clamp down their goldfish bowls and exhaust the air to what they considered comfortable. If I'd lent a hand with this job once, I'd done it fifty times and it still seemed as wacky as ever. It isn't right that guys should be happy breathing in short whiffs.

Jay Score lumbered lithely into the armory just as I'd got all the clients decorated like Christmas trees. He leaned his three hundred pounds on the tubular barrier, which promptly groaned. He got off it quickly. His strong face was impassive as ever, his eyes brilliant with their unearthly light.

Shaking the barrer to see if it was wrecked, I told him, "The trouble with you is that you don't know your own strength."

"No?" he inquired, with utter lack of tone. He turned his attention to the others. "The skipper wants you to be extra careful. We can't permit any copy of what happened to Haines and his crew. Don't fly below one thousand feet, keep the autocamera running, keep eyes skinned and beat it back here immediately if you find anything worth reporting."

"Sure, Jay." Molders slung a couple of ammo belts over one arm. "We'll be careful."

They trailed out. Shortly, the lifeboat broke free with a squeaky parody of the *Marathon*'s deep-throated, sonorous drumming. It curved sharply into the green light, soared over the huge trees and diminished to a dot. Brennand came back, stood by the port, watched the boat vanish.

"McNulty's as leery as an old maid with a penitentiary out back."

"He's got plenty of reason," I pointed out. "He's got all the explaining to do when we return."

A smirk passed over his bilious complexion, and he went on, "I took a walk to the noisy end and found that a couple of stern-gang punks have beaten us all to it. They're outside playing duck-on-the-rock."

"Playing what?" I yelped.

"Duck-on-the-rock," he repeated, enjoying himself.

I beat it to stern, Brannand following with a wide grin. Sure enough, two of those dirty mechanics who polish the tail had pulled a fast one. They must have crawled out through a main driver not yet cool. Standing ankle-deep in the green growths, the pair of them were ribbing each other and shying pebbles at a small rock poised on top of a boulder. You'd have thought this was a Sunday-school picnic.

"Does the skipper know about this?"

"You bet he doesn't! Think he'd pick that pair of unshaven bums for first out?"

One of the couple turned, saw us staring at him through the port. He smiled toothily, shouted something we could not hear, jumped nine feet into the air, smacked his chest with a grimy hand. I gathered that the gravity was low, the oxygen high, and that he was feeling top notch. Brennand's face suggested that he was sorely tempted to crawl through a tube and join in the fun.

"McNulty'll skin those hoodlums," I said.

"Can't blame them. The artificial gravity's still on, the ship's full of fog and we've come a long, long way. It'll be great to get out. I could do some sand-castling myself."

"There isn't any sand."

The pair outside became tired of the rock, got themselves a supply of pebbles from somewhere down among the growths, advanced toward a big bush growing fifty yards from the *Marathon's* stern. The farther out they went, the more they were likely to be spotted from the skipper's lair, but they didn't care a hoot. They knew McNulty couldn't do much more than lecture them.

This bush stood between ten and twelve feet high, had a very thick mass of bright-green foliage at the top of a thin, willowy trunk. One of the approaching pair got a couple of yards ahead of the other, slung a pebble at the bush, struck it fair and square in the middle of the foliage. What happened then was so swift that we had the utmost difficulty in following it.

The pebble crashed into the foliage, the entire bush whipped over as if its trunk were a steel spring. A trio of tiny creatures fell out of its leaves, dropped from sight in the herbage below. The bush stood as before, undisturbed except for a minute quivering in its topmost branches. But the guy who'd flung the missile lay flat on his face. His following companion had stopped and was gaping like one petrified by the unexpected.

"Hey," squawked Brennand, "what happened there?"

Outside, the one who'd fallen flat stirred, rolled over, sat up and started picking at himself. The other one got to him, helped him pick. No sound came into the ship, so we couldn't hear what they might have been talking about or the oaths they were certainly using. The picking finished, the smitten one came unsteadily erect. His balance was lousy, and his companion supported him as they started back to the ship. Behind them, the bush stood as imperturbably as ever, even its vague quivers having died out.

Halfway to the *Marathon* the pebble-thrower teetered, went white. Then he licked his lips and keeled over. The other one looked anxiously back toward the bush as if he wouldn't have been surprised to find it charging them. Bending down, he got the body in a fireman's hitch, struggled with it toward the midway air lock. Jay Score met him before he'd heaved his load ten steps. Jay strode powerfully and confidently through the carpet of green, took the limp form from the other's arms, carried it like it was nothing. We raced toward bow to find out what had happened.

Jay brushed past us, carried his burden into our tiny surgery where Wally Simcox, Sām's sidekick, started working on the patient. The other guy hung around outside the door and looked sick. He looked even sicker when Captain McNulty came along and stabbed him with a stare before he went inside.

After half a minute, the skipper shoved out a red, irate face and bellowed, "Go tell Steve to order that boat back at once. He's to warn Sam he's urgently needed."

Pelting to the radio room, I passed the message on. Steve's eyebrows circumnavigated his face as he flicked a switch and cuddled the microphone to his chest. He rattled off the message, listened to the reply.

"They're returning at once."

Going back, I said to the uneasy duck-on-the-rock enthusiast, "What happened, stupid?"

He flinched. "That bush made a target of him and filled his area with darts. Long thin ones, like thorns. All over his face and neck and through his clothes. One of 'em made a pinhole in his ear, but they didn't get his eyes."

"Hell!" mouthed Brennand.

"A bunch of them whisked past me on my left, fell twenty feet behind. I heard 'em buzz like bees." He swallowed hard, shuffled his feet around. "It must have flung fifty or more. Guess I was lucky."

McNulty came out then. He looked pretty fierce, and the escapee promptly changed his mind about being lucky. The skipper said to him, very slowly and deliberately, "I'll deal with you later!" The look he passed across was enough to scorch the pants off a space cop. We watched his portly form parade down the passage.

The victim registered bitterness, scrammed to his post at stern. Next minute, the lifeboat made one complete circle overhead, descended with a thin zoom ending in a heavy *swish*. Its crew poured aboard the *Marathon* while the derricks clanked and rattled as they swung the lifeboat's twelve-ton bulk into the mother ship.

Sam was in the surgery an hour, came out shaking his head. "He's gone. We could do nothing for him."

"You mean he's—dead?"

"Yes. There's some sort of vegetable poison in those darts. It's virulent. We've no antidote for it. It seems to create blood clots, a condition of thromboses." He rubbed a weary hand over his crisp, curly hair, added, "I hate having to report this to the skipper."

We followed him toward bow. I stuck my eye to the peephole in the starboard air lock as I passed and had a look at what the Martians were doing. Kli Dreen and Kli Morg were playing chess with three others watching them. As usual, Sug Farn was asleep in one corner. It takes a Martian to be bored by adventure and to sweat with excitement over a slow-motion game like chess. They always did have an inverted sense of values.

Kli Dreen kept one saucerlike eye on the board while the other glanced idly at my face framed in the peephole. His two-way look gave me the meemies. I've heard that chameleons can swivel them independently, but no chameleon could do it so violently that the spectacle tied your own optic nerves in knots. I chased after Brennand and Sam. There was a strong smell of trouble up at that end.

II

The skipper fairly rocketed on getting Sam's report. His voice resounded loud and complainingly through the slightly open door.

"Hardly landed and already there's a casualty in the log . . . utter foolhardiness . . . more than a silly prank . . . disregard of standing orders . . . sheer indiscipline." He paused while he took a breath. "The responsibility is mine. Jay, summon the ship's company."

The general call sounded throughout the ship as Jay Score pressed the stud. We barged in, the rest following close behind, the Martians arriving last. Eyeing us sourly, McNulty strutted up and down, lectured us at some length. We'd been picked as the crew of the *Marathon* because we were believed

to be cool, calculating, well-disciplined individuals who'd
come of age and had long outgrown such infantile attractions
as duck-on-the-rock.

"Not to mention chess," he added, his manner decidedly
jaundiced.

Kli Dreen started, looked around to see whether the others
heard this piece of incredible blasphemy. Nobody spoke in
denial.

"Mind you," continued the skipper, thinking again, "I'm no
killjoy, but it is necessary to emphasize that there's a time
and place for everything." The Martians rallied. "And so,"
McNulty went on, "I want you always to—"

The ship's phone shrilled and cut him short. He had three
phones on his desk, and he gaped at them as if his ears were
telling him blatant lies. The ship's company looked each other
over to see who was missing. They were all supposed to be
there.

McNulty suddenly decided that to answer the phone would
be a simple way to solve the mystery. Grabbing up an instrument, he shouted, "Yes?" One of the other phones whirred,
proving him a bad picker. He slammed down the one he was
holding, took up another, repeated, "Yes?"

The phone made squeaky noises against his ear while his
florid features underwent the most peculiar contortions. "Who?
What?" he said, incredulously. "What awoke you?" His eyes
bugged out. "Somebody knocking at the door?" He planted the
phone with the air of a sleepwalker, then spoke weakly to Jay
Score. "That was Sug Farn. He complains that he's been
disturbed from a siesta by somebody hammering on the turnscrew of the storrad lock." Finding a chair, he flopped into it,
breathed asthmatically. His still popping eyes found Steve
Gregory, and he snapped, "For heaven's sake, man, control
those eyebrows of yours!"

Steve pushed one up, pulled one down, opened his mouth,
and tried to look contrite. The result was imbecilic. Jay Score
bent over the skipper, conversed with him in smooth under-
tones. McNulty nodded tiredly. Jay came erect, addressed us.

"All right men, get back to your stations. The Martians had
better don their helmets. We'll install a pom-pom in that lock
and have the armed lifeboat crew standing ready. Then we'll
open the lock."

That was sensible enough. You could see anyone approaching the ship in broad daylight, but you couldn't see

them once they'd got close up. The side ports didn't allow a sharp enough angle, besides which anyone standing under the lock would be shielded by the vessel's bulge. Nobody mentioned it, but the skipper had made an error in holding a revival meeting without keeping watch. Unless the hammerers chose to move farther out there was no way of getting a gander at them except by opening. And we weren't going to cook the dinner and make the beds before seeing what was outside, not after that nasty experience when intelligent machines had started to disassemble the ship around us.

Well, the dozy Sug Farn got pushed out of his corner and sent off for his goldfish bowl. We erected the pom-pom, its eighth barrel lined dead center on the closed door of the lock. Something made half a dozen loud clunks on the door as we finished. It sounded to me like a shower of flung stones.

Slowly the door spun along its worm and drew aside. A bright shaft of green light poured through, also a dollop of air that made me feel like a healthy hippopotamus. At the same time, Chief Engineer Douglas switched off the artificial gravity and we all dropped to two-thirds normal weight.

We watched the green illuminated opening so intently and anxiously that it was easy to imagine an animated metal coffin suddenly clambering through, its front lenses staring glassily. But there came no whir of hidden machinery, no menacing clank of metal arms and legs, nothing except the sigh of invigorating wind in the distant trees, the rustle of blown grasses and a queer, faraway throbbing that I couldn't identify.

So silent was everyone that Jepson's regular breathing was loud over my shoulder. The pom-pom gunner squatted in his metal seat, his hard eyes focused along the sights, his finger ready on the trigger, his right- and left-hand feeders ready with reserve belts. All three were busy with wads of gum. Then I heard a soft pad-pad of feet moving in the grass below the lock.

We all knew that McNulty would throw a fit if anyone walked out to the rim. He still nursed memories of the last time somebody did just that and got snatched out. So we stayed put like a gang of dummies, waiting, waiting. Presently, there sounded a querulous gabble beneath the opening. A smooth rock the size of a melon flew through the gap, missing Jepson by a few inches, shattered against the back wall.

Skipper or no skipper, I got fed up, hefted my needler in my right hand, prowled half-bent along the footwalk cut through the threads of the air-lock opening. I reached the rim which was about nine feet above ground level, shoved out my inquiring face. Molders pressed close behind me. The muffled throbbing was clearer than ever, but just as elusive.

Beneath me stood a band of six beings who were startlingly human in general appearance. Same bodily contours, same limbs and digits, same features. They differed from us mostly in that their skins were coarse and crinkly, a dull, dead green in color, and that they had a peculiar organ like the head of a green and fleshy chrysanthemum growing out of their chests. Their eyes were sharp and jet-black, they jerked them about with monkeylike alertness.

For all these differences, our similarity was so surprising that I stood staring at them while they stood staring back at me. Then one of them shrilled something in the singsong tones of an agitated Chinese, swung his right arm, did his best to bash out what I use for brains. I ducked, heard the missile swish over my hair. Molders also ducked it, involuntarily pushed against me. The thing crashed somewhere inside the lock, I heard someone spit a lurid oath just as I overbalanced and fell out.

Clinging grimly to the needle ray, I flopped into soft greenery, rolled like mad and bounced to my feet. At any instant, I expected to see a shower of meteors as I got slugged. But the six weren't there. They were fifty yards away and moving fast, making for the forest in long, agile leaps that would have shamed a hungry kangaroo. It would have been easy to have brought two or three of them down, but McNulty would have crucified me for that. Earth laws were strict about treatment of extramundane aborigines.

Molders dropped down beside me, followed by Jepson, Wilson, and Kli Yang. Wilson had his owl-eye camera with a color filter over the lens. He was wild with excitement.

"I got them from the fourth port. I made two shots as they scrammed."

"Humph!" Molders stared around. He was a big, burly, phlegmatic man who looked more like a Scandinavian brewer than a space bug. "Let's follow them to the edge of the forest."

"Yeah," agreed Jepson, heartily. He wouldn't have been so hearty if he'd known what was coming to him. Stamping his feet in the springy turf, he took a lungful of the oxygen-rich air. "This is our chance for a legitimate walk."

We started off without delay, knowing it wouldn't be long before the skipper began baying for us to come back. There was no man so hard to convince that risks have to be taken and that casualties are the price of knowledge, nor was there any man who went so far determined to do so little.

Reaching the verge of the forest, the six green ones stopped and watched our approach. If they were quick to beat it when caught out in the open, they weren't so quick when in the shadow of the trees which, for some unknown reason, inspired them with confidence. Turning his back to us, one of them doubled himself, peered at us from between his knees. It seemed senseless.

"What's that for?" growled Jepson.

Wilson sniggered dirtily, and said, "The Arab's farewell to his steed. It must be of cosmic significance."

"I could have scalded his seat if I'd been quick," remarked Jepson, aggrievedly. Then he put his foot in a hole and fell on his face.

The green ones set up a howl of glee, flung a volley of stones which all fell far short. We began to run, going along in great bounds. The low gravity wasn't spoiled by the thick blanket of air which, of course, pressed equally in all directions. Our weight was down so that we went along several laps ahead of Olympic champions. Five of the green ones promptly faded into the forest; the sixth shot like a squirrel up the trunk of the nearest tree. Their behavior told that they'd reason for regarding the trees as safe refuge against all assault.

We stopped about eighty yards from that tree which, for all we knew, might have been ready for us with a monster load of darts. Our minds recalled what one bush had done. Scattering in a thin line, each ready to flop at the first untoward motion, we edged cautiously toward it. Nothing happened. We went nearer. Still nothing happened. In this manner we got well beneath its branches and close to its trunk. There was a strange fragrance like that of a mixture of pineapple and cinnamon. The elusive throbbing was stronger than ever.

It was a big, imposing tree. Its dark green, fibrous trunk, seven feet in diameter, soared up to twenty-five feet before it split into strong, lengthy branches each of which terminated in one huge, spatulate leaf. Looking at that trunk, it was difficult to tell how our quarry had fled up it, but he'd performed the feat like an adept.

All the same, we couldn't see him. Carefully, we went around the tree, gazing up into its great branches through which the green light filtered in large mosaic patterns. There was not a sign of him. No doubt about it, he was somewhere up there, but he simply couldn't be spotted by us. There wasn't any way in which he could have passed from this tree to its nearest neighbor, neither could he have come down. Our view up this lump of alien timber was fairly good considering the peculiar light, but the more we stared the more invisible he remained.

"That's a puzzler!" Jepson stepped well away from the trunk, seeking a better angle of view.

With a mighty *swoosh* a branch above his head drove down. Its spatulate leaf smacked him squarely in the back and a waft of pineapple and cinnamon went all over the place. Just as swiftly, the branch went up, carrying Jepson high into the air. Swearing like a tail mechanic, he struggled furiously while we gathered below him. He was stuck to the underside of that great leaf, gradually became covered in thick, yellowy-green goo as he writhed. The stuff must have been fifty times stickier than birdlime.

Together we roared at him to keep still before he got the deadly junk spread all over his face. Already his clothes were covered with it, his left arm tied up in it. He looked a mess. It was obvious that once he smeared it over his mouth and nostrils he'd stick up there and quietly suffocate.

Molders had a try at getting up the trunk, found it impossible. He edged out to have a look upward, came in when he noticed another leaf in a strategic position. The safest place was beneath the unfortunate Jepson. A little over twenty feet up, the goo was slowly spreading over its victim and I reckoned that in half an hour he'd be completely covered—in much less if he wriggled around. All this time the dull pulsations continued as if ticking off the last moments of the doomed. They made me think of jungle drums heard through thick walls.

Gesturing to the golden cylinder which was the *Marathon*

lying five hundred yards away in the glade, Wilson said, "Let's beat it back and get ropes and steel dogs. We'll soon bring him down."

"No," I answered. "We'll get him down a darned sight faster than that." Whereupon I aimed my needle ray at the point where Jepson's leaf joined the branch. The beam lanced forth at full strength.

The leaf dropped off and the tree went mad. Jepson fell into soft, springy undergrowth, the leaf still firmly fastened to his back. He landed with a wild yelp and a flood of curses. While we all lay flat, frantically trying to bury ourselves deeper, the tree thrashed around, its gum-laden spatulates hungry for vengeance.

One persistent branch kept beating within a yard of my head as I tried to shove said top-piece below ground. I hated the stink of pineapple and cinnamon that permeated the air. And it made me sweat to think how my lungs would strain, my eyes pop, and my heart burst if I got a dollop of that junk slap in the face. I'd sooner've been neatly needled.

The tree ended its wild larruping, stood like a dreaming giant liable to wake into frenzy at any moment. Crawling to Jepson, we dragged him out of reach. He couldn't walk, his jackboots and the legs of his pants being firmly stuck together. His left arm was just as securely gummed to his side. He was in an awful pickle, cursed steadily and without pause for breath or thought. We'd never suspected him of such fluency. But we got him into the safety of the glade, and it was there I thought up a few words he'd overlooked.

II

Molders stolidly said nothing, contenting himself with listening to Jepson and me. Molders had helped me do the dragging and now neither of us could let go. We were fixed to the original victim, bonded like brothers but not talking like brothers. There was nothing to do but carry Jepson bodily with our hands remaining on the most inconvenient parts of his anatomy. He had to go horizontally and face downward, as if he were a drunk getting frog-marched to barracks. He was still adorned with the leaf. He was still reciting.

The task wasn't lightened by that young fool Wilson who thought there was something funny in other people's misfortunes. He followed us, snapping his accursed camera which I could have stuffed down his gullet with the greatest of pleasure. He was too happy about the fact that there wasn't any goo on him.

Jay Score, Brennand, Armstrong, Petersen, and Drake met us as we lumbered awkwardly, across the sward. They looked curiously at Jepson, listened to him with much respect. We warned them not to touch. The pair of us weren't feeling too sprightly by the time we reached the *Marathon*. Jepson's weight was only two-thirds normal, but after five hundred yards he seemed like the last remains of a glutinous mammoth.

We dumped him on the grass below the open lock, perforce sitting with him. The faint booming sound was still coming out of the forest. Jay went inside the ship, brought out Sam and Wally to see what they could do about the superadhesive. The stuff was stiffening, growing gradually harder. My hands and fingers felt as if they'd been set into glassite gloves.

Sam and Wally tried cold water, lukewarm water, and hot water, but none of it did any good. Chief Engineer Douglas obliged them with a bottle of rocket fuel. That didn't work either. They had a go with some special gasoline which Steve Gregory kept for the crew's cigarette lighters. They wasted their time. That gasoline could play hell with rubber, but it couldn't dissolve this stuff.

"Stick it, fellers!" advised Wilson, cackling loudly. Jepson made sulphuric mention of this idiot's parents. I enlarged upon his grandparents. Jepson turned to the subject of his nonexistent progeny. Molders looked stolid, said nothing. "You sure are in a fix," went on Wilson. "By gum!"

Then Sam came out with some iodine. It didn't work, but it did make a terrible stink. Molders permitted his face to look slightly pained. Some nitric acid caused bubbles on the surface of the semi-hard goo, but did no more than that. It was risky stuff to use, anyway. Frowning, Sam went back to look for something else, passed Jay Score coming out to see how we were doing. Jay stumbled as he got near, a strange thing for him to do considering his superhuman sense of balance. His solid three hundred pounds nudged young Wilson between the shoulder blades and that grinning ape promptly flopped against Jepson's legs. Wilson struggled and changed his tune, but stayed stuck. Jepson gave him the sardonic haha, and the other didn't enjoy it a bit.

Picking up the dropped camera, Jay dangled it in one powerful hand, said contritely, "I never missed a step before. It is most unfortunate."

"Unfortunate, hell!" yelled Wilson.

Sam came out with a big glass jar, dribbled its contents over my gooey hands. The ghastly green covering at once thinned into a weak slime and my hands came free.

"Ammonia," remarked Sam. He needn't have mentioned it—I could smell the pungent stuff. It was a good solvent, and he soon had us cleaned up.

Then I chased Wilson three times around the ship. He was too fast for me. We were just about to go aboard to tell our tale to the skipper when that tree started threshing again. You could see its deadly branches beating the air and hear the violent *swoosh* of them even at that distance. Pausing beneath the lock, we watched the spectacle wonderingly. Suddenly, Jay Score spoke, his voice metallic, harsh.

"Where's Kli Yang?"

None of us knew. Now I came to think about it, I couldn't recall him being with us while we dragged Jepson home. The last I remembered of him was when he stood beside me under that tree and his saucer eyes gave me the creeps by carefully scanning two opposite branches at once. Armstrong shot into the ship, came out with the report that Kli Yang definitely wasn't there. His own eyes as saucerlike as the missing Martian's, Wilson said that he didn't remember Kli Yang coming out of the forest. Upon which we snatched up our needlers and made for that tree at the run. All the while, the tree continued to larrup around like a crazy thing, tied down by its own roots.

Reaching the monstrous growth, we made a circle just beyond the sweep of its treacherous leaves, had a look to see where the Martian was wrapped in glue. He wasn't wrapped in glue. We found him forty feet up the trunk, five of his powerful tentacles clamped around its girth, the other five embracing the green native we'd pursued. His captive was struggling wildly and futilely, all the time yelling a high-pitched stream of gibberish.

Carefully, Kli Yang edged down the trunk. The way he looked and moved made him resemble an impossible cross between a college professor and an educated octopus. His eyes rolling with terror, the native battered at Kli's glassite helmet. Kli blandly ignored the hostility, reached the branch that had caught Jepson, didn't descend any farther. Still grasping the furiously objecting green one, he crept along the whipping limb until he reached its leafless end. At that point, he and the native were being waved up and down in twenty-five-feet sweeps.

Timing himself, he cast off at the lowermost point of one beat, scuttled from reach before another eager branch could swat him. There was a singing howl from the nearer parts of the forest and something that looked like a blue-green coconut shot out of the shadows and broke at Drake's feet. The thing was as thin and brittle as an empty eggshell, had a white inner surface, and contained nothing. Kli Yang took no notice of the howls or the missile, bore his still struggling captive toward the *Marathon*.

Hanging back, Drake peered curiously at the coconut or whatever it was, struck the fragments of shell with his boot. He caught the full benefit of something invisible that was floating up from it, sucked in his cheeks, screwed up his eyes and backed away. Then he retched. He did it so violently that he fell over as he ran. We'd the sense to pick him up and rush him after Kli without getting too nosy about what had bitten him. He continued to regurgitate all the way across the grass, recovered just as we came under the ship's bulging side.

"Holy smoke!" he wheezed, "what a stench! I'd make a skunk smell like the rose of the animal world." He wiped his lips. "My stomach turned right over."

Looking up Kli, we found that his captive had been conducted to the galley for a peacemaking feed. Kli dragged off his helmet, said, "That tree wasn't so difficult for me to mount. It walloped around as I went up, but it couldn't get at anything on its own trunk." He sniffed, rubbed his flat, Red Planet face with the flexible tip of a great tentacle. "Don't know how you bipeds can swallow this soup which you're pleased to regard as air."

"Where'd you find the greenie, Kli?" asked Brennand.

"He was stuck to the trunk more than forty feet up. His whole front fitted nearly into an indentation shaped like himself, and his back matched the trunk so perfectly that I couldn't see him until he moved uneasily as I got near him." He picked up the helmet. "It was a most wonderful sample of camouflage." He looked at the helmet with one eye, kept the other on the interested Brennand, made a gesture of disgust. "How about pulling down the pressure some place where higher forms of life can live in peace?"

"We'll pump out the port lock," Brennand promised. "And don't be so all-fired snooty, you caricature of a rubber spider."

"Bah!" said Kli, with great dignity. "Who invented chess? And who can't even play duck-on-the-rock without grabbing the grief?" With that insulting reference to Terrestrial inexpertness at chess, he slapped on his glassite dome. I pumped it down for him. "Thanks!" he said, through the diaghragm.

Now to get the low-down on the greenie.

Captain McNulty himself interviewed the native. The skipper sat grandly behind his metal desk, eyed the jittery captive with a mixture of pomposity and kindliness. The native stood before him, his black optics jerking around fearfully. At that close range you could see he was wearing a loincloth that matched his own skin. His back was several shades darker than his front, coarser, more fibrous, with little nodules here and there—perfect simulation of the surface of the trunk of the tree in which he'd sought refuge. Even his loincloth was darker at the back than at the front. His feet were broad and bare; the toes double-jointed and as long as the fingers of his hands. Except for the loincloth, he was completely naked and had no weapons. The queer chrysanthemum growing out of his chest attracted all eyes.

"Has he been given a meal?" asked the skipper, full of solicitude.

"He was offered one," Jay told him. "He refused it. As far as I can make out, he wants to go back to his tree."

"Hm-m-m," grunted McNulty. "In due time, in due time." He assumed the expression of a benevolent uncle, said to the native, "What's your name?"

The green one grasped the note of interrogation, waved his arms, broke into an untranslatable tirade. On and on he went, helping his gabble with many emphatic but incomprehensible gestures. His language was very liquid, his voice singsong.

"I see," murmured McNulty as the flood of talk petered out. He blinked at Jay Score. "Think this fellow is telepathic, like those lobster things were?"

"It is much to be doubted. I'd put him at the level of a Congo pygmy—maybe lower. He doesn't even possess a simple spear, let alone bow and arrow or a blowpipe."

"Yes, that's how he looks to me." Still maintaining his soothingly paternal air, McNulty went on, "All right, Jay. There's no common basis on which we can gain his understanding at the start, so I guess we'll have to create one. We'll dig up a natural linguist, set him to learning the rudiments of this fellow's language and teaching him some of ours."

"I've got the advantage of a mechanical memory—let me have a try," suggested Jay. He approached the green native, his huge, well-proportioned body moving quietly on the sponge-rubber cushions of his dogs. The native didn't like his size or his bearing; neither did he approve of those brightly lit eyes. He backed away from Jay, backed right to the wall, his optics darting hither and thither.

Jay stopped as he saw the other's fear, slapped his own top-piece with a hand that could have knocked mine clean off my neck. He said, "Head." He did it half a dozen times, repeating, "Head, head."

The green one wasn't so stupid; he caught on, faltered, "*Mah.*"

Touching his own head again, Jay said, inquiringly, "*Mah?*"

"*Bya!*" lilted the other, starting to recover his composure.

"See, it's dead easy," approved McNulty. "*Mah*—head; *bya*—yes."

"Not necessarily," Jay contradicted. "It all depends upon how his mind translated my action. *Mah* might mean head, face, man, hair, god, mind, thought, or alien, or even the color black. If he's thinking of my hair and his own, then *mah* probably does mean black, while *bya* may mean not yes, but green."

"Oh, I hadn't thought of that." The skipper looked crushed.

"We'll have to carry on with this performance until we've picked up enough words to form lame sentences. Then we can deduce further meanings from the context. Give me a few days."

"Go ahead. Do your best, Jay. We can't expect to be able to talk turkey in the first five minutes. It isn't reasonable."

Taking our prisoner to the rest room, Jay summoned Minshull and Petersen. He thought three might just as well learn something as one. Minshull and Petersen were both hot on languages, speaking Esperanto, Ido, Venusian, low Martian, and high Martian. They were the only ones aboard the ship

who could give our chess maniacs a boiling in their own
lingo.

I found Sam in the armory, waiting to hand in the stuff
he'd taken out, and I said to him, "What did you see from
the lifeboat, Sam?"

"Not so much. We weren't out long enough. Didn't get
more than a hundred and twenty miles away. There was forest,
nothing but forest with glades here and there. A couple of
glades were the size of counties. The biggest of them lay at the
end of a long lake. There were several rivers and streams."

"Any signs of life?"

"None." He gestured down the passage toward the rest
room where Jay and the others were cross-examining the native. "It seems there's superior life in the forest, but you can
detect no signs of it from above. Wilson's processing his
reel—I doubt whether his camera caught anything that we
missed."

"Ah, well," I said, "one twenty miles in one direction is
nothing from which to estimate a world. I don't let myself be
deluded, not since that drummer sold me a can of striped
paint."

He chuckled. "Didn't it come out?"

"I laid it wrong side up," I told him.

It was right in the middle of that bantering that a powerful
idea smote me. I followed him out of the armory, made a
rush to the radio room. Steve Gregory was sitting by his instruments trying to look busy doing nothing. I was all set to
wake him with my brain wave.

IV

As Steve looked up inquiringly, I said to him, "Hey, how
about combing the bands?"

"Uh?"

"Remember those weird whistles and waterfalls you picked
up on Mechanistria? Well, if anyone's radiating here, couldn't
you detect 'em?"

"Sure." He kept his bushy eyebrows still for once, but
spoiled it by waggling his ears. "If anyone was radiating."

"Go ahead and find out. It'll tell us something. What're
you waiting for?"

"Have you kept those needlers cleaned and charged?" he
asked.

I stared at him. "You bet I have! They're always ready for action. That's my job."

"And this one's mine," he said, dryly. He waved the ears again. "You're hours behind the times. I searched the ether immediately when we landed, got nothing but a faint hiss on twelve point three meters. It was Rigel's characteristic discharge and came from that way. D'you think I'm that snake-armed snorer Sug Farn?"

"No, I don't. Sorry, Steve—it just struck me as a bright idea."

"Oh, it's O.K., sergeant," he said, amiably. "Every man to his job and every tail mechanic to his dirt." Idly he twiddled the shining dials of his slow-motion selectors.

The loudspeaker coughed as if it were clearing its throat, then announced in sharp tones, *"Pip-pip-whop! Pip-pip-whop!"*

Nothing could have been better calculated to upset the determined serenity of his brows. I'll swear that after they'd entered his hair they continued over the top, down the back and lodged under his collar.

"Morse," he said, in the complaining tone of a hurt child.

"I always thought Morse was a code, not a mode," I remarked. "Anyway, if it is Morse, you'll be able to translate it." I paused as the loudspeaker shouted me down with, *"Pip-pipper-pee-eep-whop!"* then I concluded, "Every cat to his ash can."

" 'Tain't Morse," he contradicted himself. "But it's spark signals." He might have frowned if it hadn't taken too long to drag the brows back. Giving me one of those tragic looks you get sometimes, he snatched a pad, started recording the impulses.

The spacesuits, pom-pom chargers and other things had to be done, so I left him, returned to the armory, got on with my work. He was still fiddling around when darkness fell. So were Jay and his gang, but not for long.

The sun sank, its long, greenish streamers faded from the sky and a velvet pall covered the forest and the glade. I ambled along the passage toward the gallery and was passing the rest room when its door jerked open and the green native burst out. His face was desperate, his legs going as if there were a thousand international smackers tied to the tape. Minshull yelped somewhere back of him as he jumped full tilt into my ready arms. The greenie squirmed like an eel, beat at my face, tried to kick my legs off my torso with his bare feet. His rough, harsh body exuded a weak odor of pineapple and cinnamon.

The others pounced out, got him tight, talked to him in halting words until he relaxed. His eyes shifty, anxious, he jabbered excitedly to Jay Score, making urgent gestures and waving his woody arms around in a way that reminded me of branches beating the air. Jay soothed him with fair if faltering speech. It looked as if they'd picked up enough words to get along, though not enough to understand each other perfectly. Still, they were managing.

Eventually, Jay said to Petersen, "Tell the skipper I want to let Kala go."

Petersen cleared off, came back in a minute. "He says do whatever you think is best."

"Good." Conducting the native to the opening of the starboard lock, Jay yapped to him briefly, let him go. The greenie dived off the rim. Someone in the forest must have owed him for a loincloth because his feet made rapid brushing sounds as he fled across the turf. Jay stood on the rim, his flaming orbs staring into outer gloom.

"Why let him go, Jay?"

Turning, he said to me, "I've tried to persuade him to come back at sunup. He may, or he may not—it remains to be seen. We didn't have time to get much out of him, but his language is exceedingly simple and we picked up enough of it to learn that he calls himself Kala of the tribe of Ka. All members of his tribe are named Ka-something, such as Kalee, Ka'noo, or Kaheer."

"Something like the Martians with their Klis and Leids and Sugs," I remarked.

"Something," he agreed, not caring what the Martians might think of being compared with the green aborigines. "He also told us that every man has his tree, every gnat its lichen. I can't understand what he means by that, but he satisfied me that his life depended upon his being with his tree during darkness. It was imperative. I tried to delay him, but his need was almost pitiful. He was willing to die rather than be away from his tree."

"Sounds silly to me." I blew my nose, grinned widely. "It sounds even sillier to Jepson."

Jay stared again into the deep murkiness from which came

strange, nocturnal scents and those everlasting pulsations. Quietly, he said, "I also learned that there are others in the dark, others mightier than the Ka. They have much *gamish*."

"They have what?"

"Much *gamish*," he repeated. "That word defeated me. He used it again and again. He said that the *Marathon* had much *gamish*, I had much *gamish* and that Kli Yang had very much *gamish*. Captain McNulty, it appeared, had only a little. The Ka have none at all."

"Was it something of which he was afraid?"

"Not exactly. As far as I could make out, anything unusual or surprising or unique is chock-full of *gamish*. Anything just abnormal has a lesser amount of *gamish*. Anything ordinary has none at all."

"This," I said, "goes to show the difficulties of communication. It isn't as easy as the people back home think it ought to be."

"No, it isn't." His gleaming optics shifted toward Armstrong leaning against the pom-pom. "You doing this guard?"

"Until twelve. Kelly follows me."

Picking Kelly for guard was poor psychology. That tattooed specimen was welded to a three-foot spanner and in any hot moment was liable to wield said instrument in preference to such new-fangled articles as pom-poms and needlers. Rumor had it that he'd held the lump of iron at his wedding and that his wife had gained a divorce on account of the thing's effect on her morale. My private opinion was that Kelly had a Neanderthal mind.

"We'll shut the lock," decided Jay, "fresh air or no fresh air." That was characteristic of him, and what made him seem so human—he could mention fresh air as if he used it himself. The casual way he did it made you forget that he'd never taken a breath since the day old Knud Johanssen stood him on his dogs. "Let's plug in the turnscrew." Turning his back upon the throbbing gloom, he started to walk into the lighted lock, treading carefully in the cutout of the threads.

A piping voice sprang from the darkness; it ejaculated, "*Nou baiders!*"

Jay stopped dead. His eyes were glowing. Feet padded outside just underneath the lock. Something spherical and glassy soared through the worm, went over Jay's left shoulder, broke to shards on the top recoil chamber of the pom-pom. A thin, golden liquid splashed around, vaporized instantly.

Reversing, Jay faced the black opening. Armstrong got to the wall, put out a thumb to jab the general alarm stud. Without touching the stud, Armstrong went down as if batted by an invisible club. My needler out, its muzzle extended, I began to move cautiously forward, saw the glittering thread of the worm framing a picture of Jay standing against the ebony background. It was a hell of a mistake—I should have gone for that stud. Three steps, and the whole picture swelled like a blown bubble, the circle widened, the threads of the worm became broad and deep with Jay as a gigantic shape in the middle. The bubble burst and I went down as soggily as Armstrong had done.

Don't know how long I stayed that way, for when I opened my eyes it was with the faint memory of hearing much shouting and stamping of feet around my prostrate form. Things must have happened over and all around me while I lay like a corpse. Now I was still flat. I reposed full length on deep, dew-soaked turf with the throbbing forest close on my left, the indifferent stars peering at me from the vault of night. I was bound up like an Egyptian mummy. Jepson was another mummy at one side of me; Armstrong and several more at the other.

Several hundreds of yards away, noises were still spoiling the silence of the night, a mixture of occasional Terrestrial oaths and many queer, alien pipings. The *Marathon* lay over there; all that could be seen of her in the general blackness was the funnel of light pouring from her open lock. The light flickered, waxed and waned, once or twice was momentarily obliterated. There was a struggle on that shaft of light which became blocked as the fight swayed to and fro.

Jepson was snoring as if it were Saturday night in the old home town, but Armstrong was in full possession of his wits and tongue. He cursed luridly. Rolling over, he started to chew at the knots of Blaine's bindings. Something vaguely human emerged silently from the darkness, smote downward. Armstrong went quiet.

Blinking my eyes, I adapted them enough to make out many more noiseless shapes standing around us. Keeping still and behaving myself, I thought noncomplimentary thoughts about McNulty, the *Marathon*, old Flettner who'd invented the ship and all the public-spirited guys who backed him

morally and financially. I'd always had the feeling that sooner
or later they would be the death of me.

Deep down inside me, a tiny voice said, "Sergeant, d'you
remember that promise you made your mother about obscene
language? D'you remember when you gave that guppy a can
of condensed milk for a pinfire opal not as big as the city
clock? Repent, sergeant, while there yet is time!"

The distant pipings arose crescendo, the few earthly voices
died out. There sounded occasional smashings of light, brittle
things. More shapes brought more bodies, dumped them
beside us, melted back into the gloom. I wish I could have
counted the catch, but darkness didn't permit it. All the newcomers were unconscious. They revived rapidly. I could recognize Brennand's angry voice and the skipper's asthmatic
breathing.

A blue star shone through the thin fringe of a drifting
cloud as the fight ended. The succeeding pause was ghastly; a
solemn, brooding silence broken only by the scuffle of many
feet through the grass and the steady pumping in the forest.

Forms gathered around us in large number. The glade was
full of them. Hands lifted me, felt my bonds, tossed me into
a wicker hammock. I went up shoulder-high, was borne
along. You'd have thought I was a defunct wart hog being
toted in some sportsman's line of native porters. Just meat—
that was me. Just a trophy of the chase. I wondered whether
God would confront me with that guppy.

The caravan filed into the forest, my direction of progress
being head first. Another hammock followed my feet and I
could sense rather than see a string of them farther behind.
Jepson was the sardine following me; he went along making a
loud recitation about how he'd got tied up ever since he
landed in this unprintable world. Curving warily around one
dim tree, our line marched boldly under the next, dodged the
third. How the deuce our bearers could tell one growth from
another in this lousy light was beyond my comprehension.

We'd just got deep into the deeper darkness when a
tremendous explosion sounded way back in the glade and a
column of fire lit up the whole sky. Even the fire looked
faintly green. Our line stopped. Two or three hundred voices
cheeped querulously, running from the front past me to a
hundred yards farther back. "They've blown up the good old
Marathon," thought I. "Ah, well, all things come to an end,
including the flimsiest hope of returning home."

The squeakers were drowned out as the noisy pillar of flame built itself up to a roar. My hammock started to jump as its bearers reacted. The way they put on the pace had to be experienced to be believed; I almost flew along, dodging this tree, but not that, sometimes avoiding half-seen growths that weren't trees at all. My heart was in my boots.

The bellowing back in the glade suddenly ended in a mighty thump, and a crimson spear flung itself into the sky and stabbed the clouds. It was a spectacle I'd seen before: it was a spaceship going up. It was the *Marathon*!

Were these creatures so talented that they could pick up a thoroughly strange vessel and take it wherever they wanted it? Were these the beings described as superior to the Ka? The whole thing was incongruous—expert astronauts carrying their prisoners in wicker hammocks. Besides, the way they'd jabbered and put on the pace suggested that the *Marathon's* spurt of life had taken them by surprise. The mystery was one I couldn't solve.

While the fiery trail of the spaceship arced northward, our party pressed hurriedly on. There was one stop during which our captors congregated together, but their continual piping suggested that they hadn't stopped for a meal. Twenty minutes afterward there was another halt and a hell of a row in front. Guards kept close to us while a short distance ahead sounded a vocal uproar in which many voices vied with a loud mewing and much beating of great branches. I tried to imagine a bright green tiger.

Things went *phut-phut* and the mewing ended in a choking cough. The sound of whipping branches died away. We moved on, making a wide curve around a monstrous growth that I strained in vain to see. If only this world had possessed a moon. But there was no moon. There were only the stars and the clouds and the forest from which came that all-pervading beat.

Dawn broke as the line warily bent away from a small clump of apparently innocent briers. We came to the bank of a wide river. Here, we could give our guards the once-over as they shepherded bearers and burdens down the bank. They were creatures very much like the Ka, only taller, more slender, with big, intelligent eyes. They had the same fibrous skins, grayer, not so green, and the same chrysanthemums on their chests. Unlike the Ka, their middles were clothed in pleated garments, they had harness of woven fiber, and wooden accounterments which included things like complicated blow-guns and bowl-shaped vessels having a bulbous container in the base. A few also bore panniers holding small spheres like the one that had laid me flat in the air lock.

Craning my head, I tried to see more, but could only discern Jepson in the next hammock and Brennand in the one behind that. The next instant, my hammock was unceremoniously dumped by the water's brink, Jepson's beside mine, the rest in a level row.

Jepson screwed round his head, looked at me, and said, "The punks!"

"Take it easy," I suggested. "If we play with them, they may give us more rope."

"And," he said, viciously, "I don't like guys who try to be funny at the wrong time."

"I wasn't trying to be funny," I snapped. "We're all bound to hold our own opinions, aren't we?"

"There you go again!" He writhed around on his hammock, tried to stretch his fastenings. "Some day I'll bind you!"

It's no use talking with a guy like that, so I didn't answer. The light waxed stronger, shone greenly through the thin, green mist hanging over the green river. I could now see Blaine and Minshull tied up beyond Armstrong, and the portly form of McNulty beyond them. We'd traveled about two hours.

Ten of our captors went along the line opening jackets and shirts, baring our chests. They had with them a supply of the bowls with bulbous containers. Two of them pawed my uniform apart, got my chest exposed, stared at it like Anthony stared at Cleopatra. Something about it struck them as wonderful, and it wasn't my reserve beard. It didn't require much brains to tell that they missed my chrysanthemum and couldn't see how I'd got through life without it. They called their fellows, the whole gang debated the subject while I lay like a sacrificial virgin. Then they decided that they'd struck a new line of research and went hot along the trail.

Seizing Blaine and the boob who'd played duck-on-the-rock, they untied them, stripped them down to the raw, examined them as if they were prize cattle at an agricultural exhibition. One of them prodded Blaine in the solar plexus, whereat he jumped the fellow with a savage whoop and brought him down. The other nudist joined in. Armstrong, who never had been a ninety-pound weakling, promptly burst his bonds, came up dark-faced with the effort and roared into the fray. Fragments of his mangled hammock swung and bounced on his beefy back.

All along the line the rest of us made mighty efforts to break free, but in vain. Green ones centered on the scene of the struggle, brittle spheres plopped all around the three madly fighting Earthmen. The tail mechanic and Blaine collapsed together, going down as if in a sleep. Armstrong shuddered and roared, teetered and pulled himself to, held out long enough to toss two natives into the river and slug the daylights out of a third. Then he, too, dropped.

V

The green ones dragged their fellows from the river, dressed the slumber-wrapped Blaine and the other, added Armstrong, tied all three securely. Once more they conferred together. I couldn't make head or tail of their canary talk, but I got the notion that, in their opinion, we had an uncertain quantity of *gamish*.

My bonds began to irk. I'd have given much for the chance to go into action and bash a few green heads. Twisting myself, I used a lackluster eye to survey a tiny shrub growing near the side of the hammock. The shrub jiggled its midget branches and emitted a smell of burned caramel. Local vegetation was all movement and stinks.

Abruptly, the green ones ended their talk, crowded down to the bank of the river. A flotilla of long, narrow, shapely vessels swept around the bend, foamed under projecting branches of great trees, cut in to the bank. We were carted aboard, five prisoners to the boat. Thrusting away from the bank, our crew of twenty pulled and pushed rhythmically at a row of ten wooden levers on each side of the boat, drove the vessel upstream. We went along at a fair pace, left a shallow wake on the surface of the sluggish river.

"I had a grandfather who was a missionary," I told Jepson. "He got himself in trouble like this."

"So what?"

"He went to pot," I said.

"So can you," snapped Jepson. He strained futilely at his bonds.

For lack of anything better to do, I watched the way in which our crew handled our vessel, came to the conclusion that the levers worked two large pumps or a battery of small ones, and that the vessel got along by sucking in water at the bow and blowing it out at the stern. Later, I found I was wrong. Their method was much simpler than that. The levers connected with twenty split-bladed paddles jutting horizontally a foot or two below the water line. The two flaps of the blades closed together as each paddle drove forward, opened as it swept backward. By this means they got along a good deal faster than they could have done with oars since the subsurface paddles only moved forward and back with their weight on the boat—they didn't have to be raised, turned and dipped by the muscles of the rowers.

The sun climbed higher as we progressed steadily upriver. On the second bend, the river split, its current moving more rapidly at either side of a rocky islet about a hundred yards long. A group of four huge trees stood at the upstream end of the islet, their trunks and limbs a somber green that verged on black. Each of them had one horizontal spray of branches above which the trunk continued to a feathery crest forty feet higher. Every branch ended in half a dozen powerful twigs which curved downward like the fingers of a clutching hand.

Their crews speeding up the levers, the string of boats took the right-hand channel over which reached the largest of those great branches. As the first boat's prow came underneath, the branch twitched its fingers hungrily. It was no illusion; I saw it as clearly as I can see my trip bonus when they slide it toward me across the mahogany. That limb was getting all set to grab, and from its size and spread I reckoned it could pluck the entire boatload out of the water and do things of which I didn't care to think.

But it didn't do it. Just as that boat entered the danger area its helmsman stood up, bawled a string of gibberish at the tree. The fingers relaxed. The helmsman of the next boat did the same. And the next. Then mine. Flat on my back, as ready for action as a corpse, I gaped at that enormous neckwringer while all too slowly it came on, passed above and fell behind. Our helmsman went silent; the one in the following boat took up the tale. There was dampness on my spine.

Five miles farther on, we made for the shore. My head was toward that side. I didn't get a view of the buildings until the greenies contemptuously tossed out my hammock, released me from the thing, stood me on my feet. I promptly lost balance and sat down. Temporarily, my dogs were dead. Rubbing them to restore the circulation, my curious eyes examined this dump that might have been anything from a one-horse hamlet to a veritable metropolis.

The buildings were made of light green wood, all cylindrical, of uniform height and diameter, and each had a big tree growing through its middle. The foliage of each tree extended farther than the radius of each house, thus effectively hiding it from overhead view. Nothing could have been better calculated to conceal the place from the air, though there wasn't any reason to suppose that the inhabitants feared any menace from above.

Still, the way in which trees and buildings shared the same sites made it quite impossible to estimate the size of the place, for beyond the nearer screen of buildings were trees, trees and more trees, each of which may have shielded a house. I couldn't tell whether I was looking at a kraal or at the riverside suburb of some place running right over the horizon. It was little wonder that the exploring lifeboat had observed nothing but forest. Its crew could have scouted over an area holding a population of many millions and have thought it nothing but jungle.

Their weapons ready, their eyes alert, a horde of the green ones clustered around us while some of them finished the task of releasing the prisoners. The fact that we'd arrived in a thing like the *Marathon* didn't awe them one little bit. My feet were obedient now, so I lugged on my jackboots, stood up and looked around. It was then that I got two shocks.

The first hit me as I scanned my companions in misery. They consisted of little more than half the complement of the *Marathon*. The rest weren't there. One hammock held a still, lax figure that I recognized as the body of the guy who'd caught the darts soon after we landed. Upon another reposed the awake but dreamy, disinterested form of Sug Farn. But he was the only Martian present. None of the others were there. Neither were Chief Douglas, Bannister, Kane, Richards, Kelly, Jay Score, Steve Gregory, young Wilson, and a dozen others.

Were they dead? It didn't seem so—else why should the greenies have transported one body and not the others? Had they escaped, or did they form a second party of prisoners that had been taken elsewhere? There was no way of determining their fate, yet it was strange that they should be missing.

I nudged Jepson. "Hey, have you noticed—"

Came a sudden roar over that river and all the green ones stared upward and gesticulated with their weapons. They made mouth motions, but the roar drowned them out. Whirling around, I could feel my eyes bugging as the *Marathon's* sleek pinnace dived within a few feet of the surface of the river, soared upward again. It vanished over the treetops, drummed into the distance.

Then I could hear it sweeping round in a wide circle. Its note accelerated as it went into another dive, it shot back into view, swooped so low that it touched the surface of the water, whisked a shower of green droplets behind it and sent a small wash lapping into the bank. Then it was gone in another swift and uproarious soar, bulleting past at such a rate that it was impossible to see the pilot's cabin.

Jepson spat on his fist, gave the greenies a sour eye, and said, "They've got it coming to them, the lice!"

"*Tut!*" I chided.

"As for you," he went on. He didn't get a chance to say more because a tall, thin, mean-looking greenie suddenly picked on him.

This one gave him a contemptuous shove in the chest and piped something on a rising note of interrogation.

"Don't you do that to me!" snarled Jepson, giving an answering shove.

The green one staggered backward, recovered his balance, kicked out with his right leg. I thought he was trying to give Jepson a crack on the shins, but he wasn't. He was throwing something with his foot and what he threw was alive. All I could see of it was something that may or may not have been a tiny snake. It had no more length and thickness than a pencil and, for a change, it wasn't green but a bright orange color relieved by small, black spots. It landed on Jepson's chest, bit him, then flicked down his front so fast that I could hardly follow it. Reaching the ground, it made the grass fairly whip aside as it streaked back to its owner.

Curling around the green one's ankle, it went supine, looking exactly like a harmless leg ornament. A very small number of the other natives were wearing similar objects all of which were orange and black excepting one which was yellow and black.

Jepson bugged his eyes, opened his mouth, but emitted no sound. He teetered. The guy wearing the yellow and black lump of wickedness was standing right at my side watching Jepson with academic interest. I broke his neck. The way it snapped reminded me of a rotten broomstick. That thing on his leg left him the moment he was mutton, but fast as it moved it was too late. Jepson fell onto his face just as my jackboot scrunched the thing into the turf.

There was a hullabaloo all around me. I could hear McNulty's anxious voice yelping, "Men! Men!" Even at a time like this the crackpot could dwell on the vision of himself being demoted for tolerating maltreatment of natives. Armstrong kept bawling, "Another bugger!" and each time there followed a loud splash in the river. Things were going *phut-phut* and spheres were crashing again. Jepson lay like one dead while combatants stumbled over his body. Brennand barged up against me. He was breathing in quick puffs and trying to gouge a black eye out of a green face.

By this time I'd got myself another aborigine and proceeded to take him apart. I tried to imagine that he was a fried chicken of which I never seem to get any more than the piece that goes last over the fence. He was hard to hold, this greenie, and bounced around like a rubber ball. Over his swaying shoulder I could see Sug Farn juggling with five at once and envied him the anacondas he used for limbs. My opponent stabbed his fingers into the chrysanthemum I didn't possess, looked surprised at his own forgetfulness, was still trying to think of something else as he went into the river.

Then half a dozen spheres cracked open at my feet and the last I remember hearing was Armstrong bellowing just before a splash. The last I remember seeing was Sug Farn suddenly shooting out a spare tentacle he'd temporarily overlooked and using it to arrange that of the six greenies who jumped me only five landed. The other one was still going up as I went down.

For some reason I didn't pass out as I'd done before. Maybe I only got a half-dose of whatever the spheres gave forth, or perhaps they contained a different mixture. All I know is that I went down with five aborigines aboard my ribs, the skies spun crazily, my brains turned to porridge.

Then, astonishingly, I was awake, my upper limbs again tightly bound.

Over to the left a group of natives made a heaving pile atop some forms that I couldn't see but could easily hear. Armstrong was doing some championship hog-calling underneath that bunch which, after a couple of hectic minutes, broke apart to reveal his tied body along with those of Blaine and Sug Farn. On my right lay Jepson, his limbs quite free, but the lower ones apparently helpless. There was now no sign of the pinnace.

Without further ado the greenies whisked us across the sward and five miles deep into the forest, or city, or whatever it ought to be called. Two of them bore Jepson in a sort of wicker hamper. There were still as many trees as houses. Here and there a few impassive citizens came to the doors of their abodes and watched us dragging on our way. You'd have thought we were the sole surviving specimens of the dodo.

Minshull and McNulty were right behind me in this death parade, and I heard the latter say, pontifically, "I shall speak to their leader about this. I shall point out to him that all these unfortunate struggles are the inevitable result of his own people's bellicosity."

"Undoubtedly," afforded Minshull, with a touch of sardonic heartiness.

"Making all allowances for mutual difficulties of understanding," McNulty went on, "I still think that we are entitled to be received with a modicum of courtesy."

"Quite," said Minshull. His voice was now solemn, like that of the president of a mortician's convention. "And we consider that our reception left much to be desired."

"Precisely my point," said the skipper.

"And any further hostilities would be most deplorable," continued Minshull.

"Of course!" McNulty enthused.

"In which event we'll tear the guts out of every greenie on this stinking planet."

"Eh?" McNulty paused in his pace. His voice went up in pitch.

"Nothing," lied Minshull, amiably. "I didn't even open my mouth."

What the outraged shipmaster intended to say remained a mystery, for at this point a greenie caught him lagging and prodded him on. With an angry snort, he speeded up, moving in introspective silence from then on.

Presently, we emerged from a long, orderly line of tree-shrouded homes and entered a glade fully twice as large as that in which the missing *Marathon* had made its landing. It was roughly circular, its surface level and carpeted with close-growing moss of a rich, emerald green. The sun, now well up in the sky, poured a flood of pale-green beams into this strange amphitheater around the fringes of which clustered a horde of silent, expectant natives.

The middle of the glade captured out attention. Here, as outstanding as the biggest skyscraper in the old home town, soared a veritable monster among trees. How high it went was quite impossible to estimate, but it was large enough to make Terra's giant redwoods look puny by comparison. Its bole was a full forty feet in diameter, and the spread of its oaklike branches looked immense even though they were way, way up there. So enormous was this mighty growth that we just couldn't keep our eyes off it. If these transcosmic Zulus were going to hang us, well, they sure intended to do it high and handsome. Our kicking bodies wouldn't look more than a few struggling bugs dangling between Earth and heaven.

Minshull must have been afflicted by the same thought, for I heard him say to McNulty, "There's the Christmas tree! We're the ornaments. They'll draw lots for us, and the boob who gets the ace of spades will be the fairy at the top."

"Don't be morbid," snapped McNulty. "They'll do nothing so illegal."

Then a native pointed at the positive skipper and six pounced on him before he could dilate further on the subject of intercosmic law. With complete disregard for all the customs which the victim held holy, they bore him toward the waiting tree.

VI

Up to that moment we'd failed to notice the drumming sound which thundered dully from all around the glade. It was strong now, and held a sinister quality in its muffled, insistent beat. The weird, elusive sound had been with us from the start; we'd got used to it, had become unconscious of it in the same way that one becomes insensitive to the ticking of a

familiar clock. But now, perhaps because it lent emphasis to
the dramatic scene, we were keenly aware of that deadly
throb, throb, throb.

The green light made the skipper's face ghastly as he went
forward. All the same, he still managed to lend importance to
his characteristic strut, and his features had the air of one
who has unshakable faith in the virtue of sweet reason-
ableness. I've never encountered a man with more confidence
in the law. As he walked forward, I know he was supported
by the profound conviction that these poor people could do
nothing drastic with him unless they first filled in the necessary forms and got them properly stamped and signed. Whenever McNulty died, it was going to be with official approval.

Halfway to the tree the skipper and his guard were met by
nine tall natives. The latter were dressed in no way different
from their fellows, yet, in some vague manner, managed to
convey the impression that they were beings apart from the
common herd. Witch doctors, decided my agitated mind.

Those holding McNulty promptly handed him over to the
newcomers, then beat it toward the fringe of the glade as if
the devil himself had appeared in the middle. There wasn't
any devil; there was only that monstrous tree. Still, I knew
what some growths could and did do in this green-wrapped
world and it was highly probable that this, the grandpappy of
all trees, was capable of some unique wickedness. Of that
lump of statuesque timber one thing was certain—it possessed
a damned good dollop of *gamish.*

Briskly, the nine stripped McNulty to the waist. He was
talking to them all the time, but he was too far away for us
to get the gist of his lecture, and his captors took not the
slightest notice. Again they examined his chest, conferred
among themselves, abruptly started dragging him nearer to
the tree. McNulty resisted with appropriate dignity. Picking
him up bodily, they carried him forward.

Armstrong said, in harsh tones, "We've still got legs,
haven't we?" and forthwith kicked his nearest guardian's feet
from beneath him.

But before any of us could follow his example and start
another useless melee an interruption came from the sky.
Upon the steady drumming from the forest was superimposed
another fiercer, more rapid roll which quickly merged its
beats to a rising howl. The howl waxed to an explosive roar

as, swift and silvery, the pinnace swooped low over the fateful tree.

Something dropped from the belly of the bulleting boat, something which blew out to mushroomlike shape, hesitated in its fall, then lowered gently into the head of the tree. It was a parachute! I could see a figure hanging in its harness just before he was swallowed in the deeps of that elevated foliage. The distance made it quite impossible to recognize this invader from above.

The nine who were bearing McNulty dropped him unceremoniously on the sward, gazed expectantly at the tree. Strangely enough, aerial manifestations filled these natives more with curiosity than fear. The tree stood unmoving. Suddenly, amid its top branches, the thin beam of a needle ray lanced forth, touched a large branch at its junction with the trunk, and severed it. The amputated limb went whirling to the ground.

At once a thousand budlike protuberances, which lay concealed between the leaves of the tree swelled up as if they were blown balloons, reached the size of giant pumpkins, and burst with a fusillade of dull pops. They gave out a light yellow mist, exuding the stuff at such a rate that the entire tree was clouded with it in less than one minute. All the natives within sight hooted like a gang of owls, turned and ran. McNulty's nine guardians also called off the ceremony they'd had in mind and started after their fellows. The needle caught two of them before they'd gone ten steps; the remaining seven doubled their pace. McNulty was left struggling with the bonds around his wrists while slowly the mist crawled toward him.

Again the beam speared high up in the tree which had grown dim within the envelope of its own fog, and again a branch went to the ground. The last native had faded from sight. The creeping mist was now within thirty yards of the skipper who was standing and watching it like a man fascinated. His wrists were still tied to his sides. Deep inside the mist the popping sounds continued, though not as rapidly.

Yelling at the witless McNulty to make use of his nether limbs, we struggled furiously with our own and one another's bonds. McNulty responded no more than to shuffle backward a few yards. By a superhuman effort Armstrong burst free, snatched a jackknife from his pants pocket, started cutting our arms loose. Minshull and Blaine, the first two thus relieved, immediately raced to McNulty who was posing within ten yards of the mist like a portly Ajax defying the power of alien gods. They dragged him back.

Just as we'd all got rid of our bonds the pinnace came around in another wide sweep, vanished behind the column of yellow cloud and thundered away into the distance. We gave it a hoarse cheer. Then from the mist strode a great figure dragging a limp body with each hand. It was Jay Score. He had a tiny two-way radio on his back.

He came toward us, big, powerful, his eyes aflame with their everlasting fires, released his grip on the pair of cadavers, said, "Look—this is what that vapor will do to you unless you move out plenty fast!"

We looked. These things were the remains of the two natives he'd needled, but the needlers had not caused that awful rotting of the flesh. Both leprous objects were too far gone to be corpses, not far enough to be skeletons. They were mere rags of flesh and half-eaten organs on frames of festering bone. It was easy to see what would have happened to Jay had he been composed of flesh and blood, or had he been a breather.

"Back to the river," advised Jay, "even if we have to fight our way through. The *Marathon's* going to land on the front. We must reach her at all costs."

"And remember, men," put in McNulty, "I want no unnecessary slaughter."

That was a hell of a laugh. Our sole weapons now consisted of Jay's needler, Armstrong's jacknife, and our fists. Behind us, already very near and creeping steadily nearer, was the mist of death. Between us and the river lay the greenie metropolis with its unknown number of inhabitants armed with unknown devices. Veritably we were between a yellow devil and a green sea.

We started off, Jay in the lead, McNulty and the burly Armstrong following. Behind them, two men carried Jepson who could use his tongue even if not his legs. Two more bore the body which our attackers had borne all the way from the ship. Without opposition or mishap we got a couple of hundred yards deep into the trees and there we buried the corpse of the man who was first to set foot on this soil. He went from sight with the limp silence of the dead while all around us the forest throbbed.

In the next hundred yards we were compelled to bury another. The surviving duck-on-the-rock player, sobered by the end of his buddy, took the lead as a form of penance. We were marching slowly and cautiously, our eyes alert for hidden natives, our wits ready for any untoward move by a dart-throwing bush or a goo-smearing branch.

The man in front swerved away from one tree which topped an empty and silent greenie abode. His full attention was upon the vacant entrance to that house, and he failed to be wary of another tree under which he had moved. This growth was of medium size, had a silvery green bark, long, ornamental leaves from which dangled sprays of stringy threads. The ends of the threads came within four feet of the ground. He brushed against two of them. Came a sharp, bluish flash of light, a smell of ozone and scorched hair, and he dropped. He'd been electrocuted as thoroughly as if smitten by a stroke of lightning.

Mist or no mist, we carried him back the hundred yards we'd just traversed, buried him beside his comrade. That job was done in the nick of time. The crawling leprosy was at our very heels as we resumed our way. High in the almost concealed sky the sun poured down its limpid rays and made mosaic patterns through overhead leaves.

Giving a wide berth to this latest menace, which we named the voltree, we hit the end of Main Street. Here, we had the advantage in one way, though not in another. The houses stood dead in line and well apart; we could march along the center of the route beneath the wider gap of sky and be beyond reach of this planet's bellicose vegetation. But this made our march exposed to attack from any direction by any natives who might be determined to oppose our escape. We'd have to do the trip, one way or the other, with our necks stuck out a yard.

Sug Farn said to me, "You know, I've an idea well worth developing."

"What is it?" I demanded, hopefully.

"Supposing that we had twelve squares a side," he suggested, "we could then have four more pawns and four new master pieces. I propose to call the latter 'archers.' They would move two squares forward, and could take opponents one square sidewise. Wouldn't that make a beautifully complicated game?"

"You," I told him, "may go drown yourself!"

"As I should have known, your mental appreciation is poor." So saying, he extracted a bottle of *hooloo* scent which somehow he'd managed to retain through all the turmoil, moved away from me, and sniffed it in a deliberately offensive manner. I don't give a damn what anybody says—we don't smell like Martians say we do! These octopuses are downright liars.

Stopping both our progress and argument, Jay Score growled, "I guess this'll do." Unhitching his portable radio, he tuned it up, said into its microphone. "That you, Steve?" A pause, then, "Yes, we're waiting about a quarter of a mile on the river side of the glade. No, there's been no opposition— yet. But it'll come, it'll come. O.K., we'll wait." Another pause. "We'll give it guidance by sound."

Turning his attention from the radio to the sky, but with one earpiece still in action, he listened intently. We all listened. For a while there was nothing but that *throb, throb, throb* which never ceased upon this crazy world, but presently came a faraway drone like the hum of an approaching bumblebee.

Jay snatched at the mike. "We've got you. You're coming nearer." The drone grew louder. "Nearer, nearer." He waited a moment. "Now you're away to one side." The drone drifted off. "No, you're swerved the wrong way." Another brief wait. The distant sound suddenly grew strong. "Heading correctly now." The drone swelled to a roar. "Right!" yelled Jay. "You're almost on us!"

He looked expectantly upward, and we followed his gaze as one man. The next instant the pinnace raced across the sky gap at such a pace that it had come and gone in less time than it takes to draw one breath. But those aboard must have seen us, for the little vessel zoomed around in a wide, graceful arc, hit the main stem a couple of miles farther down, and came up it at terrific speed. This time, we could watch it most of the way, and we yelled at it as if we were a gang of excited kids.

"Got us?" inquired Jay of the microphone. "All right, try it on the next run."

Again the pinnace swept around, struck its former path, tore the air as it traveled toward us. It was like a monster shell from some old-time cannon. Things fell from its underside as it neared us, bundles and packages in a parachuted stream. The stuff came down as manna from heaven while the sower passed uproariously on and dug a hole in the northern sky. But for these infernal trees the pinnace could have landed and snatched the lot of us from danger's grasp.

Eagerly we pounced on the supplies, tearing covers open and dragging out the contents. Spacesuits for all. Well, they'd preserve us from various forms of gaseous unpleasantness. Needlers, oiled and loaded, together with reserves of excitants. A small case, all sponge rubber and cotton wool, containing half a dozen atomic bombs. An ampoule of iodine and a first-aid pack apiece.

One large bundle had become lodged high up in the branches of a tree, or rather its parachute had become entangled and it was dangling enticingly from the ropes. Praying that it contained nothing liable to blast the earth from beneath us, we needled the ropes and brought it down. It proved to hold a good supply of concentrated rations and a three-gallon can of pineapple juice.

Packing the chutes and shouldering the supplies, we started off. The first mile was easy: just trees, trees, trees and abandoned houses. It was on this part of the journey that I noticed that it was always the same type of tree which surmounted a house. There was no abode built around any of those gootrees or voltrees of whose powers we now knew too well. Whether those particular trees were innocuous was something nobody seemed inclined to discover, but it was here that Minshull discovered in them the source of that everlasting throbbing.

Disregarding McNulty, who was clucking at him like an agitated hen, he tiptoed into one empty house, his needler held forward in readiness for trouble. A minute later he came out, said that the building was deserted, but that the tree in its center was booming like a tribal tom-tom. He'd put his ear to its trunk and had heard the beating of its mighty heart.

That started a dissertation by McNulty, his subject being our legal right to mutilate or otherwise harm the trees of this planet. If, in fact, they were semisentient, then in law they had the status of aborigines and as such were subject to subsection so-and-so, paragraph such 'n such of the Intercosmic Code governing planetary relations. He got down to this with gusto and with typical disregard for the fact that he might be boiled in oil by nightfall.

When he paused for breath, Jay Score said, evenly, "Skipper, maybe these people have laws of their own and are about to enforce them!" He pointed straight ahead.

I followed his unemotional finger, then frantically poured myself into my spacesuit. This, I thought, is it! The long arm of justice was about to face me with that poor guppy.

VII

What awaited us about half a mile ahead was a vanguard of enormous, snakelike things fully as thick as my body and about a hundred feet in length. They were writhing in our general direction, their movements peculiarly stiff and lacking in sinuosity. Behind them, also moving awkwardly forward, was a small army of bushes deceivingly harmless in appearance. And behind those, hooting with the courage of those who now feel themselves secure, was a great horde of natives. The progress of this nightmarish crowd was determined by the pace of the snakish objects in front, and these crept forward in tortuous manner as if they were trying to move a hundred times faster than nature had intended them to move.

Aghast at this crazy spectacle, we stopped. The creepers came steadily on and somehow managed to convey an impression of tremendous strength awaiting sudden release. The nearer they got, the bigger they looked, and when they were a mere three hundred yards away I knew that any one of them could embrace a bunch of six of us and do more to us than any boa constrictor ever did to a hapless goat.

These were the wild ones of a vast and semisentient forest. I knew it instinctively, and I could hear them faintly mewing as they came on. These, then, were my bright green tigers, samples of the thing our captors had slaughtered in the emerald jungle. But they could be tamed, their strength and fury kept on tap. This tribe had done it. Veritably, they were higher than the Ka.

"I think I can just about make this distance," said Jay Score when the intervening space had shrunk to two hundred yards.

Nonchalantly, he thumbed an atomic bomb which could have made an awful mess of the *Marathon*. His chief weakness was that he never could appreciate the power of things that go bang. So he juggled it around in a way that made me wish him someplace the other end of the cosmos, and just when I was about to burst into tears, he threw it. His powerful right arm whistled in the air as he flung the missile in a great arc.

We flattened. The earth heaved like the belly of a sick man. Huge clods of plasma and lumps of green, fibrous stuff geysered, hung momentarily in midair, then showered all around us. We got up, raced forward a hundred yards, went prone as Jay tossed another. This one made me think of volcanoes. Its blast nearly pushed me back into my boots. The uproar had scarcely ceased when the pinnace reappeared, dived upon the rear ranks of the foe, and let them have a couple there. More disruption. It tied me in knots to see what went up.

"Now!" yelled Jay. Grabbing the handicapped Jepson, he tossed him upon one shoulder and pounced forward. We drove with him as one man.

Our first obstacle was a great crater bottomed with tired and steaming earth and some mutilated yellow worms. Cutting around the edges of this, I leaped a six-foot length of blasted creeper which, even in death, continued to jerk spasmodically and horribly. There were many more odd lengths writhing between here and the next crater. All were greener than any complexion, and bristled with hair-like tendrils which squirmed around as if seeking the life that had gone. The one hundred yards between craters we covered in record time, Jay still in the lead despite his heavy burden. I was sweating like a tormented bull, and I thanked my lucky star for the low gravity which enabled us to keep up this frantic pace.

Again we split and raced around the rim of the second crater. This brought us nose to nose with the enemy, and after that, all was confusion.

A bush got me. Sheer Terrestrialism made me disregard the darned thing despite all my recent experiences. I had my eyes off it, and in an instant it had shifted to one side, wrapped itself around my legs and brought me down. I went prostrate, unharmed but cursing, and the bush methodically sprinkled my space fabric with a fine gray powder. Then a long, leatherish tentacle snaked from behind me, ripped the bush from my form, tore it to pieces.

"Thanks, Sug Farn!" I breathed, got up, and charged on.

A second bellicose growth collapsed before my needler and the potent ray carried on another sixty or seventy yards and roasted the guts of a yelling, gesticulating native. Sug snatched a third bush, scattered it with scorn. The powder it emitted did not seem to affect him.

Jay was now twenty yards ahead. He paused, flung a bomb, dropped, got up and raced on, Jepson still grasped in his mighty left arm. The pinnace howled overhead, dived, created wholesale slaughter in the enemy's rear. A needle ray spurted from behind me, lanced dangerously close to my helmet, and burned a bush. I could hear in my phone a constant and monotonous cursing as I pounded along. On my right, a great tree lashed furiously and toppled headlong, but I had neither time nor inclination to look at it.

Then a snake got Blaine. How it had survived, alone among its blasted fellows, was a mystery. It lay jerking exactly like all the other tattered bits and pieces, but it was still in one long lump and, as Blaine jumped it, the thing curled viciously, wound around him. He shrieked into his mouthpiece, and the sound of his dying was terrible to hear. His spacesuit sank in and his blood spurted out between the folds. The sound and the sight shocked me so much that I stopped abruptly, and Armstrong blundered into me from behind.

"Get going!" he roared. With his needler he sliced the green constrictor, segmenting it with savage gusto. We charged on, perforce leaving behind Blaine's crushed and broken corpse.

Now we were through the fronting ranks and into the natives whose numbers miraculously had thinned. Brittle globes plopped all around our thudding feet, but their gaseous contents were as harmless as summer air. We were protected and, in any case, we were moving too fast to get a whiff. I needled three greenies in rapid succession, saw Jay tear off the head of another without as much as pausing in his heavy onrush.

We were gasping with exertion when unexpectedly the foe gave up. The remaining natives melted into their protecting forest just as the pinnace roared vengefully toward them again. Our way was clear. Not slackening our pace in the slightest, and with eyes alert and weapons ready, we raced to the water front, and there, lying in the great space of bright green sward, found the sweetest sight in the entire cosmos— the *Marathon*!

It was here that Sug Farn put a scare into us, for as we sprinted joyfully toward the open port, he beat us to it, held up the stump of a tentacle, said, "It would be as well if we do not enter—yet."

"Why not?" demanded Jay. His cold, glowing eyes settled on the Martian's stump. "What the devil happened to you?"

"I was forced to shed a limb," said Sug Farn, mentioning it with the air of one to whom shedding a limb is like taking off a hat. "It was that powder. It was made of a million insects. It crawls around and it eats. It was eating me. Look at yourselves!"

By hokey, he was right! Now that I came to look at it, I could see small clusters of gray powder changing shape on my spacesuit. It was moving around. Sooner or later, it would eat its way through—and then start on me. I've never felt lousier in my life. So, keeping watch upon the fringe of the forest, we had to spend an impatient and sweaty half-hour roasting each other's suits with needlers turned to wide jet and low power. I was cooked by the time the last microscopic louse dropped off.

Young Wilson seized the opportunity to dig out a movie camera and record our communal decontamination. This, I knew, eventually would be shown to an amused world sitting in armchair comfort far, far from the troubles surrounding Rigel. Secretly, I wished that a few surviving bugs would somehow manage to get around with the film. With a more official air, he also got shots of the forest, the river, and a couple of upturned boats with all their bivalve paddles exposed. Then, thankfully, we all piled into the spaceship.

The pinnace was lugged aboard and the *Marathon* blew off pronto. I don't think there's ever been a time when I felt more like a million dollars than I did when normal, glorious light came through the ports and the bilious green coloring faded from our faces. With Brennand, I watched this strange, eerie world sink below us, and I can't say I was sorry to see it drop.

Jay came along, said, "Sergeant, we're not making any further landings. The skipper's decided to return to Terra at once and make a full report."

"Why?" asked Brennand. He gestured below. "We've come away with practically nothing worth having!"

"McNulty thinks we've learned quite enough." The rhythmic hum of the stern tubes sounded through his momentary silence. "He sayd he's conducting an exploratory expedition and not managing a slaughterhouse. He's had enough and is thinking of offering his resignation."

"The dunderhead!" said Brennand, with total lack of reverence.

"What have we learned, if anything?" I asked.

"Well, we know that life on that planet is mostly symbiotic," Jay replied. "There, different forms of life share their existence and their faculties. Men share with trees, each according to his kind. The communal point is that queer chest organ."

"Drugs for blood," said Brennand. "Bah!"

"But," Jay went on. "There were some higher than the Ka and their kind, some so high and godlike that they could depart from their trees and travel the globe, by day or by night. They could milk their trees, transport their nourishment and absorb it from bowls. Of the partnership imposed upon them, they had gained the mastery, and, in the estimation of this planet, they alone were free!"

"How fallen are the mighty," I commented.

"Not so," Jay contradicted. "We have killed, but not conquered. The world is still theirs. We are retiring, with our losses—and we still have Jepson to cure!" He turned away.

A thought struck me, and I said to him, "Hey, what happened during that assault on the ship? And how did you keep track of us?"

"It was a losing fight, so we blew free," he replied. "After that, we followed you very easily." His eyes were always inscrutably aflame, but I will swear that there was a touch of humor in them as he went on. "You had Sug Farn with you. We had Kli Yang and the rest." He tapped his head suggestively. "The Martians have much *gamish*."

"Hell, telepathy!" yelped Brennand. "I forgot all about that. Sug Farn never said a word. That cross-eyed spider just slept every chance he got!"

"Nevertheless," said Jay, "he was constantly in touch with his fellows!"

He went along the passage, rounded the corner. Then the warning alarm sounded, and Brennand and I clung like brothers while the ship switched to Flettner drive. The green world faded to a dot with swiftness that never failed to astound me. We took fresh hold on ourselves, rubbed our distorted innards into shape. Then Brennand went to the valve of the storrad air lock, turned the control, watched the pressure gauge crawl from three pounds to fifteen.

"The Martians are inside there," I pointed out. "And they won't like that."

"I don't want 'em to like it. I'll teach those rubber caricatures to hold out on me!"

"McNulty won't like it either."

"Who cares what McNulty likes!" he yelled. Then McNulty himself came around the corner, walking with portly dignity, and Brennand promptly added, in a still louder voice, "You ought to be a darned sight more respectful and refer to him as the skipper."

When you travel the void, never mind the ship—pick the guys who're going to accompany you in it!

THE VEIL OF ASTELLAR
Thrilling Wonder Stories
Spring

by Leigh Brackett

The vivid stories of Leigh Brackett first reached the science fiction magazines in 1940, and she soon became a regular contributor to the genre, particularly in the pages of Planet Stories *and* Thrilling Wonder Stories. *Many of her best works were novella length and therefore infrequently reprinted, but a collection of her finest short fiction is available as* The Best of Leigh Brackett, *edited by her late husband, Edmond Hamilton.*

"The Veil of Astellar" is a haunting story of love and the price of love, whose protagonist (according to Ed Hamilton) was probably modeled after Humphrey Bogart.

(So much depends upon timing. When the movie actor James Dean died, he got two obscure inches somewhere in the newspaper interior. After his death, a couple of pictures came out posthumously and he became a national craze. Could he have come back to life and died again two years later, he would have gotten the complete Elvis Presley treatment. Similarly, when Leigh Brackett was writing science fiction in the Forties, she was published only in the minor magazines such as Planet *and* Thrilling Wonder. *Her reputation grew, however, and by the time she was a star of acknowledged first magnitude she was writing for Hollywood. Could her stories of the Forties have been written in the Sixties instead, the best magazines in the field would have clawed at each other for the privilege of publishing them.—I.A.)*

Foreword

A little over a year ago, Solar Arbitrary Time, a message rocket dropped into the receiving chute at the Interworld Space Authority headquarters on Mars.

In it was a manuscript, telling a story so strange and terrible that it was difficult to believe that any sane human being could have been guilty of such crimes.

However, through a year of careful investigation, the story has been authenticated beyond doubt, and now the ISA has authorized its release to the public, just exactly as it was taken from the battered rocket.

The Veil—the light that came from nowhere to swallow ships—has disappeared. Spacemen all over the solar system, tramp traders and captains of luxury liners alike, have welcomed this knowledge as only men can who have lived in constant peril. The Veil is gone, and with it some of the crushing terror of the Alien Beyond.

We know its full name now—the Veil of Astellar.

We know the place of its origin: a world outlawed from space and time. We know the reason for its being. Through this story, written in the agony of one man's soul, we know these things—and we know the manner of the Veil's destruction.

1

Corpse at the Canal

There had been a brawl at Madam Kan's, on the Jekkara Low-Canal. Some little Martian glory-holer had got too high on thil, and pretty soon the spiked knuckle-dusters they use around there began to flash, and the little Martian had pulled his last feed-valve.

They threw what was left of him out onto the stones of the embankment almost at my feet. I suppose that was why I stopped—because I had to, or trip over him. And then I stared.

The thin red sunlight came down out of a clear green sky. Red sand whispered in the desert beyond the city walls, and red-brown water ran slow and sullen in the canal. The Martian lay twisted over on his back, with his torn throat spilling the reddest red of all across the dirty stones.

He was dead. He had green eyes, wide open, and he was dead.

I stood by him. I don't know how long. There wasn't any time. No sunlight shimmered now, no sense of people passing, no sound—nothing!

Nothing but his dead face looking up at me; green-eyed, with his lips pulled back off his white teeth.

I didn't know him. Alive, he was just another Martian snipe. Dead, he was just meat.

Dead, the Martian trash!

No time. Just a dead man's face, smiling.

And then something touched me. Thought, a sudden bursting flame of it, hit my mind, drawing it back like a magnet drawing heavy steel. Somebody's thought, directed at me. A raw, sick horror, a fear, and a compassion so deep it shook my heart— One clear, sharp thrust of word-images came to me now.

"He looks like Lucifer crying for Heaven," the message said. "His eyes. Oh, Dark Angel, his eyes!"

I shut those eyes. Sweat broke cold on me, I swayed, and then I made the world come back into focus again. Sunlight, sand, noise and stench and people crowding, the thunder of rockets from the spaceport two Mars miles away. All in focus. I looked up and saw the girl.

She was standing just beyond the dead man, almost touching him. There was a young fellow with her. I saw him vaguely, but he didn't matter then. Nothing mattered but the girl. She was wearing a blue dress, and she was staring at me with a smoke-gray gaze out of a face as white as stripped bone.

The sunlight and the noise and people went away again, leaving me alone with her. I felt the locket burn me under my spaceman's black, and my heart seemed to stop beating.

"Missy," I said. "Missy."

"Like Lucifer, but Lucifer turned saint," her mind was saying.

I laughed of a sudden, short and harsh. The world came back in place and stayed there, and so did I.

Missy. Missy, bosh! Missy's been dead a long, long time.

It was the red hair that fooled me. The same dark red hair, straight and heavy as a horse's tail, coiled on her white neck, and her smoke-gray eyes. Something, too, about her freckles and the way her mouth pulled up on one side as though it couldn't stop smiling.

Otherwise, she didn't look much like Missy. She was taller and bonier. Life had kicked her around some, and she showed it. Missy never had worn that tired, grim look. I don't know whether she had developed a tough, unbreakable character, like the girl before me, either. I couldn't read minds, then.

This girl, looking at me, had a lot in her mind that she wouldn't want known. I didn't like the idea of her catching me in a rare off-moment.

"What do you babies think you're doing here?" I said.

The young man answered me. He was a lot like her—plain, simple, a lot tougher inside than he looked—a kid who had learned how to take punishment and go on fighting. He was sick now, and angry, and a little scared.

"We thought, in broad daylight it would be safe," he answered.

"Day or night, it's all the same to this hole. I'd get out."

Without moving, the girl was still looking at me, not even realizing that she was doing it. "White hair," she was thinking. "But he isn't old. Not much older than Brad, in spite of the lines. Suffering, not age."

"You're off the *Queen of Jupiter,* aren't you?" I asked them.

I knew they were. The *Queen* was the only passenger tub in Jekkara then. I was interested only because she looked like Missy. But Missy had been dead a long time.

The young man she thought of as Brad spoke.

"Yes," he said. "We're going out to Jupiter, to the colonies." He pulled at the girl gently. "Come on, Virgie. We'd better go back to the ship."

I was sweating, and cold. Colder than the corpse at my feet. I laughed, but not loud.

"Yes," I said. "Get back to the ship, where it's safe."

The girl hadn't stirred, hadn't taken her eyes off me.

Still afraid, not so compassionate now, but still with her mind on me.

"His eyes burn," she was thinking. "What color are they? No color, really. Just dark and cold and burning. They've looked into horror—and heaven . . ."

I let her look into them. She flushed after a while, and I smiled. She was angry, but she couldn't look away, and I held her, smiling, until the young man pulled her again, not so gently.

"Come on, Virgie."

She broke free from me then, turning with an angular, coltish grace. My stomach felt like somebody stabbed it, suddenly. The way she held her head . . .

She looked back at me, sullenly, not wanting to.

"You remind me of someone," she said. "Are you from the *Queen of Jupiter,* too?"

Her voice was like Missy's. Deeper, maybe. Throatier. But enough like it.

"Yeah. Spaceman, First Class."

"Then maybe that's where I noticed you." She turned the wedding ring on her finger, not thinking about it, and frowned. "What's your name?"

"Goat," I said. "J. Goat."

"Jay Goat," she repeated. "What an odd name. But it's not unusual. I wonder why it interests me so much."

"Come on, Virgie," Brad said crossly.

I didn't give her any help. I looked at her until she flushed crimson and turned away. I read her thoughts. They were worth reading.

She and Brad went off toward the spaceport, walking close together, back to the *Queen of Jupiter,* and I stumbled over the dead Martian at my feet.

The pinched grayness had crawled in over his face. His green eyes were glazed and already sunken, and his blood was turning dark on the stones. Just another corpse.

I laughed. I put my black boot under the twist of his back and pushed him off into the sullen, red-brown water, and I laughed because my own blood was still hot and beating in me so hard it hurt.

He was dead, so I let him go.

I smiled at the splash and the fading ripples. "She was

wrong," I thought. "It isn't Jay. It's just plain J. Goat. J for Judas."

There were about ten Mars hours to kill before the *Queen* blasted off. I had a good run at the getak tables in Madam Kan's. She found me some special desert-cactus brandy and a Venusian girl with a hide like polished emerald and golden eyes.

She danced for me, and she knew how. It wasn't a bad ten hours, for a Jekkara dive.

Missy, the dead Martian, and the girl named Virgie went down in my subconscious where they belonged, and didn't leave even a ripple. Things like that are like the pain of an old wound when you twist it. They get you for a minute, but they don't last. They aren't important any more.

Things can change. You planet-bound people build your four little walls of thought and roof them in with convention, and you think there's nothing else. But space is big, and there are other worlds, and other ways. You can learn them. Even you. Try it, and see.

I finished the fiery green brandy. I filled the hollow between the Venusian dancer's emerald breasts with Martian silver and kissed her, and went away with a faint taste of fish on my lips, back toward the spaceport.

I walked. It was night, with a thin, cold wind rustling the sand and the low moons spilling silver and wild black shadows across the dunes. I could see my aura glowing, pale gold against the silver.

I felt swell. The only thing I thought about concerning the *Queen of Jupiter* was that pretty soon my job would be finished and I'd be paid.

I stretched with a pleasure you wouldn't know anything about, and it was a wonderful thing to be alive.

It was lonely out there on the moonswept desert a mile from the spaceport, when Gallery stepped out from behind a ruined tower that might have been a lighthouse once, when the desert was a sea.

Gallery was king-snipe of the glory hole. He was Black Irish, and moderately drunk, and his extra-sensory perception was quivering in him like a sensitive diaphragm. I knew he could see my aura. Very faintly, and not with his eyes, but enough. I knew he had seen it the first time he met me, when I signed aboard the *Queen of Jupiter* on Venus.

You meet them like that occasionally. Celts especially, and Romanies, both Earth and Martian, and a couple of tribes of Venusians. Extra-sensory perception is born into them. Mostly it's crude, but it can get in your way.

It was in my way now. Gallery had four inches on me, and about thirty pounds, and the whisky he'd drunk was just enough to make him fast, mean, and dangerous. His fists were large.

"You ain't human," he said softly.

He was smiling. He might have been making love to me, with his smile and his beautiful soft voice. The sweat on his face made it look like polished wood in the moonlight.

"No, Gallery," I said. "Not any more. Not for a long time."

He swayed slightly, over his flexed knees. I could see his eyes. The blueness was washed out of them by the moonlight. There was only fear left, hard and shining.

His voice was still soft, still singing. "What are you, then? And what will you be wantin' with the ship?"

"Nothing with the ship, Gallery. Only with the people on her. And as to what I am, what difference does it make?"

"None," said Gallery. "None. Because I'm going to kill you, now."

I laughed, not making any sound.

He nodded his black head slowly. "Show me your teeth, if you will. You'll be showin' them to the desert sky soon, out of a picked skull."

He opened his hands. The racing moonlight showed me a silver crucifix in each of his palms.

"No, Gallery," I said softly. "Maybe you could call me a vampire, but I'm not that kind."

He closed his hands again over the crosses and started forward, one slow step at a time. I could hear his boots in the blowing sand. I didn't move.

"You can't kill me, Gallery."

He didn't stop. He didn't speak. The sweat was trickling down his skin. He was afraid, but he didn't stop.

"You'll die here, Gallery, without a priest."

He didn't stop.

"Go on to the town, Gallery. Hide there till the *Queen's* gone. You'll be safe. Do you love the others enough to die for them?"

He stopped, then. He frowned, like a puzzled kid. It was a new thought.

I got the answer before he said it.

"What does love have to do with it? They're people."

He came on again, and I opened my eyes, wide.

"Gallery," I said.

He was close. Close enough so I could smell the raw whisky on his breath. I looked up into his face. I caught his eyes and held them, and he stopped, slowly, dragging his feet as though all of a sudden there were weights on them.

I held his eyes. I could hear his thoughts. They were the same. They're always the same.

He raised his fists up, too slowly, as though he might be lifting a man's weight on each of them. His lips drew back. I could see the wet shine of his teeth and hear the labored breath go between them, hoarse and rough.

I smiled at him, and held his eyes with mine.

He went down to his knees. Inch by inch, fighting me, but down. A big man with sweat on his face and blue eyes that couldn't look away. His hands opened. The silver crosses fell out and lay there glittering on the sand.

His head went back. The cords roped out in his neck and jerked, and then suddenly he fell over on his side and lay still.

"My heart," he whispered. "You've stopped it."

That's the only way. What they feel about us is instinct, and even psycho-surgery won't touch that. Besides, there's never time.

He couldn't breathe now. He couldn't speak, but I heard his thoughts. I picked the crucifixes out of the sand and folded his fingers over them.

He managed to turn his head a little and look at me. He tried to speak, but again it was his thought I answered.

"Into the Veil, Gallery," I whispered. "That's where I'm leading the *Queen*."

I saw his eyes widen and fix. The last thought he had was—well, never mind that. I dragged him back into the ruined tower where no one would be likely to find him for a long time, and started on again for the spaceport. And then I stopped.

He'd dropped the crosses again. They were lying in the path with the moonlight on them, and I picked them up, thinking I'd throw them out into the blowing sand where they wouldn't be seen.

I didn't. I stood holding them. They didn't burn my flesh. I laughed.

Yeah. I laughed. But I couldn't look at them.

I went back in the tower and stretched Gallery on his back with his hands crossed on his chest, and closed his eyes. I laid a crucifix on each of his eyelids and went out, this time for good.

Shirina said once that you could never understand a human mind completely no matter how well you knew it. That's where the suffering comes in. You feel fine, everything's beautiful, and then all of a sudden a trapdoor comes open somewhere in your brain, and you remember.

Not often, and you learn to kick them shut, fast. But even so, Flack is the only one of us that still has dark hair, and he never had a soul to begin with.

Well, I kicked the door shut on Gallery and his crosses, and half an hour later the *Queen of Jupiter* blasted off for the Jovian colonies, and a landing she was never going to make.

2

Voyage into Doom

Nothing happened until we hit the outer fringe of the Asteroid Belt. I'd kept watch on the minds of my crewmates, and I knew Gallery hadn't mentioned me to anyone else. You don't go around telling people that the guy in the next bunk gives off a yellow glow and isn't human, unless you want to wind up in a straitjacket. Especially when such things are something you sense but can't see, like electricity.

When we came into the danger zone inside the Belt, they set the precautionary watches at the emergency locks on the passenger decks, and I was assigned to one of them. I went up to take my station.

Just at the top of the companionway I felt the first faint reaction of my skin, and my aura began to pulse and brighten.

I went on to the Number Two lock and sat down.

I hadn't been on the passenger deck before. The *Queen of*

Jupiter was an old tub from the Triangle trade, refitted for deep-space hauling. She held together, and that's all. She was carrying a heavy cargo of food, seed, clothing, and farm supplies, and about five hundred families trying for a fresh start in the Jovian colonies.

I remembered the first time I saw Jupiter. The first time any man from Earth ever saw Jupiter. That was long ago.

Now the deck was jammed. Men, women, kids, mattresses, bags, bundles, and what have you. Martians, Venusians, Terrans, all piled in together, making a howling racket and smelling very high in the combined heat of the sun and the press of bodies.

My skin was tingling and beginning to crawl. My aura was brighter.

I saw the girl. The girl named Virgie with her thick red hair and her colt's way of moving. She and her husband were minding a wiry, green-eyed Martian baby while its mother tried to sleep, and they were both thinking the same thing.

"Maybe, someday when things are better, we'll have one of our own."

I remember thinking that Missy would have looked like that holding our kid, if we'd ever had one.

My aura pulsed and glowed.

I watched the little worlds flash by, still far ahead of the ship, all sizes, from pebbles to habitable planetoids, glittering in the raw sunlight and black as space on their shadow sides. People crowded up around the ports, and I got to looking at one old man standing almost beside me.

He had space stamped all over him, in the way he carried his lean frame and the lines in his leathery face, and the hungry-hound look of his eyes watching the Belt. An old rocket-hustler who had done plenty in his day, and remembered it all.

And then Virgie came up. Of all the women on deck it had to be Virgie. Brad was with her, and she was still holding the baby. She had her back to me, looking out.

"It's wonderful," she said softly. "Oh, Brad, just look at it!"

"Wonderful, and deadly," the old spaceman said to himself. He looked around and smiled at Virgie. "Your first trip out?"

"Yes, for both of us. I suppose we're very starry-eyed about it, but it's strange." She made a little helpless gesture.

"I know. There aren't any words for it." He turned back to the port. His voice and his face were blank, but I could read his mind.

"I used to kick the supply ships through to the first settlement, fifty years ago," he said. "There were ten of us, doing that. I'm the only one left."

"The Belt was dangerous then, before they got the Rosson deflectors," Brad said.

"The Belt," said the old man softly, "only got three of them."

Virgie lifted her red head. "Then what . . ."

The old man didn't hear her. His thoughts were way off.

"Six of the best men in space, and then, eleven years ago, my son," he said, to no one.

A woman standing beside him turned her head. I saw the wide, raw shine of terror in her eyes, and the sudden stiffness of her lips.

"The Veil?" she whispered. "That's what you mean, isn't it? The Veil?"

The old man tried to shut her up, but Virgie broke in.

"What about the Veil?" she asked. "I've heard of it, vaguely. What is it?"

The Martian baby was absorbed in a silver chain she wore around her neck. I remember thinking it looked familiar. Probably she'd had it on the first time I saw her. My aura glowed, a hot bright gold.

The woman's voice, answering, had an eerie quality of distance in it, like an echo. She was staring out of the port now.

"Nobody knows," she said. "It can't be found, or traced, or tested at all. My brother is a spaceman. He saw it once from a great distance, reaching from nowhere to swallow a ship. A veil of light. It faded, and the ship was gone! My brother saw it out here, close to the Belt."

"There's no more reason to expect it here than anywhere," the old spaceman said roughly. "It's taken ships as far in as Earth's orbit. There's no reason to be afraid."

My aura burned around me like a cloud of golden light, and my skin was alive with a subtle current.

The green-eyed Martian baby yanked the silver chain suddenly and crowed, holding its hands high. The thing on the end of the chain, that had been hidden under Virgie's dress, spun slowly round and round, and drew my eyes, and held them.

I must have made some sound, because Virgie looked around and saw me. I don't know what she thought. I didn't know anything for a long time, except that I was cold, as though some of the dead, black space outside had come in through the port somehow and touched me.

The shiny thing spun on the end of the silver chain, and the green-eyed baby watched it, and I watched it.

After that there was darkness, with me standing in the middle of it quite still, and cold, cold, cold!

Virgie's voice came through the darkness, calm, casual, as though none of it mattered at all.

"I've remembered who it is you made me think of, Mr. Goat," she said. "I'm afraid I was rather rude that day on Mars, but the resemblance puzzled me. Look."

A white object came into my shell of ice and blackness. It was a strong white hand, reddened across the knuckles with work, holding something in the palm. Something that burned with a clear, terrible light of its own. Her voice went on, so very quietly.

"This locket, Mr. Goat. It's ancient. Over three hundred years old. It belonged to an ancestor of mine, and the family has kept it ever since. It's rather a lovely story. She married a young spaceman. In those days, of course, space flight was still new and dangerous, and this young man loved it as much as he did his wife. His name was Stephen Vance. That's his picture. That's why I thought I had seen you somewhere before, and why I asked your name. I think the resemblance is quite striking, don't you?"

"Yes," I said. "Yes, it is."

"The girl is his wife, and of course, the original owner of the locket. He called her Missy. It's engraved on the back of the locket. Anyway, he had a chance to make the first flight from Mars to Jupiter, and Missy knew how much it meant to him. She knew that something of him would die if he didn't go, and so she let him. He didn't know how soon the baby they'd both wanted so much would arrive, for she didn't tell him that. Because she knew he wouldn't go if she did.

"So Stephen had two lockets made, this one and another just like it. He told her they'd make a link between them, he and Missy, that nothing could break. Sometime, somehow, he'd come back to her, no matter what happened. Then he went to Jupiter. He died there. His ship was never found.

"But Missy went on wearing the locket and praying. And when she died she gave it to her daughter. It grew into a sort of family tradition. That's why I have it now."

Her voice trailed off, drowsily, with a faint note of surprise. Her hand and the locket went away, and there was a great stillness all around me, a great peace.

I brought my arms up across my face. I stiffened, and I tried to say something, words I used to say a long, long time ago. They wouldn't come. They won't, when you go into the Beyond Place.

I took my hands away, and I could see again. I didn't touch the locket around my neck. I could feel it against my breast, like the cold of space, searing me.

Virgie lay at my feet. She still held the baby in the bend of one arm. Its round brown face was turned to hers, smiling a little. Brad lay beside them, with one arm flung across them both.

The locket lay on the gentle curve of Virgie's breast, face up, still open, rising and falling slowly to the lift of her breathing.

They don't suffer. Remember that. They don't suffer. They don't even know. They sleep, and their dreams are happy. Remember, please! Not one of them has suffered, or been afraid.

I stood alone in that silent ship. There were no stars beyond the port now, no little worlds riding the Belt. There was only a veil of light wrapped close around the ship, a soft web of green and purple and gold and blue spun on a shimmering gray woof that was no color at all, and held there with threads of scarlet.

There was the familiar dimming of the electrics inside the ship. The people slept on the broad deck. I could hear their breathing, soft and slow and peaceful. My aura burned like a golden cloud around me, and inside it my body beat and pulsed with life.

I looked down at the locket, at Missy's face. If you'd told me. Oh Missy, if you'd only told me, I could have saved you!

Virgie's red hair, dark and straight and heavy in her white

neck. Virgie's smoke-gray eyes, half open and dreaming. Missy's hair. Missy's eyes.

Mine. Part of my flesh, part of my bone, part of my blood. Part of the life that still beat and pulsed inside me.

Three hundred years.

"Oh, if I could only pray!" I thought.

I knelt down beside her. I put out my hand. The golden light came out of the flesh and veiled her face. I took my hand away and got up, slowly. More slowly than Gallery fell when he died.

The shimmer of the Veil was all through the ship, now. In the air, in every atom of its wood and metal. I moved in it, a shining golden thing, alive and young, in a silent, sleeping world.

Three hundred years, and Missy was dead, and now the locket had brought her back.

Did Judas feel like this when the rope tore the life out of him?

But Judas died.

I walked in silence, wrapped in my golden cloud, and my heartbeats shook me like the blows of a man's fist. A strong heart. A young, strong heart.

The ship swerved slowly, drawn out of its arc of free fall toward Jupiter. The auxiliaries had not been cut in yet for the Belt. The Veil just closed around the hull and drew it, easily.

It's just an application of will-power. Teleportation, the strength of mind and thought amplified by the X-crystals and directed like a radio beam. The release of energy between the force of thought and the force of gravity causes the light, the visible thing that spacemen call the Veil. The hypnotic sleep-impulse is sent the same way, through the X-crystals on Astellar.

Shirina says it's a simple thing, a child's trick, in its own space-time matrix. All it requires is a focal point to guide it, a special vibration it can follow like a torch in the void, such as the aura around flesh, human or not, that has bathed in the Cloud.

A Judas goat, to lead the sheep to slaughter.

I walked in my golden light. The pleasure of subtle energies pricked and flared across my skin. I was going home.

And Missy was still alive. Three hundred years, and she

was still alive. Her blood and mine, alive together in a girl named Virgie.

And I was taking her to Astellar, the world its own dimension didn't want.

I guess it was the stopping of the current across my skin that roused me, half an eternity later. My aura had paled to its normal faintness. I heard the faint grating ring of metal on stone, and I knew the *Queen of Jupiter* had made her last landing. I was home.

I was sitting on the edge of my own bunk. I didn't know how I got there. I was holding my head on my clenched fists, and when I opened them my own locket fell out. There was blood on my palms.

I got up and walked through the silence, through the hard impersonal glare of the electrics, to the nearest airlock, and went out.

The *Queen of Jupiter* lay in a rounded cradle of rock, worn smooth. Back at the top of the chute the space doors were closed, and the last echo of the air pumps was dying away against the low roof of the cavern. The rock is a pale translucent green, carved and polished into beauty that stabs you breathless, no matter how many times you see it.

Astellar is a little world, only about half the size of Vesta. Outside it's nothing but black slag, without even a trace of mineral to attract a tramp miner. When they want to they can bend the light around it so that the finest spacescope can't find it, and the same thought-force that makes the Veil can move Astellar where they wish it to go.

Since traffic through the Belt has grown fairly heavy, they haven't moved it much. They haven't had to.

I went across the cavern in the pale green light. There's a wide ramp that goes up from the floor like the sweep of an angel's wing. Flack was waiting for me near the foot of it, outlined in the faint gold of his aura.

"Hi, Steve," he said, and looked at the *Queen of Jupiter* with his queer gray eyes. His hair was as black as mine used to be, his skin space-burned dark and leathery. His eyes looked out of the darkness like pale spots of moonlight, faintly luminous and without a soul.

I knew Flack before he became one of us, and I thought then that he was less human than the Astellarians.

"A good haul this time, Steve?" he asked.

"Yeah." I tried to get past him. He caught my arm.

"Hey—what's eating you?" he said.

"Nothing."

I shook him off. He smiled and stepped in front of me. A big man, as big as Gallery and a lot tougher, with a mind that could meet mine on an equal footing.

"Don't give me that, Stevie. Something's—he-ey!" He pushed my chin up suddenly, and his pale eyes glowed and narrowed.

"What's this?" he said. "Tears?"

He stared at me a minute, slack-jawed, and then he began to laugh. I hit him.

3

Wages of Evil

Flack went sprawling backward onto the lucent stone. I went by him up the curve of the ramp. I went fast, but it was already too late.

The airlocks of the *Queen of Jupiter* opened behind me.

I stopped. I stopped the way Gallery did in the blowing Martian sand, slowly, dragging weights on my feet. I didn't want to. I didn't want to turn around, but there was nothing I could do about it. My body turned, by itself.

Flack was on his feet again, leaning up against the carved green wall, looking at me. Blood ran out over his lip and down his chin. He got out a handkerchief and held it over his mouth, and his eyes never left me, pale and still and glowing. The golden aura made a halo round his dark head, like the painting of a saint.

Beyond him the locks of the ship were open, and the people were coming out.

In their niche on the fourth level of Astellar the X-crystals were pulsing from pale gray to a black as endless and alien as the Coal Sack. Behind them was a mind, kindly and gentle, thinking, and the human cargo of the *Queen* heard its thoughts.

They came out of the locks, walking steadily but without haste. They formed into a loose column and came across the green translucent floor of the cavern and up the ramp. Walking easily, their breathing deep and quiet, their eyes half open and full of dreams.

Up the long sweeping ribbon of pale green stone, past Flack, past me, and into the hall beyond. They didn't see anything but their dreams. They smiled a little. They were happy, and not afraid.

Virgie still carried the baby, drowsing in her arms, and Brad was still beside her. The locket had turned with her movements, hiding the pictures, showing me only its silver back.

I watched them go. The hall beyond the ramp was gem-cut from milky crystal and inlaid with metals that came from another dimension, radioactive metals that filled the crystal walls and the air between them with softened, misty fire.

They went slowly into the veil of mist and fire, and were gone.

Flack spoke softly. "Steve."

I turned back toward the sound of his voice. There was a strange blur over everything, but I could see the yellow glow of his aura, the dark strength of him outlined against the pale green rock. He hadn't moved. He hadn't taken his cold light eyes away from me.

I had left my mind naked, unguarded, and I knew before he spoke that Flack had read it.

He spoke through his bruised lips.

"You're thinking you won't go into the Cloud again, because of that girl," he whispered. "You're thinking there must be some way to save her. But there isn't, and you wouldn't save her if you could. And you'll go into the Cloud again, Stevie. Twelve hours from now, when it's time, you'll walk into the Cloud with the rest of us. And do you know why?"

His voice grew soft as the touch of a dove, with a sound of laughter under it.

"Because you're afraid to die, Stevie, just like the rest of us. Even me, Flack, the guy that never had a soul. I never believed in any god but myself and I love life. But sometimes I look at a corpse lying in the street of some human sinkhole and curse it with all my heart because it didn't have to be afraid.

"You'll go into the Cloud, because the Cloud is all that keeps you alive. And you won't care about the red-haired girl, Stevie. You wouldn't care if it was Missy herself giving her life to you, because you're afraid. We're not human any longer, Steve. We've gone beyond. We've sinned—sins there aren't even any names for·in this dimension. And no matter what we believe in, or deny, we're afraid.

"Afraid to die, Stevie. All of us. Afraid to die!"

His words frightened me. I couldn't forget them. I was remembering them even when I saw Shirina.

"I've found a new dimension, Stevie," Shirina said lazily. "A little one, between the Eighth and Ninth. It's so little we missed it before. We'll explore it, after the Cloud."

She led me in our favorite room. It was cut from a crystal so black and deep that it was like being in outer space, and if you looked long enough you could see strange nebulae, far off, and galaxies that never were except in dreams.

"How long before it's time?" I asked her.

"An hour, perhaps less. Poor Stevie. It'll be over soon, and you'll forget."

Her mind touched mine gently, with an intimate sweetness and comfort far beyond the touch of hands. She'd been doing that for hours, soothing the fever and the pain out of my thoughts. I lay without moving, sprawled on a couch so soft it was like a cloud. I could see the glow and shimmer of Shirina against the darkness without turning my head.

I don't know how to describe Shirina. Physically she was close enough to humanity. The differences in structure were more subtle than mere shape. They were—well, they were right, and exotic, and beautiful in a way there aren't any words for.

She, and her race, had no need of clothing. Their lazy, sinuous bodies had a fleecy covering that wasn't fur or feathers or tendrils but something of all three. They had no true color. They changed according to light, in an endless spectrum of loveliness that went far beyond the range you humans know.

Now, in the dark, Shirina's aura glowed like warm pearl. I could see her face, faintly, the queer peaked triangular bones covered with skin softer than a hummingbird's breast, the dead-black, bottomless eyes, the crest of delicate antennae tipped with tiny balls of light like diamonds burning under gauze.

Her thoughts clung around me gently. "There's no need to worry, Stevie," she was thinking. "The girl will go last. It's all arranged. You will enter the Cloud first of all, and there won't be the smallest vibration of her to touch you."

"But she'll touch somebody, Shirina," I groaned. "And it makes it all different, somehow, even with the others. Time doesn't seem to mean much. She's—she's like my own kid."

Shirina answered aloud, patiently. "But she isn't. Your daughter was born three hundred years ago. Three hundred years, that is, for your body. For you there isn't any reckoning. Time is different in every dimension. We've spent a thousand years in some of them, and more than that."

Yes. I could remember those alien years. Dimensional walls are no barrier to thought. You lie under the X-crystals and watch them pulse from mist-gray to depthless black. Your mind is sucked out of you and projected along a tight beam of carefully planned vibration, and presently you're in another space, another time.

You can take over any body that pleases you, for as long as you want. You can go between planets, between suns, between galaxies, just by thinking about it. You can see things, do things, taste experiences that all the languages of our space-time continuum put together have no words for.

Shirina and I had done a lot of wandering, a lot of seeing, and a lot of tasting. And the interlocking universes are infinite.

"I can't help worrying, Shirina," I told her. "I don't want to feel like this, but I can't help it. Right now I'm human. Just plain Steve Vance of Beverly Hills, California, on the planet Earth. I can't bear my memories."

My throat closed up. I was sick, and covered with cold sweat, and closer to going crazy than ever before in all my Satan-knows-how-many years.

Shirina's voice came through the darkness. It was like a bird-call, a flute, a ripple of water over stones, and like nothing that any of you ever heard or ever will hear.

"Stevie," she said. "Listen to me. You're not human any more. You haven't been human since the first time you walked in the Cloud. You have no more contact with those people than they have with the beasts they raise for slaughter."

"But I can't help remembering."

"All right. Remember, then. Remember how from birth you were different from other men. How you had to go on and out, to see things no man had ever seen before, to fight space itself with your heart and your ship and your two hands."

I could recall it. The first man to dare the Belt, the first man to see Jupiter blazing in his swarm of moons.

"That's why, when we caught you in the Veil and brought you to Astellar, we saved you from the Cloud. You had something rare—a strength, a sweep of vision and desire. You could give us something we wanted, an easier contact with human ships. And in return, we gave you life and freedom."

She paused, and added softly, "And myself, Stevie."

"Shirina!" A lot of things met and mingled in our thoughts. Emotions born of alien bodies we had shared. Memories of battle and beauty, of terror and love, under suns that never burned afterward, even in one's dreams. I can't explain it. There aren't any words.

"Shirina, help me!"

Shirina's mind cradled mine like a mother's arms.

"You weren't to blame in the beginning, Stevie. We did it to you under hypnosis, so that your brain could assimilate the change gradually, without shock. I led you myself into our world, like someone leading a child, and when you were finally freed, much time had passed. You had gone beyond humanity. Far beyond."

"I could have stopped. I could have refused to go into the Cloud again, when I knew what it was. I could have refused to be a Judas goat, leading the sheep to slaughter."

"Then why didn't you?"

"Because I had what I wanted," I said slowly. "What I'd always wanted and never had a name for. Power and freedom such as no man ever had. I liked having it. When I thought about you and the things we could do together, and the things I could do alone, I'd have led the whole solar system into the Veil, and be hanged to it."

I drew a harsh, tight breath and wiped the sweat from my palms.

"And besides, I didn't feel human any longer. I wouldn't hurt them any more than I'd have mistreated a dog when I was still a man. But I didn't belong to them anymore."

"Then why is it different now?"

"I don't know. It just is. When I think of Virgie going under the crystals, and me walking in the Cloud, it's too much."

"You've seen their bodies afterward," Shirina said gently. "Not one atom is touched or changed, and they smile. There's no easier or kinder death in Creation."

"I know," I said. "I know. But Virgie is my own."

She'd walk under the X-crystals, smiling, with her red hair dark and shining and her smoke-gray eyes half open and full of dreams. She'd still have the baby in her arms, and Brad would walk beside her. And the X-crystals would pulse and burn with black strange fires, and she would lie down, still smiling, and that would be all.

All, forever, for Virgie and Brad and the green-eyed Martian baby.

But the life that had been in their bodies, the force that no man has a name for that makes the breath and blood and heat of living flesh, the ultimate vibration of the human soul—that life-force would rise up from the crystals, up into the chamber of the Cloud. And Shirina, and Shirina's people, and the four other men like me that weren't human any longer, would walk in it so that we could live.

It hadn't really hit me before. It doesn't. You think of it at first but it doesn't mean anything. There's no semantic referent for "soul" or "ego" or "life-force." You don't see anything, you don't have any contact with the dead. You don't even think much of death.

All you know is you walk into a radiant Cloud, and you feel like a god, and you don't think of the human side of it because you aren't human any longer.

"No wonder they threw you out of your own dimension!" I cried out.

Shirina sighed. "They called us vampires; parasites—sybaritic monsters who lived only for sensation and pleasure. And they cast us into darkness. Well, perhaps they were right. I don't know. But we never hurt or frightened anyone, and when I think of the things they did to their own people, in blood and fear and hate, I'm terrified."

She rose and came and stood over me, glowing like warm pearl against the space-deep crystal. The tiny tips of diamond fire burned on her antennae, and her eyes were like black stars.

I put out my hands to her. She took them, and her touch

broke down my control. I was crying suddenly, not making any sound.

"Right or wrong, Stevie, you're one of us now," she said gently. "I'm sorry this happened. I would have spared you, if you'd let me put your mind to sleep until it was over. But you've got to understand that. You left them, the humans, behind you, and you can never, never go back."

After a long time I spoke. "I know, I understand."

I felt her sigh and shiver, and then she drew back, still holding my hands.

"It's time now, Stevie."

I got up, slowly, and then I stopped. Shirina caught her breath suddenly.

"Steve, my hands! You're hurting me!"

I let them go. "Flack," I said, not talking to anybody. "He knew my weakness. At root and base, no matter how much I talk, I'm going into the Cloud again because I'm afraid. That's why I'll always go into the Cloud when it's time. Because I've sinned so deeply I'm afraid to die."

"What is sin?" Shirina whispered.

"God knows. God only knows."

I brought her bird-soft body into my arms and kissed her, brushing my lips across the shining down of her cheek to her little crimson mouth. There was the faint, bitter taste of my tears in the kiss, and then I laughed, softly.

I pulled the chain and locket from around my neck and dropped them on the floor, and we went out together, to the Cloud.

4

Curtain of Darkness

We walked through the halls of Astellar, like people in the heart of a many-colored jewel. Halls of amber and amethyst and cinnabar, of dragon-green and gray the color of morning mist, and colors there are no names for in this dimension.

The others joined us, coming from the crystal cells where they spent their time. Shirina's people, velvet-eyed and gentle, with their crowns of fire-tipped antennae. They were like a living rainbow in the jewel-light of the halls.

Flack and myself and the three others—only five men, in

all the time Astellar had been in our dimension, with the kind of minds Shirina's people wanted—wore our spaceman's black, walking in our golden auras.

I saw Flack looking at me, but I didn't meet his eyes.

We came finally, to the place of the Cloud, in the center of Astellar. The plain ebon-colored doors stood open. Beyond them there was a mist like curdled sunshine, motes of pure, bright, gilded radiance, coiling and dancing in a cloud of living light.

Shirina took my hand. I knew she wanted to keep me from thinking about the place below, where still through hypnotic command the men and women and children from the *Queen of Jupiter* were walking under the X-crystals to their last long sleep.

I held her, tightly, and we stepped through into the Cloud.

The light closed us in. We walked on something that was not rock, nor anything tangible, but a vibration of force from the X-crystals that held us on a tingling, buoyant web. And the golden, living light clung to us, caressing, spilling over the skin in tiny rippling waves of fire.

I was hungry for it. My body stretched, lifting up. I walked on the vibrant web of power under my feet, my head up, the breath stopped in my throat, every separate atom of my flesh rejuvenated, throbbing and blazing and pulsing with life.

Life!

And then it hit me.

I didn't want it to. I thought I had it down, down for good where it couldn't bother me any more. I thought I'd made my peace with whatever soul I'd had, or lost. I didn't want to think.

But I did. It struck me, suddenly. Like a meteor crashing a ship in space, like the first naked blaze of the sun when you clear the Darkside peaks of Mercury. Like death, the ultimate, final thing you can't dodge or get around.

I knew what that life was and where it came from, and how it had changed me.

It was Virgie. Virgie with her blasted red hair and her smoke-gray eyes, and Missy's life in her, and mine. Why did she have to be sent? Why did I have to meet her beside that dead Martian, on the Jekkara Low-Canal?

But I had met her. And suddenly I knew. I knew!

I don't remember what I did. I must have wrenched loose from Shirina's hand. I felt her startled thought touch my brain, and then it broke away and I was running through the golden Cloud, toward the exit beyond. Running without control, running at top speed.

I think I tried to scream. I don't know. I was clean crazy. But I can remember even then that I sensed somebody running beside me, pacing me through the brilliant blindness of the Cloud.

I plunged out into the hall beyond. It was blue like still deep water, and empty. I ran. I didn't want to run. Some sane corner of my mind cried out to Shirina for help, but she couldn't get through the shrieking chaos of the rest of it. I ran.

And somebody ran behind me. I didn't turn around. I didn't care. I hardly knew it. But somebody ran behind me, on long fleet legs.

Down the blue hall, and into another one that was all flame-color shot with gray, and down that to a curving ramp cut from dark amber that dropped to the level below.

The level where the X-crystals were.

I rushed down the amber path, bounding like a stag with the hounds close behind, through a crystal silence that threw the sound of my breathing back at me, harsh and tearing. There was a circular place at the bottom of the ramp where four hallways met, a place jewel-carved in somber, depthless purple.

I came into it, and from three of the hall mouths men stepped out to meet me. Men with young faces and snow-white hair, and naked bodies burning gold against the purple.

I stopped in the center of the floor. I heard bare feet racing on the ramp behind me, and I knew without looking who it was.

Flack. He circled and fixed me with his cold strange eyes, like moonlight in his dark face. Somewhere he had found a blaster.

He held it on me. Not on my head or heart, but at my middle.

"I thought you might blow your top, Stevie," he said. "So we kind of stood by, in case you'd try something."

I stood still. I didn't have any feelings. I was beyond that. I was crazy—clean, stark crazy, thinking of time and the crystals pulsing just beyond my reach.

"Get out of my way," I warned him.

Flack smiled. There was no humor in it. The three men moved in a little behind him. They looked at Flack and they looked at me, and they didn't like any of it, but they were afraid.

Afraid to die, like all of us. Even Flack, who never had a soul.

Flack acted like someone being patient with a naughty child.

"Will you come back with us, Stevie, or do I blow your insides out, here and now?" he asked me.

I looked at his cold, queer eyes. "You'd like that."

"Yeah." He ran the red tip of his tongue over his swollen lips. "Yeah. But I'm letting you choose."

"All right," I said. "All right, I'll choose."

I was crazy. I jumped him.

I hit him first with my mind. Flack was strong, but I was fifty years older in the Cloud than he was, and Shirina had taught me things. I gathered all the force I had and let him have it, and he had to marshal his own thought-force to fight it off, so that for a second he couldn't manage the blaster with his conscious mind.

Instinctive reflex sent a crimson stream of deadly power smoking past me when I dived in low. It seared my skin, but that was all.

We fell, threshing, on the purple stone. Flack was strong. He was bigger than I, and heavier, and viciously mean. He beat most of the sense out of me, but I had caught his gun wrist and wouldn't let go. The three others took their golden auras back a little toward the hall mouths, afraid the blaster might let off and hit them.

They thought Flack could handle me, and they were afraid. So they drew back and used their minds on me, trying to hammer me down.

I don't know yet why they couldn't. I guess it was because of a lot of things, Shirina's teaching, my greater age, and the fact that I wasn't thinking consciously of anything. I was just a thing that had started some place and was going through.

Sometimes I wish they had broken me. Sometimes I wish Flack had burned me down on the purple stone.

I shook off their thought-blows. I took the pounding of Flack's big fist and the savaging of his feet and knees, and put all my strength into bending his arm. I yanked it away from me, and up and around where I wanted it.

I got it there. He made his last play. He broke his heart on it, and it didn't do him any good. I saw his eyes, stretched wide in his dark face. I can still see them.

I got my finger past his and pressed the firing stud.

I got up and walked across the floor, carrying the blaster. The three others spread out, warily, ringing me. Naked men glowing gold against the purple stone, their eyes hard, animal-bright with fear.

I blasted one through the head just as his muscles tensed for the leap. The others came in, fast. They knocked me down, and time was passing, and the people walking slowly under the crystals with dreams in their eyes.

I kicked one man under the jaw and broke his neck, and the other tried to take the gun away. I had just come from the Cloud, and he hadn't. I was strong with the life that pulsed up from the X-crystals. I forced his arms back and pressed the stud again, trying not to see his eyes.

And these were my friends. Men I drank and laughed with, and went with sometimes to worlds beyond this universe.

I went on, down a hall the color of a Martian dawn. I was empty. I didn't feel or think. There was a pain a long way off, and blood in my mouth, but such things didn't matter.

I came to the place where the crystals were and stopped.

A lot of them had walked under the crystals. Almost half of the five hundred families from the *Queen of Jupiter*. They lay still on the black floor, and there was plenty of room. They didn't crowd the others coming after them, a slow, quiet stream of human beings with dreams in their eyes.

The crystals hung in a wide circle, tilting slightly inward. They pulsed with a blackness that was beyond mere dark, a negative thing as blazing and tangible as sunlight. The angle of tilt and the tuning of the facets against one another made the difference in the result, whether projecting the Veil, or motive power, or hypnosis, or serving as a gateway to another time and space.

Or sucking the power of life from human bodies.

I could see the pale shimmer of force in the center, a sort

of vortex between the limitless, burning, black facets that rose from the quiet bodies to the chamber of the Cloud above.

I could see the faces of the dead. They were still smiling.

The controls were on the other side. I ran. I was dead inside, as dead as the corpses on the floor, but I ran. I remember thinking it was funny to run when you were dead. I kept on the outside of the crystals and ran with all my strength to the controls.

I saw Virgie. She was way back in the procession, and she was just as I knew she'd be, with Brad beside her and the green-eyed baby still in her arms, asleep.

Virgie, with her gleaming red hair and Missy's eyes!

I grabbed the controls and wrenched them over, and the shimmering vortex disappeared. I spun the great hexagonal wheel and notched it for full-power hypnosis, and ran out onto the floor, among the dead.

I told the living what to do. I didn't waken them. They turned and went back the way they came, back toward the *Queen of Jupiter*, running hard and still smiling, still not afraid.

I went back to the wheel and turned it again, to a notch marked in their danger-color, and then I followed the last of the humans into the hall. At the doorway I turned and raised my blaster.

I saw Shirina standing under the radiant blackness of the crystals, halfway around the curving wall.

I felt her mind touch mine, and then drew back, slowly, the way you take your hand away from someone you loved that has just died. I looked at her eyes. I had to.

Why did I do what I did? What did I care about red hair and smoke-gray eyes, and the three-hundred-year diluted blood of a girl named Missy? I wasn't human any longer. What did I care?

We were apart, Shirina and I. We had gone away from each other and we couldn't touch, even to say good-bye. I caught a faint echo of her thought.

"Oh, Stevie, there were still so many things to do!"

Her great luminous black eyes shining with tears, her jewel-tipped antennae dulled and drooping. And yet I knew what she was going to do.

I couldn't see the crystals, suddenly. I couldn't see anything. I knew there was never going to be anything I wanted to see again. I raised the blaster and fired it full power into one of the hanging crystals, and then I ran.

I felt the bolt of Shirina's lethal thought strike my brain, and weaken, and shatter on something in her own mind, at its source. I ran, a dead thing going on leaden feet, in a halo of golden light.

Behind me the X-crystals, upset by the blaster in their fullest sympathy of power, began to split and crack and tear the world of Astellar to bits.

I don't know much about what happened. I ran and ran, on the heels of the humans who still lived, but I was beyond thinking or feeling. I have vague memories of hallways lined with cells of jewel-toned crystal, halls of amber and amethyst and cinnabar, of dragon-green and gray the color of morning mist, and colors there are no names for in this dimension.

Hallways that cracked and split behind me, falling in upon themselves, shards of broken rainbows. And above that the scream of power from the X-crystals, wrenching and tearing at Astellar.

Then something I heard with my mind, and not my ears. Shirina's people, dying in the wreckage.

My mind was stunned, but not stunned enough. I could still hear. I can still hear.

The *Queen of Jupiter* was safe. The outward-moving vibration hadn't reached her yet. We got aboard her, and I opened the space doors and blasted her off myself, because the skipper and the first and second officers were asleep for good on Astellar.

I didn't watch the death of Astellar. Only after a long time I looked back, and it was gone, and there was only a cloud of bright dust shimmering in the raw sunlight.

I set the Iron Mike for Space Authority headquarters on Mars and turned on the automatic AC warning beam. Then I left the *Queen of Jupiter* in the Number 4 lifeboat, B deck.

That's where I am now, writing this, somewhere between Mars and the Belt. I didn't see Virgie before I went. I didn't see any of them, but especially Virgie. They'll be awake now. I hope their lives are worth what they cost.

Astellar is gone. The Veil is gone. You don't have to be afraid any more. I'm going to put this manuscript in a message rocket and send it on, so you'll know you don't have to fear. I don't know why I care.

I don't know why I'm writing this at all, unless—Bosh, I
know! Why lie? At this stage of the game, why lie?

I'm alive now. I'm a young man. But the Cloud that kept
me that way is gone, and presently I shall grow old, too old,
very quickly, and die. And I'm afraid to die.

Somewhere in the solar system there must be somebody
willing to pray for me. They used to teach me, when I was a
kid, that prayer helped. I want somebody to pray for my
soul, because I can't do it for myself.

If I were glad of what I've done, if I had changed, perhaps
then I could pray.

But I've gone beyond humanity, and I can't turn back.

Maybe prayer doesn't matter. Maybe there's nothing beyond death but oblivion. I hope so! If I could only stop
being, stop thinking, stop remembering.

I hope to all the gods of all the universes that death is the
end. But I don't know, and I'm afraid.

Afraid. Judas—Judas—Judas! I betrayed two worlds, and
there couldn't be a hell deeper than the one I live in now.
And still I'm afraid.

Why? Why should I care what happens to me? I destroyed
Astellar. I destroyed Shirina, whom I loved better than any-
thing in Creation. I destroyed my friends, my comrades—and
I have destroyed myself.

And you're not worth it. Not all the human cattle that
breed in the solar system were worth Astellar, and Shirina,
and the things we did beyond space and time, together.

Why did I give Missy that locket?

Why did I have to meet Virgie, with her red hair?

Why did I remember? Why did I care? Why did I do what
I did?

Why was I ever born?

CITY

Astounding,
May

by Clifford D. Simak (1904-   )

Clifford D. Simak first appeared in the science fiction magazines with "The World of the Red Sun," in Wonder Stories *in 1931, so he was a veteran sf writer with thirteen years experience when "City" was published. Although well-known in the field, he was not considered on a level with Heinlein, the Kuttners, van Vogt, and others. This evaluation began to change with the three stories in this book and more that followed, and Cliff Simak emerged in the 1950s as one of the great talents in all of science fiction.*

"City" was the first of a series that with additional linking material appeared in book form (as City*) in 1952, and walked off with the second International Fantasy Award in 1953, defeating such tough competition as Kurt Vonnegut's* Player Piano. *Written at a time when the impact of urbanization on modern life was not being discussed in either general or scholarly publications, Simak's emphasis on the pastoral life and rural values proved immensely popular. These themes are still central to his work, which is appearing regularly, even though the author is in his mid-seventies.*

(This is the first time a story of Cliff's appears in this series, so I haven't had a chance to mention before what he meant to me. "The World of the Red Sun" was a story that pinned my 11-year-old self to the wall when it first appeared. It was one of the stories I told to my fellow junior-high-school students when they gathered round me for the only kind of science fiction they could afford. It wasn't

*till years afterward, after Cliff had become a good
friend of mine, that I discovered he had written it.
And, as Marty said, it was his first published story.
He was one of the few pre-Campbell writers who
could grow and become a great Campbell
writer.—I.A.)*

Gramp Stevens sat in a lawn chair, watching the mower at
work, feeling the warm, soft sunshine seep into his bones.
The mower reached the edge of the lawn, clucked to itself
like a contented hen, made a neat turn and trundled down
another swath. The bag holding the clippings bulged.

Suddenly the mower stopped and clicked excitedly. A
panel in its side snapped open and a cranelike arm reached
out. Grasping steel fingers fished around in the grass, came
up triumphantly with a stone clutched tightly, dropped the
stone into a small container, disappeared back into the panel
again. The lawn mower gurgled, purred on again, following
its swath.

Gramp grumbled at it with suspicion.

"Some day," he told himself, "that dadburned thing is going to miss a lick and have a nervous breakdown."

He lay back in the chair and stared up at the sun-washed
sky. A helicopter skimmed far overhead. From somewhere inside the house a radio came to life and a torturing clash of
music poured out. Gramp, hearing it, shivered and hunkered
lower in the chair.

Young Charlie was settling down for a twitch session. Dad-
burn the kid.

The lawn mower chuckled past and Gramp squinted at it
maliciously.

"Automatic," he told the sky. "Ever' blasted thing is automatic now. Getting so you just take a machine off in a corner
and whisper in its ear and it scurries off to do the job."

His daughter's voice came to him out the window, pitched
to carry above the music.

"Father!"

Gramp stirred uneasily. "Yes, Betty."

"Now, father, you see you move when that lawn mower

gets to you. Don't try to out-stubborn it. After all, it's only a machine. Last time you just sat there and made it cut around you. I never saw the beat of you."

He didn't answer, letting his head nod a bit, hoping she would think he was asleep and let him be.

"Father," she shrilled, "did you hear me?"

He saw it was no good. "Sure, I heard you," he told her. "I was just fixing to move."

He rose slowly to his feet, leaning heavily on his cane. Might make her feel sorry for the way she treated him when she saw how old and feeble he was getting. He'd have to be careful, though. If she knew he didn't need the cane at all, she'd be finding jobs for him to do and, on the other hand, if he laid it on too thick, she'd be having that fool doctor in to pester him again.

Grumbling, he moved the chair out into that portion of the lawn that had been cut. The mower, rolling past, chortled at him fiendishly.

"Some day," Gramp told it, "I'm going to take a swipe at you and bust a gear or two."

The mower hooted at him and went serenely down the lawn.

From somewhere down the grassy street came a jangling of metal, a stuttered coughing.

Gramp, ready to sit down, straightened up and listened.

The sound came more clearly, the rumbling backfire of a balky engine, the clatter of loose metallic parts.

"An automobile!" yelped Gramp. "An automobile, by cracky!"

He started to gallop for the gate, suddenly remembered that he was feeble and subsided to a rapid hobble.

"Must be that crazy Ole Johnson," he told himself. "He's the only one left that's got a car. Just too dadburned stubborn to give it up."

It was Ole.

Gramp reached the gate in time to see the rusty, dilapidated old machine come bumping around the corner, rocking and chugging along the unused street. Steam hissed from the overheated radiator and a cloud of blue smoke issued from the exhaust, which had lost its muffler five years or more ago.

Ole sat stolidly behind the wheel, squinting, trying to duck the roughest places, although that was hard to do, for weeds

and grass had overrun the streets and it was hard to see what
might be underneath them.

Gramp waved his cane.

"Hi, Ole," he shouted.

Ole pulled up, setting the emergency brake. The car
gasped, shuddered, coughed, died with a horrible sigh.

"What you burning?" asked Gramp.

"Little bit of everything," said Ole. "Kerosene, some old
tractor oil I found out in a barrel, some rubbing alcohol."

Gramp regarded the fugitive machine with forthright admi-
ration. "Them was the days," he said. "Had one myself; used
to be able to do a hundred miles an hour."

"Still O.K.," said Ole. "If you could only find the stuff to
run them or get the parts to fix them. Up to three, four years
ago I used to be able to get enough gasoline, but ain't seen
none for a long time now. Quit making it, I guess. No use
having gasoline, they tell me, when you have atomic power."

"Sure," said Gramp. "Guess maybe that's right, but you
can't smell atomic power. Sweetest thing I know, the smell of
burning gasoline. These here helicopters and other gadgets
they got took all the romance out of traveling, somehow."

He squinted at the barrels and baskets piled in the back
seat.

"Got some vegetables?" he asked.

"Yup," said Ole. "Some sweet corn and early potatoes and
a few baskets of tomatoes. Thought maybe I could sell
them."

Gramp shook his head. "You won't, Ole. They won't buy
them. Folks has got the notion that this new hydroponics stuff
is the only garden sass that's fit to eat. Sanitary, they say, and
better flavored."

"Wouldn't give a hoot in a tin cup for all they grow in
them tanks they got," Ole declared, belligerently. "Don't taste
right to me, somehow. Like I tell Martha, food's got to be
raised in the soil to have any character."

He reached down to turn over the ignition switch.

"Don't know as it's worth trying to get the stuff to town,"
he said, "the way they keep the roads. Or the way they don't
keep them, rather. Twenty years ago the state highway out
there was a strip of good concrete and they kept it patched
and plowed it every winter. Did anything, spent any amount
of money to keep it open. And now they just forgot about it.

The concrete's all broken up and some of it has washed out. Brambles are growing in it. Had to get out and cut away a tree that fell across it one place this morning."

"Ain't it the truth," agreed Gramp.

The car exploded into life, coughing and choking. A cloud of dense blue smoke rolled out from under it. With a jerk it stirred to life and lumbered down the street.

Gramp clumped back to his chair and found it dripping wet. The automatic mower, having finished its cutting job, had rolled out the hose, was sprinkling the lawn.

Muttering venom, Gramp stalked around the corner of the house and sat down on the bench beside the back porch. He didn't like to sit there, but it was the only place he was safe from the hunk of machinery out in front.

For one thing, the view from the bench was slightly depressing, fronting as it did on street after street of vacant, deserted houses and weed-grown, unkempt yards.

It had one advantage, however. From the bench he could pretend he was slightly deaf and not hear the twitch music the radio was blaring out.

A voice called from the front yard.

"Bill! Bill, where be you?"

Gramp twisted around.

"Here I am, Mark. Back of the house. Hiding from that dadburned mower."

Mark Bailey limped around the corner of the house, cigarette threatening to set fire to his bushy whiskers.

"Bit early for the game, ain't you?" asked Gramp.

"Can't play no game today," said Mark.

He hobbled over and sat down beside Gramp on the bench.

"We're leaving," he said.

Gramp whirled on him. "You're leaving!"

"Yeah. Moving out into the country. Lucinda finally talked Herb into it. Never gave him a minute's peace, I guess. Said everyone was moving away to one of them nice country estates and she didn't see no reason why we couldn't."

Gramp gulped. "Where to?"

"Don't rightly know," said Mark. "Ain't been there myself. Up north some place. Up on one of the lakes. Got ten acres of land. Lucinda wanted a hundred, but Herb put down his

foot and said ten was enough. After all, one city lot was
enough for all these years."

"Betty was pestering Johnny, too," said Gramp, "but he's
holding out **aga**inst her. Says he simply can't do it. Says it
wouldn't look right, him the secretary of the Chamber of
Commerce and all, if he went moving away from the city."

"Folks are crazy," Mark declared. "Plumb crazy."

"That's a fact," Gramp agreed. "Country crazy, that's what
they are. Look across there."

He waved his hand at the streets of vacant houses. "Can
remember the time when those places were as pretty a bunch
of homes as you ever laid your eyes on. Good neighbors, they
were. Women ran across from one back door to another to
trade recipes. And the men folks would go out to cut the
grass and pretty soon the mowers would all be sitting idle and
the men would be ganged up, chewing the fat. Friendly
people, Mark. But look at it now."

Mark stirred uneasily. "Got to be getting back, Bill. Just
sneaked over to let you know we were lighting out. Lucinda's
got me packing. She'd be sore if she knew I'd run out."

Gramp rose stiffly and held out his hand. "I'll be seeing
you again? You be over for one last game?"

Mark shook his head. "Afraid not, Bill."

They shook hands awkwardly, abashed. "Sure will miss
them games," said Mark.

"Me, too," said Gramp. "I won't have nobody once you're
gone."

"So long, Bill," said Mark.

"So long," said Gramp.

He stood and watched his friend hobble around the house,
felt the cold claw of loneliness reach out and touch him with
icy fingers. A terrible loneliness. The loneliness of age—of
age and the outdated. Fiercely, Gramp admitted it. He was
outdated. He belonged to another age. He had outstripped his
time, lived beyond his years.

Eyes misty, he fumbled for the cane that lay against the
bench, slowly made his way toward the sagging gate that
opened onto the deserted street back of the house.

The years had moved too fast. Years that had brought the
family plane and helicopter, leaving the auto to rust in some
forgotten place, the unused roads to fall into disrepair. Years

that had virtually wiped out the tilling of the soil with the rise of hydroponics. Years that had brought cheap land with the disappearance of the farm as an economic unit, had sent city people scurrying out into the country where each man, for less than the price of a city lot, might own broad acres. Years that had revolutionized the construction of homes to a point where families simply walked away from their old homes to the new ones that could be bought, custom-made, for less than half the price of a prewar structure and could be changed at small cost, to accommodate need of additional space or just a passing whim.

Gramp sniffed. Houses that could be changed each year, just like one would shift around the furniture. What kind of living was that?

He plodded slowly down the dusty path that was all that remained of what a few years before had been a busy residential street. A street of ghosts, Gramp told himself—of furtive, little ghosts that whispered in the night. Ghosts of playing children, ghosts of upset tricycles and canted coaster wagons. Ghosts of gossiping housewives. Ghosts of shouted greetings. Ghosts of flaming fireplaces and chimneys smoking of a winter night.

Little puffs of dust rose around his feet and whitened the cuffs of his trousers.

There was the old Adams place across the way. Adams had been mighty proud of it, he remembered. Gray field stone front and picture windows. Now the stone was green with creeping moss and the broken windows gaped with ghastly leer. Weeds choked the lawn and blotted out the stoop. An elm tree was pushing its branches against the gable. Gramp could remember the day Adams had planted that elm tree.

For a moment he stood there in the grass-grown street, feet in the dust, both hands clutching the curve of his cane, eyes closed.

Through the fog of years he heard the cry of playing children, the barking of Conrad's yapping pooch from down the street. And there was Adams, stripped to the waist, plying the shovel, scooping out the hole, with the elm tree, roots wrapped in burlap, lying on the lawn.

May, 1946. Forty-four years ago. Just after he and Adams had come home from the war together.

Footsteps padded in the dust and Gramp, startled, opened
his eyes.

Before him stood a young man. A man of thirty, perhaps.
Maybe a bit less.

"Good morning," said Gramp.

"I hope," said the young man, "that I didn't startle you."

"You saw me standing here," asked Gramp, "like a danged
fool, with my eyes shut?"

The young man nodded.

"I was remembering," said Gramp.

"You live around here?"

"Just down the street. The last one in this part of the
city."

"Perhaps you can help me then."

"Try me," said Gramp.

The young man stammered. "Well, you see, it's like this.
I'm on a sort of . . . well, you might call it a sentimental pil-
grimage—"

"I understand," said Gramp. "So am I."

"My name is Adams," said the young man. "My grandfather used to live around here somewhere. I wonder—"

"Right over there," said Gramp.

Together they stood and stared at the house.

"It was a nice place once," Gramp told him. "Your
granddaddy planted that tree right after he came home from
the war. I was with him all through the war and we came
home together. That was a day for you . . ."

"It's a pity," said young Adams. "A pity . . ."

But Gramp didn't seem to hear him. "Your granddaddy?"
he asked. "I seem to have lost track of him."

"He's dead," said young Adams. "Quite a number of years
ago."

"He was messed up with atomic power," said Gramp.

"That's right," said Adams proudly. "Got into it just as
soon as it was released to industry. Right after the Moscow
agreement."

"Right after they decided," said Gramp, "they couldn't
fight a war."

"That's right," said Adams.

"It's pretty hard to fight a war," said Gramp, "when there's
nothing you can aim at."

"You mean the cities," said Adams.

"Sure," said Gramp, "and there's a funny thing about it. Wave all the atom bombs you wanted to and you couldn't scare them out. But give them cheap land and family planes and they scattered just like so many dadburned rabbits."

John J. Webster was striding up the broad stone steps of the city hall when the walking scarecrow carrying a rifle under his arm caught up with him and stopped him.

"Howdy, Mr. Webster," said the scarecrow.

Webster stared, then recognition crinkled his face.

"It's Levi," he said. "How are things going, Levi?"

Levi Lewis grinned with snagged teeth. "Fair to middling. Gardens are coming along and the young rabbits are getting to be good eating."

"You aren't getting mixed up in any of the hell raising that's being laid to the *houses?*" asked Webster.

"No, sir," declared Levi. "Ain't none of us Squatters mixed up in any wrongdoing. We're law-abiding, God-fearing people, we are. Only reason we're there is we can't make a living no place else. And us living in them places other people up and left ain't harming no one. Police are just blaming us for the thievery and other things that's going on, knowing we can't protect ourselves. They're making us the goats."

"I'm glad to hear that," said Webster. "The chief wants to burn the *houses.*"

"If he tries that," said Levi, "he'll run against something he ain't counting on. They run us off our farms with this tank farming of theirs but they ain't going to run us any farther."

He spat across the steps.

"Wouldn't happen you might have some jingling money on you?" he asked. "I'm fresh out of cartridges and with them rabbits coming up—"

Webster thrust his fingers into a vest pocket, pulled out a half dollar.

Levi grinned. "That's obliging of you, Mr. Webster. I'll bring a mess of squirrels, come fall."

The Squatter touched his hat with two fingers and retreated down the steps, sun glinting on the rifle barrel. Webster turned up the steps again.

The city council session already was in full swing when he walked into the chamber.

Police Chief Jim Maxwell was standing by the table and Mayor Paul Carter was talking.

"Don't you think you may be acting a bit hastily, Jim, in urging such a course of action with the *houses?*"

"No, I don't," declared the chief. "Except for a couple of dozen or so, none of those houses are occupied by their rightful owners, or rather, their original owners. Every one of them belongs to the city now through tax forfeiture. And they are nothing but an eyesore and a menace. They have no value. Not even salvage value. Wood? We don't use wood any more. Plastics are better. Stone? We use steel instead of stone. Not a single one of those houses has any material of marketable value.

"And in the meantime they are becoming the haunts of petty criminals and undesirable elements. Grown up with vegetation as the residential sections are, they make a perfect hideout for all types of criminals. A man commits a crime and heads straight for the *houses*—once there he's safe, for I could send a thousand men in there and he could elude them all.

"They aren't worth the expense of tearing down. And yet they are, if not a menace, at least a nuisance. We should get rid of them and fire is the cheapest, quickest way. We'd use all precautions."

"What about the legal angle?" asked the mayor.

"I checked into that. A man has a right to destroy his own property in any way he may see fit so long as it endangers no one else's. The same law, I suppose, would apply to a municipality."

Alderman Thomas Griffin sprang to his feet.

"You'd alienate a lot of people," he declared. "You'd be burning down a lot of old homesteads. People still have some sentimental attachments—"

"If they cared for them," snapped the chief, "why didn't they pay the taxes and take care of them? Why did they go running off to the country, just leaving the houses standing. Ask Webster here. He can tell you what success he had trying to interest the people in their ancestral homes."

"You're talking about that Old Home Week farce," said Griffin. "It failed. Of course, it failed. Webster spread it on so thick that they gagged on it. That's what a Chamber of Commerce mentality always does."

Alderman Forrest King spoke up angrily. "There's nothing wrong with a Chamber of Commerce, Griffin. Simply because you failed in business is no reason . . ."

Griffin ignored him. "The day of high pressure is over, gentlemen. The day of high pressure is gone forever. Bally-hoo is something that is dead and buried.

"The day when you could have tall-corn days or dollar days or dream up some fake celebration and deck the place up with bunting and pull in big crowds that were ready to spend money is past these many years. Only you fellows don't seem to know it.

"The success of such stunts as that was its appeal to mob psychology and civic loyalty. You can't have civic loyalty with a city dying on its feet. You can't appeal to mob psychology when there is no mob—when every man, or nearly every man has the solitude of forty acres."

"Gentlemen," pleaded the mayor. "Gentlemen, this is distinctly out of order."

King sputtered into life, walloped the table.

"No, let's have it out. Webster is over there. Perhaps he can tell us what he thinks."

Webster stirred uncomfortably. "I scarcely believe," he said, "I have anything to say."

"Forget it," snapped Griffin and sat down.

But King still stood, face crimson, his mouth trembling with anger.

"Webster!" he shouted.

Webster shook his head. "You came here with one of your big ideas," shouted King. "You were going to lay it before the council. Step up, man, and speak your piece."

Webster rose slowly, grim-lipped.

"Perhaps you're too thick-skulled," he told King, "to know why I resent the way you have behaved."

King gasped, then exploded. "Thick-skulled! You would say that to me. We've worked together and I've helped you. You've never called me that before . . . you've—"

"I've never called you that before," said Webster, levelly. "Naturally not. I wanted to keep my job."

"Well, you haven't got a job," roared King. "From this minute on, you haven't got a job."

"Shut up," said Webster.

King stared at him, bewildered, as if someone had slapped him across the face.

"And sit down," said Webster, and his voice bit through the room like a sharp-edged knife.

King's knees caved beneath him and he sat down abruptly. The silence was brittle.

"I have something to say," said Webster. "Something that should have been said long ago. Something all of you should hear. That I should be the one who would tell it to you is the one thing that astounds me. And yet, perhaps, as one who has worked in the interests of this city for almost fifteen years, I am the logical one to speak the truth.

"Alderman Griffin said the city is dying on its feet and his statement is correct. There is but one fault I would find with it and that is its understatement. The city . . . this city, any city . . . already is dead.

"The city is an anachronism. It has outlived its usefulness. Hydroponics and the helicopter spelled its downfall. In the first instance the city was a tribal place, an area where the tribe banded together for mutual protection. In later years a wall was thrown around it for additional protection. Then the wall finally disappeared but the city lived on because of the conveniences which it offered trade and commerce. It continued into modern times because people were compelled to live close to their jobs and the jobs were in the city.

"But today that is no longer true. With the family plane, one hundred miles today is a shorter distance than five miles back in 1930. Men can fly several hundred miles to work and fly home when the day is done. There is no longer any need for them to live cooped up in a city.

"The automobile started the trend and the family plane finished it. Even in the first part of the century the trend was noticeable—a movement away from the city with its taxes and its stuffiness, a move toward the suburb and close-in acreages. Lack of adequate transportation, lack of finances held many to the city. But now, with tank farming destroying the value of land, a man can buy a huge acreage in the country for less than he could a city lot forty years ago. With planes powered by atomics there is no longer any transportation problem."

He paused and the silence held. The mayor wore a shocked

look. King's lips moved, but no words came. Griffin was smiling.

"So what have we?" asked Webster. "I'll tell you what we have. Street after street, block after block, of deserted houses, houses that the people just up and walked away from. Why should they have stayed? What could the city offer them? None of the things that it offered the generations before them, for progress had wiped out the need of the city's benefits. They lost something, some monetary consideration, of course, when they left the houses. But the fact that they could buy a house twice as good for half as much, the fact that they could live as they wished to live, that they could develop what amounts to family estates after the best tradition set them by the wealthy of a generation ago—all these things outweighed the leaving of their homes.

"And what have we left? A few blocks of business houses. A few acres of industrial plants. A city government geared to take care of a million people without the million people. A budget that has run the taxes so high that eventually even business houses will move to escape those taxes. Tax forfeitures that have left us loaded with worthless property. That's what we have left.

"If you think any Chamber of Commerce, any ballyhoo, any hare-brained scheme will give you the answers, you're crazy. There is only one answer and that is simple. The city as a human institution is dead. It may struggle on a few more years, but that is all."

"Mr. Webster—" said the mayor.

But Webster paid him no attention.

"But for what happened today," he said, "I would have stayed on and played doll house with you. I would have gone on pretending that the city was a going concern. Would have gone on kidding myself and you. But there is, gentlemen, such a thing as human dignity."

The icy silence broke down in the rustling of papers, the muffled cough of some embarrassed listener.

But Webster was not through.

"The city failed," he said, "and it is well it failed. Instead of sitting here in mourning above its broken body you should rise to your feet and shout your thanks it failed.

"For if this city had not outlived its usefulness, as did every other city—if the cities of the world had not been deserted, they would have been destroyed. There would have been a war, gentlemen, an atomic war. Have you forgotten the 1950's and the 60's? Have you forgotten waking up at night and listening for the bomb to come, knowing that you would not hear it when it came, knowing that you would never hear again, if it did come?

"But the cities were deserted and industry was dispersed and there were no targets and there was no war.

"Some of you gentlemen," he said, "many of you gentlemen, are alive today because the people left your city.

"Now, for God's sake, let it stay dead. Be happy that it's dead. It's the best thing that ever happened in all human history."

John J. Webster turned on his heel and left the room.

Outside on the broad stone steps, he stopped and stared up at the cloudless sky, saw the pigeons wheeling above the turrets and spires of the city hall.

He shook himself mentally, like a dog coming out of a pool.

He had been a fool, of course. Now he'd have to hunt for a job and it might take time to find one. He was getting a bit old to be hunting for a job.

But despite his thoughts, a little tune rose unbidden to his lips. He walked away briskly, lips pursed, whistling soundlessly.

No more hypocrisy. No more lying awake nights wondering what to do—knowing that the city was dead, knowing that what he did was a useless task, feeling like a heel for taking a salary that he knew he wasn't earning. Sensing the strange, nagging frustration of a worker who knows his work is nonproductive.

He strode toward the parking lot, heading for his helicopter.

Now, maybe, he told himself, they could move out into the country the way Betty wanted to. Maybe he could spend his evenings tramping land that belonged to him. A place with a stream. Definitely it had to have a stream he could stock with trout.

He made a mental note to go up into the attic and check his fly equipment.

Martha Johnson was waiting at the barnyard gate when the old car chugged down the lane.

Ole got out stiffly, face rimmed with weariness.

"Sell anything?" asked Martha.

Ole shook his head. "It ain't no use. They won't buy farm-raised stuff. Just laughed at me. Showed me ears of corn twice as big as the ones I had, just as sweet and with more even rows. Showed me melons that had almost no rind at all. Better tasting, too, they said."

He kicked at a clod and it exploded into dust.

"There ain't no getting around it," he declared. "Tank farming has ruined us."

"Maybe we better fix to sell the farm," suggested Martha.

Ole said nothing.

"You could get a job on a tank farm," she said. "Harry did. Likes it real well."

Ole shook his head.

"Or maybe a gardener," said Martha. "You would make a right smart gardener. Ritzy folks that's moved out to big estates like to have gardeners to take care of flowers and things. More classy than doing it with machines."

Ole shook his head again. "Couldn't stand to mess around with flowers," he declared. "Not after raising corn for more than twenty years."

"Maybe," said Martha, "we could have one of them little planes. And running water in the house. And a bathtub instead of taking a bath in the old washtub by the kitchen fire."

"Couldn't run a plane," objected Ole.

"Sure you could," said Martha. "Simple to run, they are. Why, them Anderson kids ain't no more than knee-high to a cricket and they fly one all over. One of them got fooling around and fell out once, but——"

"I got to think about it," said Ole desperately. "I got to think."

He swung away, vaulted a fence, headed for the fields. Martha stood beside the car and watched him go. One lone tear rolled down her dusty cheek.

"Mr. Taylor is waiting for you," said the girl.

John J. Webster stammered. "But I haven't been here before. He didn't know I was coming."

"Mr. Taylor," insisted the girl, "is waiting for you."
She nodded her head toward the door. It read:

Bureau of Human Adjustment

"But I came here to get a job," protested Webster. "I didn't come to be adjusted or anything. This is the World Committee's placement service, isn't it?"

"That is right," the girl declared. "Won't you see Mr. Taylor?"

"Since you insist," said Webster.

The girl clicked over a switch, spoke into the intercommunicator. "Mr. Webster is here, sir."

"Send him in," said a voice.

Hat in hand, Webster walked through the door.

The man behind the desk had white hair but a young man's face. He motioned toward a chair.

"You've been trying to find a job," he said.

"Yes," said Webster, "but—"

"Please sit down," said Taylor. "If you're thinking about that sign on the door, forget it. We'll not try to adjust you."

"I couldn't find a job," said Webster. "I've hunted for weeks and no one would have me. So, finally, I came here."

"You didn't want to come here?"

"No, frankly, I didn't. A placement service. It has, well . . . it has an implication I do not like."

Taylor smiled. "The terminology may be unfortunate. You're thinking of the employment services of the old days. The places where men went when they were desperate for work. The government operated places that tried to find work for men so they wouldn't become public charges."

"I'm desperate enough," confessed Webster. "But I still have a pride that made it hard to come. But, finally, there was nothing else to do. You see, I turned traitor—"

"You mean," said Taylor, "that you told the truth. Even when it cost you your job. The business world, not only here, but all over the world is not ready for that truth. The businessman still clings to the city myth, to the myth of salesmanship. In time to come he will realize he doesn't need the city, that service and honest values will bring him more substantial business than salesmanship ever did.

"I've wondered, Webster, just what made you do what you did?"

"I was sick of it," said Webster. "Sick of watching men blundering along with their eyes tight shut. Sick of seeing an old tradition being kept alive when it should have been laid away. Sick of King's simpering civic enthusiasm when all cause for enthusiasm had vanished."

Taylor nodded. "Webster, do you think you could adjust human beings?"

Webster merely stared.

"I mean it," said Taylor. "The World Committee has been doing it for years, quietly, unobtrusively. Even many of the people who have been adjusted don't know they have been adjusted.

"Changes such as have come since the creation of the World Committee out of the old United Nations has meant much human maladjustment. The advent of workable atomic power took jobs away from hundreds of thousands. They had to be trained and guided into new jobs, some with the new atomics, some into other lines of work. The advent of tank farming swept the farmers off their land. They, perhaps, have supplied us with our greatest problem, for other than the special knowledge needed to grow crops and handle animals, they had no skills. Most of them had no wish for acquiring skills. Most of them were bitterly resentful at having been forced from the livelihood which they inherited from their forebears. And being natural individualists, they offered the toughest psychological problems of any other class."

"Many of them," declared Webster, "still are at loose ends. There's a hundred or more of them squatting out in the *houses*, living from hand to mouth. Shooting a few rabbits and a few squirrels, doing some fishing, raising vegetables and picking wild fruit. Engaging in a little petty thievery now and then and doing occasional begging on the uptown streets."

"You know these people?" asked Taylor.

"I know some of them," said Webster. "One of them brings me squirrels and rabbits on occasions. To make up for it, he bums ammunition money."

"They'd resent being adjusted, wouldn't they?"

"Violently," said Webster.

"You know a farmer by the name of Ole Johnson? Still sticking to his farm, still unreconstructed?"

Webster nodded.

"What if you tried to adjust him?"

"He'd run me off the farm," said Webster.

"Men like Ole and the Squatters," said Taylor, "are our special problems now. Most of the rest of the world is fairly well-adjusted, fairly well settled into the groove of the present. Some of them are doing a lot of moaning about the past, but that's just for effect. You couldn't drive them back to their old ways of life.

"Years ago, with the advent of industrial atomics in fact, the World Committee faced a hard decision. Should changes that spelled progress in the world be brought about gradually to allow the people to adjust themselves naturally, or should they be developed as quickly as possible, with the committee aiding in the necessary human adjustment? It was decided, rightly or wrongly, that progress should come first, regardless of its effect upon the people. The decision in the main has proved a wise one.

"We knew, of course, that in many instances, this readjustment could not be made too openly. In some cases, as in large groups of workers who had been displaced, it was possible, but in most individual cases, such as our friend Ole, it was not. These people must be helped to find themselves in this new world, but they must not know that they're being helped. To let them know would destroy confidence and dignity, and human dignity is the keystone of any civilization."

"I knew, of course, about the readjustments made within industry itself," said Webster, "but I had not heard of the individual cases."

"We could not advertise it," Taylor said. "It's practically undercover."

"But why are you telling me all this now?"

"Because we'd like you to come in with us. Have a hand at adjusting Ole to start with. Maybe see what could be done about the Squatters next."

"I don't know—" said Webster.

"We'd been waiting for you to come in," said Taylor. "We knew you'd finally have to come here. Any chance you might have had at any kind of job would have been queered by King. He passed the word along. You're blackballed by every

Chamber of Commerce and every civic group in the world today."

"Probably I have no choice," said Webster.

"We don't want you to feel that way about it," Taylor said. "Take a while to think it over, then come back. Even if you don't want the job we'll find you another one—in spite of King."

Outside the office, Webster found a scarecrow figure waiting for him. It was Levi Lewis, snaggle-toothed grin wiped off, rifle under his arm.

"Some of the boys said they seen you go in here," he explained. "So I waited for you."

"What's the trouble?" Webster asked, for Levi's face spoke eloquently of trouble.

"It's them police," said Levi. He spat disgustedly.

"The police," said Webster, and his heart sank as he said the words. For he knew what the trouble was.

"Yeah," said Levi. "They're fixing to burn us out."

"So the council finally gave in," said Webster.

"I just came from police headquarters," declared Levi. "I told them they better go easy. I told them there'd be guts strewed all over the place if they tried it. I got the boys posted all around the place with orders not to shoot till they're sure of hitting."

"You can't do that, Levi," said Webster, sharply.

"I can't!" retorted Levi. "I done it already. They drove us off the farms, forced us to sell because we couldn't make a living. And they aren't driving us no farther. We either stay here or we die here. And the only way they'll burn us out is when there's no one left to stop them."

He shucked up his pants and spat again.

"And we ain't the only ones that feel that way," he declared. "Gramp is out there with us."

"Gramp!"

"Sure, Gramp. The old guy that lives with you. He's sort of taken over as our commanding general. Says he remembers tricks from the war them police have never heard of. He sent some of the boys over to one of them Legion halls to swipe a cannon. Says he knows where we can get some shells for it from the museum. Says we'll get it all set up and then send word that if the police make a move we'll shell the loop."

"Look, Levi, will you do something for me?"

"Sure will, Mr. Webster."

"Will you go in and ask for a Mr. Taylor? Insist on seeing him. Tell him I'm already on the job."

"Sure will, but where are you going?"

"I'm going up to the city hall."

"Sure you don't want me along?"

"No," declared Webster. "I'll do better alone. And, Levi—"

"Yes."

"Tell Gramp to hold up his artillery. Don't shoot unless he has to—but if he has, to lay it on the line."

"The mayor is busy," said Raymond Brown, his secretary.

"That's what you think," said Webster, starting for the door.

"You can't go in there, Webster," yelled Brown.

He leaped from his chair, came charging around the desk, reaching for Webster. Webster swung broadside with his arm, caught Brown across the chest, swept him back against the desk. The desk skidded and Brown waved his arms, lost his balance, thudded to the floor.

Webster jerked open the mayor's door.

The mayor's feet thumped off his desk. "I told Brown—" he said.

Webster nodded. "And Brown told me. What's the matter, Carter. Afraid King might find out I was here? Afraid of being corrupted by some good ideas?"

"What do you want?" snapped Carter.

"I understand the police are going to burn the *houses*."

"That's right," declared the mayor, righteously. "They're a menace to the community."

"What community?"

"Look here, Webster—"

"You know there's no community. Just a few of you lousy politicians who stick around so you can claim residence, so you can be sure of being elected every year and drag down your salaries. It's getting to the point where all you have to do is vote for one another. The people who work in the stores and shops, even those who do the meanest jobs in the factories, don't live inside the city limits. The businessmen quit the city long ago. They do business here, but they aren't residents."

"But this is still a city," declared the mayor.

"I didn't come to argue that with you," said Webster. "I came to try to make you see that you're doing wrong by burning those houses. Even if you don't realize it, the *houses* are homes to people who have no other homes. People who have come to this city to seek sanctuary, who have found refuge with us. In a measure, they are our responsibility."

"They're not our responsibility," gritted the mayor. "Whatever happens to them is their own hard luck. We didn't ask them here. We don't want them here. They contribute nothing to the community. You're going to tell me they're misfits. Well, can I help that? You're going to say they can't find jobs. And I'll tell you they could find jobs if they tried to find them. There's work to be done, there's always work to be done. They've been filled up with this new world talk and they figure it's up to someone to find the place that suits them and the job that suits them."

"You sound like a rugged individualist," said Webster.

"You say that like you think it's funny," yapped the mayor.

"I do think it's funny," said Webster. "Funny, and tragic, that anyone should think that way today."

"The world would be a lot better off with some rugged individualism," snapped the mayor. "Look at the men who have gone places—"

"Meaning yourself?" asked Webster.

"You might take me, for example," Carter agreed. "I worked hard. I took advantage of opportunity. I had some foresight. I did—"

"You mean you licked the correct boots and stepped in the proper faces," said Webster. "You're the shining example of the kind of people the world doesn't want today. You positively smell musty, your ideas are so old. You're the last of the politicians, Carter, just as I was the last of the Chamber of Commerce secretaries. Only you don't know it yet. I did. I got out. Even when it cost me something, I got out, because I had to save my self-respect. Your kind of politics is dead. They are dead because any tinhorn with a loud mouth and a brassy front could gain power by appeal to mob psychology. And you haven't got mob psychology any more. You can't have mob psychology when people don't give a damn what happens to a thing that's dead already—a political system that broke down under its own weight."

"Get out of here," screamed Carter. "Get out before I have the cops come and throw you out."

"You forget," said Webster, "that I came in to talk about the *houses*."

"It won't do you any good," snarled Carter. "You can stand and talk till doomsday for all the good it does. Those *houses* burn. That's final."

"How would you like to see the loop a mass of rubble?" asked Webster.

"Your comparison," said Carter, "is grotesque."

"I wasn't talking about comparisons," said Webster.

"You weren't—" The mayor stared at him. "What were you talking about then?"

"Only this," said Webster. "The second the first torch touches the *houses*, the first shell will land on the city hall. And the second one will hit the First National. They'll go down the line, the biggest targets first."

Carter gaped. Then a flush of anger crawled from his throat up into his face.

"It won't work, Webster," he snapped. "You can't bluff me. Any cock-and-bull story like that—"

"It's no cock-and-bull story," declared Webster. "Those men have cannon out there. Pieces from in front of Legion halls, from the museums. And they have men who know how to work them. They wouldn't need them, really. It's practically point-blank range. Like shooting the broadside of a barn."

Carter reached for the radio, but Webster stopped him with an upraised hand.

"Better think a minute, Carter, before you go flying off the handle. You're on a spot. Go ahead with your plan and you have a battle on your hands. The *houses* may burn but the loop is wrecked. The businessmen will have your scalp for that."

Carter's hand retreated from the radio.

From far away came the sharp crack of a rifle.

"Better call them off," warned Webster.

Carter's face twisted with indecision.

Another rifle shot, another and another.

"Pretty soon," said Webster, "it will have gone too far. So far that you can't stop it."

A thudding blast rattled the windows of the room. Carter leaped from his chair.

Webster felt suddenly cold and weak. But he fought to keep his face straight and his voice calm.

Carter was staring out the window, like a man of stone.

"I'm afraid," said Webster, "that it's gone too far already."

The radio on the desk chirped insistently, red light flashing.

Carter reached out a trembling hand and snapped it on.

"Carter," a voice was saying. "Carter. Carter."

Webster recognized that voice—the bull-throated tone of Police Chief Jim Maxwell.

"What is it?" asked Carter.

"They had a big gun," said Maxwell. "It exploded when they tried to fire it. Ammunition no good, I guess."

"One gun?" asked Carter. "Only one gun?"

"I don't see any others."

"I heard rifle fire," said Carter.

"Yeah, they did some shooting at us. Wounded a couple of the boys. But they've pulled back now. Deeper into the brush. No shooting now."

"O.K.," said Carter, "go ahead and start the fires."

Webster started forward. "Ask him, ask him—"

But Carter clicked the switch and the radio went dead.

"What was it you want to ask?"

"Nothing," said Webster. "Nothing that amounted to anything."

He couldn't tell Carter that Gramp had been the one who knew about firing big guns. Couldn't tell him that when the gun exploded Gramp had been there.

He'd have to get out of here, get over to the gun as quickly as possible.

"It was a good bluff, Webster," Carter was saying. "A good bluff, but it petered out."

The mayor turned to the window that faced toward the *houses*.

"No more firing," he said. "They gave up quick."

"You'll be lucky," snapped Webster, "if six of your policemen come back alive. Those men with the rifles are out in the brush and they can pick the eye out of a squirrel at a hundred yards."

Feet pounded in the corridor outside, two pairs of feet racing toward the door.

The mayor whirled from his window and Webster pivoted around.

"Gramp!" he yelled.

"Hi, Johnny," puffed Gramp, skidding to a stop.

The man behind Gramp was a young man and he was waving something in his hand—a sheaf of papers that rustled as he waved them.

"What do you want?" asked the mayor.

"Plenty," said Gramp.

He stood for a moment, catching back his breath, and said between puffs:

"Meet my friend, Henry Adams."

"Adams?" asked the mayor.

"Sure," said Gramp. "His granddaddy used to live here. Out on Twenty-seventh Street."

"Oh," said the mayor and it was as if someone had smacked him with a brick. "Oh, you mean F. J. Adams."

"Bet your boots," said Gramp. "Him and me, we were in the war together. Used to keep me awake nights telling me about his boy back home."

Carter nodded to Henry Adams. "As mayor of the city," he said, trying to regain some of his dignity, "I welcome you to—"

"It's not a particularly fitting welcome," Adams said. "I understand you are burning my property."

"Your property!" The mayor choked and his eyes stared in disbelief at the sheaf of papers Adams waved at him.

"Yeah, his property," shrilled Gramp. "He just bought it. We just come from the treasurer's office. Paid all the back taxes and penalties and all the other things you legal thieves thought up to slap against them houses."

"But, but—" the mayor was grasping for words, gasping for breath. "Not all of it. Perhaps just the old Adams property."

"Lock, stock and barrel," said Gramp, triumphantly.

"And now," said Adams to the mayor, "if you would kindly tell your men to stop destroying my property."

Carter bent over the desk and fumbled at the radio, his hands suddenly all thumbs.

"Maxwell," he shouted. "Maxwell. Maxwell."

"What do you want?" Maxwell yelled back.

"Stop setting those fires," yelled Carter. "Start putting them out. Call the fire department. Do anything. But stop those fires."

"Cripes," said Maxwell, "I wish you'd make up your mind."

"You do what I tell you," screamed the mayor. "You put out those fires."

"All right," said Maxwell. "All right. Keep your shirt on. But the boys won't like it. They won't like getting shot at to do something you change your mind about."

Carter straightened from the radio.

"Let me assure you, Mr. Adams," he said, "that this is all a big mistake."

"It is," Adams declared solemnly. "A very great mistake, mayor. The biggest one you ever made."

For a moment the two of them stood there, looking across the room at one another.

"Tomorrow," said Adams, "I shall file a petition with the courts asking dissolution of the city charter. As owner of the greatest portion of the land included in the corporate limits, both from the standpoint of area and valuation, I understand I have a perfect legal right to do that."

The mayor gulped, finally brought out some words.

"Upon what grounds?" he asked.

"Upon the grounds," said Adams, "that there is no further need of it. I do not believe I shall have too hard a time to prove my case."

"But . . . but . . . that means . . ."

"Yeah," said Gramp, "you know what it means. It means you are out right on your ear."

"A park," said Gramp, waving his arm over the wilderness that once had been the residential section of the city. "A park so that people can remember how their old folks lived."

The three of them stood on Tower Hill, with the rusty old water tower looming above them, its sturdy steel legs planted in a sea of waist-high grass.

"Not a park, exactly," explained Henry Adams. "A

memorial, rather. A memorial to an era of communal life
that will be forgotten in another hundred years. A preserva-
tion of a number of peculiar types of construction that arose
to suit certain conditions and each man's particular tastes. No
slavery to any architectural concepts, but an effort made to
achieve better living. In another hundred years men will walk
through those houses down there with the same feeling of respect and awe they have when they go into a museum today.
It will be to them something out of what amounts to a primeval age, a stepping-stone on the way to the better, fuller life.
Artists will spend their lives transferring those old houses to
their canvasses. Writers of historical novels will come here
for the breath of authenticity."

"But you said you meant to restore all the houses, make
the lawns and gardens exactly like they were before," said
Webster. "That will take a fortune. And, after that, another
fortune to keep them in shape."

"I have too much money," said Adams. "Entirely too
much money. Remember, my grandfather and father got into
atomics on the ground floor."

"Best crap player I ever knew, your granddaddy was," said
Gramp. "Used to take me for a cleaning every pay day."

"In the old days," said Adams, "when a man had too much
money, there were other things he could do with it. Organized charities, for example. Or medical research or something like that. But there are no organized charities today.
Not enough business to keep them going. And since the
World Committee has hit its stride, there is ample money for
all the research, medical or otherwise, anyone might wish to
do.

"I didn't plan this thing when I came back to see my
grandfather's old house. Just wanted to see it, that was all.
He'd told me so much about it. How he planted the tree in
the front lawn. And the rose garden he had out back.

"And then I saw it. And it was a mocking ghost. It was
something that had been left behind. Something that had
meant a lot to someone and had been left behind. Standing
there in front of that house with Gramp that day, it came to
me that I could do nothing better than preserve for posterity
a cross section of the life their ancestors lived."

A thin blue thread of smoke rose above the trees far below.

Webster pointed to it. "What about them?"

"The Squatters stay," said Adams, "if they want to. There will be plenty of work for them to do. And there'll always be a house or two that they can have to live in.

"There's just one thing that bothers me. I can't be here all the time myself. I'll need someone to manage the project. It'll be a lifelong job."

He looked at Webster.

"Go ahead, Johnny," said Gramp.

Webster shook his head. "Betty's got her heart set on that place out in the country."

"You wouldn't have to stay here," said Adams. "You could fly in every day."

From the foot of the hill came a hail.

"It's Ole," yelled Gramp.

He waved his cane. "Hi, Ole. Come on up."

They watched Ole striding up the hill, waiting for him, silently.

"Wanted to talk to you, Johnny," said Ole. "Got an idea. Waked me out of a sound sleep last night."

"Go ahead," said Webster.

Ole glanced at Adams. "He's all right," said Webster. "He's Henry Adams. Maybe you remember his grandfather, old F. J."

"I remember him," said Ole. "Nuts about atomic power, he was. How did he make out?"

"He made out rather well," said Adams.

"Glad to hear that," Ole said. "Guess I was wrong. Said he never would amount to nothing. Daydreamed all the time."

"How about that idea?" Webster asked.

"You heard about dude ranches, ain't you?" Ole asked. Webster nodded.

"Place," said Ole, "where people used to go and pretend they were cowboys. Pleased them because they really didn't know all the hard work there was in ranching and figured it was romantic-like to ride horses and—"

"Look," asked Webster, "you aren't figuring on turning your farm into a dude ranch, are you?"

"Nope," said Ole. "Not a dude ranch. Dude farm, maybe. Folks don't know too much about farms any more, since there ain't hardly no farms. And they'll read about the frost being on the pumpkin and how pretty a—"

Webster stared at Ole. "They'd go for it, Ole," he declared. "They'd kill one another in the rush to spend their vacation on a real, honest-to-God, old-time farm."

Out of a clump of bushes down the hillside burst a shining thing that chattered and gurgled and screeched, blades flashing, a cranelike arm waving.

"What the—" asked Adams.

"It's that dadburned lawn mower!" yelped Gramp. "I always knew the day would come when it would strip a gear and go completely off its nut!"

ARENA

Astounding,
June

by Fredric Brown

Readers of earlier volumes in this series will be familiar with the multi-talented Fredric Brown, whose sharp, witty, and frequently profound stories graced the pages of many science fiction and mystery magazines during his long career. His satirical humor was one of his strongest attributes, and he maintained an amazingly high standard of quality in his work, which ranged from the short-short story to the novel.

"Arena" is perhaps his most famous story and rightly so, an exciting and yet humanistic account of mortal combat between an Earthman and alien with the survival of their respective battle fleets at stake. Written in the midst of World War II, it manages to be respectful to "the other side" at a time of total war in the present of the writer, never as easy task.

(One of the games one can play with science fiction (or with literature in general) is to trace back the treatment of themes. This is not to say Writer A deliberately copies a story written by Writer B a generation before, or is even consciously influenced by him. However, a successful story makes a dent in literary history; one that influences literary thought thereafter. There was an extremely moving story by Barry Longyear called "Enemy Mine" (which will be a certain inclusion when we reach 1979 in this series) that pitted a human against an alien in a particularly subtle way—and I couldn't help but think of "Arena."—I.A.)

409

Carson opened his eyes and found himself looking upward
into a flickering blue dimness.

It was hot, and he was lying on sand, and a sharp rock
embedded in the sand was hurting his back. He rolled over to
his side, off the rock, and then pushed himself up to a sitting
position.

"I'm crazy," he thought. "Crazy—or dead—or something."
The sand was blue, bright blue. And there wasn't any such
thing as bright blue sand on Earth or any of the planets.

Blue sand.

Blue sand under a blue dome that wasn't the sky nor yet a
room, but a circumscribed area—somehow he knew it was
circumscribed and finite even though he couldn't see to the
top of it.

He picked up some of the sand in his hand and let it run
through his fingers. It trickled down onto his bare leg. *Bare?*

Naked. He was stark naked, and already his body was
dripping perspiration from the enervating heat, coated blue
with sand wherever sand had touched it.

But elsewhere his body was white.

He thought: Then this sand is really blue. If it seemed blue
only because of the blue light, then I'd be blue also. But I'm
white, so the sand *is* blue. *Blue sand.* There isn't any blue
sand. There isn't any place like this place I'm in.

Sweat was running down in his eyes.

It was hot, hotter than hell. Only hell—the hell of the ancients—was supposed to be red and not blue.

But if this place wasn't hell, what was it? Only Mercury,
among the planets, had heat like this and this wasn't Mercury. And Mercury was some four billion miles from—

It came back to him then, where he'd been. In the little
one-man scouter, outside the orbit of Pluto, scouting a scant
million miles to one side of the Earth Armada drawn up in
battle array there to intercept the Outsiders.

That sudden strident nerve-shattering ringing of the alarm
bell when the rival scouter—the Outsider ship—had come
within range of his detectors—

No one knew who the Outsiders were, what they looked

like, from what far galaxy they came, other than that it was in the general direction of the Pleiades.

First, sporadic raids on Earth colonies and outposts. Isolated battles between Earth patrols and small groups of Outsider spaceships; battles sometimes won and sometimes lost, but never to date resulting in the capture of an alien vessel. Nor had any member of a raided colony ever survived to describe the Outsiders who had left the ships, if indeed they had left them.

Not a too-serious menace, at first, for the raids had not been too numerous or destructive. And individually, the ships had proved slightly inferior in armament to the best of Earth's fighters, although somewhat superior in speed and maneuverability. A sufficient edge in speed, in fact, to give the Outsiders their choice of running or fighting, unless surrounded.

Nevertheless, Earth had prepared for serious trouble, for a showdown, building the mightiest armada of all time. It had been waiting now, that armada, for a long time. But now the showdown was coming.

Scouts twenty billion miles out had detected the approach of a mighty fleet—a showdown fleet—of the Outsiders. Those scouts had never come back, but their radiotronic messages had. And now Earth's armada, all ten thousand ships and half-million fighting spacemen, was out there, outside Pluto's orbit, waiting to intercept and battle to the death.

And an even battle it was going to be, judging by the advance reports of the men of the far picket line who had given their lives to report—before they had died—on the size and strength of the alien fleet.

Anybody's battle, with the mastery of the solar system hanging in the balance, on an even chance. A last and *only* chance, for Earth and all her colonies lay at the utter mercy of the Outsiders if they ran that gauntlet—

Oh yes. Bob Carson remembered now.

Not that it explained blue sand and flickering blueness. But that strident alarming of the bell and his leap for the control panel. His frenzied fumbling as he strapped himself into the seat. The dot in the visiplate that grew larger.

The dryness of his mouth. The awful knowledge that this was *it*. For him, at least, although the main fleets were still out of range of one another.

This, his first taste of battle. Within three seconds or less he'd be victorious, or a charred cinder. Dead.

Three seconds—that's how long a space-battle lasted. Time enough to count to three slowly, and then you'd won or you were dead. One hit completely took care of a lightly armed and armored little one-man craft like a scouter.

Frantically—as, unconsciously, his dry lips shaped the word "One"—he worked at the controls to keep that growing dot centered on the crossed spiderwebs of the visiplate. His hands doing that, while his right foot hovered over the pedal that would fire the bolt. The single bolt of concentrated hell that had to hit—or else. There wouldn't be time for any second shot.

"Two." He didn't know he'd said that, either. The dot in the visiplate wasn't a dot now. Only a few thousand miles away, it showed up in the magnification of the plate as though it were only a few hundred yards off. It was a sleek, fast little scouter, about the size of his.

And an alien ship, all right.

"Thr—" His foot touched the bolt-release pedal—

And then the Outsider had swerved suddenly and was off the crosshairs. Carson punched keys frantically, to follow.

For a tenth of a second, it was out of the visiplate entirely, and then as the nose of his scouter swung after it, he saw it again, diving straight toward the ground.

The ground?

It was an optical illusion of some sort. It *had* to be, that planet—or whatever it was—that now covered the visiplate. Whatever it was, it couldn't be there. Couldn't possibly. There *wasn't* any planet nearer than Neptune three billion miles away—with Pluto around on the opposite side of the distant pinpoint sun.

His *detectors! They* hadn't shown any object of planetary dimensions, even of asteroid dimensions. They still didn't.

So it couldn't be there, that whatever-it-was he was diving into, only a few hundred miles below him.

And in his sudden anxiety to keep from crashing, he forgot even the Outsider ship. He fired the front braking rockets, and even as the sudden change of speed slammed him forward against the seat straps, he fired full right for an emergency turn. Pushed them down and *held* them down, knowing that he needed everything the ship had to keep from crashing and that a turn that sudden would black him out for a moment.

It did black him out.

And that was all. Now he was sitting in hot blue sand, stark naked but otherwise unhurt. No sign of his spaceship and—for that matter—no sign of *space*. That curve overhead wasn't a sky, whatever else it was.

He scrambled to his feet.

Gravity seemed a little more than Earth-normal. Not much more.

Flat sand stretching away, a few scrawny bushes in clumps here and there. The bushes were blue, too, but in varying shades, some lighter than the blue of the sand, some darker.

Out from under the nearest bush ran a little thing that was like a lizard, except that it had more than four legs. It was blue, too. Bright blue. It saw him and ran back again under the bush.

He looked up again, trying to decide what was overhead. It wasn't exactly a roof, but it was dome-shaped. It flickered and was hard to look at. But definitely, it curved down to the ground, to the blue sand, all around him.

He wasn't far from being under the center of the dome. At a guess, it was a hundred yards to the nearest wall, if it was a wall. It was as though a blue hemisphere of *something*, about two hundred and fifty yards in circumference, was inverted over the flat expanse of the sand.

And everything blue, except one object. Over near a far curving wall there was a red object. Roughly spherical, it seemed to be about a yard in diameter. Too far for him to see clearly through the flickering blueness. But, unaccountably, he shuddered.

He wiped sweat from his forehead, or tried to, with the back of his hand.

Was this a dream, a nightmare? This heat, this sand, that vague feeling of horror he felt when he looked toward that red thing?

A dream? No, one didn't go to sleep and dream in the midst of a battle in space.

Death? No, never. If there were immortality, it wouldn't be a senseless thing like this, a thing of blue heat and blue sand and a red horror.

Then he heard the voice—

Inside his head he heard it, not with his ears. It came from nowhere or everywhere.

"*Through spaces and dimensions wandering,*" rang the words in his mind, "*and in this space and this time I find two peoples about to wage a war that would exterminate one and so weaken the other that it would retrogress and never fulfill its destiny, but decay and return to mindless dust whence it came. And I say this must not happen.*"

"Who . . . what are you?" Carson didn't say it aloud, but the question formed itself in his brain.

"*You would not understand completely. I am—*" There was a pause as though the voice sought—in Carson's brain—for a word that wasn't there, a word he didn't know. "*I am the end of evolution of a race so old the time can not be expressed in words that have meaning to your mind. A race fused into a single entity, eternal—*

"*An entity such as your primitive race might become*"—again the groping for a word—"*time from now. So might the race you call, in your mind, the Outsiders. So I intervene in the battle to come, the battle between fleets so evenly matched that destruction of both races will result. One must survive. One must progress and evolve.*"

"One?" thought Carson. "Mine, or—?"

"*It is in my power to stop the war, to send the Outsiders back to their galaxy. But they would return, or your race would sooner or later follow them there. Only by remaining in this space and time to intervene constantly could I prevent them from destroying one another, and I cannot remain.*

"*So I shall intervene now. I shall destroy one fleet completely without loss to the other. One civilization shall thus survive.*"

Nightmare. This had to be nightmare, Carson thought. But he knew it wasn't.

It was too mad, too impossible, to be anything but real.

He didn't dare ask *the* question—*which?* But his thoughts asked it for him.

"*The stronger shall survive,*" said the voice. "*That I can not—and would not—change. I merely intervene to make it a complete victory, not*"—groping again—"*not Pyrrhic victory to a broken race.*

"*From the outskirts of the not-yet battle I plucked two individuals, you and an Outsider. I see from your mind that in*

your early history of nationalisms battles between champions,
to decide issues between races, were not unknown.

"*You and your opponent are here pitted against one an-*
other, naked and unarmed, under conditions equally unfamil-
iar to you both, equally unpleasant to you both. There is no
time limit, for here there is no time. The survivor is the
champion of his race. That race survives."

"But—" Carson's protest was too inarticulate for expression, but the voice answered it.

"*It is fair. The conditions are such, that the accident of*
physical strength will not completely decide the issue. There
is a barrier. You will understand. Brain-power and courage
will be more important than strength. Most especially cour-
age, which is the will to survive."

"But while this goes on, the fleets will—"

"*No, you are in another space, another time. For as long*
as you are here, time stands still in the universe you know. I
see you wonder whether this place is real. It is, and it is not.
As I—to your limited understanding—am and am not real.
My existence is mental and not physical. You saw me as a
planet; it could have been as a dustmote or a sun.

"*But to you this place is now real. What you suffer here*
will be real. And if you die here, your death will be real. If
you die, your failure will be the end of your race. That is
enough for you to know."

And then the voice was gone.

Again he was alone, but not alone. For as Carson looked
up, he saw that the red thing, the red sphere of horror which
he now knew was the Outsider, was rolling toward him.

Rolling.

It seemed to have no legs or arms that he could see, no
features. It rolled across the blue sand with the fluid quickness of a drop of mercury. And before it, in some manner he
could not understand, came a paralyzing wave of nauseating,
retching, horrid hatred.

Carson looked about him frantically. A stone, lying in the
sand a few feet away, was the nearest thing to a weapon. It
wasn't large, but it had sharp edges, like a slab of flint. It
looked a bit like blue flint.

He picked it up, and crouched to receive the attack. It was
coming fast, faster than he could run.

No time to think out how he was going to fight it, and how

anyway could he plan to battle a creature whose strength, whose characteristics, whose method of fighting he did not know? Rolling so fast, it looked more than ever like a perfect sphere.

Ten yards away. Five. And then it stopped.

Rather, it *was stopped*. Abruptly the near side of it flattened as though it had run up against an invisible wall. It bounced, actually bounced back.

Then it rolled forward again, but more slowly, more cautiously. It stopped again, at the same place. It tried again, a few yards to one side.

There was a barrier there of some sort. It clicked, then, in Carson's mind. That thought projected into his mind by the Entity who had brought them here: "—accident of physical strength will not completely decide the issue. There is a barrier."

A force-field, of course. Not the Netzian Field, known to Earth science, for that glowed and emitted a crackling sound. This one was invisible, silent.

It was a wall that ran from side to side of the inverted hemisphere; Carson didn't have to verify that himself. The Roller was doing that: rolling sideways along the barrier, seeking a break in it that wasn't there.

Carson took half a dozen steps forward, his left hand groping out before him, and then his hand touched the barrier. It felt smooth, yielding, like a sheet of rubber rather than like glass. Warm to his touch, but no warmer than the sand underfoot. And it was completely invisible, even at close range.

He dropped the stone and put both hands against it, pushing. It seemed to yield, just a trifle. But no farther than that trifle, even when he pushed with all his weight. It felt like a sheet of rubber backed up by steel. Limited resiliency, and then firm strength.

He stood on tiptoe and reached as high as he could and the barrier was still there.

He saw the Roller coming back, having reached one side of the arena. That feeling of nausea hit Carson again, and he stepped back from the barrier as it went by. It didn't stop.

But did the barrier stop at ground level? Carson knelt down and burrowed in the sand. It was soft, light, easy to dig in. At two feet down the barrier was still there.

The Roller was coming back again. Obviously, it couldn't find a way through at either side.

There must be a way through, Carson thought. *Some* way we can get at each other, else this duel is meaningless.

But no hurry now, in finding that out. There was something to try first. The Roller was back now, and it stopped just across the barrier, only six feet away. It seemed to be studying him, although for the life of him, Carson couldn't find external evidence of sense organs on the thing. Nothing that looked like eyes or ears, or even a mouth. There was though, he saw now, a series of grooves—perhaps a dozen of them altogether, and he saw two tentacles suddenly push out from two of the grooves and dip into the sand as though testing its consistency. Tentacles about an inch in diameter and perhaps a foot and a half long.

But the tentacles were retractable into the grooves and were kept there except when not in use. They were retracted when the thing rolled and seemed to have nothing to do with its method of locomotion. That, as far as Carson could judge, seemed to be accomplished by some shifting—just *how* he couldn't even imagine—of its center of gravity.

He shuddered as he looked at the thing. It was alien, utterly alien, horribly different from anything on Earth or any of the life forms found on the other solar planets. Instinctively, somehow, he knew its mind was as alien as its body.

But he had to try. If it had no telepathic powers at all, the attempt was foredoomed to failure, yet he thought it had such powers. There had, at any rate, been a projection of something that was not physical at the time a few minutes ago when it had first started for him. An almost tangible wave of hatred.

If it could project that, perhaps it could read his mind as well, sufficiently for his purpose.

Deliberately, Carson picked up the rock that had been his only weapon, then tossed it down again in a gesture of relinquishment and raised his empty hands, palms up, before him.

He spoke aloud, knowing that although the words would be meaningless to the creature before him, speaking them would focus his own thoughts more completely upon the message.

"Can we not have peace between us?" he said, his voice sounding strange in the utter stillness. "The Entity who brought us here has told us what must happen if our races fight—extinction of one and weakening and retrogression of the other. The battle between them, said the Entity, depends upon what we do here. Why can not we agree to an eternal peace—your race to its galaxy, we to ours?"

Carson blanked out his mind to receive a reply.

It came, and it staggered him back physically. He actually recoiled several steps in sheer horror at the depth and intensity of the hatred and lust-to-kill of the red images that had been projected at him. Not as articulate words—as had come to him the thoughts of the Entity—but as wave upon wave of fierce emotion.

For a moment that seemed an eternity he had to struggle against the mental impact of that hatred, fight to clear his mind of it and drive out the alien thoughts to which he had given admittance by blanking his own thoughts. He wanted to retch.

Slowly his mind cleared as, slowly, the mind of a man wakening from nightmare clears away the fear-fabric of which the dream was woven. He was breathing hard and he felt weaker, but he could think.

He stood studying the Roller. It had been motionless during the mental duel it had so nearly won. Now it rolled a few feet to one side, to the nearest of the blue bushes. Three tentacles whipped out of their grooves and began to investigate the bush.

"O.K.," Carson said, "so it's war then." He managed a wry grin. "If I got your answer straight, peace doesn't appeal to you." And, because he was, after all, a quite young man and couldn't resist the impulse to be dramatic, he added, "To the death!"

But his voice, in that utter silence, sounded very silly, even to himself. It came to him, then, that this *was* to the death. Not only his own death or that of the red spherical thing which he now thought of as the Roller, but death to the entire race of one or the other of them. The end of the human race, if he failed.

It made him suddenly very humble and very afraid to think that. More than to think it, to *know* it. Somehow, with a knowledge that was above even faith, he knew that the Enity who had arranged this duel had told the truth about its intentions and its powers. It wasn't kidding.

The future of humanity depended upon *him*. It was an awful thing to realize, and he wrenched his mind away from it. He had to concentrate on the situation at hand.

There had to be some way of getting through the barrier, or of killing through the barrier.

Mentally? He hoped that wasn't all, for the Roller obviously had stronger telepathic powers than the primitive, undeveloped ones of the human race. Or did it?

He had been able to drive the thoughts of the Roller out of his own mind; could it drive out his? If its ability to project was stronger, might not its receptivity mechanism be more vulnerable?

He stared at it and endeavored to concentrate and focus all his thoughts upon it.

"Die," he thought. *"You are going to die. You are dying. You are—"*

He tried variations on it, and mental pictures. Sweat stood out on his forehead and he found himself trembling with the intensity of the effort. But the Roller went ahead with its investigation of the bush, as utterly unaffected as though Carson had been reciting the multiplication table.

So *that* was no good.

He felt a bit weak and dizzy from the heat and his strenuous effort at concentration. He sat down on the blue sand to rest and gave his full attention to watching and studying the Roller. By close study, perhaps, he could judge its strength and detect its weaknesses, learn things that would be valuable to know when and if they should come to grips.

It was breaking off twigs. Carson watched carefully, trying to judge just how hard it worked to do that. Later, he thought, he could find a similar bush on his own side, break off twigs of equal thickness himself, and gain a comparison of physical strength between his own arms and hands and those tentacles.

The twigs broke off hard; the Roller was having to struggle with each one, he saw. Each tentacle, he saw, bifurcated at the tip into two fingers, each tipped by a nail or claw. The claws didn't seem to be particularly long or dangerous. No more so than his own fingernails, if they were let to grow a bit.

No, on the whole, it didn't look too tough to handle physically. Unless, of course, that bush was made of pretty tough

stuff. Carson looked around him and, yes, right within reach
was another bush of identically the same type.

He reached over and snapped off a twig. It was brittle,
easy to break. Of course, the Roller might have been faking
deliberately but he didn't think so.

On the other hand, where was it vulnerable? Just how
would he go about killing it, if he got the chance? He went
back to studying it. The outer hide looked pretty tough. He'd
need a sharp weapon of some sort. He picked up the piece of
rock again. It was about twelve inches long, narrow, and
fairly sharp on one end. If it chipped like flint, he could
make a serviceable knife out of it.

The Roller was continuing its investigations of the bushes.
It rolled again, to the nearest one of another type. A little
blue lizard, many-legged like the one Carson had seen on his
side of the barrier, darted out from under the bush.

A tentacle of the Roller lashed out and caught it, picked it
up. Another tentacle whipped over and began to pull legs off
the lizard, as coldly and calmly as it had pulled twigs off the
bush. The creature struggled frantically and emitted a shrill
squealing sound that was the first sound Carson had heard
here other than the sound of his own voice.

Carson shuddered and wanted to turn his eyes away. But
he made himself continue to watch; anything he could learn
about his opponent might prove valuable. Even this
knowledge of its unnecessary cruelty. Particularly, he thought
with a sudden vicious surge of emotion, this knowledge of its
unnecessary cruelty. It would make it a pleasure to kill the
thing, if and when the chance came.

He steeled himself to watch the dismembering of the lizard, for that very reason.

But he felt glad when, with half its legs gone, the lizard
quit squealing and struggling and lay limp and dead in the
Roller's grasp.

It didn't continue with the rest of the legs. Contemptuously
it tossed the dead lizard away from it, in Carson's direction.
It arced through the air between them and landed at his feet.

It had come through the barrier! The barrier wasn't there
any more!

Carson was on his feet in a flash, the knife gripped tightly
in his hand, and leaped forward. He'd settle this thing here
and now! With the barrier gone—

But it wasn't gone. He found that out the hard way, running head on into it and nearly knocking himself silly. He bounced back, and fell.

And as he sat up, shaking his head to clear it, he saw something coming through the air toward him, and to duck it, he threw himself flat again on the sand, and to one side. He got his body out of the way, but there was a sudden sharp pain in the calf of his left leg.

He rolled backward, ignoring the pain, and scrambled to his feet. It was a rock, he saw now, that had struck him. And the Roller was picking up another one now, swinging it back gripped between two tentacles, getting ready to throw again.

It sailed through the air toward him, but he was easily able to step out of its way. The Roller, apparently, could throw straight, but not hard nor far. The first rock had struck him only because he had been sitting down and had not seen it coming until it was almost upon him.

Even as he stepped aside from that weak second throw, Carson drew back his right arm and let fly with the rock that was still in his hand. If missiles, he thought with sudden elation, can cross the barrier, then two can play at the game of throwing them. And the good right arm of an Earthman—

He couldn't miss a three-foot sphere at only four-yard range, and he didn't miss. The rock whizzed straight, and with a speed several times that of the missiles the Roller had thrown. It hit dead center, but it hit flat, unfortunately, instead of point first.

But it hit with a resounding thump, and obviously it hurt. The Roller had been reaching for another rock, but it changed its mind and got out of there instead. By the time Carson could pick up and throw another rock, the Roller was forty yards back from the barrier and going strong.

His second throw missed by feet, and his third throw was short. The Roller was back out of range—at least out of range of a missile heavy enough to be damaging.

Carson grinned. That round had been his. Except—

He quit grinning as he bent over to examine the calf of his leg. A jagged edge of the stone had made a pretty deep cut, several inches long. It was bleeding freely, but he didn't think it had gone deep enough to hit an artery. If it stopped bleeding of its own accord, well and good. If not, he was in for trouble.

Finding out one thing, though, took precedence over that
cut. The nature of the barrier.

He went forward to it again, this time groping with his
hands before him. He found it; then holding one hand against
it, he tossed a handful of sand at it with the other hand. The
sand went right through. His hand didn't.

Organic matter versus inorganic? No, because the dead lizard had gone through it, and a lizard, alive or dead, was certainly organic. Plant life? He broke off a twig and poked it at
the barrier. The twig went through, with no resistance, but
when his fingers gripping the twig came to the barrier, they
were stopped.

He couldn't get through it, nor could the Roller. But rocks
and sand and a dead lizard—

How about a live lizard? He went hunting, under bushes,
until he found one, and caught it. He tossed it gently against
the barrier and it bounced back and scurried away across the
blue sand.

That gave him the answer, in so far as he could determine
it now. The screen was a barrier to living things. Dead or
inorganic matter could cross it.

That off his mind, Carson looked at his injured leg again.
The bleeding was lessening, which meant he wouldn't need to
worry about making a tourniquet. But he should find some
water, if any was available, to clean the wound.

Water—the thought of it made him realize that he was getting awfully thirsty. He'd *have* to find water, in case this contest turned out to be a protracted one.

Limping slightly now, he started off to make a full circuit
of his half of the arena. Guiding himself with one hand along
the barrier, he walked to his right until he came to the curving sidewall. It was visible, a dull blue-gray at close range,
and the surface of it felt just like the central barrier.

He experimented by tossing a handful of sand at it, and
the sand reached the wall and disappeared as it went through.
The hemispherical shell was a force-field, too. But an opaque
one, instead of transparent like the barrier.

He followed it around until he came back to the barrier,
and walked back along the barrier to the point from which
he'd started.

No sign of water.

Worried now, he started a series of zigzags back and forth

between the barrier and the wall, covering the intervening space thoroughly.

No water. Blue sand, blue bushes, and intolerable heat. Nothing else.

It must be his imagination, he told himself angrily, that he was suffering *that* much from thirst. How long had he been here? Of course, no time at all, according to his own space-time frame. The Entity had told him time stood still out there, while he was here. But his body processes went on here, just the same. And according to his body's reckoning, how long had he been here? Three or four hours, perhaps. Certainly not long enough to be suffering seriously from thirst.

But he was suffering from it; his throat dry and parched. Probably the intense heat was the cause. It was *hot!* A hundred and thirty Fahrenheit, at a guess. A dry, still heat without the slightest movement of air.

He was limping rather badly, and utterly fagged out when he'd finished the futile exploration of his domain.

He stared across at the motionless Roller and hoped it was as miserable as he was. And quite possibly it wasn't enjoying this, either. The Entity had said the conditions here were equally unfamiliar and equally uncomfortable for both of them. Maybe the Roller came from a planet where two hundred degree heat was the norm. Maybe it was freezing while he was roasting.

Maybe the air was as much too thick for it as it was too thin for him. For the exertion of his explorations had left him panting. The atmosphere here, he realized now, was not much thicker than that on Mars.

No water.

That meant a deadline, for him at any rate. Unless he could find a way to cross that barrier or to kill his enemy from this side of it, thirst would kill him eventually.

It gave him a feeling of desperate urgency. He *must* hurry.

But he made himself sit down a moment to rest, to think.

What was there to do? Nothing, and yet so many things. The several varieties of bushes, for example. They didn't look promising, but he'd have to examine them for possibilities. And his leg—he'd have to do something about that, even without water to clean it. Gather ammunition in the form of rocks. Find a rock that would make a good knife.

His leg hurt rather badly now, and he decided that came first. One type of bush had leaves—or things rather similar to leaves. He pulled off a handful of them and decided, after examination, to take a chance on them. He used them to clean off the sand and dirt and caked blood, then made a pad of fresh leaves and tied it over the wound with tendrils from the same bush.

The tendrils proved unexpectedly tough and strong. They were slender, and soft and pliable, yet he couldn't break them at all. He had to saw them off the bush with the sharp edge of a piece of the blue flint. Some of the thickest ones were over a foot long, and he filed away in his memory, for future reference, the fact that a bunch of the thick ones, tied together, would make a pretty serviceable rope. Maybe he'd be able to think of a use for rope.

Next, he made himself a knife. The blue flint *did* chip. From a foot-long splinter of it, he fashioned himself a crude but lethal weapon. And of tendrils from the bush, he made himself a rope belt through which he could thrust the flint knife, to keep it with him all the time and yet have his hands free.

He went back to studying the bushes. There were three other types. One was leafless, dry, brittle, rather like a dried tumbleweed. Another was of soft, crumbly wood, almost like punk. It looked and felt as though it would make excellent tinder for a fire. The third type was the most nearly woodlike. It had fragile leaves that wilted at a touch, but the stalks, although short, were straight and strong.

It was horribly, unbearably hot.

He limped up to the barrier, felt to make sure that it was still there. It was.

He stood watching the Roller for a while. It was keeping a safe distance back from the barrier, out of effective stone-throwing range. It was moving around back there, doing something. He couldn't tell what it was doing.

Once it stopped moving, came a little closer, and seemed to concentrate its attention on him. Again Carson had to fight off a wave of nausea. He threw a stone at it and the Roller retreated and went back to whatever it had been doing before.

At least he could make it keep its distance.

And, he thought bitterly, a devil of a lot of good *that* did him. Just the same, he spent the next hour or two gathering stones of suitable size for throwing, and making several neat piles of them, near his side of the barrier.

His throat burned now. It was difficult for him to think about anything except water.

But he *had* to think about other things. About getting through that barrier, under or over it, getting *at* that red sphere and killing it before this place of heat and thirst killed him first.

The barrier went to the wall upon either side, but how high and how far under the sand?

For just a moment, Carson's mind was too fuzzy to think out how he could find out either of those things. Idly, sitting there in the hot sand—and he didn't remember sitting down—he watched a blue lizard crawl from the shelter of one bush to the shelter of another.

From under the second bush, it looked out at him.

Carson grinned at it. Maybe he was getting a bit punch-drunk, because he remembered suddenly the old story of the desert-colonists on Mars, taken from an older desert story of Earth— "Pretty soon you get so lonesome you find yourself talking to the lizards, and then not so long after that you find the lizards talking back to you—"

He should have been concentrating, of course, on how to kill the Roller, but instead he grinned at the lizard and said, "Hello, there."

The lizard took a few steps toward him. "Hello," it said.

Carson was stunned for a moment, and then he put back his head and roared with laughter. It didn't hurt his throat to do so, either; he hadn't been *that* thirsty.

Why not? Why should the Entity who thought up this nightmare of a place not have a sense of humor, along with the other powers he has? Talking lizards, equipped to talk back in my own language, if I talk to them— It's a nice touch.

He grinned at the lizard and said, "Come on over." But the lizard turned and ran away, scurrying from bush to bush until it was out of sight.

He was thirsty again.

And he had to *do* something. He couldn't win this contest by sitting here sweating and feeling miserable. He had to *do* something. But what?

Get through the barrier. But he couldn't get through it, or over it. But was he certain he couldn't get under? And come to think of it, didn't one sometimes find water by digging? Two birds with one stone—

Painfully now, Carson limped up to the barrier and started digging, scooping up sand a double handful at a time. It was slow, hard work because the sand ran in at the edges and the deeper he got the bigger in diameter the hole had to be. How many hours it took him, he didn't know, but he hit bedrock four feet down. Dry bedrock; no sign of water.

And the force-field of the barrier went down clear to the bedrock. No dice. No water. Nothing.

He crawled out of the hole and lay there panting, and then raised his head to look across and see what the Roller was doing. It must be doing something back there.

It was. It was making something out of wood from the bushes, tied together with tendrils. A queerly shaped framework about four feet high and roughly square. To see it better, Carson climbed up onto the mound of sand he had excavated from the hole, and stood there staring.

There were two long levers sticking out of the back of it, one with a cup-shaped affair on the end of it. Seemed to be some sort of a catapult, Carson thought.

Sure enough, the Roller was lifting a sizable rock into the cup-shaped outfit. One of his tentacles moved the other lever up and down for a while, and then he turned the machine slightly as though aiming it and the lever with the stone flew up and forward.

The stone arced several yards over Carson's head, so far away that he didn't have to duck, but he judged the distance it had traveled, and whistled softly. He couldn't throw a rock that weight more than half that distance. And even retreating to the rear of his domain wouldn't put him out of range of that machine, if the Roller shoved it forward almost to the barrier.

Another rock whizzed over. Not quite so far away this time.

That thing could be dangerous, he decided. Maybe he'd better do something about it.

Moving from side to side along the barrier, so the catapult couldn't bracket him, he whaled a dozen rocks at it. But that wasn't going to be any good, he saw. They had to be light rocks, or he couldn't throw them that far. If they hit the framework, they bounced off harmlessly. And the Roller had no difficulty, at that distance, in moving aside from those that came near it.

Besides, his arm was tiring badly. He ached all over from sheer weariness. If he could only rest a while without having to duck rocks from that catapult at regular intervals of maybe thirty seconds each—

He stumbled back to the rear of the arena. Then he saw even that wasn't any good. The rocks reached back there, too, only there were longer intervals between them, as though it took longer to wind up the mechanism, whatever it was, of the catapult.

Wearily he dragged himself back to the barrier again. Several times he fell and could barely rise to his feet to go on. He was, he knew, near the limit of his endurance. Yet he didn't dare stop moving now, until and unless he could put that catapult out of action. If he fell asleep, he'd never wake up.

One of the stones from it gave him the first glimmer of an idea. It struck upon one of the piles of stones he'd gathered together near the barrier to use as ammunition, and it struck sparks.

Sparks. Fire. Primitive man had made fire by striking sparks, and with some of those dry crumbly bushes as tinder—

Luckily, a bush of that type was near him. He broke it off, took it over to the pile of stones, then patiently hit one stone against another until a spark touched the punklike wood of the bush. It went up in flames so fast that it singed his eyebrows and was burned to an ash within seconds.

But he had the idea now, and within minutes he had a little fire going in the lee of the mound of sand he'd made digging the hole an hour or two ago. Tinder bushes had started it, and other bushes which burned, but more slowly, kept it a steady flame.

The tough wirelike tendrils didn't burn readily; that made the fire-bombs easy to make and throw. A bundle of faggots tied about a small stone to give it weight and a loop of the tendril to swing it by.

He made half a dozen of them before he lighted and threw the first. It went wide, and the Roller started a quick retreat, pulling the catapult after him. But Carson had the others ready and threw them in rapid succession. The fourth wedged in the catapult's framework, and did the trick. The Roller tried desperately to put out the spreading blaze by throwing sand, but its clawed tentacles would take only a spoonful at a time and his efforts were ineffectual. The catapult burned.

The Roller moved safely away from the fire and seemed to concentrate its attention on Carson and again he felt that wave of hatred and nausea. But more weakly; either the Roller itself was weakening or Carson had learned how to protect himself against the mental attack.

He thumbed his nose at it and then sent it scuttling back to safety by throwing a stone. The Roller went clear to the back of its half of the arena and started pulling up bushes again. Probably it was going to make another catapult.

Carson verified—for the hundredth time—that the barrier was still operating, and then found himself sitting in the sand beside it because he was suddenly too weak to stand up.

His leg throbbed steadily now and the pangs of thirst were severe. But those things paled beside the utter physical exhaustion that gripped his entire body.

And the heat.

Hell must be like this, he thought. The hell that the ancients had believed in. He fought to stay awake, and yet staying awake seemed futile, for there was nothing he could do. Nothing, while the barrier remained impregnable and the Roller stayed back out of range.

But there must be *something*. He tried to remember things he had read in books of archaeology about the methods of fighting used back in the days before metal and plastic. The stone missile, that had come first, he thought. Well, that he already had.

The only improvement on it would be a catapult, such as the Roller had made. But he'd never be able to make one, with the tiny bits of wood available from the bushes—no single piece longer than a foot or so. Certainly he could figure out a mechanism for one, but he didn't have the endurance left for a task that would take days.

Days? But the Roller had made one. Had they been here days already? Then he remembered that the Roller had many tentacles to work with and undoubtedly could do such work faster than he.

And besides, a catapult wouldn't decide the issue. He had to do better than that.

Bow and arrow? No; he'd tried archery once and knew his own ineptness with a bow. Even with a modern sportsman's durasteel weapon, made for accuracy. With such a crude, pieced-together outfit as he could make here, he doubted if he could shoot as far as he could throw a rock, and knew he couldn't shoot as straight.

Spear? Well, he *could* make that. It would be useless as a throwing weapon at any distance, but would be a handy thing at close range, if he ever got to close range.

And making one would give him something to do. Help keep his mind from wandering, as it was beginning to do. Sometimes now, he had to concentrate a while before he could remember why he was here, why he had to kill the Roller.

Luckily he was still beside one of the piles of stones. He sorted through it until he found one shaped roughly like a spearhead. With a smaller stone he began to chip it into shape, fashioning sharp shoulders on the sides so that if it penetrated it would not pull out again.

Like a harpoon? There was something in that idea, he thought. A harpoon was better than a spear, maybe, for this crazy contest. If he could once get it into the Roller, and had a rope on it, he could pull the Roller up against the barrier and the stone blade of his knife would reach through that barrier, even if his hands wouldn't.

The shaft was harder to make than the head. But by splitting and joining the main stems of four of the bushes, and wrapping the joints with the tough but thin tendrils, he got a strong shaft about four feet long, and tied the stone head in a notch cut in the end.

It was crude, but strong.

And the rope. With the thin tough tendrils he made himself twenty feet of line. It was light and didn't look strong, but he knew it would hold his weight and to spare. He tied one end of it to the shaft of the harpoon and the other end about his right wrist. At least, if he threw his harpoon across the barrier, he'd be able to pull it back if he missed.

Then when he had tied the last knot and there was nothing more he could do, the heat and the weariness and the pain in his leg and the dreadful thirst were suddenly a thousand times worse than they had been before.

He tried to stand up, to see what the Roller was doing now, and found he couldn't get to his feet. On the third try, he got as far as his knees and then fell flat again.

"I've got to sleep," he thought. "If a showdown came now, I'd be helpless. He could come up here and kill me, if he knew. I've got to regain some strength."

Slowly, painfully, he crawled back away from the barrier. Ten yards, twenty—

The jar of something thudding against the sand near him waked him from a confused and horrible dream to a more confused and more horrible reality, and he opened his eyes again to blue radiance over blue sand.

How long had he slept? A minute? A day?

Another stone thudded nearer and threw sand on him. He got his arms under him and sat up. He turned around and saw the Roller twenty yards away, at the barrier.

It rolled away hastily as he sat up, not stopping until it was as far away as it could get.

He'd fallen asleep too soon, he realized, while he was still in range of the Roller's throwing ability. Seeing him lying motionless, it had dared come up to the barrier to throw at him. Luckily, it didn't realize how weak he was, or it could have stayed there and kept on throwing stones.

Had he slept long? He didn't think so, because he felt just as he had before. Not rested at all, no thirstier, no different. Probably he'd been there only a few minutes.

He started crawling again, this time forcing himself to keep going until he was as far as he could go, until the colorless, opaque wall of the arena's outer shell was only a yard away.

Then things slipped away again—

When he awoke, nothing about him was changed, but this time he knew that he had slept a long time.

The first thing he became aware of was the inside of his mouth; it was dry, caked. His tongue was swollen.

Something was wrong, he knew, as he returned slowly to full awareness. He felt less tired, the stage of utter exhaustion had passed. The sleep had taken care of that.

But there was pain, agonizing pain. It wasn't until he tried to move that he knew that it came from his leg.

He raised his head and looked down at it. It was swollen

terribly below the knee and the swelling showed even halfway up his thigh. The plant tendrils he had used to tie on the protective pad of leaves now cut deeply into the swollen flesh.

To get his knife under that imbedded lashing would have been impossible. Fortunately, the final knot was over the shin bone, in front, where the vine cut in less deeply than elsewhere. He was able, after an agonizing effort, to untie the knot.

A look under the pad of leaves told him the worst. Infection and blood poisoning, both pretty bad and getting worse.

And without drugs, without cloth, without even *water,* there wasn't a thing he could do about it.

Not a thing, except *die,* when the poison had spread through his system.

He knew it was hopeless, then, and that he'd lost.

And with him, humanity. When he died here, out there in the universe he knew, all his friends, everybody, would die too. And Earth and the colonized planets would be the home of the red, rolling, alien Outsiders. Creatures out of nightmare, things without a human attribute, who picked lizards apart for the fun of it.

It was the thought of that which gave him courage to start crawling, almost blindly in pain, toward the barrier again. Not crawling on hands and knees this time, but pulling himself along only by his arms and hands.

A chance in a million, that maybe he'd have strength left, when he got there, to throw his harpoon-spear just *once,* and with deadly effect, if—on another chance in a million—the Roller would come up to the barrier. Or if the barrier was gone, now.

It took him years, it seemed, to get there.

The barrier wasn't gone. It was as impassable as when he'd first felt it.

And the Roller wasn't at the barrier. By raising up on his elbows, he could see it at the back of its part of the arena, working on a wooden framework that was a half-completed duplicate of the catapult he'd destroyed.

It was moving slowly now. Undoubtedly it had weakened, too.

But Carson doubted that it would ever need that second catapult. He'd be dead, he thought, before it was finished.

If he could attract it to the barrier, now, while he was still alive— He waved an arm and tried to shout, but his parched throat would make no sound.

Or if he could get through the barrier—

His mind must have slipped for a moment, for he found himself beating his fists against the barrier in futile rage, made himself stop.

He closed his eyes, tried to make himself calm.

"Hello," said the voice.

It was a small, thin voice. It sounded like—

He opened his eyes and turned his head. It *was* a lizard.

"Go away," Carson wanted to say. "Go away; you're not really there, or you're there but not really talking. I'm imagining things again."

But he couldn't talk; his throat and tongue were past all speech with the dryness. He closed his eyes again.

"Hurt," said the voice. "Kill. Hurt—kill. Come."

He opened his eyes again. The blue ten-legged lizard was still there. It ran a little way along the barrier, came back, started off again, and came back.

"Hurt," it said. "Kill. Come."

Again it started off, and came back. Obviously it wanted Carson to follow it along the barrier.

He closed his eyes again. The voice kept on. The same three meaningless words. Each time he opened his eyes, it ran off and came back.

"Hurt. Kill. Come."

Carson groaned. There would be no peace unless he followed the blasted thing. As it wanted him to.

He followed it, crawling. Another sound, a high-pitched squealing, came to his ears and grew louder.

There was something lying in the sand, writhing, squealing. Something small, blue, that looked like a lizard and yet didn't—

Then he saw what it was—the lizard whose legs the Roller had pulled off, so long ago. But it wasn't dead; it had come back to life and was wriggling and screaming in agony.

"Hurt," said the other lizard. "Hurt. Kill. Kill."

Carson understood. He took the flint knife from his belt and killed the tortured creature. The live lizard scurried off quickly.

Carson turned back to the barrier. He leaned his hands and head against it and watched the Roller, far back, working on the new catapult.

"I could get that far," he thought, "if I could get through. If I could get through, I might win yet. It looks weak, too. I might—"

And then there was another reaction of black hopelessness, when pain sapped his will and he wished that he were dead. He envied the lizard he'd just killed. It didn't have to live on and suffer. And he did. It would be hours, it might be days, before the blood poisoning killed him.

If only he could use that knife on himself—

But he knew he wouldn't. As long as he was alive, there was the millionth chance—.

He was straining, pushing on the barrier with the flat of his hands, and he noticed his arms, how thin and scrawny they were now. He must really have been here a long time, for days, to get as thin as that.

How much longer now, before he died? How much more heat and thirst and pain could flesh stand?

For a little while he was almost hysterical again, and then came a time of deep calm, and a thought that was startling.

The lizard he had just killed. *It had crossed the barrier, still alive*. It had come from the Roller's side; the Roller had pulled off its legs and then tossed it contemptuously at him and it had come through the barrier. He'd thought, because the lizard was dead.

But it hadn't been dead; it had been unconscious.

A live lizard couldn't go through the barrier, but an unconscious one could. The barrier was not a barrier, then, to living flesh, but to conscious flesh. It was a *mental* projection, a *mental* hazard.

And with that thought, Carson started crawling along the barrier to make his last desperate gamble. A hope so forlorn that only a dying man would have dared try it.

No use weighing the odds of success. Not when, if he didn't try it, those odds were infinitely to zero.

He crawled along the barrier to the dune of sand, about four feet high, which he'd scooped out in trying—how many days ago?—to dig under the barrier or to reach water.

That mound was right at the barrier, its farther slope half
on one side of the barrier, half on the other.

Taking with him a rock from the pile nearby, he climbed
up to the top of the dune and over the top, and lay there
against the barrier, his weight leaning against it so that if the
barrier were taken away he'd roll on down the short slope,
into the enemy territory.

He checked to be sure that the knife was safely in his rope
belt, that the harpoon was in the crook of his left arm and
that the twenty-foot rope fastened to it and to his wrist.

Then with his right hand he raised the rock with which he
would hit himself on the head. Luck would have to be with
him on that blow; it would have to be hard enough to knock
him out, but not hard enough to knock him out for long.

He had a hunch that the Roller was watching him, and
would see him roll down through the barrier, and come to investigate. It would think he was dead, he hoped—he thought
it had probably drawn the same deduction about the nature
of the barrier that he had drawn. But it would come cautiously. He would have a little time—

He struck.

Pain brought him back to consciousness. A sudden, sharp
pain in his hip that was different from the throbbing pain in
his head and the throbbing pain in his leg.

But he had, thinking things out before he had struck himself, anticipated that very pain, even hoped for it, and had
steeled himself against awakening with a sudden movement.

He lay still, but opened his eyes just a slit, and saw that he
had guessed right. The Roller was coming closer. It was
twenty feet away and the pain that had awakened him was
the stone it had tossed to see whether he was alive or dead.

He lay still. It came closer, fifteen feet away, and stopped
again. Carson scarcely breathed.

As nearly as possible, he was keeping his mind a blank, lest
its telepathic ability detect consciousness in him. And with his
mind blanked out that way, the impact of its thoughts upon
his mind was nearly soul-shattering.

He felt sheer horror at the utter *alienness*, the *differentness*
of those thoughts. Things that he felt but could not understand and could never express, because no terrestrial language

had words, no terrestrial mind had images to fit them. The mind of a spider, he thought, or the mind of a praying mantis or a Martian sand-serpent, raised to intelligence and put in telepathic rapport with human minds, would be a homely familiar thing, compared to this.

He understood now that the Entity had been right: Man or Roller, and the universe was not a place that could hold them both. Further apart than god and devil, there could never be even a balance between them.

Closer. Carson waited until it was only feet away, until its clawed tentacles reached out—

Oblivious to agony now, he sat up, raised and flung the harpoon with all the strength that remained to him. Or he thought it was all; sudden final strength flooded through him, along with a sudden forgetfulness of pain as definite as a nerve block.

As the Roller, deeply stabbed by the harpoon, rolled away, Carson tried to get to his feet to run after it. He couldn't do that; he fell, but kept crawling.

It reached the end of the rope, and he was jerked forward by the pull on his wrist. It dragged him a few feet and then stopped. Carson kept on going, pulling himself toward it hand over hand along the rope.

It stopped there, writhing tentacles trying in vain to pull out the harpoon. It seemed to shudder and quiver, and then it must have realized that it couldn't get away, for it rolled back toward him, clawed tentacles reaching out.

Stone knife in hand, he met it. He stabbed, again and again, while those horrid claws ripped skin and flesh and muscle from his body.

He stabbed and slashed, and at last it was still.

A bell was ringing, and it took him a while after he'd opened his eyes to tell where he was and what it was. He was strapped into the seat of his scouter, and the visiplate before him showed only empty space. No Outsider ship and no impossible planet.

The bell was the communications plate signal; someone wanted him to switch power into the receiver. Purely reflex action enabled him to reach forward and throw the lever.

The face of Brander, captain of the *Magellan*, mother-ship

of his group of scouters, flashed into the screen. His face was pale and his black eyes glowing with excitement.

"*Magellan* to Carson," he snapped. "Come on in. The flight's over. We've won!"

The screen went blank; Brander would be signaling the other scouters of his command.

Slowly, Carson set the controls for the return. Slowly, unbelievingly, he unstrapped himself from the seat and went back to get a drink at the cold-water tank. For some reason, he was unbelievably thirsty. He drank six glasses.

He leaned there against the wall, trying to think.

Had it happened? He was in good health, sound, uninjured. His thirst had been mental rather than physical; his throat hadn't been dry. His leg—

He pulled up his trouser leg and looked at the calf. There was a long white scar there, but a perfectly healed scar. It hadn't been there before. He zipped open the front of his shirt and saw that his chest and abdomen were criss-crossed with tiny, almost unnoticeable, perfectly healed scars.

It *had* happened.

The scouter, under automatic control, was already entering the hatch of the mother-ship. The grapples pulled it into its individual lock, and a moment later a buzzer indicated that the lock was airfilled. Carson opened the hatch and stepped outside, went through the double door of the lock.

He went right to Brander's office, went in, and saluted.

Brander still looked dizzily dazed. "Hi, Carson," he said. "What you missed! What a show!"

"What happened, sir?"

"Don't know, exactly. We fired one salvo, and their whole fleet went up in dust! Whatever it was jumped from ship to ship in a flash, even the ones we hadn't aimed at and that were out of range! The whole fleet disintegrated before our eyes, and we didn't get the paint of a single ship scratched!

"We can't even claim credit for it. Must have been some unstable component in the metal they used, and our sighting shot just set it off. Man, oh man, too bad you missed all the excitement."

Carson managed to grin. It was a sickly ghost of a grin, for it would be days before he'd be over the mental impact of his experience, but the captain wasn't watching, and didn't notice.

"Yes, sir," he said. Common sense, more than modesty, told him he'd be branded forever as the worst liar in space if he ever said any more than that. "Yes, sir, too bad I missed all the excitement."

HUDDLING PLACE

Astounding,

July

by Clifford D. Simak

The second of the City Series that brought fame and honors to Cliff Simak, "Huddling Place" is a wonderful story about an important problem—that of breaking away, of starting something entirely new, and of leaving the familiar for the unknown. Few writers have brought the emotion and pathos to this experience achieved by Simak in this moving and quite profound story.

(In 1938, Cliff published "Rule 18" (which I would have fought to include had we not started this series in the year 1939) and I slammed it in a letter to the editor. Cliff wrote to me (initiating a life-long correspondence and asked if I could explain what was wrong with it. I reread it and discovered there was nothing wrong with it. I had simply not read it with sufficient attention. I told him this in all humility and then I went further. So much did I admire the story on rereading that I consciously adopted Cliff's style as best I could and clung to it ever since. It is a pleasant memory that at the Nebula Awards Dinner at which Cliff was honored as Grand Master, I served as Toastmaster. (He is the favorite science fiction writer of my wife, Janet Jeppson, and marriage to me didn't shake her allegiance to him in the least.)—I.A.)

The drizzle sifted from the leaden skies, like smoke drifting through the bare-branched trees. It softened the hedges and hazed the outlines of the buildings and blotted out the distance. It glinted on the metallic skins of the silent robots and silvered the shoulders of the three humans listening to the intonations of the black-garbed man, who read from the book cupped between his hands.

"*For I am the Resurrection and the Life—*"

The moss-mellowed graven figure that reared above the door of the crypt seemed straining upward, every crystal of its yearning body reaching toward something that no one else could see. Straining as it had strained since that day of long ago when men had chipped it from the granite to adorn the family tomb with a symbolism that had pleased the first John J. Webster in the last years he held of life.

"*And whosoever liveth and believeth in Me—*"

Jerome A. Webster felt his son's fingers tighten on his arm, heard the muffled sobbing of his mother, saw the lines of robots standing rigid, heads bowed in respect to the master they had served. The master who now was going home—to the final home of all.

Numbly, Jerome A. Webster wondered if they understood—if they understood life and death—if they understood what it meant that Nelson F. Webster lay there in the casket, that a man with a book intoned words above him.

Nelson F. Webster, fourth of the line of Websters who had lived on these acres, had lived and died here, scarcely leaving, and now was going to his final rest in that place the first of them had prepared for the rest of them—for that long line of shadowy descendants who would live here and cherish the things and the ways and the life that the first John J. Webster had established.

Jerome A. Webster felt his jaw muscles tighten, felt a little tremor run across his body. For a moment his eyes burned and the casket blurred in his sight and the words the man in black was saying were one with the wind that whispered in the pines standing sentinel for the dead. Within his brain remembrance marched—remembrance of a gray-haired man stalking the hills and fields, sniffing the breeze of an early morning, standing, legs braced, before the flaring fireplace with a glass of brandy in his hand.

Pride—the pride of land and life, and the humility and greatness that quiet living breeds within a man. Contentment of casual leisure and surety of purpose. Independence of assured security, comfort of familiar surroundings, freedom of broad acres.

Thomas Webster was jiggling his elbow. "Father," he was whispering. "Father."

The service was over. The black-garbed man had closed his book. Six robots stepped forward, lifted the casket.

Slowly the three followed the casket into the crypt, stood silently as the robots slid it into its receptacle, closed the tiny door and affixed the plate that read:

NELSON F. WEBSTER
2034-2117

That was all. Just the name and dates. And that, Jerome A. Webster found himself thinking, was enough. There was nothing else that needed to be there. That was all those others had. The ones that called the family roll—starting with William Stevens, 1920-1999. Gramp Stevens, they had called him, Webster remembered. Father of the wife of that first John J. Webster, who was here himself—1951-2020. And after him his son, Charles F. Webster, 1980-2060. And his son, John J. II, 2004-2086. Webster could remember John J. II—a grandfather who had slept beside the fire with his pipe hanging from his mouth, eternally threatening to set his whiskers aflame.

Webster's eyes strayed to another plate. Mary Webster, the mother of the boy here at his side. And yet not a boy. He kept forgetting that Thomas was twenty now, in a week or so would be leaving for Mars, even as in his younger days he, too, had gone to Mars.

All here together, he told himself. The Websters and their wives and children. Here in death together as they had lived together, sleeping in the pride and security of bronze and marble with the pines outside and the symbolic figure above the age-greened door.

The robots were waiting, standing silently, their task fulfilled.

His mother looked at him.

"You're the head of the family now, my son," she told him.

He reached out and hugged her close against his side. Head of the family—what was left of it. Just the three of them now. His mother and his son. And his son would be leaving soon, going out to Mars. But he would come back. Come back with a wife, perhaps, and the family would go on. The family wouldn't stay at three. Most of the big house wouldn't stay closed off, as it now was closed off. There had been a time when it had rung with the life of a dozen units of the family, living in their separate apartments under one big roof. That time, he knew, would come again.

The three of them turned and left the crypt, took the path back to the house, looming like a huge gray shadow in the midst.

A fire blazed in the hearth and the book lay upon his desk. Jerome A. Webster reached out and picked it up, read the title once again:

Martian Physiology, With Especial Reference to the Brain by Jerome A. Webster, M.D.

Thick and authoritative—the work of a lifetime. Standing almost alone in its field. Based upon the data gathered during those five plague years on Mars—years when he had labored almost day and night with his fellow colleagues of the World Committee's medical commission, dispatched on an errand of mercy to the neighboring planet.

A tap sounded on the door.

"Come in," he called.

The door opened and a robot glided in.

"Your whiskey, sir."

"Thank you, Jenkins," Webster said.

"The minister, sir," said Jenkins, "has left."

"Oh, yes. I presume that you took care of him."

"I did, sir. Gave him the usual fee and offered him a drink. He refused the drink."

"That was a social error," Webster told him. "Ministers don't drink."

"I'm sorry, sir. I didn't know. He asked me to ask you to come to church sometime."

"Eh?"

"I told him, sir, that you never went anywhere."

"That was quite right, Jenkins," said Webster. "None of us go anywhere."

Jenkins headed for the door, stopped before he got there, turned around. "If I may say so, sir, that was a touching

service at the crypt. Your father was a fine human, the finest
ever was. The robots were saying the service was very fitting.
Dignified like, sir. He would have liked it had he known."

"My father," said Webster, "would be even more pleased
to hear you say that, Jenkins."

"Thank you, sir," said Jenkins, and went out.

Webster sat with the whisky and the book and fire—felt
the comfort of the well-known room close in about him, felt
the refuge that was in it.

This was home. It had been home for the Websters since
that day when the first John J. had come here and built the
first unit of the sprawling house. John J. had chosen it because it had a trout stream, or so he always said. But it was
something more than that. It must have been, Webster told
himself, something more than that.

Or perhaps, at first, it had only been the trout stream.
The trout stream and the trees and meadows, the rocky ridge
where the mist drifted in each morning from the river.
Maybe the rest of it had grown, grown gradually through the
years, through years of family association until the very soil
was soaked with something that approached, but wasn't quite,
tradition. Something that made each tree, each rock, each
foot of soil a Webster tree or rock or clod of soil. It all belonged.

John J., the first John J., had come after the breakup of
the cities, after men had forsaken, once and for all, the twentieth century huddling places, had broken free of the tribal
instinct to stick together in one cave or in one clearing
against a common foe or a common fear. An instinct that
had become outmoded, for there were no fears or foes. Man
revolting against the herd instinct economic and social conditions had impressed upon him in ages past. A new security
and a new sufficiency had made it possible to break away.

The trend had started back in the twentieth century, more
than two hundred years before, when men moved to country
homes to get fresh air and elbow room and a graciousness in
life that communal existence, in its strictest sense, never had
given them.

And here was the end result. A quiet living. A peace that
could only come with good things. The sort of life that men
had yearned for years to have. A manorial existence, based

on old family homes and leisurely acres, with atomics supplying power and robots in place of serfs.

Webster smiled at the fireplace with its blazing wood. That was an anachronism, but a good one—something that Man had brought forward from the caves. Useless, because atomic heating was better—but more pleasant. One couldn't sit and watch atomics and dream and build castles in the flames.

Even the crypt out there, where they had put his father that afternoon. That was family, too. All of a piece with the rest of it. The somber pride and leisured life and peace. In the old days the dead were buried in vast plots all together, stranger cheek by jowl with stranger—

He never goes anywhere.

That is what Jenkins had told the minister.

And that was right. For what need was there to go anywhere? It all was here. By simply twirling a dial one could talk face-to-face with anyone one wished, could go, by sense, if not in body, anywhere one wished. Could attend the theater or hear a concert or browse in a library halfway around the world. Could transact any business one might need to transact without rising from one's chair.

Webster drank the whisky, then swung to the dialed machine beside his desk.

He spun dials from memory without resorting to the log. He knew where he was going.

His finger flipped a toggle and the room melted away—or seemed to melt. There was left the chair within which he sat, part of the desk, part of the machine itself and that was all.

The chair was on a hillside swept with golden grass and dotted with scraggly, wind-twisted trees, a hillside that straggled down to a lake nestling in the grip of purple mountain spurs. The spurs, darkened in long streaks with the bluish-green of distant pine, climbed in staggering stairs, melting into the blue-tinged snow-capped peaks that reared beyond and above them in jagged saw-toothed outline.

The wind talked harshly in the crouching trees and ripped the long grass in sudden gusts. The last rays of the sun struck fire from the distant peaks.

Solitude and grandeur, the long sweep of tumbled land, the cuddled lake, the knifelike shadows on the far-off ranges.

Webster sat easily in his chair, eyes squinting at the peaks.

A voice said almost at his shoulder: "May I come in?"

A soft, sibilant voice, wholly unhuman. But one that Webster knew.

He nodded his head. "By all means, Juwain."

He turned slightly and saw the elaborate crouching pedestal, the furry, soft-eyed figure of the Martian squatting on it. Other alien furniture loomed indistinctly beyond the pedestal, half-guessed furniture from that dwelling out on Mars.

The Martian flipped a furry hand toward the mountain range.

"You love this," he said. "You can understand it. And I can understand how you understand it, but to me there is more terror than beauty in it. It is something we could never have on Mars."

Webster reached out a hand, but the Martian stopped him.

"Leave it on," he said. "I know why you came here. I would not have come at a time like this except I thought perhaps an old friend—"

"It is kind of you," said Webster. "I am glad that you have come."

"Your father," said Juwain, "was a great man. I remember how you used to talk to me of him, those years you spent on Mars. You said then you would come back sometime. Why is it you've never come?"

"Why," said Webster, "I just never—"

"Do not tell me," said the Martian. "I already know."

"My son," said Webster, "is going to Mars in a few days. I shall have him call on you."

"That would be a pleasure," said Juwain. "I shall be expecting him."

He stirred uneasily on the crouching pedestal. "Perhaps he carries on tradition."

"No," said Webster. "He is studying engineering. He never cared for surgery."

"He has a right," observed the Martian, "to follow the life that he has chosen. Still, one might be permitted to wish."

"One could," Webster agreed. "But that is over and done with. Perhaps he will be a great engineer. Space structure. Talks of ships out to the stars."

"Perhaps," suggested Juwain, "your family has done enough for medical science. You and your father—"

"And his father," said Webster, "before him."

"Your book," declared Juwain, "has put Mars in debt to you. It may focus more attention on Martian specialization. My people do not make good doctors. They have no background for it. Queer how the minds of races run. Queer that Mars never thought of medicine—literally never thought of it. Supplied the need with a cult of fatalism. While even in your early history, when men still lived in caves—"

"There are many things," said Webster, "that you thought of and we didn't. Things we wonder now how we ever missed. Abilities that you developed and we do not have. Take your own specialty, philosophy. But different than ours. A science, while ours never was more than ordered fumbling. Yours an orderly, logical development of philosophy, workable, practical, applicable, an actual tool."

Juwain started to speak, hesitated, then when ahead. "I am near to something, something that may be new and startling. Something that will be a tool for you humans as well as for the Martians. I've worked on it for years, starting with certain mental concepts that first were suggested to me with arrival of the Earthmen. I have said nothing, for I could not be sure."

"And now," suggested Webster, "you are sure."

"Not quite," said Juwain. "Not positive. But almost."

They sat in silence, watching the mountains and the lake. A bird came and sat in one of the scraggly trees and sang. Dark clouds piled up behind the mountain ranges and the snow-tipped peaks stood out like graven stone. The sun sank in a lake of crimson, hushed finally to the glow of a fire burned low.

A tap sounded from a door and Webster stirred in his chair, suddenly brought back to the reality of the study, of the chair beneath him.

Juwain was gone. The old philosopher had come and sat an hour of contemplation with his friend and then had quietly slipped away.

The rap came again.

Webster leaned forward, snapped the toggle and the mountains vanished; the room became a room again. Dusk filtered through the high windows and the fire was a rosy flicker in the ashes.

"Come in," said Webster.

Jenkins opened the door. "Dinner is served, sir," he said.

"Thank you," said Webster. He rose slowly from the chair.

"Your place, sir," said Jenkins, "is laid at the head of the table."

"Ah, yes," said Webster. "Thank you, Jenkins. Thank you very much, for reminding me."

Webster stood on the broad ramp of the space field and watched the shape that dwindled in the sky with faint flickering points of red lancing through the wintry sunlight.

For long minutes after the shape was gone he stood there, hands gripping the railing in front of him, eyes still staring up into the sky.

His lips moved and they said: "Good-bye, son"; but there was no sound.

Slowly he came alive to his surroundings. Knew that people moved about the ramp, saw that the landing field seemed to stretch interminably to the far horizon, dotted here and there with hump-backed things that were waiting spaceships. Scooting tractors worked near one hangar, clearing away the last of the snowfall of the night before.

Webster shivered and thought that it was queer, for the noonday sun was warm. And shivered again.

Slowly he turned away from the railing and headed for the administration building. And for one brain-wrenching moment he felt a sudden fear—an unreasonable and embarrassing fear of that stretch of concrete that formed the ramp. A fear that left him shaking mentally as he drove his feet toward the waiting door.

A man walked toward him, briefcase swinging in his hand and Webster, eyeing him, wished fervently that the man would not speak to him.

The man did not speak, passed him with scarcely a glance, and Webster felt relief.

If he were back home, Webster told himself, he would have finished lunch, would now be ready to lie down for his midday nap. The fire would be blazing on the hearth and the flicker of the flames would be reflected from the andirons. Jenkins would bring him a liqueur and would say a word or two—inconsequential conversation.

He hurried toward the door, quickening his step, anxious to get away from the bare-cold expanse of the massive ramp.

Funny how he had felt about Thomas. Natural, of course,

that he should have hated to see him go. But entirely unnatural that he should, in those last few minutes, find such horror welling up within him. Horror of the trip through space, horror of the alien land of Mars—although Mars was scarcely alien any longer. For more than a century now Earthmen had known it, had fought it, lived with it; some of them had even grown to love it.

But it had only been utter will power that had prevented him, in those last few seconds before the ship had taken off, from running out into the field, shrieking for Thomas to come back, shrieking for him not to go.

And that, of course, never would have done. It would have been exhibitionism, disgraceful and humiliating—the sort of thing a Webster could not do.

After all, he told himself, a trip to Mars was no great adventure, not any longer. There had been a day when it had been, but that day was gone forever. He, himself, in his earlier days had made a trip to Mars, had stayed there for five long years. That had been—he gasped when he thought of it—that had been almost thirty years ago.

The babble and hum of the lobby hit him in the face as the robot attendant opened the door for him, and in that babble ran a vein of something that was almost terror. For a moment he hesitated, then stepped inside. The door closed softly behind him.

He stayed close to the wall to keep out of people's way, headed for a chair in one corner. He sat down and huddled back, forcing his body deep into the cushions, watching the milling humanity that seethed out in the room.

Shrill people, hurrying people, people with strange, unneighborly faces. Strangers—every one of them. Not a face he knew. People going places. Heading out for the planets. Anxious to be off. Worried about last details. Rushing here and there.

Out of the crowd loomed a familiar face. Webster hunched forward.

"Jenkins!" he shouted, and then was sorry for the shout, although no one seemed to notice.

The robot moved toward him, stood before him.

"Tell Raymond," said Webster, "that I must return immediately. Tell him to bring the 'copter in front at once."

"I am sorry, sir," said Jenkins, "but we cannot leave at

once. The mechanics found a flaw in the atomics chamber. They are installing a new one. It will take several hours."

"Surely," said Webster, impatiently, "that could wait until some other time."

"The mechanic said not, sir," Jenkins told him. "It might go at any minute. The entire charge of power——"

"Yes, yes," agreed Webster. "I suppose so."

He fidgeted with his hat. "I just remembered," he said, "something I must do. Something that must be done at once. I must get home. I can't wait several hours."

He hitched forward to the edge of the chair, eyes staring at the milling crowd.

Faces—faces—

"Perhaps you could televise," suggested Jenkins. "One of the robots might be able to do it. There is a booth——"

"Wait, Jenkins," said Webster. He hesitated a moment. "There is nothing to do back home. Nothing at all. But I must get there. I can't stay here. If I have to, I'll go crazy. I was frightened out there on the ramp. I'm bewildered and confused here. I have a feeling—a strange, terrible feeling. Jenkins, I——"

"I understand, sir," said Jenkins. "Your father had it, too."

Webster gasped. "My father?"

"Yes, sir, that is why he never went anywhere. He was about your age, sir, when he found it out. He tried to make a trip to Europe and he couldn't. He got halfway there and turned back. He had a name for it."

Webster sat in stricken silence.

"A name for it," he finally said. "Of course there's a name for it. My father had it. My grandfather—did he have it, too?"

"I wouldn't know that, sir," said Jenkins. "I wasn't created until after your grandfather was an elderly man. But he may have. He never went anywhere, either."

"You understand, then," said Webster. "You know how it is. I feel like I'm going to be sick—physically ill. See if you can charter a 'copter—anything, just so we get home."

"Yes, sir," said Jenkins.

He started off and Webster called him back.

"Jenkins, does anyone else know about this? Anyone——"

"No, sir," said Jenkins. "Your father never mentioned it and I felt, somehow, that he wouldn't wish me to."

"Thank you, Jenkins," said Webster.

Webster huddled back into his chair again, feeling desolate and alone and misplaced. Alone in a humming lobby that pulsed with life—a loneliness that tore at him, that left him limp and weak.

Homesickness. Downright, shameful homesickness, he told himself. Something that boys are supposed to feel when they first leave home, when they first go out to meet the world.

There was a fancy word for it—agoraphobia, the morbid dread of being in the midst of open spaces—from the Greek root for the fear—literally, of the market place.

If he crossed the room to the television booth, he could put in a call, talk with his mother or one of the robots—or, better yet, just sit and look at the place until Jenkins came for him.

He started to rise, then sank back in the chair again. It was no dice. Just talking to someone or looking in on the place wasn't being there. He couldn't smell the pines in the wintry air, or hear familiar snow crunch on the walk beneath his feet or reach out a hand and touch one of the massive oaks that grew along the path. He couldn't feel the heat of the fire or sense the sure, deft touch of belonging, of being one with a tract of ground and the things upon it.

And yet—perhaps it would help. Not much, maybe, but some. He started to rise from the chair again and froze. The few short steps to the booth held terror, a terrible, overwhelming terror. If he crossed them, he would have to run. Run to escape the watching eyes, the unfamiliar sounds, the agonizing nearness of strange faces.

Abruptly he sat down.

A woman's shrill voice cut across the lobby and he shrank away from it. He felt terrible. He felt like hell. He wished Jenkins would get a hustle on.

The first breath of spring came through the window, filling the study with the promise of melting snows, of coming leaves and flowers, of north-bound wedges of waterfowl streaming through the blue, of trout that lurked in pools waiting for the fly.

Webster lifted his eyes from the sheaf of papers on his desk, sniffed the breeze, felt the cool whisper of it on his cheek. His hand reached out for the brandy glass, found it empty, and put it back.

He bent back above the papers once again, picked up a pencil and crossed out a word.

Critically, he read the final paragraphs:

The fact that of the two hundred fifty men who were invited to visit me, presumably on missions of more than ordinary importance, only three were able to come, does not necessarily prove that all but those three are victims of agoraphobia. Some may have had legitimate reasons for being unable to accept my invitation. But it does indicate a growing unwillingness of men living under the mode of Earth existence set up following the breakup of the cities to move from familiar places, a deepening instinct to stay among the scenes and possessions which in their mind have become associated with contentment and graciousness of life.

What the result of such a trend will be, no one can clearly indicate since it applies to only a small portion of Earth's population. Among the larger families economic pressure forces some of the sons to seek their fortunes either in other parts of the Earth or on one of the other planets. Many others deliberately seek adventure and opportunity in space, while still others become associated with professions or trades which make a sedentary existence impossible.

He flipped the page over, went on to the last one.

It was a good paper, he knew, but it could not be published, not just yet. Perhaps after he had died. No one, so far as he could determine, had ever so much as realized the trend, had taken as matter of course the fact that men seldom left their homes. Why, after all, should they leave their homes?

The televisor muttered at his elbow and he reached out to flip the toggle.

The room faded and he was face-to-face with a man who sat behind a desk, almost as if he sat on the opposite side of Webster's desk. A gray-haired man with sad eyes behind heavy lenses.

For a moment Webster stared, memory tugging at him.

"Could it be——" he asked and the man smiled gravely.

"I have changed," he said. "So have you. My name is Clayborne. Remember? The Martian medical commission—"

"Clayborne! I'd often thought of you. You stayed on Mars."

Clayborne nodded. "I've read your book, doctor. It is a real contribution. I've often thought one should be written, wanted to myself, but I didn't have the time. Just as well I didn't. You did a better job. Especially on the brain."

"The Martian brain," Webster told him "always intrigued me. Certain peculiarities. I'm afraid I spent more of those five years taking notes on it than I should have. There was other work to do."

"A good thing you did," said Clayborne. "That's why I'm calling you now. I have a patient—a brain operation. Only you can handle it."

Webster gasped, his hands trembling. "You'll bring him here?"

Clayborne shook his head. "He cannot be moved. You know him, I believe. Juwain, the philosopher."

"Juwain!" said Webster. "He's one of my best friends. We talked together just a couple of days ago."

"The attack was sudden," said Clayborne. "He's been asking for you."

Webster was silent and cold—cold with a chill that crept upon him from some unguessed place. Cold that sent perspiration out upon his forehead, that knotted his fists.

"If you start immediately," said Clayborne, "you can be here on time. I've already arranged with the World Committee to have a ship at your disposal instantly. The utmost speed is necessary."

"But," said Webster, "but . . . I cannot come."

"You can't come!"

"It's impossible," said Webster. "I doubt in any case that I am needed. Surely, you yourself—"

"I can't," said Clayborne. "No one can but you. No one else has the knowledge. You hold Juwain's life in your hands. If you come, he lives. If you don't, he dies."

"I can't go into space," said Webster.

"Anyone can go into space," snapped Clayborne. "It's not like it used to be. Conditioning of any sort desired is available."

"But you don't understand," pleaded Webster. "You—"

"No, I don't," said Clayborne. "Frankly, I don't. That anyone should refuse to save the life of his friend—"

The two men stared at one another for a long moment, neither speaking.

"I shall tell the committee to send the ship straight to your home," said Clayborne finally. "I hope by that time you will see your way clear to come."

Clayborne faded and the wall came into view again—the wall and books, the fireplace and the paintings, the well-loved furniture, the promise of spring that came through the open window.

Webster sat frozen in his chair, staring at the wall in front of him.

Juwain, the furry, wrinkled face, the sibilant whisper, the friendliness and understanding that were his. Juwain, grasping the stuff that dreams are made of and shaping them into logic, into rules of life and conduct. Juwain, using philosophy as a tool, as a science, as a stepping stone to better living.

Webster dropped his face into his hands and fought the agony that welled up within him.

Clayborne had not understood. One could not expect him to understand since there was no way for him to know. And even knowing, would he understand? Even he, Webster, would not have understood it in someone else until he had discovered it in himself—the terrible fear of leaving his own fire, his own land, his own possessions, the little symbolisms that he had erected. And yet, not he, himself, alone, but those other Websters as well. Starting with the first John J. Men and women who had set up a cult of life, a tradition of behavior.

He, Jerome A. Webster, had gone to Mars when he was a young man, and had not felt or suspected the psychological poison that ran through his veins. Even as Thomas a few months ago had gone to Mars. But thirty years of quiet life here in the retreat that the Websters called a home had brought it forth, had developed it without his even knowing it. There had, in fact, been no opportunity to know it.

It was clear how it had developed—clear as crystal now. Habit and mental pattern and a happiness association with certain things—things that had no actual value in themselves, but had been assigned a value, a definite, concrete value by one family through five generations.

No wonder other places seemed alien, no wonder other horizons held a hint of horror in their sweep.

And there was nothing one could do about it—nothing, that is, unless one cut down every tree and burned the house and changed the course of waterways. Even that might not do it—even that—

The televisor purred and Webster lifted his head from his hands, reached out and thumbed the tumbler.

The room became a flare of white, but there was no image. A voice said: "Secret call. Secret call."

Webster slid back a panel in the machine, spun a pair of dials, heard the hum of power surge into a screen that blocked out the room.

"Secrecy established," he said.

The white flare snapped out and a man sat across the desk from him. A man he had seen many times before in televised addresses, in his daily paper.

Henderson, president of the World Committee.

"I have had a call from Clayborne," said Henderson.

Webster nodded without speaking.

"He tells me you refuse to go to Mars."

"I have not refused," said Webster. "When Clayborne cut off the question was left open. I had told him it was impossible for me to go, but he had rejected that, did not seem to understand."

"Webster, you must go," said Henderson. "You are the only man with the necessary knowledge of the Martian brain to perform this operation. If it were a simple operation, perhaps someone else could do it. But not one such as this."

"That maybe true," said Webster, "but—"

"It's not just a question of saving a life," said Henderson. "Even a life of so distinguished a personage as Juwain. It involves even more than that. Juwain is a friend of yours. Perhaps he hinted of something he has found."

"Yes," said Webster. "Yes, he did. A new concept of philosophy."

"A concept," declared Henderson, "that we cannot do without. A concept that will remake the solar system, that will put mankind ahead a hundred thousand years in the space of two generations. A new direction of purpose that will aim toward a goal we heretofore had not suspected, had not even known existed. A brand new truth, you see. One that never before had occurred to anyone."

Webster's hand gripped the edge of the desk until his knuckles stood out white.

"If Juwain dies," said Henderson, "that concept dies with him. Maybe lost forever."

"I'll try," said Webster. I'll try—"

Henderson's eyes were hard. "Is that the best you can do?"

"That is the best," said Webster.

"But, man, you must have a reason! Some explanation."

"None," said Webster, "that I would care to give."

Deliberately he reached out and flipped up the switch.

Webster sat at the desk and held his hands in front of him, staring at them. Hands that had skill, held knowledge. Hands that could save a life if he could get them to Mars. Hands that could save for the solar system, for mankind, for the Martians an idea—a new idea—that would advance them a hundred thousand years in the next two generations.

But hands chained by a phobia that grew out of his quiet life. Decadence—a strangely beautiful—and deadly—decadence.

Man had forsaken the teeming cities, the huddling place, two hundred years ago. He had done with the old foes and the ancient fears that kept him around the common campfire, had left behind the hobgoblins that had walked with him from the caves.

And yet—and yet.

Here was another huddling place. Not a huddling place for one's body, but one's mind. A psychological campfire that still held a man within the circle of its light.

Still, Webster knew, he must leave that fire. As the men had done with the cities two centuries before, he must walk off and leave it. And he must not look back.

He had to go to Mars—or at least start for Mars. There was no question there, at all. He had to go.

Whether he would survive the trip, whether he could perform the operation once he had arrived, he did not know. He wondered vaguely whether agoraphobia could be fatal. In its most exaggerated form, he supposed it could.

He reached out a hand to ring, then hesitated. No use having Jenkins pack. He would do it himself—something to keep him busy until the ship arrived.

From the top shelf of the wardrobe in the bedroom, he took down a bag and saw that it was dusty. He blew on it, but the dust still clung. It had been there for too many years.

As he packed, the room argued with him, talked in that mute tongue with which inanimate but familiar things may converse with a man.

"You can't go," said the room. "You can't go off and leave me."

And Webster argued back, half pleading, half explaining, "I have to go. Can't you understand? It's a friend, an old friend. I will be coming back."

Packing done, Webster returned to the study, slumped into his chair.

He must go and yet he couldn't go. But when the ship arrived, when the time had come, he knew that he would walk out of the house and toward the waiting ship.

He steeled his mind to that, tried to set it in a rigid pattern, tried to blank out everything but the thought that he was leaving.

Things in the room intruded on his brain, as if they were part of a conspiracy to keep him there. Things that he saw as if he were seeing them for the first time. Old, remembered things that suddenly were new. The chronometer that showed both Earthian and Martian time, the days of the month, the phases of the moon. The picture of his dead wife on the desk. The trophy he had won at prep school. The framed short snorter bill that had cost him ten bucks on his trip to Mars.

He stared at them, half unwilling at first, then eagerly, storing up the memory of them in his brain. Seeing them as separate components of a room he had accepted all these years as a finished whole, never realizing what a multitude of things went to make it up.

Dusk was falling, the dusk of early spring, a dusk that smelled of early pussy willows.

The ship should have arrived long ago. He caught himself listening for it, even as he realized that he would not hear it. A ship, driven by atomic motors, was silent except when it gathered speed. Landing and taking off, it floated like thistledown, with not a murmur in it.

It would be here soon. It would have to be here soon or he

could never go. Much longer to wait, he knew, and his high-keyed resolution would crumble like a mound of dust in beating rain. Not much longer could he hold his purpose against the pleading of the room, against the flicker of the fire, against the murmur of the land where five generations of Websters had lived their lives and died.

He shut his eyes and fought down the chill that crept across his body. He couldn't let it get him now, he told himself. He had to stick it out. When the ship arrived he still must be able to get up and walk out the door to the waiting port.

A tap came on the door.

"Come in," Webster called.

It was Jenkins, the light from the fireplace flickering on his shining metal hide.

"Had you called earlier, sir?" he asked.

Webster shook his head.

"I was afraid you might have," Jenkins explained, "and wondered why I didn't come. There was a most extraordinary occurrence, sir. Two men came with a ship and said they wanted you to go to Mars."

"They are here," said Webster. "Why didn't you call me?"

He struggled to his feet.

"I didn't think, sir," said Jenkins, "that you would want to be bothered. It was so preposterous. I finally made them understand you could not possibly want to go to Mars."

Webster stiffened, felt chill fear gripping at his heart. Hands groping for the edge of the desk, he sat down in the chair, sensed the walls of the room closing in about him, a trap that would never let him go.

KINDNESS

Astounding,

October

by Lester Del Rey (1915-   )

*Lester Del Rey has appeared frequently in this
series, and justifiably so, because the first half of the
1940's were productive years for him, years that
saw him bring a quiet strength and emotionality to
science fiction. It is probable that this story was influenced by the events of World War II and the na-
tionalism that often produces conflict. "Kindness"
raises important questions about what it means to
be "normal" (and* different), *an issue that would be
later addressed frequently in science fiction, most
notably by writers as different from Del Rey as
Robert Sheckley and Philip K. Dick.*

*(I think it's time to tell my favorite Lester Del
Rey story because it deals with the one time when I
clearly got the last word in a verbal exchange with
him. A couple of years ago, I was describing one of
my father's teachings. My father would say to me,
"Don't think, Isaac, that if you associate with bums,
you will make those bums into good people. No!
Those bums will make you into a bum." Upon
which Lester said, "So why do you still associate
with bums, Isaac?" To which I answered instantly,
"Because I love you, Lester." Everyone laughed and
even Lester was so busy laughing he had not time
to think of a riposte.—I.A.)*

The wind eddied idly around the corner and past the se-
cluded park bench. It caught fitfully at the paper on the

457

ground, turning the pages, then picked up a section and blew
away with it, leaving gaudy-colored comics uppermost.
Danny moved forward into the sunlight, his eyes dropping to
the children's page exposed.

But it was no use; he made no effort to pick up the paper.
In a world where even the children's comics needed explaining, there could be nothing of interest to the last living *homo
sapiens*—the last normal man in the world. His foot kicked
the paper away, under the bench where it would no longer
remind him of his deficiencies. There had been a time when
he had tried to reason slowly over the omitted steps of logic
and find the points behind such things, sometimes successfully, more often not; but now he left it to the quick, intuitive
thinking of those about him. Nothing fell flatter than a joke
that had to be reasoned out slowly.

Homo sapiens! The type of man who had come out of the
caves and built a world of atomic power, electronics and
other old-time wonders—thinking man, as it translated from
the Latin. In the dim past, when his ancestors had owned the
world, they had made a joke of it, shortening it to homo sap,
and laughing, because there had been no other species to
rival them. Now it was no longer a joke.

Normal man had been only a "sap" to *homo intelligens*—
intelligent man—who was now the master of the world.
Danny was only a left-over, the last normal man in a world
of supermen, hating the fact that he had been born, and that
his mother had died at his birth to leave him only loneliness
as his heritage.

He drew farther back on the bench as the steps of a young
couple reached his ears, pulling his hat down to avoid recognition. But they went by, preoccupied with their own affairs,
leaving only a scattered bit of conversation in his ears. He
turned it over in his mind, trying senselessly to decode it.

Impossible! Even the casual talk contained too many steps
of logic left out. Homo intelligens had a new way of thinking,
above reason, where all the long, painful steps of logic could
be jumped instantly. They could arrive at a correct picture of
the whole from little scattered bits of information. Just as
man had once invented logic to replace the trial-and-error
thinking that most animals have, so homo intelligens had
learned to use intuition. They could look at the first page of
an old-time book and immediately know the whole of it,

since the little tricks of the author would connect in their intuitive minds and at once build up all the missing links. They didn't even have to try—they just looked, and knew. It was like Newton looking at an apple falling and immediately seeing why the planets circled the sun, and realizing the laws of gravitation; but these new men did it all the time, not just at those rare intervals as it had worked for homo sapiens once.

Man was gone, except for Danny, and he too had to leave this world of supermen. Somehow, soon, those escape plans must be completed, before the last of his little courage was gone! He stirred restlessly, and the little coins in his pocket set up a faint jingling sound. More charity, or occupational therapy! For six hours a day, five days a week, he worked in a little office, painfully doing routine work that could probably have been done better by machinery. Oh, they assured him that his manual skill was as great as theirs and that it was needed, but he could never be sure. In their unfailing kindness, they had probably decided it was better for him to live as normally as they could let him, and then had created the job to fit what he could do.

Other footsteps came down the little path, but he did not look up, until they stopped. "Hi, Danny! You weren't at the library, and Miss Larsen said, pay day, weather, and all, I'd find you here. How's everything?"

Outwardly, Jack Thorpe's body might have been the twin of Danny's own well-muscled one, and the smiling face above it bore no distinguishing characteristics. The mutation that changed man to superman had been within, a quicker, more complex relation of brain cell to brain cell that had no outward signs. Danny nodded at Jack, drawing over reluctantly to make room on the bench for this man who had been his playmate when they were both too young for the difference to matter much.

He did not ask the reason behind the librarian's knowledge of his whereabouts; so far as he knew, there was no particular pattern to his coming here, but to the others there must be one. He found he could even smile at their ability to foretell his plans.

"Hi, Jack! Fine. I thought you were on Mars."

Thorpe frowned, as if an effort were needed to remember that the boy beside him was different, and his words bore the careful phrasing of all those who spoke to Danny. "I finished that, for the time being; I'm supposed to report to Venus next. They're having trouble getting an even balance of boys and girls there, you know. Thought you might want to come along. You've never been Outside, and you were always bugs about those old space stories, I remember."

"I still am, Jack. But—" He knew what it meant, of course. Those who looked after him behind the scenes had detected his growing discontent, and were hoping to distract him with this chance to see the places his father had conquered in the heyday of his race. But he had no wish to see them as they now were, filled with the busy work of the new men; it was better to imagine them as they had once been, rather than see reality. And the ship was *here;* there could be no chance for escape from those other worlds.

Jack nodded quickly, with the almost telepathic understanding of his race. "Of course. Suit yourself, fellow. Going up to the Heights? Miss Larsen says she has something for you."

"Not yet, Jack. I thought I might look at—drop by the old museum."

"Oh." Thorpe got up slowly, brushing his suit with idle fingers. "Danny!"

"Uh?"

"I probably know you better than anyone else, fellow, so—" He hesitated, shrugged, and went on. "Don't mind if I jump to conclusions; I won't talk out of turn. But best of luck—and good-bye, Danny."

He was gone, almost instantly, leaving Danny's heart stuck in his throat. A few words, a facial expression, probably some childhood memories, and Danny might as well have revealed his most cherished secret hope in shouted words! How many others knew of his interest in the old ship in the museum and his carefully made plot to escape this kindly, charity-filled torture world?

He crushed a cigarette under his heel, trying to forget the thought. Jack had played with him as a child, and the others hadn't. He'd have to base his hopes on that and be even more careful never to think of the idea around others. In the meantime he'd stay away from the ship! Perhaps in that way Thorpe's subtle warning might work in his favor—provided the man had meant his promise of silence.

Danny forced his doubts away, grimly conscious that he dared not lose hope in this last desperate scheme for independence and self-respect; the other way offered only despair and listless hopelessness, the same empty death from an acute inferiority complex that had claimed the diminishing numbers of his own kind and left him as the last, lonely specimen. Somehow, he'd succeed, and in the meantime, he would go to the library and leave the museum strictly alone.

There was a throng of people leaving the library as Danny came up the escalator, but either they did not recognize him with his hat pulled low or sensed his desire for anonymity and pretended not to know him. He slipped into one of the less used hallways and made his way toward the historic documents section, where Miss Larsen was putting away the reading tapes and preparing to leave.

But she tossed them aside quickly as he came in and smiled up at him, the rich, warm smile of her people. "Hello, Danny! Did your friend find you all right?"

"Mm-hmm. He said you had something for me."

"I have." There was pleasure in her face as she turned back toward the desk behind her to come up with a small wrapped parcel. For the thousandth time, he caught himself wishing she were of his race and quenching the feeling as he realized what her attitude must really be. To her, the small talk from his race's past was a subject of historic interest, no more. And he was just a dull-witted hangover from ancient days. "Guess what?"

But in spite of himself, his face lighted up, both at the game and the package. "The magazines! The lost issues of *Space Trails?*" There had been only the first installment of a story extant, and yet that single part had set his pulses throbbing as few of the other ancient stories of his ancestors' conquest of space had done. Now, with the missing sections, life would be filled with zest for a few more hours as he followed the fictional exploits of a conqueror who had known no fear of keener minds.

"Not quite, Danny, but almost. We couldn't locate even a trace of them, but I gave the first installment to Bryant Kenning last week, and he finished it for you." Her voice was apologetic. "Of course the words won't be quite identical, but Kenning swears that the story is undoubtedly exactly the same in structure as it would have been, and the style is duplicated almost perfectly!"

Like that! Kenning had taken the first pages of a novel that had meant weeks and months of thought to some ancient writer and had found in them the whole plot, clearly revealed, instantly his! A night's labor had been needed to duplicate it, probably—a disagreeable and boring piece of work, but not a difficult one! Danny did not question the accuracy of the duplication, since Kenning was their greatest historical novelist. But the pleasure went out of the game.

He took the package, noting that some illustrator had even copied the old artist's style, and that it was set up to match the original format. "Thank you, Miss Larsen. I'm sorry to put all of you to so much trouble. And it was nice of Mr. Kenning!"

Her face had fallen with his, but she pretended not to notice. "He wanted to do it—volunteered when he heard we were searching for the missing copies. And if there are any others with pieces missing, Danny, he wants you to let him know. You two are about the only ones who use this division now; why don't you drop by and see him? If you'd like to go tonight—"

"Thanks. But I'll read this tonight, instead. Tell him I'm very grateful, though, will you?" But he paused, wondering again whether he dared ask for tapes on the history of the asteroids; no, there would be too much risk of her guessing, either now or later. He dared not trust any of them with a hint of his plan.

Miss Larsen smiled again, half winking at him. "Okay, Danny, I'll tell him. 'Night!"

Outside, with the cool of evening beginning to fall, Danny found his way into the untraveled quarters and let his feet guide him. Once, as a group came toward him, he crossed the street without thinking and went on. The package under his arm grew heavy and he shifted it, torn between a desire to find what had happened to the hero and a disgust at his own *sapiens* brain for not knowing. Probably, in the long run, he'd end up by going home and reading it, but for the moment he was content to let his feet carry him along idly, holding most of his thoughts in abeyance.

Another small park was in his path, and he crossed it slowly, the babble of small children's voices only partly heard until he came up to them, two boys and a girl. The supervisor, who should have had them back at the Center, was a dim shape in the far shadows, with another, dimmer shape beside her, leaving the five-year-olds happily engaged in the ancient pastime of getting dirty and impressing each other.

Danny stopped, a slow smile creeping over his lips. At that age, their intuitive ability was just beginning to develop, and their little games and pretenses made sense, acting on him like a tonic. Vaguely, he remembered his own friends of that age beginning uncertainly to acquire the trick of seeming to know everything, and his worries at being left behind. For a time, the occasional flashes of intuition that had always blessed even *homo sapiens* gave him hope, but eventually the supervisor had been forced to tell him that he was different, and why. Now he thrust those painful memories aside and slipped quietly forward into the game.

They accepted him with the easy nonchalance of children who have no repressions, feverishly trying to build their sand castles higher than his; but in that, his experience was greater than theirs, and his judgment of the damp stuff was surer. A perverse glow of accomplishment grew inside him as he added still another story to the towering structure and built a bridge, propped up with sticks and leaves, leading to it.

Then the lights came on, illuminating the sandbox and those inside it and dispelling the shadows of dusk. The smaller of the two boys glanced up, really seeing him for the first time. "Oh, you're Danny Black, ain't you? I seen your pi'ture. Judy, Bobby, look! It's that man—"

But their voices faded out as he ran off through the park and into the deserted byways again, clutching the package to him. Fool! To delight in beating children at a useless game, or to be surprised that they should know him! He slowed to a walk, twitching his lips at the thought that by now the supervisor would be reprimanding them for their thoughtlessness. And still his feet went on, unguided.

It was inevitable, of course, that they should lead him to the museum, where all his secret hopes centered, but he was surprised to look up and see it before him. And then he was glad. Surely they could read nothing into his visit, unpremeditated, just before the place closed. He caught his breath, forced his face into lines of mere casual interest, and went inside, down the long corridors, and to the hall of the ship.

She rested there, pointed slightly skyward, sleek and immense even in a room designed to appear like the distant reaches of space. For six hundred feet, gleaming metal formed a smooth frictionless surface that slid gracefully from the blunt bow back toward the narrow stern with its blackened ion jets.

This, Danny knew, was the last and greatest of the space liners his people had built at the height of their glory. And even before her, the mutation that made the new race of men had been caused by the radiations of deep space, and the results were spreading. For a time, as the log book indicated this ship had sailed out to Mars, to Venus, and to the other points of man's empire, while the tension slowly mounted at home. There had never been another wholly *sapient*-designed ship, for the new race was spreading, making its greater intelligence felt, with the invert-matter rocket replacing this older, less efficient ion rocket which the ship carried. Eventually, unable to compete with the new models, she had been retired from service and junked, while the war between the new and old race passed by her and buried her under tons of rubble, leaving no memory of her existence.

And now, carefully excavated from the old ruins of the drydock where she had lain so long, she had been enthroned in state for the last year, here in the Museum of Sapient History, while all Danny's hopes and prayers had centered around her. There was still a feeling of awe in him as he started slowly across the carpeted floor toward the open lock and the lighted interior.

"Danny!" The sudden word interrupted him, bringing him about with a guilty start, but it was only Professor Kirk, and he relaxed again. The old archaeologist came toward him, his smile barely visible in the half-light of the immense dome. "I'd about given you up, boy, and started out. But I happened to look back and see you. Thought you might be interested in some information I just came onto today."

"Information about the ship?"

"What else? Here, come on inside her and into the lounge—I have a few privileges here, and we might as well be comfortable. You know, as I grow older, I find myself appreciating your ancestors' ideas of comfort, Danny. Sort of a pity our own culture is too new for much luxuriousness yet."
Of all the new race, Kirk seemed the most completely at ease

before Danny, partly because of his age, and partly because they had shared the same enthusiasm for the great ship when it had first arrived.

Now he settled back into one of the old divans, using his immunity to ordinary rules to light a cigarette and pass one to the younger man. "You know all the supplies and things in the ship have puzzled us both, and we couldn't find any record of them? The log ends when they put the old ship up for junking, you remember; and we couldn't figure out why all this had been restored and restocked, ready for some long voyage to somewhere. Well, it came to light in some further excavations they've completed. Danny, your people did that, during the war; or really, after they'd lost the war to us!"

Danny's back straightened. The war was a period of history he'd avoided thinking about, though he knew the outlines of it. With *homo intelligens* increasing and pressing the older race aside by the laws of survival, his people had made a final desperate bid for supremacy. And while the new race had not wanted the war, they had been forced finally to fight back with as little mercy as had been shown them; and since they had the tremendous advantage of the new intuitive thinking, there had been only thousands left of the original billions of the old race when its brief course was finished. It had been inevitable probably, from the first mutation, but it was not something Danny cared to think of. Now he nodded, and let the other continue.

"Your ancestors, Danny, were beaten then, but they weren't completely crushed, and they put about the last bit of energy they had into rebuilding this ship—the only navigable one left them—and restocking it. They were going to go out somewhere, they didn't know quite where, even to another solar system, and take some of the old race for a new start, away from us. It was their last bid for survival, and it failed when my people learned of it and blasted the docks down over the ship, but it was a glorious failure, boy! I thought you'd want to know."

Danny's thoughts focused slowly. "You mean everything on the ship is of my people? But surely the provisions wouldn't have remained usable after all this time?"

"They did, though; the tests we made proved that conclusively. Your people knew how to preserve things as well as we do, and they expected to be drifting in the ship for half a century, maybe. They'll be usable a thousand years from now." He chucked his cigarette across the room and chuckled in pleased surprise when it fell accurately into a snuffer. "I stuck around, really, to tell you, and I've kept the papers over at the school for you to see. Why not come over with me now?"

"Not tonight, sir. I'd rather stay here a little longer."

Professor Kirk nodded, pulling himself up reluctantly. "As you wish . . . I know how you feel, and I'm sorry about their moving the ship, too. We'll miss her, Danny!"

"Moving the ship?"

"Hadn't you heard? I thought that's why you came around at this hour. They want her over in London, and they're bringing one of the old Lunar ships here to replace her. Too bad!" He touched the walls thoughtfully, drawing his hands down and across the rich nap of the seat. "Well, don't stay too long, and turn her lights out before you leave. Place'll be closed in half an hour. 'Night, Danny."

" 'Night, Professor." Danny sat frozen on the soft seat, listening to the slow tread of the old man and the beating of his own heart. They were moving the ship, ripping his plans to shreds, leaving him stranded in this world of a new race, where even the children were sorry for him.

It had meant so much, even to feel that somehow he would escape, some day! Impatiently, he snapped off the lights, feeling closer to the ship in the privacy of the dark, where no watchman could see his emotion. For a year now he had built his life around the idea of taking this ship out and away, to leave the new race far behind. Long, carefully casual months of work had been spent in learning her structure, finding all her stores, assuring himself bit by bit from a hundred old books that he could operate her.

She had been almost designed for the job, built to be operated by one man, even a cripple, in an emergency, and nearly everything was automatic. Only the problem of a destination had remained, since the planets were all swarming with the others, but the ship's log had suggested the answer even to that.

Once there had been rich men among his people who sought novelty and seclusion, and found them among the larger asteroids; money and science had built them artificial gravities and given them atmospheres, powered by atomic-energy plants that should last forever. Now the rich men were undoubtedly dead, and the new race had abandoned such useless things. Surely, somewhere among the asteroids, there should have been a haven for him, made safe by the very numbers of the little worlds that could discourage almost any search.

Danny heard a guard go by, and slowly got to his feet, to go out again into a world that would no longer hold even that hope. It had been a lovely plan to dream on, a necessary dream. Then the sound of the great doors came to his ears, closing! The Professor had forgotten to tell them of his presence! And—!

All right, so he didn't know the history of all those little worlds; perhaps he would have to hunt through them, one by one, to find a suitable home. Did it matter? In every other way, he could never be more ready. For a moment only, he hesitated; then his hands fumbled with the great lock's control switch, and it swung shut quietly in the dark, shutting the sound of his running feet from outside ears.

The lights came on silently as he found the navigation chair and sank into it. Little lights that spelled out the readiness of the ship. "Ship sealed . . . Air Okay . . . Power, Automatic . . . Engine, Automatic. . . ." Half a hundred little lights and dials that told the story of a ship waiting for his hand. He moved the course plotter slowly along the tiny atmospheric map until it reached the top of the stratosphere; the big star map moved slowly out, with the pointer in his fingers tracing an irregular, jagged line that would lead him somewhere toward the asteroids, well away from the present position of Mars, and yet could offer no clue. Later, he could set the analyzers to finding the present location of some chosen asteroid and determine his course more accurately, but all that mattered now was to get away, beyond all tracing, before his loss could be reported.

Seconds later his fingers pressed down savagely on the main power switch, and there was a lurch of starting, followed by another slight one as the walls of the museum crumpled before the savage force of the great ion rockets. On the map, a tiny spot of light appeared, marking the ship's changing position. The world was behind him now, and there was no one to look at his efforts in kindly pity or remind him of his weakness. Only blind fate was against him, and his ancestors had met and conquered that long before.

A bell rang, indicating the end of the atmosphere, and the big automatic pilot began clucking contentedly, emitting a louder cluck now and then as it found the irregularities in the unorthodox course he had charted and swung the ship to follow. Danny watched it, satisfied that it was working. His ancestors may have been capable of reason only, but they had built machines that were almost intuitive, as the ship about him testified. His head was higher as he turned back to the kitchen, and there was a bit of a swagger to his walk.

The food was still good. He wolfed it down, remembering that supper had been forgotten, and leafing slowly through the big log book which recorded the long voyages made by the ship, searching through it for each casual reference to the asteroids, Ceres, Palas, Vesta, some of the ones referred to by nicknames or numbers? Which ones?

But he had decided by the time he stood once again in the navigation room, watching the aloof immensity of space; out here it was relieved only by the tiny hot pinpoints that must be stars, colored, small and intense as no stars could be through an atmosphere. It would be one of the numbered planetoids, referred to also as "The Dane's" in the log. The word was meaningless, but it seemed to have been one of the newer and more completely terranized, though not the very newest where any search would surely start.

He set the automatic analyzer to running from the key number in the manual and watched it for a time, but it ground on slowly, tracing through all the years that had passed. For a time, he fiddled with the radio, before he remembered that it operated on a wave form no longer used. It was just as well; his severance from the new race would be all the more final.

Still the analyzer ground on. Space lost its novelty, and the operation of the pilot ceased to interest him. He wandered back through the ship toward the lounge, to spy the parcel where he had dropped and forgotten it. There was nothing else to do.

And once begun, he forgot his doubts at the fact that it was Kenning's story, not the original; there was the same sweep to the tale, the same warm and human characters, the same drive of a race that had felt the mastership of destiny so long ago. Small wonder the readers of that time had named it the greatest epic of space to be written!

Once he stopped, as the analyzer reached its conclusions and bonged softly, to set the controls on the automatic for the little world that might be his home, with luck. And then the ship moved on, no longer veering, but making the slightly curved path its selectors found most suitable, while Danny read further, huddled over the story in the navigator's chair, feeling a new and greater kinship with the characters of the story. He was no longer a poor Earthbound charity case, but a man and an adventurer with them!

His nerves were tingling when the tale came to its end, and he let it drop onto the floor from tired fingers. Under his hand, a light had sprung up, but he was oblivious to it, until a crashing gong sounded over him, jerking him from the chair. There had been such a gong described in the story. . . .

And the meaning was the same. His eyes made out the red letters that glared accusingly from the control panel: RADIATION AT TEN O'CLOCK HORIZ—SHIP INDICATED!

Danny's fingers were on the master switch and cutting off all life except pseudogravity from the ship as the thought penetrated. The other ship was not hard to find from the observation window; the great streak of an invert-matter rocket glowed hotly out there, pointed apparently back to Earth—probably the *Callisto!*

For a second he was sure they had spotted him, but the flicker must have been only a minor correction to adjust for the trail continued. He had no knowledge of the new ships and whether they carried warning signals or not, but apparently they must have dispensed with such things. The streak vanished into the distance, and the letters on the panel that had marked it changing position went dead. Danny waited until the fullest amplification showed no response before throwing power on again. The small glow of the ion rocket would be invisible at the distance, surely.

Nothing further seemed to occur; there was a contented purr from the pilot and the faint sleepy hum of raw power from the rear, but no bells or sudden sounds. Slowly, his head fell forward over the navigator's table, and his heavy breathing mixed with the low sounds of the room. The ship went on about its business as it had been designed to do. Its course was charted, even to the old landing sweep, and it needed no further attention.

That was proved when the slow ringing of a bell woke Danny, while the board blinked in time to it: Destination! Destination! Destination Reached!

He shut off everything, rubbing the sleep from his eyes, and looked out. Above, there was weak but warm sunlight streaming down from a bluish sky that held a few small clouds suspended close to the ground. Beyond the ship, where it lay on a neglected sandy landing field, was the green of grass and the wild profusion of a forest. The horizon dropped off sharply, reminding him that it was only a tiny world, but otherwise it might have been Earth. He spotted an unkempt hangar ahead and applied weak power to the underjets, testing until they moved the ship slowly forward and inside, out of the view of any above.

Then he was at the lock, fumbling with the switch. As it opened, he could smell the clean fragrance of growing things, and there was the sound of birds nearby. A rabbit hopped leisurely out from underfoot as he stumbled eagerly out to the sunlight, and weeds and underbrush had already spread to cover the buildings about him. For a moment, he sighed; it had been too easy, this discovery of a heaven on the first wild try.

But the sight of the buildings drove back the doubt. Once, surrounded by a pretentious formal garden, this had been a great stone mansion, now falling into ruins. Beside it and farther from him, a smaller house had been built, seemingly from the wreckage. That was still whole, though ivy had grown over it and half covered the door that came open at the touch of his fingers.

There was still a faint glow to the heaters that drew power from the great atomic plant that gave this little world a perpetual semblance of Earthliness, but a coating of dust was everywhere. The furnishings, though, were in good condition. He scanned them, recognizing some as similar to the pieces in the museum, and the products of his race. One by one he studied them—his fortune, and now his home!

On the table, a book was dropped casually, and there was a sheet of paper propped against it, with what looked like a girl's rough handwriting on it. Curiosity carried him closer, until he could make it out, through the dust that clung even after he shook it.

> Dad:
>   Charley Summers found a wrecked ship of those things, and came for me. We'll be living high on 13. Come on over, if your jets will make it, and meet your son-in-law.

There was no date, nothing to indicate whether "Dad" had returned, or what had happened to them. But Danny dropped it reverently back on the table, looking out across the landing strip as if to see a worn old ship crawl in through the brief twilight that was falling over the tiny world. "Those things" could only be the new race, after the war; and that meant that here was the final outpost of his people. The note might be ten years or half a dozen centuries old—but his people had been here, fighting on and managing to live, after Earth had been lost to them. If they could, so could he!

And unlikely though it seemed, there might possibly be more of them out there somewhere. Perhaps the race was still surviving in spite of time and trouble and even *homo intelligens*.

Danny's eyes were moist as he stepped back from the door and the darkness outside to begin cleaning his new home. If any were there, he'd find them. And if not—

Well, he was still a member of a great and daring race that could never know defeat so long as a single man might live. He would never forget that.

Back on Earth, Bryant Kenning nodded slowly to the small group as he put the communicator back, and his eyes were a bit sad in spite of the smile that lighted his face. "The Director's scout is back, and he did choose 'The Dane's.' Poor kid. I'd begun to think we waited too long, and that he never would make it. Another six months—and he'd have died like a flower out of the sun! Yet I was sure it would work when Miss Larsen showed me that story, with its mythical planetoid-paradises. A rather clever story, if you like pseudohistory. I hope the one I prepared was its equal."

"For historical inaccuracy, fully its equal." But the amusement in old Professor Kirk's voice did not reach his lips.

"Well, he swallowed our lies and ran off with the ship we built him. I hope he's happy, for a while at least."

Miss Larsen folded her things together and prepared to leave. "Poor kid! He was sweet, in a pathetic sort of way. I wish that girl we were working on had turned out better; maybe this wouldn't have been necessary then. See me home, Jack?"

The two older men watched Larsen and Thorpe leave, and silence and tobacco smoke filled the room. Finally Kenning shrugged and turned to face the professor.

"By now he's found the note. I wonder if it was a good idea, after all? When I first came across it in that old story, I was thinking of Jack's preliminary report on Number 67, but now I don't know; she's an unknown quantity, at best. Anyhow, I meant it for kindness."

"Kindness! Kindness to repay with a few million credits and a few thousands of hours of work—plus a lie here and there—for all that we owe the boy's race!" The professor's voice was tired, as he dumped the contents of his pipe into a snuffer, and strode over slowly toward the great window that looked out on the night sky. "I wonder sometimes, Bryant, what kindness Neanderthaler found when the last one came to die. Or whether the race that will follow us when the darkness falls on us will have something better than such kindness."

The novelist shook his head doubtfully, and there was silence again as they looked out across the world and toward the stars.

DESERTION

Astounding,
November

by Clifford D. Simak

*The fourth of the City series ("Census" appeared
in Astounding in September), "Desertion" is the
best of a wonderful group, written in direct response to the news of what was happening in the
Nazi-run death camps in Europe.*

*This is one of the great stories about the diffi-
culty of making choices in all of literature, and
contains one of the great last lines in the history of
science fiction.*

*(Clearly, 1944 was Simak's big year. This is the
third time I've had to talk about him in this volume,
after his total absence in the first five of the series. I
suppose it's time to own up to a small sin of mine.
Since my association with him has been almost entirely by way of correspondence (I met him in person only three times in forty-two years of friendship
and then only for a few hours each time), I never
had occasion to use or hear his last name expressed
in sound. (Even when we did meet I called him
Cliff.) The result is that, for some reason, I assumed
the "i" in his last name was long and thought of him
always as SIGH-mak. Actually, the "i" is short and
it is SIM-ak. It may seem a small thing but I am always irritated when anyone mispronounces my
name and I should be equally careful of others'
names. Fortunately, Cliff is so sweet-tempered a fellow, I can't conceive of him being annoyed at me
for so venial a crim—I mean, crime.—I.A.)*

Four men, two by two, had gone into the howling maelstrom that was Jupiter and had not returned. They had walked into the keening gale—or rather, they had loped, bellies low against the ground, wet sides gleaming in the rain.

For they did not go in the shape of men.

Now the fifth man stood before the desk of Kent Fowler, head of Dome No. 3, Jovian Survey Commission.

Under Fowler's desk, old Towser scratched a flea, then settled down to sleep again.

Harold Allen, Fowler saw with a sudden pang, was young—too young. He had the easy confidence of youth, the straight back and straight eyes, the face of one who never had known fear. And that was strange. For men in the domes of Jupiter did know fear—fear and humility. It was hard for man to reconcile his puny self with the mighty forces of the monstrous planet.

"You understand," said Fowler, "that you need not do this. You understand that you need not go."

It was formula, of course. The other four had been told the same thing, but they had gone. This fifth one, Fowler knew, would go too. But suddenly he felt a dull hope stir within him that Allen wouldn't go.

"When do I start?" asked Allen.

There was a time when Fowler might have taken quiet pride in that answer, but not now. He frowned briefly.

"Within the hour," he said.

Allen stood waiting, quietly.

"Four other men have gone out and have not returned," said Fowler. "You know that, of course. We want you to return. We don't want you going off on any heroic rescue expedition. The main thing, the only thing, is that you come back, that you prove man can live in a Jovian form. Go to the first survey stake, no farther, then come back. Don't take any chances. Don't investigate anything. Just come back."

Allen nodded. "I understand all that."

"Miss Stanley will operate the converter," Fowler went on. "You need have no fear on that particular point. The other men were converted without mishap. They left the converter

in apparently perfect condition. You will be in thoroughly competent hands. Miss Stanley is the best qualified conversion operator in the Solar System. She has had experience on most of the other planets. That is why she's here."

Allen grinned at the woman and Fowler saw something flicker across Miss Stanley's face—something that might have been pity, or rage—or just plain fear. But it was gone again and she was smiling back at the youth who stood before the desk. Smiling in that prim, schoolteacherish way she had of smiling, almost as if she hated herself for doing it.

"I shall be looking forward," said Allen, "to my conversion."

And the way he said it, he made it all a joke, a vast, ironic joke.

But it was no joke.

It was serious business, deadly serious. Upon these tests, Fowler knew, depended the fate of men on Jupiter. If the tests succeeded, the resources of the giant planet would be thrown open. Man would take over Jupiter as he already had taken over the smaller planets. And if they failed—

If they failed, man would continue to be chained and hampered by the terrific pressure, the greater force of gravity, the weird chemistry of the planet. He would continue to be shut within the domes, unable to set actual foot upon the planet, unable to see it with direct, unaided vision, forced to rely upon the awkward tractors and the televisor, forced to work with clumsy tools and mechanisms or through the medium of robots that themselves were clumsy.

For man, unprotected and in his natural form, would be blotted out by Jupiter's terrific pressure of fifteen thousand pounds per square inch, pressure that made Terrestrial sea bottoms seem a vacuum by comparison.

Even the strongest metal Earthmen could devise couldn't exist under pressure such as that, under the pressure and the alkaline rains that forever swept the planet. It grew brittle and flaky, crumbling like clay, or it ran away in little streams and puddles of ammonia salts. Only by stepping up the toughness and strength of that metal, by increasing its electronic tension, could it be made to withstand the weight of thousands of miles of swirling, choking gases that made up the atmosphere. And even when that was done, everything

had to be coated with tough quartz to keep away the rain—
the bitter rain that was liquid ammonia.

Fowler sat listening to the engines in the sub-floor of the
dome. Engines that ran on endlessly, the dome never quiet of
them. They had to run and keep on running. For if they
stopped, the power flowing into the metal walls of the dome
would stop, the electronic tension would ease up and that
would be the end of everything.

Towser roused himself under Fowler's desk and scratched
another flea, his leg thumping hard against the floor.

"Is there anything else?" asked Allen.

Fowler shook his head. "Perhaps there's something you
want to do," he said. "Perhaps you—"

He had meant to say write a letter and he was glad he
caught himself quick enough so he didn't say it.

Allen looked at his watch. "I'll be there on time," he said.
He swung around and headed for the door.

Fowler knew Miss Stanley was watching him and he didn't
want to turn and meet her eyes. He fumbled with a sheaf of
papers on the desk before him.

"How long are you going to keep this up?" asked Miss
Stanley and she bit off each word with a vicious snap.

He swung around in his chair and faced her then. Her lips
were drawn into a straight, thin line, her hair seemed skinned
back from her forehead tighter than ever, giving her face that
queer, almost startling death-mask quality.

He tried to make his voice cool and level. "As long as
there's any need of it," he said. "As long as there's any
hope."

"You're going to keep on sentencing them to death," she
said. "You're going to keep marching them out face to face
with Jupiter. You're going to sit in here safe and comfortable
and send them out to die."

"There is no room for sentimentality, Miss Stanley," Fowler said, trying to keep the note of anger from his voice.
"You know as well as I do why we're doing this. You realize
that man in his own form simply cannot cope with Jupiter.
The only answer is to turn men into the sort of things that
can cope with it. We've done it on the other planets.

"If a few men die, but we finally succeed, the price is
small. Through the ages men have thrown away their lives on

foolish things, for foolish reasons. Why should we hesitate, then, at a little death in a thing as great as this?"

Miss Stanley sat stiff and straight, hands folded in her lap, the lights shining on her graying hair and Fowler, watching her, tried to imagine what she might feel, what she might be thinking. He wasn't exactly afraid of her, but he didn't feel quite comfortable when she was around. Those sharp blue eyes saw too much, her hands looked far too competent. She should be somebody's Aunt sitting in a rocking chair with her knitting needles. But she wasn't. She was the top-notch conversion unit operator in the Solar System and she didn't like the way he was doing things.

"There is something wrong, Mr. Fowler," she declared.

"Precisely," agreed Fowler. "That's why I'm sending young Allen out alone. He may find out what it is."

"And if he doesn't?"

"I'll send someone else."

She rose slowly from her chair, started toward the door, then stopped before his desk.

"Some day," she said, "you will be a great man. You never let a chance go by. This is your chance. You knew it was when this dome was picked for the tests. If you put it through, you'll go up a notch or two. No matter how many men may die, you'll go up a notch or two."

"Miss Stanley," he said and his voice was curt, "young Allen is going out soon. Please be sure that your machine—"

"My machine," she told him, icily, "is not to blame. It operates along the coordinates the biologists set up."

He sat hunched at his desk, listening to her footsteps go down the corridor.

What she said was true, of course. The biologists had set up the coordinates. But the biologists could be wrong. Just a hairbreadth of difference, one iota of digression and the converter would be sending out something that wasn't the thing they meant to send. A mutant that might crack up, go haywire, come unstuck under some condition or stress of circumstance wholly unsuspected.

For man didn't know much about what was going on outside. Only what his instruments told him was going on. And the samplings of those happenings furnished by those instruments and mechanisms had been no more than samplings, for Jupiter was unbelievably large and the domes were very few.

Even the work of the biologists in getting the data on the Lopers, apparently the highest form of Jovian life, had involved more than three years of intensive study and after that two years of checking to make sure. Work that could have been done on Earth in a week or two. But work that, in this case, couldn't be done on Earth at all, for one couldn't take a Jovian life form to Earth. The pressure here on Jupiter couldn't be duplicated outside of Jupiter and at Earth pressure and temperature the Lopers would simply have disappeared in a puff of gas.

Yet it was work that had to be done if man ever hoped to go about Jupiter in the life form of the Lopers. For before the converter could change a man to another life form, every detailed physical characteristic of that life form must be known—surely and positively, with no chance of mistake.

Allen did not come back.

The tractors, combing the nearby terrain, found no trace of him, unless the skulking thing reported by one of the drivers had been the missing Earthman in Loper form.

The biologists sneered their most accomplished academic sneers when Fowler suggested the coordinates might be wrong. Carefully they pointed out that the coordinates worked. When a man was put into the converter and the switch was thrown, the man became a Loper. He left the machine and moved away, out of sight, into the soupy atmosphere.

Some quirk, Fowler had suggested; some tiny deviation from the thing a Loper should be, some minor defect. If there were, the biologists said, it would take years to find it.

And Fowler knew that they were right.

So there were five men now instead of four and Harold Allen had walked out into Jupiter for nothing at all. It was as if he'd never gone so far as knowledge was concerned.

Fowler reached across his desk and picked up the personal file, a thin sheaf of papers neatly clipped together. It was a thing he dreaded but a thing he had to do. Somehow the reason for these strange disappearances must be found. And there was no other way than to send out more men.

He sat for a moment listening to the howling of the wind above the dome, the everlasting thundering gale that swept across the planet in boiling, twisting wrath.

Was there some threat out there, he asked himself? Some
danger they did not know about? Something that lay in wait
and gobbled up the Lopers, making no distinction between
Lopers that were *bona fide* and Lopers that were men? To
the gobblers, of course, it would make no difference.

Or had there been a basic fault in selecting the Lopers as
the type of life best fitted for existence on the surface of the
planet? The evident intelligence of the Lopers, he knew, had
been one factor in that determination. For if the thing man
became did not have capacity for intelligence, man could not
for long retain his own intelligence in such a guise.

Had the biologists let that one factor weigh too heavily,
using it to offset some other factor that might be unsatisfactory, even disastrous? It didn't seem likely. Stiffnecked as they
might be, the biologists knew their business.

Or was the whole thing impossible, doomed from the very
start? Conversion to other life forms had worked on other
planets, but that did not necessarily mean it would work on
Jupiter. Perhaps man's intelligence could not function correctly through the sensory apparatus provided Jovian life.
Perhaps the Lopers were so alien there was no common
ground for human knowledge and the Jovian conception of
existence to meet and work together.

Or the fault might lie with man, be inherent with the race.
Some mental aberration which, coupled with what they found
outside, wouldn't let them come back. Although it might not
be an aberration, not in the human sense. Perhaps just one
ordinary human mental trait, accepted as commonplace on
Earth, would be so violently at odds with Jovian existence
that it would blast all human intelligence and sanity.

Claws rattled and clicked down the corridor. Listening to
them, Fowler smiled wanly. It was Towser coming back from
the kitchen, where he had gone to see his friend, the cook.

Towser came into the room, carrying a bone. He wagged
his tail at Fowler and flopped down beside the desk, bone between his paws. For a long moment his rheumy old eyes regarded his master and Fowler reached down a hand to ruffle
a ragged ear.

"You still like me, Towser?" Fowler asked and Towser
thumped his tail.

"You're the only one," said Fowler. "All through the dome they're cussing me. Calling me a murderer, more than likely."

He straightened and swung back to the desk. His hand reached out and picked up the file.

Bennett? Bennett had a girl waiting for him back on Earth.

Andrews? Andrews was planning on going back to Mars Tech just as soon as he earned enough to see him through a year.

Olson? Olson was nearing pension age. All the time telling the boys how he was going to settle down and grow roses.

Carefully, Fowler laid the file back on the desk.

Sentencing men to death. Miss Stanley had said that, her pale lips scarcely moving in her parchment face. Marching men out to die while he, Fowler, sat here safe and comfortable.

They were saying it all through the dome, no doubt, especially since Allen had failed to return. They wouldn't say it to his face, of course. Even the man or men he called before this desk and told they were the next to go, wouldn't say it to him.

They would only say: "When do we start?" For that was formula.

But he would see it in their eyes.

He picked up the file again. Bennett, Andrews, Olson. There were others, but there was no use in going on.

Kent Fowler knew that he couldn't do it, couldn't face them, couldn't send more men out to die.

He leaned forward and flipped up the toggle on the intercommunicator.

"Yes, Mr. Fowler."

"Miss Stanley, please."

He waited for Miss Stanley, listening to Towser chewing half-heartedly on the bone. Towser's teeth were getting bad.

"Miss Stanley," said Miss Stanley's voice.

"Just wanted to tell you, Miss Stanley, to get ready for two more."

"Aren't you afraid," asked Miss Stanley, "that you'll run out of them? Sending out one at a time, they'd last longer, give you twice the satisfaction."

"One of them," said Fowler, "will be a dog."

"A dog!"

"Yes, Towser."

He heard the quick, cold rage that iced her voice. "Your own dog! He's been with you all these years—"

"That's the point," said Fowler. "Towser would be unhappy if I left him behind."

It was not the Jupiter he had known through the televisor. He had expected it to be different, but not like this. He had expected a hell of ammonia rain and stinking fumes and the deafening, thundering tumult of the storm. He had expected swirling clouds and fog and the snarling flicker of monstrous thunderbolts.

He had not expected the lashing downpour would be reduced to drifting purple mist that moved like fleeing shadows over a red and purple sward. He had not even guessed the snaking bolts of lightning would be flares of pure ecstasy across a painted sky.

Waiting for Towser, Fowler flexed the muscles of his body, amazed at the smooth, sleek strength he found. Not a bad body, he decided, and grimaced at remembering how he had pitied the Lopers when he glimpsed them through the television screen.

For it had been hard to imagine a living organism based upon ammonia and hydrogen rather than upon water and oxygen, hard to believe that such a form of life could know the same quick thrill of life that humankind could know. Hard to conceive of life out in the soupy maelstrom that was Jupiter, not knowing, of course, that through Jovian eyes it was no soupy maelstrom at all.

The wind brushed against him with what seemed gentle fingers and he remembered with a start that by Earth standards the wind was a roaring gale, a two-hundred-mile an hour howler laden with deadly gases.

Pleasant scents seeped into his body. And yet scarcely scents, for it was not the sense of smell as he remembered it. It was as if his whole being were soaking up the sensation of lavender—and yet not lavender. It was something, he knew, for which he had no word, undoubtedly the first of many enigmas in terminology. For the words he knew, the thought symbols that served him as an Earthman would not serve him as a Jovian.

The lock in the side of the dome opened and Towser came tumbling out—at least he thought it must be Towser.

He started to call to the dog, his mind shaping the words he meant to say. But he couldn't say them. There was no way to say them. He had nothing to say them with.

For a moment his mind swirled in muddy terror, a blind fear that eddied in little puffs of panic through his brain.

How did Jovians talk? How—

Suddenly he was aware of Towser, intensely aware of the bumbling, eager friendliness of the shaggy animal that had followed him from Earth to many planets. As if the thing that was Towser had reached out and for a moment sat within his brain.

And out of the bubbling welcome that he sensed, came words.

"Hiya, pal."

Not words really, better than words. Thought symbols in his brain, communicated thought symbols that had shades of meaning words could never have.

"Hiya, Towser," he said.

"I feel good," said Towser. "Like I was a pup. Lately I've been feeling pretty punk. Legs stiffening up on me and teeth wearing down to almost nothing. Hard to mumble a bone with teeth like that. Besides, the fleas give me hell. Used to be I never paid much attention to them. A couple of fleas more or less never meant much in my early days."

"But . . . but—" Fowler's thoughts tumbled awkwardly. "You're talking to me!"

"Sure thing," said Towser. "I always talked to you, but you couldn't hear me. I tried to say things to you, but I couldn't make the grade."

"I understood you sometimes," Fowler said.

"Not very well," said Towser. "You knew when I wanted food and when I wanted a drink and when I wanted out, but that's about all you ever managed."

"I'm sorry," Fowler said.

"Forget it," Towser told him. "I'll race you to the cliff."

For the first time, Fowler saw the cliff, apparently many miles away, but with a strange crystalline beauty that sparkled in the shadow of the many-colored clouds.

Fowler hesitated. "It's a long way—"

"Ah, come on," said Towser and even as he said it he started for the cliff.

Fowler followed, testing his legs, testing the strength in that new body of his, a bit doubtful at first, amazed a moment later, then running with a sheer joyousness that was one with the red and purple sward, with the drifting smoke of the rain across the land.

As he ran the consciousness of music came to him, a music that beat into his body, that surged throughout his being, that lifted him on wings of silver speed. Music like bells might make from some steeple on a sunny, springtime hill.

As the cliff drew nearer the music deepened and filled the universe with a spray of magic sound. And he knew the music came from the tumbling waterfall that feathered down the face of the shining cliff.

Only, he knew, it was no waterfall, but an ammonia-fall and the cliff was white because it was oxygen, solidified.

He skidded to a stop beside Towser where the waterfall broke into a glittering rainbow of many hundred colors. Literally many hundred, for here, he saw, was no shading of one primary to another as human beings saw, but a clear-cut selectivity that broke the prism down to its last ultimate classification.

"The music," said Towser.

"Yes, what about it?"

"The music," said Towser, "is vibrations. Vibrations of water falling."

"But, Towser, you don't know about vibrations."

"Yes, I do," contended Towser. "It just popped into my head."

Fowler gulped mentally. "Just popped!"

And suddenly, within his own head, he held a formula—the formula for a process that would make metal to withstand the pressure of Jupiter.

He stared, astounded, at the waterfall and swiftly his mind took the many colors and placed them in their exact sequence in the spectrum. Just like that. Just out of blue sky. Out of nothing, for he knew nothing either of metals or of colors.

"Towser," he cried. "Towser, something's happening to us!"

"Yeah, I know," said Towser.

"It's our brains," said Fowler. "We're using them, all of them, down to the last hidden corner. Using them to figure out things we should have known all the time. Maybe the brains of Earth things naturally are slow and foggy. Maybe we are the morons of the universe. Maybe we are fixed so we have to do things the hard way."

And, in the new sharp clarity of thought that seemed to grip him, he knew that it would not only be the matter of colors in a waterfall or metals that would resist the pressure of Jupiter, he sensed other things, things not yet quite clear. A vague whispering that hinted of greater things, of mysteries beyond the pale of human thought, beyond even the pale of human imagination. Mysteries, fact, logic built on reasoning. Things that any brain should know if it used all its reasoning power.

"We're still mostly Earth," he said. "We're just beginning to learn a few of the things we are to know—a few of the things that were kept from us as human beings, perhaps because we were human beings. Because our human bodies were poor bodies. Poorly equipped for thinking, poorly equipped in certain senses that one has to have to know. Perhaps even lacking in certain senses that are necessary to true knowledge."

He stared back at the dome, a tiny black thing dwarfed by the distance.

Back there were men who couldn't see the beauty that was Jupiter. Men who thought that swirling clouds and lashing rain obscured the face of the planet. Unseeing human eyes. Poor eyes. Eyes that could not see the beauty in the clouds, that could not see through the storms. Bodies that could not feel the thrill of trilling music stemming from the rush of broken water.

Men who walked alone, in terrible loneliness, talking with their tongue like Boy Scouts wigwagging out their messages, unable to reach out and touch one another's mind as he could reach out and touch Towser's mind. Shut off forever from that personal, intimate contact with other living things.

He, Fowler, had expected terror inspired by alien things out here on the surface, had expected to cower before the threat of unknown things, had steeled himself against disgust of a situation that was not of Earth.

But instead he had found something greater than man had ever known. A swifter, surer body. A sense of exhilaration, a deeper sense of life. A sharper mind. A world of beauty that even the dreamers of the Earth had not yet imagined.

"Let's get going," Towser urged.

"Where do you want to go?"

"Anywhere," said Towser. "Just start going and see where we end up. I have a feeling . . . well, a feeling—"

"Yes, I know," said Fowler.

For he had the feeling, too. The feeling of high destiny. A certain sense of greatness. A knowledge that somewhere off beyond the horizons lay adventure and things greater than adventure.

Those other five had felt it, too. Had felt the urge to go and see, the compelling sense that here lay a life of fullness and of knowledge.

That, he knew, was why they had not returned.

"I won't go back," said Towser.

"We can't let them down," said Fowler.

Fowler took a step or two, back toward the dome, then stopped.

Back to the dome. Back to that aching, poison-laden body that he left. It hadn't seemed aching before, but now he knew it was.

Back to the fuzzy brain. Back to muddled thinking. Back to the flapping mouths that formed signals others understood. Back to eyes that now would be worse than no sight at all. Back to squalor, back to crawling, back to ignorance.

"Perhaps some day," he said, muttering to himself.

"We got a lot to do and a lot to see," said Towser. "We got a lot to learn. We'll find things—"

Yes, they could find things. Civilizations, perhaps. Civilizations that would make the civilization of man seem puny by comparison. Beauty and more important—an understanding of that beauty. And a comradeship no one had ever known before—that no man, no dog had ever known before.

And life. The quickness of life after what seemed a drugged existence.

"I can't go back," said Towser.

"Nor I," said Fowler.

"They would turn me back into a dog," said Towser.

"And me," said Fowler, "back into a man."

WHEN THE BOUGH BREAKS

Astounding,
November

by "Lewis Padgett" (Henry Kuttner, 1914-1958, and C. L. Moore) (1911-   )

Henry Kuttner and C. L. Moore continued the brilliant streak of productivity and quality they had started earlier in the 1940's in 1944, with stories like "Housing Problem" (Charm, October), "Trophy" (Thrilling Wonder Stories, Winter), and "The Children's Hour" (Astounding, March), But their great collaborative effort of the year was "When the Bough Breaks," a powerful story somewhat similar to their "Mimsy Were the Borogoves" of the previous year. It is frequently argued that great fiction captures the tragic nature of life—if so, this story has greatness written all over it.

(I am frequently asked whether a scientific education is an essential for writing science fiction. One might think it was but clearly it isn't since excellent science fiction is written by writers who lack such an education. As examples I have cited Fredric Brown among the earlier generation and Harlan Ellison (whose stories, will start appearing in due course as we proceed with these volumes) in the newer generation. It occurs to me that Henry Kuttner and C. L. Moore are additional examples. Mind you, this doesn't mean they are scientifically ignorant; that would indeed disqualify them. It does mean, however, that what science they needed, they picked up for themselves and that they knew very well how to keep their needs to a minimum and yet do marvelously well.—I.A.)

They were surprised at getting the apartment, what with high rents and written-in clauses in the lease, and Joe Calderon felt himself lucky to be only ten minutes' subway ride from the University. His wife, Myra, fluffed up her red hair in a distracted fashion and said that landlords presumably expected parthenogenesis in their tenants, if that was what she meant. Anyhow, it was where an organism split in two and the result was two mature specimens. Calderon grinned, said, "Binary fission, chump," and watched young Alexander, aged eighteen months, backing up on all fours across the carpet, preparatory to assuming a standing position on his fat bow-legs.

It was a pleasant apartment, at that. The sun came into it at times, and there were more rooms than they had any right to expect, for the price. The next-door neighbor, a billowy blonde who talked of little except her migraine, said that it was hard to keep tenants in 4-D. It wasn't exactly haunted, but it had the queerest visitors. The last lessee, an insurance man who drank heavily, moved out one day talking about little men who came ringing the bell at all hours asking for a Mr. Pott, or somebody like that. Not until some time later did Joe identify Pott with Cauldron—or Calderon.

They were sitting on the couch in a pleased manner, looking at Alexander. He was quite a baby. Like all infants, he had a collar of fat at the back of his neck, and his legs, Calderon said, were like two vast and trunkless limbs of stone—at least they gave that effect. The eyes stopped at their incredible bulging pinkness, fascinated. Alexander laughed like a fool, rose to his feet, and staggered drunkenly toward his parents, muttering unintelligible gibberish. "Madman," Myra said fondly, and tossed the child a floppy velvet pig of whom he was enamored.

"So we're all set for the winter," Calderon said. He was a tall, thin, harassed-looking man, a fine research physicist, and very much interested in his work at the University. Myra was a rather fragile red head, with a tilted nose and sardonic red-brown eyes. She made deprecatory noises.

"If we can get a maid. Otherwise I'll char."

"You sound like a lost soul," Calderon said. "What do you mean, you'll char?"

"Like a charwoman. Sweep, cook, clean. Babies are a great trial. Still, they're worth it."

"Not in front of Alexander. He'll get above himself."

The doorbell rang. Calderon uncoiled himself, wandered vaguely across the room, and opened the door. He blinked at nothing. Then he lowered his gaze somewhat, and what he saw was sufficient to make him stare a little.

Four tiny men were standing in the hall. That is, they were tiny below the brows. Their craniums were immense, watermelon large and watermelon shaped, or else they were wearing abnormally huge helmets of glistening metal. Their faces were wizened, peaked tiny masks that were nests of lines and wrinkles. Their clothes were garish, unpleasantly colored, and seemed to be made of paper.

"Oh?" Calderon said blankly.

Swift looks were exchanged among the four. One of them said, "Are you Joseph Calderon?"

"Yeah."

"We," said the most wrinkled of the quartet, "are your son's descendants. He's a super child. We're here to educate him."

"Yes," Calderon said. "Yes, of course. I . . . *listen!*"

"To what?"

"Super—"

"There he is," another dwarf cried. "It's Alexander! We've hit the right time at last!" He scuttled past Calderon's legs and into the room. Calderon made a few futile snatches, but the small men easily evaded him. When he turned, they were gathered around Alexander. Myra had drawn up her legs under her and was watching with an amazed expression.

"Look at that," a dwarf said. "See his potential tefeetzie?" It sounded like tefeetzie.

"But his skull, Bordent," another put in. "That's the important part. The vyrings are almost perfectly coblastably."

"Beautiful," Bordent acknowledged. He leaned forward. Alexander reached forward into the nest of wrinkles, seized Bordent's nose, and twisted painfully. Bordent bore it stoically until the grip relaxed.

"Undeveloped," he said tolerantly. "We'll develop him."

Myra sprang from the couch, picked up her child, and

stood at bay, facing the little men. "Joe," she said, "are you going to stand for this? Who are these bad-mannered goblins?"

"Lord knows," Calderon said. He moistened his lips. "What kind of a gag is that? Who sent you?"

"Alexander," Bordent said. "From the year . . . ah . . . about 2450, reckoning roughly. He's practically immortal. Only violence can kill one of the Supers, and there's none of that in 2450."

Calderon sighed. "No, I mean it. A gag's a gag. But—"

"Time and again we've tried. In 1940, 1944, 1947—all around this era. We were either too early or too late. But now we've hit on the right time sector. It's our job to educate Alexander. You should feel proud of being his parents. We worship you, you know. Father and mother of the new race."

"Tuh!" Calderon said. "Come off it!"

"They need proof, Dobish," someone said. "Remember, this is their first inkling that Alexander is homo superior."

"Homo nuts," Myra said. "Alexander's a perfectly normal baby."

"He's perfectly supernormal," Dobish said. "We're his descendants."

"That makes you a superman," Calderon said skeptically, eyeing the small man.

"Not in toto. There aren't many of the X Free type. The biological norm is specialization. Only a few are straight-line super. Some specialize in logic, others in vervainity, others—like us—are guides. If we were X Free supers, you couldn't stand there and talk to us. Or look at us. We're only parts. Those like Alexander are the glorious whole."

"Oh, send them away," Myra said, getting tired of it. "I feel like a Thurber woman."

Calderon nodded. "O.K. Blow, gentlemen. Take a powder, I mean it."

"Yes," Dobish said, "they need proof. What'll we do? Skyskinate?"

"Too twisty," Bordent objected. "Object lesson, eh? The stiller."

"Stiller?" Myra asked.

Bordent took an object from his paper clothes and spun it in his hands. His fingers were all double-jointed. Calderon felt a tiny electric shock go through him.

"Joe," Myra said, white-faced. "I can't move."

"Neither can I. Take it easy. This is . . . it's—" He slowed and stopped.

"Sit down," Bordent said, still twirling the object. Calderon and Myra backed up to the couch and sat down. Their tongues froze with the rest of them.

Dobish came over, clambered up, and pried Alexander out of his mother's grip. Horror moved in her eyes.

"We won't hurt him," Dobish said. "We just want to give him his first lesson. Have you got the basics, Finn?"

"In the bag." Finn extracted a foot-long bag from his garments. Things came out of that bag. They came out incredibly. Soon the carpet was littered with stuff—problematical in design, nature, and use. Calderon recognized a tesseract.

The fourth dwarf, whose name, it turned out, was Quat, smiled consolingly at the distressed parents. "You watch. You can't learn; you've not got the potential. You're homo saps. But Alexander, now—"

Alexander was in one of his moods. He was diabolically gay. With the devil-possession of all babies, he refused to collaborate. He crept rapidly backwards. He burst into loud, squalling sobs. He regarded his feet with amazed joy. He stuffed his fist into his mouth and cried bitterly at the result. He talked about invisible things in a soft, cryptic monotone. He punched Dobish in the eye.

The little men had inexhaustible patience. Two hours later they were through. Calderon couldn't see that Alexander had learned much.

Bordent twirled the object again. He nodded affably, and led the retreat. The four little men went out of the apartment, and a moment later Calderon and Myra could move.

She jumped up, staggering on numbed legs, seized Alexander, and collapsed on the couch. Calderon rushed to the door and flung it open. The hall was empty.

"Joe—" Myra said, her voice small and afraid. Calderon came back and smoothed her hair. He looked down at the bright fuzzy head of Alexander.

"Joe. We've got to do—do something."

"I don't know," he said. "If it happened—"

"It happened. They took those things with them. Alexander. Oh!"

"They didn't try to hurt him," Calderon said hesitatingly.

"Our *baby*! He's no superchild."

"Well," Calderon said, "I'll get out my revolver. What else can I do?"

"I'll do something," Myra promised. "Nasty little goblins! I'll do something, just wait."

And yet there wasn't a great deal they could do.

Tacitly they ignored the subject the next day. But at 4 P.M., the same time as the original visitation, they were with Alexander in a theater, watching the latest technicolor film. The four little men could scarcely find them here—

Calderon felt Myra stiffen, and even as he turned, he suspected the worst. Myra sprang up, her breath catching. Her fingers tightened on his arm.

"He's gone!"

"G-gone?"

"He just vanished. I was holding him . . . let's get out of here."

"Maybe you dropped him," Calderon said inanely, and lit a match. There were cries from behind. Myra was already pushing her way toward the aisle. There were no babies under the seat, and Calderon caught up with his wife in the lobby.

"He disappeared," Myra was babbling. "Like that. Maybe he's in the future, Joe, what'll we do?"

Calderon, through some miracle, got a taxi. "We'll go home. That's the most likely place. I hope."

"Yes. Of course it is. Give me a cigarette."

"He'll be in the apartment—"

He was, squatting on his haunches, taking a decided interest in the gadget Quat was demonstrating. The gadget was a gayly-colored egg beater with four-dimensional attachments, and it talked in a thin, high voice. Not in English.

Bordent flipped out the stiller and began to twirl it as the couple came in. Calderon got hold of Myra's arms and held her back. "Hold on," he said urgently. "That isn't necessary. We won't try anything."

"Joe!" Myra tried to wriggle free. "Are you going to let them—"

"Quiet!" he said. "Bordent, put that thing down. We want to talk to you."

"Well—if you promise not to interrupt—"

"We promise." Calderon forcibly led Myra to the couch and held her there. "Look, darling. Alexander's all right. They're not hurting him."

"Hurt him, indeed!" Finn said. "He'd skin us alive in the future if we hurt him in the past."

"Be quiet," Bordent commanded. He seemed to be the leader of the four. "I'm glad you're cooperating, Joseph Calderon. It goes against my grain to use force on a demigod. After all, you're *Alexander's* father."

Alexander put out a fat paw and tried to touch the whirling rainbow egg beater. He seemed to be fascinated. Quat said, "The kivelish is sparkling. Shall I vastinate?"

"Not too fast," Bordent said. "He'll be rational in a week, and then we can speed up the process. Now, Calderon, please relax. Anything you want?"

"A drink."

"They mean alcohol," Finn said. "The Rubaiyat mentions it, remember?"

"Rubaiyat?"

"The singing red gem in Twelve Library."

"Oh, yes," Bordent said. "That one. I was thinking of the Yahveh slab, the one with the thunder effects. Do you want to make some alcohol, Finn?"

Calderon swallowed. "Don't bother. I have some in that sideboard. May I—"

"You're not *prisoners*." Bordent's voice was shocked. "It's just that we've got to make you listen to a few explanations, and after that—well, it'll be different."

Myra shook her head when Calderon handed her a drink, but he scowled at her meaningly. "You won't feel it. Go ahead."

She hadn't once taken her gaze from Alexander. The baby was imitating the thin noise of the egg beater now. It was subtly unpleasant.

"The ray is working," Quat said. "The viewer shows some slight cortical resistance, though."

"Angle the power," Bordent told him.

Alexander said, "Modjewabba?"

"What's that?" Myra asked in a strained voice. "Super language?"

Bordent smiled at her. "No, just baby talk."

Alexander burst into sobs. Myra said, "Super baby or not,

when he cries like that, there's a good reason. Does your
tutoring extend to that point?"

"Certainly," Quat said calmly. He and Finn carried
Alexander out. Bordent smiled again.

"You're beginning to believe," he said. "That helps."

Calderon drank, feeling the hot fumes of whisky along the
backs of his cheeks. His stomach was crawling with cold
uneasiness.

"If you were human—" he said doubtfully.

"If we were, we wouldn't be here. The old order changeth.
It had to start sometime. Alexander is the first homo superior."

"But why us?" Myra asked.

"Genetics. You've both worked with radioactivity and certain short-wave radiations that effected the germ plasm. The
mutation just happened. It'll happen again from now on. But
you happen to be the first. You'll die, but Alexander will live
on. Perhaps a thousand years."

Calderon said, "This business of coming from the future
... you say Alexander sent you?"

"The adult Alexander. The mature superman. It's a different culture, of course—beyond your comprehension. Alexander is one of the X Frees. He said to me, through the
interpreting-machine, of course, 'Bordent, I wasn't recognized
as a super till I was thirty years old. I had only ordinary
homo sap development till then. I didn't know my potential
myself. And that's bad.' It *is* bad, you know." Bordent
digressed. "The full capabilities of an organism can't emerge
unless it's given the fullest chance of expansion from birth
on. Or at least from infancy. Alexander said to me, 'It's
about five hundred years ago that I was born. Take a few
guides and go into the past. Locate me as an infant. Give me
specialized training, from the beginning. I think it'll expand
me.'"

"The past," Calderon said. "You mean it's plastic?"

"Well, it affects the future. You can't alter the past without
altering the future, too. But things tend to drift back. There's
a temporal norm, a general level. In the original time sector,
Alexander wasn't visited by us. Now that's changed. So the
future will be changed. But not tremendously. No crucial
temporal apexes are involved, no keystones. The only result

will be that the mature Alexander will have his potential more fully realized."

Alexander was carried back into the room, beaming. Quat resumed his lesson with the egg beater.

"There isn't a great deal you can do about it," Bordent said. "I think you realize that now."

Myra said, "Is Alexander going to look like you?" Her face was strained.

"Oh, no. He's a perfect physical specimen. I've never seen him, of course, but—"

Calderon said, "Heir to all the ages. Myra, are you beginning to get the idea?"

"Yes. A superman. But he's our baby."

"He'll remain so," Bordent put in anxiously. "We don't want to remove him from the beneficial home and parental influence. An infant needs that. In fact, tolerance for the young is an evolutionary trait aimed at providing for the superman's appearance, just as the vanishing appendix is such a preparation. At certain eras of history mankind is receptive to the preparation of the new race. It's never been quite successful before—there were anthropological miscarriages, so to speak. My squeevers, it's *important!* Infants are awfully irritating. They're helpless for a very long time, a great trial to the patience of the parents—the lower the order of the animal, the faster the infant develops. With mankind, it takes years for the young to reach an independent state. So the parental tolerance increases in proportion. The superchild won't mature, actually, till he's about twenty."

Myra said, "Alexander will still be a baby then?"

"He'll have the physical standards of an eight-year-old specimen of homo sap. Mentally . . . well, call it irrationality. He won't be leveled out to an intellectual or emotional norm. He won't be sane, any more than any baby is. Selectivity takes quite a while to develop. But his peaks will be far, far above the peaks of, say, *you* as a child."

"Thanks," Calderon said.

"His horizons will be broader. His mind is capable of grasping and assimilating far more than yours. The world is really his oyster. He won't be limited. But it'll take a while for his mind, his personality, to shake down."

"I want another drink," Myra said.

Calderon got it. Alexander inserted his thumb in Quat's eye and tried to gouge it out. Quat submitted passively.

"Alexander!" Myra said.

"Sit still," Bordent said. "Quat's tolerance in this regard is naturally more highly developed than yours."

"If he puts Quat's eye out," Calderon said, "it'll be just too bad."

"Quat isn't important, compared to Alexander. He knows it, too."

Luckily for Quat's binocular vision, Alexander suddenly tired of his new toy and fell to staring at the egg beater again. Dobish and Finn leaned over the baby and looked at him. But there was more to it than that, Calderon felt.

"Induced telepathy," Bordent said. "It takes a long time to develop, but we're starting now. I tell you, it was a relief to hit the right time at last. I've rung this doorbell at least a hundred times. But never till now——"

"Move," Alexander said clearly. "Real. Move."

Bordent nodded. "Enough for today. We'll be here again tomorrow. You'll be ready?"

"As ready," Myra said, "as we'll ever be, I suppose." She finished her drink.

They got fairly high that night and talked it over. Their arguments were biased by their realization of the four little men's obvious resources. Neither doubted any more. They knew that Bordent and his companions had come from five hundred years in the future, at the command of a future Alexander who had matured into a fine specimen of superman.

"Amazing, isn't it?" Myra said. "That fat little blob in the bedroom turning into a twelfth-power Quiz Kid."

"Well, it's got to start somewhere. As Bordent pointed out."

"And as long as he isn't going to look like those goblins—ugh!"

"He'll be super. Deucalion and what's-her-name—that's us. Parents of a new race."

"I feel funny," Myra said. "As though I'd given birth to a moose."

"That could never happen," Calderon said consolingly. "Have another slug."

"It might as well have happened. Alexander is a swoose."

"Swoose?"

"I can use that goblin's doubletalk, too. Vopishly woggle in the grand foyer. So there."

"It's a language to them," Calderon said.

"Alexander's going to talk English. I've got my rights."

"Well, Bordent doesn't seem anxious to infringe on them. He said Alexander needed a home environment."

"That's the only reason I haven't gone crazy," Myra said. "As long as he . . . they . . . don't take our baby away from us—"

A week later it was thoroughly clear that Bordent had no intention of encroaching on parental rights—at least, any more than was necessary, for two hours a day. During that period the four little men fulfilled their orders by cramming Alexander with all the knowledge his infantile but super brain could hold. They did not depend on blocks or nursery rhymes or the abacus. Their weapons in the battle were cryptic, futuristic, but effective. And they taught Alexander, there was no doubt of that. As B-$_1$ poured on a plant's roots forces growth, so the vitamin teaching of the dwarfs soaked into Alexander, and his potentially superhuman brain responded, expanding with brilliant, erratic speed.

He had talked intelligibly on the fourth day. On the seventh day he was easily able to hold conversations, though his baby muscles, lingually undeveloped, tired easily. His cheeks were still sucking-disks; he was not yet fully human, except in sporadic flashes. Yet those flashes came oftener now, and closer together.

The carpet was a mess. The little men no longer took their equipment back with them; they left it for Alexander to use. The infant crept—he no longer bothered to walk much, for he could crawl with more efficiency—among the Objects, selected some of them, and put them together. Myra had gone out to shop. The little men wouldn't show up for half an hour. Calderon, tired from his day's work at the University, fingered a highball and looked at his offspring.

"Alexander," he said.

Alexander didn't answer. He fitted a gadget to a Thing, inserted it peculiarly in a Something Else, and sat back with an air of satisfaction. Then—"Yes?" he said. It wasn't perfect pronunciation, but it was unmistakable. Alexander talked somewhat like a toothless old man.

"What are you doing?" Calderon said.

"No."

"What's that?"

"No."

"No?"

"I understand it," Alexander said. "That's enough."

"I see." Calderon regarded the prodigy with faint apprehension. "You don't want to tell me."

"No."

"Well, all right."

"Get me a drink," Alexander said. For a moment Calderon had a mad idea that the infant was demanding a highball. Then he sighed, rose, and returned with a bottle.

"Milk," Alexander said, refusing the potation.

"You said a drink. Water's a drink, isn't it?" My God, Calderon thought, I'm arguing with the kid. I'm treating him like . . . like an adult. But he isn't. He's a fat little baby squatting on his behind on the carpet, playing with a tinkertoy.

The tinkertoy said something in a thin voice. Alexander murmured, "Repeat." The tinkertoy did.

Calderon said, "What was that?"

"No."

"Nuts." Calderon went out to the kitchen and got milk. He poured himself another shot. This was like having relatives drop in suddenly—relatives you hadn't seen for ten years. How the devil did you *act* with a superchild?

He stayed in the kitchen, after supplying Alexander with his milk. Presently Myra's key turned in the outer door. Her cry brought Calderon hurrying.

Alexander was vomiting, with the air of a research man absorbed in a fascinating phenomenon.

"Alexander!" Myra cried. "Darling, are you sick?"

"No," Alexander said. "I'm testing my regurgitative process. I must learn to control my digestive organs."

Calderon leaned against the door, grinning crookedly. "Yeah. You'd better start now, too."

"I'm finished," Alexander said. "Clean it up."

Three days later the infant decided that his lungs needed developing. He cried. He cried at all hours, with interesting variations—whoops, squalls, wails, and high-pitched bellows. Nor would he stop till he was satisfied. The neighbors complained. Myra said, "Darling, is there a pin sticking you? Let me look—"

"Go away," Alexander said. "You're too warm. Open the window. I want fresh air."

"Yes, d-darling. Of course." She came back to bed and Calderon put his arm around her. He knew there would be shadows under her eyes in the morning. In his crib Alexander cried on.

So it went. The four little men came daily and gave Alexander his lessons. They were pleased with the infant's progress. They did not complain when Alexander indulged in his idiosyncrasies, such as batting them heavily on the nose or ripping their paper garments to shreds. Bordent tapped his metal helmet and smiled triumphantly at Calderon.

"He's coming along. He's developing."

"I'm wondering. What about discipline?"

Alexander looked up from his rapport with Quat. "Homo sap discipline doesn't apply to me, Joseph Calderon."

"Don't call me Joseph Calderon. I'm your father, after all."

"A primitive biological necessity. You are not sufficiently well developed to provide the discipline I require. Your purpose is to give me parental care."

"Which makes me an incubator," Calderon said.

"But a deified one," Bordent soothed him. "Practically a logos. The father of the new race."

"I feel more like Prometheus," the father of the new race said dourly. "He was helpful, too. And he ended up with a vulture eating his liver."

"You will learn a great deal from Alexander."

"He says I'm incapable of understanding it."

"Well, aren't you?"

"Sure. I'm just the papa bird," Calderon said, and subsided into a sad silence, watching Alexander, under Quat's tutelary eye, put together a gadget of shimmering glass and twisted metal. Bordent said suddenly, "Quat! Be careful of the egg!" And Finn seized a bluish ovoid just before Alexander's chubby hand could grasp it.

"It isn't dangerous," Quat said. "It isn't connected."

"He might have connected it."

"I want that," Alexander said. "Give it to me."

"Not yet, Alexander," Bordent refused. "You must learn the correct way of connecting it first. Otherwise it might harm you."

"I could do it."

"You are not logical enough to balance your capabilities and lacks as yet. Later it will be safe. I think now, perhaps, a little philosophy, Dobish—eh?"

Dobish squatted and went en rapport with Alexander. Myra came out of the kitchen, took a quick look at the tableau, and retreated. Calderon followed her out.

"I will never get used to it if I live a thousand years," she said with slow emphasis, hacking at the doughy rim of a pie. "He's my baby only when he's asleep."

"We won't live a thousand years," Calderon told her. "Alexander will, though. I wish we could get a maid."

"I tried again today," Myra said wearily. "No use. They're all in war plants. I mention a baby—"

"You can't do all this alone."

"You help," she said, "when you can. But you're working hard too, fella. It won't be forever."

"I wonder if we had another baby . . . if—"

Her sober gaze met his. "I've wondered that, too. But I should think mutations aren't as cheap as that. Once in a lifetime. Still, we don't know."

"Well, it doesn't matter now, anyway. One infant's enough for the moment."

Myra glanced toward the door. "Everything all right in there? Take a look. I worry."

"It's all right."

"I know, but the blue egg—Bordent said it was dangerous, you know. I heard him."

Calderon peeped through the door-crack. The four dwarfs were sitting facing Alexander, whose eyes were closed. Now they opened. The infant scowled at Calderon.

"Stay out," he requested. "You're breaking the rapport."

"I'm so sorry," Calderon said, retreating. "He's O.K., Myra. His own dictatorial little self."

"Well, he *is* a superman," she said doubtfully.

"No. He's a super-baby. There's all the difference."

"His latest trick," Myra said, busy with the oven, "is

riddles. Or something like riddles. I feel so small when he catches me up. But he says it's good for his ego. It compensates for his physical frailness."

"Riddles, eh? I know a few too."

"They won't work on Alexander," Myra said, with grim assurance.

Nor did they. "What goes up a chimney up?" was treated with the contempt it deserved; Alexander examined his father's riddles, turned them over in his logical mind, analyzed them for flaws in semantics and logic, and rejected them. Or else he answered them, with such fine accuracy that Calderon was too embarrassed to give the correct answers. He was reduced to asking why a raven was like a writing desk, and since not even the Mad Hatter had been able to answer his own riddle, was slightly terrified to find himself listening to a dissertation on comparative ornithology. After that, he let Alexander needle him with infantile gags about the relations of gamma rays to photons, and tried to be philosophical. There are few things as irritating as a child's riddles. His mocking triumph pulverizes itself into the dust in which you grovel.

"Oh, leave your father alone," Myra said, coming in with her hair disarranged. "He's trying to read the paper."

"That news is unimportant."

"I'm reading the comics," Calderon said. "I want to see if the Katzenjammers get even with the Captain for hanging them under a waterfall."

"The formula for the humor of an incongruity predicament," Alexander began learnedly, but Calderon disgustedly went into the bedroom, where Myra joined him. "He's asking me riddles again," she said. "Let's see what the Katzenjammers did."

"You look rather miserable. Got a cold?"

"I'm not wearing make-up. Alexander says the smell makes him ill."

"So what? He's no petunia."

"Well," Myra said, "he does get ill. But of course he does it on purpose."

"Listen. There he goes again. What now?"

But Alexander merely wanted an audience. He had found a new way of making imbecilic noises with his fingers and

lips. At times the child's normal phases were more trying
than his super periods. After a month had passed, however,
Calderon felt that the worst was yet to come. Alexander had
progressed into fields of knowledge hitherto untouched by
homo sap, and he had developed a leechlike habit of sucking
his father's brains dry of every scrap of knowledge the
wretched man possessed.

It was the same with Myra. The world was indeed Alexander's oyster. He had an insatiable curiosity about everything,
and there was no longer any privacy in the apartment. Calderon took to locking the bedroom door against his son at
night—Alexander's crib was now in another room—but furious squalls might waken him at any hour.

In the midst of preparing dinner, Myra would be forced to
stop and explain the caloric mysteries of the oven to Alexander. He learned all she knew, took a jump into more abstruse
aspects of the matter, and sneered at her ignorance. He found
out Calderon was a physicist, a fact which the man had
hitherto kept carefully concealed, and thereafter pumped his
father dry. He asked questions about geodetics and geopolitics. He inquired about monotremes and monorails. He was
curious about biremes and biology. And he was skeptical,
doubting the depth of his father's knowledge. "But," he said,
"you and Myra Calderon are my closest contacts with homo
sap as yet, and it's a beginning. Put out that cigarette. It isn't
good for my lungs."

"All right," Calderon said. He rose wearily, with his usual
feeling these days of being driven from room to room of the
apartment, and went in search of Myra. "Bordent's about
due. We can go out somewhere, O.K.?"

"Swell." She was at the mirror, fixing her hair, in a trice.
"I need a permanent. If I only had the time—!"

"I'll take off tomorrow and stay here. You need a rest."

"Darling, no. The exams are coming up. You simply can't
do it."

Alexander yelled. It developed that he wanted his mother
to sing for him. He was curious about the tonal range of
homo sap and the probable emotional and soporific effect of
lullabies. Calderon mixed himself a drink, sat in the kitchen
and smoked, and thought about the glorious destiny of his
son. When Myra stopped singing, he listened for Alexander's

wails, but there was no sound till a slightly hysterical Myra burst in on him, dithering and wide-eyed.

"Joe!" She fell into Calderon's arms. "Quick, give me a drink or . . . or hold me tight or something."

"What is it?" He thrust the bottle into her hands, went to the door, and looked out. "Alexander? He's quiet. Eating candy."

Myra didn't bother with a glass. The bottle's neck clicked against her teeth. "Look at me. Just look at me. I'm a mess."

"What happened?"

"Oh, nothing. Nothing at all. Alexander's turned into a black magician, that's all." She dropped into a chair and passed a palm across her forehead. "Do you know what that genius son of ours just did?"

"Bit you," Calderon hazarded, not doubting it for a minute.

"Worse, far worse. He started asking me for candy. I said there wasn't any in the house. He told me to go down to the grocery for some. I said I'd have to get dressed first, and I was too tired."

"Why didn't you ask me to go?"

"I didn't have the chance. Before I could say boo that infantile Merlin waved a magic wand or something. I . . . I was down at the grocery. Behind the candy counter."

Calderon blinked. "Induced amnesia?"

"There wasn't any time-lapse. It was just *phweet*—and there I was. In this rag of a dress, without a speck of make-up on, and my hair coming down in tassels. Mrs. Busherman was there, too, buying a chicken—that cat across the hall. She was kind enough to tell me I ought to take more care of myself. Meow," Myra ended furiously.

"Good Lord."

"Teleportation. That's what Alexander says it is. Something new he's picked up. I'm not going to stand for it, Joe. I'm not a rag doll, after all." She was half hysterical.

Calderon went into the next room and stood regarding his child. There was chocolate smeared around Alexander's mouth.

"Listen, wise guy," he said. "You leave your mother alone, hear me?"

"I didn't hurt her," the prodigy pointed out, in a blobby voice. "I was simply being efficient."

"Well, don't be so efficient. Where did you learn that trick, anyhow?"

"Teleportation? Quat showed me last night. He can't do it himself, but I'm X Free super, so I can. The power isn't disciplined yet. If I'd tried to teleport Myra Calderon over to Jersey, say, I might have dropped her in the Hudson by mistake."

Calderon muttered something uncomplimentary. Alexander said, "Is that an Anglo-Saxon derivative?"

"Never mind about that. You shouldn't have all that chocolate, anyway. You'll make yourself sick. You've already made your mother sick. And you nauseate me."

"Go away," Alexander said. "I want to concentrate on the taste."

"No. I said you'd make yourself sick. Chocolate's too rich for you. Give it here. You've had enough." Calderon reached for the paper sack. Alexander disappeared. In the kitchen Myra shrieked.

Calderon moaned despondently, and turned. As he had expected, Alexander was in the kitchen, on top of the stove, hoggishly stuffing candy into his mouth. Myra was concentrating on the bottle.

"What a household," Calderon said. "The baby teleporting himself all over the apartment, you getting stewed in the kitchen, and me heading for a nervous breakdown." He started to laugh. "O.K., Alexander. You can keep the candy. I know when to shorten my defensive lines strategically."

"Myra Calderon," Alexander said. "I want to go back into the other room."

"Fly in," Calderon suggested. "Here, I'll carry you."

"Not you. Her. She has a better rhythm when she walks."

"Staggers, you mean," Myra said, but she obediently put aside the bottle, got up, and laid hold of Alexander. She went out. Calderon was not much surprised to hear her scream a moment later. When he joined the happy family, Myra was sitting on the floor, rubbing her arms and biting her lips. Alexander was laughing.

"What now?"

"He-he sh-shocked me," Myra said in a child's voice. "He's

like an electric eel. He d-did it on purpose, too. Oh, Alexander, will you *stop* laughing!"

"You fell down," the infant crowed in triumph. "You yelled and fell down."

Calderon looked at Myra, and his mouth tightened. "Did you do that on purpose?" he asked.

"Yes. She fell down. She looked funny."

"You're going to look a lot funnier in a minute. X Free super or not, what you need is a good paddling."

"Joe—" Myra said.

"Never mind. He's got to learn to be considerate of the rights of others."

"I'm homo superior," Alexander said, with the air of one clinching on argument.

"It's homo posterior I'm going to deal with," Calderon announced, and attempted to capture his son. There was a stinging blaze of jolting nervous energy that blasted up through his synapses; he went backwards ignominiously, and slammed into the wall, cracking his head hard against it. Alexander laughed like an idiot.

"You fell down too," he crowed. "You look funny."

"Joe," Myra said. "Joe. Are you hurt?"

Calderone said sourly that he supposed he'd survive. Though, he added, it would probably be wise to lay in a few splints and a supply of blood plasma. "In case he gets interested in vivisection."

Myra regarded Alexander with troubled speculation. "You're kidding, I hope."

"I hope so, too."

"Well—here's Bordent. Let's talk to him."

Calderon answered the door. The four little men came in solemnly. They wasted no time. They gathered about Alexander, unfolded fresh apparatus from the recesses of their paper clothes, and set to work. The infant said, "I teleported *her* about eight thousand feet."

"That far, eh?" Quat said. "Were you fatigued at all?"

"Not a bit."

Calderon dragged Bordent aside. "I want to talk to you. I think Alexander needs a spanking."

"By voraster!" the dwarf said, shocked. "But he's *Alexander*! He's X Free type super!"

"Not yet. He's still a baby."

"But a superbaby. No, no, Joseph Calderon. I must tell you again that disciplinary measures can be applied only by sufficiently intelligent authorities."

"You?"

"Oh, not yet," Bordent said. "We don't want to overwork him. There's a limit even to super brain power, especially in the very formative period. He's got enough to do, and his attitudes for social contacts won't need forming for a while yet."

Myra joined them. "I don't agree with you there. Like all babies, he's antisocial. He may have superhuman powers but he's subhuman as far as mental and emotional balance go."

"Yeah," Calderon agreed. "This business of giving us electric shocks—"

"He's only playing," Bordent said.

"And teleportation. Suppose he teleports me to Times Square when I'm taking a shower?"

"It's only his play. He's a baby still."

"But what about us?"

"You have the hereditary characteristic of parental tolerance," Bordent explained. "As I told you before, Alexander and his race are the reason why tolerance was created in the first place. There's no great need for it with homo sap. I mean there's a wide space between normal tolerance and normal provocation. An ordinary baby may try his parents severely for a few moments at a time, but that's about all. The provocation is far too small to require the tremendous store of tolerance the parents have. But with the X Free type, it's a different matter."

"There a limit even to tolerance," Calderon said. "I'm wondering about a crèche."

Bordent shook his shiny metallic-sheathed head. "He needs you."

"But," Myra said, "but! Can't you give him just a little discipline?"

"Oh, it isn't necessary. His mind's still immature, and he must concentrate on more important things. You'll tolerate him."

"It's not as though he's our baby any more," she murmured. "He's not Alexander."

"But he is. That's just it. *He's Alexander!*"

"Look, it's normal for a mother to want to hug her baby.

But how can she do that if she expects him to throw her halfway across the room?"

Calderon was brooding. "Will he pick up more . . . more super powers as he goes along?"

"Why, yes. Naturally."

"He's a menace to life and limb. I still say he needs discipline. Next time I'll wear rubber gloves."

"That won't help," Bordent said, frowning. "Besides, I must insist . . . no, Joseph Calderon, it won't do. You mustn't interfere. You're not capable of giving him the right sort of discipline—which he doesn't need yet anyway."

"Just one spanking," Calderon said wistfully. "Not for revenge. Only to show him he's got to consider the rights of others."

"He'll learn to consider the rights of other X Free supers. You must not attempt anything of the sort. A spanking— even if you succeeded, which is far from probable—might warp him psychologically. We are his tutors, his mentors. We must *protect* him. You understand?"

"I think so," Calderon said slowly. "That's a threat."

"You are Alexander's parents, but it's Alexander who is important. If I must apply disciplinary measures to you, I must."

"Oh, forget it," Myra sighed. "Joe, let's go out and walk in the park while Bordent's here."

"Be back in two hours," the little man said. "Good-bye."

As time went past, Calderon could not decide whether Alexander's moronic phrases or his periods of keen intelligence were more irritating. The prodigy had learned new powers; the worst of that was that Calderon never knew what to expect, or when some astounding gag would be sprung on him. Such as the time when a mess of sticky taffy had materialized in his bed, filched from the grocery by deft teleportation. Alexander thought it was very funny. He laughed.

And, when Calderon refused to go to the store to buy candy because he said he had no money—"Now don't try to teleport me. I'm broke."—Alexander had utilized mental energy, warping gravity lines shockingly. Calderon found himself hanging upside-down in midair, being shaken, while loose coins cascaded out of his pocket. He went after the candy.

Humor is a developed sense, stemming basically from cruelty. The more primitive a mind, the less selectivity exists. A cannibal would probably be profoundly amused by the squirmings of his victim in the seething kettle. A man slips on a banana peel and breaks his back. The adult stops laughing at that point, the child does not. And a civilized ego finds embarrassment as acutely distressing as physical pain. A baby, a child, a moron, is incapable of practicing empathy. He cannot identify himself with another individual. He is regrettably autistic; his own rules are arbitrary, and garbage strewn around the bedroom was funny to neither Myra nor Calderon.

There was a little stranger in the house. Nobody rejoiced. Except Alexander. He had a lot of fun.

"No privacy," Calderon said. "He materializes everywhere, at all hours. Darling, I wish you'd see a doctor."

"What would he advise?" Myra asked. "Rest, that's all. Do you realize it's been two months since Bordent took over?"

"And we've made marvelous progress," Bordent said, coming over to them. Quat was en rapport with Alexander on the carpet, while the other two dwarfs prepared the makings of a new gadget. "Or, rather, Alexander has made remarkable progress."

"We need a rest," Calderon growled. "If I lose my job, who'll support that genius of yours?" Myra looked at her husband quickly, noting the possessive pronoun he had used.

Bordent was concerned. "You are in difficulty?"

"The Dean's spoken to me once or twice. I can't control my classes any more. I'm too irritable."

"You don't need to expend tolerance on your students. As for money, we can keep you supplied. I'll arrange to get some negotiable currency for you."

"But I want to work. I like my job."

"Alexander is your job."

"I need a maid," Myra said, looking hopeless. "Can't you make me a robot or something? Alexander scares every maid I've managed to hire. They won't stay a day in this madhouse."

"A mechanical intelligence would have a bad effect on Alexander," Bordent said. "No."

"I wish we could have guests in once in a while. Or go out visiting. Or just be alone," Myra sighed.

"Some day Alexander will be mature, and you'll reap your

reward. The parents of Alexander. Did I ever tell you that we
have images of you two in the Great Fogy Hall?"

"They must look terrible," Calderon said. "I know we do
now."

"Be patient. Consider the destiny of your son."

"I do. Often. But he gets a little wearing sometimes. That's
quite an understatement."

"Which is where tolerance comes in," Bordent said.
"Nature planned well for the new race."

"Mm-m-m."

"He is working on sixth-dimensional abstractions now. Everything is progressing beautifully."

"Yeah," Calderon said. And he went away, muttering, to
join Myra in the kitchen.

Alexander worked with facility at his gadgets, his pudgy
fingers already stronger and surer. He still had an illicit passion for the blue ovoid, but under Bordent's watchful eye he
could use it only along the restricted lines laid out by his
mentors. When the lesson was finished, Quat selected a few
of the objects and locked them in a cupboard, as was his custom. The rest he left on the carpet to provide exercise for
Alexander's ingenuity.

"He develops," Bordent said. "Today we've made a great
step."

Myra and Calderon came in time to hear this. "What goes?"
he asked.

"A psychic bloc-removal. Alexander will no longer need to
sleep."

"What?" Myra said.

"He won't require sleep. It's an artificial habit anyway. The
super race has no need of it."

"He won't sleep any more, eh?" Calderon said. He had
grown a little pale.

"Correct. He'll develop faster now, twice as fast."

At 3:30 A.M. Calderon and Myra lay in bed, wide awake,
looking through the open door into the full blaze of light
where Alexander played. Seen there clearly, as if upon a
lighted stage, he did not look quite like himself any more.
The difference was subtle, but it was there. Under the golden
down his head had changed shape slightly, and there was a
look of intelligence and purpose upon the blobby features. It

was not an attractive look. It didn't belong there. It made
Alexander look less like a super-baby than a debased oldster.
All a child's normal cruelty and selfishness—perfectly
healthy, natural traits in the developing infant—flickered
across Alexander's face as he played absorbedly with solid
crystal blocks which he was fitting into one another like a
Chinese puzzle. It was quite a shocking face to watch.

Calderon heard Myra sigh beside him.

"He isn't our Alexander any more," she said. "Not a bit."

Alexander glanced up and his face suddenly suffused. The
look of paradoxical age and degeneracy upon it vanished as
he opened his mouth and bawled with rage, tossing the blocks
in all directions. Calderon watched one roll through the bedroom door and come to rest upon the carpet, spilling out of
its solidity a cascade of smaller and smaller solid blocks that
tumbled winking toward him. Alexander's cries filled the
apartment. After a moment windows began to slam across
the court, and presently the phone rang. Calderon reached
for it, sighing.

When he hung up he looked across at Myra and grimaced.
Above the steady roars he said, "Well, we have notice to
move."

Myra said, "Oh. Oh, well."

"That about covers it."

They were silent for a moment. Then Calderon said,
"Nineteen years more of it. I thing we can expect about that.
They did say he'd mature at twenty, didn't they?"

"He'll be an orphan long before then," Myra groaned.
"Oh, my head! I think I caught cold when he teleported us
up to the roof just before dinner. Joe, do you suppose we're
the first parents who ever got . . . got caught like this?"

"What do you mean?"

"I mean, was there ever another super-baby before Alexander? It does seem like a waste of a lot of tolerance if we're
the first to need it."

"We could use a lot more. We'll need a lot." He said nothing more for awhile, but he lay there thinking and trying not
to hear his super-child's rhythmic howling. Tolerance. Every
parent needed a great deal of it. Every child was intolerable
from time to time. The race had certainly needed parental
love in vast quantities to permit its infants to survive. But no
parents before had ever been tried consistently up to the very

last degree of tolerance. No parents before had ever had to face twenty years of it, day and night, strained to the final notch. Parental love is a great and all-encompassing emotion, but—

"I wonder," he said thoughtfully. "I wonder if we *are* the first."

Myra's speculations had been veering. "I suppose it's like tonsils and appendix," she murmured. "They've outlived their use, but they still hang on. This tolerance is vestigial in reverse. It's been hanging on all these millenniums, waiting for Alexander."

"Maybe. I wonder— Still, if there ever had been an Alexander before now, we'd have heard of him. So—"

Myra rose on one elbow and looked at her husband. "You think so?" she said softly. "I'm not so sure. I think it might have happened before."

Alexander suddenly quieted. The apartment rang with silence for a moment. Then a familiar voice, without words, spoke in both their brains simultaneously.

"Get me some more milk. And I want it just warm, not hot."

Joe and Myra looked at one another again, speechless. Myra sighed and pushed the covers back. "I'll go this time," she said. "Something new, eh? I—"

"Don't dawdle," said the wordless voice, and Myra jumped and gave a little shriek. Electricity crackled audibly through the room, and Alexander's bawling laughter was heard through the doorway.

"He's about as civilized now as a well-trained monkey, I suppose," Joe remarked, getting out of bed. "I'll go. You crawl back in. And in another year he may reach the elevation of a bushman. After that, if we're still alive, we'll have the pleasure of living with a super-powered cannibal. Eventually he may work up to the level of practical joker. That ought to be interesting." He went out, muttering to himself.

Ten minutes later, returning to bed, Joe found Myra clasping her knees and looking into space.

"We aren't the first, Joe," she said, not glancing at him. "I've been thinking. I'm pretty sure we aren't."

"But we've never heard of any supermen developing—"

She turned her head and gave him a long, thoughtful look. "No," she said.

They were silent. Then, "Yes, I see what you mean," he nodded.

Something crashed in the living room. Alexander chuckled and the sound of splintering wood was loud in the silence of the night. Another window banged somewhere outside.

"There's a breaking point," Myra said quietly. "There's got to be."

"Saturation," Joe murmured. "Tolerance saturation—or something. It could have happened."

Alexander trundled into sight, clutching something blue. He sat down and began to fiddle with bright wires. Myra rose suddenly.

"Joe, he's got that blue egg! He must have broken into the cupboard."

Calderon said, "But Quat told him—"

"It's dangerous!"

Alexander looked at them, grinned, and bent the wires into a cradle-shape the size of the egg.

Calderon found himself out of bed and halfway to the door. He stopped before he reached it. "You know," he said slowly, "he might hurt himself with that thing."

"We'll have to get it away from him," Myra agreed, heaving herself up with tired reluctance.

"Look at him," Calderon urged. "Just look."

Alexander was dealing competently with the wires, his hands flickering into sight and out again as he balanced a tesseract beneath the cradle. That curious veil of knowledge gave his chubby face the debased look of senility which they had come to know so well.

"This will go on and on, you know," Calderon murmured. "Tomorrow he'll look a little less like himself than today. Next week—next month—what will he be like in a year?"

"I know." Myra's voice was an echo. "Still, I suppose we'll have to—" Her voice trailed to a halt. She stood barefoot beside her husband, watching.

"I suppose the gadget will be finished," she said, "once he connects up that last wire. We ought to take it away from him."

"Think we could?"

"We ought to try."

They looked at each other. Calderon said, "It looks like an Easter egg. I never heard of an Easter egg hurting anybody."

"I suppose we're doing him a favor, really," Myra said in a low voice. "A burnt child dreads the fire. Once a kid burns himself on a match, he stays away from matches."

They stood in silence, watching.

It took Alexander about three more minutes to succeed in his design, whatever it was. The results were phenomenally effective. There was a flash of white light, a crackle of split air, and Alexander vanished in the dazzle, leaving only a faint burnt smell behind him.

When the two could see again, they blinked distrustfully at the empty place. "Teleportation?" Myra whispered dazedly.

"I'll make sure." Calderon crossed the floor and stood looking down at a damp spot on the carpet, with Alexander's shoes in it. He said, "No. Not teleportation." Then he took a long breath. "He's gone, all right. So he never grew up and sent Bordent back in time to move in on us. It never happened."

"We weren't the first," Myra said in an unsteady, bemused voice. "There's a breaking point, that's all. How sorry I feel for the first parents who don't reach it!"

She turned away suddenly, but not so suddenly that he could not see she was crying. He hesitated, watching the door. He thought he had better not follow her just yet.

KILLDOZER!

Astounding,
November

by Theodore Sturgeon (1918-   )

Ted Sturgeon returned to the pages of Astounding *after an absence of several years with this thrilling masterpiece. "Possession" stories are usually the province of fantasy, but since the possessor in this case is an alien intelligence, "Killdozer!" qualifies as science fiction. The theme of man vs. machine is an old one in science fiction, but it has rarely been treated with as much skill as it is here. Sturgeon was a heavy machine operator and knew of what he wrote. The story was filmed (a made-for-television production) in 1974 but failed to capture the dramatic tension of the original.*

(World War II meant a fall-off in the output of a number of science fiction's leading authors. The years 1942 to 1945, for instance, saw Robert Heinlein, Sprague de Camp and myself working on the same floor of the same building at the U.S. Navy Yard in Philadelphia. It meant that Bob and Sprague wrote virtually nothing for three years (though I myself managed to find spare time in which to continue my Foundation series and my positronic robot stories). Ted Sturgeon was another one of the fall-offs (and it all drove poor John Campbell half-crazy, as you can well imagine). When Ted came back, however, it was with his best straight science fiction piece, the one you are about to read, so maybe it was all for the best.—I.A.)

*Before the race was the deluge, and before the deluge an-
other race, whose nature it is not for mankind to understand.
Not unearthly, not alien, for this was their earth and their
home.*

*There was a war between this race, which was a great one,
and another. The other was truly alien, a sentient cloudform,
an intelligent grouping of tangible electrons. It was spawned in
mighty machines by some accident of a science before our ab-
original conception of its complexities. And the machines, servants of the people, became the people's masters, and great
were the battles that followed. The electron-beings had the
power to warp the delicate balances of atom-structure, and
their life-medium was metal, which they permeated and used
to their own ends. Each weapon the people developed was
possessed and turned against them, until a time when the remnants of that vast civilization found a defense—*

*An insulator. The terminal product or by-product of all en-
ergy research—neutronium.*

*In its shelter they developed a weapon. What it was we shall
never know, and our race will live—or we shall know, and our
race will perish as theirs perished. For, to destroy the enemy,
it got out of hand and its measureless power destroyed them
with it, and their cities, and their possessed machines. The
very earth dissolved in flame, the crust writhed and shook and
the ocean boiled. Nothing escaped it, nothing that we know as
life, and nothing of the pseudolife that had evolved within the
mysterious force-fields of their incomprehensible machines,
save one hardy mutant.*

*Mutant it was, and ironically this one alone could have
been killed by the first simple measures used against its
kind—but it was past time for simple expediences. It was an
organized electron-field possessing intelligence and mobility
and a will to destroy, and little else. Stunned by the holocaust,
it drifted over the grumbling globe, and in a lull in the violence of the forces gone wild on Earth, sank to the steaming
ground in its half-conscious exhaustion. There it found shelter—shelter built by and for its dead enemies. An envelope of
neutronium. It drifted in, and its consciousness at last fell to*

its lowest ebb. And there it lay while the neutronium, with its strange constant flux, its interminable striving for perfect balance, extended itself and closed the opening. And thereafter in the turbulent eons that followed, the envelope tossed like a gray bubble on the surface of the roiling sphere, for no substance on Earth would have it or combine with it.

The ages came and went, and chemical action and reaction did their mysterious work, and once again there was life and evolution. And a tribe found the mass of neutronium, which is not a substance but a static force, and were awed by its aura of indescribable chill, and they worshiped it and built a temple around it and made sacrifices to it. And ice and fire and the seas came and went, and the land rose and fell as the years went by, until the ruined temple was on a knoll, and the knoll was an island. Islanders came and went, lived and built and died, and races forgot. So now, somewhere in the Pacific to the west of the archipelago called Islas Revillagigeda, there was an uninhabited island. And one day—

Chub Horton and Tom Jaeger stood watching the *Sprite* and her squat tow of three cargo lighters dwindle over the glassy sea. The big ocean-going towboat and her charges seemed to be moving out of focus rather than traveling away. Chub spat cleanly around the cigar that grew out of the corner of his mouth.

"That's that for three weeks. How's it feel to be a guinea pig?"

"We'll get it done." Tom had little crinkles all around the outer ends of his eyes. He was a head taller than Chub and rangy, and not so tough, and he was a real operator. Choosing him as a foreman for the experiment had been wise, for he was competent and he commanded respect. The theory of airfield construction that they were testing appealed vastly to him, for here were no officers-in-charge, no government inspectors, no timekeeping or reports. The government had allowed the company a temporary land grant, and the idea was to put production-line techniques into the layout and grading of the project. There were six operators and two mechanics and more than a million dollars' worth of the best equipment that money could buy. Government acceptance was to be on a partially completed basis, and contingent on government standards. The theory obviated both gold-bricking and graft, and neatly sidestepped the manpower shortage. "When that blacktopping crew gets here, I reckon we'll be ready for 'em," said Tom.

He turned and scanned the island with an operator's vision and saw it as it was, and in all the stages it would pass through, and as it would look when they had finished, with four thousand feet of clean-draining runway, hard-packed shoulders, four acres of plane-park, the access road and the short taxiway. He saw the lay of each lift that the power shovel would cut as it brought down the marl bluff, and the ruins on top of it that would give them stone to haul down the salt-flat to the little swamp at the other end, there to be walked in by the dozers.

"We got time to walk the shovel up there to the bluff before dark."

They walked down the beach toward the outcropping where the equipment stood surrounded by crates and drums of supplies. The three tractors were ticking over quietly, the two-cycle Diesel chuckling through their mufflers and the big D-7 whacking away its metronomic compression knock on every easy revolution. The Dumptors were lined up and silent, for they would not be ready to work until the shovel was ready to load them. They looked like a mechanical interpretation of Dr. Dolittle's "Pushme-pullyou," the fantastic animal with two front ends. They had two large driving wheels and two small steerable wheels. The motor and the driver's seat were side by side over the front—or smaller—wheels; but the driver faced the dump body between the big rear wheels, exactly the opposite of the way he would sit in a dump truck. Hence, in traveling from shovel to dumping-ground, the operator drove backwards, looking over his shoulder, and in dumping he backed the machine up but he himself traveled forward—quite a trick for fourteen hours a day! The shovel squatted in the midst of all the others, its great hulk looming over them, humped there with its boom low and its iron chin on the ground, like some great tired dinosaur.

Rivera, the Puerto Rican mechanic, looked up grinning as Tom and Chub approached, and stuck a bleeder wrench into the top pocket of his coveralls.

"She says 'Sigalo,' " he said, his white teeth flashlighting out of the smear of grease across his mouth. "She says she wan' to get dirt on dis paint." He kicked the blade of the Seven with his heel.

Tom sent the grin back—always a surprising thing in his grave face.

"That Seven'll do that, and she'll take a good deal off her bitin' edge along with the paint before we're through. Get in the saddle, Goony. Build a ramp off the rocks down to the flat there, and blade us off some humps from here to the bluff yonder. We're walking the dipper up there."

The Puerto Rican was in the seat before Tom had finished, and with a roar the Seven spun in its length and moved back along the outcropping to the inland edge. Rivera dropped his blade and the sandy marl curled and piled up in front of the dozer, loading the blade and running off in two even rolls at the ends. He shoved the load toward the rocky edge, the Seven revving down as it took the load, *blat blat blatting* and pulling like a supercharged ox as it fired slowly enough for them to count the revolutions.

"She's a hunk of machine," said Tom.

"A hunk of operator, too," gruffed Chub, and added, "for a mechanic."

"The boy's all right," said Kelly. He was standing there with them, watching the Puerto Rican operate the dozer, as if he had been there all along, which was the way Kelly always arrived places. He was tall, slim, with green eyes too long and an easy stretch to the way he moved, like an attenuated cat. He said, "Never thought I'd see the day when equipment was shipped set up ready to run like this. Guess no one ever thought of it before."

"There's times when heavy equipment has to be unloaded in a hurry these days," Tom said. "If they can do it with tanks, they can do it with construction equipment. We're doin' it to build something instead, is all. Kelly, crank up the shovel. It's oiled. We're walking it over to the bluff."

Kelly swung up into the cab of the big dipper-stick and, diddling the governor control, pulled up the starting handle. The Murphy Diesel snorted and settled down into a thudding idle. Kelly got into the saddle, set up the throttle a little, and began to boom up.

"I still can't get over it," said Chub. "Not more'n a year ago we'd a had two hundred men on a job like this."

Tom smiled. "Yeah, and the first thing we'd have done

would be to build an office building, and then quarters. Me, I'll take this way. No timekeepers, no equipment-use reports, no progress and yardage summaries, no nothin' but eight men, a million bucks worth of equipment, an' three weeks. A shovel an' a mess of tool crates'll keep the rain off us, an' army field rations'll keep our bellies full. We'll get it done, we'll get out and we'll get paid."

Rivera finished the ramp, turned the Seven around and climbed it, walking the new fill down. At the top he dropped his blade, floated it, and backed down the ramp, smoothing out the rolls. At a wave from Tom he started out across the shore, angling up toward the bluff, beating out the humps and carrying fill into the hollows. As he worked, he sang, feeling the beat of the mighty motor, the micrometric obedience of that vast implacable machine.

"Why doesn't that monkey stick to his grease guns?"

Tom turned and took the chewed end of a match stick out of his mouth. He said nothing, because he had for some time been trying to make a habit of saying nothing to Joe Dennis. Dennis was an ex-accountant, drafted out of an office at the last gasp of a defunct project in the West Indies. He had become an operator because they needed operators badly. He had been released with alacrity from the office because of his propensity for small office politics. It was a game he still played, and completely aside from his boiled-looking red face and his slightly womanish walk, he was out of place in the field; for boot-licking and back-stabbing accomplish even less out on the field than they do in an office. Tom, trying so hard to keep his mind on his work, had to admit to himself that of all Dennis' annoying traits the worst was that he was good a pan operator as could be found anywhere, and no one could deny it.

Dennis certainly didn't.

"I've seen the day when anyone catching one of those goonies so much as sitting on a machine during lunch, would kick his fanny," Dennis groused. "Now they give 'em a man's work and a man's pay."

"*Doin'* a man's work, ain't he?" Tom said.

"He's a Puerto Rican!"

Tom turned and looked at him levelly. "Where was it you said *you* come from," he mused. "Oh yeah. Georgia."

"What do you mean by that?"

Tom was already striding away. "Tell you as soon as I have to," he flung back over his shoulder. Dennis went back to watching the Seven.

Tom glanced at the ramp and then waved Kelly on. Kelly set his house-brake so the shovel could not swing, put her into travel gear, and shoved the swing lever forward. With a crackling of drive chains and a massive scrunching of compacting coral sand, the shovel's great flat pads carried her over and down the ramp. As she tipped over the peak of the ramp the heavy manganese steel bucket-door gaped open and closed, like a hungry mouth, slamming up against the bucket until suddenly it latched shut and was quiet. The big Murphy Diesel crooned hollowly under compression as the machine ran downgrade and then the sensitive governor took hold and it took up its belly-beating thud.

Peebles was standing by one of the door-pan combines, sucking on his pipe and looking out to sea. He was grizzled and heavy, and from under the bushiest gray brows looked the calmest gray eyes Tom had ever seen. Peebles had never gotten angry at a machine—a rare trait in a born mechanic—and in fifty-odd years he had learned it was even less use getting angry at a man. Because no matter what, you could always fix what was wrong with a machine. He said around his pipestem:

"Hope you'll give me back my boy, there."

Tom's lips quirked in a little grin. There had been an understanding between old Peebles and himself ever since they had met. It was one of those things which exists unspoken—they knew little about each other because they had never found it necessary to make small talk to keep their friendship extant. It was enough to know that each could expect the best from the other, without persuasion.

"Rivera?" Tom asked. "I'll chase him back as soon as he finishes that service road for the dipper-stick. Why—got anything on?"

"Not much. Want to get that arc welder drained and flushed and set up a grounded table in case you guys tear anything up." He paused. "Besides, the kid's filling his head up with too many things at once. Mechanicing is one thing; operating is something else."

"Hasn't got in his way much so far, has it?"

"Nope. Don't aim t' let it, either. 'Less you need him."

Tom swung up on the pan tractor. "I don't need him that bad, Peeby. If you want some help in the meantime, get Dennis."

Peebles said nothing. He spat. He didn't say anything at all.

"What's the matter with Dennis?" Tom wanted to know.

"Look yonder," said Peebles, waving his pipestem. Out on the beach Dennis was talking to Chub, in Dennis' indefatigable style, standing beside Chub, one hand on Chub's shoulder. As they watched they saw Dennis call his side-kick, Al Knowles.

"Dennis talks too much," said Peebles. "That most generally don't amount to much, but that Dennis, he sometimes *says* too much. Ain't got what it takes to run a show, and knows it. Makes up for by messin' in between folks."

"He's harmless," said Tom.

Still looking up the beach, Peebles said slowly:

"Is, so far."

Tom started to say something, then shrugged. "I'll send you Rivera," he said, and opened the throttle. Like a huge electric dynamo, the two-cycle motor whined to a crescendo. Tom lifted the dozer with a small lever by his right thigh and raised the pan with the long control sprouting out from behind his shoulder. He moved off, setting the rear gate of the scraper so that anything the blade bit would run off to the side instead of loading into the pan. He slapped the tractor into sixth gear and whined up to and around the crawling shovel, cutting neatly in under the boom and running on ahead with his scraper blade just touching the ground, dragging to a fine grade the service road Rivera had cut.

Dennis was saying, "It's that little Hitler stuff. Why should I take that kind of talk? 'You come from Georgia,' he says. What is he—a Yankee or something?"

"A crackah f'm Macon," chortled Al Knowles, who came from Georgia, too. He was tall and stringy and round-shouldered. All of his skill was in his hands and feet, brains being a commodity he had lived without all his life until he had met Dennis and used him as a reasonable facsimile thereof.

"Tom didn't mean nothing by it," said Chub.

"No, he didn't mean nothin'. Only that we do what he says the way he says it, specially if he finds a way we don't like it.

You wouldn't do like that, Chub. Al, think Chub would carry
on thataway?"

"Sure wouldn't," said Al, feeling it expected of him.

"Nuts," said Chub, pleased and uncomfortable, and thinking, what have I got against Tom?—not knowing, not liking
Tom as well as he had. "Tom's the man here, Dennis. We got
a job to do—let's skit and git. Man can take anything for a
lousy six weeks."

"Oh, sho'," said Al.

"Man can take just so much," Dennis said. "What they put
a man like that on top for, Chub? What's the matter with
you? Don't you know grading and drainage as good as Tom?
Can Tom stake out a side hill like you can?"

"Sure, sure, but what's the difference, long as we get a field
built? An' anyhow, hell with bein' the boss-man. Who gets
the blame if things don't run right, anyway?"

Dennis stepped back, taking his hand off Chub's shoulder,
and stuck an elbow in Al's ribs.

"You see that, Al? Now there's a smart man. That's the
thing Uncle Tom didn't bargain for. Chub, you can count on
Al and me to do just that little thing."

"Do just what little thing?" asked Chub, genuinely puzzled.

"Like you said. If the job goes wrong, the boss gets
blamed. So if the boss don't behave, the job goes wrong."

"Uh-huh," agreed Al with the conviction of mental sim-
plicity.

Chub double-took this extraordinary logical process and
grasped wildly at anger as the conversation slid out from under him. "I didn't say any such thing! This job is goin' to get
done, no matter what! Hitler ain't hangin' no iron cross on
me or anybody else around here if I can help it."

"Tha's the ol' fight," feinted Dennis. "We'll show that guy
what we think of his kind of sabotage."

"You talk too much," said Chub and escaped with the
remnants of coherence. Every time he talked with Dennis he
walked away feeling as if he had an unwanted membership
card stuck in his pocket that he couldn't throw away with a
clear conscience.

Rivera ran his road up under the bluff, swung the Seven
around, punched out the master clutch and throttled down,
idling. Tom was making his pass with the pan, and as he ap-

proached, Rivera slipped out of the seat and behind the tractor, laying a sensitive hand on the final drive casing and sprocket bushings, checking for overheating. Tom pulled alongside and beckoned him up on the pan tractor.

"*Que pase,* Goony? Anything wrong?"

Rivera shook his head and grinned. "Nothing wrong. She is perfect, that '*De Siete.*' She—"

"That what? 'Daisy Etta'?"

"*De siete.* In Spanish, D-7. It means something in English?"

"Got you wrong," smiled Tom. "But Daisy Etta is a girl's name in English, all the same."

He shifted the pan tractor into neutral and engaged the clutch, and jumped off the machine. Rivera followed. They climbed aboard the Seven, Tom at the controls.

Rivera said "Daisy Etta," and grinned so widely that a soft little chuckling noise came from behind his back teeth. He reached out his hand, crooked his little finger around one of the tall steering clutch levers, and pulled it all the way back. Tom laughed outright.

"You got something there," he said. "The easiest runnin' cat ever built. Hydraulic steerin' clutches and brakes that'll bring you to a dead stop if you spit on 'em. Forward an' reverse lever so's you got all your speeds front and backwards. A little different from the old jobs. They had no booster springs, eight-ten years ago; took a sixty-pound pull to get a steerin' clutch back. Cuttin' a side-hill with an angle-dozer really was a job in them days. You try it sometime, dozin' with one hand, holdin' her nose out o' the bank with the other, ten hours a day. And what'd it get you? Eighty cents an hour an' "—Tom took his cigarette and butted the fiery end out against the horny palm of his hand—"these."

"*Santa Maria!*"

"Want to talk to you, Goony. Want to look over the bluff, too, at that stone up there. It'll take Kelly pret' near an hour to get this far and sumped in, anyhow."

They started up the slope, Tom feeling the ground under the four-foot brush, taking her up in a zigzag course like a hairpin road on a mountainside. Though the Seven carried a muffler on the exhaust stack that stuck up out of the hood before them, the blat of four big cylinders hauling fourteen tons of steel upgrade could outshout any man's conversation, so they sat without talking, Tom driving, Rivera watching his hands flick over the controls.

The bluff started in a low ridge running almost the length of the little island, like a lopsided backbone. Toward the center it rose abruptly, sent a wing out toward the rocky outcropping at the beach where their equipment had been unloaded, and then rose again to a small, almost square plateau area, half a mile square. It was humpy and rough until they could see all of it, when they realized how incredibly level it was, under the brush and ruins that covered it. In the center—and exactly in the center they realized suddenly—was a low, overgrown mound. Tom threw out the clutch and revved her down.

"Survey report said there was stone up here," Tom said, vaulting out of the seat. "Let's walk around some."

They walked toward the knoll, Tom's eyes casting about as he went. He stooped down into the heavy, short grass and scooped up a piece of stone, blue-gray, hard and brittle.

"Rivera—look at this. This is what the report was talking about. See—more of it. All in small pieces, though. We need big stuff for the bog if we can get it."

"Good stone?" asked Rivera.

"Yes, boy—but it don't belong here. Th' whole island's sand and marl and sandstone on the outcrop down yonder. This here's a bluestone, like diamond clay. Harder'n blazes. I never saw this stuff on a marl hill before. Or near one. Anyhow, root around and see if there is any big stuff."

They walked on. Rivera suddenly dipped down and pulled grass aside.

"Tom—here's a beeg one."

Tom came over and looked down at the corner of stone sticking up out of the topsoil. "Yeh. Goony, get your girlfriend over here and we'll root it out."

Rivera sprinted back to the idling dozer and climbed aboard. He brought the machine over to where Tom waited, stopped, stood up and peered over the front of the machine to locate the stone, then sat down and shifted gears. Before he could move the machine Tom was on the fender beside him, checking him with a hand on his arm.

"No, boy—no. Not third. First. And half throttle. That's it. Don't try to bash a rock out of the ground. Go on up to it easy; set your blade against it, lift it out, don't boot it out.

Take it with the middle of your blade, not the corner—get the load on both hydraulic cylinders. Who told you to do like that?"

"No one tol' me, Tom. I see a man do it, I do it."

"Yeah? Who was it?"

"Dennis, but—"

"Listen, Goony, if you want to learn anything from Dennis, watch him while he's on a pan. He dozes like he talks. That reminds me—what I wanted to talk to you about. You ever have any trouble with him?"

Rivera spread his hands. "How I have trouble when he never talk to me?"

"Well, that's all right then. You keep it that way. Dennis is O.K., I guess, but you better keep away from him."

He went on to tell the boy then about what Peebles had said concerning being an operator and a mechanic at the same time. Rivera's lean dark face fell, and his hand strayed to the blade control, touching it lightly, feeling the composition grip and the machined locknuts that held it. When Tom had quite finished he said:

"O.K., Tom—if you want, you break 'em, I feex 'em. But if you wan' help some time, I run *Daisy Etta* for you, no?"

"Sure, kid, sure. But don't forget, no man can do everything."

"You can do everything," said the boy.

Tom leaped off the machine and Rivera shifted into first and crept up to the stone, setting the blade gently against it. Taking the load, the mighty engine audibly bunched its muscles; Rivera opened the throttle a little and the machine set solidly against the stone, the tracks slipping, digging into the ground, piling loose earth up behind. Tom raised a fist, thumb up, and the boy began lifting his blade. The Seven lowered her snout like an ox pulling through mud; the front of the tracks buried themselves deeper and the blade slipped upward an inch on the rock, as if it were on a ratchet. The stone shifted, and suddenly heaved itself up out of the earth that covered it, bulging the sod aside like a ship's slow bow wave. And the blade lost its grip and slipped over the stone. Rivera slapped out the master clutch within an ace of letting the mass of it poke through his radiator core. Reversing, he set the blade against it again and rolled it at last into daylight.

Tom stood staring at it, scratching the back of his neck. Rivera got off the machine and stood beside him. For a long time they said nothing.

The stone was roughly rectangular, shaped like a brick with one end cut at about a thirty-degree angle. And on the angled face was a square-cut ridge, like the tongue on a piece of milled lumber. The stone was about 3 × 2 × 2 feet, and must have weighed six or seven hundred pounds.

"Now that," said Tom, bug-eyed, "didn't grow *here,* and if it did it never grew that way."

"*Una piedra de una casa,*" said Rivera softly. "Tom, there was a building here, no?"

Tom turned suddenly to look at the knoll.

"There is a building here—or what's left of it. Lord on'y knows how old—"

They stood there in the slowly dwindling light, staring at the knoll; and there came upon them a feeling of oppression, as if there were no wind and no sound anywhere. And yet there was wind, and behind them *Daisy Etta* whacked away with her muttering idle, and nothing had changed and—was that it? That nothing had changed? That nothing would change, or could, here?

Tom opened his mouth twice to speak, and couldn't, or didn't want to—he didn't know which. Rivera slumped down suddenly on his hunkers, back erect, and his eyes wide.

It grew very cold. "It's cold," Tom said, and his voice sounded harsh to him. And the wind blew warm on them, the earth was warm under Rivera's knees. The cold was not a lack of heat, but a lack of something else—warmth, but the specific warmth of life-force, perhaps. The feeling of oppression grew, as if their recognition of the strangeness of the place had started it, and their increasing sensitivity to it made it grow.

Rivera said something, quietly, in Spanish.

"What are you looking at?" asked Tom.

Rivera started violently, threw up an arm, as if to ward off the crash of Tom's voice.

"I . . . there is nothin' to see, Tom. I feel this way wance before. I dunno—" He shook his head, his eyes wide and blank. "An' after, there was being wan hell of a thunderstorm—" His voice petered out.

Tom took his shoulder and hauled him roughly to his feet. "Goony! You slap-happy?"

The boy smiled, almost gently. The down on his upper lip held little spheres of sweat. "I ain' nothin', Tom. I'm jus' scare like hell."

"You scare yourself right back up there on that cat and git to work," Tom roared. More quietly then he said, "I know there's something—wrong—here, Goony, but that ain't goin' to get us a runway built. Anyhow, I know what to do about a dawg 'at gits gun-shy. Ought to be able to do as much fer you. Git along to th' mound now and see if it ain't a cache o' big stone for us. We got a swamp down there to fill."

Rivera hesitated, started to speak, swallowed and then walked slowly over to the Seven. Tom stood watching him, closing his mind to the impalpable pressure of something, somewhere near, making his guts cold.

The bulldozer nosed over to the mound, grunting, reminding Tom suddenly that the machine's Spanish slang name was *puerco*—pig, boar. Rivera angled into the edge of the mound with the cutting corner of the blade. Dirt and brush curled up, fell away from the mound and loaded from the bank side, out along the moldboard. The boy finished his pass along the mound, carried the load past it and wasted it out on the flat, turned around and started back again.

Ten minutes later Rivera struck stone, the manganese steel screaming along it, a puff of gray dust spouting from the cutting corner. Tom knelt and examined it after the machine had passed. It was the same kind of stone they had found out on the flat—and shaped the same way. But here it was a wall, the angled faces of the block ends obviously tongued and grooved together.

Cold, cold as—

Tom took one deep breath and wiped sweat out of his eyes.

"I don't care," he whispered, "I got to have that stone. I got to fill me a swamp." He stood back and motioned to Rivera to blade into a chipped crevice in the buried wall.

The Seven swung into the wall and stopped while Rivera shifted into first, throttled down and lowered his blade. Tom looked up into his face. The boy's lips were white. He eased in the master clutch, the blade dipped and the corner swung neatly into the crevice.

The dozer blatted protestingly and began to crab sideways, pivoting on the end of the blade. Tom jumped out of the way, ran around behind the machine, which was almost parallel with the wall now, and stood in the clear, one hand ready to signal, his eyes on the straining blade. And then everything happened at once.

With a toothy snap the block started and came free, pivoting outward from its square end, bringing with it its neighbor. The block above them dropped, and the whole mound seemed to settle. And *something* whooshed out of the black hole where the rocks had been. Something like a fog, but not a fog that could be seen, something huge that could not be measured. With it came a gust of that cold which was not cold, and the smell of ozone, and the prickling crackle of a mighty static discharge.

Tom was fifty feet from the wall before he knew he had moved. He stopped and saw the Seven suddenly buck like a wild stallion, once, and Rivera turning over twice in the air. Tom shouted some meaningless syllable and tore over to the boy, where he sprawled in the rough grass, lifted him in his arms, and ran. Only then did he realize that he was running from the machine.

It was like a mad thing. Its moldboard rose and fell. It curved away from the mound, howling governor gone wild, controls flailing. The blade dug repeatedly into the earth, gouging it up in great dips through which the tractor plunged, clanking and bellowing furiously. It raced away in a great irregular arc, turned and came snorting back to the mound, where it beat at the buried wall, slewed and scraped and roared.

Tom reached the edge of the plateau sobbing for breath, and kneeling, laid the boy gently down on the grass.

"Goony, boy . . . hey—"

The long silken eyelashes fluttered, lifted. Something wrenched in Tom as he saw the eyes, rolled right back so that only the whites showed. Rivera drew a long quivering breath which caught suddenly. He coughed twice, threw his head from side to side so violently that Tom took it between his hands and steadied it.

"*Ay . . . Maria madre . . . que ha me pasado,* Tom—w'at has happen to me?"

"Fell off the Seven, stupid. You . . . how you feel?"

Rivera scrabbled at the ground, got his elbows half under him, then sank back weakly. "Feel O.K. Headache like hell. W-w'at happen to my feets?"

"Feet? They hurt?"

"No hurt—" The young face went gray, the lips tightened with effort. "No, nothin', Tom."

"You can't move 'em?"

Rivera shook his head, still trying. Tom stood up. "You take it easy. I'll go get Kelly. Be right back."

He walked away quickly and when Rivera called to him he did not turn around. Tom had seen a man with a broken back before.

At the edge of the little plateau Tom stopped, listening. In the deepening twilight he could see the bulldozer standing by the mound. The motor was running; she had not stalled herself. But what stopped Tom was that she wasn't idling, but revving up and down as if an impatient hand were on the throttle—*hroom hroooom,* running up and up far faster than even a broken governor should permit, then coasting down to near silence, broken by the explosive punctuation of sharp and irregular firing. Then it would run up and up again, almost screaming, sustaining a r.p.m. that threatened every moving part, shaking the great machine like some deadly ague.

Tom walked swiftly toward the Seven, a puzzled and grim frown on his weatherbeaten face. Governors break down occasionally, and once in a while you will have a motor tear itself to pieces, revving up out of control. But it will either do that or it will rev down and quit. If an operator is fool enough to leave his machine with the master clutch engaged, the machine will take off and run the way the Seven had— but it will not turn unless the blade corner catches in something unresisting, and then the chances are very strong that it will stall. But in any case, it was past reason for any machine to act this way, revving up and down, running, turning, lifting and dropping the blade.

The motor slowed as he approached, and at last settled

down into something like a steady and regular idle. Tom had the sudden crazy impression that it was watching him. He shrugged off the feeling, walked up and laid a hand on the fender.

The Seven reacted like a wild stallion. The big Diesel roared, and Tom distinctly saw the master clutch lever snap back over center. He leaped clear, expecting the machine to jolt forward, but apparently it was in a reverse gear, for it shot backward, one track locked, and the near end of the blade swung in a swift vicious arc, breezing a bare fraction of an inch past his hip as he danced back out of the way.

And as if it had bounced off a wall, the tractor had shifted and was bearing down on him, the twelve-foot blade rising, the two big headlights looming over him on their bowlegged supports, looking like the protruding eyes of some mighty toad. Tom had no choice but to leap straight up and grasp the top of the blade in his two hands, leaning back hard to brace his feet against the curved moldboard. The blade dropped and sank into the soft topsoil, digging a deep little swale in the ground. The earth loading on the moldboard rose and churned around Tom's legs; he stepped wildly, keeping them clear of the rolling drag of it. Up came the blade then, leaving a four-foot pile at the edge of the pit; down and up the tractor raced as the tracks went into it; up and up as they climbed the pile of dirt. A quick balance and overbalance as the machine lurched up and over like a motorcycle taking a jump off a ramp, and then a spine-shaking crash as fourteen tons of metal smashed blade-first into the ground.

Part of the leather from Tom's tough palms stayed with the blade as he was flung off. He went head over heels backwards, but had his feet gathered and sprang as they touched the ground; for he knew that no machine could bury its blade like that and get out easily. He leaped to the top of the blade, got one hand on the radiator cap, vaulted. Perversely, the cap broke from its hinge and came away in his hand, in that split instant when only that hand rested on anything. Off balance, he landed on his shoulder with his legs flailing the air, his body sliding off the hood's smooth shoulder toward the track now churning the earth beneath. He made a wild grab at the air intake pipe, barely had it in his fingers when the dozer freed itself and shot backwards up and over the hump. Again that breathless flight pivoting over the top, and the clanking crash as the machine landed, this time almost flat on its tracks.

The jolt tore Tom's hand away, and as he slid back over the hood the crook of his elbow caught the exhaust stack, the dull red metal biting into his flesh. He grunted and clamped the arm around it. His momentum carried him around it, and his feet crashed into the steering clutch levers. Hooking one with his instep, he doubled his legs and whipped himself back, scrabbling at the smooth warm metal, crawling frantically backward until he finally fell heavily into the seat.

"Now," he gritted through a red wall of pain, "you're gonna git operated." And he kicked out the master clutch.

The motor wailed, with the load taken off so suddenly. Tom grasped the throttle, his thumb clamped down on the ratchet release, and he shoved the lever forward to shut off the fuel.

It wouldn't shut off; it went down to a slow idle, but it wouldn't shut off.

"There's one thing you can't do without," he muttered, "compression."

He stood up and leaned around the dash, reaching for the compression-release lever. As he came up out of the seat, the engine revved up again. He turned to the throttle, which had snapped back into the "open" position. As his hand touched it the master clutch lever snapped in and the howling machine lurched forward with a jerk that snapped his head on his shoulders and threw him heavily back into the seat. He snatched at the hydraulic blade control and threw it to "float" position; and then as the falling moldboard touched the ground, into "power down." The cutting edge bit into the ground and the engine began to labor. Holding the blade control, he pushed the throttle forward with his other hand. One of the steering clutch levers whipped back and struck him agonizingly on the kneecap. He involuntarily let go of the blade control and the moldboard began to rise. The engine began to turn faster and he realized that it was not responding to the throttle. Cursing, he leaped to his feet; the suddenly flailing levers struck him three times in the groin before he could get between them.

Blind with pain, Tom clung gasping to the dash. The oil-pressure gauge fell off the dash to his right, with a tinkling of broken glass, and from its broken quarter-inch line scalding oil drenched him. The shock of it snapped back his wavering consciousness. Ignoring the blows of the left steering clutch and the master clutch which had started the same mad punching, he bent over the left end of the dash and grasped the compression lever. The tractor rushed forward and spun sickeningly, and Tom knew he was thrown. But as he felt himself leave the decking his hand punched the compression lever down. The great valves at the cylinder heads opened and locked open; atomized fuel and superheated air chattered out, and as Tom's head and shoulders struck the ground the great wild machine rolled to a stop, stood silently except for the grumble of water boiling in the cooling system.

Minutes later Tom raised his head and groaned. He rolled over and sat up, his chin on his knees, washed by wave after wave of pain. As they gradually subsided, he crawled to the machine and pulled himself to his feet, hand over hand on the track. And groggily he began to cripple the tractor, at least for the night.

He opened the cock under the fuel tank, left the warm yellow fluid gushing out on the ground. He opened the drain on the reservoir by the injection pump. He found a piece of wire in the crank box and with it tied down the compression release lever. He crawled up on the machine, wrenched the hood and ball jar off the air intake precleaner, pulled off his shirt and stuffed it down the pipe. He pushed the throttle all the way forward and locked it with the locking pin. And he shut off the fuel on the main line from the tank to the pump.

Then he climbed heavily to the ground and slogged back to the edge of the plateau where he had left Rivera.

They didn't know Tom was hurt until an hour and a half later—there had been too much to do—rigging a stretcher for the Puerto Rican, building him a shelter, an engine crate with an Army pup tent for a roof. They brought out the first-aid kit and the medical books and did what they could—tied and splinted and dosed with an opiate. Tom was a mass of bruises, and his right arm, where it had hooked the exhaust stack, was a flayed mass. They fixed him up then, old Peebles handling the sulfa powder and bandages like a trained nurse. And only then was there talk.

"I've seen a man thrown off a pan," said Dennis, as they

sat around the coffee urn munching C rations. "Sittin' up on the armrest on a cat, looking backwards. Cat hit a rock and bucked. Threw him off on the track. Stretched him out ten feet long." He in-whistled some coffee to dilute the mouthful of food he had been talking around, and masticated noisily. "Man's a fool to set up there on one side of his butt even on a pan. Can't see why th' goony was doin' it on a dozer."

"He wasn't," said Tom.

Kelly rubbed his pointed jaw. "He set flat on th' seat an' was th'owed?"

"That's right."

After an unbelieving silence Dennis said, "What was he doin'—drivin' over sixty?"

Tom looked around the circle of faces lit up by the over-artificial brilliance of a pressure lantern, and wondered what the reaction would be if he told it all just as it was. He had to say something, and it didn't look as if it could be the truth.

"He was workin'," he said finally. "Bucking stone out of the wall of an old building up on the mesa there. One turned loose an' as it did the governor must've gone haywire. She bucked like a loco hoss and run off."

"Run off?"

Tom opened his mouth and closed it again, and just nodded.

Dennis said, "Well, reckon that's what happens when you put a mechanic to operatin'."

"That had nothin' to do with it," Tom snapped.

Peebles spoke up quickly. "Tom—what about the Seven? Broke up any?"

"Some," said Tom. "Better look at the steering clutches. An' she was hot."

"Head's cracked," said Harris, a burly young man with shoulders like a buffalo and a famous thirst.

"How do you know?"

"Saw it when Al and me went up with the stretcher to get the kid while you all were building the shelter. Hot water runnin' down the side of the block."

"You mean you walked all the way out to the mound to look at that tractor while the kid was lyin' there? I told you where he was!"

"Out to the mound!" Al Knowles's bulging eyes teetered

out of their sockets. "We found that cat stalled twenty feet away from where the kid was!"

"What!"

"That's right, Tom," said Harris. "What's eatin' you? Where'd you leave it?"

"I told you . . . by the mound . . . the ol' building we cut into."

"Leave the startin' motor runnin'?"

"Starting motor?" Tom's mind caught the picture of the small, two-cylinder gasoline engine bolted to the side of the big diesel's crankcase, coupled through a Bendix gear and clutch to the flywheel of the diesel to crank it. He remembered his last glance at the still machine, silent but for the sound of water boiling. "Hell no!"

Al and Harris exchanged a glance. "I guess you were sort of slap-happy at the time, Tom," Harris said, not unkindly. "When we were halfway up the hill we heard it, and you know you can't mistake that racket. Sounded like it was under a load."

Tom beat softly at his temples with his clenched fists. "I left that machine dead," he said quietly. "I got compression off her and tied down the lever. I even stuffed my shirt in the intake. I drained the tank. But—I didn't touch the starting motor."

Peebles wanted to know why he had gone to all that trouble. Tom just looked vaguely at him and shook his head. "I shoulda pulled the wires. I never thought about the starting motor," he whispered. Then, "Harris—you say you found the starting motor running when you got to the top?"

"No—she was stalled. And hot—awmighty hot. I'd say the startin' motor was seized up tight. That must be it, Tom. You left the startin' motor runnin' and somehow engaged the clutch an' Bendix." His voice lost conviction as he said it—it takes seventeen separate motions to start a tractor of this type. "Anyhow, she was in gear an' crawled along on the little motor."

"I done that once," said Chub. "Broke a con rod on an Eight, on a highway job. Walked her about three-quarters of a mile on the startin' motor that way. Only I had to stop every hundred yards and let her cool down some."

Not without sarcasm, Dennis said, "Seems to me like the

Seven was out to get th' goony. Made one pass at him and then went back to finish the job."

Al Knowles haw-hawed extravagantly.

Tom stood up, shaking his head, and went off among the crates to the hospital they had jury-rigged for the kid.

A dim light was burning inside, and Rivera lay very still, with his eyes closed. Tom leaned in the doorway—the open end of the engine crate—and watched him for a moment. Behind him he could hear the murmur of the crew's voices; the night was otherwise windless and still. Rivera's face was the peculiar color that olive skin takes when drained of blood. Tom looked at his chest and for a panicky moment thought he could discern no movement there. He entered and put a hand over the boy's heart. Rivera shivered, his eyes flew open, and he drew a sudden breath which caught raggedly at the back of his throat. "Tom . . . Tom!" he cried weakly.

"O. K., Goony . . . *que pasa?*"

"She comeen back . . . Tom!"

"Who?"

"*El de siete.*"

Daisy Etta—"She ain't comin' back, kiddo. You're off the mesa now. Keep your chin up, fella."

Rivera's dark, doped eyes stared up at him without expression. Tom moved back and the eyes continued to stare. They weren't seeing anything. "Go to sleep," he whispered. The eyes closed instantly.

Kelly was saying that nobody ever got hurt on a construction job unless somebody was dumb. "An' most times you don't realize how dumb what you're doin' is until somebody does get hurt."

"The dumb part was gettin' a kid, an' not even an operator at that, up on a machine," said Dennis in his smuggest voice.

"I heard you try to sing that song before," said old Peebles quietly. "I hate to have to point out anything like this to a man because it don't do any good to make comparisons. But I've worked with that fella Rivera for a long time now, an' I've seen 'em as good but doggone few better. As far as you're concerned, you're O. K. on a pan, but the kid could give you cards and spades and still make you look like a cost accountant on a dozer."

Dennis half rose and mouthed something filthy. He looked

at Al Knowles for backing and got it. He looked around the circle and got none. Peebles lounged back, sucking on his pipe, watching from under those bristling brows. Dennis subsided, running now on another tack.

"So what does that prove? The better you say he is, the less reason he had to fall off a cat and get himself hurt."

"I haven't got the thing straight yet," said Chub, in a voice whose tone indicated "I hate to admit it, but—"

About this time Tom returned, like a sleepwalker, standing with the brilliant pressure lantern between him and Dennis. Dennis rambled right on, not knowing he was anywhere near: "That's something you never will find out. That Puerto Rican is a pretty husky kid. Could be Tom said somethin' he didn't like an' he tried to put a knife in Tom's back. They all do, y'know. Tom didn't get all that bashin' around just stoppin' a machine. They must've went round an' round for a while an' the goony wound up with a busted back. Tom sets the dozer to walk him down while he lies there and comes on down here and tries to tell us—" His voice fluttered to a stop as Tom loomed over him.

Tom grabbed the pan operator up by the slack of his shirt front with his uninjured arm and shook him like an empty burlap bag.

"Skunk," he growled. "I oughta lower th' boom on you." He set Dennis on his feet and backhanded his face with the edge of his forearm. Dennis went down—cowered down, rather than fell. "Aw, Tom, I was just talkin'. Just a joke, Tom, I was just—"

"Yellow, too," snarled Tom, stepping forward, raising a solid Texan boot. Peebles barked "Tom!" and the foot came back to the ground.

"Out o' my sight," rumbled the foreman. "Git!"

Dennis got. Al Knowles said vaguely, "Naow, Tom, y'all cain't—"

"You, y'wall-eyed string bean!" Tom raved, his voice harsh and strained. "Go 'long with yer Siamese twin!"

"O. K., O. K.," said Al, white-faced, and disappeared into the dark after Dennis.

"Nuts to this," said Chub. "I'm turnin' in." He went to a crate and hauled out a mosquito-hooded sleeping bag and went off without another word. Harris and Kelly, who were both on their feet, sat down again. Old Peebles hadn't moved.

Tom stood staring out into the dark, his arms straight at his sides, his fists knotted.

"Sit down," said Peebles gently. Tom turned and stared at him.

"Sit down. I can't change that dressing 'less you do." He pointed at the bandage around Tom's elbow. It was red, a widening stain, the tattered tissues having parted as the big Georgian bunched his infuriated muscles. He sat down.

"Talkin' about dumbness," said Harris calmly, as Peebles went to work, "I was about to say that I got the record. I done the dumbest thing anybody ever did on a machine. You can't top it."

"I could," said Kelly. "Runnin' a crane dragline once. Put her in boom gear and started to boom her up. Had an eighty-five-foot stick on her. Machine was standing on wooden mats in th' middle of a swamp. Heard the motor miss and got out of the saddle to look at the filer-glass. Messed around back there longer than I figured, and the boom went straight up in the air and fell backwards over the cab. Th' jolt tilted my mats an' she slid backwards slowly and stately as you please, butt-first into the mud. Buried up to the eyeballs, she was." He laughed quietly. "Looked like a ditching machine!"

"I still say I done the dumbest thing ever, bar none," said Harris. "It was on a river job, widening a channel. I come back to work from a three-day binge, still rum-dumb. Got up on a dozer an' was workin' around on the edge of a twenty-foot cliff. Down at the foot of the cliff was a big hickory tree, an' growin' right along the edge was a great big limb. I got the dopey idea I should break it off. I put one track on the limb and the other on the cliff edge and run out away from the trunk. I was about halfway out, an' the branch saggin' some, before I thought what would happen if it broke. Just about then it did break. You know hickory—if it breaks at all it breaks altogether. So down we go into thirty feet of water—me an' the cat. I got out from under somehow. When all them bubbles stopped comin' up I swum around lookin' down at it. I was still paddlin' around when the superintendent came rushin' up. He wants to know what's up. I yell at him, 'Look down there, the way that water is movin' an' shiftin', looks like the cat is workin' down there.' He pursed his lips and *tsk tsked*. My, that man said some nasty things to me."

"Where'd you get your next job?" Kelly exploded.

"Oh, he didn't fire me," said Harris soberly. "Said he couldn't afford to fire a man as dumb as that. Said he wanted me around to look at whenever he felt bad."

Tom said, "Thanks, you guys. That's as good a way as any of sayin' that everybody makes mistakes." He stood up, examining the new dressing, turning his arm in front of the lantern. "You all can think what you please, but I don't recollect there was any dumbness went on on that mesa this evenin'. That's finished with, anyway. Do I have to say that Dennis's idea about it is all wet?"

Haris said one foul word that completely disposed of Dennis and anything he might say.

Peebles said, "It'll be all right. Dennis an' his pop-eyed friend'll hang together, but they don't amount to anything. Chub'll do whatever he's argued into."

"So you got 'em all lined up, hey?" Tom shrugged. "In the meantime, are we going to get an airfield built?"

"We'll get it built," Peebles said. "Only—Tom, I got no right to give you any advice, but go easy on the rough stuff after this. It does a lot of harm."

"I will if I can," said Tom gruffly. They broke up and turned in.

Peebles was right. It did do harm. It made Dennis use the word "murder" when they found, in the morning, that Rivera had died during the night.

The work progressed in spite of everything that had happened. With equipment like that, it's hard to slow things down. Kelly bit two cubic yards out of the bluff with every swing of the big shovel, and Dumptors are the fastest short-haul earth movers yet devised. Dennis kept the service road clean for them with his pan, and Tom and Chub spelled each other on the bulldozer they had detached from its pan to make up for the lack of the Seven, spending their alternate periods with transit and stakes. Peebles was rod-man for the surveys, and in between times worked on setting up his field shop, keeping the water cooler and battery chargers running, and lining up his forge and welding tables. The operators fueled and serviced their own equipment, and there was little delay. Rocks and marl came out of the growing cavity in the side of the central mesa—a whole third of it had to come out—were spun down to the edge of the swamp, which lay across the lower end of the projected runway, in the hornet-howling dump-tractors, their big driving wheels churned up vast clouds of dust, and were dumped and spread and walked in by the whining two-cycle dozer. When muck began to pile up in front of the fill, it was blasted out of the way with carefully placed charges of sixty percent dynamite and the craters filled with rocks, stone from the ruins, and surfaced with easily compacting marl, run out of a clean deposit by the pan.

And when he had his shop set up, Peebles went up the hill to get the Seven. When he got to it he just stood there for a moment scratching his head, and then, shaking his head, he ambled back down the hill and went for Tom.

"Been looking at the Seven," he said, when he had flagged the moaning two-cycle and Tom had climbed off.

"What'd you find?"

Peebles held out an arm. "A list as long as that." He shook his head. "Tom, what really happened up there?"

"Governor went haywire and she run away," Tom said promptly, deadpan.

"Yeah, but—" For a long moment he held Tom's gaze. Then he sighed. "O. K., Tom. Anyhow, I can't do a thing up there. We'll have to bring her back and I'll have to have this tractor to tow her down. And first I have to have some help—the track idler adjustment bolt's busted and the right track is off the track rollers."

"Oh-h-h. So that's why she couldn't get to the kid, running on the starting motor. Track would hardly turn, hey?"

"It's a miracle she ran as far as she did. That track is really jammed up. Riding right up on the roller flanges. And that ain't the half of it. The head's gone, like Harris said, and Lord only knows what I'll find when I open her up."

"Why bother?"

"What?"

"We can get along without that dozer," said Tom suddenly. "Leave her where she is. There's lots more for you to do."

"But what for?"

"Well, there's no call to go to all that trouble."

Peebles scratched the side of his nose and said, "I got a new head, track master pins—even a spare starting motor. I

got tools to make what I don't stock." He pointed at the long
row of dumps left by the hurtling dump-tractors while they
had been talking. "You got a pan tied up because you're
using this machine to doze with, and you can't tell me you
can't use another one. You're gonna have to shut down one
or two o' those Dumptors if you go on like this."

"I had all that figured out as soon as I opened my mouth,"
Tom said sullenly. "Let's go."

They climbed on the tractor and took off, stopping for a
moment at the beach outcropping to pick up a cable and
some tools.

Daisy Etta sat at the edge of the mesa, glowering out of
her stilted headlights at the soft sward which still bore the
impression of a young body and the tramplings of the
stretcher-bearers. Her general aspect was woebegone—there
were scratches on her olive-drab paint and the bright metal of
the scratches was already dulled red by the earliest powder-
rust. And though the ground was level, she was not, for her
right track was off its lower rollers, and she stood slightly
canted, like a man who has had a broken hip. And whatever
passed for consciousness within her mulled over that paradox
of the bulldozer that every operator must go through while he
is learning his own machine.

It is the most difficult thing of all for the beginner to understand, that paradox. A bulldozer is a crawling powerhouse,
a behemoth of noise and toughness, the nearest thing to the
famous irresistible force. The beginner, awed and with the
pictures of unconquerable Army tanks printed on his mind
from the newsreels, takes all in his stride and with a sense of
limitless power treats all obstacles alike, not knowing the
fragility of a cast-iron radiator core, the mortality of tempered manganese, the friability of overheated babbitt, and
most of all, the ease with which a tractor can bury itself in
mud. Climbing off to stare at a machine which he has
reduced in twenty seconds to a useless hulk, or which was
running a half-minute before on ground where it now has its
tracks out of sight, he has that sense of guilty disappointment
which overcomes any man on having made an error in judgment.

So, as she stood, *Daisy Etta* was broken and useless. These
soft persistent bipeds had built her, and if they were like any

other race that built machines, they could care for them. The ability to reverse the tension of a spring, or twist a control rod, or reduce to zero the friction in a nut and lock-washer, was not enough to repair the crack in a cylinder head nor bearings welded to a crankshaft in an overheated starting motor. There had been a lesson to learn. It had been learned. *Daisy Etta* would be repaired, and the next time—well, at least she would know her own weaknesses.

Tom swung the two-cycle machine and edged in next to the Seven, with the edge of his blade all but touching *Daisy Etta's* push-beam. They got off and Peebles bent over the drum-tight right track.

"Watch yourself," said Tom.

"Watch what?"

"Oh—nothin', I guess." He circled the machine, trained eyes probing over frame and fittings. He stepped forward suddenly and grasped the fuel-tank drain cock. It was closed. He opened it; golden oil gushed out. He shut it off, climbed up on the machine and opened the fuel cap on top of the tank. He pulled out the bayonet gauge, wiped it in the crook of his knee, dipped and withdrew it.

The tank was more than three quarters full.

"What's the matter?" asked Peebles, staring curiously at Tom's drawn face.

"Peeby, I opened the cock to drain this tank. I left it with oil runnin' out on the ground. She shut herself off."

"Now, Tom, you're lettin' this thing get you down. You just thought you did. I've seen a main-line valve shut itself off when it's worn bad, but only 'cause the fuel pump pulls it shut when the motor's runnin'. But not a gravity drain."

"Main-line valve?" Tom pulled the seat up and looked. One glance was enough to show him that this one was open.

"She opened this one, too."

"O. K.—O. K. Don't look at me like that!" Peebles was as near to exasperation as he could possibly get. "What difference does it make?"

Tom did not answer. He was not the type of man who, when faced with something beyond his understanding, would begin to doubt his own sanity. His was a dogged insistence that what he saw and sensed was what had actually happened. In him was none of the fainting fear of madness that another, more sensitive, man might feel. He doubted neither himself nor his evidence, and so could free his mind for searching out the consuming "why" of a problem. He knew instinctively that to share "unbelievable" happenings with anyone else, even if they had really occurred, was to put even further obstacles in his way. So he kept his clamlike silence and stubbornly, watchfully, investigated.

The slipped track was so tightly drawn up on the roller flanges that there could be no question of pulling the master pin and opening the track up. It would have to be worked back in place—a very delicate operation, for a little force applied in the wrong direction would be enough to run the track off altogether. To complicate things, the blade of the Seven was down on the ground and would have to be lifted before the machine could be maneuvered, and its hydraulic hoist was useless without the motor.

Peebles unhooked twenty feet of half-inch cable from the rear of the smaller dozer, scratched a hole in the ground under the Seven's blade, and pushed the eye of the cable through. Climbing over the moldboard, he slipped the eye on to the big towing hook bolted to the underside of the belly-guard. The other end of the cable he threw out on the ground in front of the machine. Tom mounted the other dozer and swung into place, ready to tow. Peebles hooked the cable onto Tom's drawbar, hopped up on the Seven. He put her in neutral, disengaged the master clutch, and put the blade control over into "float" position, then raised an arm.

Tom perched upon the armrest of his machine, looking backwards, moved slowly, taking up the slack in the cable. It straightened and grew taut, and as it did it forced the Seven's blade upward. Peebles waved for slack and put the blade control into "hold." The cable bellied downward away from the blade.

"Hydraulic system's O. K., anyhow," called Peebles, as Tom throttled down. "Move over and take a strain to the right, sharp as you can without fouling the cable on the track. We'll see if we can walk this track back on."

Tom backed up, cut sharply to the right, and drew the cable out almost at right angles to the other machine. Peebles held the right track of the Seven with the brake and released both steering clutches. The left track now could turn free, the right not at all. Tom was running at a quarter throttle in his lowest gear, so that his machine barely crept along, taking the strain. The Seven shook gently and began to pivot on the taut right track, unbelievable foot-pounds of energy coming to bear on the front of the track where it rode high up on the idler wheel. Peebles released the right brake with his foot and applied it again in a series of skilled, deft jerks. The track would move a few inches and stop again, force being applied forward and sideways alternately, urging the track persuasively back in place. Then, a little jolt and she was in, riding true on the five truck rollers, the two track carrier rollers, the driving sprocket and the idler.

Peebles got off and stuck his head in between the sprocket and the rear carrier, squinting down and sideways to see if there were any broken flanges or roller bushes. Tom came over and pulled him out by the seat of his trousers. "Time enough for that when you get her in the shop," he said, masking his nervousness. "Reckon she'll roll?"

"She'll roll. I never saw a track in that condition come back that easy. By gosh, it's as if she was tryin' to help!"

"They'll do it sometimes," said Tom stiffly. "You better take the tow-tractor, Peeby. I'll stay with this'n."

"Anything you say."

And cautiously they took the steep slope down, Tom barely holding the brakes, giving the other machine a straight pull all the way. And so they brought *Daisy Etta* down to Peebles's outdoor shop, where they pulled her cylinder head off, took off her starting motor, pulled out a burned clutch facing, had her quite helpless—

And put her together again.

"I tell you it was outright, cold-blooded murder," said Dennis hotly. "An' here we are takin' orders from a guy like that. What are we goin' to do about it?" They were standing by the cooler—Dennis had run his machine there to waylay Chub.

Chub Horton's cigar went down and up like a semaphore with a short circuit. "We'll skip it. The blacktopping crew will be here in another two weeks or so, an' we can make a report. Besides, I don't know what happened up there any more than you do. In the meantime we got a runway to build."

"You don't know what happened up there? Chub, you're a smart man. Smart enough to run this job better than Tom

Jaeger even if he wasn't crazy. And you're surely smart
enough not to believe all that cock and bull about that tractor
runnin' out from under that grease-monkey. Listen—" he
leaned forward and tapped Chub's chest. "He said it was the
governor. I saw that governor myself an' heard ol' Peebles
say there wasn't a thing wrong with it. Th' throttle control
rod had slipped off its yoke, yeah—but you know what a
tractor will do when the throttle control goes out. It'll idle or
stall. It won't run away, whatever."

"Well, maybe so, but—"

"But nothin'! A guy that'll commit murder ain't sane. If he
did it once, he can do it again and I ain't fixin' to let that
happen to me."

Two things crossed Chub's steady but not too bright mind
at this. One was that Dennis, whom he did not like but could
not shake, was trying to force him into something that he did
not want to do. The other was that under all of his swift talk
Dennis was scared spitless.

"What do you want to do—call up the sheriff?"

Dennis ha-ha-ed appreciatively—one of the reasons he was
so hard to shake. "I'll tell you what we can do. As long as we
have you here, he isn't the only man who knows the work. If
we stop takin' orders from him, you can give 'em as good or
better. An' there won't be anything he can do about it."

"Doggone it, Dennis," said Chub, with sudden exasperation. "What do you think you're doin'—handin' me over the
keys to the kingdom or something? What do you want to see
me bossin' around here for?" He stood up. "Suppose we did
what you said? Would it get the field built any quicker?
Would it get me any more money in my pay envelope? What
do you think I want—glory? I passed up a chance to run for
councilman once. You think I'd raise a finger to get a bunch
of mugs to do what I say—when they do it anyway?"

"Aw, Chub—I wouldn't cause trouble just for the fun of it.
That's not what I mean at all. But unless we do something
about that guy we ain't safe. Can't you get that through your
head?"

"Listen, windy. If a man keeps busy enough he can't get
into no trouble. That goes for Tom—you might keep that in
mind. But it goes for you, too. Get back up on that rig an'
get back to the marl pit." Dennis, completely taken by surprise, turned to his machine.

"It's a pity you can't move earth with your mouth," said Chub, as he walked off. "They could have left you to do this job singlehanded."

Chub walked slowly toward the outcropping, switching at beach pebbles with a grade stake and swearing to himself. He was essentially a simple man and believed in the simplest possible approach to everything. He liked a job where he could do everything required and where nothing turned up to complicate things. He had been in the grading business for a long time as an operator and survey party boss, and he was remarkable for one thing—he had always held aloof from the cliques and internecine politics that are the breath of life to most construction men. He was disturbed and troubled at the back-stabbing that went on around him on various jobs. If it was blunt, he was disgusted, and subtlety simply left him floundering and bewildered. He was stupid enough so that his basic honesty manifested itself in his speech and actions, and he had learned that complete honesty in dealing with men above and below him was almost invariably painful to all concerned, but he had not the wit to act otherwise, and did not try to. If he had a bad tooth, he had it pulled out as soon as he could. If he got a raw deal from a superintendent over him, that superintendent would get told exactly what the trouble was, and if he didn't like it, there were other jobs. And if the pulling and hauling of cliques got in his hair, he had always said so and left. Or he had sounded off and stayed; his completely selfish reaction to things that got in the way of his work had earned him a lot of regard from men he had worked under. And so, in this instance, he had no hesitation about choosing a course of action. Only—how did you go about asking a man if he was a murderer?

He found the foreman with an enormous wrench in his hand, tightening up the new track adjustment bolt they had installed in the Seven.

"Hey, Chub! Glad you turned up. Let's get a piece of pipe over the end of this thing and really bear down." Chub went for the pipe, and they fitted it over the handle of the four-foot wrench and hauled until the sweat ran down their backs, Tom checking the track clearance occasionally with a crowbar. He finally called it good enough and they stood there in the sun gasping for breath.

"Tom," panted Chub, "did you kill that Puerto Rican?"

Tom's head came up as if someone had burned the back of his neck with a cigarette.

"Because," said Chub, "if you did you can't go on runnin' this job."

Tom said, "That's a lousy thing to kid about."

"You know I ain't kiddin'. Well, did you?"

"No!" Tom sat down on a keg, wiped his face with a bandanna. "What's got into you?"

"I just wanted to know. Some of the boys are worried about it."

Tom's eyes narrowed. "Some of the boys, huh? I think I get it. Listen to me, Chub. Rivera was killed by that thing there." He thumbed over his shoulder at the Seven, which was standing ready now, awaiting only the building of a broken cutting corner on the blade. Peebles was winding up the welding machine as he spoke. "If you mean, did I put him up on the machine before he was thrown, the answer is yes. That much I killed him, and don't think I don't feel it. I had a hunch something was wrong up there, but I couldn't put my finger on it and I certainly didn't think anybody was going to get hurt."

"Well, what was wrong?"

"I still don't know." Tom stood up. "I'm tired of beatin' around the bush, Chub, and I don't much care any more what anybody thinks. There's somethin' wrong with that Seven, something that wasn't built into her. They don't make tractors better'n that one, but whatever it was happened up there on the mesa has queered this one. Now go ahead and think what you like, and dream up any story you want to tell the boys. In the meantime you can pass the word—nobody runs that machine but me, understand? Nobody!"

"Tom—"

Tom's patience broke. "That's all I'm going to say about it! If anybody else gets hurt, it's going to be me, understand? What more do you want?"

He strode off, boiling. Chub stared after him, and after a long moment reached up and took the cigar from his lips. Only then did he realize that he had bitten it in two; half the butt was still inside his mouth. He spat and stood there, shaking his head.

"How's she going, Peeby?"

Peebles looked up from the welding machine. "Hi, Chub, have her ready for you in twenty minutes." He gauged the distance between the welding machine and the big tractor. "I should have forty feet of cable," he said, looking at the festoons of arc and ground cables that hung from the storage hooks in the back of the welder. "Don't want to get a tractor over here to move the thing, and don't feel like cranking up the Seven just to get it close enough." He separated the arc cable and threw it aside, walked to the tractor, paying the ground cable off his arm. He threw out the last of his slack and grasped the ground clamp when he was eight feet from the machine. Taking it in his left hand, he pulled hard, reaching out with his right to grasp the moldboard of the Seven, trying to get it far enough to clamp on to the machine.

Chub stood there watching him, chewing on his cigar, absentmindedly diddling with the controls on the arc-welder. He pressed the starter button, and the six-cylinder motor responded with a purr. He spun the work-selector dials idly, threw the arc generator switch—

A bolt of incredible energy, thin, searing, blue-white, left the rod-holder at his feet, stretched itself *fifty feet* across to Peebles, whose fingers had just touched the moldboard of the tractor. Peebles's head and shoulders were surrounded for a second by a violet nimbus, and then he folded over and dropped. A circuit breaker clacked behind the control board of the welder, but too late. The Seven rolled slowly backward, without firing, on level ground, until it brought up against a road-roller.

Chub's cigar was gone, and he didn't notice it. He had the knuckles of his right hand in his mouth, and his teeth sunk into the pudgy flesh. His eyes protruded; he crouched there and quivered, literally frightened out of his mind. For old Peebles was almost burned in two.

They buried him next to Rivera. There wasn't much talk afterwards; the old man had been a lot closer to all of them than they had realized until now. Harris, for once in his rum-dumb, lighthearted life, was quiet and serious, and Kelly's walk seemed to lose some of its litheness. Hour after hour Dennis's flabby mouth worked, and he bit at his lower lip until it was swollen and tender. Al Knowles seemed more or less unaffected, as was to be expected from a man who had something less than the brains of a chicken. Chub Horton had snapped out of it after a couple of hours and was very nearly himself again. And in Tom Jaeger swirled a black, furious anger at this unknowable curse that had struck the camp.

And they kept working. There was nothing else to do. The shovel kept up its rhythmic swing and dig, swing and dump, and the Dumptors screamed back and forth between it and the little that there was left of the swamp. The upper end of the runway was grassed off; Chub and Tom set grade stakes and Dennis began the long job of cutting and filling the humpy surface with his pan. Harris manned the other and followed him, a cut behind. The shape of the runway emerged from the land, and then that of the paralleling taxiway; and three days went by. The horror of Peebles's death wore off enough so that they could talk about it, and very little of the talk helped anybody. Tom took his spells at everything, changing over with Kelly to give him a rest from the shovel, making a few rounds with a pan, putting in hours on a Dumptor. His arm was healing slowly but clean, and he worked grimly in spite of it, taking a perverse sort of pleasure from the pain of it. Every man on the job watched his machine with the solicitude of a mother with her firstborn; a serious breakdown would have been disastrous without a highly skilled mechanic.

The only concession that Tom allowed himself in regard to Peebles's death was to corner Kelly one afternoon and ask him about the welding machine. Part of Kelly's rather patchy past had been spent in a technical college, where he had studied electrical engineering and women. He had learned a little of the former and enough of the latter to get him thrown out on his ear. So, on the off-chance that he might know something about the freak arc, Tom put it to him.

Kelly pulled off his high-gauntlet gloves and batted sandflies with them. "What sort of an arc was that? Boy, you got me there. Did you ever hear of a welding machine doing like that before?"

"I did not. A welding machine just don't have that sort o' push. I saw a man get a full jolt from a 400-amp welder once, an' although it sat him down it didn't hurt him any."

"It's not amperage that kills people," said Kelly, "it's volt-

age. Voltage is the pressure behind a current, you know.
Take an amount of water, call it amperage. If I throw it in
your face, it won't hurt you. If I put it through a small hose
you'll feel it. But if I pump it through the tiny holes on a
diesel injector nozzle at about twelve hundred pounds, it'll
draw blood. But a welding arc generator just is not wound to
build up that kind of voltage. I can't see where any short circuit anywhere through the armature or field windings could
do such a thing."

"From what Chub said, he had been foolin' around with
the work selector. I don't think anyone touched the dials after
it happened. The selector dial was run all the way over to the
low-current application segment, and the current control was
around the halfway mark. That's not enough juice to get you
a good bead with a quarter-inch rod, let alone kill somebody—or roll a tractor back thirty feet on level ground."

"Or jump fifty feet," said Kelly. "It would take thousands
of volts to generate an arc like that."

"Is it possible that something in the Seven could have
pulled that arc? I mean, suppose the arc wasn't driven over,
but was drawn over? I tell you, she was hot for four hours
after that."

Kelly shook his head. "Never heard of any such thing.
Look, just to have something to call them, we call direct current terminals positive and negative, and just because it works
in theory we say that current flows from negative to positive.
There couldn't be any more positive attraction in one elec-
trode than there is negative drive in the other; see what I
mean?"

"There couldn't be some freak condition that would cause
a sort of oversize positive field? I mean one that would suck
out the negative flow all in a heap, make it smash through
under a lot of pressure like the water you were talking about
through an injector nozzle?"

"No, Tom. It just don't work that way, far as anyone
knows. I dunno, though—there are some things about static
electricity that nobody understands. All I can say is that what
happened couldn't happen and if it did it couldn't have killed
Peebles. And you know the answer to that."

Tom glanced away at the upper end of the runway, where
the two graves were. There was bitterness and turbulent anger
naked there for a moment, an he turned and walked away

without another word. And when he went back to have another look at the welding machine, *Daisy Etta* was gone.

Al Knowles and Harris squatted together near the water cooler.

"Bad," said Harris.

"Nevah saw anythin' like it," said Al. "Ol' Tom come back f'm the shop theah jus' *raisin'* Cain. 'Weah's 'at Seven gone? Weah's 'at Seven?' I never heered sech cah'ins on."

"Dennis did take it, huh?"

"Sho' did."

Harris said, "He came spoutin' around to me a while back, Dennis did. Chub'd told him Tom said for everybody to stay off that machine. Dennis was mad as a wet hen. Said Tom was carryin' that kind o' business too far. Said there was probably somethin' about the Seven Tom didn't want us to find out. Might incriminate him. Dennis is ready to say Tom killed the kid."

"Reckon he did, Harris?"

Harris shook his head. "I've known Tom too long to think that. If he won't tell us what really happened up on the mesa, he has a reason for it. How'd Dennis come to take the dozer?"

"Blew a front tire on his pan. Came back heah to git anothah rig—maybe a Dumptor. Saw th' Seven standin' theah ready to go. Stood theah lookin' at it and cussin' Tom. Said he was tired of bashin' his kindeys t'pieces on them othah rigs an' bedamned if he wouldn't take suthin' that rode good fo' a change. I tol' him ol' Tom'd raise th' roof when he found him on it. He had a couple mo' things t'say 'bout Tom then."

"I didn't think he had the guts to take the rig."

"Aw, he talked hisself blind mad."

They looked up as Chub Horton trotted up, panting. "Hey, you guys, come on. We better get up there to Dennis."

"What's wrong?" asked Harris, climbing to his feet.

"Tom passed me a minute ago lookin' like the wrath o' God and hightallin' it for the swamp fill. I asked him what was the matter and he hollered that Dennis had took the Seven. Said he was always talkin' about murder, and he'd get his fill of it foolin' around that machine." Chub went wall-eyed, licked his lips beside his cigar.

"Oh-oh," said Harris quietly. "That's the wrong kind o' talk for just now."

"You don't suppose he—"

"Come on!"

They saw Tom before they were halfway there. He was walking slowly, with his head down. Harris shouted. Tom raised his face, stopped, stood there waiting with a peculiarly slumped stance.

"Where's Dennis?" barked Chub.

Tom waited until they were almost up to him and then weakly raised an arm and thumbed over his shoulder. His face was green.

"Tom—is he—"

Tom nodded, and swayed a little. His granite jaw was slack.

"Al, stay with him. He's sick. Harris, let's go."

Tom was sick, then and there. Very. Al stood gaping at him, fascinated.

Chub and Harris found Dennis. All of twelve square feet of him, ground and churned and rolled out into a torn-up patch of earth. *Daisy Etta* was gone.

Back at the outcropping, they sat with Tom while Al Knowles took a Dumptor and roared away to get Kelly.

"You saw him?" he said dully after a time.

Harris said, "Yeh."

The screaming Dumptor and a mountainous cloud of dust arrived, Kelly driving, Al holding on with a death-grip to the dump-bed guards. Kelly flung himself off, ran to Tom. "Tom—what is all this? Dennis dead? And you . . . you—"

Tom's head came up slowly, the slackness going out of his long face, a light suddenly coming into his eyes. Until this moment it had not crossed his mind what these men might think.

"I—what?"

"Al says you killed him."

Tom's eyes flicked at Al Knowles, and Al winced as if the glance had been a quirt.

Harris said, "What about it, Tom?"

"Nothing about it. He was killed by that Seven. You saw that for yourself."

"I stuck with you all along," said Harris slowly. "I took everything you said and believed it."

"This is too strong for you?" Tom asked.

Harris nodded. "Too strong, Tom."

Tom looked at the grim circle of faces and laughed suddenly. He stood up, put his back against a tall crate. "What do you plan to do about it?"

There was a silence. "You think I went up there and knocked that windbag off the machine and ran over him?" More silence. "Listen. I went up there and saw what you saw. He was dead before I got there. That's not good enough either?" He paused and licked his lips. "So after I killed him I got up on the tractor and drove it far enough away so you couldn't see or hear it when you got there. And then I sprouted wings and flew back so's I was halfway here when you met me—*ten minutes* after I spoke to Chub on my way up!"

Kelly said vaguely, "Tractor?"

"Well," said Tom harshly to Harris, "was the tractor there when you and Chub went up and saw Dennis?"

"No—"

Chub smacked his thigh suddenly. "You could've drove it into the swamp, Tom."

Tom said angrily, "I'm wastin' my time. You guys got it all figured out. Why ask me anything at all?"

"Aw, take it easy," said Kelly. "We just want the facts. Just what did happen? You met Chub and told him that Dennis would get all the murderin' he could take if he messed around that machine. That right?"

"That's right."

"Then what?"

"Then the machine murdered him."

Chub, with remarkable patience, asked, "What did you mean the day Peebles was killed when you said that something had queered the Seven up there on the mesa?"

Tom said furiously, "I meant what I said. You guys are set to crucify me for this and I can't stop you. Well, listen. Something's got into that Seven. I don't know what it is and I don't think I ever will know. I thought that after she smashed herself up that it was finished with. I had an idea that when we had her torn down and helpless we should have left her that way. I was dead right but it's too late now. She's killed

Rivera and she's killed Dennis and she sure had something to do with killing Peebles. And my idea is that she won't stop as long as there's a human being alive on this island."

"Whaddaya know!" said Chub.

"Sure, Tom, sure," said Kelly quietly. "That tractor is out to get us. But don't worry; we'll catch it and tear it down. Just don't you worry about it any more; it'll be all right."

"That's right, Tom," said Harris. "You just take it easy around camp for a couple of days till you feel better. Chub and the rest of us will handle things for you. You had too much sun."

"You're a swell bunch of fellows," gritted Tom, with the deepest sarcasm. "You want to live," he shouted, "git out there and throw that maverick bulldozer!"

"That maverick bulldozer is at the bottom of the swamp where you put it," growled Chub. His head lowered and he started to move in. "Sure we want to live. The best way to do that is to put you where you can't kill anybody else. *Get him!*"

He leaped. Tom straightened him with his left and crossed with his right. Chub went down, tripping Harris. Al Knowles scuttled to a toolbox and dipped out a fourteen-inch crescent wrench. He circled around, keeping out of trouble, trying to look useful. Tom loosened a haymaker at Kelly, whose head seemed to withdraw like a turtle's; it whistled over, throwing Tom badly off balance. Harris, still on his knees, tackled Tom's legs; Chub hit him in the small of the back with a meaty shoulder, and Tom went flat on his face. Al Knowles, holding the wrench in both hands, swept it up and back like a baseball bat; at the top of its swing Kelly reached over, snatched it out of his hands and tapped Tom delicately behind the ear with it. Tom went limp.

It was late, but nobody seemed to feel like sleeping. They sat around the pressure lantern, talking idly. Chub and Kelly played an inconsequential game of casino, forgetting to pick up their points; Harris paced up and down like a man in a cell, and Al Knowles was squinched up close to the light, his eyes wide and watching, watching—

"I need a drink," said Harris.

"Tens," said one of the casino players.

Al Knowles said, "We shoulda killed him. We oughta kill him now."

"There's been too much killin' already," said Chub. "Shut up, you." And to Kelly, "With big casino," sweeping up cards.

Kelly caught his wrist and grinned. "Big casino's the ten of diamonds, not the ten of hearts. Remember?"

"Oh."

"How long before the blacktopping crew will be here?" quavered Al Knowles.

"Twelve days," said Harris. "And they better bring some likker."

"Hey, you guys."

They fell silent.

"Hey!"

"It's Tom," said Kelly. "Building sixes, Chub."

"I'm gonna go kick his ribs in," said Knowles, not moving.

"I heard that," said the voice from the darkness. "If I wasn't hogtied—"

"We know what you'd do," said Chub. "How much proof do you think we need?"

"Chub, you don't have to do any more to him!" It was Kelly, flinging his cards down and getting up. "Tom, you want water?"

"Yes."

"Siddown, siddown," said Chub.

"Let him lie there and bleed," Al Knowles said.

"Nuts!" Kelly went and filled a cup and brought it to Tom. The big Georgian was tied thoroughly, wrists together, taut rope between elbows and elbows behind his back, so that his hands were immovable over his solar plexus. His knees and ankles were bound as well, although Knowles' little idea of a short rope between ankles and throat hadn't been used.

"Thanks, Kelly." Tom drank greedily, Kelly holding his head. "Goes good." He drank more. "What hit me?"

"One of the boys. 'Bout the time you said the cat was haunted."

"Oh, yeah." Tom rolled his head and blinked with pain.

"Any sense asking you if you blame us?"

"Kelly, does somebody else have to get killed before you guys wake up?"

"None of us figure there will be any more killin'—now."

The rest of the men drifted up. "He willing to talk sense?" Chub wanted to know.

Al Knowles laughed, "Hyuk! Hyuk! Don't he look dangerous now!"

Harris said suddenly, "Al, I'm gonna hafta tape your mouth with the skin off your neck."

"Am I the kind of guy that makes up ghost stories?"

"Never have that I know of, Tom." Harris kneeled down beside him. "Never killed anyone before, either."

"Oh, get away from me. Get away," said Tom tiredly.

"Get up and make us," jeered Al.

Harris got up and backhanded him across the mouth. Al squeaked, took three steps backward and tripped over a drum of grease. "I told you," said Harris almost plaintively. "I *told* you, Al."

Tom stopped the bumble of comment. "Shut up!" he hissed. "SHUT UP!" he roared.

They shut.

"Chub," said Tom, rapidly, evenly, "what did you say I did with that Seven?"

"Buried it in the swamp."

"Yeh. Listen."

"Listen at what?"

"Be quiet and listen!"

So they listened. It was another still, windless night, with a thin crescent of moon showing nothing true in the black and muffled silver landscape. The smallest whisper of surf drifted up from the beach, and from far off to the right, where the swamp was, a scandalized frog croaked protest at the manhandling of his mudhole. But the sound that crept down, freezing their bones, came from the bluff behind their camp.

It was the unmistakable staccato of a starting engine.

"The Seven!"

" 'At's right, Chub," said Tom.

"Wh-who's crankin' her up?"

"Are we all here?"

"All but Peebles and Dennis and Rivera," said Tom.

"It's Dennis's ghost," moaned Al.

Chub snapped, "Shut up, lamebrain."

"She's shifted to diesel," said Kelly, listening.

"She'll be here in a minute," said Tom. "Y'know, fellas, we

can't all be crazy, but you're about to have a time convincin' yourself of it."

"You like this, doncha?"

"Some ways. Rivera used to call that machine *Daisy Etta*, 'cause she's *de siete* in Spig. *Daisy Etta*, she wants her a man."

"Tom," said Harris, "I wish you'd stop that chatterin'. You make me nervous."

"I got to do somethin'. I can't run," Tom drawled.

"We're going to have a look," said Chub. "If there's nobody on that cat, we'll turn you loose."

"Mighty white of you. Reckon you'll get back before she does?"

"We'll get back. Harris, come with me. We'll get one of the pan tractors. They can outrun a Seven. Kelly, take Al and get the other one."

"Dennis's machine has a flat tire on the pan," said Al's quavering voice.

"Pull the pin and cut the cables, then! Git!" Kelly and Al Knowles ran off.

"Good huntin', Chub."

Chub went to him, bent over. "I think I'm goin' to have to apologize to you, Tom."

"No you ain't. I'd a done the same. Get along now, if you think you got to. But hurry back."

"I got to. An' I'll hurry back."

Harris said, "Don't go 'way, boy." Tom returned the grin, and they were gone. But they didn't hurry back. They didn't come back at all.

It was Kelly who came pounding back, with Al Knowles on his heels, a half hour later. "Al—gimme your knife."

He went to work on the ropes. His face was drawn.

"I could see some of it," whispered Tom. "Chub and Harris?"

Kelly nodded. "There wasn't nobody on the Seven like you said." He said it as if there were nothing else in his mind, as if the most rigid self-control was keeping him from saying it over and over.

"I could see the lights," said Tom. "A tractor angling up the hill. Pretty soon another, crossing it, lighting up the whole slope."

"We heard it idling up there somewhere," Kelly said. "Olive-drab paint—couldn't see it."

"I saw the pan tractor turn over—oh, four, five times down the hill. It stopped, lights still burning. Then something hit it and rolled it again. That sure blacked it out. What turned it over first?"

"The Seven. Hanging up there just at the brow of the bluff. Waited until Chub and Harris were about to pass, sixty, seventy feet below. Tipped over the edge and rolled down on them with her clutches out. Must've been going thirty miles an hour when she hit. Broadside. They never had a chance. Followed the pan as it rolled down the hill and when it stopped booted it again."

"Want me to rub yo' ankles?" asked Al.

"You! Get outa my sight!"

"Aw, Tom—" whimpered Al.

"Skip it, Tom," said Kelly. "There ain't enough of us left to carry on that way. Al, you mind your manners from here on out, hear?"

"Ah jes' wanted to tell y'all. I knew you weren't lyin' 'bout Dennis, Tom, if only I'd stopped to think. I recollect when Dennis said he'd take that tractuh out . . . 'membah, Kelly? . . . He went an' got the crank and walked around to th' side of th' machine and stuck it in th' hole. It was barely in theah befo' the startin' engine kicked off. 'Whadda ya know!' he says t'me. 'She started by here'f! I nevah pulled that handle!' And I said, 'She sho' rarin' t'go!' "

"You pick a fine time to 'recollec' ' something," gritted Tom. "C'mon—let's get out of here."

"Where to?"

"What do you know that a Seven can't move or get up on?"

"That's a large order. A big rock, maybe."

"Ain't nothing that big around here," said Tom.

Kelly thought a minute, then snapped his fingers. "Up on the top of my last cut with the shovel," he said. "It's fourteen feet if it's an inch. I was pullin' out small rock an' topsoil, and Chub told me to drop back and dip out marl from a pocket there. I sumped in back of the original cut and took out a whole mess o' marl. That left a big neck of earth sticking thirty feet or so out of the cliff. The narrowest part is only about four feet wide. If *Daisy Etta* tries to get us from the top, she'll straddle the neck and hang herself. If she tries to get us from below, she can't get traction to climb; it's too lose and too steep."

"And what happens if she builds herself a ramp?"

"We'll be gone from there."

"Let's go."

Al agitated for the choice of a Dumptor because of its speed, but was howled down. Tom wanted something that could not get a flat tire and that would need something really powerful to turn it over. They took the two-cycle pan tractor with the bulldozer blade that had been Dennis's machine and crept out into the darkness.

It was nearly six hours later that *Daisy Etta* came and woke them up. Night was receding before a paleness in the east, and a fresh ocean breeze had sprung up. Kelly had taken the first lookout and Al the second, letting Tom rest the night out. And Tom was far too tired to argue the arrangement. Al had immediately fallen asleep on his watch, but fear had such a sure, cold hold on his vitals that the first faint growl of the big diesel engine snapped him erect. He tottered on the edge of the tall neck of earth that they slept on and squeaked as he scrabbled to get his balance.

"What's giving?" asked Kelly, instantly wide awake.

"It's coming," blubbered Al. "Oh my, oh my—"

Kelly stood up and stared into the fresh, dark dawn. The motor boomed hollowly, in a peculiar way heard twice at the same time as it was thrown to them and echoed back by the bluffs under and around them.

"It's coming and what are we goin' to do?" chanted Al. "What is going to happen?"

"My head is going to fall off," said Tom sleepily. He rolled to a sitting position, holding the brutalized member between his hands. "If that egg behind my ear hatches, it'll come out a full-sized jack-hammer." He looked at Kelly. "Where is she?"

"Don't rightly know," said Kelly. "Somewhere down around the camp."

"Probably pickin' up our scent."

"Figure it can do that?"

"I figure it can do anything," said Tom. "Al, stop your moanin'."

The sun slipped its scarlet edge into the thin slot between sea and sky, and rosy light gave each rock and tree a shape

and a shadow. Kelly's gaze swept back and forth, back and
forth, until, minutes later, he saw movement.

"There she is!"

"Where?"

"Down by the grease rack."

Tom rose and stared. "What's she doin'?"

After an interval Kelly said, "She's workin'. Diggin' a
swale in front of the fuel drums."

"You don't say. Don't tell me she's goin' to give herself a
grease job."

"She don't need it. She was completely greased and new oil
put in the crankcase after we set her up. But she might need
fuel."

"Not more'n half a tank."

"Well, maybe she figures she's got a lot of work to do today." As Kelly said this Al began to blubber. They ignored
him.

The fuel drums were piled in a pyramid at the edge of the
camp, in forty-four-gallon drums piled on their sides. The
Seven was moving back and forth in front of them, close up,
making pass after pass, gouging earth up and wasting it out
past the pile. She soon had a huge pit scooped out, about
fourteen feet wide, six feet deep and thirty feet long, right at
the very edge of the pile of drums.

"What you reckon she's playin' at?"

"Search me. She seems to want fuel, but I don't . . . look
at that! She's stopped in the hole; she's pivoting, smashing the
top corner of the moldboard into one of the drums on the
bottom!"

Tom scraped the stubble on his jaw with his nails. "An'
you wonder how much that critter can do! Why, she's got the
whole thing figured out. She knows if she tried to punch a
hole in a fuel drum that she'd only kick it around. If she did
knock a hole in it, how's she going to lift it? She's not
equipped to handle hose, so . . . see? Look at her now! She
just gets herself lower than the bottom drum on the pile, and
punches a hole. She can do that then, with the whole weight
of the pile holding it down. Then she backs her tank under
the stream of fuel runnin' out!"

"How'd she get the cap off?"

Tom snorted and told them how the radiator cap had come

off its hinges as he vaulted over the hood the day Rivera was hurt.

"You know," he said after a moment's thought, "if she knew as much then as she does now, I'd be snoozin' beside Rivera and Peebles. She just didn't know her way around then. She run herself like she'd never run before. She's learned plenty since."

"She has," said Kelly, "and here's where she uses it on us. She's headed this way."

She was. Straight out across the roughed-out runway she came, grinding along over the dew-sprinkled earth, yesterday's dust swirling up from under her tracks. Crossing the shoulder line, she took the rougher ground skillfully, angling up over the occasional swags in the earth, by-passing stones, riding free and fast and easily. It was the first time Tom had actually seen her clearly running without an operator, and his flesh crept as he watched. The machine was unnatural, her outline somehow unreal and dreamlike purely through the lack of the small silhouette of a man in the saddle. She looked hulked, compact, dangerous.

"What are we gonna do?" wailed Al Knowles.

"We're gonna sit and wait," said Kelly, "and you're gonna shut your trap. We won't know for five minutes yet whether she's going to go after us from down below or from up here."

"If you want to leave," said Tom gently, "go right ahead." Al sat down.

Kelly looked down at his beloved power shovel, sitting squat and unlovely in the cut below them and away to their right. "How do you reckon she'd stand up against the dipper stick?"

"If it ever came to a rough-and-tumble," said Tom, "I'd say it would be just too bad for *Daisy Etta*. But she wouldn't fight. There's no way you could get the shovel within punchin' range; *Daisy*'d just stand there and laugh at you."

"I can't see her now," whined Al.

Tom looked. "She's taken the bluff. She's going to try it from up here. I move we sit tight and see if she's foolish enough to try to walk out here over that narrow neck. If she does, she'll drop on her belly with one truck on each side. Probably turn herself over trying to dig out."

The wait then was interminable. Back over the hill they could hear the laboring motor; twice they heard the machine

stop momentárily to shift gears. Once they looked at each
other hopefully as the sound rose to a series of bellowing
roars, as if she were backing and filling; then they realized
that she was trying to take some particularly steep part of the
bank and having trouble getting traction. But she made it; the
motor revved up as she made the brow of the hill, and she
shifted into fourth gear and came lumbering out into the
open. She lurched up to the edge of the cut, stopped,
throttled down, dropped her blade on the ground and stood
there idling. Al Knowles backed away to the very edge of
the tongue of earth they stood on, his eyes practically on
stalks.

"O.K.—put up or shut up," Kelly called across harshly.

"She's looking the situation over," said Tom. "That narrow
pathway don't fool her a bit."

Daisy Etta's blade began to rise, and stopped just clear of
the ground. She shifted without clashing her gears, began to
back slowly, still at little more than an idle.

"She's gonna jump!" screamed Al. "I'm gettin' out of
here!"

"Stay here, you fool," shouted Kelly. "She can't get us as
long as we're up here! If you go down, she'll hunt you down
like a rabbit."

The blast of the Seven's motor was the last straw for Al.
He squeaked and hopped over the edge, scrambling and sliding down the almost sheer face of the cut. He hit the bottom
running.

Daisy Etta lowered her blade and raised her snout and
growled forward, the blade loading. Six, seven, seven and a
half cubic yards of dirt piled up in front of her as she neared
the edge. The loaded blade bit into the narrow pathway that
led out to their perch. It was almost all soft, white, crumbly
marl, and the great machine sank nose down into it, the monstrous overload of topsoil spilling down on each side.

"She's going to bury herself!" shouted Kelly.

"No—wait." Tom caught his arm. "She's trying to turn—
she made it! She made it! She's ramping herself down to the
flat!"

"She is—and she's cut us off from the bluff!"

The bulldozer, blade raised as high as it could possibly go,
the hydraulic rod gleaming clean in the early light, freed herself of the last of her tremendous load, spun around and

headed back upward, sinking her blade again. She made one more pass between them and the bluff, making a cut now far too wide for them to jump, particularly to the cumbly footing at the bluff's edge. Once down again, she turned to face their haven, now an isolated pillar of marl, and revved down, waiting.

"I never thought of this," said Kelly guiltily. "I knew we'd be safe from her ramping up, and I never thought she'd try it the other way!"

"Skip it. In the meantime, here we sit. What happens—do we wait up here until she idles out of fuel, or do we starve to death?"

"Oh, this won't be a siege, Tom. That thing's too much of a killer. Where's Al? I wonder if he's got guts enough to make a pass near here with our tractor and draw her off?"

"He had just guts enough to take our tractor and head out," said Tom. "Didn't you know?"

"He took our—*what?*" Kelly looked out toward where they had left their machine the night before. It was gone. "Why the dirty little yellow rat!"

"No sense cussin'," said Tom steadily, interrupting what he knew was the beginning of some really flowery language. "What else could you expect?"

Daisy Etta decided, apparently, how to go about removing their splendid isolation. She uttered the snort of too-quick throttle, and moved into their peak with a corner of her blade, cutting out a huge swipe, undercutting the material over it so that it fell on her side and track as she passed. Eight inches disappeared from that side of their little plateau.

"Oh-oh. That won't do a-tall," said Tom.

"Fixin' to dig us down," said Kelly grimly. "Take her about twenty minutes. Tom, I say leave."

"It won't be healthy. You just got no idea how fast that thing can move now. Don't forget, she's a good deal more than she was when she had a man runnin' her. She can shift from high to reverse to fifth speed forward like that"—he snapped his fingers—"and she can pivot faster'n you can blink and throw that blade just where she wants it."

The tractor passed under them, bellowing, and their little table was suddenly a foot shorter.

"Awright," said Kelly. "So what do you want to do? Stay here and let her dig the ground out from under our feet?"

"I'm just warning you," said Tom. "Now listen. We'll wait until she's taking a load. It'll take her a second to get rid of it when she knows we're gone. We'll split—she can't get both of us. You head out in the open, try to circle the curve of the bluff and get where you can climb it. Then come back over here to the cut. A man can scramble off a fourteen-foot cut faster'n any tractor ever built. I'll cut in close to the cut, down at the bottom. If she takes after you, I'll get clear all right. If she takes after me, I'll try to make the shovel and at least give her a run for her money. I can play hide an' seek in an' around and under that dipper-stick all day if she wants to play."

"Why me out in the open?"

"Don't you think those long laigs o' yours can outrun her in that distance?"

"Reckon they got to," grinned Kelly. "O.K., Tom."

They waited tensely. *Daisy Etta* backed close by, started another pass. As the motor blatted under the load, Tom said, "Now!" and they jumped. Kelly, catlike as always, landed on his feet. Tom, whose knees and ankles were black and blue with rope bruises, took two staggering steps and fell. Kelly scooped him to his feet as the dozer's steel prow came around the bank. Instantly she was in fifth gear and howling down at them. Kelly flung himself to the left and Tom to the right, and they pounded away, Kelly out toward the runway, Tom straight for the shovel. *Daisy Etta* let them diverge for a moment, keeping her course, trying to pursue both; then she evidently sized Tom up as the slower, for she swung toward him. The instant's hesitation was all Tom needed to get the little lead necessary. He tore up to the shovel, his legs going like pistons, and dived down between the shovel's tracks.

As he hit the ground, the big manganese-steel moldboard hit the right track of the shovel, and the impact set all forty-seven tons of the great machine quivering. But Tom did not stop. He scrabbled his way under the rig, stood up behind it, leaped and caught the sill of the rear window, clapped his other hand on it, drew himself up and tumbled inside. Here he was safe for the moment; the huge tracks themselves were higher than the Seven's blade could rise, and the floor of the cab was a good sixteen inches higher than the top of the track. Tom went to the cab door and peeped outside. The tractor had drawn off and was idling.

"Study away," gritted Tom, and went to the big Murphy diesel. He unhurriedly checked the oil with the bayonet gauge, replaced it, took the governor cut-out rod from its rack and inserted it in the governor casing. He set the master throttle at the halfway mark, pulled up the starter-handle, twitched the cut-out. The motor spat a wad of blue smoke out of its hooded exhaust and caught. Tom put the rod back, studied the fuel-flow glass and pressure gauges, and then went to the door and looked out again. The Seven had not moved, but it was revving up and down in that uneven fashion it had shown up on the mesa. Tom had the extraordinary idea that it was gathering itself to spring. He slipped into the saddle, threw the master clutch. The big gears that half-filled the cab obediently began to turn. He kicked the brake locks loose with his heels, let his feet rest lightly on the pedals as they rose.

Then he reached over his head and snapped back the throttle. As the Murphy picked up he grasped both hoist and swing levers and pulled them back. The engine howled; the two-yard bucket came up off the ground with a sudden jolt as the cold friction grabbed it. The big machine swung hard to the right; Tom snapped his hoist lever forward and checked the bucket's rise with his foot on the brake. He shoved the crowd lever forward; the bucket ran out to the end of its reach, and the heel of the bucket wiped across the Seven's hood, taking with it the exhaust stack, muffler and all, and the pre-cleaner on the air intake. Tom cursed. He had figured on the machine's leaping backward. If it had, he would have smashed the cast-iron radiator core. But she had stood still, making a split-second decision.

Now she moved, though, and quickly. With that incredibly fast shifting, she leaped backwards and pivoted out of range before Tom could check the shovel's mad swing. The heavy swing-friction blocks smoked acridly as the machine slowed, stopped and swung back. Tom checked her as he was facing the Seven, hoisted his bucket a few feet, and rehauled, bringing it about halfway back, ready for anything. The four great dipper-teeth gleamed in the sun. Tom ran a practiced eye over cables, boom and dipper-stick, liking the black polish of crater compound on the sliding parts, the easy tension of well-greased cables and links. The huge machine stood strong, ready and profoundly subservient for all its brute power.

Tom looked searchingly at the Seven's ruined engine hood. The gaping end of the broken air-intake pipe stared back at him. "Aha!" he said. "A few cupfuls of nice dry marl down there'll give you something to chew on."

Keeping a wary eye on the tractor, he swung into the bank, dropped his bucket and plunged it into the marl. He crowded it deep, and the Murphy yelled for help but kept on pushing. At the peak of the load a terrific jar rocked him in the saddle. He looked back over his shoulder through the door and saw the Seven backing off again. She had run up and delivered a terrific punch to the counterweight at the back of the cab. Tom grinned tightly. She'd have to do better than that. There was nothing back there but eight or ten tons of solid steel. And he didn't much care at the moment whether or not she scratched his paint.

He swung back again, white marl running away on both sides of the heaped bucket. The shovel rode perfectly now, for a shovel is counterweighted to balance true when standing level with the bucket loaded. The hoist and swing frictions and the brake linings had heated and dried themselves of the night's condensation moisture, and she answered the controls in a way that delighted the operator in him. He handled the swing lever lightly, back to swing to the right, forward to swing to the left, following the slow dance the Seven had started to do, stepping warily back and forth like a fighter looking for an opening. Tom kept the bucket between himself and the tractor, knowing that she could not hurl a tool that was built to smash hard rock for twenty hours a day and like it.

Daisy Etta bellowed and rushed in. Tom snapped the hoist lever back hard, and the bucket rose, letting the tractor run underneath. Tom punched the bucket trip, and the great steel jaw opened, cascading marl down on the broken hood. The tractor's fan blew it back in a huge billowing cloud. The instant that it took Tom to check and dump was enough, however, for the tractor to dance back out of the way, for when he tried to drop it on the machine to smash the coiled injector tubes on top of the engine block, she was gone.

The dust cleared away, and the tractor moved in again, feinted to the left, then swung her blade at the bucket, which was just clear of the ground. Tom swung to meet her, her feint having gotten her in a little closer than he liked, and bucket met blade with a shower of sparks and a clank that could be heard for half a mile. She had come in with her blade high, and Tom let out a wordless shout as he saw the A-frame brace behind the blade had caught between two of his dipper-teeth. He snatched at his hoist lever and the bucket came up, lifting with it the whole front end of the bulldozer.

Daisy Etta plunged up and down and her tracks dug violently into the earth as she raised and lowered her blade, trying to shake herself free. Tom rehauled, trying to bring the tractor in closer, for the boom was set too low to attempt to lift such a dead weight. As it was, the shovel's off track was trying its best to get off the ground. But the crowd and rehaul frictions could not handle her alone; they began to heat and slip.

Tom hoisted a little; the shovel's off track came up a foot off the ground. Tom cursed and let the bucket drop, and in an instant the dozer was free and running clear. Tom swung wildly at her, missed. The dozer came in on a long curve; Tom swung to meet her again, took a vicious swipe at her which she took on her blade. But this time she did not withdraw after being hit, but bored right in, carrying the bucket before her. Before Tom realized what she was doing, his bucket was around in front of the tracks and between them, on the ground. It was as swift and skillful a maneuver as could be imagined, and it left the shovel without the ability to swing as long as *Daisy Etta* could hold the bucket trapped between the tracks.

Tom crowded furiously, but that succeeded only in lifting the boom higher in the air, since there is nothing to hold a boom down but its own weight. Hoisting did nothing but make his frictions smoke and rev the engine down dangerously close to the stalling point.

Tom swore again and reached down to the cluster of small levers at his left. These were the gears. On this type of shovel, the swing lever controls everything except crowd and hoist. With the swing lever, the operator, having selected his gear, controls the travel—that is, power to the tracks—in forward and reverse; booming up and booming down; and swinging. The machine can do only one of these things at a time. If she is in travel gear, she cannot swing. If she is in swing gear, she cannot boom up or down. Not once in years of operating would this inability bother an operator; now, however, nothing was normal.

Tom pushed the swing gear control down and pulled up on the travel. The clutches involved were jaw clutches, not frictions, so that he had to throttle down to an idle before he could make the castellations mesh. As the Murphy revved down, *Daisy Etta* took it as a signal that something could be done about it, and she shoved furiously into the bucket. But Tom had all controls in neutral and all she succeeded in doing was to dig herself in, her sharp new cleats spinning deep into the dirt.

Tom set his throttle up again and shoved the swing lever forward. There was a vast crackling of drive chains; and the big tracks started to turn.

Daisy Etta had sharp cleats; her pads were twenty inches wide and her tracks were fourteen feet long, and there were fourteen tons of steel on them. The shovel's big flat pads were three feet wide and twenty feet long, and forty-seven tons aboard. There was simply no comparison. The Murphy bellowed the fact that the work was hard, but gave no indications of stalling. *Daisy Etta* performed the incredible feat of shifting into a forward gear while she was moving backwards, but it did her no good. Round and round her tracks went, trying to drive her forward, gouging deep; and slowly and surely she was forced backward toward the cut wall by the shovel.

Tom heard a sound that was not part of a straining machine; he looked out and saw Kelly up on top of the cut, smoking, swinging his feet over the edge, making punching motions with his hands as if he had a ringside seat at a big fight—which he certainly had.

Tom now offered the dozer little choice. If she did not turn aside before him, she would be borne back against the bank and her fuel tank crushed. There was every possibility that, having her pinned there, Tom would have time to raise his bucket over her and smash her to pieces. And if she turned before she was forced against the bank, she would have to free Tom's bucket. This she had to do.

The Murphy gave him warning, but not enough. It crooned as the load came off, and Tom knew then that the dozer was shifting into a reverse gear. He whipped the hoist lever back, and the bucket rose as the dozer backed away from him. He crowded it out and let it come smashing down—and missed. For the tractor danced aside—and while he was in travel gear he could not swing to follow it. *Daisy Etta* charged then, put one track on the bank and went over almost on her beam-ends, throwing one end of her blade high in the air. So totally unexpected was it that Tom was quite unprepared. The tractor flung itself on the bucket, and the cutting edge of the blade dropped between the dipper teeth. This time there was the whole weight of the tractor to hold it there. There would be no way for her to free herself—but at the same time she had trapped the bucket so far out from the center pin of the shovel that Tom couldn't hoist without overbalancing and turning the monster over.

Daisy Etta ground away in reverse, dragging the bucket out until it was checked by the bumper-blocks. Then she began to crab sideways, up against the bank and when Tom tried tentatively to rehaul, she shifted and came right with him, burying one whole end of her blade deep into the bank.

Stalemate. She had hung herself up on the bucket, and she had immobilized it. Tom tried to rehaul, but the tractor's anchorage in the bank was too solid. He tried to swing, to hoist. All the overworked frictions could possibly give out was smoke. Tom grunted and throttled to an idle, leaned out the window. *Daisy Etta* was idling too, loudly without her muffler, the stackless exhaust giving out an ugly flat sound. But after the roar of the two great motors the partial silence was deafening.

Kelly called down, "Double knockout, hey?"

"Looks like it. What say we see if we can't get close enough to her to quiet her down some?"

Kelly shrugged. "I dunno. If she's really stopped herself, it's the first time. I respect that rig, Tom. She wouldn't have got herself into that spot if she didn't have an ace up her sleeve."

"Look at her, man! Suppose she was a civilized bulldozer and you had to get her out of there. She can't raise her blade high enough to free it from those dipper-teeth, y'know. Think you'd be able to do it?"

"It might take several seconds," Kelly drawled. "She's sure high and dry."

"O.K., let's spike her guns."

"Like what?"

"Like taking a bar and prying out her tubing." He referred to the coiled brass tubing that carried the fuel, under pressure, from the pump to the injectors. There were many feet of it, running from the pump reservoir, stacked in expansion coils over the cylinder head.

As he spoke *Daisy Etta*'s idle burst into that maniac revving up and down characteristic of her.

"What do you know!" Tom called above the racket. "Eavesdropping!"

Kelly slid down the cut, stood up on the track of the shovel and poked his head in the window. "Well, you want to get a bar and try?"

"Let's go!"

Tom went to the toolbox and pulled out the pinch bar that Kelly used to replace cables on his machine, and swung to the ground. They approached the tractor warily. She revved up as they came near, began to shudder. The front end rose and dropped and the tracks began to turn as she tried to twist out of the vise her blade had dropped into.

"Take it easy, sister," said Tom. "You'll just bury yourself. Set still and take it, now, like a good girl. You got it comin'."

"Be careful," said Kelly. Tom hefted the bar and laid a hand on the fender.

The tractor literally shivered, and from the rubber hose connection at the top of the radiator, a blinding stream of hot water shot out. It fanned and caught them both full in the face. They staggered back, cursing.

"You O.K. Tom?" Kelly gasped a moment later. He had got most of it across the mouth and cheek. Tom was on his knees, his shirt tail out, blotting at his face.

"My eyes . . . oh, my eyes—"

"Let's see!" Kelly dropped down beside him and took him by the wrists, gently removing Tom's hands from his face. He whistled. "Come on," he gritted. He helped Tom up and led him away a few feet. "Stay here," he said hoarsely. He turned, walked back toward the dozer, picking up the pinch-bar. "You dirty——!" he yelled, and flung it like a javelin at the tube coils. It was a little high. It struck the ruined hood, made a deep dent in the metal. The dent promptly inverted with a loud *thung-g-g!* and flung the bar back at him. He ducked; it whistled over his head and caught Tom in the calves of his legs. He went down like a poled ox, but staggered to his feet again.

"Come on!" Kelly snarled, and taking Tom's arm, hustled him around the turn of the cut. "Sit down! I'll be right back."

"Where you going? Kelly—be careful!"

"Careful and how!"

Kelly's long legs ate up the distance back to the shovel. He swung into the cab, reached back over the motor and set up the master throttle all the way. Stepping up behind the saddle, he opened the running throttle and the Murphy howled. Then he hauled back on the hoist lever until it knuckled in, turned and leaped off the machine in one supple motion.

The hoist drum turned and took up slack; the cable straightened as it took the strain. The bucket stirred under the dead weight of the bulldozer that rested on it; and slowly, then, the great flat tracks began to lift their rear ends off the ground. The great obedient mass of machinery teetered forward on the tips of her tracks, the Murphy revved down and under the incredible load, but it kept the strain. A strand of the two-part hoist cable broke and whipped around, singing; and then she was balanced—over-balanced—

And the shovel had hauled herself right over and had fallen with an earth-shaking crash. The boom, eight tons of solid steel, clanged down onto the blade of the bulldozer, and lay there, crushing it down tightly onto the imprisoning row of dipper-teeth.

Daisy Etta sat there, not trying to move now, racing her motor impotently. Kelly strutted past her, thumbing his nose, and went back to Tom.

"Kelly! I thought you were never coming back! What happened?"

"Shovel pulled herself over on her nose."

"Good boy! Fall on the tractor?"

"Nup. But the boom's laying across the top of her blade. Caught like a rat in a trap."

"Better watch out the rat don't chew its leg off to get out," said Tom, drily. "Still runnin', is she?"

"Yep. But we'll fix that in a hurry."

"Sure. Sure. How?"

"How? I dunno. Dynamite, maybe. How's the optics?"

Tom opened one a trifle and grunted. "Rough. I can see a

little, though. My eyelids are parboiled, mostly. Dynamite, you say? Well—"

Tom sat back against the bank and stretched out his legs. "I tell you, Kelly, I been too blessed busy these last few hours to think much, but there's one thing that keeps comin' back to me—somethin' I was mullin' over long before the rest of you guys knew anything was up at all, except that Rivera had got hurt in some way I wouldn't tell you all about. But I don't reckon you'll call me crazy if I open my mouth now and let it all run out?"

"From now on," Kelly said fervently, "nobody's crazy. After this I'll believe anything."

"O.K. Well, about that tractor. What do you suppose has got into her?"

"Search me. I dunno."

"No—don't say that. I just got an idea we can't stop at 'I dunno.' We got to figure all the angles on this thing before we know just what to do about it. Let's just get this thing lined up. When did it start? On the mesa. How? Rivera was opening an old building with the Seven. This thing came out of there. Now here's what I'm getting at. We can dope these things out about it: It's intelligent. It can only get into a machine and not into a man. It—"

"What about that? How do you know it can't?"

"Because it had the chance to and didn't. I was standing right by the opening when it kited out. Rivera was upon the machine at the time. It didn't directly harm either of us. It got into the tractor, and the tractor did. By the same token, it can't hurt a man when it's out of a machine, but that's all it wants to do when it's in one. O.K.?"

"To get on: once it's in one machine it can't get out again. We know that because it had plenty of chances and didn't take them. That scuffle with the dipper-stick, f'r instance. My face woulda been plenty red if it had taken over the shovel—and you can bet it would have if it could."

"I got you so far. But what are we going to do about it?"

"That's the thing. You see, I don't think it's enough to wreck the tractor. We might burn it, blast it, take whatever it was that got into it up on the mesa."

"That makes sense. But I don't see what else we can do than just break up the dozer. We haven't got a line on actually what the thing is."

"I think we have. Remember I asked you all those screwy questions about the arc that killed Peebles. Well, when that happened, I recollected a flock of other things. One—when it got out of that hole up there, I smelled that smell that you notice when you're welding; sometimes when lightning strikes real close."

"Ozone," said Kelly.

"Yeah—ozone. Then, it likes metal, not flesh. But most of all, there was that arc. Now, that was absolutely screwy. You know as well as I do—better—that an arc generator simply don't have the push to do a thing like that. It can't kill a man, and it can't throw an arc no fifty feet. But it did. An' that's why I asked you if there could be something—a field, or some such—that could *suck* current out of a generator, all at once, faster than it could flow. Because this thing's electrical; it fits all around."

"Electronic," said Kelly doubtfully, thoughtfully.

"I wouldn't know. Now then. When Peebles was killed, a funny thing happened. Remember what Chub said? The Seven moved back—straight back, about thirty feet, until it bumped into a roadroller that was standing behind it. It did that with no fuel in the starting engine—without even using the starting engine, for that matter—and with the compression valves locked open!

"Kelly, that thing in the dozer can't do much, when you come right down to it. It couldn't fix itself up after the joyride on the mesa. It can't make the machine do too much more than the machine can do ordinarily. What it actually can do, seems to me, is to make a spring push instead of pull, like the control levers, and make a fitting slip when it's supposed to hold, like the ratchet on the throttle lever. It can turn a shaft, like the way it cranks its own starting motor. But if it was so all-fired high-powered, it wouldn't have to use the starting motor! The absolute biggest job it's done so far, seems to me, was when it walked back from that welding machine when Peebles got his. Now, why did it do that just then?"

"Reckon it didn't like the brimstone smell, like it says in the Good Book," said Kelly sourly.

"That's pretty close, seems to me. Look, Kelly—this thing *feels* things. I mean, it can get sore. If it couldn't it never woulda kept driving in at the shovel like that. It can think. But if it can do all those things, then it can be *scared!*"

"Scared? Why should it be scared?"

"Listen. Something went on in that thing when the arc hit it. What's that I read in a magazine once about heat—something about molecules runnin' around with their heads cut off when they got hot?"

"Molecules do. They go into rapid motion when heat is applied. But—"

"But nothin'. That machine was hot for four hours after that. But she was hot in a funny way. Not just around the place where the arc hit, like as if it was a welding arc. But hot all over—from the moldboard to the fuel-tank cap. Hot everywhere. And just as hot behind the final drive housings as she was at the top of the blade where the poor guy put his hand.

"And look at this." Tom was getting excited, as his words crystallized his ideas. "She was scared—scared enough to back off from that welder, putting everything she could into it, to get back from that welding machine. And after that, she was sick. I say that because in the whole time she's had that whatever-ya-call-it in her, she's never been near men without trying to kill them, except for those two days after the arc hit her. She had juice enough to start herself when Dennis came around with the crank, but she still needed someone to run her till she got her strength back."

"But why didn't she turn and smash up the welder when Dennis took her?"

"One of two things. She didn't have the strength, or she didn't have the guts. She was scared, maybe, and wanted out of there, away from that thing."

"But she had all night to go back for it!"

"Still scared. Or . . . oh, *that's* it! She had other things to do first. Her main idea is to kill men—there's no other way you can figure it. It's what she was built to do. Not the tractor—they don't build 'em sweeter'n that machine; but the thing that's runnin' it."

"What *is* that thing?" Kelly mused. "Coming out of that old building—temple—what have you—how old is it? How long was it there? What kept it in there?"

"What kept it in there was some funny gray stuff that lined the inside of the buildin'," said Tom. "It was like rock, an' it was like smoke.

"It was a color that scared you to look at it, and it gave

Rivera and me the creeps when we got near it. Don't ask me what it was. I went up there to look at it, and it's gone. Gone from the building, anyhow. There was a little lump of it on the ground. I don't know whether that was a hunk of it, or all of it rolled up into a ball. I get the creeps again thinkin' about it."

Kelly stood up. "Well, the heck with it. We been beatin' our gums up here too long anyhow. There's just enough sense in what you say to make me want to try something nonsensical, if you see what I mean. If that welder can sweat the Ol' Nick out of that tractor, I'm on. Especially from fifty feet away. There should be a Dumptor around here somewhere; let's move from here. Can you navigate now?"

"Reckon so, a little." Tom rose and together they followed the cut until they came on the Dumptor. They climbed on, cranked it up and headed toward camp.

About halfway there Kelly looked back, gasped, and putting his mouth close to Tom's ear, bellowed against the scream of the motor, "Tom! 'Member what you said about the rat in the trap biting off a leg?"

Tom nodded.

"Well, *Daisy* did too! She's left her blade an' pushbeams an' she's followin' us in!"

They howled into the camp, gasping against the dust that followed when they pulled up by the welder.

Kelly said, "You cast around and see if you can find a drawpin to hook that rig up to the Dumptor with. I'm goin' after some water an' chow!"

Tom grinned. Imagine old Kelly forgetting that a Dumptor had no drawbar! He groped around to a toolbox, peering out of the narrow slit beneath swollen lids, felt behind it and located a shackle. He climbed up on the Dumptor, turned it around and backed up to the welding machine. He passed the shackle through the ring at the end of the steering tongue of the welder, screwed in the pin and dropped the shackle over the front towing hook of the Dumptor. A dumptor being what it is, having no real front and no real rear, and direct reversing gears in all speeds, it was no trouble to drive it "backwards" for a change.

Kelly came pounding back, out of breath. "Fix it? Good. Shackle? No drawbar! *Daisy's* closin' up fast; I say let's take

the beach. We'll be concealed until we have a good lead out
o' this pocket, and the going's pretty fair, long as we don't
bury this jalopy in the sand."

"Good," said Tom as they climbed on and he accepted an
open tin of K. "Only go easy; bump around too much and
the welder'll slip off the hook. An' I somehow don't want to
lose it just now."

They took off, zooming up the beach. A quarter of a mile
up, they sighted the Seven across the flat. It immediately
turned and took a course that would intercept them.

"Here she comes," shouted Kelly, and stepped down hard
on the accelerator. Tom leaned over the back of the seat,
keeping his eye on their tow. "Hey! Take it easy! Watch it!
"Hey!"

But it was too late. The tongue of the welding machine responded to that one bump too many. The shackle jumped up
off the hook, the welder lurched wildly, slewed hard to the
left. The tongue dropped to the sand and dug in; the machine
rolled up on it and snapped it off, finally stopped, leaning
crazily askew. By a miracle it did not quite turn over.

Kelly tramped on the brakes and both their heads did their
utmost to snap off their shoulders. They leaped off and ran
back to the welder. It was intact, but towing it was now out
of the question.

"If there's going to be a showdown, it's gotta be here."

The beach here was about thirty yards wide, the sand almost level, and undercut banks of sawgrass forming the land-
ward edge in a series of little hummocks and headlands.
While Tom stayed with the machine, testing starter and generator contacts, Kelly walked up one of the little mounds,
stood up on it and scanned the beach back the way he had
come. Suddenly he began to shout and wave his arms.

"What's got into you?"

"It's Al!" Kelly called back. "With the pan tractor!"

Tom dropped what he was doing, and came to stand beside
Kelly. "Where's the Seven? I can't see."

"Turned on the beach and followin' our track. Al! Al! You
little skunk, c'mere!"

Tom could now dimly make out the pan tractor cutting
across directly toward them and the beach.

"He don't see *Daisy Etta*," remarked Kelly disgustedly, "or
he'd sure be headin' the other way."

Fifty yards away Al pulled up and throttled down. Kelly shouted and waved to him. Al stood up on the machine, cupped his hands around his mouth. "Where's the Seven?"

"Never mind that! Come here with that tractor!"

Al stayed where he was. Kelly cursed and started out after him.

"You stay away from me," he said when Kelly was closer.

"I ain't got time for you now," said Kelly. "Bring that tractor down to the beach."

"Where's that *Daisy Etta*?" Al's voice was oddly strained.

"Right behind us." Kelly thumbed over his shoulder. "On the beach."

Al's bulging eyes clicked wide almost audibly. He turned on his heel and jumped off the machine and started to run. Kelly uttered a wordless syllable that was somehow more obscene than anything else he had ever uttered, and vaulted into the seat of the machine. "Hey!" he bellowed after Al's rapidly diminishing figure. "You're runnin' right into her." Al appeared not to hear, but went pelting down the beach.

Kelly put her into fifth gear and poured on the throttle. As the tractor began to move he whacked out the master clutch, snatched the overdrive lever back to put her into sixth, rammed the clutch in again, all so fast that she did not have time to stop rolling. Bucking and jumping over the rough ground, the fast machine whined for the beach.

Tom was fumbling back to the welder, his ears telling him better than his eyes how close the Seven was—for she was certainly no nightingale, particularly without her exhaust stack. Kelly reached the machine as he did.

"Get behind it," snapped Tom. "I'll jam the tierod with the shackle, and you see if you can't bunt her up into that pocket between these two hummocks. Only take it easy—you don't want to tear up that generator. Where's Al?"

"Don't ask me. He run down the beach to meet *Daisy*."

"He *what*?"

The whine of the two-cycle drowned out Kelly's answer, if any. He got behind the welder and set his blade against it. Then in a low gear, slipping his clutch in a little, he slowly nudged the machine toward the place Tom had indicated. It was a little hollow in between two projecting banks. The surf and the high-tide mark dipped inland here to match it; the water was only a few feet away.

Tom raised his arm and Kelly stopped. From the other side of the projecting shelf, out of their sight now, came the flat roar of the Seven's exhaust. Kelly sprang off the tractor and went to help Tom, who was furiously throwing out coils of cable from the rack back of the welder. "What's the game?"

"We got to ground that Seven some way," panted Tom. He threw the last bit of cable out to clear it of kinks and turned to the panel. "How was it—about sixty volts and the amperage on 'special application'?" He spun the dials, pressed the starter button. The motor responded instantly. Kelly scooped up ground clamp and rod holder and tapped them together. The solenoid governor picked up the load and the motor hummed as a good live spark took the jump.

"Good," said Tom, switching off the generator. "Come on, Lieutenant General Electric, figure me out a way to ground that maverick."

Kelly tightened his lips, shook his head. "I dunno—unless somebody actually clamps this thing on her."

"No, boy, can't do that. If one of us gets killed—"

Kelly tossed the ground clamp idly, his lithe body taut. "Don't give me that, Tom. You know I'm elected because you can't see good enough yet to handle it. You know you'd do it if you could. You—"

He stopped short, for the steadily increasing roar of the approaching Seven had stopped, was blatting away now in that extraordinary irregular throttling that *Daisy Etta* affected.

"Now, what's got into her?"

Kelly broke away and scrambled up the bank. "Tom!" he gasped. "Tom—come up here!"

Tom followed, and they lay side by side, peering out over the top of the escarpment at the remarkable tableau.

Daisy Etta was standing on the beach, near the water, not moving. Before her, twenty or thirty feet away, stood Al Knowles, his arms out in front of him, talking a blue streak. *Daisy* made far too much racket for them to hear what he was saying.

"Do you reckon he's got guts enough to stall her off for us?" said Tom.

"If he has, it's the queerest thing that's happened yet on his old island," Kelly breathed, "an' that's saying something."

The Seven revved up till she shook, and then throttled back. She ran down so low then that they thought she had shut herself down, but she caught on the last two revolutions and began to idle quietly. And then they could hear.

Al's voice was high, hysterical. "—I come t' he'p you, I come t' he'p you, don' kill me, I'll he'p you—" He took a step forward; the dozer snorted and he fell to his knees. "I'll wash you an' grease you and change yo' ile," he said in a high singsong.

"The guy's not human," said Kelly wonderingly.

"He ain't housebroke either," Tom chuckled.

"—lemme he'p you. I'll fix you when you break down. I'll he'p you kill those other guys—"

"She don't need any help!" said Tom.

"The louse," growled Kelly. "The rotten little double-crossing polecat!" He stood up. "Hey, you Al! Come out o' that. I mean now! If she don't get you I will, if you don't move."

Al was crying now. "Shut up!" he screamed. "I know who's bawss hereabouts, an' so do you!" He pointed at the tractor. "She'll kill us all off'n we don't do what she wants!" He turned back to the machine. "I'll k-kill 'em fo' you. I'll wash you and shine you up and f-fix yo' hood. I'll put yo' blade back on. . . ."

Tom reached out and caught Kelly's leg as the tall man started out, blind mad. "Git back here," he barked. "What you want to do—get killed for the privilege of pinnin' his ears back?"

Kelly subsided and came back, threw himself down beside Tom, put his face in his hands. He was quivering with rage.

"Don't take on so," Tom said. "The man's plumb loco. You can't argue with him any more'n you can with *Daisy,* there. If he's got to get his, *Daisy*'ll give it to him."

"Aw, Tom, it ain't that. I know he ain't worth it, but I can't sit up here and watch him get himself killed. I can't, Tom."

Tom thumped him on the shoulder, because there were simply no words to be said. Suddenly he stiffened, snapped his fingers.

"There's our ground," he said urgently, pointing seaward. "The water—the wet beach where the surf runs. If we can get our ground clamp out there and her somewhere near it—"

"Ground the pan tractor. Run it out into the water. It ought to reach—partway, anyhow."

"That's it—c'mon."

They slid down the bank, snatched up the ground clamp, attached it to the frame of the pan tractor.

"I'll take it," said Tom, and as Kelly opened his mouth, Tom shoved him back against the welding machine. "No time to argue," he snapped, swung on to the machine, slapped her in gear and was off. Kelly took a step toward the tractor, and then his quick eye saw a bight of the ground cable about to foul a wheel of the welder. He stooped and threw it off, spread out the rest of it so it would pay off clear. Tom, with the incredible single-mindedness of the trained operator, watched only the black line of the trailing cable on the sand behind him. When it straightened, he stopped. The front of the tracks were sloshing in the gentle surf. He climbed off the side away from the Seven and tried to see. There was movement, and the growl of her motor now running at a bit more than idle, but he could not distinguish much.

Kelly picked up the rod-holder and went to peer around the head of the protruding bank. Al was on his feet, still crooning hysterically, sidling over toward *Daisy Etta*. Kelly ducked back, threw the switch on the arc generator, climbed the bank and crawled along through the sawgrass paralleling the beach until the holder in his hand tugged and he knew he had reached the end of the cable. He looked out at the beach; measured carefully with his eye the arc he would travel if he left his position and, keeping the cable taut, went out on the beach. At no point would he come within seventy feet of the possessed machine, let alone fifty. She had to be drawn in closer. And she had to be maneuvered out to the wet sand, or in the water—

Al Knowles, encouraged by the machine's apparent decision not to move, approached, though warily, and still running off at the mouth. "—we'll kill'em off an' then we'll keep it a secret and th' bahges'll come an' take us offen th' island and we'll go to anothah job an' kill us lots mo' . . . an' when yo' tracks git dry an' squeak we'll wet 'em up with blood, and you'll be rightly king o' th' hill . . . look yondah, look yondah, *Daisy Etta*, see them theah, by the otheh tractuh, theah they are, kill 'em, *Daisy*, kill 'em, *Daisy*, an' lemme he'p . . . heah me. *Daisy*, heah me, say you heah me—" and the motor roared in response. Al laid a timid hand on the radiator guard, leaning far over to do it, and the tractor still stood there grumbling but not moving. Al stepped back, motioned with his arm, began to walk off slowly toward the pan tractor, looking backwards as he did so like a man training a dog. "C'mon, c'mon, theah's one theah, le's *kill'm, kill'm, kill'm. . . .*"

And with a snort the tractor revved up and followed.

Kelly licked his lips without effect because his tongue was dry, too. The madman passed him, walking straight up the center of the beach, and the tractor, now no longer a bull-dozer, followed him; and there the sand was bone dry, sun-dried, dried to powder. As the tractor passed him, Kelly got up on all fours, went over the edge of the bank onto the beach, crouched there.

Al crooned, "I love ya, honey, I love ya, 'deed I do—"

Kelly ran crouching, like a man under machine-gun fire, making himself as small as possible and feeling as big as a barn door. The torn-up sand where the tractor had passed was under his feet now; he stopped, afraid to get much closer, afraid that a weakened, badly grounded arc might leap from the holder in his hand and serve only to alarm and infuriate the thing in the tractor. And just then Al saw him.

"There!" he screamed; and the tractor pulled up short. "Behind you! Get'm, *Daisy! Kill'm, kill'm, kill'm.*"

Kelly stood up almost wearily, fury and frustration too much to be borne. "In the water," he yelled, because it was what his whole being wanted. "Get'er in the water! Wet her tracks, Al!"

"*Kill'm, kill'm—*"

As the tractor started to turn, there was a commotion over by the pan tractor. It was Tom, jumping, shouting, waving his arms, swearing. He ran out from behind his machine, straight at the Seven. *Daisy Etta*'s motor roared and she swung to meet him, Al barely dancing back out of the way. Tom cut sharply, sand spouting under his pumping feet, and ran straight into the water. He went out to about waist deep, suddenly disappeared. He surfaced, spluttering, still trying to shout. Kelly took a better grip on his rod holder and rushed.

Daisy Etta, in following Tom's crazy rush, had swung in beside the pan tractor, not fifteen feet away; and she, too, was now in the surf. Kelly closed up the distance as fast as his long legs would let him; and as he approached to within that crucial fifty feet, Al Knowles hit him.

Al was frothing at the mouth, gibbering. The two men hit full tilt; Al's head caught Kelly in the midriff as he missed a straightarm, and the breath went out of him in one great *whoosh!* Kelly went down like tall timber, the whole world turned to one swirling red-gray haze. Al flung himself on the bigger man, clawing, smacking, too berserk to ball his fists.

"Ah'm go' to kill you," he gurgled. "She'll git one, I'll git t'other, an' then she'll know——"

Kelly covered his face with his arms, and as some wind was sucked at last into his laboring lungs, he flung them upward and sat up in one mighty surge. Al was hurled upward and to one side, and as he hit the ground Kelly reached out a long arm, and twisted his fingers into the man's coarse hair, raised him up, and came across with his other fist in a punch that would have killed him had it landed square. But Al managed to jerk to one side enough so that it only amputated a cheek. He fell and lay still. Kelly scrambled madly around in the sand for his welding-rod holder, found it and began to run again. He couldn't see Tom at all now, and the Seven was standing in the surf, moving slowly from side to side, backing out, ravening. Kelly held the rod-clamp and its trailing cable blindly before him and ran straight at the machine. And then it came—that thin, soundless bolt of energy. But this time it had its full force, for poor old Peebles's body had not been the ground that this swirling water offered. *Daisy Etta* literally leaped backwards toward him, and the water around her tracks spouted upward in hot steam. The sound of her engine ran up and up, broke, took on the rhythmic, uneven beat of a swing drummer. She threw herself from side to side like a cat with a bag over its head. Kelly stepped a little closer, hoping for another bolt to come from the clamp in his hand, but there was none, for——

"The circuit breaker!" cried Kelly.

He threw the holder up on the deck plate of the Seven in front of the seat, and ran across the little beach to the welder. He reached behind the switchboard, got his thumb on the contact hinge and jammed it down.

Daisy Etta leaped again, and then again, and suddenly her motor stopped. Heat in turbulent waves blurred the air over

her. The little gas tank for the starting motor went out with
a cannon's roar, and the big fuel tank, still holding thirty-odd
gallons of diesel oil followed. It puffed itself open rather than
exploded, and threw a great curtain of flame over the ground
behind the machine. Motor or no motor, then, Kelly distinctly saw the tractor shudder convulsively. There was a
crawling movement of the whole frame, a slight wave of motion away from the fuel tank, approaching the front of the
machine, and moving upward from the tracks. It culminated
in the crown of the radiator core, just in front of the radiator
cap; and suddenly an area of six or seven square inches literally *blurred* around the edges. For a second, then, it was normal, and finally it slumped molten, and liquid metal ran
down the sides, throwing out little sparks as it encountered
what was left of the charred paint. And only then was Kelly
conscious of agony in his left hand. He looked down. The
welding machine's generator had stopped, though the motor
was still turning, having smashed the friable coupling on its
drive shaft. Smoke poured from the generator, which had become little more than a heap of slag. Kelly did not scream,
though, until he looked and saw what had happened to his
hand—

When he could see straight again, he called for Tom, and
there was no answer. At last he saw something out in the
water, and plunged in after it. The splash of cold salt water
on his left hand he hardly felt, for the numbness of shock
'had set in. He grabbed at Tom's shirt with his good hand,
and then the ground seemed to pull itself out from under his
feet. That was it, then—a deep hole right off the beach. The
Seven had run right to the edge of it, had kept Tom there out
of his depth and—

He flailed wildly, struck out for the beach, so near and so
hard to get to. He gulped a stinging lungful of brine, and
only the lovely shock of his knee striking solid beach kept
him from giving up to the luxury of choking to death. Sobbing with effort, he dragged Tom's dead weight inshore and
clear of the surf. It was then that he became conscious of a
child's shrill weeping; for a mad moment he thought it was
himself, and then he looked and saw that it was Al Knowles.
He left Tom and went over to the broken creature.

"Get up, you," he snarled. The weeping only got louder.
Kelly rolled him over on his back—he was quite unresist-

ing—and belted him back and forth across the mouth until
Al began to choke. Then he hauled him to his feet and led
him over to Tom.

"Kneel down, scum. Put one of your knees between his
knees." Al stood still. Kelly hit him again and he did as he
was told.

"Put your hands on his lower ribs. There. O.K. Lean, you
rat. Now sit back." He sat down, holding his left wrist in his
right hand, letting the blood drop from the ruined hand.
"Lean. Hold it—sit back. Lean. Sit. Lean. Sit."

Soon Tom sighed and began to vomit weakly, and after
that he was all right.

This is the story of *Daisy Etta,* the bulldozer that went
mad and had a life of its own, and not the story of the flat-
top *Marokuru* of the Imperial Japanese Navy, which has
been told elsewhere. But there is a connection. You will
remember how the *Marokuru* was cut off from its base by the
concentrated attack on Truk, how it slipped far to the south
and east and was sunk nearer to our shores than any other
Jap warship in the whole course of the war. And you will
remember how a squadron of five planes, having been separated by three vertical miles of water from their flight deck,
turned east with their bombloads and droned away for a
suicide mission. You read that they bombed a minor airfield
in the outside of Panama's far-flung defenses, and all hands
crashed in the best sacrificial fashion.

Well, that was no airfield, no matter what it might have
looked like from the air. It was simply a roughly graded runway, white marl against brown scrub-grass.

The planes came two days after the death of *Daisy Etta,* as
Tom and Kelly sat in the shadow of the pile of fuel drums,
down in the coolness of the swag that *Daisy* had dug there to
fuel herself. They were poring over paper and pencil, trying
to complete the impossible task of making a written statement of what had happened on the island, and why they and
their company had failed to complete their contract. They
had found Chub and Harris, and had buried them next to the
other three. Al Knowles was tied up in the camp, because
they had heard him raving in his sleep, and it seemed he
could not believe that *Daisy* was dead and he still wanted to

go around killing operators for her. They knew that there must be an investigation, and they knew just how far their story would go; and having escaped a monster like *Daisy Etta*, life was far too sweet for them to want to be shot for sabotage. And murder.

The first stick of bombs struck three hundred yards behind them at the edge of the camp, and at the same instant a plane whistled low over their heads, and that was the first they knew about it. They ran to Al Knowles and untied his feet and the three of them headed for the bush. They found refuge, strangely enough, inside the mound where *Daisy Etta* had first met her possessor.

"Bless their black little hearts," said Kelly as he and Tom stood on the bluff and looked at the flaming wreckage of a camp and five medium bombers below them. And he took the statement they had been sweating out and tore it across.

"But what about him?" said Tom, pointing at Al Knowles, who was sitting on the ground, playing with his fingers. "He'll still spill the whole thing, no matter if we do try to blame it all on the bombing."

"What's the matter with that?" said Kelly.

Tom thought a minute, then grinned. "Why, nothing! That's just the sort of thing they'll expect from him!"

NO WOMAN BORN

Astounding,

December

by C. L. Moore

The mid-1940's were truly great years in the writing career of Catherine L. Moore, both individually and in collaboration with her husband, Henry Kuttner. This story was (we think) hers alone, and it is certainly her finest solo effort. The concept of the "cyborg," part-machine and part-human, had existed in science fiction before this story was published, but no one had explored the potential of the idea until "No Woman Born." It was also one of the first to examine the future of the arts in science fiction, and a classic story of anguish and rebirth.

(A couple of years ago, I attended a science fiction convention at which Catherine Moore was scheduled to speak. I was eager to see her for I had met her only once and that was thirty-five years before. She looked amazingly youthful still, and gave a good talk. It was delightful to see how lightly the years rested upon her. It helped, I am sure, that she was married again, and happily. Why not? Poor Hank had been dead for twenty years. —And yet, no one dating back to the older days of science fiction could think of Moore without Kuttner or Kuttner without Moore and I sat there feeling dissociated. How could they have been separated— I.A.)

She had been the loveliest creature whose image ever moved along the airways. John Harris, who was once her

584

manager, remembered doggedly how beautiful she had been as he rose in the silent elevator toward the room where Deirdre sat waiting for him.

Since the theater fire that had destroyed her a year ago, he had never been quite able to let himself remember her beauty clearly, except when some old poster, half in tatters, flaunted her face at him, or a maudlin memorial program flashed her image unexpectedly across the television screen. But now he had to remember.

The elevator came to a sighing stop and the door slid open. John Harris hesitated. He knew in his mind that he had to go on, but his reluctant muscles almost refused him. He was thinking helplessly, as he had not allowed himself to think until this moment, of the fabulous grace that had poured through her wonderful dancer's body, remembering her soft and husky voice with the little burr in it that had fascinated the audiences of the whole world.

There had never been anyone so beautiful.

In times before her, other actresses had been lovely and adulated, but never before Deirdre's day had the entire world been able to take one woman so wholly to its heart. So few outside the capitals had ever seen Bernhardt or the fabulous Jersey Lily. And the beauties of the movie screen had had to limit their audiences to those who could reach the theaters. But Deirdre's image had once moved glowingly across the television screens of every home in the civilized world. And in many outside the bounds of civilization. Her soft, husky songs had sounded in the depths of jungles, her lovely, languorous body had woven its patterns of rhythm in desert tents and polar huts. The whole world knew every smooth motion of her body and every cadence of her voice, and the way a subtle radiance had seemed to go on behind her features when she smiled.

And the whole world had mourned her when she died in the theater fire.

Harris could not quite think of her as other than dead, though he knew what sat waiting him in the room ahead. He kept remembering the old words James Stephens wrote long ago for another Deirdre, also lovely and beloved and unforgotten after two thousand years.

The time comes when our hearts sink utterly,
When we remember Deirdre and her tale,
And that her lips are dust. . . .
There has been again no woman born
Who was so beautiful; not one so beautiful
Of all the women born—

That wasn't quite true, of course—there had been one. Or
maybe, after all, this Deirdre who died only a year ago had
not been beautiful in the sense of perfection. He thought the
other one might not have been either, for there are always
women with perfection of feature in the world, and they are
not the ones that legend remembers. It was the light within,
shining through her charming, imperfect features, that had
made this Deirdre's face so lovely. No one else he had ever
seen had anything like the magic of the lost Deirdre.

Let all men go apart and mourn together—
No man can ever love her. Not a man
Can dream to be her lover. . . . No man say—
What could one say to her? There are no words
That one could say to her.

No, no words at all. And it was going to be impossible to
go through with this. Harris knew it overwhelmingly just as
his finger touched the buzzer. But the door opened almost instantly, and then it was too late.

Maltzer stood just inside, peering out through his heavy
spectacles. You could see how tensely he had been waiting.
Harris was a little shocked to see that the man was trembling.
It was hard to think of the confident and imperturbable Maltzer, whom he had known briefly a year ago, as shaken like
this. He wondered if Deirdre herself were as tremulous with
sheer nerves—but it was not time yet to let himself think of
that.

"Come in, come in," Maltzer said irritably. There was no
reason for irritation. The year's work, so much of it in
secrecy and solitude, must have tried him physically and
mentally to the very breaking point.

"She all right?" Harris asked inanely, stepping inside.

"Oh yes . . . yes, *she's* all right." Maltzer bit his thumbnail
and glanced over his shoulder at an inner door, where Harris
guessed she would be waiting.

"No," Maltzer said, as he took an involuntary step toward it. "We'd better have a talk first. Come over and sit down. Drink?"

Harris nodded, and watched Maltzer's hands tremble as he tilted the decanter. The man was clearly on the very verge of collapse, and Harris felt a sudden cold uncertainty open up in him in the one place where until now he had been oddly confident.

"She *is* all right?" he demanded, taking the glass.

"Oh yes, she's perfect. She's so confident it scares me." Maltzer gulped his drink and poured another before he sat down.

"What's wrong, then?"

"Nothing, I guess. Or . . . well, I don't know. I'm not sure anymore. I've worked toward this meeting for nearly a year, but now—well, I'm not sure it's time yet. I'm just not sure."

He stared at Harris, his eyes large and blurred behind the lenses. He was a thin, wire-taut man with all the bone and sinew showing plainly beneath the dark skin of his face. Thinner now than he had been a year ago when Harris saw him last.

"I've been too close to her," he said now. "I have no perspective anymore. All I can see is my own work. And I'm just not sure that's ready yet for you or anyone to see."

"She thinks so?"

"I never saw a woman so confident." Maltzer drank, the glass clicking on his teeth. He looked up suddenly through the distorting lenses. "Of course a failure now would mean—well, absolute collapse," he said.

Harris nodded. He was thinking of the year of incredibly painstaking work that lay behind this meeting, the immense fund of knowledge, of infinite patience, the secret collaboration of artists, sculptors, designers, scientists, and the genius of Maltzer governing them all as an orchestra conductor governs his players.

He was thinking too, with a certain unreasoning jealousy, of the strange, cold, passionless intimacy between Maltzer and Deirdre in that year, a closer intimacy than any two humans can ever have shared before. In a sense the Deirdre whom he saw in a few minutes would *be* Maltzer, just as he thought he detected in Maltzer now and then small manner-

isms of inflection and motion that had been **Deirdre's own.**
There had been between them a sort of unimaginable marriage stranger than anything that could ever have taken place
before.

"—so many complications," Maltzer was saying in his worried voice with its faintest possible echo of Deirdre's lovely,
cadenced rhythm. (The sweet, soft huskiness he would never
hear again.) "There was shock, of course. Terrible shock.
And a great fear of fire. We had to conquer that before we
could take the first steps. But we did it. When you go in
you'll probably find her sitting before the fire." He caught the
startled question in Harris' eyes and smiled. "No, she can't
feel the warmth now, of course. But she likes to watch the
flames. She's mastered any abnormal fear of them quite beautifully."

"She can—" Harris hesitated. "Her eyesight's normal
now?"

"Perfect," Maltzer said. "Perfect vision was fairly simple to
provide. After all, that sort of thing has already been worked
out, in other connections. I might even say her vision's a little
better than perfect, from our own standpoint." He shook his
head irritably. "I'm not worried about the mechanics of the
thing. Luckily they got to her before the brain was touched at
all. Shock was the only danger to her sensory centers, and we
took care of all that first of all, as soon as communication
could be established. Even so, it needed great courage on her
part. Great courage." He was silent for a moment, staring
into his empty glass.

"Harris," he said suddenly, without looking up, "have I
made a mistake? Should we have let her die?"

Harris shook his head helplessly. It was an unanswerable
question. It had tormented the whole world for a year now.
There had been hundreds of answers and thousands of words
written on the subject. Has anyone the right to preserve a
brain alive when its body is destroyed? Even if a new body
can be provided, necessarily so very unlike the old?

"It's not that she's—ugly—now," Maltzer went on hurriedly, as if afraid of an answer. "Metal isn't ugly. And
Deirdre . . . well, you'll see. I tell you, I can't see myself. I
know the whole mechanism so well—it's just mechanics to
me. Maybe she's—grotesque. I don't know. Often I've wished
I hadn't been on the spot, with all my ideas, just when the

fire broke out. Or that it could have been anyone but Deirdre. She was so beautiful— Still, if it had been someone else I think the whole thing might have failed completely. It takes more than just an uninjured brain. It takes strength and courage beyond common, and—well, something more. Something—unquenchable. Deirdre has it. She's still Deirdre. In a way she's still beautiful. But I'm not sure anybody but myself could see that. And you know what she plans?"

"No—what?"

"She's going back on the air-screen."

Harris looked at him in stunned disbelief.

"She *is* still beautiful," Maltzer told him fiercely. "She's got courage, and a serenity that amazes me. And she isn't in the least worried or resentful about what's happened. Or afraid what the verdict of the public will be. But I am, Harris. I'm terrified."

They looked at each other for a moment more, neither speaking. Then Maltzer shrugged and stood up.

"She's in there," he said, gesturing with his glass.

Harris turned without a word, not giving himself time to hesitate. He crossed toward the inner door.

The room was full of a soft, clear, indirect light that climaxed in the fire crackling on a white tiled hearth. Harris paused inside the door, his heart beating thickly. He did not see her for a moment. It was a perfectly commonplace room, bright, light, with pleasant furniture, and flowers on the tables. Their perfume was sweet on the clear air. He did not see Deirdre.

Then a chair by the fire creaked as she shifted her weight in it. The high back hid her, but she spoke. And for one dreadful moment it was the voice of an automaton that sounded in the room, metallic, without inflection.

"Hel-lo—" said the voice. Then she laughed and tried again. And it was the old, familiar, sweet huskiness he had not hoped to hear again as long as he lived.

In spite of himself he said, "Deirdre!" and her image rose before him as if she herself had risen unchanged from the chair, tall, golden, swaying a little with her wonderful dancer's poise, the lovely, imperfect features lighted by the glow that made them beautiful. It was the cruelest thing his memory could have done to him. And yet the voice—after that one lapse, the voice was perfect.

"Come and look at me, John," she said.

He crossed the floor slowly, forcing himself to move. That instant's flash of vivid recollection had nearly wrecked his hard-won composure. He tried to keep his mind perfectly blank as he came at last to the verge of seeing what no one but Maltzer had so far seen or known about in its entirety. No one at all had known what shape would be forged to clothe the most beautiful woman on Earth, now that her beauty was gone.

He had envisioned many shapes. Great, lurching robot forms, cylindrical, with hinged arms and legs. A glass case with the brain floating in it and appendages to serve its needs. Grotesque visions, like nightmares come nearly true. And each more inadequate than the last, for what metal shape could possibly do more than house ungraciously the mind and brain that had once enchanted a whole world?

Then he came around the wing of the chair, and saw her.

The human brain is often too complicated a mechanism to function perfectly. Harris's brain was called upon now to perform a very elaborate series of shifting impressions. First, incongruously, he remembered a curious inhuman figure he had once glimpsed leaning over the fence rail outside a farmhouse. For an instant the shape had stood up, integrated, ungainly, impossibly human, before the glancing eye resolved it into an arrangement of brooms and buckets. What the eye had found only roughly humanoid, the suggestible brain had accepted fully formed. It was thus now, with Deirdre.

The first impression that his eyes and mind took from sight of her was shocked and incredulous, for his brain said to him unbelievingly, *"This is Deirdre! She hasn't changed at all!"*

Then the shift of perspective took over, and even more shockingly, eye and brain said, "No, not Deirdre—not human. Nothing but metal coils. Not Deirdre at all—" And that was the worst. It was like waking from a dream of someone beloved and lost, and facing anew, after that heartbreaking reassurance of sleep, the inflexible fact that nothing can bring the lost to life again. Deirdre was gone, and this was only machinery heaped in a flowered chair.

Then the machinery moved, exquisitely, smoothly, with a grace as familiar as the swaying form he remembered. The sweet, husky voice of Deirdre said,

"It's me, John darling. It really is, you know."

And it was.

That was the third metamorphosis, and the final one. Illusion steadied and became factual, real. It was Deirdre.

He sat down bonelessly. He had no muscles. He looked at her speechless and unthinking, letting his senses take in the sight of her without trying to rationalize what he saw.

She was golden still. They had kept that much of her, the first impression of warmth and color which had once belonged to her sleek hair and the apricot tints of her skin. But they had had the good sense to go no further. They had not tried to make a wax image of the lost Deirdre. (*No woman born who was so beautiful—Not one so beautiful, of all the women born—*)

And so she had no face. She had only a smooth, delicately modeled ovoid for her head, with a . . . a sort of crescent-shaped mask across the frontal area where her eyes would have been if she had needed eyes. A narrow, curved quarter-moon, with the horns turned upward. It was filled in with something translucent, like cloudy crystal, and tinted the aquamarine of the eyes Deirdre used to have. Through that, then, she saw the world. Through that she looked without eyes, and behind it, as behind the eyes of a human—she was.

Except for that, she had no features. And it had been wise of those who designed her, he realized now. Subconsciously he had been dreading some clumsy attempt at human features that might creak like a marionette's in parodies of animation. The eyes, perhaps, had had to open in the same place upon her head, and at the same distance apart, to make easy for her an adjustment to the stereoscopic vision she used to have. But he was glad they had not given her two eye-shaped openings with glass marbles inside them. The mask was better.

(Oddly enough, he did not once think of the naked brain that must lie inside the metal. The mask was symbol enough for the woman within. It was enigmatic; you did not know if her gaze was on you searchingly, or wholly withdrawn. And it had no variations of brilliance such as once had played across the incomparable mobility of Deirdre's face. But eyes, even human eyes, are as a matter of fact enigmatic enough. They have no expression except what the lids impart; they take all animation from the features. We automatically watch the eyes of the friend we speak with, but if he happens to be

lying down so that he speaks across his shoulder and his face
is upside-down to us, quite as automatically we watch the
mouth. The gaze keeps shifting nervously between mouth and
eyes in their reversed order, for it is the position in the face,
not the feature itself, which we are accustomed to accept as
the seat of the soul. Deirdre's mask was in that proper place;
it was easy to accept it as a mask over eyes.)

She had, Harris realized as the first shock quieted, a very
beautifully shaped head—a bare, golden skull. She turned it a
little, gracefully upon her neck of metal, and he saw that the
artist who shaped it had given her the most delicate suggestion of cheekbones, narrowing in the blankness below the
mask to the hint of a human face. Not too much. Just
enough so that when the head turned you saw by its modeling that it had moved, lending perspective and foreshorten-
ing to the expressionless golden helmet. Light did not slip
uninterrupted as if over the surface of a golden egg. Brancusi
himself had never made anything more simple or more subtle
than the modeling of Deirdre's head.

But all expression, of course, was gone. All expression had
gone up in the smoke of the theater fire, with the lovely, mobile, radiant features which had meant Deirdre.

As for her body, he could not see its shape. A garment hid
her. But they had made no incongruous attempt to give her
back the clothing that once had made her famous. Even the
softness of cloth would have called the mind too sharply to
the remembrance that no human body lay beneath the folds,
nor does metal need the incongruity of cloth for its protection. Yet without garments, he realized, she would have
looked oddly naked, since her new body was humanoid, not
angular machinery.

The designer had solved his paradox by giving her a robe
of very fine metal mesh. It hung from the gentle slope of her
shoulders in straight, pliant folds like a longer Grecian
chlamys, flexible, yet with weight enough of its own not to
cling too revealingly to whatever metal shape lay beneath.

The arms they had given her were left bare, and the feet
and ankles. And Maltzer had performed his greatest miracle
in the limbs of the new Deirdre. It was a mechanical miracle
basically, but the eye appreciated first that he had also
showed supreme artistry and understanding.

Her arms were pale shining gold, tapered smoothly, without modeling, and flexible their whole length in diminishing metal bracelets fitting one inside the other clear down to the slim, round wrists. The hands were more nearly human than any other feature about her, though they, too, were fitted together in delicate, small sections that slid upon one another with the flexibility almost of flesh. The fingers' bases were solider than human, and the fingers themselves tapered to longer tips.

Her feet, too, beneath the tapering broader rings of the metal ankles, had been constructed upon the model of human feet. Their finely tooled sliding segments gave her an arch and a heel and a flexible forward section formed almost like the *sollerets* of medieval armor.

She looked, indeed, very much like a creature in armor, with her delicately plated limbs and her featureless head like a helmet with a visor of glass, and her robe of chain-mail. But no knight in armor ever moved as Deirdre moved, or wore his armor upon a body of such inhumanly fine proportions. Only a knight from another world, or a knight of Oberon's court, might have shared that delicate likeness.

Briefly he had been surprised at the smallness and exquisite proportions of her. He had been expecting the ponderous mass of such robots as he had seen, wholly automatons. And then he realized that for them, much of the space had to be devoted to the inadequate mechanical brains that guided them about their duties. Deirdre's brain still preserved and proved the craftsmanship of an artisan far defter than man. Only the body was of metal, and it did not seem complex, though he had not yet been told how it was motivated.

Harris had no idea how long he sat staring at the figure in the cushioned chair. She was still lovely—indeed, she was still Deirdre—and as he looked he let the careful schooling of his face relax. There was no need to hide his thoughts from her.

She stirred upon the cushions, the long, flexible arms moving with a litheness that was not quite human. The motion disturbed him as the body itself had not, and in spite of himself his face froze a little. He had the feeling that from behind the crescent mask she was watching him very closely.

Slowly she rose.

The motion was very smooth. Also it was serpentine, as if the body beneath the coat of mail were made in the same interlocking sections as her limbs. He had expected and feared mechanical rigidity; nothing had prepared him for this more than human suppleness.

She stood quietly, letting the heavy mailed folds of her garment settle about her. They fell together with a faint ringing sound, like small bells far off, and hung beautifully in pale golden, sculptured folds. He had risen automatically as she did. Now he faced her, staring. He had never seen her stand perfectly still, and she was not doing it now. She swayed just a bit, vitality burning inextinguishably in her brain as once it had burned in her body, and stolid immobility was as impossible for her as it had always been. The golden garment caught points of light from the fire and glimmered at him with tiny reflections as she moved.

Then she put her featureless helmeted head a little to one side, and he heard her laughter as familiar in its small, throaty, intimate sound as he had ever heard it from her living throat. And every gesture, every attitude, every flowing of motion into motion was so utterly Deirdre that the overwhelming illusion swept his mind again and this was the flesh-and-blood woman as clearly as if he saw her standing there whole once more, like Phoenix from the fire.

"Well, John," she said in the soft, husky, amused voice he remembered perfectly. "Well, John, is it I?" She knew it was. Perfect assurance sounded in the voice. "The shock will wear off, you know. It'll be easier and easier as time goes on. I'm quite used to myself now. See?"

She turned away from him and crossed the room smoothly, with the old, poised, dancer's glide, to the mirror that paneled one side of the room. And before it, as he had so often seen her preen before, he watched her preening now, running flexible metallic hands down the folds of her metal garment, turning to admire herself over one metal shoulder, making the mailed folds tinkle and sway as she struck an arabesque position before the glass.

His knees let him down into the chair she had vacated. Mingled shock and relief loosened all his muscles in him, and she was more poised and confident than he.

"It's a miracle," he said with conviction. "It's *you*. But I don't see how—" He had meant, "—how, without face or body—" but clearly he could not finish that sentence.

She finished it for him in her own mind, and answered without self-consciousness. "It's motion, mostly," she said, still admiring her own suppleness in the mirror. "See?" And very lightly on her springy, armored feet she flashed through an enchaînement of brilliant steps, swinging round with a pirouette to face him. "That was what Maltzer and I worked out between us, after I began to get myself under control again." Her voice was somber for a moment, remembering a dark time in the past. Then she went on, "It wasn't easy, of course, but it was fascinating. You'll never guess how fascinating, John! We knew we couldn't work out anything like a facsimile of the way I used to look, so we had to find some other basis to build on. And motion is the other basis of recognition, after actual physical likeness."

She moved lightly across the carpet toward the window and stood looking down, her featureless face averted a little and the light shining across the delicately hinted curves of the cheekbones.

"Luckily," she said, her voice amused, "I never was beautiful. It was all—well, vivacity, I suppose, and muscular co-ordination. Years and years of training, and all of it engraved here"—she struck her golden helmet a light, ringing blow with golden knuckles—"in the habit patterns grooved into my brain. So this body . . . did he tell you? . . . works entirely through the brain. Electromagnetic currents flowing along from ring to ring, like this." She rippled a boneless arm at him with a motion like flowing water. "Nothing holds me to-gether—nothing!—except muscles of magnetic currents. And if I'd been somebody else—somebody who moved differently, why the flexible rings would have moved differently too, guided by the impulse from another brain. I'm not conscious of doing anything I haven't always done. The same impulses that used to go out to my muscles go out now to—this." And she made a shuddering, serpentine motion of both arms at him, like a Cambodian dancer, and then laughed wholeheart-edly, the sound of it ringing through the room with such full-throated merriment that he could not help seeing again the familiar face crinkled with pleasure, the white teeth shin-ing. "It's all perfectly subconscious now," she told him. "It took lots of practice at first, of course, but now even my signature looks just as it always did—the coordination is duplicated that delicately." She rippled her arms at him again and chuckled.

"But the voice, too," Harris protested inadequately. "It's *your* voice, Deirdre."

"The voice isn't only a matter of throat construction and breath control, my darling Johnnie! At least, so Professor Maltzer assured me a year ago, and I certainly haven't any reason to doubt him!" She laughed again. She was laughing a little too much, with a touch of the bright, hysteric overexcitement he remembered so well. But if any woman ever had reason for mild hysteria, surely Deirdre had it now.

The laughter rippled and ended, and she went on, her voice eager. "He says voice control is almost wholly a matter of hearing what you produce, once you've got adequate mechanism, of course. That's why deaf people, with the same vocal chords as ever, let their voices change completely and lose all inflection when they've been deaf long enough. And luckily, you see, I'm not deaf!"

She swung around to him, the folds of her robe twinkling and ringing, and rippled up and up a clear, true scale to a lovely high note, and then cascaded down again like water over a falls. But she left him no time for applause. "Perfectly simple, you see. All it took was a little matter of genius from the professor to get it worked out for me! He started with a new variation of the old Vodor you must remember hearing about, years ago. Originally, of course, the thing was ponderous. You know how it worked—speech broken down to a few basic sounds and built up again in combinations produced from a keyboard. I think originally the sounds were a sort of *ktch* and a *shooshing* noise, but we've got it all worked to a flexibility and range quite as good as human now. All I do is—well, mentally play on the keyboard of my . . . my sound-unit, I suppose it's called. It's much more complicated than that, of course, but I've learned to do it unconsciously. And I regulate it by ear, quite automatically now. If you were—*here*—instead of me, and you'd had the same practice, your own voice would be coming out of the same keyboard and diaphragm instead of mine. It's all a matter of the brain patterns that operated the body and now operate the machinery. They send out very strong impulses that are stepped up as much as necessary somewhere or other in here—" Her hands waved vaguely over the mesh-robed body.

She was silent a moment, looking out the window. Then she turned away and crossed the floor to the fire, sinking

again into the flowered chair. Her helmet-skull turned its
mask to face him and he could feel a quiet scrutiny behind
the aquamarine of its gaze.

"It's—odd," she said, "being here in this . . . this . . . instead of a body. But not as odd or as alien as you might
think. I've thought about it a lot—I've had plenty of time to
think—and I've begun to realize what a tremendous force the
human ego really is. I'm not sure I want to suggest it has any
mystical power it can impress on mechanical things, but it
does seem to have a power of some sort. It does instill its
own force into inanimate objects, and they take on a personality of their own. People do impress their personalities on
the houses they live in, you know. I've noticed that often.
Even empty rooms. And it happens with other things too, especially, I think, with inanimate things that men depend on
for their lives. Ships, for instance—they always have personalities of their own.

"And planes—in wars you always hear of planes crippled
too badly to fly, but struggling back anyhow with their crews.
Even guns acquire a sort of ego. Ships and guns and planes
are 'she' to the men who operate them and depend on them
for their lives. It's as if machinery with complicated moving
parts almost simulates life, and does acquire from the men
who used it—well, not exactly life, of course—but a personality. I don't know what. Maybe it absorbs some of the actual
electrical impulses their brains throw off, especially in times
of stress.

"Well, after awhile I began to accept the idea that this new
body of mine could behave at least as responsively as a ship
or a plane. Quite apart from the fact that my own brain controls its 'muscles.' I believe there's an affinity between men
and the machines they make. They make them out of their
own brains, really, a sort of mental conception and gestation,
and the result responds to the minds that created them, and
to all human minds that understand and manipulate them."

She stirred uneasily and smoothed a flexible hand along her
mesh-robed metal thigh. "So this is myself," she said.
"Metal—but me. And it grows more and more myself the
longer I live in it. It's my house and the machine my life depends on, but much more intimately in each case than any
real house or machine ever was before to any other human.
And you know, I wonder if in time I'll forget what flesh felt

like—my own flesh, when I touched it like this—and the metal against the metal will be so much the same I'll never even notice?"

Harris did not try to answer her. He sat without moving, watching her expressionless face. In a moment she went on.

"I'll tell you the best thing, John," she said, her voice softening to the old intimacy he remembered so well that he could see superimposed upon the blank skull the warm, intent look that belonged with the voice. "I'm not going to live forever. It may not sound like a—best thing—but it is, John. You know, for a while that was the worst of all, after I knew I was—after I woke up again. The thought of living on and on in a body that wasn't mine, seeing everyone I knew grow old and die, and not being able to stop—

"But Maltzer says my brain will probably wear out quite normally—except, of course, that I won't have to worry about looking old!—and when it gets tired and stops, the body I'm in won't be any longer. The magnetic muscles that hold it into my own shape and motions will let go when the brain lets go, and there'll be nothing but a . . . a pile of disconnected rings. If they ever assemble it again, it won't be me." She hesitated. "I like that, John," she said, and he felt from behind the mask a searching of his face.

He knew and understood that somber satisfaction. He could not put it into words; neither of them wanted to do that. But he understood. It was the conviction of mortality, in spite of her immortal body. She was not cut off from the rest of her race in the essence of their humanity, for though she wore a body of steel and they perishable flesh, yet she must perish too, and the same fears and faiths still united her to mortals and humans, though she wore the body of Oberon's inhuman knight. Even in her death she must be unique—dissolution in a shower of tinkling and clashing rings, he thought, and almost envied her the finality and beauty of that particular death—but afterward, oneness with humanity in however much or little awaited them all. So she could feel that this exile in metal was only temporary, in spite of everything.

(And providing, of course, that the mind inside the metal did not veer from its inherited humanity as the years went by. A dweller in a house may impress his personality upon the walls, but subtly the walls too, may impress their own shape upon the ego of the man. Neither of them thought of that, at the time.)

Deirdre sat a moment longer in silence. Then the mood vanished and she rose again, spinning so that the robe belled out ringing about her ankles. She rippled another scale up and down, faultlessly and with the same familiar sweetness of tone that had made her famous.

"So I'm going right back on the stage, John," she said serenely. "I can still sing. I can still dance. I'm still myself in everything that matters, and I can't imagine doing anything else for the rest of my life."

He could not answer without stammering a little. "Do you think . . . will they accept you, Deirdre? After all—"

"They'll accept me," she said in that confident voice. "Oh, they'll come to see a freak at first, of course, but they'll stay to watch—Deirdre. And come back again and again just as they always did. You'll see, my dear."

But hearing her sureness, suddenly Harris himself was unsure. Maltzer had not been, either. She was so regally confident, and disappointment would be so deadly a blow at all that remained of her—

She was so delicate a being now, really. Nothing but a glowing and radiant mind poised in metal, dominating it, bending the steel to the illusion of her lost loveliness with a sheer self-confidence that gleamed through the metal body. But the brain sat delicately on its base of reason. She had been through intolerable stresses already, perhaps more terrible depths of despair and self-knowledge than any human brain had yet endured before her, for—since Lazarus himself—who had come back from the dead?

But if the world did not accept her as beautiful, what then? If they laughed, or pitied her, or came only to watch a jointed freak performing as if on strings where the loveliness of Deirdre had once enchanted them, what then? And he could not be perfectly sure they would not. He had known her too well in the flesh to see her objectively even now, in metal. Every inflection of her voice called up the vivid memory of the face that had flashed its evanescent beauty in some look to match the tone. She was Deirdre to Harris simply because she had been so intimately familiar in every pose and attitude, through so many years. But people who knew her only slightly, or saw her for the first time in metal—what would they see?

A marionette? Or the real grace and loveliness shining through?

He had no possible way of knowing. He saw her too clearly as she had been to see her now at all, except so linked with the past that she was not wholly metal. And he knew what Maltzer feared, for Maltzer's psychic blindness toward her lay at the other extreme. He had never known Deirdre except as a machine, and he could not see her objectively any more than Harris could. To Maltzer she was pure metal, a robot his own hands and brain had devised, mysteriously animated by the mind of Deirdre, to be sure, but to all outward seeming a thing of metal solely. He had worked so long over each intricate part of her body, he knew so well how every jointure in it was put together, that he could not see the whole. He had studied many film records of her, of course, as she used to be, in order to gauge the accuracy of his facsimile, but this thing he had made was a copy only. He was too close to Deirdre to see her. And Harris, in a way, was too far. The indomitable Deirdre herself shone so vividly through the metal that his mind kept superimposing one upon the other.

How would an audience react to her? Where in the scale between these two extremes would their verdict fall?

For Deirdre, there was only one possible answer.

"I'm not worried," Deirdre said serenely, and spread her golden hands to the fire to watch lights dancing in reflection upon their shining surfaces. "I'm still myself. I've always had . . . well, power over my audiences. Any good performer knows when he's got it. Mine isn't gone. I can still give them what I always gave, only now with greater variations and more depths than I ever have done before. Why, look—" She gave a little wriggle of excitement.

"You know the arabesque principle—getting the longest possible distance from fingertip to toetip with a long, slow curve through the whole length? And the brace of the other leg and arm giving contrast? Well, look at me. I don't work on hinges now. I can make every motion a long curve if I want to. My body's different enough now to work out a whole new school of dancing. Of course there'll be things I used to do that I won't attempt now—no more dancing *sur les pointes,* for instance—but the new things will more than balance the loss. I've been practicing. Do you know I can turn a hundred *fouettés* now without a flaw? And I think I could go right on and turn a thousand, if I wanted."

She made the firelight flash on her hands, and her robe rang musically as she moved her shoulders a little. "I've already worked out one new dance for myself," she said. "God knows I'm no choreographer, but I did want to experiment first. Later, you know, really creative men like Massanchine or Fokhileff may want to do something entirely new for me—a whole new sequence of movements based on a new technique. And music—that could be quite different, too. Oh, there's no end to the possibilities! Even my voice has more range and power. Luckily I'm not an actress—it would be silly to try to play Camille or Juliet with a cast of ordinary people. Not that I couldn't, you know." She turned her head to stare at Harris through the mask of glass. "I honestly think I could. But it isn't necessary. There's too much else. Oh, I'm not worried!"

"Maltzer's worried," Harris reminded her.

She swung away from the fire, her metal robe ringing, and into her voice came the old note of distress that went with a furrowing of her forehead and a sideways tilt of the head. The head went sideways as it had always done, and he could see the furrowed brow almost as clearly as if flesh still clothed her.

"I know. And I'm worried about him, John. He's worked so awfully hard over me. This is the doldrums now, the letdown period, I suppose. I know what's on his mind. He's afraid I'll look just the same to the world as I look to him. Tooled metal. He's in a position no one ever quite achieved before, isn't he? Rather like God." Her voice rippled a little with amusement. "I suppose to God we must look like a collection of cells and corpuscles ourselves. But Maltzer lacks a god's detached viewpoint."

"He can't see you as I do, anyhow." Harris was choosing his words with difficulty. "I wonder, though—would it help him any if you postponed your debut awhile? You've been with him too closely, I think. You don't quite realize how near a breakdown he is. I was shocked when I saw him just now."

The golden head shook. "No. He's close to a breaking

point, maybe, but I think the only cure's action. He wants me to retire and stay out of sight, John. Always. He's afraid for anyone to see me except a few old friends who remember me as I was. People he can trust to be—kind." She laughed. It was very strange to hear that ripple of mirth from the blank, unfeatured skull. Harris was seized with sudden panic at the thought of what reaction it might evoke in an audience of strangers. As if he had spoken the fear aloud, her voice denied it. "I don't need kindness. And it's no kindness to Maltzer to hide me under a bushel. He *has* worked too hard, I know. He's driven himself to a breaking point. But it'll be a complete negation of all he's worked for if I hide myself now. You don't know what a tremendous lot of geniuses and artistry went into me, John. The whole idea from the start was to recreate what I'd lost so that it could be proved that beauty and talent need not be sacrificed by the destruction of parts or all the body.

"It wasn't only for me that we meant to prove that. There'll be others who suffer injuries that once might have ruined them. This was to end all suffering like that forever. It was Maltzer's gift to the whole race as well as to me. He's really a humanitarian, John, like most great men. He'd never have given up a year of his life to this work if it had been for any one individual alone. He was seeing thousands of others beyond me as he worked. And I won't let him ruin all he's achieved because he's afraid to prove it now he's got it. The whole wonderful achievement will be worthless if I don't take the final step. I think his breakdown, in the end, would be worse and more final if I never tried than if I tried and failed."

Harris sat in silence. There was no answer he could make to that. He hoped the little twinge of shamefaced jealousy he suddenly felt did not show, as he was reminded anew of the intimacy closer than marriage which had of necessity bound these two together. And he knew that any reaction of his would in its way be almost as prejudiced as Maltzer's, for a reason at once the same and entirely opposite. Except that he himself came fresh to the problem, while Maltzer's viewpoint was colored by a year of overwork and physical and mental exhaustion.

"What are you going to do?" he asked.

She was standing before the fire when he spoke, swaying

just a little so that highlights danced all along her golden body. Now she turned with a serpentine grace and sank into the cushioned chair beside her. It came to him suddenly that she was much more than humanly graceful—quite as much as he had once feared she would be less than human.

"I've already arranged for a performance," she told him, her voice a little shaken with a familiar mixture of excitement and defiance.

Harris sat up with a start. "How? Where? There hasn't been any publicity at all yet, has there? I didn't know—"

"Now, now, Johnnie," her amused voice soothed him. "You'll be handling everything just as usual once I get started back to work—that is, if you still want to. But this I've arranged for myself. It's going to be a surprise. I . . . I felt it had to be a surprise." She wriggled a little among the cushions. "Audience psychology is something I've always felt rather than known, and I do feel this is the way it ought to be done. There's no precedent. Nothing like this ever happened before. I'll have to go by my own intuition."

"You mean it's to be a complete surprise?"

"I think it must be. I don't want the audience coming in with preconceived ideas. I want them to see me exactly as I am now *first*, before they know who or what they're seeing. They must realize I can still give as good a performance as ever before they remember and compare it with my past performances. I don't want them to come ready to pity my handicaps—I haven't got any!—or full of morbid curiosity. So I'm going on the air after the regular eight-o'clock telecast of the feature from Teleo City. I'm just going to do one specialty in the usual vaude program. It's all been arranged. They'll build up to it, of course, as the highlight of the evening, but they aren't to say who I am until the end of the performance—if the audience hasn't recognized me already, by then."

"Audience?"

"Of course. Surely you haven't forgotten they still play to a theater audience at Teleo City? That's why I want to make my debut there. I've always played better when there were people in the studio, so I could gauge reactions. I think most performers do. Anyhow, it's all arranged."

"Does Maltzer know?"

She wriggled uncomfortably. "Not yet."

"But he'll have to give his permission too, won't he? I mean—"

"Now look, John! That's another idea you and Maltzer will have to get out of your minds. I don't belong to him. In a way he's just been my doctor through a long illness, but I'm free to discharge him whenever I choose. If there were ever any legal disagreement, I suppose he'd be entitled to quite a lot of money for the work he's done on my new body—for the body itself, really, since it's his own machine, in one sense. But he doesn't own it, or me. I'm not sure just how the question would be decided by the courts—there again, we've got a problem without precedent. The body may be his work, but the brain that makes it something more than a collection of metal rings is *me,* and he couldn't restrain me against my will even if he wanted to. Not legally, and not—" She hesitated oddly and looked away. For the first time Harris was aware of something beneath the surface of her mind which was quite strange to him.

"Well, anyhow," she went on, "that question won't come up. Maltzer and I have been much too close in the past year to clash over anything as essential as this. He knows in his heart that I'm right, and he won't try to restrain me. His work won't be completed until I do what I was built to do. And I intend to do it."

That strange little quiver of something—something un-Deirdre—which had so briefly trembled beneath the surface of familiarity stuck in Harris's mind as something he must recall and examine later. Now he said only, "All right. I suppose I agree with you. How soon are you going to do it?"

She turned her head so that even the glass mask through which she looked out at the world was foreshortened away from him, and the golden helmet with its hint of sculptured cheekbone was entirely enigmatic.

"Tonight," she said.

Maltzer's thin hand shook so badly that he could not turn the dial. He tried twice and then laughed nervously and shrugged at Harris.

"You get her," he said.

Harris glanced at his watch. "It isn't time yet. She won't be on for half an hour."

Maltzer made a gesture of violent impatience. "Get it, get it!"

Harris shrugged a little in turn and twisted the dial. On the tilted screen above them shadows and sound blurred together and then clarified into a somber medieval hall, vast, vaulted, people in bright costumes moving like pygmies through its dimness. Since the play concerned Mary of Scotland, the actors were dressed in something approximating Elizabethan garb, but as every era tends to translate costume into terms of the current fashions, the women's hair was dressed in a style that would have startled Elizabeth, and their footgear was entirely anachronistic.

The hall dissolved and a face swam up into soft focus upon the screen. The dark, lush beauty of the actress who was playing the Stuart queen glowed at them in velvety perfection from the clouds of her pearl-strewn hair. Maltzer groaned.

"She's competing with *that*," he said hollowly.

"You think she can't?"

Maltzer slapped the chair arms with angry palms. Then the quivering of his fingers seemed suddenly to strike him, and he muttered to himself, "Look at 'em! I'm not even fit to handle a hammer and saw." But the mutter was an aside. "Of course she can't compete," he cried irritably. "She hasn't any sex. She isn't female any more. She doesn't know that yet, but she'll learn."

Harris stared at him, feeling a little stunned. Somehow the thought had not occurred to him before at all, so vividly had the illusion of the old Deirdre hung about the new one.

"She's an abstraction now," Maltzer went on, drumming his palms upon the chair in quick, nervous rhythms. "I don't know what it'll do to her, but there'll be change. Remember Abelard? She's lost everything that made her essentially what the public wanted, and she's going to find it out the hard way. After that—" He grimaced savagely and was silent.

"She hasn't lost everything," Harris defended. "She can dance and sing as well as ever, maybe better. She still has grace and charm and—"

"Yes, but where did the grace and charm come from? Not out of the habit patterns in her brain. No, out of human contacts, out of all the things that stimulate sensitive minds to creativeness. And she's lost three of her five senses. Everything she can't see and hear is gone. One of the strongest stimuli to a woman of her type was the knowledge of sex competition. You know how she sparkled when a man came into the room? All that's gone, and it was an essential. You know how liquor stimulated her? She's lost that. She couldn't taste food or drink even if she needed it. Perfume, flowers, all the odors we respond to mean nothing to her now. She can't feel anything with tactual delicacy any more. She used to surround herself with luxuries—she drew her stimuli from them—and that's all gone too. She's withdrawn from all physical contacts."

He squinted at the screen, not seeing it, his face drawn into lines like the lines of a skull. All flesh seemed to have dissolved off his bones in the past year, and Harris thought almost jealously that even in that way he seemed to be drawing nearer Deirdre in her fleshlessness with every passing week.

"Sight," Maltzer said, "is the most highly civilized of the senses. It was the last to come. The other senses tie us in closely with the very roots of life; I think we perceive with them more keenly than we know. The things we realize through taste and smell and feeling stimulate directly, without a detour through the centers of conscious thought. You know how often a taste or odor will recall a memory to you so subtly you don't know exactly what caused it? We need those primitive senses to tie us in with nature and the race. Through those ties Deirdre drew her vitality without realizing it. Sight is a cold, intellectual thing compared with the other senses. But it's all she has to draw on now. She isn't a human being any more, and I think what humanity is left in her will drain out little by little and never be replaced. Abelard, in a way, was a prototype. But Deirdre's loss is complete."

"She isn't human," Harris agreed slowly. "But she isn't pure robot either. She's something somewhere between the two, and I think it's a mistake to try to guess just where, or what the outcome will be."

"I don't have to guess," Maltzer said in a grim voice. "I know. I wish I'd let her die. I've done something to her a thousand times worse than the fire ever could. I should have let her die in it."

"Wait," said Harris. "Wait and see. I think you're wrong."

On the television screen Mary of Scotland climbed the

scaffold to her doom, the gown of traditional scarlet clinging warmly to supple young curves as anachronistic in their way as the slippers beneath the gown, for—as everyone but play-wrights knows—Mary was well into middle age before she died. Gracefully this latter-day Mary bent her head, sweeping the long hair aside, kneeling to the block.

Maltzer watched stonily, seeing another woman entirely.

"I shouldn't have let her," he was muttering. "I shouldn't have let her do it."

"Do you really think you'd have stopped her if you could?" Harris asked quietly. And the other man after a moment's pause shook his head jerkily.

"No, I suppose not. I keep thinking if I worked and waited a little longer maybe I could make it easier for her, but—no, I suppose not. She's got to face them sooner or later, being herself." He stood up abruptly, shoving back his chair. "If she only weren't so . . . so frail. She doesn't realize how deli-cately poised her very sanity is. We gave her what we could—the artists and the designers and I, all gave our very best—but she's so pitifully handicapped even with all we could do. She'll always be an abstraction and a . . . a freak, cut off from the world by handicaps worse in their way than anything any human being ever suffered before. Sooner or later she'll realize it. And then—" He began to pace up and down with quick, uneven steps, striking his hands together. His face was twitching with a little *tic* that drew up one eye to a squint and released it again at irregular intervals. Harris could see how very near collapse the man was.

"Can you imagine what it's like?" Maltzer demanded fiercely. "Penned into a mechanical body like that, shut out from all human contacts except what leaks in by way of sight and sound? To know you aren't human any longer? She's been through shocks enough already. When that shock fully hits her—"

"Shut up," said Harris roughly. "You won't do her any good if you break down yourself. Look—the vaude's starting."

Great golden curtains had swept together over the unhappy Queen of Scotland and were parting again now, all sorrow and frustration wiped away once more as cleanly as the pass-ing centuries had already expunged them. Now a line of tiny dancers under the tremendous arch of the stage kicked and pranced with the precision of little mechanical dolls too small

and perfect to be real. Vision rushed down upon them and
swept along the row, face after stiffly smiling face racketing
by like fence pickets. Then the sight rose into the rafters and
looked down upon them from a great height, the grotesquely
foreshortened figures still prancing in perfect rhythm even
from this inhuman angle.

There was applause from an invisible audience. Then
someone came out and did a dance with lighted torches that
streamed long, weaving ribbons of fire among clouds of what
looked like cotton wool but was most probably asbestos. Then
a company in gorgeous pseudo-period costumes postured its
way through the new singing ballet form of dance, roughly
following a plot which had been announced as *Les Sylphides,*
but had little in common with it. Afterward the precision
dancers came on again, solemn and charming as performing
dolls.

Maltzer began to show signs of dangerous tension as act
succeeded act. Deirdre's was to be the last, of course. It
seemed very long indeed before a face in close-up blotted out
the stage, and a master of ceremonies with features like an
amiable marionette's announced a very special number as the
finale. His voice was almost cracking with excitement—perhaps he, too, had not been told until a moment before what
lay in store for the audience.

Neither of the listening men heard what it was he said, but
both were conscious of a certain indefinable excitement rising
among the audience, murmurs and rustlings and a mounting
anticipation as if time had run backward here and knowledge
of the great surprise had already broken upon them.

Then the golden curtains appeared again. They quivered
and swept apart on long upward arcs, and between them the
stage was full of a shimmering golden haze. It was, Harris realized in a moment, simply a series of gauze curtains, but the
effect was one of strange and wonderful anticipation, as if
something very splendid must be hidden in the haze. The
world might have looked like this on the first morning of
creation, before heaven and earth took form in the mind of
God. It was a singularly fortunate choice of stage set in its
symbolism, though Harris wondered how much necessity had
figured in its selection, for there could not have been much
time to prepare an elaborate set.

The audience sat perfectly silent, and the air was tense.

This was no ordinary pause before an act. No one had been told, surely, and yet they seemed to guess—

The shimmering haze trembled and began to thin, veil by veil. Beyond was darkness, and what looked like a row of shining pillars set in a balustrade that began gradually to take shape as the haze drew back in shining folds. Now they could see that the balustrade curved up from left and right to the hand of a sweep of stairs. Stage and stairs were carpeted in black velvet; black velvet draperies hung just ajar behind the balcony, with a glimpse of dark sky beyond them trembling with dim synthetic stars.

The last curtain of golden gauze withdrew. The stage was empty. Or it seemed empty. But even through the aerial distances between this screen and the place it mirrored, Harris thought that the audience was not waiting for the performer to come on from the wings. There was no rustling, no coughing, no sense of impatience. A presence upon the stage was in command from the first drawing of the curtains; it filled the theater with its calm domination. It gauged its timing, holding the audience as a conductor with lifted baton gathers and holds the eyes of his orchestra.

For a moment everything was motionless upon the stage. Then, at the head of the stairs, where the two curves of the pillared balustrade swept together, a figure stirred.

Until that moment she had seemed another shining column in the row. Now she swayed deliberately, light catching and winking and running molten along her limbs and her robe of metal mesh. She swayed just enough to show that she was there. Then, with every eye upon her, she stood quietly to let them look their fill. The screen did not swoop to a close-up upon her. Her enigma remained inviolate and the television watchers saw her no more clearly than the audience in the theater.

Many must have thought her at first some wonderfully animate robot, hung perhaps from wires invisible against the velvet, for certainly she was no woman dressed in metal—her proportions were too thin and fine for that. And perhaps the impression of robotism was what she meant to convey at first. She stood quiet, swaying just a little, a masked and inscrutable figure, faceless, very slender in her robe that hung in folds as pure as a Grecian chlamys, though she did not look Grecian at all. In the visored golden helmet and the robe of mail that odd likeness to knighthood was there again, with its implications of medieval richness behind the simple lines. Except that in her exquisite slimness she called to mind no human figure in armor, not even the comparative delicacy of a St. Joan. It was the chivalry and delicacy of some other world implicit in her outlines.

A breath of surprise had rippled over the audience when she moved. Now they were tensely silent again, waiting. And the tension, the anticipation, was far deeper than any mood the scene itself could ever have evoked. Even those who thought her a manikin seemed to feel the forerunning of greater revelations.

Now she swayed and came slowly down the steps, moving with a suppleness just a little better than human. The swaying strengthened. By the time she reached the stage floor she was dancing. But it was no dance that any human creature could ever have performed. The long, slow, languorous rhythms of her body would have been impossible to a figure hinged at its joints as human figures hinge. (Harris remembered incredulously that he had feared once to find her jointed like a mechanical robot. But it was humanity that seemed, by contrast, jointed and mechanical now.)

The languor and the rhythm of her patterns looked impromptu, as all good dances should, but Harris knew what hours of composition and rehearsal must lie behind it, what laborious graving into her brain of strange new pathways, the first to replace the old ones and govern the mastery of metal limbs.

To and fro over the velvet carpet, against the velvet background, she wove the intricacies of her serpentine dance, leisurely and yet with such hypnotic effect that the air seemed full of looping rhythms, as if her long, tapering limbs had left their own replicas hanging upon the air and fading only slowly as she moved away. In her mind, Harris knew, the stage was a whole, a background to be filled in completely with the measured patterns of her dance, and she seemed almost to project that completed pattern to her audience so that they saw her everywhere at once, her golden rhythms fading upon the air long after she had gone.

Now there was music, looping and hanging in echoes after her like the shining festoons she wove with her body. But it was no orchestral music. She was humming, deep and sweet and wordlessly, as she glided her easy, intricate path about the stage. And the volume of the music was amazing. It seemed to fill the theater, and it was not amplified by hidden loudspeakers. You could tell that. Somehow, until you heard the music she made, you had never realized before the subtle distortions that amplification puts into music. This was utterly pure and true as perhaps no ear in all her audience had ever heard music before.

While she danced the audience did not seem to breathe. Perhaps they were beginning already to suspect who and what it was that moved before them without any fanfare of the publicity they had been half-expecting for weeks now. And yet, without the publicity, it was not easy to believe the dancer they watched was not some cunningly motivated manikin swinging on unseen wires about the stage.

Nothing she had done yet had been human. The dance was no dance a human being could have performed. The music she hummed came from a throat without vocal chords. But now the long, slow rhythms were drawing to their close, the pattern tightening in to a finale. And she ended as inhumanly as she had danced, willing them not to interrupt her with applause, dominating them now as she had always done. For her implication here was that a machine might have performed the dance, and a machine expects no applause. If they thought unseen operators had put her through those wonderful paces, they would wait for the operators to appear for their bows. But the audience was obedient. It sat silently, waiting for what came next. But its silence was tense and breathless.

The dance ended as it had begun. Slowly, almost carelessly, she swung up the velvet stairs, moving with rhythms as perfect as her music. But when she reached the head of the stairs she turned to face her audience, and for a moment stood motionless, like a creature of metal, without volition, the hands of the operator slack upon its strings.

Then, startlingly, she laughed.

It was lovely laughter, low and sweet and full-throated. She threw her head back and let her body sway and her shoulders shake, and the laughter, like the music, filled the theater, gaining volume from the great hollow of the roof and sounding in the ears of every listener, not loud, but as intimately as if each sat alone with the woman who laughed.

And she was a woman now. Humanity had dropped over her like a tangible garment. No one who had ever heard that laughter before could mistake it here. But before the reality of who she was had quite time to dawn upon her listeners she let the laughter deepen into music, as no human voice could have done. She was humming a familiar refrain close in the ear of every hearer. And the humming in turn swung into words. She sang in her clear, light, lovely voice:

"The yellow rose of Eden, is blooming in my heart—"

It was Deirdre's song. She had sung it first upon the airways a month before the theater fire that had consumed her. It was a commonplace little melody, simple enough to take first place in the fancy of a nation that had always liked its songs simple. But it had a certain sincerity too, and no taint of the vulgarity of tune and rhythm that foredooms so many popular songs to oblivion after their novelty fades.

No one else was ever able to sing it quite as Deirdre did. It had been identified with her so closely that though for awhile after her accident singers tried to make it a memorial for her, they failed so conspicuously to give it her unmistakable flair that the song died from their sheer inability to sing it. No one ever hummed the tune without thinking of her and the pleasant, nostalgic sadness of something lovely and lost.

But it was not a sad song now. If anyone had doubted whose brain and ego motivated this shining metal suppleness, they could doubt no longer. For the voice was Deirdre, and the song. And the lovely, poised grace of her mannerisms that made up recognition as certainly as sight of a familiar face.

She had not finished the first line of her song before the audience knew her.

And they did not let her finish. The accolade of their interruption was a tribute more eloquent than polite waiting could ever have been. First a breath of incredulity rippled over the theater, and a long, sighing gasp that reminded Harris irrelevantly as he listened of the gasp which still goes up from matinee audiences at the first glimpse of the fabulous Valentino, so many generations dead. But this gasp did not sigh itself away and vanish. Tremendous tension lay behind it, and the rising tide of excitement rippled up in little murmurs and spatterings of applause that ran together into one overwhelming roar. It shook the theater. The television screen trembled and blurred a little to the volume of that transmitted applause.

Silenced before it, Deirdre stood gesturing on the stage, bowing and bowing as the noise rolled up about her, shaking perceptibly with the triumph of her own emotion.

Harris had an intolerable feeling that she was smiling radiantly and that the tears were pouring down her cheeks. He even thought, just as Maltzer leaned forward to switch off the screen, that she was blowing kisses over the audience in the time-honored gesture of the grateful actress, her golden arms shining as she scattered kisses abroad from the featureless helmet, the face that had no mouth.

"Well?" Harris said, not without triumph.

Maltzer shook his head jerkily, the glasses unsteady on his nose so that the blurred eyes behind them seemed to shift.

"Of course they applauded, you fool," he said in a savage voice. "I might have known they would under this setup. It doesn't prove anything. Oh she was smart to surprise them—I admit that. But they were applauding themselves as much as her. Excitement, gratitude for letting them in on a historic performance, mass hysteria—*you* know. It's from now on the test will come, and this hasn't helped any to prepare her for it. Morbid curiosity when the news gets out—people laughing when she forgets she isn't human. And they will, you know. There are always those who will. And the novelty wearing off. The slow draining away of humanity for lack of contact with any human stimuli any more—"

Harris remembered suddenly and reluctantly the moment that afternoon which he had shunted aside mentally, to consider later. The sense of something unfamiliar beneath the surface of Deirdre's speech. Was Maltzer right? Was the drainage already at work? Or was there something deeper than this obvious answer to the question? Certainly she had been through experiences too terrible for ordinary people to comprehend. Scars might still remain. Or, with her body, had she put on a strange, metallic something of the mind, that spoke to no sense which human minds could answer?

For a few minutes neither of them spoke. Then Maltzer rose abruptly and stood looking down at Harris with an abstract scowl.

"I wish you'd go now," he said.

Harris glanced up at him, startled. Maltzer began to pace again, his steps quick and uneven. Over his shoulder he said,

"I've made up my mind, Harris. I've got to put a stop to this."

Harris rose. "Listen," he said. "Tell me one thing. What makes you so certain you're right? Can you deny that most of it's speculation—hearsay evidence? Remember, I talked to Deirdre, and she was just as sure as you are in the opposite direction. Have you any real reason for what you think?"

Maltzer took his glasses off and rubbed his nose carefully, taking a long time about it. He seemed reluctant to answer. But when he did, at last, there was a confidence in his voice Harris had not expected.

"I have a reason," he said. "But you won't believe it. Nobody would."

"Try me."

Maltzer shook his head. "Nobody *could* believe it. No two people were ever in quite the same relationship before as Deirdre and I have been. I helped her come back out of complete—oblivion. I knew her before she had voice or hearing. She was only a frantic mind when I first made contact with her, half insane with all that had happened and fear of what would happen next. In a very literal sense she was reborn out of that condition, and I had to guide her through every step of the way. I came to know her thoughts before she thought them. And once you've been that close to another mind, you don't lose the contact easily." He put the glasses back on and looked blurrily at Harris through the heavy lenses. "Deirdre is worried," he said. "I know it. You won't believe me, but I can—well, sense it. I tell you, I've been too close to her very mind itself to make any mistake. You don't see it, maybe. Maybe even she doesn't know it yet. But the worry's there. When I'm with her, I feel it. And I don't want it to come any nearer the surface of her mind than it's come already. I'm going to put a stop to this before it's too late."

Harris had no comment for that. It was too entirely outside his own experience. He said nothing for a moment. Then he asked simply, "How?"

"I'm not sure yet. I've got to decide before she comes back. And I want to see her alone."

"I think you're wrong," Harris told him quietly. "I think you're imagining things. I don't think you *can* stop her."

Maltzer gave him a slanted glance. "I can stop her," he said, in a curious voice. He went on quickly, "She has enough already—she's nearly human. She can live normally as other people live, without going back on the screen. Maybe this taste of it will be enough. I've got to convince her it is. If she retires now, she'll never guess how cruel her own audiences could be, and maybe that deep sense of—distress, uneasiness, whatever it is—won't come to the surface. It mustn't. She's too fragile to stand that." He slapped his hands together sharply. "I've got to stop her. For her own sake I've got to do it!" He swung round again to face Harris. "Will you go now?"

Never in his life had Harris wanted less to leave a place. Briefly he thought of saying simply, "No I won't." But he had to admit in his own mind that Maltzer was at least partly right. This was a matter between Deirdre and her creator, the culmination, perhaps, of that year's long intimacy so like marriage that this final trial for supremacy was a need he recognized.

He would not, he thought, forbid the showdown if he could. Perhaps the whole year had been building up to this one moment between them in which one or the other must prove himself victor. Neither was very well stable just now, after the long strain of the year past. It might very well be that the mental salvation of one or both hinged upon the outcome of the clash. But because each was so strongly motivated not by selfish concern but by solicitude for the other in this strange combat, Harris knew he must leave them to settle the thing alone.

He was in the street and hailing a taxi before the full significance of something Maltzer had said came to him. *"I can stop her,"* he had declared, with an odd inflection in his voice.

Suddenly Harris felt cold. Maltzer had made her—of course he could stop her if he chose. Was there some key in that supple golden body that could immobilize it at its maker's will? Could she be imprisoned in that cage of her own body? No body before in all history, he thought, could have been designed more truly to be a prison for its mind than Deirdre's, if Maltzer chose to turn the key that locked her in. There must be many ways to do it. He could simply withhold whatever source of nourishment kept her brain alive, if that were the way he chose.

But Harris could not believe he would do it. The man wasn't insane. He would not defeat his own purpose. His determination rose from his solicitude for Deirdre; he would not even in the last extremity try to save her by imprisoning her in the jail of her own skull.

For a moment Harris hesitated on the curb, almost turning back. But what could he do? Even granting that Maltzer would resort to such tactics, self-defeating in their very nature, how could any man on earth prevent him if he did it subtly enough? But he never would. Harris knew he never would. He got into his cab slowly, frowning. He would see them both tomorrow.

He did not. Harris was swamped with excited calls about yesterday's performance, but the message he was awaiting did not come. The day went by very slowly. Toward evening he surrendered and called Maltzer's apartment.

It was Deirdre's face that answered, and for once he saw no remembered features superimposed upon the blankness of her helmet. Masked and faceless, she looked at him inscrutably.

"Is everything all right?" he asked, a little uncomfortable.

"Yes, of course," she said, and her voice was a bit metallic for the first time, as if she were thinking so deeply of some other matter that she did not trouble to pitch it properly. "I had a long talk with Maltzer last night, if that's what you mean. You know what he wants. But nothing's been decided yet."

Harris felt oddly rebuffed by the sudden realization of the metal of her. It was impossible to read anything from face or voice. Each had its mask.

"What are you going to do?" he asked.

"Exactly as I'd planned," she told him, without inflection.

Harris floundered a little. Then, with an effort at practicality, he said, "Do you want me to go to work on bookings, then?"

She shook the delicately modeled skull. "Not yet. You saw

the reviews today, of course. They—*did* like me." It was an understatement, and for the first time a note of warmth sounded in her voice. But the preoccupation was still there, too. "I'd already planned to make them wait awhile after my first performance," she went on. "A couple of weeks, anyhow. You remember that little farm of mine in Jersey, John? I'm going over today. I won't see anyone except the servants there. Not even Maltzer. Not even you. I've got a lot to think about. Maltzer has agreed to let everything go until we've both thought things over. He's taking a rest, too. I'll see you the moment I get back, John. Is that all right?"

She blanked out almost before he had time to nod and while the beginning of a stammered argument was still on his lips. He sat there staring at the screen.

The two weeks that went by before Maltzer called him again were the longest Harris had ever spent. He thought of many things in the interval. He believed he could sense in that last talk with Deirdre something of the inner unrest that Maltzer had spoken of—more an abstraction than a distress, but some thought had occupied her mind which she would not—or was it that she could not?—share even with her closest confidants. He even wondered whether, if her mind was as delicately poised as Maltzer feared, one would ever know whether or not it had slipped. There was so little evidence one way or the other in the unchanging outward form of her.

Most of all he wondered what two weeks in a new environment would do to her untried body and newly patterned brain. If Maltzer were right, then there might be some perceptible—drainage—by the time they met again. He tried not to think of that.

Maltzer televised him on the morning set for her return. He looked very bad. The rest must have been no rest at all. His face was almost a skull now, and the blurred eyes behind their lenses burned. But he seemed curiously at peace, in spite of his appearance. Harris thought he had reached some decision, but whatever it was had not stopped his hands from shaking or the nervous *tic* that drew his face sideways into a grimace at intervals.

"Come over," he said briefly, without preamble. "She'll be here in half an hour." And he blanked out without waiting for an answer.

When Harris arrived, he was standing by the window looking down and steadying his trembling hands on the sill.

"I can't stop her," he said in a monotone, and again without preamble. Harris had the impression that for the two weeks his thoughts must have run over and over the same track, until any spoken word was simply a vocal interlude in the circling of his mind. "I couldn't do it. I even tried threats, but she knew I didn't mean them. There's only one way out Harris." He glanced up briefly, hollow-eyed behind the lenses. "Never mind. I'll tell you later."

"Did you explain everything to her that you did to me?"

"Nearly all. I even taxed her with that . . . that sense of distress I *know* she feels. She denied it. She was lying. We both knew. It was worse after the performance than before. When I saw her that night, I tell you I *knew*—she senses something wrong, but she won't admit it." He shrugged. "Well—"

Faintly in the silence they heard the humming of the elevator descending from the helicopter platform on the roof. Both men turned to the door.

She had not changed at all. Foolishly, Harris was a little surprised. Then he caught himself and remembered that she would never change—never, until she died. He himself might grow white-haired and senile; she would move before him then as she moved now, supple, golden, enigmatic.

Still, he thought she caught her breath a little when she saw Maltzer and the depths of his swift degeneration. She had no breath to catch, but her voice was shaken as she greeted them.

"I'm glad you're both here," she said, a slight hesitation in her speech. "It's a wonderful day outside. Jersey was glorious. I'd forgotten how lovely it is in summer. Was the sanitarium any good, Maltzer?"

He jerked his head irritably and did not answer. She went on talking in a light voice, skimming the surface, saying nothing important.

This time Harris saw her as he supposed her audiences would, eventually, when the surprise had worn off and the image of the living Deirdre faded from memory. She was all metal now, the Deirdre they would know from today on. And she was not less lovely. She was not even less human—yet.

Her motion was a miracle of flexible grace, a pouring of suppleness along every limb. (From now on, Harris realized suddenly, it was her body and not her face that would have mobility to express emotion; she must act with her limbs and her lithe, robed torso.)

But there was something wrong. Harris sensed it almost tangibly in her inflections, her elusiveness, the way she fenced with words. This was what Maltzer had meant, this was what Harris himself had felt just before she left for the country. Only now it was strong—certain. Between them and the old Deirdre whose voice still spoke to them a veil of—detachment—had been drawn. Behind it she was in distress. Somehow, somewhere, she had made some discovery that affected her profoundly. And Harris was terribly afraid that he knew what the discovery must be. Maltzer was right.

He was still leaning against the window, staring out unseeingly over the vast panorama of New York, webbed with traffic bridges, winking with sunlit glass, its vertinginous distances plunging downward into the blue shadows of Earthlevel. He said now, breaking into the light-voiced chatter, "Are you all right, Deirdre?"

She laughed. It was lovely laughter. She moved lithely across the room, sunlight glinting on her musical mailed robe, and stooped to a cigarette box on a table. Her fingers were deft.

"Have one?" she said, and carried the box to Maltzer. He let her put the brown cylinder between his lips and hold a light to it, but he did not seem to be noticing what he did. She replaced the box and then crossed to a mirror on the far wall and began experimenting with a series of gliding ripples that wove patterns of pale gold in the glass. "Of course I'm all right," she said.

"You're lying."

Deirdre did not turn. She was watching him in the mirror, but the ripple of her motion went on slowly, languorously, undisturbed.

"No," she told them both.

Maltzer drew deeply on his cigarette. Then with a hard pull he unsealed the window and tossed the smoking stub far out over the gulfs below. He said, "You can't deceive me, Deirdre." His voice was suddenly, quite calm. "I created you,

my dear. I know. I've sensed that uneasiness in you growing
and growing for a long while now. It's much stronger today
than it was two weeks ago. Something happened to you in the
country. I don't know what it was, but you've changed. Will
you admit to yourself what it is, Deirdre? Have you realized
yet that you must not go back on the screen?"

"Why, no," said Deirdre, still not looking at him except
obliquely, in the glass. Her gestures were slower now, weaving lazy patterns in the air. "No, I haven't changed my
mind."

She was all metal—outwardly. She was taking unfair advantage of her own metal-hood. She had withdrawn far
within, behind the mask of her voice and her facelessness.
Even her body, whose involuntary motions might have betrayed what she was feeling, in the only way she could be
subject to betrayal now, she was putting through ritual motions that disguised it completely. As long as these looping,
weaving patterns occupied her, no one had any way of
guessing even from her motion what went on in the hidden
brain inside her helmet.

Harris was struck suddenly and for the first time with the
completeness of her withdrawal. When he had seen her last in
this apartment she had been wholly Deirdre, not masked at
all, overflowing the metal with the warmth and ardor of the
woman he had known so well. Since then—since the performance on the stage—he had not seen the familiar Deirdre
again. Passionately he wondered why. Had she begun to suspect even in her moment of triumph what a fickle master an
audience could be? Had she caught, perhaps, the sound of
whispers and laughter among some small portion of her
watchers, though the great majority praised her?

Or was Maltzer right? Perhaps Harris's first interview with
her had been the last bright burning of the lost Deirdre, animated by excitement and the pleasure of meeting after so
long a time, animation summoned up in a last strong effort to
convince him. Now she was gone, but whether in self-protection against the possible cruelties of human beings, or to withdraw to metal-hood, he could not guess. Humanity might be
draining out of her fast, and the brassy taint of metal per-
meating the brain it housed.

Maltzer laid his trembling hand on the edge of the opened

window and looked out. He said in a deepened voice, the querulous note gone for the first time: "I've made a terrible mistake, Deirdre. I've done you irreparable harm." He paused a moment, but Deirdre said nothing. Harris dared not speak. In a moment Maltzer went on. "I've made you vulnerable, and given you no weapons to fight your enemies with. And the human race is your enemy, my dear, whether you admit it now or later. I think you know that. I think it's why you're so silent. I think you must have suspected it on the stage two weeks ago, and verified it in Jersey while you were gone. They're going to hate you, after a while, because you are still beautiful, and they're going to persecute you because you are different—and helpless. Once the novelty wears off, my dear, your audience will be simply a mob."

He was not looking at her. He has bent forward a little, looking out the window and down. His hair stirred in the wind that blew very strongly up this high, and whined thinly around the open edge of the glass.

"I meant what I did for you," he said, "to be for everyone who meets with accidents that might have ruined them. I should have known my gift would mean worse ruin than any mutilation could be. I know now that there's only one legitimate way a human being can create life. When he tries another way, as I did, he has a lesson to learn. Remember the lesson of the student Frankenstein? He learned, too. In a way, he was lucky—the way he learned. He didn't have to watch what happened afterward. Maybe he wouldn't have had the courage—I know I haven't."

Harris found himself standing without remembering that he rose. He knew suddenly what was about to happen. He understood Maltzer's air of resolution, his new, unnatural calm. He knew, even, why Maltzer had asked him here today, so that Deirdre might not be left alone. For he remembered that Frankenstein, too, had paid with his life for the unlawful creation of life.

Maltzer was leaning head and shoulders from the window now, looking down with almost hypnotized fascination. His voice came back to them remotely in the breeze, as if a barrier already lay between them.

Deirdre had not moved. Her expressionless mask, in the mirror, watched him calmly. She *must* have understood. Yet she gave no sign, except that the weaving of her arms had almost stopped now, she moved so slowly. Like a dance seen in a nightmare, under water.

It was impossible, of course, for her to express any emotion. The fact that her face showed none now should not, in fairness, be held against her. But she watched so wholly without feeling— Neither of them moved toward the window. A false step, now, might send him over. They were quiet, listening to his voice.

"We who bring life into the world unlawfully," said Maltzer, almost thoughtfully, "must make room for it by withdrawing our own. That seems to be an inflexible rule. It works automatically. The thing we create makes living unbearable. No, it's nothing you can help, my dear. I've asked you to do something I created you incapable of doing. I made you to perform a function, and I've been asking you to forgo the one thing you were made to do. I believe that if you do it, it will destroy you, but the whole guilt is mine, not yours. I'm not even asking you to give up the screen, anymore. I know you can't, and live. But I can't live and watch you. I put all my skill and all my love in one final masterpiece, and I can't bear to watch it destroyed. I can't live and watch you do only what I made you to do, and ruin yourself because you must do it.

"But before I go, I have to make sure you understand." He leaned a little farther, looking down, and his voice grew more remote as the glass came between them. He was saying almost unbearable things now, but very distantly, in a cool, passionless tone filtered through wind and glass and with the distant humming of the city mingled with it, so that the words were curiously robbed of poignancy. "I can be a coward," he said, "and escape the consequences of what I've done, but I can't go and leave you—not understanding. It would be even worse than the thought of your failure, to think of you bewildered and confused when the mob turns on you. What I'm telling you, my dear, won't be any real news—I think you sense it already, though you may not admit it to yourself. We've been too close to lie to each other, Deirdre—I know when you aren't telling the truth. I know the distress that's been growing in your mind. You are not wholly human, my dear. I think you know that. In so many

ways, in spite of all I could do, you must always be less than
human. You've lost the senses of perception that kept you in
touch with humanity. Sight and hearing are all that remain,
and sight, as I've said before, was the last and coldest of the
senses to develop. And you're so delicately poised on a sort
of thin edge of reason. You're only a clear, glowing mind an-
imating a metal body, like a candle flame in a glass. And as
precariously vulnerable to the wind."

He paused. "Try not to let them ruin you completely," he
said after a while. "When they turn against you, when they
find out you're more helpless than they—I wish I could have
made you stronger, Deirdre. But I couldn't. I had too much
skill for your good and mine, but not quite enough skill for
that."

He was silent again, briefly, looking down. He was balanced precariously now, more than halfway over the sill and
supported only by one hand on the glass. Harris watched
with an agonized uncertainty, not sure whether a sudden leap
might catch him in time or send him over. Deirdre was still
weaving her golden patterns, slowly and unchangingly,
watching the mirror and its reflection, her face and masked
eyes enigmatic.

"I wish one thing, though," Maltzer said in his remote
voice. "I wish—before I finish—that you'd tell me the truth,
Deirdre. I'd be happier if I were sure I'd—reached you. Do
you understand what I've said? Do you believe me? Because
if you don't, then I know you're lost beyond all hope. If
you'll admit your own doubt—and I know you do doubt—I
can think there may be a chance for you after all. Were you
lying to me, Deirdre? Do you know how . . . how wrong I've
made you?"

There was silence. Then very softly, a breath of sound,
Deirdre answered. The voice seemed to hang in midair, because she had no lips to move and localize it for the imagination.

"Will you listen, Maltzer?" she asked.

"I'll wait," he said. "Go on. Yes or no?"

Slowly she let her arms drop to her sides. Very smoothly
and quietly she turned from the mirror and faced him. She
swayed a little, making her metal robe ring.

"I'll answer you," she said. "But I don't think I'll answer

that. Not with yes or no, anyhow. I'm going to walk a little, Maltzer. I have something to tell you, and I can't talk standing still. Will you let me move about without—going over?"

He nodded distantly. "You can't interfere from that distance," he said. "But keep the distance. What do you want to say?"

She began to pace a little way up and down her end of the room, moving with liquid ease. The table with the cigarette box was in her way, and she pushed it aside carefully, watching Maltzer and making no swift motions to startle him.

"I'm not—well, sub-human," she said, a faint note of indignation in her voice. "I'll prove it in a minute, but I want to say something else first. You must promise to wait and listen. There's a flaw in your argument, and I resent it. I'm not a Frankenstein monster made out of dead flesh. I'm myself—alive. You didn't create my life, you only preserved it. I'm not a robot, with compulsions built into me that I have to obey. I'm free-willed and independent, and Maltzer—I'm human."

Harris had relaxed a little. She knew what she was doing. He had no idea what she planned, but he was willing to wait now. She was not the indifferent automaton he had thought. He watched her come to the table again in a lap of her pacing, and stoop over it, her eyeless mask turned to Maltzer to make sure a variation of her movement did not startle him.

"I'm human," she repeated, her voice humming faintly and very sweetly. "Do you think I'm not?" she asked, straightening and facing them both. And then suddenly, almost overwhelmingly, the warmth and the old ardent charm were radiant all around her. She was robot no longer, enigmatic no longer. Harris could see as clearly as in their first meeting the remembered flesh still gracious and beautiful as her voice evoked his memory. She stood swaying a little, as she had always swayed, her head on one side, and she was chuckling at them both. It was such a soft and lovely sound, so warmly familiar.

"Of course I'm myself," she told them, and as the words sounded in their ears neither of them could doubt it. There was hypnosis in her voice. She turned away and began to pace again, and so powerful was the human personality which she had called up about her that it beat out at them in deep pulses, as if her body were a furnace to send out those comforting waves of warmth. "I have handicaps, I know," she said. "But my audiences will never know. I won't let them know. I think you'll believe me, both of you, when I say I could play Juliet just as I am now, with a cast of ordinary people, and make the world accept it. Do you think I could, John? Maltzer, don't you believe I could?"

She paused at the far end of her pacing path and turned to face them, and they both stared at her without speaking. To Harris she was the Deirdre he had always known, pale gold, exquisitely graceful in remembered postures, the inner radiance of her shining through metal as brilliantly as it had ever shone through flesh. He did not wonder, now, if it were real. Later he would think again that it might be only a disguise, something like a garment she had put off with her lost body, to wear again only when she chose. Now the spell of her compelling charm was too strong for wonder. He watched, convinced for the moment that she was all she seemed to be. She could play Juliet if she said she could. She could sway a whole audience as easily as she swayed himself. Indeed, there was something about her just now more convincingly human than anything he had noticed before. He realized that in a split second of awareness before he saw what it was.

She was looking at Maltzer. He, too, watched, spellbound in spite of himself, not dissenting. She glanced from one to the other. Then she put back her head and laughter came welling and choking from her in a great, full-throated tide. She shook in the strength of it. Harris could almost see her round throat pulsing with the sweet low-pitched waves of laughter that were shaking her—honest mirth, with a little derision in it.

Then she lifted one arm and tossed her cigarette into the empty fireplace.

Harris choked, and his mind went blank for one moment of blind denial. He had not sat here watching a robot smoke and accepting it as normal. He could not! And yet he had. That had been the final touch of conviction which swayed his hypnotized mind into accepting her humanity. And she had done it so deftly, so naturally, wearing her radiant humanity with such rightness, that his watching mind had not even questioned what she did.

He glanced at Maltzer. The man was still halfway over the window ledge, but through the opening of the window he, too, was staring in stupefied disbelief and Harris knew they had shared the same delusion.

Deirdre was still shaking a little with laughter. "Well," she demanded, the rich chuckling making her voice quiver, "am I all robot, after all?"

Harris opened his mouth to speak, but he did not utter a word. This was not his show. The byplay lay wholly between Deirdre and Maltzer; he must not interfere. He turned his head to the window and waited.

And Maltzer for a moment seemed shaken in his conviction.

"You . . . you *are* an actress," he admitted slowly. "But I . . . I'm not convinced I'm wrong. I think—" He paused. The querulous note was in his voice again, and he seemed racked once more by the old doubts and dismay. Then Harris saw him stiffen. He saw the resolution come back, and understood why it had come. Maltzer had gone too far already upon the cold and lonely path he had chosen to turn back, even for stronger evidence than this. He had reached his conclusions only after mental turmoil too terrible to face again. Safety and peace lay in the course he had steeled himself to follow. He was too tired, too exhausted by months of conflict, to retrace his path and begin all over. Harris could see him groping for a way out, and in a moment he saw him find it.

"That was a trick," he said hollowly. "Maybe you could play it on a larger audience, too. Maybe you have more tricks to use. I might be wrong. But Deirdre"—his voice grew urgent—"you haven't answered the one thing I've got to know. You can't answer it. You *do* feel—dismay. You've learned your own inadequacy, however well you can hide it from us—even from us. I *know*. Can you deny that, Deirdre?"

She was not laughing now. She let her arms fall, and the flexible golden body seemed to droop a little all over, as if the brain that a moment before had been sending out strong, sure waves of confidence had slackened its power, and the intangible muscles of her limbs slackened with it. Some of the glowing humanity began to fade. It receded within her and was gone, as if the fire in the furnace of her body were sinking and cooling.

"Maltzer," she said uncertainly, "I can't answer that—yet. I can't—"

And then, while they waited in anxiety for her to finish the sentence, she *blazed*. She ceased to be a figure in stasis—she *blazed*.

It was something no eyes could watch and translate into terms the brain could follow; her motion was too swift. Maltzer in the window was a whole long room-length away. He had thought himself safe at such a distance, knowing no normal human being could reach him before he moved. But Deirdre was neither normal nor human.

In the same instant she stood drooping by the mirror she was simultaneously at Maltzer's side. Her motion negated time and destroyed space. And as a glowing cigarette tip in the dark describes closed circles before the eye when the holder moves it swiftly, so Deirdre blazed in one continuous flash of golden motion across the room.

But curiously, she was not blurred. Harris, watching, felt his mind go blank again, but less in surprise than because no normal eyes and brain could perceive what it was he looked at.

(In that moment of intolerable suspense his complex human brain paused suddenly, annihilating time in its own way, and withdrew to a cool corner of its own to analyze in a flashing second what it was he had just seen. The brain could do it timelessly; words are slow. But he knew he had watched a sort of tesseract of human motion, a parable of fourth-dimensional activity. A one-dimensional point, moved through space, creates a two-dimensional line, which in motion creates a three-dimensional cube. Theoretically the cube, in motion, would produce a fourth-dimensional figure. No human creature had ever seen a figure of three dimensions moved through space and time before—until this moment. She had not blurred; every motion she made was distinct, but not like moving figures on a strip of film. Not like anything that those who use our language had ever seen before, or created words to express. The mind saw, but without perceiving. Neither words nor thoughts could resolve what happened into terms for human brains. And perhaps she had not actually and

literally moved through the fourth dimension. Perhaps—since
Harris was able to see her—it had been almost and not quite
that unimaginable thing. But it was close enough.)

While to the slow mind's eye she was still standing at the
far end of the room, she was already at Maltzer's side, her
long, flexible fingers gentle but very firm upon his arms. She
waited—

The room shimmered. There was sudden violent heat
beating upon Harris's face. Then the air steadied again and
Deirdre was saying softly, in a mournful whisper: "I'm
sorry—I had to do it. I'm sorry—I didn't mean you to
know—"

Time caught up with Harris. He saw it overtake Maltzer
too, saw the man jerk convulsively away from the grasping
hands, in a ludicrously futile effort to forestall what had already happened. Even thought was slow, compared with
Deirdre's swiftness.

The sharp outward jerk was strong. It was strong enough
to break the grasp of human hands and catapult Maltzer
out and down into the swimming gulfs of New York. The
mind leaped ahead to a logical conclusion and saw him
twisting and turning and diminishing with dreadful rapidity to
a tiny point of darkness that dropped away through sunlight
toward the shadows near the earth. The mind even conjured
up a shrill, thin cry that plummeted away with the falling
body and hung behind it in the shaken air.

But the mind was reckoning on human factors.

Very gently and smoothly Deirdre lifted Maltzer from the
window sill and with effortless ease carried him well back
into the safety of the room. She set him down before a sofa
and her golden fingers unwrapped themselves from his arms
slowly, so that he could regain control of his own body before she released him.

He sank to the sofa without a word. Nobody spoke for an
unmeasurable length of time. Harris could not. Deirdre
waited patiently. It was Maltzer who regained speech first,
and it came back on the old track, as if his mind had not yet
relinquished the rut it had worn so deep.

"All right," he said breathlessly. "All right, you can stop
me this time. But I know, you see. I know! You can't hide

your feeling from me, Deirdre. I know the trouble you feel. And next time—next time I won't wait to talk!"

Deirdre made the sound of a sigh. She had no lungs to expel the breath she was imitating, but it was hard to realize that. It was hard to understand why she was not panting heavily from the terrible exertion of the past minutes; the mind knew why, but could not accept the reason. She was still too human.

"You still don't see," she said. "Think, Maltzer, think!"

There was a hassock beside the sofa. She sank upon it gracefully, clasping her robed knees, her head tilted back to watch Maltzer's face. She saw only stunned stupidity on it now; he had passed through too much emotional storm to think at all.

"All right," she told him. "Listen—I'll admit it. You're right. I *am* unhappy. I do know what you said was true—but not for the reason you think. Humanity and I are far apart, and drawing farther. The gap will be hard to bridge. Do you hear me, Maltzer?"

Harris saw the tremendous effort that went into Maltzer's wakening. He saw the man pull his mind back into focus and sit up on the sofa with weary stiffness.

"You . . . you do admit it, then?" he asked in a bewildered voice.

Deirdre shook her head sharply.

"Do you still think of me as delicate?" she demanded. "Do you know I carried you here at arm's length halfway across the room? Do you realize you weigh *nothing* to me? I could"—she glanced around the room and gestured with sudden, rather appalling violence—"tear this building down," she said quietly. "I could tear my way through these walls, I think. I've found no limit yet to the strength I can put forth if I try." She held up her golden hands and looked at them. "The metal would break, perhaps," she said reflectively, "but then, I have no feeling—"

Maltzer gasped, *"Deirdre—"*

She looked up with what must have been a smile. It sounded clearly in her voice. "Oh, I won't. I wouldn't have to do it with my hands, if I wanted. Look—listen!"

She put her head back and a deep, vibrating hum gathered and grew in what one still thought of as her throat. It deepened swiftly and the ears began to ring. It was deeper, and the furniture vibrated. The walls began almost imperceptibly to shake. The room was full and bursting with a sound that shook every atom upon its neighbor with a terrible, disrupting force.

The sound ceased. The humming died. Then Deirdre laughed and made another and quite differently pitched sound. It seemed to reach out like an arm in one straight direction—toward the window. The opened panel shook. Deirdre intensified her hum, and slowly, within-perceptible jolts that merged into smoothness, the window jarred itself shut.

"You see?" Deirdre said. "You see?"

But still Maltzer could only stare. Harris was staring too, his mind beginning slowly to accept what she implied. Both were too stunned to leap ahead to any conclusions yet.

Deirdre rose impatiently and began to pace again, in a ringing of metal robe and a twinkling of reflected lights. She was pantherlike in her suppleness. They could see the power behind that lithe motion now; they no longer thought of her as helpless, but they were far still from grasping the truth.

"You were wrong about me, Maltzer," she said with an effort at patience in her voice. "But you were right too, in a way you didn't guess. I'm not afraid of humanity. I haven't anything to fear from them. Why"—her voice took on a tinge of contempt—"already I've set a fashion in women's clothing. By next week you won't see a woman on the street without a mask like mine, and every dress that isn't cut like a chlamys will be out of style. I'm not afraid of humanity! I won't lose touch with them unless I want to. I've learned a lot—I've learned too much already."

Her voice faded for a moment, and Harris had a quick and appalling vision of her experimenting in the solitude of her farm, testing the range of her voice, testing her eyesight—could she see microscopically and telescopically?—and was her hearing as abnormally flexible as her voice?

"You were afraid I had lost feeling and scent and taste," she went on, still pacing with that powerful, tigerish tread. "Hearing and sight would not be enough, you think? But why do you think sight is the last of the senses? It may be the latest, Maltzer—Harris—*but why do you think it's the last?*"

She may not have whispered that. Perhaps it was only their hearing that made it seem thin and distant, as the brain contracted and would not let the thought come through in its stunning entirety.

"No," Deirdre said, "I haven't lost contact with the human race. I never will, unless I want to. It's too easy . . . too easy."

She was watching her shining feet as she paced, and her masked face was averted. Sorrow sounded in her soft voice now.

"I didn't mean to let you know," she said. "I never would have, if this hadn't happened. But I couldn't let you go believing you'd failed. You made a perfect machine, Maltzer. More perfect than you knew."

"But Deirdre—" breathed Maltzer, his eyes fascinated and still incredulous upon her, "but Deirdre, if we did succeed—what's wrong? I can feel it now—I've felt it all along. You're so unhappy—you still are. Why, Deirdre?"

She lifted her head and looked at him, eyelessly, but with a piercing stare.

"Why are you so sure of that?" she asked gently.

"You think I could be mistaken, knowing you as I do? But I'm not Frankenstein . . . you say my creation's flawless. Then what—"

"Could you ever duplicate this body?" she asked.

Maltzer glanced down at his shaking hands. "I don't know. I doubt it. I—"

"Could anyone else?"

He was silent. Deirdre answered for him. "I don't believe anyone could. I think I was an accident. A sort of mutation halfway between flesh and metal. Something accidental and . . . and unnatural, turning off on a wrong course of evolution that never reaches a dead end. Another brain in a body like this might die or go mad, as you thought I would. The synapses are too delicate. You were—call it lucky—with me. From what I know now, I don't think a . . . a baroque like me could happen again." She paused a moment. "What you did was kindle the fire for the Phoenix, in a way. And the Phoenix rises perfect and renewed from its own ashes. Do you remember why it had to reproduce itself that way?"

Maltzer shook his head.

"I'll tell you," she said. "It was because there was only one Phoenix. Only one in the whole world."

They looked at each other in silence. Then Deirdre shrugged a little.

"He always came out of the fire perfect, of course. I'm not weak, Maltzer. You needn't let that thought bother you any more. I'm not vulnerable and helpless. I'm not sub-human." She laughed dryly. "I suppose," she said, "that I'm—super-human."

"But—not happy."

"I'm afraid. It isn't unhappiness, Maltzer—it's fear. I don't want to draw so far away from the human race. I wish I needn't. That's why I'm going back on the stage—to keep in touch with them while I can. But I wish there could be others like me. I'm . . . I'm lonely, Maltzer."

Silence again. Then Maltzer said, in a voice as distant as when he had spoken to them through glass, over gulfs as deep as oblivion: "Then I am Frankenstein, after all."

"Perhaps you are," Deirdre said very softly. "I don't know. Perhaps you are."

She turned away and moved smoothly, powerfully, down the room to the window. Now that Harris knew, he could almost hear the sheer power purring along her limbs as she walked. She leaned the golden forehead against the glass—it clinked faintly, with a musical sound—and looked down into the depths Maltzer had hung above. Her voice was reflective as she looked into those dizzy spaces which had offered oblivion to her creator.

"There's one limit I can think of," she said, almost inaudibly. "Only one. My brain will wear out in another forty years or so. Between now and then I'll learn . . . I'll change . . . I'll know more than I can guess today. I'll change— That's frightening. I don't like to think about that." She laid a curved golden hand on the latch and pushed the window open a little, very easily. Wind whined around its edge. "I could put a stop to it now, if I wanted," she said. "If I wanted. But I can't, really. There's so much still untried. My brain's human, and no human brain could leave such possibilities untested. I wonder, though . . . I do wonder—"

Her voice was soft and familiar in Harris's ears, the voice Deirdre had spoken and sung with, sweetly enough to enchant a world. But as preoccupation came over her a certain flatness crept into the sound. When she was not listening to her own voice, it did not keep quite to the pitch of trueness. It sounded as if she spoke in a room of brass, and echoes from the walls resounded in the tones that spoke there.

"I wonder," she repeated, the distant taint of metal already in her voice.